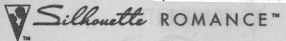
Silhouette ROMANCE™

What's a single dad to do when he needs a wife by next Thursday?

Who's a confirmed bachelor to call when he finds a baby on his doorstep?

How does a plain Jane in love with her gorgeous boss get him to notice her?

From classic love stories to romantic comedies to emotional heart tuggers, **Silhouette Romance** offers six irresistible novels every month by some of your favorite authors!
Such as...beloved bestsellers **Diana Palmer,
Annette Broadrick, Suzanne Carey, Elizabeth August** and **Marie Ferrarella,** to name just a few—and some sure to become favorites!

Fabulous Fathers...Bundles of Joy...Miniseries...
Months of blushing brides and convenient weddings...
Holiday celebrations... You'll find all this and much more in
Silhouette Romance—always emotional, always enjoyable, always about love!

SR-GEN

Mikal Romanov—the anything-but-ordinary father next door

Sloan McQuade—the hard-edged troubleshooter with anything but women on his mind

Miguel Hidalgo—the "late" idealistic revolutionary who was anything but dead

When it comes to giving it up for love, these men wrote the book.

Surrender!

What would *you* do for love?

KATHLEEN EAGLE
is a transplant from New England to Minnesota
via a twenty-year sojourn in North Dakota.
Following a long career as a high school English
teacher, she saw her first novel published in 1984.
She's been writing books for Silhouette and
Harlequin ever since, most of them national
bestsellers. She also writes bestselling mainstream
novels and has received numerous awards from
Romantic Times, Affaire de Coeur and Romance
Writers of America, including the prestigious
RITA Award. Her husband Clyde's Lakota heritage
has enriched her own life as well as her writing.
The Eagles have three children.

Kathleen Eagle

Surrender!

To Bonnie
and Jan Milella,
who are always at the ready

SILHOUETTE BOOKS

SURRENDER, SURRENDER

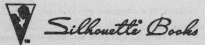

Published by Silhouette Books
America's Publisher of Contemporary Romance

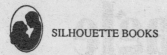

SILHOUETTE BOOKS

by Request

SURRENDER!

Copyright © 1995 by Harlequin Books S.A.

ISBN 0-373-20116-8

The publisher acknowledges the copyright holders of the individual works as follows:

CANDLES IN THE NIGHT
Copyright © 1988 by Kathleen Eagle

MORE THAN A MIRACLE
Copyright © 1988 by Kathleen Eagle

PAINTBOX MORNING
Copyright © 1989 by Kathleen Eagle

CONTENTS

A Note from Kathleen Eagle

Dear Reader,

I've yet to write a series that started out to be more than
one book. Whenever I've written connected books they've
evolved when secondary characters have caught my fancy
and lured me more deeply into their lives. The DeColores
trilogy started out with two seemingly ordinary people
living in my very down-to-earth hometown—at the time—
of Bismarck, North Dakota, who got caught up in
extraordinary circumstances just as they were falling in
love with each other—an extraordinary event in itself.
Being whisked away to a fictitious Caribbean island was,
for me, a little like a Peter Pan adventure, where Morgan
finds herself risking everything for Mikal, who is far from
just an ordinary guy.

Morgan and Mikal found passion and adventure on the
island of DeColores, and I found several characters who
were intriguing enough to demand their own stories.
Elizabeth, the mysterious woman who was separated from
her child; McQuade, the hard-edged troubleshooter who
had no room in his heart for a woman; Miguel, the
idealistic revolutionary betrayed by his comrades. As it
turned out, there was passion and adventure on that little
island far beyond my first imaginings. So I just kept right
on imagining. Since the three novels were published in
two different lines over the course of more than a year,
I'm really pleased that they're available again, all in one
volume.

The name "DeColores" was inspired by a wonderful
Spanish folk song that celebrates love, faith and diversity
symbolized by the colors of the rainbow. It has come to be
a joyous greeting, almost an embrace.

DeColores, dear friend, and happy reading!

CANDLES IN THE NIGHT

Kathleen Eagle

For David,
my firstborn

Chapter One

Mikal Romanov reminded himself that he was a patient man as he studied the pictures in Miss Kramer's outer office. There was a watercolor of a prairie schoolhouse, a print of Ben Franklin's portrait, a framed copy of the Declaration of Independence, and John Donne's "No Man is an Island" quotation in decorative calligraphy. Heady stuff, he thought. Franklin and Donne were admirable men, and patient, too, no doubt.

Miss Kramer was on the phone, or so the secretary had told him. She'd be with him in just a moment. He glanced at his watch. That had been ten minutes ago. He'd give the lady another five. His patience notwithstanding, he'd never enjoyed sitting in the principal's office.

Studying the knowing look in Ben Franklin's piercing eyes, Mikal absently drew a quarter from his pocket and flipped it with his thumb. On the third flip, the coin escaped him, rolling under a chair near the inner office's closed door. Mikal squatted and reached for the quarter just as the office door opened. He hesitated, turned his head and encountered first a pair of black pumps, then sleek ankles, and finally two very silky, sexy legs. They were such great legs that he had no desire to lift his eyes any higher.

"Mr. Romanov?"

Mikal glanced up quickly. Her eyes were cold, but her face matched her legs—unmistakably feminine. He smiled. "How do you do, Miss Kramer? I thought it would be simplest just to cower right from the start."

"I see." The smile she returned was patient. "You were expecting the worst?"

"Much worse." He dared another glance at her legs as he uncoiled his own, rising slowly to tower over her. "But not *the* worst. The worst was Mr. Pross, the principal who saw to it that I was benched on a regular basis."

"Did you turn the lab mice loose, too?"

"No. My son can take credit for thinking that one up on his own." She was the epitome of primness. She looked as if she needed a wicked grin, so he gave her one. "But I did sell tickets to the peephole into the girls' locker room. I paid for the damages on that one, too."

"Somehow I think those damages might have been irreparable." She lifted an admonishing eyebrow. "Please come into my office, Mr. Romanov."

Her voice, low and dignified, carried such foreboding that he hastened to explain. "We couldn't really see much. It was just the idea."

"Sit down, Mr. Romanov," she instructed, again with the patience of someone accustomed to being the only adult in the room. He watched her move crisply around her desk and sit down. Her dark hair was pinned neatly at the back of her head. She wore a charcoal-gray tailored suit, and the only hint of frivolity Mikal detected in her outfit was the small ruffle on the high collar of her wine-colored blouse. The ruffle dipped when she lowered her chin to look at some papers on her desk—papers that undoubtedly recounted David's education from birth through the eighth grade. Another narrow ruffle framed her wrist as she turned a page. She wore no jewelry, no nail polish, and her nails were sensibly trimmed. Only the small bit of burgundy ruffle was there to accent the softness of her slight hand. She was lovely, but she was probably one of the few women who preferred to be considered attractive or distinguished. "Attractive" fell short of describing her, and Mikal figured she was about thirty years too young for "distinguished."

Morgan folded her hands on top of the pile of papers—which had nothing to do with David Romanov. She took a long, slow breath before looking across the desk at the man who had, surprisingly, seated himself in the seat she'd indicated. She'd expected him to take another chair or to stand in the doorway—anything but what she'd suggested. She knew how rebels behaved.

"The mice are not the reason I've requested this meeting," Morgan began, lifting her chin first, then her eyes. "David will be required to pay for them, and for the cost of exterminating them."

Mikal winced, squirming as his son had surely done when he'd been sitting in the same chair. "The mice had to be exterminated?"

She dipped her chin in solemn confirmation. "One of them turned up in the home economics lab. The teacher was certain we had an infestation, and we do have health codes to consider. I've explained to David that he must bear those expenses, and I hope you won't bail him out on that. It should be his responsibility."

"I realize that." She was lovely, yes, but he was beginning to chafe a little. Didn't she think he knew how to raise his own kid?

"Good. The real problem here, Mr. Romanov, is the recent decline in David's academic efforts. Several of his teachers have reported a marked change in attitude. He hasn't been doing his assignments. Report cards will be out soon, and I'm afraid David's grades won't be as good as they have been in the past."

Morgan watched the effect the news had on Mikal Romanov's face. His brow furrowed, and he fixed his eyes on her. "What kind of change in attitude? He's not giving his teachers any trouble, is he?"

"David is never rude, of course. He's a very pleasant boy—personable and well-mannered." That assurance brought relief and then, predictably, satisfaction to the father's face. "He's simply not doing his job here."

Mikal shook his head slowly. "I guess I've eased up on him lately. I've been leaving it up to him to get his homework done. I'll get back on his case."

"Mr. Romanov, your son is very bright. He's been in the gifted and talented program, and his teachers know his potential. We try very hard to—"

"Yes, I know. You try hard; I try hard; and David works like hell when it catches his fancy." Mikal offered an apologetic smile and an open-handed gesture. He'd fought this battle over his son before. "He doesn't always respond to traditional methods of teaching."

"We're aware of that," Morgan assured him, laying her palms carefully on the papers in front of her. "But no matter how talented an individual may be, there are certain responsibilities we all have, certain mundane tasks we all must perform every day. Chores, paperwork, schedules—we all learn to deal with those things or we go down in the mire of our own disorganization.''

His laughter caught her off guard, and she gave him a wide-eyed stare. ''Now you're talking about David's old man,'' Mikal confessed, shifting in his chair.

''We start talking organization, and *he's* the one who gets on *my* case.''

''I see.'' Morgan folded her hands and studied the even row of her knuckles. She saw a great deal, and that made it difficult to keep a steady eye on the man. He was casually dressed in a yellow sweater vest, and a brown corduroy sports jacket, with corduroy pants, and he looked completely comfortable. His tawny hair curled around his ears and tumbled over his forehead in a style that probably required only the use of his fingers as a comb. He smiled easily, laughed even more easily, and his clear blue eyes invited her to laugh with him—even *at* him, if she'd succumb to the temptation. But she wouldn't. He was undoubtedly as charming as he was handsome, but concern for a student's well-being was not a matter to be charmed away. ''David may fail English this quarter.''

Mikal laughed again, and this time Morgan frowned at him. He dismissed the threat with a wave of his hand. ''David reads as much as I do. His writing may be a little undisciplined, but he's only thirteen. He's creative; what more can you ask?''

''He isn't doing his work, Mr. Romanov. His vocabulary assignments—''

''He has an excellent vocabulary.'' This point was couched in a less jovial tone.

''I realize that, but he is not doing his vocabulary *assignments*. He may be a creative writer, but he isn't writing. We cannot evaluate what we cannot see.''

Mikal's hands went up in surrender. "Okay. You're right. No excuses. We'll talk this over and get it straightened out. I didn't realize he'd slacked off this much. Maybe I haven't spent enough time with him lately."

Guilt. Morgan had seen a lot of it in her work, and she knew it weighed heavily on parents. Her job wasn't easy, but she imagined that being a father was much harder, especially for a single man. She remembered David's bid for sympathy when she'd had him in her office. "I don't have a mother, Miss Kramer. He's all I've got, and we've gotten to the point where we don't even speak the same language. He's literally not of this world."

"Not of this world" was probably putting it mildly. From what she'd heard, the man had his head in the clouds. All for a good cause, of course. Morgan smiled, remembering her middleman's role. "Your son is very proud of you. In fact, I think he feels you're a bit larger than life, and he's afraid he can't measure up."

He was surprised by her statement, as well as by her smile, which was warming up a little. "Measure up to what? The work I do best doesn't pay, and I can't find much time for what I do second best—which pays only when I do it." Mikal lifted a shoulder and smiled again. "*That's* lack of organization, Miss Kramer. David sees me in my natural state, and it isn't larger than life, believe me."

There was something admirable in his honest admission, and Morgan caught his eye in a frank exchange. He wasn't a saint. Neither was he a great sinner. He was a man, concerned about his son and willing to tell Morgan the long and the short of his existence in order to clarify the situation. David's father was just like any other father.

Hardly, she reminded herself. His voice said "believe me" but his eyes were more effective than his words. Their crystal-blue honesty could suck a listener in before the man opened his mouth. And Morgan was not about to forget the kind of man he was. Charming dreamers were her Achilles' heel.

"David lists his father's occupation as 'writer,' but that isn't the real source of your fame," Morgan said, allowing herself, against her better judgment, to show an interest in his activities. "I think . . . that is, I'm sure the whole *community* shares David's pride in your . . . your work."

"If you're talking about Freedom International, it's the work of a lot of people, and all of them deserve commendations. I feel a little self-conscious about being singled out."

"They gave you a big write-up in the paper."

"It was a nice honor, but it could have been divided a hundred ways." He shifted again in his chair. The man who had been completely at ease had suddenly become uncomfortable. Morgan noticed that his size overwhelmed the small chair she had given him. If she could have done it without making him even more self-conscious, she would have offered him a different one.

"But you seem to be an eloquent spokesman, Mr. Romanov. From what I've read, your organization has been instrumental in securing freedom for a number of political prisoners."

He shrugged. "We can't always get them out, but we find that sometimes just by drawing attention to them, we can improve conditions."

"Do you travel much for your work?" She knew full well that he must, and she wondered how that affected David.

"Some. I also write a lot of letters, draft a lot of petitions." He cocked his head to the side and smiled. "Would you care to sign one? I have two with me—one protesting the proposed new missile base and the other . . ." He laid a hand over one side of his jacket, but his smile said that he knew better than to reach inside.

"Another time, maybe. My concern right now is for David's attitude and what influences may be affecting it adversely." Rolling her chair back from the desk, Morgan put more distance between them as she made a gable of her hands, her habitual "discussion" gesture, and launched into a personal aside as impersonally as she could manage. "You see, I believe I understand David's viewpoint even better than you do. My father is a minister—a missionary, in fact. His work is his life, and his ideals are impeccable. It's very difficult for a child—" eyeing the man quickly, she saw that he was interested "—*any* child, to assert his own need when the needs of...of hungry people—" she risked another glance "—of people who are imprisoned unjustly, are at stake. Sometimes a child does whatever he thinks is necessary to get his father's attention." She hastened to add, "Unconsciously, of course."

"Are you thinking maybe I'm letting my causes take precedence over my son?"

She didn't answer. Her eyes became a mirror and he saw the reflection of all his worries, all the doubts he'd had since the death of David's mother some ten years ago. "It's for David that I do what I do," he said quietly. "I love my son, and I want to give him a better world."

Morgan glanced away, taking the time to put that beautiful ideal into perspective. She returned to the matter-of-fact approach. "I appreciate that, Mr. Romanov. Someday David will, too. My concern is with giving him a better education, and I think you need to be aware that he hasn't been cooperating with that effort lately."

"I think he's playing a game with both of us, Miss Kramer. I'll find out what it is and see that he stops."

She stood, and he followed suit, watching her move around the desk as she explained, "What seems like a game to us might be serious business for David. Children's minds work in mysterious ways."

As she stepped in front of him, reaching for the door, Mikal noticed the small wisps of hair that fringed the back of her neck, defying the restrictions her severe hairstyle tried to impose on them. They looked soft, and he had a sudden urge to blow on them and make them flutter—just to see if she had a giggle in her. He smiled, believing she might. He suspected David believed she did, too. David was probably after somebody's attention, all right, but not his dad's.

"I appreciate your taking the time—"

"My time belongs to the students," she said, offering her hand. "I can't let a problem like David's slip by me."

Of that he had no doubt. He took her hand in his and pressed it, palm to palm, in a gesture that in no way suggested a final goodbye. She looked up, and he took stock of the features she couldn't play down—the fine bone structure, the translucent white skin, the brown-green eyes. If David harbored a crush on this woman, it was well-founded, Mikal decided. "I'll call you in a week or so," he promised, "to see if we're making progress."

"Yes," Morgan managed in a voice much smaller than it had been during the entire meeting, "that will be fine."

Morgan closed the door and leaned her back against it. She felt a little weak-kneed because . . . well, the man *was* charming. Predictably so, she reminded herself, moving toward her desk and sitting down. She pulled a three-day-old copy of the *Tribune* from the bottom drawer. Recent publicity had probably given David's father folk-hero status in some circles across the country, but the people of Bismarck were generally conservative. He'd made the news with a presidential commendation for his work with Freedom International, but the headline was dwarfed by the one announcing a hike in hog prices.

The photograph of Mikal Romanov with two other members of the organization confirmed her idea that he was not obsessed with appearances, but that he exuded a kind of magnetism, something that drew the eye to his face. Handsome, yes, but more than that he was...an idealist, Morgan told herself as she leaned back in her chair, putting some distance between herself and the picture. A cockeyed optimist. An aging hippie. The man was zealous in his pursuit of causes—world peace, freedom for political prisoners, affirmative action, clean water. Morgan knew the type. Buoyed up by their own charisma, men like him were completely impractical, totally unpredictable, and produced very little in the way of tangible results.

No wonder David was acting up. At his age he needed less zeal and more stability. He was a very clever young man, but the same battle raged within him as in every thirteen-year-old. He wanted to grow up, but he didn't want to leave childhood behind. Morgan smiled, remembering the boy's wide-eyed expression of innocence when she'd confronted him with the charges against him.

"The fault, Miss Kramer, is not in my stars, but in my father." She'd told him to try that one on his English teacher. "Really," he'd insisted. "The man is driving me crazy. Which explained my insane behavior: Independence day for the white mice in the science lab."

The boy's dark brown eyes weren't quite as overwhelming as his father's, but then he'd had fewer years to perfect the knack, and already he was hard to resist. She'd explained to him that, though he'd have to pay for the mice, her real concern was for his falling grades, which were not his father's responsibility.

David had agreed, at least in part. "I'm responsible for my grades. He's responsible for my insanity. I've become a madman."

Morgan had noticed the three books he'd set by the chair; science, math, and Salinger's *Catcher in the Rye.* "Just lately?" she'd asked.

"Salinger has nothing to do with this," David had assured her. "He's prehistoric. I'm talking major insanity here. Do you know what it's like to be the son of a saint?"

It was an interesting question. She was the daughter of one, which might be less taxing than the role of a son. She wondered what was expected of a boy whose father had been honored by the president simply for helping people. Her own father's work had received little notice, and he required none. He went right on with his mission even now, when by all rights he should have been spending a comfortable retirement with what family he had left.

"Everybody thinks he's such a great man," David had said. "At least, they say they do, but they're probably thinking he's weird. Great, but weird."

Yes, Morgan thought, for Bismarck, Mikal Romanov was a little different. He would have to move much farther east or west to find an active community of believers. *Dreamers,* Morgan amended. She wondered why he chose to stay among the practical conservatives who were the backbone of central North Dakota.

Morgan glanced at the picture in the paper and then at the small chair in front of her desk. That chair had only made him seem bigger, a circumstance made more charming by the fact that he hadn't complained. His modest squirm when she'd mentioned his award had been a nice touch, too. Despite all that, she'd dealt with the matter just as she'd intended; David would pay for the damages, and his schoolwork would be closely monitored.

Folding the newspaper in half, Morgan eyed the trashcan beside her desk, but she tucked the paper back in the bottom drawer, stopping for one more glimpse of Mikal Romanov's charming smile before she slid the drawer closed.

David stumbled over a pair of size thirteen running shoes when he came home. He wondered why he hadn't expected the shoes to be there since that was where his dad always kept them—just inside the back door, waiting to trip all comers.

That minor annoyance quickly took a back seat to the aromatic promise that filled the kitchen. David moved to the stove, lifted the lid on the steaming kettle and took a deep whiff. Hungarian goulash. The clutter at the back door was forgiven.

"Dad? You home?"

Even in stockinged feet, Mikal Romanov's approach was clearly audible. He never climbed the basement stairs; he bounded up two steps at a time. The jogging shoes or whatever else he'd left by the door were never in his way. Dressed in gray sweats, he came into the kitchen looking like the professional football player David often wished his father was. He was big enough, David thought as he turned a sheepish grin at Mikal. "Got my nose ground down at the sweatshop today. I'm starved." David inhaled dramatically. "Supper smells great."

Mikal registered the compliment with a grain of salt as he straddled a kitchen chair and folded his arms atop the back. "I got started a little late this afternoon; it'll be a while yet. Hard day, huh?"

David ducked into the refrigerator, took a quick survey and reached for the crisper drawer. "Full of the usual stuff we've done a hundred times. I hope they think of something new for high school." He came up with two apples and, with a questioning look, held one up in Mikal's direction.

"I hope so, too." Mikal gave a nod, and the apple flew through the air and whacked into his big hand. "If they don't, you will."

The refrigerator door swung closed, and David hung his head in a small act of contrition. "It's just what I said, Dad, the mice were like a mountain. They were there, waiting to be—"

"No sale on that one, David. And I think the bill you have to pay will keep you out of circulation for some time."

True, David thought, but the stunt had accomplished one thing. His dad had introduced himself to Miss Kramer. David tried to inject a note of dread into his voice. "So you had your conference with Miss Kramer today, huh?"

"We're concerned about your schoolwork, son."

David joined his father at the table and sank his teeth into the sweet red apple. *We're* concerned. He liked the sound of that. He hoped this meant his dad would be conferring with Miss Kramer on a regular basis. "It's no big deal, Dad. It's probably hormones."

"Hormones?" Mikal felt a smile coming on that he'd just as soon repress.

"Yeah, you know. I'm at that age."

"Girls becoming a distraction, are they?" Not yet, Mikal hoped. He wasn't ready to let his son's boyhood go, and he sent up a silent prayer for one more year of skateboards and vintage comic books.

"Not so much." David hooked his right ankle over his left knee and watched his own foot jiggle. Then a memory made him smile. "But it was pretty funny when that mouse jumped out of Jenny Dutton's purse in science class. You never heard such a shriek."

"Now you have to pay the piper." Mikal's smile was getting away from him as he remembered the day when the news of the locker-room peephole hit the cheerleading squad. "The Pied Piper—he was an exterminator, too, remember? And after supper you hit the books."

David offered a bony-shouldered, adolescent shrug. "No problem, Dad. I was just taking a little midsemester hiatus. So, uh…" He risked an upward glance. "What'd you think of Miss Kramer?"

Mikal considered. "I guess I thought…for a principal, she wasn't half bad." His eyebrows went up a notch as he added, "Quite fair, in fact. She could have thrown the book at us—at *you*."

"I mean…" David hedged. He didn't want to push too quickly, but he did want to know. "What did you think of…like her looks, for instance."

"'Her looks, for instance,'" Mikal repeated as he bit into his apple. David had very good taste, he thought, remembering the dark wisps of hair against the fine porcelain of her neck. "Fair," he said, adding quietly and with a wistful smile, "Fair and very, very fine."

"I think…I mean the *kids* think…I mean we *all* pretty much like her." David paused to check for reactions. His father was all ears. "She's nice, once you get to know her. Strict, you now, but good sense of humor, and fair, just like you said. And, uh, I don't know if you noticed, but…she's got a really good set of legs."

The bite of apple nearly took a wrong turn in Mikal's throat. Yes, indeed, he had noticed, and he hoped David hadn't been anywhere around when he'd been introducing himself to the lady's hemline. "She probably has nice hair, too," he volunteered, "when it's not done up in that knot."

"Probably. She said she saw your picture in the paper. I think she was kind of impressed."

"You think so?"

"Well, she asked a lot of questions about you."

Mikal swung his leg over the chair and moved to the stove. "She did, huh?" He stuck a spoon in the goulash and stirred slowly. "Hope you didn't tell her any bad stuff."

"What bad stuff? There isn't any."

Mikal ducked his head under a bank of cupboards to look at his son and grinned. "Is that Romanov diplomacy I hear?"

"Maybe a little," David admitted. "I figure it can't hurt."

"Neither can my keeping close tabs on your progress in school."

"You mean . . ."

Mikal nodded. "I mean I'll be checking in with Miss Kramer." David turned his chair toward the table and planted his chin in his hands. "Regularly. I think that's what's called for now, don't you?" Mikal asked the back of his son's head.

David managed a joyless "I guess I've got it coming" as he directed a slow Cheshire-cat grin at the opposite wall.

Chapter Two

David Romanov had given hours of thought to his prospects for family life in the immediate future, and he decided that his father's meeting with Miss Kramer had improved the outlook enormously. The dinner conversation that night more than once centered on Mikal's interest in her, and David worked her name in several times to test the waters further. His father took the bait each time. The interest was there, and David liked that idea. In fact, the more he thought about it, the better he liked it. He had only vague memories of his mother and absolutely no reservations about having his father bring another woman into the family. While Mikal dreamed of peace in his time, David dreamed of order, the kind he hoped might arrive with a woman around the house.

Figuring in his head, David concluded that Miss Kramer ought to be perfect for his father. For one thing, she made a very nice living, and although Mikal Romanov was a good man, making a lot of money was not one of the things he was good at. If the Romanovs were to have a serious bread-winner, David's father would have to marry one. Miss Kramer was efficient, ambitious and actually pretty cool for an adult. Her looks were nothing to complain about, either. In David's mind it all added up to a good prospect, one he intended to encourage. He excused himself from the table and went to his room, where dreams and schemes had a way of taking shape. He rummaged through his gym bag.

Getting a romance going required dates—at least, for the "older generation" it did. As always, his father was busy. There was a fund-raiser coming up in Philadelphia, from which Mikal had asked to be excused. He was a grass roots man, he said. He was working on a local rally and trying to write another book. But the executive board of Freedom International knew what it had in Mikal Romanov, and the members wanted his charm to work its magic in Philadelphia. He'd grumble about it, but in another couple of weeks he'd decide to go, so there wasn't much time. David sorted through a handful of printed tickets with a calculating smile on his face. His father didn't have time right now to arrange a date with Miss Kramer. David did.

The auditorium was filling up fast. It buzzed with the excitement of the friends and relatives of the children who were about to perform. Morgan scanned the crowd as she stepped down from the stage. The parents stood out from the rest, their eyes bright with anticipation, a contrast to the stage fright Morgan had just seen in the students back-stage. She'd told them to break a leg, drawing a terrible groan from Jason Rikhert, whose part called for some acrobatics.

Morgan greeted adults and children by name as she made her way toward her seat. David Romanov had sold her a ticket for "the best seat in the house." Ten-A, she reminded herself, scanning the auditorium. There it was, and there was David's father, occupying what was probably the second-best seat in the house. Morgan found herself needing a moment before taking the seat next to him with a collected "How nice to see you again, Mr. Romanov."

His grandmother's old-world training brought him to his feet quickly, and he smiled. "Miss Kramer. Is this your seat?" She nodded in response to his gesture, and since hers was to the inside, he stepped in front of it and offered his. "I'm told *this* is the best seat in the house. Be my guest."

She returned a smile, and her cheeks grew warm. "I think we bought our tickets from the same salesman."

"I have no doubt of it. What other kid would seat his father next to the school principal after he'd set the lab mice loose just the week before?"

"Just David." As she sat, Morgan smoothed her skirt with one hand, waving any concern away with the other. "But that's all taken care of, and tonight is David's night. I understand he's quite the actor."

The truth dawned slowly, but Mikal couldn't miss it when it finally arrived. David had something up his sleeve. Mikal nodded, grinning. "Much better than I'd realized."

"I usually get a chance to peek in on the dress rehearsal, but I missed it this time." The house lights dimmed. Both of them made a point of looking toward the stage, but each took a turn glancing furtively at the other as the performance got under way.

The play was a spoof of an old melodrama, and David was delightfully nefarious as the villain. Despite her egalitarian attitude toward her students, she found herself concentrating on the boy whose father's presence in the seat next to her was almost overpowering. As she watched David, Mikal's rich laughter found favor in her ears, and his eyes, when they caught hers, blazed with warmth.

The warmth was easily explained. It was his pride in his son, Morgan told herself. He glanced at her occasionally— just to see if she caught each subtle nuance of David's performance, she was sure. They were harmless glances—the kind that would only make her uncomfortable if she allowed them to. The tingling she felt inside must be imaginary.

"You're allowed to laugh out loud, Miss Kramer." Morgan turned to find Mikal leaning close to her. He glanced down at the hands clasped in her lap. "You look like you're having a little sympathetic stage fright," he whispered.

"I probably am." She returned his smile, telling herself that must be it. These were her kids.

"Do I make you nervous?" She gave him a questioning look, and he shrugged. "Just a hunch."

Morgan tried to remember what was going on up front as she made every effort to dismiss his comment. It didn't work. "Why would you think you—"

"Because you make me nervous," he whispered. He was looking at the stage, but his attention was clearly on her.

"I won't keep you after school," she promised. A "shush" from behind brought hot color to Morgan's face, and she heard Mikal's laughter above the rest. She'd missed another gag line. Yes, he definitely made her nervous.

"Join us for an ice-cream cone after the show," Mikal suggested close to her ear. "Ice cream's great for the nerves."

Absurd as that notion was, Morgan found herself agreeing to the invitation. David, on the other hand, declined. After the show was over and the accolades were handed around, he explained quickly that his friend Scott had invited several of the boys to his house for pizza. It was with a sense of great personal satisfaction that David watched his father leave the auditorium with Miss Kramer.

"This changes our options. Do you really want ice cream, or would you rather have a drink?"

Morgan's answer came after Mikal had flicked the rock and roll music off and the heater on. "Ice cream's fine."

"There'll probably be fifty chattering teenagers in every booth, along with video game sound effects and heavy-metal background music."

True. It was Friday night, and she'd earned a respite. "A drink, then."

"Have your cake and eat it, too." He flashed her a smile in passing as he directed his attention to the rearview mirror. "An ice-cream drink."

"Mmm. I'll take all three—the drink, the ice cream *and* the cake. I missed dessert tonight." He had switched from reverse to low gear and was pulling out of the parking lot when the engine made an unmistakable thunk. "Sounds like you're in for some transmission trouble," Morgan remarked.

"Wouldn't surprise me. I had radiator trouble last month. I've got over a hundred thousand miles on this old bomb." He patted the dash. "She's served gallantly."

In the dark, Morgan raised an appreciative brow. Every mile showed. "Maybe it's time for a trade-in."

"You're kidding. Nobody wants her but me."

"You're very tolerant." She'd expected flamboyant. He was a writer and an activist, a combination she would have thought would add up to his having a car with more flash, and probably another date for tonight, as well. "And... conservative, maybe?"

"Conservative!" His laughter was unreserved, rolling freely from his chest. "There's a truly insulting epithet. A lady shouldn't use such language."

"I didn't mean politically. I meant economically. Obviously you're not much of a consumer."

"The economy seems to take its course without my wholehearted participation. I think someone else has been assigned to consume my share." As he took a corner, he glanced her way. Her hair was done up neatly in a bun, and there was a heady scent of expensive perfume in the air. A diamond stud flashed in her ear as they passed under a streetlight. "Was it you?"

"I doubt it," she returned, eyeing him cautiously.

"Too bad. I was hoping it was a sensible, hard-working woman who deserved a few creature comforts and a bauble or two." Shifting into second gear, he slowed the car for a turn. "Probably some oil tycoon."

"Probably." She figured Mikal could have his share if he wanted it. In the time since he'd come to her office, she'd made a point of reading his last book. It was a collection of vignettes that were pulled together to form a powerful picture of rural life. It told of the second and third generations of immigrants to the Dakota farmlands whose road was not marked as clearly as their parents' and whose journey had become stagnant. The book had been the basis for a film, a piece that made a statement and won awards but was not a box-office hit. Mikal Romanov was clearly talented enough to write whatever he chose to. He hadn't chosen the bestseller market, or any market for that matter, for the last five years. Morgan wondered why.

The night spot Mikal chose was quiet, far removed from the idea of fifty teenagers per booth and blaring music. The decor consisted of rural-looking antiques, and the music was Viennese strings. They sat across from one another at a corner table, and the drinks they ordered were a small price to pay for the privilege of occupying such a comfortable corner of the world for a while.

"I read *The Last Barnraising*," Morgan announced. "I thought it was beautiful. I don't know why I hadn't read it before."

Mikal's eyes danced knowingly, a flicker of candlelight caught in them. "Probably because you're not a country girl anymore, or you don't want to think of yourself as one."

"I don't think I've ever thought of myself as a country girl. My family traveled a great deal when I was a child."

She'd said her father was a missionary. What she hadn't said was why she had trouble parting with that information. He remembered the way she'd glanced down at her hands and carefully enunciated the word "missionary" as though she were testing out a foreign phrase. He leaned forward, elbows on the table, arms forming a tepee over his glass. "Where did you live?"

"Everywhere that was nowhere," she said lightly. "Places that were beautiful and barren. Africa, Central America, South America. Places that draw few tourists."

"How old were you?"

"I was twelve when my mother decided it was time to come home. Until that point the missionary life was all I knew." She remembered the heat very well, remembered it especially well on cold winter days. A few minutes in a sauna brought back the humidity, but she missed the smell of damp earth and thick vegetation. "North Dakota was my mother's home. After she and I came back here, we saw much less of my father."

"He continued with his work?"

"He had to," she told him. "My father *is* his work. He used to come home more often when my mother was alive, but now..." Morgan's shrug indicated a dismissal of regret. "I think he's somewhere in the Caribbean at the moment."

Mikal nodded thoughtfully. He knew how such a thing might happen, and it wasn't what he wanted for himself. Work should be an extension of the man, not the man himself. In the shadowy candlelight he saw Morgan's regret, heard it in her voice, and it occurred to him that she cared more about her father than she was willing to admit. "You had a fantastic education, then, as the daughter of a missionary. You saw the world as most people never see it."

"Yes, I did." Most of all, she remembered the children. She remembered feeling akin to them but never really one of them. Sometimes she'd wished her father could see her as one of the suffering, because he worked so feverishly to serve them. "We have so much," he would say, "and they have so little." It made her feel guilty to envy them anything, but she did. They had her father's heart. She would never reclaim it, because he would never retire from his work. "Does your kind of work take you out of the country very often?" Morgan wondered.

Mikal shook his head as he raised his glass, sipping from it before he answered. "I have an uncle who's very much involved at the international level, and he's included me on a couple of missions. I'd rather work locally, try to get people involved. Once or twice a year I help out with a fundraiser. I know how to charm the bucks out of people's billfolds." He gave her a smile and a look that she was sure often did the job before he opened his mouth to speak.

"I see. Does this mean the drinks might be on me?"

Mikal laughed. "Absolutely not. My grandmother would turn over in her grave." He raised a forefinger. "But I warn you, if you come to a rally, you're fair game."

"Forewarned is forearmed." He could think again. She'd been fair game for the likes of him once, and she'd learned her lesson. "Romanov is Russian. Are you related to royalty?"

"Distantly, I guess. My grandparents escaped the Bolsheviks in 1917 with my uncle Yuri, the one I told you about. He was just a young child. An older brother was arrested, and no one knows what happened to him. If he were alive, he'd be in his eighties now. My dad was born in this country, here in North Dakota. My grandfather became a farmer, and my father after him. But my uncle Yuri became an agitator." Mikal's smile indicated the direction of his own sympathies. "An irritant in the world's craw, he calls himself. He was never able to find out what happened to his brother, but he helped found Freedom International. When the organization won the Nobel Peace Prize, it was my uncle Yuri who was there to accept the check."

"Did he put it to good use?"

Mikal's eyes flashed. "Freedom International puts every penny it gets to good use. Would you like a rundown?"

"I'll take your word for it," Morgan offered quickly. "I know a good social conscience when I see one."

"Because you grew up with one?"

She nodded. "How does David feel about all this?"

At the sound of his son's name, Mikal's eyes brightened again, but his brilliant, "public" smile grew softly private. "David thinks his old man's a little crazy, but he loves me just the same. I think he's going to be a computer whiz or a physicist or something. Analytical, practical and organized—that's David."

"Do those things clash with your dreams for him?"

"My dream for him is peace of mind," Mikal explained, his shrug adding that that went without saying. "I want him to be comfortable with himself and to respect the rest of us." Smiling, he used a finger to punctuate. "Including the mice in the lab and the girls in the locker room."

"Bravo. On behalf of mice and girls alike, I thank you." Mikal dipped his head in acknowledgement. Morgan's smile faded as she let her gaze drop back to her glass. "Aren't you afraid a physicist might lose sight of the ideals you've instilled if he's offered a hundred thousand dollars a year to invent better bombs?" It gave her a perverse pleasure to play the devil's advocate, and she had no idea why.

"Not David," Mikal said, no doubts in his mind. "He'll be his own man. I think I've given him that much."

Morgan nodded, but she was thinking that she was her own woman and no one had given her that. She had claimed it for herself, and she was certainly comfortable with herself. She felt a degree of kinship with David. "He's definitely an individual. I enjoy having him in my phys ed group."

Mikal's frown was an expression of his interest. "You teach a physical education class? I'd have taken you for a former social studies teacher."

"I am." Morgan smiled. How had she given herself away? It pleased her that he'd studied her closely enough to come to that conclusion. "I also teach aerobics, which is what David elected to take this quarter."

"Aerobics? I thought he'd signed up for soccer."

"That was last quarter. We just switched."

As he leaned back in his chair, Mikal digested this news as carefully as he did any foreign dish. Aerobics? David? "How's the gender ratio in aerobics class?"

"Heavy on the females, but that doesn't seem to bother David."

Mikal's slow grin indicated that he thought his son was a chip off the old block. "Wouldn't bother me, either. How do you have time to teach a phys ed class?"

"I think every principal should stay in touch with teaching. I taught a world history class until I had to give the phys ed teacher another chance at driver's ed, so I took up the slack in the gym. I'm saving myself an hour in the evening by doing my exercise during the day."

Mikal leaned forward again, concentrating on her eyes. They came to life in the candlelight. She was telling him about something she obviously considered to be one of her few self-indulgences, and she'd begun to apologize. "What do you do with that extra hour in the evening?" he asked, his voice smooth.

"I go to exercise class anyway, but at least I don't feel obligated." She gathered her nerve. "I enjoy working out."

"Why shouldn't you?"

She shrugged, and his eyes were drawn to the knot of hair at her neck. It was beginning to feather away from its anchor at the back of her head and the wispy tendrils at her temples were all the more attractive because they hadn't been styled. "I didn't used to. I started exercising because I was sitting at a desk too much. I had to push myself at first, but one night when I was shaving my legs in the shower at the Y, I found this terrible lump in my leg." His frown deepened, but she dismissed it quickly. "Right in the back of my thigh. I discovered it was a muscle. I couldn't believe it."

Mikal laughed easily, and Morgan joined him. "I wonder if they have a peephole over there. I'd love to have seen the expression on your face." When she pursed her lips in mock scolding, he added, "That's all I would have looked at—the expression on your face. I swear!"

"Nice try, Mikal, but the innocent look doesn't fool me for a minute." She was smiling again, enjoying the feeling that she had charm to return. "I've seen it too many times before."

He liked the sound of his name as it came from her throat, the *k* catching crisply on the back of her tongue. She was trying it out, testing the sound of it, deciding whether it was a name she wanted to say often. "The innocent look, huh?" he protested. "Who's been overusing it for your benefit lately?"

"Any number of boys who think they can put something over on me."

Her merriment was lovely, but it felt fragile, and Mikal wondered why. When he wondered, it was his habit to be gentle, to ask his questions in a soft voice. "Have there been men who've thought they could put something over on you?" It occurred to him suddenly that he needed to know.

She looked into his eyes, frankly assessing him. What was the source of the gentleness in his voice? Where did the softness in his eyes come from? "Not lately," she told him quietly.

"But once upon a time?"

She glanced away. "One . . . once."

"And now?" She looked back at him, questioning his boldness, and he leaned toward her, bolder still. "Is there anyone now, Morgan?"

His directness prompted hers. "No, there isn't."

"Good." He smiled and settled back in his chair. "That's good."

Morgan turned the name over and over in her mind as she prepared for bed that night. Mikal Romanov. It was a beautiful name, a fairy-tale name. It somehow matched the rich shade of blue in his eyes, a shade that ranged in texture from that of gemstones to soft velvet. Royal blue, sky blue— lofty and vast. She knew better than to let that shade lure her feet to leave the ground. It was not her color. It was a dreamy color—dancer, dramatist, dreamer's delight. Dreamers, all dreamers, should come with warning labels, she decided. Caution: Hard to Resist and Impossible to Guarantee.

She studied herself in the mirror, looking for symptoms of an overdose. She'd been down this road before. Twice in fact. Her father was a dreamer, just like this man. And Jeremy, that impossible, impractical artist she'd actually considered marrying when she was young and foolish—he was a dreamer, too. Fortunately she'd had the sense—well, *he'd* taken the initiative, but she'd had the sense to agree that it would never have worked. Don't fall in love with a dreamer, Morgan. She gave herself a hard stare and said the words aloud so that she could hear them and heed them. *"Don't fall in love with a dreamer, Morgan."*

"So, Dad, how was Miss Kramer?"

Mikal turned his head to glance first at the hand on his shoulder and then at the grinning face behind it. Was that a knowing male look? What did he mean by "How was Miss Kramer?" The kid was still getting from place to place on a skateboard, for God's sake. "She was fine when I left her."

"Come on! You know what I mean." David moved around Mikal's chair and sat down across from him. "She's not bad looking, is she?"

Mikal turned his mouth down and paused consideringly. "Not bad at all."

"Did you make any bases with her?" David wondered anxiously.

"Bases? You mean as in baseball or air force?"

Mikal's knee got a punch. "Come on, Dad. You know what I mean."

"What kind of bases are you running these days?" David's knee got a return punch.

"It's soccer season."

"Aerobics season, from what I understand."

"Well, yeah. It's good for the respiratory system." David grinned broadly. There was no such thing as a genuine sheepish grin among the Romanov men.

"How come you didn't ask me to buy you a leotard?"

"Geez, you're a tease." It was a rhyme they offered back and forth, and it was always accompanied by another playful punch. "You're not gonna tell me anything, are you?"

"I'll tell you that I had a nice evening and thank you for selling me that ticket."

David nodded, smiling. "Want a sandwich?"

"Sure." Mikal followed David's retreat to the kitchen and shot him another question as an afterthought. "Does Miss Kramer wear a leotard in aerobics class?"

It was a hazy fantasy that danced across Mikal's mind in the days that followed. Morgan Kramer in a leotard. Morgan Kramer—whom he'd seen outfitted only in crisp, high-necked propriety—jumping around to music, sweating and stretching like the exercise fanatics on TV. When David called home to say he'd forgotten his gym shorts and needed them next hour for phys ed, Mikal grinned as he hung up the phone.

David grinned back when he saw his father in the gym lobby. Mikal produced the shorts from the pocket of his jacket, and David snatched them on the run. "Gotta go, Dad. Thanks!"

Mikal watched his son melt into the flow of chattering adolescent traffic in the hallway. One bell sounded, and the halls cleared quickly. Another bell warned the two girls who burst forth from the bathroom that they were late. Mikal smiled, aware of his own impulse to move at the sound of the bell. He figured he'd give her about ten minutes. By then the class should be under way.

An alcove inside the gym gave him the advantage of being able to watch without being readily noticeable. Rock music filled the room to the rafters, and forty kids, mostly girls, followed their instructor's lead, jumping, toe-touching, hustling and hopscotching in time to the music. Her leotard was black, trimmed in pink, and it topped shiny black tights and pink legwarmers, bunched near her ankles. She wore a pink headband, and her hair was caught up in a ponytail that swayed and bounced as she led the group through a routine with her back to the alcove where Mikal stood.

"And it's punch...punch...punch. Now, reach, two, three, four. And punch. Reach it out. Stretch the waist. Stretch the back. And tabletop. Flat back. Knees bent, touch the floor. Grab the ankles, drop the head . . ."

With her head hanging somewhere below her knees, her ponytail sweeping the floor, blood rushing to her brain, and bottom uppermost, she saw him. He smiled and fluttered his fingers at her. Even upside-down, his smile was charming. Morgan missed a beat, but only one. "Nose to knee. Other nose—other *knee*—and roll it up."

Between songs she stopped the tape. "Mr. Romanov, you're welcome to come and join us!"

He gave a quick laugh. "David forgot his gym shorts. I just thought I'd take a peek."

"We love to have parents observe, Mr. Romanov, but we always try to include them in the activity." Extending her hand in invitation, she flashed him a bright smile before turning to her class. "In fact, we insist, don't we?" The chorus of "Yeah, come on!" masked Morgan's mumbled, "You should've picked social studies. You could've gotten away with listing the countries in Africa." She'd already pulled him several feet into the gym.

"But I'm not..." Mikal looked down at the sweats and running shoes that he spent many comfortable hours in and realized that he *was* dressed for this. He rolled his eyes toward the ceiling and shucked his jacket. That got him scattered applause.

"We're just getting started," Morgan said, placing Mikal in the group, front and center. "Do a little of this." She demonstrated a couple of stretches, and he followed suit. "Now go at your own pace. When your pulse rate gets too high, just jog in place."

"*When?*" Mikal figured that the gauntlet had been thrown. "Let's have some music, Miss Kramer."

Mikal was a good dancer, and he was in the habit of running every day, but he found himself flagging as the increased pace had them ponying out of one song and goose-stepping into the next. He noted that Morgan Kramer was, indeed, sweating, but she was smiling, shouting instructions and smiling again. Mikal's side began to ache, but he'd be damned if he'd let her show him up. He took a swipe at the perspiration trickling down his face and smiled back.

Just when he thought they must be finished, the kids ran for a pile of rubberized mats, and the floor exercises began. Mikal did sit-ups and crunches and bicycles until he thought his gut would split, but as long as Morgan kept smiling, he managed to smile back. The fire-hydrant kicks seemed undignified, as did the pelvic lifts. He decided that this woman couldn't count past eight, but she knew one through eight forward and backward, and she counted up and down forever just for practice while he strained his every muscle.

"And it's squeeze, squeeze, squeeze..."

Mikal stifled a groan. If he ever got his arms around her, he would do just that.

"And lift, lift, lift..."

Give me a chance, lady. I can do that, too.

"Make it work. Make it burn. Keep it up."

The woman was indefatigable. Or was she insatiable? He looked up and grinned past the sweat that threatened to stream into his eyes. Again she smiled back, her face bright with mischief, and he decided that she was probably equal parts of both. It might be worth taking the time to find out.

"One more set. And it's *one*-two-three-four-five-six-seven-eight, *two*-two-three . . ."

After the students had cleared the gym, Morgan offered Mikal a towel, which he accepted gratefully. "That's pretty good exercise," he admitted, mopping his face.

"You approve of David's choice, then?"

"Heartily." He flipped the towel over his shoulder and leaned against a wall of bleachers. "And after a workout like that, you should be able to eat as much as you want. How about dinner tonight?"

Morgan looked up, surprised. "Dinner?"

"At my place. I'm a great cook."

"I'm sure you are." Morgan glanced away and shook her head quickly. "I'm afraid I'm busy tonight."

"Tomorrow night, then."

"Um...no. There's a basketball game. I'll have to be here for... Thank you, but I can't."

Mikal considered her face for a moment, searching it for the real reasons. When she didn't offer any, he shrugged and returned her towel. "Some other time maybe. Let me know if you're ever free." He picked up his jacket, slung it over his shoulder and offered his charming smile in parting. "Thanks for the workout."

Morgan had dinner alone that night. In solitude she sipped her after-dinner coffee and read the evening paper. At least, she made an attempt to read it. Nothing sank in.

The silence in the living room was deafening, and the room she'd designed for coziness and comfort suddenly seemed cold. Why had she turned down his invitation? She'd enjoyed herself with him before, and she'd thought about him a great deal since that evening.

Too much. She'd thought about him daily, almost hourly, and that was more than she could handle. He was charming, she reminded herself, and she was being sucked right in by that charm. He was a dreamer, and the world needed a few dreamers to furnish its ideals. The world also needed a good supply of down-to-earth workers to keep its gears moving from one day to the next. Morgan was a worker. She was productive and practical. This dreamer was a distraction, nothing more.

As she turned the page of the newspaper, an advertisement caught Morgan's eye. "Awareness Rally. Freedom International. Twenty-Four Hour Candlelight Vigil." It sounded like something out of the sixties. Aging hippies trying to raise a consciousness that had all but gone to sleep in this day and age. Mikal would be at the forefront, and almost no one would pay any attention. In fact, she couldn't remember there ever having been much interest in Bismarck, except perhaps among the "transplants" from the east. Dakota prairie-dwellers' feet were, much like her own, firmly rooted in prairie sod.

Strangely she felt embarrassed for Mikal. "My dad's weird," David had said, and she wondered if he were embarrassed, too. She remembered the look on David's face when his father had joined the aerobics class, a look of pure delight. She would have expected embarrassment from a thirteen-year-old whose father had appeared in his exercise class, but there was none. "Awareness Rally," she read again, and made a mental note of the time and place.

Chapter Three

The fact that the auditorium was more than half-filled surprised Morgan. Apparently Mikal Romanov the writer was a respectable drawing card. Or perhaps some of the town was more "aware" than she had suspected. She took a chair at the back of the room as she wondered whether dreamers were born as often as the proverbial suckers. She hoped there would always be enough cynics like herself around to keep things on an even keel.

Within moments she had picked up the thread of the speech in progress. A man with a professional bearing was delineating the effects of apartheid in South Africa, punching a finger at the air as he delivered point after point. Passion for his subject and total self-absorption marked the man as a teacher, probably a college professor, Morgan thought.

As she craned her neck to survey the crowd, she recognized several professors from the local college, some clergymen, some young people who were probably students, and a few stray passersby, but she didn't see Mikal. Several people were taking notes, while others sipped coffee from disposable cups, one man clipped his nails, and another read. Some listened with interest, others with ire. Morgan chafed in her chair, not because she didn't agree with the speaker's condemnation of the apartheid system, but because she couldn't share his passion. She jumped in surprise when someone touched her shoulder.

Mikal smiled, enjoying the unguarded expression he'd caught on her face. "Glad you could come," he whispered.

"I can't stay, really. I just..."

"That's okay. You can always come back later. We've got some great speakers, and there are some people here I want you to meet. We've got about eighteen hours to go." He squeezed her shoulder. "See you later."

She watched him make his way to the front of the room as the speaker finished his remarks. Mikal claimed the audience's attention with a few words. The words themselves were not surprising, since he was only introducing another speaker, but the rich depth of his voice, his smooth delivery and the way he commanded the space he occupied drew all eyes and ears. Morgan sensed that she was not alone in her disappointment when another speaker claimed the microphone.

After a talk about an imprisoned Soviet dissident and another on political prisoners in the Middle East, a break was announced. Morgan made her way toward the door.

"Could I interest you in some lunch?"

She turned toward the sound of Mikal's voice and found him standing beside her with a half-eaten sandwich in one hand. He'd shed the sports jacket he'd been wearing and looked more himself in his brown corduroy pants and yellow sweater. Morgan glanced back at the exit door.

"We've got excellent baloney," Mikal said.

"I have no doubt of that." Her plans for the afternoon became insignificant the moment he smiled and beckoned her his way. She followed him into a small anteroom, where an urn of fresh coffee was being brewed. That much, she admitted to herself, was tempting.

The refrigerator in the corner yielded a sandwich, and there were trays piled high with cookies on one of the tables. Morgan took a paper plate and reached for the sandwich, but Mikal raised a teasing eyebrow and cocked his head toward a coffee can labeled Donations Accepted.

"I warned you," Mikal said. "At a rally you're fair game." He held the sandwich in front of her face. "How much is a choice cut of baloney worth to you, Miss Kramer?"

"I have a feeling this is a double-sided coin. Is this your own personal baloney, Mr. Romanov?"

His eyes danced. "Made from my own home-grown bull."

"So that's what I'm about to be fed." Morgan laughed, shaking her head as she fished inside her purse. "What I'm about to *pay* to be fed." She added her money to the coffee can and took the sandwich. "I don't even like baloney."

"You'll like mine."

"Do me one favor?" she asked as she added a brownie to her plate. She glanced his way and added another dollar to the can. "Don't tell me about the starving children who'd give anything for this nutritious baloney sandwich."

"You've seen them for yourself."

The disposable cup was already in her hand. With a sigh, she dipped into her purse again and let him see that she took the last of her cash from her wallet and deposited it in the can before she filled the cup with coffee.

Mikal laughed. "You're too easy."

"Once a missionary's kid, always a missionary's kid." She eyed him over the rim of her cup and saw that he was studying her in a way that made her uneasy. "You're right, of course. I *have* seen them."

"Freedom International isn't about starving children. It's about prisoners and hostages."

"Some people deserve to be imprisoned." Morgan took a seat on the vinyl couch near the refrigerator, and Mikal helped himself to a cup of coffee before joining her.

"After a fair trial and a conviction, some people do. We're talking about people who are imprisoned because they're black or Jewish or the wrong kind of Muslim, or because they disagree with the people in power."

"People like your uncle who was left behind."

"That's right," Mikal agreed, hooking an arm over the back of the couch as he settled in to relax. "People like him. I want you to meet my uncle Yuri." He smiled, and his affection for his uncle glistened in his eyes. "He's quite a character. He's been all over the world, and he has some terrific stories to tell." He cocked his head at another thought. "I'll bet your father has some, too. I'd like to meet him."

"Maybe it's your uncle and my father who should get together," Morgan suggested. "I doubt that I need to be in on any of this. I have no dreams of saving the world."

"You're doing your part. You were pretty intent on saving my kid."

He gave her a look that said he knew more about her than she did, and she swallowed a quick protest. It occurred to her that kids didn't like that look much, either, and she knew she'd used it on them. "I do my job. I'm not unrealistic about it, though. I'm in the business of educating, not saving."

"Semantics." With a wave of his hand, he dismissed the difference. "No one person can save the world, but each of us can play his part to improve the chances of its survival. Yours is with kids. And you're good at it; I know, because I've watched you."

She knew she was being charmed by a professional. Ordinarily she would take exception to being winked at, but when Mikal did it, she smiled and warmed to the compliment. "Will we see how good you are at what you do?" she asked. "I came to hear you speak."

Mikal glanced at his watch. "Stick around, then. I think I'm about out of history professors." He took a small book from the pocket of his jacket, which he left hanging on a coatrack in the corner of the room, then motioned for Morgan to join him.

Morgan headed for the rear of the room but Mikal steered her to the front with a firm hand. From her previous seat in the back she hadn't noticed the table full of large white candles, twenty-four in all. Eight of them were already aflame, and Mikal struck a match to light the ninth one before he went to the podium. He opened the small book and read.

It was poetry—stunning, offered without fanfare, without credits, without explanatory transition between pieces. Morgan had anticipated hearing Mikal's thoughts, or perhaps some anecdotes about his uncle Yuri, who was obviously one of the movement's mentors. Ideas and anecdotes she could contend with, but she didn't like poetry. It was like music; it came too close to getting under her skin. The writer behind the little book in Mikal's hands exposed too much of himself. Morgan resisted the first three poems, listening only with her intellect, but the fourth took hold of something else inside her, something she guarded jealously.

The poem spoke of being touched by harsh hands, and it evoked images of pain, then numbness. It spoke of separation and want of company. Finally it offered the poet's touch, a caring touch to soothe the mind and heal the spirit. "Don't shut me out," the poet entreated in Mikal's gentle voice. "Let me shed my tears upon your feet and dry them with my hair."

And there were more poems. Mikal Romanov, a writer himself, chose to read poetry rather than to speak his own prose. It was effective, Morgan admitted to herself. He chose poems that spoke of the despair found only in isolation and of the human heart's capacity for compassion. She wondered at the man. He appeared to be the image of masculinity, yet there was such softness in his message. What would he know of tears? Was this the most subtle refinement of his charm?

The audience stood to applaud, but Morgan came to her feet more slowly than the rest. When Mikal left the podium, she followed, curious about the small book in his hand. It was the book she followed, really, and when he finally stopped and turned to her, she reached for it without explanation. None was needed, and he handed it to her.

Breath of Freedom. Mikal Romanov. Morgan looked up and found him waiting for her comment. "That was your own poetry?" She studied the book cover again. "I thought you were a novelist."

"I am. At least, that's what I get paid for. I like to think I'm a poet, too, but not for money."

"For what, then?"

"For love." He nodded toward the book in her hand. "Proceeds from the sale of that book go to Freedom International."

Impulsively she drew it to her breast. "Where's the coffee can?"

"The book is yours."

"Oh, no, I want to pay for it."

"You don't have any money left, remember?" He smiled. "You gave all you had, Miss Kramer. That makes you entitled to charity. That book is my charity."

"Thank you." Morgan looked down at the book again, still holding it close. She was glad it wasn't returnable. The word "charity" took on new meaning, making her heart feel light. "So how's it going so far?"

Mikal raised a quizzical brow. "You mean the rally?"

Nodding, Morgan surveyed the auditorium lobby. One man was perusing the literature on a display table, and two women were talking in the far corner of the room. "Does something like this really bring in very much money?"

"The purpose of something like this is to make people aware of the injustices that abound in this world."

Her light heart wanted to giggle at his seriousness. "Really, Mikal, we're sitting in the middle of Bismarck, North Dakota. What have we got to say about what goes on in South Africa or Siberia?"

He loved that question. It was his cue to take her by the elbow, steer her over to the table and shove a fat paperback book into her hands. "We say we don't like it," he insisted. "We say we won't stand for torture or capital punishment, and when somebody gets locked up, somebody else better have a damn good reason—"

"Who's listening to us, Mikal?" Morgan noted that the man who'd been standing at the table was listening, as were the other two women, and she sobered, lowering her voice. "Opening the window and shouting 'I'm mad as hell' doesn't seem to scare the Kremlin."

"You'd be surprised. One voice may not mean much, but you add your voice to mine, and we'll be twice as loud. We write letters by the thousands, and somebody reads them."

He tapped a finger on the book he'd just handed her. "Read this and see how it works."

"Sounds like a lotta pinko bull to me."

Mikal glanced up, and Morgan turned toward the man who'd been sorting through pamphlets at the other end of the table. He was about Mikal's height, perhaps a few years younger, but he carried some extra weight in a belly that hung over his belt like a pouch. He eyed Mikal with dark suspicion.

"I seen you on TV talking about the missile site they want to build. Whose side are you on, anyway?" The man's nose, already red, seemed to darken as his face flushed with angry color. He edged closer to Mikal. "This here's the U.S. of A., and we carry a big stick. I say shoot first and ask questions later." The gum in the man's mouth snapped when he grinned. "What do you say?"

Morgan stepped back involuntarily, but Mikal seemed completely at ease, even offering the man his hand. "Mikal Romanov. I didn't catch your name."

Mikal's hand was ignored. "I didn't give it. I'm here to tell you you sound like a sissy. You want the rest of the country thinkin' we got a bunch of sissies out here in North Dakota? I went to Nam. I did my duty. Did you?"

"I...did my duty, yes. I'm doing it now. Look, maybe we should talk about this—"

Mikal's hand-on-the-shoulder gesture was shrugged off, and the man bristled. "You got something against keeping America strong, mister? What in hell's wrong with you? You look like a man, but you talk like a woman." He poked at Mikal's shoulder with his forefinger, and Morgan stiffened as she watched, her nails digging into her palms. Talk like a woman—was that the ultimate insult? "You're scared of everything, aren't you? Scared of Nam, scared of nukes."

Mikal held his ground as the man experimented with a harder tap. "Scared of me? Huh?"

"I'd be glad to—" The man had no interest in what would make Mikal glad. It was Mikal's hand on his arm that interested him, and that for only a moment before he punched Mikal in the jaw.

Morgan gasped as Mikal stepped back for balance, raising a hand to his cheek. "You good for anything but talk, Mister Peacenik? Huh?"

Mikal dodged a second punch and caught the man's arm on the third try. "You need to cool off, friend," Mikal said quietly as he moved the man toward the door. "Anytime you want to talk, we'll talk, but I won't fight with you."

"Yeah, that's what I thought. Talk's cheap, mister. Take your hands—"

"But fighting's too expensive." Mikal moved the man through the door using, as far as Morgan could tell, nothing more than a hold on his arm. When Mikal returned, he was rubbing his jaw and shaking his head. He caught Morgan's concerned look and gave her half a smile. "Could have been worse. I've got a steel jaw and a glass nose."

"I guess it's a good thing you didn't hit him back, then," she said, craning her neck for a closer look at his jaw.

"Disappointed?" He moved his jaw from side to side a couple of times, and she heard it crack.

"Of course not. Are you okay?"

"I think everything's back in place."

"Aren't you going to call the police?"

"Not unless he comes back." The incredulous look on her face made him laugh. "You're thinking the script should've called for me to take at least one parting shot at him once I got him outside. You like John Wayne movies?"

"Not particularly." Morgan smiled. "I prefer Woody Allen."

"Me, too." But I like your smile even more, he thought. He decided she'd spend this night with him even though they'd have to share it with a cause less sensual than the one that had nagged him ever since he'd first laid eyes on her legs. "I don't suppose you brought your leotard along?"

"My leotard?"

"I've got a job for you."

He touched her, and Morgan lifted her chin, listening. His hand on her shoulder made it impossible for her to do less, and she wasn't inclined to shrug it off. She had a feeling that before the night was over she would learn that once Mikal Romanov had a listener, chances were he had a new sympathizer for the cause.

Morgan wasn't ready to distribute pamphlets, but the job Mikal gave her didn't require any soulsearching. Keeping the participants alert by leading them in a little exercise seemed a small request. A leotard was hardly necessary. Her red blouse was soft and comfortable, and she'd worn loose-fitting slacks. All she asked for was some music and some floor space. It seemed a little silly to start her session by lighting the fifteenth candle, but Mikal insisted that it was part of the tradition. As she led the exercises, she looked to the back of the room and caught him stretching to the right when she'd said left. She smiled when he switched.

He looked up, grinning, and gave her a helpless shrug. So what if he was too tired to remember which side was the left? He'd gotten Morgan Kramer to light a candle.

The numbers had thinned to a few of the hardiest and most dedicated by the wee hours of morning. Morgan told herself she qualified for hardy and dedicated, though not necessarily to this cause. As the crowd diminished in size, the speeches became discussions. Morgan found herself enjoying the people she met and becoming interested in their views. There was even a sing-along. By request, Mikal read more poetry, and Morgan took out her copy of the book and followed his words. She was drawn to his compassion because he spoke of more than the isolation of the physical prisoner. He decried the mental prisons that plagued all human lives.

The end of the vigil came too quickly for Morgan, and when most of the others had left, she sat near the front of the auditorium and watched twenty-four bobbing flames. The first few candles had to be replaced after they'd burned down. Her father had loved to use candles in his churches, and she remembered making them with her mother for Christmas once. It had been a sultry Advent season that year, and all the candles, improperly stored, had melted. She remembered thinking it was too hot to make candles, but Mother had said it wouldn't be Christmas without them.

"What would you usually be doing this early on a Sunday morning?"

Morgan looked up quickly. Mikal lowered himself to the floor and settled, cross-legged, next to her. The mention of regular Sunday activity aroused a deep-seated vestige of guilt in her brain. Years ago she'd risen earlier on Sunday than any other day. "Sleeping," she confessed.

"How about breakfast?"

"I couldn't even scramble a decent egg at this point."

"Neither could I. Let's go catch the sunrise and then find a pancake house," he suggested.

"I'm broke," she reminded him.

Mikal checked his pocket. "I'm not; which just goes to prove that when you give all you have—"

"It turns up in somebody else's pocket."

He shook his head. "You'll be provided for somehow."

"Where's David?" Morgan asked.

"At his Aunt Peg's." He turned his eyes toward the row of candles. "Sleeping. We'll roust him out and take him along."

Morgan nodded, but she said, "It's too soon to roust him yet, though."

"Yes, you're right. Not before sunrise. There's no need to rush."

Mikal waited, wondering what was on her mind. She was a private woman. Hauntingly beautiful, to be sure, but that wasn't what drew him to her. She tried to keep her beauty private. All of it. She bound her feelings as she bound her hair, and Mikal's hands itched to set both of them free.

"How often do you see your uncle Yuri?"

"As often as he can manage," Mikal told her. "Maybe three or four times a year, maybe not even that. I wish it could be more." He let her consider that piece of personal information for a moment and then he asked, "How often do see you see your father?"

"Not often at all. The older he gets, the more desperate he seems about his work. He takes so little time for himself."

"And for you?"

She was quiet for a moment. "I'm a grown woman. A father isn't a crucial factor in my life."

"Anymore," he added for her. "You could visit him. You have free time in the summer."

"He asks me to do that every year." She sighed as she poked her finger into a warm bit of melted wax at the base of a candle. "But he has his children, and I have mine."

"Maybe you're both more desperate about your work as the time passes."

Morgan frowned, considering, and then she shook her head quickly, wondering how she could give such a thought any credence at all. Fatigue, she decided. "I have sensible, attainable goals. There's no reason for me to be desperate."

"I see. Do I seem desperate to you?"

"No," she admitted. The commitment was there, but his demeanor was never anything but casual.

"How about my goals? Do they strike you as sensible and attainable?"

"I guess I don't see how they can be."

"And I guess I think they'd better be or we're all in a lot of trouble." He smiled and shrugged. "But I may not see them realized, not in my lifetime. The man who designed Notre Dame Cathedral didn't see his project finished, either. He knew it would take a hundred years to build, but that didn't stop him from giving it all he had."

"But he was working on something tangible. He could control the mortar and stone, put it where he wanted it, make it amount to something. My father and your uncle—" she looked at him steadily "—and you, Mikal Romanov, you're all off on a canoe trip, and you haven't got a paddle. Even if you make a little headway, the current's bound to shift, and you'll be back where you started. You can't really change anything. You don't have access to the right buttons."

"Do you?"

"I don't claim to be able to push any buttons."

"When David was in trouble, you called me. Didn't you think I was the right button? I can't make David learn, any more than you can. All we can do is try to shed some light on the choices, offer some awareness." Mikal moved closer. He closed his hands over Morgan's arms, his eyes never leaving hers. His voice was a soft, warm sound within the darkened room. "How much control do we have, Morgan? Kids have ideas of their own. Laws change. Governments topple overnight. Mortar cracks."

The candlelight flickered in Mikal's eyes, and Morgan was mesmerized. She struggled for words, any words. "We can control ourselves. We can make our decisions rationally, based on—"

"I've decided to kiss you," he said, lowering his head. "I'll try to do it rationally."

She watched his mouth's slow descent until she felt his breath on her face, and then she let her eyes drift shut. There was no question of turning away, even though some stubborn thing inside her protested as she lifted her chin for the tentative touch of his lips to hers. It was his kiss, his message, his gift to her. He pulled her closer and gave more deeply, and she accepted. By nature he was generous, and she was reserved. It was all she could do at the moment just to accept. His kiss tasted of the promise that he had so much to give to someone who could give in return, and her heart drummed out the words "I can do it," while her brain flashed "Control" in red warning lights.

Mikal could almost hear the argument he knew was going on inside Morgan's head, but her lips felt warm against his and her mouth tasted sweet. It had been years since he'd tasted anything so sweet this early in the morning. She revived him with a quick rush of energy, and he wished he had the power to transport them somewhere else. The hell with being rational. He slid one hand up to her shoulder, then to her neck, folding his fingers around the back of her head to hold her still.

"How's that for rational?" he whispered against her lips.

"Not so good," she managed. "But as kisses go, it was superb."

"It was controlled, believe me." He sat back and smiled. "Raised a little awareness in you, though, didn't it?" She glanced away, and he chuckled. "Raised mine, too. Shall we make a wish and blow out the candles?"

Morgan looked to the twenty-four bright flames, the sole source of light in the dark, empty auditorium. The room was forbidding, except for the warm space she shared with Mikal in the candlelight. Her one wish at that moment was to keep the candles burning.

The sky was beginning to lighten when Mikal pulled the car off the road onto a bluff above a lazy bend in the Missouri River. The sign said that Fort Lincoln State Park was closed for the season, but Mikal wasn't interested in reconstructed blockhouses or earth lodges. He was interested in the painted prairie sky and the reflection of dawn drifting in the water below. Zipping up the jacket he'd taken from the backseat, he opened the door on the passenger's side and reached for Morgan's hand.

"Should we be here?" she asked in a hushed tone. Gravel ground too loudly underfoot, and the slamming of the car door announced their intention to trespass. "The police hang out here—" she lowered her voice quickly as if conspiring to commit some mischief "—waiting for speeders."

"And parkers," he whispered. "But we're neither."

"The car *is* parked . . ." She glanced back over her shoulder as she allowed him to lead her up a grassy hill. Dry leaves crackled under her shoes.

"We're not in it." He picked up his pace once they reached higher ground. "So we're not parkers. Am I going too fast for you?"

"Not at all," she said as she doubled her steps to keep up with his long-legged stride. Heavens, yes, he was going too fast for her, but she seemed to be moving at the same pace.

"Then we're not speeders."

"But the park is closed," she whispered. "I don't think we're supposed to . . ." Her step never faltered as she followed his lead.

"There's a spot over here, just beyond the buffalo berry bushes."

A fine, white mist hugged the riverbanks as night receded and soft light claimed the jagged horizon. Morgan stood beside Mikal, their breath shooting out in small, white puffs into the vastness of a high-plains morning while they drank deeply of pine-scented air. The river reflected the pink-and-orange sky and made it ripple and shimmer in late fall's last hurrah. In the distance stood barren buttes, deep purple shadows against the expectant sky. Off to the right the river stretched southward, its tree-lined banks cutting a ribbon of contrasts through the grassland. The city lay to the left, lights blinking. In those fragile moments, soft blue haze sifted through the valley like powder. Then crimson cracks widened in the sky and its seams were split by the rays of the rising sun.

Morgan shivered, and Mikal put his arm around her shoulders. She felt tucked-in and cozy, and she slipped her hand beneath his jacket and held him at the waist. "I don't feel like I'm trespassing," she said quietly.

He smiled as he unzipped his jacket. "You aren't. In fact—" he took her hands and slid them under his jacket, directing them around his back "—if your hands are cold, come inside and let me warm them for you."

She spread her fingers and felt the cabled pattern of his sweater. She wanted time to count the cotton stitches under her palms. "It's beautiful here, Mikal."

Gone was the coolness he'd once seen in those hazel eyes. Gold and green glinted in them now, the two shades rivaling one another for dominance like precious gems in neighboring settings. Dazzled, he closed his eyes and pulled her close, tucking her shoulders under his arms and laying his cheek against her hair. "Stay as long as you like," he murmured.

"I mean..." She couldn't let herself say what she meant. The warmth of his body was beautiful, and the intimacy of sharing the space inside his jacket was beautiful, and it would take her hours to count the stitches and memorize the heady scent of his skin. "I mean this spot. But it might be embarrassing if someone catches us here."

"I'll keep a lookout," he promised.

"Perfect place for a lookout," she observed, burying her nose in his jacket's pile lining.

"That's what the Mandan Indians said when they were packing the dirt over log frames to make their lodges here."

"And probably what the soldiers said when they put up their blockhouses."

He could see for miles, and he knew that if he climbed to the top of the hill that stood at his back, he could see forever. High places gave him a sense of power, and holding this woman in his arms put the depths of his feelings in touch with the height of his strength. He sensed that others had been here before him, holding their women, watching the hills change color and relishing the vitality of it all.

"The soldiers had it tough here," he mused. "Of course, Custer and the other officers had their wives with them, but the ordinary soldiers..." He looked across the river at a place where the traders might have peddled their rotgut whiskey. "They'd cross the river and get drunk to try to ward off the loneliness. Sometimes they drowned trying to get back, or they died of alcohol poisoning."

Morgan glanced up, then followed his gaze to the mist-shrouded trees across the river. "I don't suppose there was much for them to do besides watch and wait."

"And listen to the wind," he said. "It's good to keep busy when you're..." He caught himself as he'd learned to do whenever he felt melancholy, and he put those thoughts aside. He was in touch with life and the strength of the hills and Morgan. Her dark brown hair was smooth and soft, pinned to the back of her head and glistening with hints of naughty red in the early-morning sun. "It's good to be here with you," he told her, and he lifted his hands to the back of her head.

"Mikal..." she whispered quickly. But she didn't move away. She felt secure with her hair in its coil, but there was a coil in her stomach, too. It relaxed a notch each time he spoke, each time he touched her.

"Let me," he insisted. "It's morning; time to comb it out. Let me do that." He used his fingers, and the long, brown hair slipped through them like water—soft and cool. His breath caught in his chest, and he kissed her hard, her hair clutched in his hands.

Her lips trembled when he released them. Her breath came quickly; her eyes were closed. "We should go before..."

"Yes," he assured her, touching her cheek. "We have to get back."

David wished his dad would go away and let him sleep. He and his uncle Bill had been up half the night working on the computer. Dad was always hyped up after an all-night rally, and he always wanted to talk. David wanted to rest. He wanted to scrunch down deep and wallow in the luxury of sleeping in. He wasn't interested in food, either. He wasn't interested in...

"Miss Kramer?" David lowered the covers from his face. "What was she doing there?"

"Just curious, I guess. But she got hooked. You and I are taking her out to breakfast."

"Hooked? Miss Kramer?" David braced himself on his elbows as his jeans landed across his legs.

"Well, she stayed to the end. I'd say that was hooked. Wouldn't you?"

"I'd say she might be interested, but I wouldn't count on her being hooked already. She's pretty cagey." David swung his feet over the side of the bed and reached for his jeans. He knew darn well they were talking about two different interests and two different kinds of "hooked," but that wasn't important. What *was* important was that... "Is she here now?"

"She's downstairs talking to Aunt Peg." Mikal sat on the bed and braced his palms on his knees. "What do you mean by cagey?"

"Well, you know—pretty sharp. Like you can't put anything over on her." As he zipped his jeans, David took a quick survey of his father's yellow pullover and cords. "Don't you have anything better than that to wear?"

Mikal had to look down to remember what he'd put on almost a day and a half earlier. "What's wrong with this? It's comfortable."

David picked up a comb and answered Mikal's reflection in the mirror. "That's the problem, Dad. You look too comfortable. Adults are supposed to look starched. You know what I mean?"

David's shirt, hanging neatly over the back of a chair, caught Mikal's eye and he nodded thoughtfully. Peg had undoubtedly ironed the shirt and put it there for him the night before. At home David was responsible for his own laundry, and he often did Mikal's, as well. "I know what you mean. But I'm not starched, and I doubt if I can convince Miss Kramer that I am." He smiled. "What with her being so cagey and all."

"I guess not." He tossed the comb, then grinned when Mikal caught it. "Maybe she'd settle for neat and clean."

"Maybe she would."

Chapter Four

He marked the days on the wall
small scratches in gray cement
The man who had warned the world
the voice of the voiceless
Alone, undernourished, he could have survived
The cold, the damp, the lash could not kill him
But for want of paper and pencil
He starved

Morgan closed the book and set it aside. Not satisfied, she tossed a magazine over it and picked up the newspaper. It had been days since she'd read the paper thoroughly. She was shirking her duty to keep herself informed, and all because of that little book. She'd read it and reread it, but it kept drawing her again. She had to get back on track.

"Diplomat Disappears in Middle East." "Senate Debates Arms Sale." "Assassination in Latin America." "Unrest on the Island of De Colores." De Colores? Her father was there. How could there be unrest on an island paradise? Why not? Morgan asked herself, flipping to another page. There was trouble everywhere else. Trouble in Bismarck. "School Board Divided Over Building Proposal." Morgan sighed, turning the page again. She'd be in an overcrowded building forever. "Dow Jones Up." Sure. Somebody was making money on all this misery.

Somebody was... Morgan closed the newspaper. She had to be careful. She was even beginning to think like Mikal. Not that she *disagreed* with him, but passive agreement on distant issues was enough. It was the school board's decision that affected her. Those other things were just food for thought. Active agreement with Mikal could mean...action. And to what end? Mikal hadn't published anything in five years. He was totally impractical.

He was disturbing. His poetry had become a fixation for her. He knew people's minds. He knew the imprisoned dissident who died because he couldn't write. He knew the exile, the refugee, the immigrant. And he knew loneliness. He'd called her once since the rally and invited her to dinner, but she'd been busy so the invitation had been left open. She wondered if he was aware of her loneliness. She regarded it as a private matter, but he knew people's minds, and it disturbed Morgan that he might know hers.

There was absolutely nothing in the refrigerator worth eating, and there was absolutely no restaurant in town worth going to tonight. Morgan's stomach was empty. She was actually hungry, and she had an open invitation for dinner. She called Mikal.

"Come on in. We'll put you to work." Mikal's once-white butcher apron hung from his neck like a knee-length bib, covering jeans and a fisherman's-knit sweater. Morgan handed him her coat and checked her watch. "We started without you, but we're not very far along. Find a place for this, David.''

She watched her coat go from hand to hand, returned David's greeting, then checked her watch again. She was on time. ''Started without me?''

''We're working on the crepes.'' Mikal took another apron from a drawer, shook it out and draped it over Morgan's head. ''You haven't missed much.'' Turning her around by the shoulders, he leaned close to her ear, chuckling while he tied the apron around her waist. ''You weren't expecting to be waited on, were you?''

''I expected to get here in time for the first course.''

''You did. Would I deny you the best part of a meal?''

''Dessert?''

''Preparation! You want to know what you're eating, don't you?''

Morgan sniffed the air, which was tangy with the smell of tomato sauce and Italian sausage. It was a smell that went with the kitchen, which was traditional in design and functional in decor. Gleaming copper-bottomed pots and pans were suspended from a rack in the middle of the room, and there was a wooden chopping block, along with crockery and a wide variety of utensils. Individually potted herbs grew in the windowsill. ''Spaghetti?''

''Cannelloni. I was sure you wouldn't want to miss flipping the crepes.''

Frowning, she thought for a moment. ''I don't think I've ever flipped a crepe. But I warn you, I can't turn an egg without breaking the yolk.''

''Aha! Raw material,'' Mikal exclaimed, rolling the words with an unidentifiable foreign accent. With one arm he guided Morgan toward the stove while he gestured flamboyantly with the other. ''A pupil to be molded like a soft piece of dough, shaped to my specifications. 'Tis a consummation devoutly to be wished.''

"Your wish may be very different after you see what I can do to a pancake." The batter caught her eye, and she took the spoon out of it and watched the thin stuff drip back into the bowl.

Mikal caught her hand. "*Crepes,* not pancakes. Don't tease the batter. See how you make it cry?"

"I think we have a serious case of infantile personification here." Smiling, she laid the back of her hand on his forehead. "Any other symptoms?"

"Fever?"

"I can feel a twinge, yes," she decided.

"This could ruin my career. Any suggestions?"

"Bite your tongue when you feel another bout coming on."

"The cure could ruin me, as well. On with the crepes?"

"On with the crepes. What's my assignment?"

"Observe, my dear pupil. Let there be fire." Gas flames leaped to life under the crepe pan's round bottom.

"And there was fire," Morgan observed.

David rounded the corner of the island counter and peered past Mikal's shoulder into the pan. "You're in for a treat, Miss Kramer. Dad could turn the soles of your shoes into something delicious."

Without looking up from stirring the batter, Mikal muttered, "Don't give away the chef's secrets."

"I think I *do* want to know what I'm eating."

"Pay no attention to the kid. I haven't done fillet of sole since I got my first book advance."

"No, but you've done leg of frog and arm of octopus," David put in. "Mrs. Kopeke called a while ago and wondered if something was burning up here and why it didn't smell like steak, since it sounds like we have company."

Mikal rolled his eyes toward the ceiling and gave a good-natured chuckle. "Mrs. Kopeke lives in our basement apartment," he told Morgan. "And we're not having steak because it's no challenge. Miss Kramer needs to learn to flip crepes."

"You don't flip crepes?" David asked seriously.

"Uh, no, I haven't..."

"You see, David? This kind of deprivation is rampant, even in our own city. Pancakes. That's all they know." Morgan searched for a comeback, but Mikal dismissed the attempt with "We're here to help you, Miss Kramer. Watch carefully."

He used a crepe pan as deftly as most men used a razor. One flick of the wrist and the pan was coated with batter. Another flick of the spatula and the crepe was turned perfectly. A final flick and it was out of the pan. Morgan tried to repeat the process, but with less success. Mikal coaxed her to try again, and she improved with practice. She knew she could never match his dexterity with a chopping knife, and she marveled that nothing was measured before it went into his bowls.

"And now for the sauce béchamel."

Morgan watched Mikal whisk flour and butter together and thought of the many times she'd burned food at this stage. She leaned toward David and put a hand on his shoulder. "I have no idea what he's talking about. Are we on camera? Is this really the 'Galloping Gourmet'?"

David laughed. "Galloping is good. That fits. I thought you adults all spoke the same language."

"I speak pretty good *Franco American*. What's sauce béchamel?"

"A little salt...and a pinch of fresh nutmeg." It was not an answer to her question; Mikal was talking to himself—or possibly to his sauce. He tasted. "Perfect."

"How do you keep from getting fat?" Morgan wondered aloud.

"When I'm cooking for four, I make just four servings."

"Four?"

"Mrs. Kopeke," David explained. "Dad's afraid she'll waste away if he doesn't feed her."

"People who live alone don't usually cook for themselves. They start getting—" Mikal glanced at Morgan's small waist "—perilously thin."

"Really?" Morgan's hand went to her flat stomach, and it answered with a growl.

"I think she's perilously hungry, Dad."

Mikal stuck a homemade breadstick in her mouth and invited her to help him stuff crepes. David took care of the table, and when all was ready, he skipped down the stairs with a plate for Mrs. Kopeke.

"What's this stuff?" she was heard to say.

"Cannelloni, Mrs. Kopeke. It's Italian."

"Doesn't he ever make anything Polish?"

"Not if I'm trying to impress somebody," Mikal muttered as he uncorked a bottle of Chianti.

The dry, thin voice at the foot of the stairs ended with, "Well, all right, I guess I can *try* it."

A door closed and David scampered up the steps. "She's gonna *try* it, Dad." The look that passed between them said this was a ritual they both enjoyed.

Morgan was impressed. Mikal was an artist with food, and the meal was an aesthetic experience. It was something to be savored slowly. "I think *I* would get fat if I ate this way all the time."

"We don't eat this way *all* the time," David said. "Dad makes good sandwiches, too."

"So do you." With obvious satisfaction, Mikal reported, "He's coming along. He makes an excellent hamburger and downright decent pizza."

"You'll be hard-pressed to find a wife who can compete with your father in the kitchen, David," Morgan said as she lifted her wineglass.

"He won't have to. He'll learn to cook the way he wants to eat." Morgan didn't miss the eyebrow Mikal raised in challenge. "Who says the woman has to excel in the kitchen?"

"Certainly not I," Morgan said with a smile.

They heard the door at the foot of the basement steps rattle, then open. "Here's your plate," Mrs. Kopeke shouted from the bottom of the stairs.

David rolled his eyes. "I'll get it," Mikal said as he pushed his chair back from the table. "You start stacking the dishes. I've got plans for Miss Kramer."

"I figured as much," Morgan groaned over her last sip of wine. "If David stacks, I'll wash, and we'll give the cook a break."

"Not dishes. Dancing," Mikal corrected over his shoulder on his way down the stairs. "Did you enjoy that, Mrs. Kopeke?"

"I don't know," the crackling voice replied slowly. "Can't really taste much anymore. Seemed like a funny way to fix pancakes."

"Those were crepes, Mrs. Kopeke, and I'm glad you liked them. How's Oscar?"

Morgan missed the reply because David was filling her in on the facts. "Oscar's a goldfish. Dad just finished wallpapering the kitchen downstairs to cheer Oscar up after Pearl died. Pearl was another goldfish."

"When does your father write?"

"When most people are sleeping. Didn't I tell you he's a saint?" Playing up his father's sainthood seemed to David to be a good idea. Someone like Miss Kramer would be impressed, maybe enough to overlook the obvious...eccentricities. Yes, eccentric sounded better than weird.

Morgan had the dishes organized into neat groups by the time Mikal came back upstairs. "Everything's under control, Mikal, although I should point out that you've used all the bowls and spoons in the place."

"Not possible," David replied. He was letting his nightly chore slip out of his hands, figuring that if Miss Kramer *wanted* to do the dishes, he was in no position to stop her. "We've got every kind of bowl, spoon and pan imaginable."

Mikal stopped in his tracks. "You're letting a guest clean up, David? Your great-grandmother would twist your ears into pretzels." He turned to Morgan. "I said dancing, not dishes."

"Dancing?"

"I want to bob with you, baby." He demonstrated a couple of steps and finally had Morgan laughing.

"If you're talking about the Ray Durkee dance, I heard it's sold out." The disc jockey's annual dance was always well-attended, but Morgan had never found the time to go.

"Ah, but I have tickets. Two." He flashed the number with his fingers.

"You had plans..."

"I had a premonition," he corrected, taking the dish towel from her hand and laying it over David's shoulder. "Is that your best sock-hop outfit? You have to dress the part for Durkee's oldies show."

Morgan reached back to untie the apron she was wearing over a slim charcoal-gray skirt and red blouse. "It's as close as I can get. I wasn't planning—"

"Good! Not planning makes it even better. I'll be ready in two minutes." Backing away, he considered her outfit once more. "I can get closer."

"Closer to what?" Morgan tried, but he had already disappeared down the hallway. At her back she heard a tentative throat-clearing.

"Uh, Miss Kramer...there must be a hundred ways to be weird—I mean *eccentric*—and I think my dad knows them all. He only practices the harmless ones, of course." He shrugged apologetically. "Embarrassing sometimes, but always harmless."

"Maybe it's because he's an artist," Morgan offered, thinking that that excuse didn't give her much comfort. She'd known an artist once before.

"Maybe."

When Mikal came out again he was outfitted as a tall, broad-shouldered version of James Dean. Morgan stifled what threatened to be an adolescent giggle, and he gave her a slow grin. His hair was several shades darker and slicked back in a pompadour. His jeans fit tighter, and his gum popped as he chewed. "Course you realize, this ain't my era, but it's the one I do best. I'm a rebel at heart."

"But *with* a cause." She was close enough to smell the oil in his hair, and she shook her head and laughed.

"Several. One of them is showing you a good time tonight. Ever been to a Durkee dance?" She shook her head again. "Sure you don't want to change clothes?"

"I have absolutely nothing..."

He patted the back of one of the kitchen chairs. "Sit right down here, ma'am. Ain't *nobody* ain't got absolutely *nothin'.*"

"That's a double negative." Morgan sat down, realizing that he was doing it again—charming her into doing something crazy.

"Quadruple negative. I think I have a positive there. Got a brush in your purse?" She nodded. "David, where did you put Miss Kramer's purse?"

"I'll get it," David offered, tossing the dish towel aside.

"Have you got a pair of clean white socks, too? And some of that red lipstick you used for that skit you did?" He slid a hairpin from Morgan's upswept hairdo. "Do you mind?"

"Since the answer seems to be no, I now ought to have my head examined."

Mikal smiled at the pleasure he felt in running his fingers through her hair. "I can do that for you while I'm at it. Looks good so far."

As David handed over her purse, she assured him, "You were right the first time. He's weird." But she handed Mikal the brush as though she were in the habit of having her hair styled in his kitchen.

Minutes later he directed her to a full-length mirror, and she stood there in amazement. He'd given her a ponytail, rolled her sleeves just above her elbows, opened the neck of her blouse and added a scarf, and put white socks with her red flats. Then he handed her a tube of lipstick called "Cherries in the Snow." She couldn't resist swishing her ponytail just once before she painted her lips bright red. When Mikal stepped up to the mirror beside her, they both laughed. Then they straightened their faces, looked at one another and laughed even harder. The principal and the poet were going out for the evening.

Nationally syndicated disc jockey Ray Durkee held an annual oldies dance in Bismarck as a benefit for the Association for Retarded Citizens, and Mikal had tickets in support of the cause. The idea of taking Morgan had occurred to him when she'd called to invite herself to his house for dinner, but he'd decided to spring it on her only after he'd plied her with good food and fairly good wine. He knew she was tempted to have fun once in a while, and he'd planned to make the fun start happening before she had time to think about it.

In her "silly outfit" Morgan was free of her staid image. Out on the dance floor she saw people she knew—parents, teachers, her hairdresser, and the couple who lived next door—and she waved gaily. Tonight she was just Morgan. Ray Durkee asked "Remember this one?" and played a vaguely familiar tune. Her feet began to move and soon she was doing steps she thought she'd forgotten long ago. She danced until her blouse stuck to her back and her feet ached from pounding against the cement floor. It was finally Mikal who begged for mercy, and because the disc jockey was taking a break, too, Morgan agreed to sit down.

"I think I've created a monster," Mikal grumbled as they made their way to the end of a long table and reclaimed their folding chairs. "Once you get going, you're unstoppable."

"Making me up to look like the queen of the hop does not make you my creator, Mr. Romanov. This is just another aerobics workout for me." Under the table Morgan slipped her shoes off and flexed her aching toes.

"Not having any fun?" He raised a mocking eyebrow. "I can get you another drink."

She shook her head. "I don't need another drink, and of course I'm having fun. I love a good workout."

"You love to dance. Admit it."

"I love to dance." Her eyes brightened as she smiled with the admission. "And I love dancing with a man who dances well, and you do, so I love dancing with you. But I haven't danced like *this* in years. I feel like a kid!''

The smile he returned held none of the innocence of hers. He leaned closer. "Great. What do you say we go out in the parking lot and neck?''

It was a joke, of course, but the familiar way he laid his arm along the back of her chair and teased her shoulder with his thumb made her shimmy on the inside just as she had on the outside while she was dancing. "If you didn't look like such a hood, I might consider it.''

"A hood? Is that better or worse than a hippie?''

"They're probably about even.'' She lifted her hand toward a lock of hair that had fallen over his forehead Presley-style. The look he gave her drew her to touch it, but the hair refused to stay where she placed it. "Which do you prefer?''

He lifted one shoulder. "One label's about as bad as the next. How do you like yuppie?''

"Would you call me that?'' she asked, uneasy with the term.

"I'd call you Morgan.'' His hand curved comfortably around her arm. "And whether you're wearing your hair this way, or all bound up at the back of your head—'' he tilted his head a little to one side, imagining ''—or maybe soft and free, the way it was the other morning, I'd call you a friend of mine. Morgan.'' The name was spoken as a special word. "Let's go for a walk.''

It was a brisk November night, and the city lights dimmed the stars' brightness. They had only to drive a short distance from town to enjoy the clear, starry sky, but neither suggested it. The crisp air felt good, Morgan thought. It cleared the head and made it seem unwise to pay undue attention to things like stars. Stars, like hair, could get to be sticky subjects.

"Do you smell smoke?"

"Smoke?" Morgan stopped, glancing around quickly.

"I could have sworn you were headed for a fire somewhere. I thought we were going for a walk." Mikal shoved his hands in his pockets and rocked back on the heels of his loafers. "What's it going to be?"

"Just a walk. I'll try to slow down."

He chuckled. "You might as well. Nobody's chasing you." Morgan looked up at him, and he laughed as he put his arm around her shoulders and slowed the pace. "Not that you aren't worth chasing. It's just that I don't think there's any chance of catching you on the run."

"What's that supposed to mean?"

"Every time I ask you out, you shy away. I have better luck if I just plant an idea in your head and wait around until it germinates."

"I don't shy away," Morgan objected, disliking the vision the words suggested of some shrinking violet. "I'm not shy."

"In some ways you are. We make each other nervous." He looked down at her and smiled. "It's kind of a good feeling, isn't it? Kind of anxious and tingly. I haven't felt that kind of nervous in a long time."

They walked in step together, hips nearly touching, as she told herself to relax under his arm so he'd have no reason to be so direct. Their footsteps echoed in the quiet of the night. "Your wife died, didn't she? How long ago?"

"Ten years."

"What happened?" She asked the question gently because she knew the passage of time didn't necessarily mean anything.

"She had leukemia." The words came in a spiritless monotone, filled with a terrible resignation Morgan had never heard before in anything Mikal said. "She was twenty-five."

"And David was only three. What a tragic loss for both of you."

"Yes." He spoke quietly, as though there was something in the night surrounding them that might be disturbed. "I loved her. I might have gone with her if it hadn't been for David." There was a pause. "And for my uncle Yuri."

"Gone with her?"

"In a sense. Not literally, of course, but I didn't want to feel anything anymore. I wanted to stay numb."

"I remember feeling that way when I lost my mother." It hadn't been that long ago, and it was still difficult to use the word "died."

"I didn't lose *her,* really, I just lost out on some time I'd counted on spending with her. At first I wouldn't let it hurt. I told myself to forget and go on with my life. But that didn't work." They had come to an empty parking lot and made a tacit agreement to turn around. Mikal hesitated, and Morgan looked up. "I had to feel the pain and then let it ease up gradually. I had to let her have a piece of my heart, a place where I could carry her comfortably.

"I think you lose somebody when you push them out of your heart, Morgan." He saw that she hadn't made the leap with him yet, from his memories to hers. "Your pride tells you not to give them another chance even though your heart's saving that place for them. Whether they're alive or dead, you'll never be comfortable with that."

Morgan was surprised. He was talking about... "My father?" He nodded. "I haven't pushed him away," she insisted.

"You refuse to see him."

"I don't *refuse* to see him; I just won't go traipsing off to Timbuktu to do it. I saw him...well, I suppose it's been...no more than four or five years."

"Timbuktu's in Africa," he pointed out. "I'd say you were due for a trip to the Caribbean."

She stared at him for a moment. It was true that he made her nervous. Shadows from the streetlights flickered over his face. He looked the part of the brooding rebel, but if this man had been a travel agent, he probably could have sold her a ticket. But she told herself that she didn't want a ticket. "I'd say I'm due for another dance."

They danced until the last record was played. Morgan had left her car at Mikal's house, and he insisted on making coffee for her before she went home. Though hers was always adequate, she had a feeling his would be excellent, and she wasn't disappointed.

"Where's David?" she asked, following Mikal into the living room. He reached under the shade of a table lamp and clicked on the switch. It was a comfortable room, one that looked as though someone had put it together years ago and it had been lived in ever since. Overstuffed furniture and overstocked bookcases dominated the area.

"He stays at Peg's when I go out for an evening. She's helped us out a lot since Sharon died. She was Sharon's big sister, and then she became mine." He joined her on the sofa. "How's the coffee?"

After another sip she said, "I think it's the best I've ever tasted. You have a secret?"

"Umm-hmm." He smiled, his eyes twinkling. "Lots of them. I don't give them out, because they only work for me."

"What is it? Eggshells? Some kind of spice?" She sipped again and concentrated on the flavor. "I think I taste some spice."

"Magic."

"Come on," she urged. "It isn't cinnamon. It must be..."

He gave an exaggerated sigh. "Believe and enjoy, Morgan Kramer. Magic is a spice that can't be bought or measured."

"Neither can your recipe for cannelloni. Nothing was measured. I don't suppose you could give out a recipe even if you wanted to."

"It's my own magic. What can I tell you?" There was little pretense of modesty in his clear blue eyes. "I can't do much with a hammer and saw, or anything worth a damn under the hood of a car, but in the kitchen I can do no wrong."

Morgan set her cup aside and reached back to take her hair down. "I like your poetry, too," she said, hoping it sounded like no more than a casual compliment. *Like* was hardly an adequate description of the way she felt about his little book.

"You've read it, then?"

She nodded. "Do you have any more?"

"One other volume in print, and sheaves of it that haven't been published. I write poetry when I need to laugh or cry or make a fool of myself over something that seems like a big deal at the time. I sweat over prose, but poetry seems to tumble out of me. I always feel good after I've gotten it out, like I've just done a triple somersault on the trapeze."

"Reading it makes me... feel things, too."

He watched her comb her fingers through the dark thickness of her hair. "What kind of things?"

"The things you express," she said as she unrolled one of her sleeves. "Joy, sorrow. Of course, they're really *your* feelings, but they're expressed in such... well, I can't help but... sympathize."

"I liked the way you said it first." He caught the hand that was fumbling with the buttons on her cuff and fastened them himself as he watched her face. "That it made you feel things. I like that better than 'sympathize.'" He slid his hands down her other arm, unfolding her sleeve as he went. "I like your hair like this, too."

She gave a small, nervous laugh. "Men always seem to like that windblown look."

"Do they?" She didn't object when he lifted one of her feet, slipped her shoe off and slowly peeled away the white sock. "Have you taken a survey?"

"No. The women's magazines do that for us." His fingers skimmed her stockinged foot as he put her shoe back on, and her stomach tightened. "As if we cared."

He switched his attentions to her other foot, but his eyes never left her face. "You have beautiful hair. I had a poet's fantasy about taking the pins out and letting it fall into my hands."

"And what's the difference between a poet's fantasy and any other man's?"

"A poet fantasizes metaphorically. 'Shall I compare thee to a summer's day?'" He dropped the second sock on the floor beside its mate and lowered her foot.

"My hair?" A good, quick comeback escaped her. He was sitting so close to her, and her feet still tingled where he'd touched them.

"I could start there." He touched the smooth hair at her temple and saw that her eyelids lowered just slightly.

"I think you did," she said, struggling to keep the words coming as his hands went to the knot in the scarf around her neck. "Then you went to my feet. What would you compare them to?"

"I don't usually do feet metaphorically." When the scarf was undone he used it, one end in each hand, to draw her to him. "I like to do lips."

Morgan had no thought of avoiding his kiss, but the greediness of it surprised her. He opened his mouth over hers and tasted her with a fiery need. She reached for him instinctively, arms winding around his neck, inhaling the scent of his hair. She grew warm, and her pulse shifted into fast-dance gear; the scarf tightened at the back of her neck as his thumbs caressed her jaw and he slanted his mouth to demand her response from a different angle.

Long-buried need welled up in him. Here was a woman he wanted to give to, and when he had given, he would want to give more. He would take her hair down again and make her comfortable with her femininity, make her feel how beautiful she was. Breathless, he laid his forehead against hers and whispered the word. "Beautiful."

"Like what?" she asked, her eyes still closed.

"Fruit ripening in the warm summer sun."

"What kind?"

He tasted again, sipping gently this time, touching her lower lip with the tip of his tongue. "Peaches," he decided. "Sweet. My favorite."

"I would have said raspberries for you," she whispered, and brushed her lips against his. "Tangy. *My* favorite."

"We should have lunch sometime." He returned her soft kiss, then planted another on her chin.

"We're not in season."

"That might be what makes us taste so good to each other. It's been a while since summer."

The truth of his statement hit her hard. He rose above her, another kiss in his eyes, and she drew back. She'd had her summer with a charming dreamer, and she knew it was a short season. "That's true," she said. "It's been a long time."

"Did the metaphor go sour?"

"No." She smiled, not completely uncomfortable with the effectiveness of his charm. "It's lovely, and I'm flattered."

"You're more than flattered," he said quietly.

She nodded and allowed herself an unsteady sigh. "I'm more than flattered. That's how I know it's time for me to go home. We can dress up and pretend for a while but, let's face it, we're not two teenagers necking on the sofa."

"Uh-uh. We're not."

She moved back on the seat, and his arm slid away from her. "Which means games are not in order. It's either friends or lovers."

"Why not both?"

"Because it wouldn't work." She rose to her feet as though convinced, but somewhere in the back of her mind she knew she wasn't. There was an obstinate part of her that didn't want to be. "I like being friends with you, though. You're a good dancer and a fantastic cook."

Mikal settled back on the sofa, giving her a slow, self-satisfied grin. "And you're still nervous. You're even a little scared."

"Maybe that's the only smart way for me to be. Thanks for the evening." She gave him an apologetic smile and turned toward the door. "Good night, Mikal."

"Good night," he called after her as the door closed behind her. He stared at the coffee she'd left behind and listened to the roar of her car engine as she fed it too much gas. "If you were so smart, Morgan Kramer, you'd realize there's only one thing that won't work with us. And that, my lady, is *just* being friends."

Chapter Five

Can I love someone else after loving you?

He'd thought it might be the beginning of something when he'd first written the line, but all it did was repeat itself, both in his mind and on the paper. Many of his poems were questions that required no answers, but this wasn't one of those. This question definitely needed an answer.

Mikal rarely discussed his wife anymore, except when David asked about her. The memories were all good ones now, and the pain was little more than a dull ache. He hadn't led a celibate life in the ten years since her death, but he'd loved no other woman. He told himself there'd been no time for that. Sharon was still with him in so many ways that he'd been able to convince himself that nothing was really missing. He was a passionate man, but he had many outlets for his passion. His writing was a testimony to that. And his life was filled with love—love for his son, for those who worked with him and shared his beliefs, for Peg and for

Yuri. He hadn't been looking for a close relationship with a woman.

Now there was Morgan. So many pictures of her came to his mind at once. There was the school principal, dressed for business, letting him know that she was concerned about his son, but that she would tolerate no more of the boy's nonsense. Then there was the exercise instructor, dressed in a leotard and convincing a gym full of preteens that working up a sweat was truly fun. Mikal smiled to himself as he remembered Morgan's story and pictured the prim and studious lady finding she'd finally built a muscle and secretly crowing at the accomplishment.

She'd come to his house as the proper dinner guest, but she'd willingly put on an apron and started cooking. She'd gone to a rally with the intention of listening to what he had to say, and she'd accepted a role in that, too. She was more flexible than she realized. He'd turned her classic outfit into a fifties costume, and she'd taken the cue, nearly dancing him under the table. And on the hill above the Missouri River, with the morning sky painting streaks all around them, she'd let him take her hair down. *That* was the image he treasured. That was the one haunting him day and night. He'd made it happen again after the dance, and he remembered how she'd looked then—relaxed, her hazel eyes soft and sleepy. She'd let her hair fall loosely around her shoulders, and her mouth had been berry-stained with the remnants of "Cherries in the Snow." She'd lifted her face to him, and he could still taste that kiss.

Mikal needed a good swift kick in the pants. His typewriter hummed, and the words, "Can I love someone else after loving you?" stared up at him. With an inaudible growl, he ripped the paper from the machine, wadded it in his fist and pitched it toward the wastepaper basket.

"Of course I can," he told the typewriter as though it had posed the question. "If I want to love somebody, I'll love somebody. Just as soon as I have the time. I have a book to finish first, and I have to. . ."

He tapped his fingers lightly against the keys, not typing, just thinking. He was well into the middle of this book. He knew when his work was good, and this was. *A Free Country* was better than *The Last Barnraising*. It was a refugee's story. The main character was a composite of a number of people he'd come to know through his work with Freedom International, people whom Uncle Yuri called "freedom seekers." Mikal knew that this would be an important book, that it was timely, and that Americans were ready to read it. He just had to write it.

He heard the phone ring, and he pushed his chair back, mumbling an expression he wouldn't want his son to hear him use. Apparently David had picked up the phone, though, so maybe he *had* heard it. When Mikal wasn't called within a few seconds, he rolled his chair back under his desk and set his fingers on the typewriter keys again. If he weren't so damned disorganized, he thought, he'd get more done.

Get organized, then, he told himself. You have so many hours for writing, so many for David, so many for consciousness-raising, and if you want to see Morgan, you have to plan for that, too. Right now, you're writing. Mikal tilted his head back and laughed at his own delusion. Above his desk was a bulletin board with notes to himself, some of them a year old. He'd tried. He'd had this conversation with himself before. David had given him an appointment book, which he'd never used. It was full of square blocks of time, and Mikal couldn't fit the flow of his life into square blocks of time. *Always* there was David, and *always* his writing, and *always* the things he believed in.

And now, too, there was Morgan. God help him, she was not going to go away. In fact, he didn't want her to. With that settled in his mind, Mikal began pecking at the typewriter.

David waited until suppertime to tell his father about the phone call. He knew he'd be in trouble. Phone calls from Uncle Yuri were not to be considered interruptions. Without looking up from his plate of eggplant made so even a kid could love it, David said, "Uncle Yuri called today."

"Uncle Yuri?" Mikal laid his fork back on his plate. "Where was I?"

"You were in the office."

"Why didn't you tell me he was on the phone? Didn't he ask for me?"

"Well, yeah," David admitted with a shrug. "I told him you were busy writing. He just wants to know if you're going to Philadelphia."

Pulling the napkin up from his lap, Mikal sighed and wiped his chin. "That fancy affair is for the national office and big-money contributors. They don't need me for that kind of stuff. I'm satisfied to do my bit at the local level. I'm no good at—"

"He says you are." Mikal gave David a helpless look, as if hoping somebody would sympathize with him. "I'm sorry, Dad, but he says they need you. That was the message."

Mikal knew what Yuri had in mind for him, and he knew that in the end he wouldn't refuse. Mikal would get the commitments. He had the knack for it. "It's over the Thanksgiving holiday, and I hate to be away from home then."

David drew lines in the melted Parmesan cheese with his fork. He knew his father played an important role in the organization's work, but he suspected there was more to this work than he'd been privy to. There'd been times when he'd had an uneasy feeling about Mikal's trips. "You don't think they need you for anything . . . special this time, do you?"

"Special?" Mikal watched as David played with his food.

"Overseas or something." Looking up at his father, David added quickly, "Like one of those investigations, or whatever they are."

"No, this is just a fund-raiser. You have to go around glad-handing everybody and being very . . ." With a sigh, Mikal admitted, "But it has to be done, and I guess I can do my share."

"You're never gonna finish that book, Dad."

"Of course I will." Mikal sipped his coffee and regarded his son thoughtfully. He hadn't discussed the full implications of his work with Freedom International because he'd always thought David was too young to understand and that he might worry unnecessarily. The next time "something special" came up, David had a right to know, Mikal decided. But this time it *was* just a fund-raiser.

"You know what I was thinking?" Mikal began, and David looked up, curious. "I was thinking of asking Miss Kramer to go with me."

"Take Miss Kramer?" From the look on David's face, Mikal might have suggested that they have something wonderful for dessert. "To Philadelphia?" Mikal nodded. "You think she'd go?"

"Why not?" A picture formed in Mikal's mind of the two of them bounding up the steps of the Philadelphia Museum of Art together. He liked what he saw.

"Yeah, why not?" David smiled as he pictured the look on Miss Kramer's face when she got a load of Mikal Romanov in a tux. His dad was one cool-looking dude when he got dressed up. "I don't think she's ever been to Philadelphia. And now that you've got her interested in Freedom

International . . ." If Miss Kramer were going on this trip, it couldn't be one of those special assignments, David told himself. "I think she'd go for it, Dad."

Mikal grinned, thinking of the art museum steps again. "So do I."

Morgan watched the airplane's wing cut through the white mist of clouds as it dipped in its final approach to the runway below. She felt her stomach flutter and wasn't sure whether to blame it on a bump in the air or the knot in her nerves. In truth it was probably neither. Her stomach had been fluttering from the first moment Mikal had suggested this trip. She'd known from the start that the whole idea had been blown through a dreamer's pipe and that she had no business climbing into his bubble and drifting off with him. She'd also known she would go.

She hadn't agreed right away, not because she was playing coy, but because her brain had insisted she give voice to a list of reasonable objections. All the while her heart had been playing jump rope in her chest. Mikal must have seen her answer in her eyes when he first offered his proposal, but he listened to all her excuses. When she ran out, he concluded, "You'll go, then?"

"You're really serious, aren't you?"

"Of course I'm serious. I want to take you to Philadelphia with me. Otherwise I don't want to go."

"But this is your job, sort of. . . . Isn't it?"

He laughed. "I don't have a job. I have a mission. I have—" he waved his hand near his temple "—a vision." She rolled her eyes and thought, *Don't remind me.* "I see the two of us running up the steps of the art museum, you in your leotard, me in my gray sweats."

"Dream on, Mr. Romanov."

He did. "I see us having dinner at a little place I know on South Street. Flowers. Candlelight. Soft music." By that time she was smiling and her heart was skipping double-dutch, which he must have sensed because he added, "An old-fashioned date, Morgan. My treat."

Now Morgan rolled her head against the high-backed seat and looked over at Mikal, who'd slept through most of the flight from Minneapolis. He'd refused the airline lunch, though Morgan had found it passable, and mumbling an apology for being poor company, he'd fallen asleep. He'd been at the typewriter most of the night, and it occurred to Morgan that for a man who didn't have a job, Mikal worked very hard. Now he slept hard, undisturbed by the change of pressure caused by the plane's descent. His chin rested on his chest as he listed toward Morgan. She thought that if she moved a little closer, his head might drop to her shoulder and he might be more comfortable. It was a whimsical urge, she told herself firmly, probably brought on by the fact that he looked almost childlike as he slept. His thick, yellow-brown hair was tumbling over his forehead, and his full lips were parted just slightly. She noticed the plush length of his eyelashes for the first time.

The plane touched down, and Mikal sat up, stretching and shaking off sleep like a lion awakening from an afternoon nap. He was, Morgan realized, the epitome of the natural man, which was probably at the root of his charm. Comfortable with himself, he put others at ease. He smiled at her, and she felt herself melt.

"I'm glad you came," he assured her, covering her hand with his. Morgan felt uneasy, as if all the sound and speed of the airplane were crowding into the pit of her stomach. "I've been anxious for you to meet Uncle Yuri, but don't let him rattle you. He's direct, impatient and dictatorial, but his insides are made of chocolate mousse."

"That sweet?"

"And that soft." Mikal grinned at the thought. "He's going to love you."

Yuri Romanov paused on his way down the concourse to check the computer screen for the gate number. With a glance at his watch, he proceeded at a pace that proudly denied any question of physical deterioration, even though he was seventy-four. There was no time in his day for stiff joints or aching muscles. He was always busy, always moving with deliberation and purpose, as he did now to await the arrival of his nephew and the woman he would bring, presumably for Yuri's approval. Yuri was anxious to see them both, and he was annoyed by the flight's delay. When Mikal's face appeared above the crowd of passengers who were streaming into the terminal, annoyance was forgotten. The old man's heart swelled with pride.

The garment bag Mikal had slung over his shoulder slipped to the floor as he reached for his uncle Yuri. Morgan snatched up the bag and draped it over the back of a chair as she watched the two big men greet each other with unreserved bear hugs, the older man bussing the younger on both cheeks. Uncle Yuri was the image of the man Mikal would be in another thirty-five years. Yuri was heavier, but his eyes were just as blue, and he had a full head of thick, white hair the same texture as Mikal's.

"Uncle Yuri, this is my friend, Morgan Kramer."

Yuri took the hand Morgan offered, but he brushed his lips over the back of it. "You're lovely, my dear, and I'm delighted." He turned to Mikal. "How good a friend?"

Mikal laughed as he retrieved Morgan's bag. "A very good friend, Uncle Yuri."

Yuri's embrace took Morgan by surprise, and her eyes widened. "A *good* friend! Welcome, welcome, dear lady.

Mikal sometimes brings his friends to see me, but always they are friends of the cause first, *then* friends of Mikal's." His smile was meant to reassure her as he surrounded her shoulders with one arm and squeezed. "You will have a fascinating and enjoyable holiday, and I promise to see that Mikal has plenty of time to spend with you."

His smile was as irresistible as his nephew's. It melted the stiffness from her shoulders as she stood pinned under his arm. "I've been looking forward to meeting you, Mr. Romanov. Mikal talks about you a great deal."

"All good, Uncle Yuri, except that whenever there's a woman around, she ends up on your arm while I carry the bags." Mikal was holding two of Morgan's and one of his own. "Morgan refused to check hers through, but I'll have to pick up one of mine at the baggage claim area."

"Very wise, my dear," Yuri said, settling Morgan's hand in the crook of his elbow. "I always refuse to let them lose mine. It can ruin a holiday when your baggage is delayed."

"If they lose my tux, I'll just have to wear something else." Mikal fell into step with Yuri and Morgan, shouldering his way past a flock of teenagers who'd just spotted someone whose arrival touched off peals of excitement.

Yuri shot Mikal a fatherly glance. "If they lose your tux, we'll get you another one."

"My poetry is more convincing if I'm allowed to read it looking the part of a poet."

"I have much more in mind for you than the reading of poetry. Do you think I would allow you to get up in front of our benefactors in blue jeans and a sweatshirt?" Yuri glanced down at Morgan and reassured them both. "He knows his job well, but he thinks it's fun to rile an old man. His grandmother would never have allowed him to appear in public without a tie, not even in Bismarck."

Morgan detected a note of disdain in the way he enunciated the last word. "Mikal's poetry sounds beautiful no matter how he's dressed."

Yuri's eyes brightened and crinkled at the corners as he gave his nephew an approving smile. She was just the kind of woman Mikal needed—warm, wise and patient. One who would give his ego the boost it needed, but not object to the time he had to spend on his work. And Mikal was needed; Yuri had work for him to do.

"You have a treasure here, Mikal. Keep her happy. I trust you turned your nose up at airline food. The hotel has excellent dining facilities. I'll see that the baggage is taken to your rooms. How was your weather in Bismarck?"

Mikal knew that North Dakota had never been Yuri's favorite place. He'd tried many times to persuade Mikal to move to the east coast, where he'd be closer to the daily business of the organization. "Great," Mikal reported. "Crisp, clean fall weather. Brisk."

Yuri laughed. "Euphemisms. I know North Dakota, dear children. I grew up there. November can be a monster, and the snow and wind can continue into May." It reminded him of Russia and the bitterly cold trip he had taken long ago to leave there. He'd been terrified at the time because his father, always a man of such courage, had been afraid of something too awful to name. Years later, when Yuri had left the Midwest for college in the east, he'd never called it home again, and he'd never missed the prairie's icy winter blasts. Its one point of interest for him was Mikal, and he couldn't understand why his nephew made his home there.

"Not this year," Mikal said, hoping to dismiss his uncle's usual indictment of North Dakota. "The weather's been fine."

Morgan took a mental back seat as she sat close to Mikal in the cab and watched the sights of the city pass by the window. While the men talked of the upcoming event, she absorbed the contrasts between the city she'd left and the one she was visiting. They were the same kind of contrasts she was beginning to sense between Mikal and his uncle—the private man who took life as it came, quietly making it fit his terms, and the man who represented an international movement, met the world with a list of demands, made noise and made news. For every urgency of Yuri's there was a quiet response from Mikal. Morgan wondered how they got along as well as they seemed to.

At the hotel the bellman took the bags as Mikal and Yuri went to the desk. "You did reserve two rooms as I asked." Mikal knew his uncle well.

"Of course, Mikal. Do you take me for a boor? I respect a lady's privacy. You have two separate rooms." He clapped a hand on Mikal's shoulder and tossed him a wink. "Adjoining, of course. She is lovely, my boy."

"It's just as I told you," Mikal said, smiling as Morgan turned from the display of paintings she'd stopped to examine. Her loveliness was a fact to which he took no exception. She was living proof that the dark-haired, fair-skinned beauty in the painting behind her could have been a reality. "She's a very good friend."

"I can see that, and I approve." Yuri gave his nephew another reassuring pat on the shoulder. "Have dinner with your good friend now. Tonight you'll have a drink with Marshal Kost and tomorrow lunch with—" he drew his notes from his breast pocket to refresh his memory "—Stan Levine. Miss Kramer would be an asset in your meeting with Levine, but not Kost. Kost is a man of purpose, and he resents distractions."

Mikal understood his uncle. Nothing in Yuri's life had ever interfered with his work. Each time they met, Mikal had to set Yuri straight on his own priorities. "Yuri, listen to me. Morgan is not here to be an asset. She's a guest. I intend to see that she enjoys herself." He crooked a finger at Yuri's notes. "Just hand over the appointments and let me deal with them."

Joining them near the desk, Morgan glanced at the paper. They were two men who shared strong beliefs, cared for one another, worked together, but whose styles were totally different. Two different sources of power. Two hands on an apparently important list.

Mikal waited for the list of appointments. "You do trust me to do my job?" he asked quietly.

Yes, Yuri thought, I've always trusted you, but you've never brought a woman along before. How will she change you? How *has* she changed you? To another man, the idea of a woman as an asset would not be offensive, but to Mikal... Yuri should have known better. "You've done well for us in this role. I would allow no one else to deal with these people."

"Nothing's changed. I know what our needs are and I know how to meet them." Yuri relinquished the list, and Mikal pocketed it with a smile. "Your ways might be as good as mine, Uncle Yuri, but they're different. We're not the same man."

The concern disappeared from Yuri's face as he laughed. "I'm too old to be the man you are. And I never had your charm, even when I might have had some of your patience. Do it your way, Mikal. It always works."

Chapter Six

Morgan liked taking her things out of a suitcase and arranging them in an orderly fashion, ready to be used. She liked having places for things, particularly herself. The fact that her room adjoined Mikal's didn't bother her. She had her own bed and her own place to unwind. Knowing that he was in the next room gave her a good feeling, because the rest of the scene promised to be foreign to her. She had attended conferences before, mostly for educators, but they had never been glamorous or high-pressure, which was what she expected from an organization courting big money. She knew she could count on Mikal to be a breath of unaffected midwestern air.

Mikal's knock came at the hallway door, not at the one between their rooms. She opened the door to find him standing there dressed in a trim, blue suit. What surprised her was not the suit itself, though she'd never seen him wear one, but the fact that he looked as comfortable in it as he did in his customary pullover. His tawny, slightly coarse hair fell into place naturally. Morgan remembered the way he'd joined her exercise class, the way he'd read his poetry for the Bismarck group, the way he'd looked when he was made up for the oldies dance. No matter how he dressed or what he did, he was always comfortable with his role. He was always Mikal. He adjusted the knot in his tie and grinned, blue eyes flashing. "Didn't think I owned one, did you?"

"I like it. It matches your eyes."

"That's what the saleswoman told me. She said I was a real knockout in this suit. Are you reeling?"

She was, but she couldn't manage a direct admission. "I'm suit-ably impressed." With a groan, he offered his arm. "Wasn't that good highbrow humor?" she teased.

"Classy as hell, Miss Kramer. You're seated at my table for the duration, no matter what Uncle Yuri says. I can use a laugh once in a while."

The table they shared for dinner was tucked in a private corner in a dimly lit dining room. The decor was so plush and the voices so hushed that Morgan felt as though she'd been wrapped in velvet. Mikal discouraged her first choice, which was steak, and suggested lack of lamb or poached salmon. She ordered stuffed fillet of beef and challenged him with an arched eyebrow. With a shrug, he opted for the fish.

"What do you think of Uncle Yuri?" Mikal asked, bracing himself both physically and mentally as he planted his elbows at the edge of the table and laced his fingers together.

"It's too early to tell," Morgan replied. "I'm still wondering what he thinks of me. I take it 'good friend' is another euphemism."

"Uncle Yuri has never been married. He contends that he can't commit himself to a marriage because of his commitment to Freedom International.'' Mikal considered the candle in the center of the table for a moment. ''I've told him that's garbage. He's loved the same woman for twenty years, and he should have married her a long time ago. Helen's a fine lady.'' He lifted his gaze to Morgan's face. ''I guess it's their business.''

''Maybe it's best. If he's not a family man, at least he never pretended to be.''

He noted the dignified way she held her chin up, shoulders squared. She wasn't thinking about Uncle Yuri. ''People make lots of commitments in the course of a lifetime, and one doesn't necessarily cancel out all the others. Your mother made some choices, too.''

''Yes, but my father...'' She saw him in her mind and the image worked on her as it always did. She missed him. ''They did stay married, though I've never understood why. When my mother died, my father truly became a widower.''

''Uncle Yuri is committed to Helen in his way, too. She knows who he is, what he is, and she's always accepted that. When he dies, she'll be a widow, whether he marries her or not. He needs to recognize that.''

''Maybe having a 'good friend' is the best he can do,'' Morgan suggested.

''Maybe.''

''Maybe he thinks every man should have at least one 'good friend.' '' She was teasing now, a smile sneaking into her eyes.

''I agree, but then 'good friend' isn't a euphemism to me. You have to take Uncle Yuri with a grain of salt. He thinks he's grooming me for something, and I think I'm pretty well groomed as it is.'' He ran a thumb under his lapel and adjusted his tie. ''What do you think?''

''I think you're a knockout.''

After dinner Morgan and Mikal strolled through the hotel's huge, glass-walled lobby, with its arching escalators and profusion of lush greenery. They window-shopped in the hotel's mall, admiring the displays in the exclusive stores. When the time came for Mikal's appointment, Morgan half hoped he'd skip it. He asked her to join him, but she professed a need for sleep before she could manage more sociability. He walked her back to her room and lingered at the door for a time, letting them both enjoy the bittersweet regret that went with their long, slow kiss and whispered goodnights.

At breakfast Morgan watched the Romanov charm go to work. She lost count of the number of people Mikal greeted. No name escaped him, and he showed a genuine interest in some aspect of each person's life when he asked about families and businesses and listened attentively to the answers. When they left the dining room, Morgan noticed that most of Mikal's meal was still on his plate.

Morgan listened to speakers during the rest of the morning, while Mikal seemed to come and go from the meeting rooms. He moved with the casual assurance of one who commanded respect and attention, though he made no demands. Nothing appeared to push him, and he never pushed. He always had an easy smile for Morgan, a comment or two about the speaker, and a way of touching her arm that suggested a special intimacy.

As Yuri had promised, they had lunch with Stan Levine, a man who enjoyed being distracted from his nervous stomach by beautiful young women. He spoke with a trace of an East European accent, and his age was hard to guess. His face had probably never looked young. Morgan accepted his barrage of compliments graciously. Mikal suffered them briefly, then turned the conversation to food.

"You kids order whatever you like," Stan said, scanning the menu with a face that looked predisposed to be disgusted. "Nothing agrees with me. There's nothing on here I can eat."

"You're sadly in need of a dietician, Stan." Mikal looked the menu over quickly.

"Oh, I've gone that route. No point in eating if the food's tasteless."

"Let me try something out on you." Mikal wrote a note to the kitchen and gave it to the waiter, along with his order and Morgan's. "If this gives you any problem, let me know. I'll be honor-bound to find a remedy."

Stan's lunch consisted of a clear soup and a chicken dish that Stan pronounced delicious. "But, you know, I can't have salt," he cautioned after the second bite.

Mikal smiled. "There isn't any."

"Mmm." Stan studied the next forkful of food as if still searching for some sign of salt, which he apparently didn't find. "Tasty. I'll take the recipe."

"I have several others," Mikal said. "Use them in good health."

"My mother would bless you for that, though she'd be surprised to find a man who could cook as well as she does." There was a faraway sadness in the older man's eyes that tugged at Morgan's heart.

"I understand you've had no contact with your mother since you came to this country," Mikal said. "How long has it been?"

"Thirty years." Stan's deep sigh seemed to pull him backward through those years, one at a time. "I've tried government agencies, the Red Cross, and I get nothing. I'm told she died, but I'm denied proof. I'm told she moved. I'm told she never existed. Never existed! I'm here, right? Therefore she existed."

"Of course," Mikal said quietly, his voice a balm even for Morgan, who suffered vicariously as she witnessed Stan Levine's anguish. "You're feeling cut off at the roots. Whether she's alive or dead, you need to know."

"I believe she was imprisoned." Stan stabbed at his food. "I'm sure of it."

"Have you been in touch with any of her friends?"

Stan shook his head, despairing, "It's so difficult to get answers out of them. Double-talk, secrets, cover-ups. I can't tell you how discouraging it is."

"Yes you can. And I can believe every word," Mikal assured him, and the man's tired eyes filled with gratitude.

"My wife tells me to give up, but I can't give up. My mother helped me escape. She had a good job, a little influence." He shrugged. "She risked it all, used it all to help me. Now I want you to help me find her." His demand became a plea. "At least help me find the truth."

Mikal laid a comforting hand on the man's forearm. "Give us all the information you have."

"Make her a high priority. Please. My contribution will be—"

Mikal waved the promise away. "Because of your mother's age, I think this will be seen as an urgent case. We need contributions, but they have nothing to do with the way our investigations are handled. You can give anonymously, and I guarantee we will be looking for your mother within a month."

Morgan felt Stan's relief. Mikal's manner was as soothing to his anxious mind as his food was to the poor man's sensitive stomach. "How good was your promise?" she asked Mikal after they'd left Stan with handshakes and good wishes.

'As good as gold. He should've come to us sooner, though. It's hard to cut through thirty years."

"It really doesn't matter how much money he can contribute?"

Mikal slipped an arm around her shoulders as they walked through the sunlit lobby. "It really doesn't matter. Donations and investigations are handled completely separately."

"But your uncle must have his hands in both pies." His frown told her she'd chosen the wrong words. "Figuratively, of course."

"His concern with both aspects of the organization is literal, though. We're audited regularly. Our overhead is consistently low in comparison with that of other charitable organizations. And what we do is vitally important, Morgan." She looked up at him, and he knew she was willing to believe him. "We keep the world's eyes open."

The same message resounded throughout the afternoon presentations. Human beings must not be put away and forgotten. Morgan recalled Mr. Levine's anguish and began to feel deeply that this was true. She listened to stories like his, each one demanding its own attention, its own personal responses. Conditions, policies and politics were discussed, questioned, even roundly debated by speakers and their audiences, but at the heart of the matter for Morgan was Mr. Levine's mother.

"We have a couple of hours before we'll have to get dolled up for tonight's banquet. How about a walk over to the park?" Mikal offered, catching up with her as she emerged from a meeting room. "You must be tired of sitting."

"I am." Hands at her waist, Morgan stretched her back and rolled her shoulders. "I'm not tired of listening, though. That doctor who lived in Swaziland was just fascinating."

He put his hand around her elbow and slid it along her silken sleeve to press his palm against hers. "I'm just fascinating, too,'' he muttered near her ear. ''You want card tricks or kisses?''

''While we're walking?''

''All three at once, if you like.'' He squeezed her hand and gave her a wink. ''That's what makes me so fascinating.''

''Mikal, may I have a word with you?''

They stopped and waited for Yuri. He was accompanied by a shorter man dressed in a conservative gray suit. Morgan felt Mikal's body stiffen before he released her hand. She glanced up and watched him force himself to relax and accept the shorter man's handshake. ''Alex,'' he acknowledged.

''It's good to have you back, Mikal.''

''Only for the fund-raiser, Alex. Nothing more.'' Morgan felt the strange current of emotion between the two men as Mikal turned to draw her into the conversation. It wasn't really outright antagonism; it was more a mutual defensiveness. ''Morgan, this is Alex Steiger, a member of the board of directors. Alex, Morgan Kramer.''

Morgan extended her hand, and Alex greeted her cordially, but he was clearly not a man to linger on the social amenities. ''If I might have a few moments with you, Mikal, there are a few matters—''

''We were just going for a walk. Perhaps tomorrow,'' Mikal suggested.

''I have to be in Washington tomorrow morning. I'm not going to ask you to negotiate any treaties, Mikal.'' Alex glanced at Yuri for confirmation, which he gave with a nod. ''Your uncle feels that we should visit with each other about some—'' he waved his hand in a dismissive gesture ''—organizational business while you're here. I've asked a couple of the members of the board to join us.''

''And I would like nothing better than to take a walk this evening,'' Yuri put in. ''If you can keep up with me, Morgan. I tend to worry that my time is short, and I forget to take it easy."

Morgan looked at Mikal and felt a stab of disappointment when he nodded. He was more than the "gladhander" for the organization that he'd claimed to be, and the meeting with Alex Steiger was to be more than a casual discussion. Mikal was being drawn away from her, and she didn't like the feeling that left her with. Lifting her chin, she beat the sensation down. "I think I can manage," Morgan said, accepting Yuri's proferred arm. "We'll take periodic pulse checks. I'll be ready by eight, Mikal."

There was something singularly stylish about the way Yuri strolled down the street with Morgan on his arm. It was like finding a man who was truly a good dancer. Morgan felt her spirits lifting and her heart warming to the man simply because the evening was balmy and the smooth, unhurried motion felt so fine.

"What's the problem between Mikal and Alex?" Morgan asked as they waited for the light at the corner.

"You're very perceptive," Yuri said without looking down at her.

"It was impossible to miss the tension there. Mikal is *never* like that."

"'Mikal is *never* like that'?" Yuri echoed with a smile. "How long have you known him?"

"Long enough," popped into Morgan's mind, much to her own surprise, but the light changed and she decided the question didn't warrant an answer.

"It doesn't matter," Yuri said, dismissing his own presumptuousness. "You'll see him as long as I have and still continue to see new beauty in him. Alex is an attorney, our specialist in international law, and a brilliant man, but he knows it's Mikal who's the heir apparent."

"Heir to whom?"

He gave her a look of patient disbelief. "To me. But, of course, Mikal resists. A grass roots man, he calls himself." With a short laugh he added, "It sounds like a group from the early sixties. Mikal Romanov, the grass roots man. Absurd!"

"Mikal is a writer," Morgan reminded him.

"He is a man who is acutely aware of everything that goes on around him. That awareness forces him to speak out in many ways. What's more important, though, is his gift for touching the heart of the matter without flourish or fanfare. He reaches people."

"So you want him to do more work for Freedom International, and that's what Alex has been assigned to talk with him about."

"Alex takes this upon himself," Yuri explained. "There are times when Mikal's talents are invaluable."

"He's here for your fund-raiser, and he's certainly reaching people. I'd say you're getting your money's worth out of him."

They had come to the edge of a park and slowed to turn around and head back. Yuri paused to make his point. "Mikal is not paid for what he does for us right now. We use his name and pay his expenses to bring him here, because, as I said, he reaches people. We want him to do more. We want him to negotiate for us on a regular basis."

"Negotiate... prisoner releases and things like that?"

"We do a great deal of negotiating for releases, improved conditions for prisoners, and so on. Sometimes in a hostage situation we'll be called in, discreetly, of course. Governments are supposed to take care of these things."

Resuming the walk, Morgan considered the pavement under her feet. "Apparently, Mikal has some choices to make."

"We have used him on a couple of occasions in the past, and he is a master. A situation is developing now that we've been unofficially invited to look into. Alex is talking to Mikal about serving on the team."

"Obviously it isn't the kind of thing Mikal wants to do."

"We understand his reasons. Mikal has a son to think about. But it is the kind of thing he does extremely well, and, as you say, he has some choices to make."

Morgan chose not to ask whether it was the kind of thing that might also be extremely dangerous. In the movies the enemy usually made an example of the guy who carried the white flag.

Mikal carried a red rose. When he appeared at her door a few minutes before eight Morgan allowed herself a moment to admire him. His black tuxedo was cut to accentuate his broad shoulders and long torso. His pleated shirtfront was ivory, which was particularly flattering to the golden tone of his skin. She stepped back, not to escape, but to draw him over the threshold.

Mikal followed, closing the door behind him. Morgan's long, sleek, red dress was stunning and very provocative in the way it moved over her slender body with silken fluidity. Her hair was caught up off her neck, leaving a long column of soft, translucent skin that he would have to touch before he could decide whether it was real or not. Wordlessly he put the long-stemmed rose in her hand and drew her into his arms, his mouth descending to give her something more. She offered no resistance. Her arms went around his neck as she lifted her body to his embrace, melted into it, then returned his gift with one of her own. With a guttural groan, he tightened his arms around her and deepened his kiss.

Their mingling breaths quickened as the kiss, given and returned, grew hot and urgent. Mikal's hands moved in slow circles over Morgan's back. The silky fabric of her dress moved with him, and he learned exactly what she wore underneath it. With his mouth he tested the softness of her neck and the sleekness of her jawline while he nuzzled the heady scent behind her ear.

"I could easily do without this banquet business," he whispered, keeping his mouth where it was.

The heat of his breath made Morgan shiver. "But we're all dressed."

"I could easily do without that, too."

"I thought you'd like this dress."

"I love it." His hand slid over her bottom as he tightened his hold. "Oh, God, I love it."

He held her against him, pillowing his hard length against the soft pliancy of her body, and she sucked in a breath, inhaling the sweet scent of the rose. "Mmm, so good," Morgan whispered.

Mikal heard music in Morgan's soft voice. Tenderly he kissed the mouth that made it. "Let's lock the door and take the phone off the hook."

Morgan brushed her fingers through the hair over his temple, and Mikal detected a hint of sadness in her smile. "I'm afraid that wouldn't take *you* off the hook."

"How can anyone so beautiful be so sensible?"

"It's not such an odd combination—" she gave him a saucy smile as she let her hand slide down his satin lapel "—in a *woman*. Incidentally you're beautiful tonight, too."

"Men aren't beautiful."

She touched his black bow tie and ran her thumbnail along a pleat in his shirt. "In the eyes of this beholder you are."

"But not sensible?"

"Dreamers don't have to be. You did say there'd be dancing after dinner?" Mikal nodded, knowing that eating a predictable banquet dinner of chicken à la king was an inevitability now. "How many contributors will you have to dance with?"

"None. I have a date."

Mikal found the chicken Kiev to be a pleasant surprise, but he ate little of it before giving his poetry reading. The crowd was moved, some to tears, and Morgan knew that he touched a chord of loss for many of them. She saw, too, that whereas at home he was the town's eccentric, here he was revered as an artist and a visionary. Watching him and listening, she remembered seeing her father surrounded by people who took his message to heart, and she felt the swelling in her own breast. She had always loved her father, and now she loved another who was just like him. There was no help for it.

Mikal kept his promise and danced with Morgan to the exclusion of all others. Surrounded by music and mirrors and chandeliers, both were too absorbed to notice another living soul. They moved over the polished floor with the grace of unconscious effort, seeing only each other. Morgan had imagined herself in such a place with such a man many times, and now she glided, light-headed from dreams rather than drinks, and enamored with Mikal's beauty.

Stan Levine joined Yuri at the bar and tipped a glass toward the waltzing couple. "I'd hoped for a dance with her," he said, "but there's a special aura about them. I couldn't cut in."

Yuri nodded, sipping his Scotch. "I'm having the same trouble."

It was later, after the last waltz had been played that Yuri joined the two for a drink beside the pool. They sat in chairs with canvas-covered cushions and talked in the hushed tones befitting the late hour. Lights at the bottom of the pool cast purling shadows on the ceiling, and Morgan could almost feel the water's warm caress.

"Where's Helen, Uncle Yuri? It's unlike her to miss the fall fund-raiser."

Smiling at his nephew, Yuri translated the message into his own terms. Mikal's lady was at his side, and he wished the same joy for the rest of the world's male population. In a few minutes, he thought, I'll leave you alone with her. "She's with her sister in Utica. Doris hasn't been well, so Helen spends more time with her. She sends you her best." He settled back in his chair and studied Mikal for a moment. "Alex tells me you aren't interested in being included on this mission."

"The whole thing sounds pretty iffy," Mikal said. "*If* there's actually been a coup, and *if* there are actually hostages, and *if* whoever's in charge will see me. We don't even know who we'd be dealing with." He offered Morgan an explanation. "It's one of those overnight revolutions, with everything still up in the air as far as who'd taken over whom. There may be American hostages."

"I haven't heard anything in the news about a revolution," Morgan said.

"It hasn't been called that yet," Mikal answered. "As I said, it's all very iffy, and it isn't my bailiwick. Let Alex handle it."

"Alex is excellent when it comes to facts, figures and codes of law, but he's no good one-on-one, Mikal. You are. You must not withhold your talents when they're so desperately needed. If our information is correct, we may be able to get these people out before the media calls them hostages and forces the new government to put on a show of strength."

Mikal watched the reflections from the water dance above his head. He spoke quietly. "We all have choices to make,

Uncle Yuri. I make mine much more carefully than I used to. My book is going well, and I want to finish it, and then I want to start another one. If I do this now, within a matter of weeks or months there'll be another mission. You take care of the politics, Uncle Yuri, you and Alex.''

Yuri turned to Morgan, looking for help. After all, didn't every woman hope her man would rise to greatness? ''The world would thank you if you would talk some sense into this man, my dear.''

Morgan looked at Mikal and saw his fatigue, familiar not because she'd seen it in his eyes before but from memories of her father. It occurred to her that it was not the work that brought this kind of weariness but the unending demands, the knowledge that meeting one need only left a thousand more. ''You were right about choices, Mikal. My father made his, my mother hers. And yours are no easier to make.''

His appreciative smile made her pulse flutter. Without taking his eyes from her, he explained to his uncle, ''We've decided you should meet Morgan's father, Uncle Yuri. He's a missionary. In fact, maybe we could all pay him a visit. I could use a Caribbean holiday along about January.'' He hastened to add, ''A real holiday, with no strings attached.''

''Is your father in the Bahamas or one of the American islands?'' Yuri asked, interested.

''Further south,'' Morgan told him. ''A little to the west of Cuba. One of those little banana republics.''

''De Colores?''

''Yes.'' The glance Yuri exchanged with Mikal puzzled her. ''Have you been there?'' she wondered.

''Uh, yes,'' Yuri answered. ''Yes, I have. Years ago. Lovely island.'' He laid a hand on Mikal's forearm as he moved to the edge of his chair, preparing to stand. ''We've very little information on this other thing, Mikal. Nothing official. I'm sure you'll want to be kept informed.''

Mikal's brow was pulled into a deep frown. "You'll be making more inquiries?"

"We're doing that now. The entire report may be unfounded, and there may be no need for our...services. You'll know the minute I do, and then..." He gave Mikal a fatherly pat on the arm before he rose to his feet. "Choices. I'll get out of your way so you can enjoy what's left of this evening." To Morgan he added, "Good night, dear lady."

With Yuri gone, Mikal reached for Morgan's hand and laced his fingers through hers. Her eyes followed the path of his arm, but she knew by the way he held her hand what look she would find when she reached his face. Still, it surprised her a little. His face was taut with an emotion that transcended desire. His eyes touched her with concern, almost compassion. She meant to ask him whether something was wrong, and her lips parted for the question, but his covered them with a hard, quick kiss. He laid his forehead against hers and whispered, "No more heavy discussions. What's left of the night belongs to us."

Chapter Seven

He knew she'd measured his promise against the time that lay before them, and she was stalling. He listened while she told him things about herself that he already knew, or at least suspected. It was the omissions that interested him, the fact that she mentioned no close friends, no ties other than professional ones. She didn't think she needed anyone, but he believed she'd come this far because she needed him. She simply hadn't admitted that to herself yet. But she would, Mikal promised himself. Since he'd met Morgan, he'd come a long way, too.

She said she wanted to see the sights tomorrow, and he promised to take her, which meant, she said, that she needed some sleep. They walked back to their rooms with slow, heavy feet, and Morgan's brain, which had been crowded with chatter, went suddenly blank. Sleep was far from her mind, and sense seemed to be, too. She didn't turn to him at the door to say good-night, as she'd imagined herself doing. But when the door closed behind her, she turned to find that he wasn't there. Her face grew instantly hot. Staring at the Do Not Disturb sign that hung on the doorknob, she felt hollow inside.

She should have been relieved, she told herself, but as she prepared for bed she thought of going to him. She thought of what she might say and how he might respond. She wanted to be with him tonight—just be with him. She'd seen him with his son, with his uncle, with others who admired him. There were so many demands made on him, so many people who laid claim to him. His dreams were too big for her, but she wanted a piece of him anyway, some small piece of him that would be hers and no one else's. Mikal never laughed at anyone or took anyone's feelings lightly, and it would be easy to go to him and admit to this preposterous need for just one small. . .

The knock at the door between their rooms reverberated all the way to her chest. Morgan pulled the door open and found him leaning against the doorframe dressed only in a pair of jeans. "I can't sleep, lady," he said, his eyes alight at the sight of her. "You're making too much racket."

"I haven't made a sound," she told him quietly, her eyes warming to the glow in his. "It must be all in your head."

She wore a black nightgown with lace that followed the curve of her breasts, and she hadn't taken her hair down yet. He was glad. He wanted to do that for her. "You're all that's in my head." He reached out to touch her cheek with the backs of his fingers. "I want to come in."

"You're welcome," she whispered, closing her eyes and relishing his touch.

"That's not easily said, is it?"

She opened her eyes to look at him as she took his hand. "It came more easily than I thought it would."

"You've given it a great deal of thought, have you?"

"My head seems to be filled with you, too."

"But you think it shouldn't be, and I thought I shouldn't press." He stepped from his room into hers, shutting the door behind him. Light from the bathroom spilled over toward the big bed in the middle of the room.

"'Should' is such a worthless word when it comes to—"

"You should let your hair down for me." One by one, he pulled the pins from her hair until it fell down her back. He combed it with his fingers. "Beautiful. Now you should just relax."

Closing her eyes once more, she lifted her chin and breathed deeply of the scent of him, enjoying his ministrations.

He pulled her close and lowered his mouth to hers, muttering "And you should put your arms around me" before he kissed her. She complied, and then there were no more "shoulds," only "woulds." She would have this much of him now. She would make a place deep inside her practical, well-organized self, and there she would cherish her piece of this beautiful dreamer. Just one night would be all she would need, one improbable and glorious night, and then he could dream on, and she would be satisfied.

His kisses were deep, hot and wholly absorbing, drawing her in, drawing her down. The sheets cooled her back, and the broad expanse of his chest warmed her breasts. She touched him to know him, the smooth feel of his back, the tension in each muscle that shifted as he moved over her. He made her neck tingle with the touch of moist lips, and then he kissed the curve of her shoulder as he slipped the strap of her nightgown out of the way of his searching mouth. Baring one breast, he nuzzled it, tongued her nipple to make it his.

"Oh," she groaned appreciatively, then whispered, "Mikal."

"Don't hold back with me, Morgan." His fingers touched her covered breast in soft circles. "Show me when it's good, and let me make it better."

"It's been so long."

"Then we'll make it last." He pushed the other strap away. "We'll make it worth the wait."

"I haven't been waiting. I haven't been *wanting* . . . ." His tongue made a diamond of the second nipple, and she caught her breath.

"You do now."

Her breast felt cool and wet after his mouth came away, but he warmed it with his breath. "I want this night with you," she confessed.

"I want your skin next to mine," he said, and took her gown away. She watched him as he looked down at her, and she knew her beauty by the light in his eyes. "I've been wanting you since we first met," he whispered, "but I had no idea . . ."

She was smooth, like silk, but every plane and curve of her body was firm. He'd felt that solidity whenever he'd held her in his arms, but her silkiness had been hidden beneath tailored suits, crisply creased slacks, neatly ironed blouses. He loved natural beauty, and he lowered his head to pay tribute to hers.

His hands were bold and gentle, and his mouth found exquisite ways to make her flesh tingle. The wanting in her became a fluid thing that coursed and eddied, pitched and plummeted wildly inside her, demanding some vital piece of Mikal. She slid her palms down his back until they met the waistband of his jeans.

"You're still dressed."

He chuckled. "A man needs to keep his pockets handy." Dropping a kiss at her temple, he whispered, "I came prepared to protect you."

"Thank you, Mikal." It seemed unnecessary to tell him that she hadn't been totally unprepared. "But this—" she hooked a finger in the back of his waistband "—*this* isn't fair," she groaned.

"Who said it had to be?" Raining small kisses over her face, he smoothed her hair with one hand and the satiny skin just below her navel with the other. He felt her finger slip inside his waistband and follows its path from his back to his belly, and he sucked in a breath. "If you're looking for fairness, you won't find it that way."

"Why not?"

"Because patience doesn't seem to be my body's greatest virtue right now."

"Who said it had to be?" She managed to flick open the snap of his jeans before he hauled her hips against his, trapping her hand before it made another move, silencing her frustrated groan with his mouth, pinning her thighs in the vise of his.

"I did," he rasped, and he thought his own demands on himself might very well drive him mad. He drank her mouth's sweetness while he traced the indentation of her waist and the proud curve of her hip. His thumb strayed over her abdomen, and when she relaxed, giving in to his hypnotic caress, he released her thighs and tucked his hand between them.

Morgan gave herself over to pleasure, dimly aware that she hadn't gotten what she wanted of him yet, but that he was at least making promises. She had only to hold on to that last corner of herself, to save it for him. He eased back, and she smiled at his look of burning passion.

"You won't let go," he said.

"Not yet. Not without you. Not this time." Each refusal was tellingly breathless. She found his zipper with one hand and opened his jeans. And then she found him inside them.

When he was as naked as she, they both became desperate. He moved over her, and she lifted herself to him, welcoming the sting of his first thrust with a small whimper, absorbing the power of the second with a sigh of pleasure.

"Oh, Morgan," came as his apology.

"It's fine, Mikal. It's been . . ."

". . . a long time. You feel so. . ."

". . . good. And you . . . oh, Mikal, you're music. You're poetry, Mikal."

"We're poetry," he whispered. "Trochaic rhythm, I think. Oh, Morgan . . ."

"Yes, yes, *yes*, Mikal . . . Mikal . . . *Mikal!*"

The litany she made of his name matched the rhythm of the poetry he made with her. It was that piece of him she took, and while she hoarded it jealously, a similar piece of her became forever his.

It was early morning and they hadn't slept. It felt too good to lie in each other's arms and touch or catch a languid look, a satisfied smile, a soft, nuzzling kiss. And tease. The teasing was delicious, Morgan thought. He did it so sweetly. Her teasing had always had a slight edge to it, and she liked his way better. It was warmer.

"Where's that muscle you told me about?" he wondered as he slid his hand around to the back of her thigh. "The one you found when you were shaving. Flex it for me so I won't have to go prowling around looking for peepholes."

"I thought you said you'd only peek to see the expression on my face."

"I lied, of course." She raised one eyebrow in mock surprise. "A diplomatic lie. Courteous, not substantive. Come on, show me."

She stretched, tightening every muscle in her legs. "A diplomatic lie? Figures."

"Ooo, nice. That muscle was definitely worth cultivating."

"Very diplomatic."

"No, that was honest admiration, Miss Kramer." He gave her kneecap a quick kiss as he ran his hand under her calf, admiring more. Then he scooted back up. "A diplomatic lie is like when I ask how you are, and you say 'fine' whether you are or not. Or—" his blue eyes softened as he looked into hers "—when I take you too suddenly, and it hurts, but you say it's fine."

"I *was* fine. I was more than fine." She smiled to convince him.

"You have a real stubborn streak."

"Oh, yes, I do have that." She touched his hair, then laid her hand along his cheek. "It's a sanity-saver when you're dealing with dreamers."

"Ahh." He nodded, registering the idea. "Dreamers." Uncomfortable with labels and categories of any kind, Mikal chafed at this one, but he suspected she had some connection to make that might be interesting. "You've dealt with guys like me before, huh?"

"I have a positive predisposition to get tangled up with guys like you, and I don't know why." Her sigh was only for effect; the way she ran an exploratory finger around the curve of his ear and along his neck said that she wasn't minding this particular entanglement. "I don't have an impractical bone in my body."

"Hmm. You say stubbornness works well for you?" She nodded. Settling back against a pile of pillows, he folded his arms across his chest. "How so?"

"It's a good mooring. When a dreamer goes drifting away to do 'his thing,' I'm still tethered right where I want to be—on good, firm, North Dakota sod."

He smiled at the image she created of herself, the lone woman clinging to her piece of grassland, which hardly coincided with the reality of the nude beauty who was sharing the bed with him at that moment. "I wasn't trying to drift away or do *my* thing. I had your pleasure in mind."

The light was dim, but he saw that she flushed. "Yes, well...we did *our* thing, and it was certainly very...pleasurable." *And I have a piece of you, Mikal Romanov.*

"Come here," he said quietly, opening his arms for her. She slid into the pocket he made for her against his side. "How many other dreamers are we talking about, Morgan? If it's just a couple, I wouldn't call it a positive predisposition."

"Besides my father, there was...Jeremy." The word fell into the air like a three-hundred-pound set of barbells.

"Jeremy?" He didn't like the name.

"Jeremy was an artist. I'm sure he still is—he was good at it."

"I don't suppose he had a practical bone in his body," Mikal ventured.

"Not one."

"But that isn't why you parted company."

"I admired Jeremy. I admired his work." She shrugged the shoulder that wasn't buried under Mikal's arm. "Jeremy admired Jeremy. Jeremy admired Jeremy's work." Lifting her chin, Morgan offered a confident smile. "I've learned a lot about big dreams."

"What have you learned?"

"That relationships tend to be dwarfed by them."

"I see." He saw the long, dark hair that fell over her shoulder and his arm, the soft, white breast pressed against his side, and the glittering hazel eyes that defied him to deny the truth in her statements. Mikal knew better than to ar-

gue with long-held convictions. He knew that he had to let
them stand for the time being while he worked around them,
gained her trust, offered himself as he was. In time she
would topple those beliefs herself.

He moved his hand over her belly and smiled. "If I were
an artist, I'd paint a portrait of you right now, Morgan.
You'd be a masterpiece with that dewy-eyed look and those
wonderful muscles." She returned the smile. "Did Jeremy
ever paint your portrait?"

"No."

"Well, there it is, positive proof." Oddly relieved, Mikal
turned on his side, easing down for a kiss. "The man was an
absolute fool."

It was a balmy day, with enough crispness in the air to
smack of November and enough sunshine to keep the chill
at bay. Morgan loved historical sights, galleries and muse-
ums, and Mikal enjoyed seeing them with her. At the foot
of the towering stairway leading to the Philadelphia art
museum they eyed one another for a moment, gauged the
distance and then raced one another up the steps. They arrived at the top with an exhilarated burst of laughter that
caught the attention of a uniformed security guard, who
wondered if they were "training for the championship."

Independence Hall was a moving experience for Morgan. Because she was an educator and a history buff, she'd
always made a point of stopping at national landmarks
whenever she traveled, but she found colonial Philadelphia's little state house to be more than just a place of historical interest. The rooms seemed too small to
accommodate so many great men at once. She could almost feel their presence as she surveyed the assembly room
with its soft colors and clean architectural lines. Washington, Jefferson, Franklin—names to be found on street signs

in every corner of the country—but they had been men once, and they'd spent untold hours in these rooms. Above the voice of the park ranger who guided them through the building, Morgan could hear echoes of people arguing, haggling, coaxing and swearing, even indulging in the mundane gossip that must have filled the hours. There had been tremendous excitement here, she realized, and terrible fear.

Morgan looked up at Mikal, who stared briefly at Washington's "rising sun" chair before turning his meditative expression her way. "They say it was pretty hot that summer in more ways than one. Wonder where we'd all be if they'd decided to go back to safer moorings and hang on to what they had."

"They couldn't have done that," Morgan decided. "They came here to do a job, and they did it."

"You don't think any of them ever had the urge to call it quits—just say the hell with King George and all the rest of it, I've got a plantation to run?"

Morgan studied the carving of the sun at the top of Washington's chair. "I'm sure they had their moments, but they were made of sturdy stuff."

"Really? Strange stuffing for guys like that."

The ranger was herding his little group of tourists along, and Morgan looked up when Mikal took her arm. "What do you mean, 'guys like that'?"

A spark of mischief danced in his eyes. "Nothing but dreamers, every last one of them."

The little house where Mikal took Morgan for lunch was over two hundred years old. It was Yuri's home and one of the few free-standing houses in the old section of the city. There were plenty of row houses along the cobblestoned streets, like those on Elfreth's Alley, which seemed like a street in miniature, built, Morgan fantasized, for people who might have been only four and a half feet tall. Yuri had acquired his house a few blocks away before restoration had been the vogue. Having renovated it according to the Historical Society's standards, he now owned a valuable piece of history.

Morgan was enchanted from the minute she stepped into the tiny parlor. Two Kennedy-style rockers faced the small brick fireplace that had once been the house's main heat source. The dining area held a table, four chairs and a breakfront hutch, and the kitchen, which had once been a pantry, was only big enough for the cook, preferably some-one half Mikal's size.

"I don't need gadgets," Mikal grumbled from the kitchen as Morgan set the table. "But I could use a little room to turn around."

"What are you trying to make in there?"

"Just a quick quiche," he called over his shoulder. Searching the cupboards required a great deal of leaning and ducking.

"Oh, Mikal, that's too much trouble. Besides, haven't you heard? Real men don't eat quiche."

He leaned back and stuck his head out into the dining room. "They don't? What do they eat?"

"Meat and potatoes."

"That's *it?*"

Morgan laughed. He looked as though he'd somehow wedged himself into a child's playhouse. If that shoulder didn't belong to the proverbial "real man," then there was no such thing. "Cold meat sandwiches for lunch, I think."

He ducked back into his niche with the assurance that "This kitchen isn't *that* small." As he worked, Morgan was never sure whether his conversation was meant for her or the food in preparation. "Spinach—great. And fresh mush-rooms. We're in luck. Well, sort of fresh. How long have you guys been hanging out here? Hmm, not bad. You're okay." Morgan heard a couple of clattering sounds, some chopping and then a muttered curse. "What do you think about a set of decent knives as a Christmas present?"

"Me?" Or the mushrooms? Morgan wondered.

"For Uncle Yuri. These are a joke."

"Are they making the spinach cry?"

He remembered admonishing her once over her treatment of crepe batter, and he laughed. "They're making *me* cry." He craned his neck around the doorway again. "But you can make me laugh again. Come on and kiss the cook."

Morgan set the last of the silverware out and moved toward the kitchen, concerned. "Did you cut yourself?"

"Would it help if I did?"

Laying her hand on the back of his neck, she touched her lips to his in sweet consolation and then repeated, "Did you?"

"No." He smiled against her lips. "But do that again."

Her next kiss was a teasing nibble, followed by a peck. "In answer to the original question, I think knives are a very practical gift."

"Bingo!" He returned her peck with more gusto. "The magic word is practical. Fork over one more stamp of approval, and you shall feast on the very finest—" she kissed him quickly, and he grinned "—lips available in the City of Brotherly Love."

"What about *sisterly* love?"

In a passable south Philly drawl he retorted, "Hey, what about it, sister? It takes two pairs of lips—y'know what I mean? I got no problem with equal billing."

"But you do have the very finest lips," she assured him, touching the lower one with her fingertip before she moved away. "I could learn to love this wonderful old house, but it seems a little small for Yuri."

"A refrigerator and a hot plate would be enough kitchen for Uncle Yuri. Bed, bookshelves, a roof over his head—that's about all he needs. He's gone a lot. We've got a little white wine here. How about a glass?"

"Only if it complements the quiche." She spotted goblets in the hutch and took two out as she wondered how soon it would be before Mikal needed as little in the way of a home as Yuri did. David would soon be old enough for a good deal of independence, and Mikal's singular talents were apparently much in demand.

"It will shower the quiche with compliments and put a little glow in your cheeks, as well." She held the glasses out to him, and he poured.

"Here's to brotherly love," she offered, glass raised.

His gaze caught hers. "Here's to...womanly love."

Glasses clinked. "And real men."

He put his arm behind her neck and drew her closer. "Who'll take womanly love—" he gave one soft kiss "—over quiche—" followed by another "—anytime." He lingered longer on the third kiss.

"I'm hungry...for quiche." There was some truth in that, she told herself as her eyes drifted open. Mikal smiled and sipped his wine, and she knew he didn't doubt she was hungry.

He showed her the rest of the house—the bedroom, bathroom and den on the second floor, and the second bedroom in the garret. All the rooms were compact and efficiently furnished, and the first and second floors were connected by a narrow, winding flight of stairs. The garret was accessible only by ladder.

They were enjoying quiche, salad and a second glass of wine when Yuri let himself in the front door. Mikal knew the reason for the intrusion when he saw his uncle's expressionless face. Yuri had suggested this stop at his house for lunch, and he'd also promised Mikal some information.

"Have you children taken in all the important sights?" Yuri asked, not bothering to take off his topcoat.

"This house is one of the important sights, Yuri. It feels like living history, sort of a..." Morgan saw that Yuri had other things on his mind, and she had an uncomfortable feeling about what they might be, an unreasonable dread of hearing them. "Have you had lunch?" she asked quickly. "The quiche is delicious."

"Thank you, no. I'll interrupt for just a few moments, and then I must get back to the hotel." He beckoned Mikal with a gesture. "Just a brief conference. We've had word, Mikal."

The two men went upstairs, leaving Morgan at the table. The food was no longer palatable. She sipped her wine and tasted fear. She heard the brusque tones men used when business became serious, but the voices upstairs were too low for her to distinguish words. Secrets were to be expected in their business, Morgan told herself. They were men who looked for the skeletons in the world's closets, and there was a lot of risk-taking in such activity. She didn't want to know, didn't *need* to know, what they were talking about—except that she had a feeling. She shivered with it. Icy nausea. Their conversation touched her somehow.

On his way out Yuri pressed Morgan's hand between both of his and offered a strangely sad smile. "You and Mikal will talk. Old men always bring complications. It's the way of the world, I'm afraid."

Morgan couldn't find an airy reply, but she clung to Yuri's hand a moment longer.

Yuri turned to Mikal. "We'll count on you, then."

"Yes."

"I'll make the arrangements. You should have a couple of hours, at least."

Morgan stared at the door Yuri had closed behind him. At the touch of Mikal's hand on her shoulder, she turned and stepped into his arms and pressed the side of her face against his sweater. "May I know where you're going?"

"Yes, but you mustn't discuss it with anyone, Morgan. I'm going to an island in the Caribbean." She lifted her head to look up at him. "De Colores."

"My father is there." She took great care with the words, because she wanted them to be the simple truth. No complications from old men or younger ones.

"I know."

"But something's happened," she concluded.

Her eyes glittered up at him, and he hated the words, hated saying them to her. "There was a quick, quiet, almost bloodless coup. It looks like they've traded their old dictator in for a new one, but we're not—"

"*Almost* bloodless?"

"He's alive, Morgan. A number of Americans are being detained by the new government. Your father is one of them."

Chapter Eight

"How do you know?"

"We have reliable contacts." The fear in her eyes cut him deeply. "The details are sketchy. Nothing has been officially released on this. The State Department wants verification, and then they'll quietly notify—"

"The next of kin," she whispered.

"They're not even sure who they're dealing with, Morgan. The former regime was pro-Western, and this one, until they establish themselves...well, they're probably on the fence right now. We just don't know."

"What kind of people are they? Pro-Western, anti-Western—Mikal! My father is a *minister*. He has nothing to do with—"

"I know." He also knew her need to lash out.

"Why does the State Department need verification? How can your people be so sure if the State Department doesn't even know for certain?"

"We're regarded with a certain trust by some who can't trust anyone else. As I said, we have reliable—"

"Contacts, yes." The idea was incredible, and she tossed her head to make it go away. "Contacts! That's spy talk, agency talk." He lifted his hand to touch her face, but she whirled away from him. "Mikal! My father is a missionary. He has nothing to do with politics." Wild-eyed, she clenched her fists at her sides, struggling against the whole insane concept. "He has a little church and a school, and he feeds children and hands out secondhand clothing, and he doesn't... These people have guns, don't they, Mikal?"

"Morgan..."

He reached for her, but she backed away. "In the news, they always look like a bunch of thugs, and they're armed to the teeth. Are these... these *revolutionaries* like that?"

"Probably. But they're not going to hurt him, Morgan. He's no good to them dead."

"'Hurt' and 'kill' are two different things." Her voice quivered, low and gravelly, in her throat. "He's not a young man. Even so, he'll look after everyone else before he looks after himself. Mikal, if it's a choice between... he'll care more what happens to the others than..."

Her hands went to her face, and he seized the opportunity to take her back into his arms. Weeping softly, she sagged against him. "I should have gone to see him... just once."

"There'll be time, Morgan."

She grabbed two handfuls of his sweater and leaned back to plead, "Take me with you, Mikal."

"No."

"Let me go with you. I promise I won't—"

"No." He took her face in his hands and held her still. "Morgan, no. Truthfully, I don't know what's going on down there."

"Then what can you do? What can *you* do, Mikal Romanov? Do you have a gun?"

"No."

"*Will* you have a gun?"

"No."

"Then how will you get my father out? He doesn't have a gun, either, and *they* have . . ." She squeezed her eyes shut and saw her father with his hands bound behind his back and the barrel of a gun inches from his head. Tears rolled down her cheeks and splashed into Mikal's palms. "Oh, Mikal, please let me . . ."

"No," he whispered. "Please let *me*. Morgan, this is part of what I do."

"What can you do?" she demanded.

"I can talk to them." He saw the disbelief in her eyes. She wanted to hear that he could leap tall buildings in a single bound, crush bricks with his bare hands, shoot from the hip with precision and grace. He wished, just for her, that he could make *talk* sound as powerful. "I speak Spanish, which is one of the reasons I've been chosen."

"And you'll just . . . talk?"

He gave her half a smile. "Would you rather I promised to blow their heads off?"

"Yes."

With a quick laugh, he wrapped his arms around her. "Then I will."

"Is that one of those diplomatic lies?"

"Yes."

She closed her eyes and sighed. "Do you really have a chance, Mikal?"

"Yes. Otherwise I wouldn't go."

"You men always expect the women to stay home and wait, worrying. I don't want to be left . . ."

"I know." He tilted her head back so that she could see for herself. He understood. "Waiting is the hard part. Keep a candle burning for me, and I'll do my best to keep in touch with you." He brushed his lips across her forehead.

"Your best?" she managed, swallowing hard. Would there be problems even keeping in touch?

"Trust me, Morgan," he whispered. "Let me take care of this."

"I'm scared, Mikal." She closed her eyes and let him taste tears on her cheeks.

"Yes, I know." He drew her closer, and she tightened her hold around his back.

"I'm scared for *you.*"

"I'll be all right," he promised before he closed his mouth over hers.

She strained to get closer, to be enveloped in the comfort of his confidence. His hands moved along the ridges of her back and settled over her buttocks, and he pressed her against him. They shared a long, deep shudder.

"Hold me, Mikal."

"I need you now."

"Yes. Let me take care of you."

Zippers were difficult, buttons barely manageable. Flesh was alive, warm to the touch, yielding. So little time, so much to give.

"Make me part of you, Morgan."

"That's what I want. That's what I've wanted."

"It's settled, then. That's what you'll have."

Chairs were pushed aside. A small braided rug received them. Hovering close to his face, she breathed his breath. Cradling his head to her breast, she let tears fall in his hair. And then they cradled each other.

"You can't leave me now, not really."

"Keep me here. Keep me inside you."

"You're safe here, Mikal. Always."

The door between their rooms had been left open. There wasn't much time, and while she packed, Morgan listened to the sounds coming from Mikal's room, doting on them. Minutes were precious. She tossed things in her bags and turned from the shoddy job she'd done to find that Mikal had done much the same. Going to his aid, she assumed charge of the tuxedo he was stuffing into a garment bag. "I'll take this with me," she decided. "It'll just be in your way."

"Thanks." He backed away as she took over, smoothing, straightening, fussing over his shirts and pants as though taking care of an untidy child. Mikal shoved his hands into his pockets, lifting one corner of his mouth in a smile. She needed to be busy. "That leaves a little room for that stuff over there."

Morgan reached for the big plastic shopping bag that lay next to Mikal's small suitcase. "New clothes?"

"Summer stuff. Uncle Yuri thinks of everything."

"I'm glad someone does." She emptied the bag on the bed and began removing tags from the short-sleeved shirts and lightweight pants. She held up a sporty cotton jacket. "Is this the proper negotiator's attire? This looks like something for the well-dressed African explorer."

"I don't know much about styles." He chuckled as he lifted the jacket's sleeve. "David would get a kick out of this. He's been critical of my jackets with the elbow patches, says I oughta get with it. What do you think? Is this 'with it'?"

She imagined him wearing the natural-colored cottons and smiled. "If it isn't, I'm sure you can set a new trend."

"You'll look in on him, won't you?" She glanced at Mikal, saw the worry in his eyes, and she nodded. "Not just at school. His Aunt Peg's not too crazy about any of this, and she'll be huffing and puffing around. He'll need to be able to talk to someone else.''

''You've called him?''

''Yes. I told him as much as I knew—more than I've told him before. He's too old to be satisfied with the promise of a souvenir.''

''What did he say?''

Mikal smiled, pride brightening his eyes. ''He told me to give 'em hell. I think he'd like me to pack a gun, too.''

It was Morgan who took Mikal's hands and held them in hers. He would bring her father home. No weapon could match what Mikal had. He was going not because he sought the challenge, but because it sought him. The man that he was couldn't *not* go.

When the phone rang they both flinched. She held his hands a moment longer but on the fourth ring he answered. There was no conversation, just Mikal's confirmation. He was nearly ready. Morgan finished his packing quickly, touching each piece of his clothing in the silent hope that when he wore it, something of her would be close to his skin. Each item that was his seemed precious. She had a wild notion that she should pack a lunch for him, knit him some socks, or give him her ring. They were the most feminine of drives—to feed a man, keep him warm, give him remembrances. She was surprised to find she had those drives in her and, for some reason, she was pleased.

''I'll be in touch,'' he promised. ''Often. And when I come back, I'll want to see you.'' He pulled her into his arms and kissed her. She held tight as he whispered, ''Immediately. And then often. Do you think that can be arranged?''

''I think you could arrange to have the sun rise in the west, Mikal. With that silver tongue of yours...''

With a growl, he pressed his lips to the side of her neck and then gently corrected, "Velvet tongue, sweet Morgan. While I'm gone, decide which parts of your beautiful being would most enjoy the touch of velvet."

While he was gone, she decided that every part of her being wanted him back home. Without fanfare or media coverage, Mikal and Yuri had left Philadelphia on a plane bound for Mexico City en route to De Colores. As she said goodbye, Morgan told herself that Mikal would bring her father back. A piece of cake for the Romanovs, she decided, a routine matter. Pull a few strings, smooth a few feathers, the right words in the right ears, and everything would be all right. It was her part that would be the most difficult to play—waiting.

In two weeks there had been two calls from Mikal. The first came from Mexico City. Mikal and Yuri were leaving for La Primavera, De Colores's capital city, by chartered plane.

"Listen, Morgan, if I can't put my calls through directly, I'll get word to you by the Red Cross. And to David through you. Okay?"

Her stomach twisted into a knot. She knew he was saying that if his mission went awry, he wanted David to get the news from her rather than from some stranger. When word had come from the State Department that her father had been "detained," Morgan was glad she already knew, glad that the initial word had come from Mikal.

"David stopped in to see me this afternoon." She tossed off a small laugh. "He seems to think you timed this Caribbean junket just right. The weather's just turned cold." Morgan tried to will the tension in her stomach away. They *volunteered* for this, she told herself. Both her father and Mikal. This was who they were, and loving them meant sitting around with her insides tied up in knots, which was not the way she intended to live the rest of her life. She would definitely cut back on loving them, both of them, when they were safe.

Though the temperature was eighty-seven degrees in Mexico, Mikal felt the cold, and he felt the knot in her stomach. "Are you cold, Morgan?"

"Yes," she said quietly. "Yes," she repeated, injecting more strength into the word. "But I'm going to turn up the heat and have a cup of tea. And I'm not going to worry, Mikal. I know you'll be successful."

"I like your outlook. I'll try not to enjoy the weather too much if you'll just remember..." Remember the sound of my voice and how you felt when you looked at me when we were alone together, how you felt when I held you, and remember "... to keep a candle burning for me."

"I'll do that, Mikal. I promise."

Two days later Morgan received a call from the Red Cross. "Mr. Romanov sends word that he has reached his destination and his business should be taken care of within a few days."

Those few days were already long past by Morgan's calculations. She had acquired the habit of eating dinner alone by candlelight, a touch that she told herself was a pleasant one, but essentially meaningless. Pleasant, too, were the candles on the mantel and in the hurricane lamps by the mirror in the entryway. She'd never lit them since she'd first hung them on the wall, but now she decided she liked to keep the light flickering inside the glass. After all, Christmas was coming, and that was the time for candles.

News of the De Colores situation was vague. Everyone seemed to be sizing up the new government, which made bold declarations of its independence. Most foreigners had been free to leave the island or stay, as they wished. Transportation problems had caused some delays in evacuation, and there were those, a few American citizens among them, who were being temporarily detained by the new government, but no mention of hostages was ever made in the media. Nor was there mention of Freedom International.

"How come he can't call us himself, then?" David demanded as he scowled at Morgan's TV screen while they watched the evening news.

"Maybe tonight he will." Morgan gave David a hopeful smile. He'd been coming over in the evenings for the past week, hoping to be there when the next call came.

"You know what he'll do, don't you? He'll just park himself on the steps of the presidential palace and wait till hell freezes over or they let those people go." With a sigh, David tossed a magazine back on the coffee table where he'd found it. "That's just the way he is. He'll get himself—" David glanced at Morgan and slouched down a little further. He felt pretty low. "I'm sorry. I know it's for your dad."

"And I know it's your dad you're worrying about, so I guess we're both in the same boat."

"All these candles remind me of one of his damn rallies." David cast another guilty glance at Morgan and slid down further. "I mean *crazy* rallies. I mean...I don't know what I mean. He does such *good* stuff, but geez..."

"You want him back here, safe and sound." Morgan's encouraging nod gave David leave to agree. "I do, too."

She meant she wanted them *both* back, and David knew that. She'd been concerned for her father and his these last weeks, and he wondered if she were as scared as he was. He searched her sympathetic expression for signs. "It's usually the guys who are dying to punch somebody's face in who won't back down," he began. "Dad's the most peaceful guy you'll ever meet, but he won't give an inch, not on some-

thing like this. What I don't understand is, if you're no
willing to punch out somebody's lights, how do you make
him give in?''

"I guess you try to persuade him to look at things from
your perspective," Morgan suggested as she folded her
arms. "Which the adversary probably couldn't manage i
his lights were punched out."

"Yeah, but sometimes..." His attention seemed to be
drawn back to the news for a moment. He took a long drink
from the cup of hot chocolate he'd been nursing as he
watched. "You know, I saw a TV special about the sixties
and they showed some film clips of the '68 Democratic
convention. My dad was there—he was just a college kid—
and sure enough, I saw him in that show. I was just sitting
there watching this riot stuff, and all of a sudden there's m
dad, being beaten with a club. I swear, Dad was twice as big
as that cop, but he didn't fight back. He was trying to shield
some other guy with his own body, when he could have just
taken that club away and broken it over the cop's head." He
mimed the motions, then turned to Morgan with a face full
of conviction. "He could have, you know."

"I'm sure he could have, but then he'd have gotten him
self arrested." She used her sensible teacher's tone for Da
vid's sake. She knew her role. But the mental image o
Mikal being beaten made her mad as hell.

"He got arrested anyway. The camera picked that up, too
I wanted to walk into that film and fight back for him."

Morgan laughed. "You weren't even born yet!"

"Yeah, I know. Wouldn't it have been great? An aveng
ing angel from the future comes back to make mincemeat
out of—" Grinning, David shook his head. "But you know
what? He'd probably have protected the cop from *me*. He'
gotten arrested a couple of times for protesting, but when h
believes in something... You know, when they organiz

those demonstrations, the people who get arrested are usually volunteers."

"Yes, I know." She'd been in on one, she remembered, a long time ago. Teachers demonstrating at the White House. She remembered being told that there would be arrests, and she had been relieved to learn that it was part of the strategy; *she* would not be arrested. She felt a pang of inexplicable guilt.

"I guess... I guess that's just Dad," David decided. "He wouldn't be Dad if he didn't care so hard."

"Care so *hard?*"

"Well, it's hard—it's *hard* getting hit over the head with a club."

"And not fighting back?" Morgan asked gently.

"Yeah, especially when you know just one good right would..." David smacked his fist into his palm, and they both laughed at the irony. David might do that. Morgan, maybe. But not Mikal. "He's not gonna change, is he? He's gonna keep on being just as weird as he's always been." Morgan nodded. "I'm glad," David concluded. "I love him just like he is."

He looked at Morgan to see if she felt the same way. The funny way her eyes glistened as she smiled made him think she probably did.

Morgan wasn't sure when she decided to go to De Colores on her own. It might have been on the spur of the moment when the Red Cross told her that they were "not currently in touch" with either Mikal or Yuri Romanov, even though conditions on the island appeared stable. It might have been on the heels of the frustrating telephone conversation with a Mr. Morris at the State Department, who assured her that he would hear if her father's situation became critical, and since he hadn't heard, it must not be.

The word "hostage" met with resounding disapproval from Mr. Morris. She might have decided when she'd reread her father's last letter, or Mikal's poetry. Ultimately it might have been David's courage that activated a little of her own. It was an impetuous move, the kind she almost never made, but when the pilot announced the little commuter plane's arrival at La Primavera, Morgan's blood surged with excitement.

The air was warm and heavy, and its salty scent captured Morgan's fancy. The sea was visible from the small landing strip, and the stretch of white sand made her wish she were on vacation. White runway, white buildings, white-capped sea and white sand—the reflected light from the noon sun was almost oppressive. Morgan followed the other passengers to the terminal.

To her surprise, the customs official let her pass with few questions. She explained that she was on vacation in Mexico, and she claimed to have friends in De Colores who worked for the Red Cross. In fact she had two names, and those seemed acceptable. The new government obviously hoped that tourism would flourish again in short order because the official said that the beaches were beautiful this time of year. Then he asked about the weather in North Dakota as he stamped her passport.

With her two small bags in hand, Morgan breathed a sigh of relief as she made her way to the street outside the small terminal. One hurdle cleared. She refused to worry about the military jeep, the canvas-covered truck and the four leering men, armed and dressed in fatigues, whose suggestions to her were clearly understandable even though she spoke no Spanish.

She took a taxi to the Red Cross office, which was adjacent to the island's one hospital. It wasn't much of a hospital, Morgan decided as she surveyed the two-story stucco building. She had higher hopes for the Red Cross, which was housed in a newer, cleaner-looking building. It was the only contact she had.

"I'm trying to locate two American citizens who are here on the island somewhere. I wonder if you can help me."

The woman behind the desk reminded Morgan of a prairie grouse, so perfectly did she blend with her surroundings—gray dress and gray hair, which matched the steel-gray desk and file cabinet and the gray walls. She looked up and offered a tight smile. "You're here under whose auspices?"

"My own," Morgan explained. "That is, I came on my own. My name is Morgan Kramer, and I'm looking for—"

The gray woman frowned. "Morgan Kramer? Have we relayed messages to you recently, Miss Kramer?"

"Yes, you have. From—"

The woman rose quickly. "Yes, I know. It was your own idea to come here?"

"Yes, I . . . I decided it wouldn't hurt to try. I wasn't getting any answers, and I—"

"Come with me, Miss Kramer." The woman indicated a path through the office, past crates and boxes of supplies marked with the familiar red cross, to a door in the back of the room. "I have a feeling you're going to be sent home," the gray woman mumbled as she rapped on the door.

A man's voice answered. "Yes, Dorothy?"

"We have a visitor."

The door opened, and Morgan half expected to see Mikal. Her heart sank at the sight of the granite-faced man whose crinkled eyebrows almost made her swallow her own resolve. "Visitor?" The frown eased from his face as the man surveyed Morgan with all the subtlety of a panther, to which she decided he could well have been akin. "I think you got off at the wrong stop, ma'am. Bermuda is east of here."

"I'm looking for someone," Morgan informed him crisply.

The man sighed and shoved his hands in the pockets of his khaki slacks. "Well, the list is pretty long at the moment, but I guess I can—"

"Mikal Romanov," Morgan said. "And Sidney Kramer. Are they being held—"

The frown returned abruptly. "Who the hell are you?"

"My name is Morgan Kramer. Reverend Kramer is my father, and Mikal is here because—"

The man with the dark scowl snatched Morgan by the arm and dragged her through the door, muttering, "Mike's girlfriend. God in heaven, what next?"

Chapter Nine

"Take a seat, Morgan. Anywhere is fine. Mind if I smoke?"

There was only one chair in the little cubicle that appeared to be the man's office. It stood behind a desk, near a small window and the back door. With that escape route handy, it seemed a good place to situate herself. "Yes, I do." The man looked surprised, but his hand dropped away from his breast pocket. "Since you seem to know something about Mikal and me, may I know who you are?"

He smiled, and his face was no longer frightening. "'May I know who you are?' You remind me of a girl I knew in Springfield. Teacher type."

"Really," she managed tightly. "There are lots of Springfields."

"And lots of girls in every one. The name's McQuade," he said, offering his hand. Morgan hesitated. "Mike's a friend of mine. His messages to you came through me."

Morgan accepted his handshake with sudden gratitude. Here was a link to Mikal. "You've seen him then? He's all right?"

"It's been more than a week since they've allowed us any contact with them. Mike and Yuri are 'guests' at the palace—at least, they were as of a week and a half ago. Your father and the others have been detained."

"Which means?"

McQuade sat on the edge of the desk and looked Morgan straight in the eye. "Which could mean anything. This is a brand-new government, which is just like a brand-new baby. We await their pleasure. And right now, they seem to be taking pleasure in keeping us waiting."

"So you just sit here?" she asked, indicating the confines of the little office.

McQuade was amused. "I suppose you came all the way from North Dakota with a better idea?"

"Well, I...I suppose I'd..." Morgan sputtered before she remembered David's suggestion, which seemed as good as any at the moment. "I guess I'll sit on the steps of that palace until they let those people go or hell freezes over, whichever comes first."

"You're sure to draw a crowd, if nothing else."

Her jaw was set, her eyes growing colder by the minute. "Have you seen my father?"

"No."

"Do you know whether he's all right? When they plan to let him go?" McQuade shook his head. "Well, can you find out?"

"Mike Romanov is over there trying to do just that."

"And you don't even know whether Mikal is all right. Where are all of these reliable contacts of yours, Mr. McQuade?"

"Contacts of *mine?*"

"Mikal says you people have such good contacts, but you can't even seem to stay in contact with your own—"

McQuade raised a hand to quell her accusations in midstream. "First of all, I'm not part of Freedom International, even though I work with them occasionally. If Mike mentioned reliable contacts, you're probably looking at them."

It was Morgan's turn to scowl. "Oh, great. So being a contact means you're just waiting to be contacted. What an absurd situation." She rose from her chair.

"Where do you think you're going?" he asked, still amused.

"You said that Mikal is a 'guest'—" the word was couched in sarcasm "—at the palace, the seat of this glorious new government, I presume. That's where I'll try next."

"Try what? Getting yourself arrested?"

"Try getting in to see someone who will tell me something about—"

"Look, lady, simmer down." His gesture indicated that she should *sit* down, as well, and she complied. "Mikal tells me that Bismarck is one of the few places left in the world where people can leave their doors unlocked and odds are they won't get ripped off, so your naïveté is forgiven."

"Naïveté!"

"But if you screw up his efforts and get anybody killed, especially him, you won't be forgiven, so let's be friends. I don't know whatever possessed you to come to De Colores, but as long as you're here, I'll try to help you. You and I will get into that palace together." Morgan settled back into the chair and nodded. "They've been putting me off for over a week now, but they'll let me back in sooner or later, because sooner or later they'll want a good report from the Red Cross."

"You work for the Red Cross, then."

"Not exactly. Let's say I'm working *with* the Red Cross right now, and let's say you're with Freedom International. You're, uh, you're Mike's secretary."

"I don't speak Spanish."

McQuade shrugged. "Yeah, well Mike . . . Mike doesn't type well. What the hell, it's worth a shot."

For two days they had met with human stone walls at the doors of the presidential palace. No one knew anything about anyone named Romanov or Kramer, no one spoke Morgan's English or McQuade's Spanish, and no one was authorized to disturb anyone who might be able to answer any of their questions. Morgan was ready to stage her promised sit-in on the steps, and McQuade was on the verge of charging the entrance with a Sherman tank, when suddenly doors began to open. Glancing at one another as they followed their escort into the palace, they wondered what magic words they had said.

"We've missed your smiling face, McQuade." The announcement came from a man whose striking Latin features were enhanced by his crisp khaki uniform. His dark eyes brightened as they passed over McQuade's stony countenance and rested on Morgan. "But I see why you've been too busy to pay us a visit in the last week. The Red Cross has yet to send us such—"

"Too busy!" McQuade exploded. "I've been getting the runaround from your goons at the gate for nearly two weeks, Colonel. What the hell is going on here? Why have I been refused admittance?"

The colonel looked genuinely puzzled. "I wasn't informed of your visits."

"And I was told that you were not to be disturbed," McQuade bit out. "Which *I* found very disturbing. Are your 'guests' receiving hospitable treatment?"

"Of course."

"May I be allowed to verify that?"

"Certainly. Mikal is with the general at the moment, and Yuri chooses to spend most of his time with our detainees. That, of course, is his privilege. Please—" he gestured toward an open door "—make yourselves comfortable. They have spent the morning together, and the general will need a rest soon. The young lady is . . . ?"

"Mikal's secretary," McQuade explained. "Morgan Remark. Morgan, this is Colonel Hidalgo."

"How do you do, Colonel?" Sliding McQuade a quick frown as she offered her hand, Morgan fully expected the colonel to kiss it, but she realized she'd seen too many movies when he merely gave her a polite handshake.

"Ordinarily Miss Remark accompanies Mikal on all his missions, but we had assumed that this one would be handled quickly." They'd moved from a foyer to a room containing a heavy wooden table surrounded by chairs. McQuade knew the routine. He pulled a chair out for Morgan, then took the one beside her.

"Mikal's messages for his family have not reached you in the last few days, then," Colonel Hidalgo surmised in his accented but flawless English.

"His family hasn't had a message in almost two weeks," McQuade said.

The colonel's apology was directed at Morgan. "I'm sure his loved ones are concerned about him. I regret that. We have no intention of frightening or harming anyone."

"That *is* good news," Morgan told him as she assumed a collected posture, folding her hands on the table in front of her.

"Just a few moments, then," the colonel promised as he took his leave.

"Remark?" Morgan whispered, sagging a little in relief at having gotten this far.

"Kramer backward," McQuade explained with a smile. "No offense. It's best not to give them any emotions to play with, so don't let them see any. You're nobody's relative."

McQuade was pacing by the time Colonel Hidalgo finally ushered Mikal through the door. Morgan remembered packing the yellow, cotton, short-sleeved shirt and beige slacks he was wearing. He looked tired, she thought as her heart yearned toward him. He saw McQuade first. "Where've you been, McQuade? I understand you brought my sec—" the sudden sight of Morgan made him break the word into senseless pieces "—re . . . tary. Morgan?"

They exchanged wordless looks, one stunned, one scared, letting reality gradually take hold and giving McQuade the moment he needed. "Your home office decided you might need Miss Remark if this is to be a long siege. For, uh, correspondence, research, whatever it is you guys do. Anyway, they sent her along, and I brought her over."

"Thank you, McQuade," Mikal managed. It didn't matter for the moment that she was in danger up to her eyebrows. In her pristine white suit, hair done up to keep her neck cool, she was a vision of beauty.

"I spoke with your son just before I left," Morgan offered, finding the nerve for a tentative smile. "He's fine. He—" she cast a quick glance at Colonel Hidalgo "—hopes you'll be home for Christmas."

The fact that she was actually there in the room with him made everything else seem slightly fuzzy, out of focus. There was no floor, no furniture, nothing but Morgan. Mikal forced himself to walk calmly to the table and take the chair across from her.

"With the two of you here and no word from you," Morgan hastened to explain, "no hint of when you might be inished with your mission, we're sort of at a standstill. Loose ends, you might say."

So beautiful, he thought. Such a breath of fresh air. Invigorating, like a prairie wind. If they let you walk out of here, Morgan, don't stop walking until the plane lands in Bismarck. But if they don't . . . oh, God, Morgan, if they don't . . . You, of all people.

"We had to be certain you were all right, Mikal." She'd never seen him angry, and she wondered if the strange look on his face was his version of it. Disapproval was certainly there, and tension. But he seemed to be all right, and if something was wrong, maybe it was . . . "And we've had no word on the others—those who were taken . . . before."

"Yuri is with the detainees as our observer," Mikal explained quietly. "They're all accounted for, and Colonel Hidalgo personally sees to it that their needs are met." Morgan gave the colonel a furtive glance. He was standing at the window, pretending to have no interest in the conversation. He seemed fairly considerate, Morgan decided, for a thug who took hostages.

"There's adequate food and medical attention, then?" McQuade put in, playing his role. Mikal's chin dipped in assent. "You're not still drinking the water, are you, Mike?"

"I've come to an understanding with the water, and I'm doing my own cooking." It was difficult not to reach across the table and touch her. "It's good that you were able to see me for yourself, Morgan. Now your job will be to set the minds back home at rest. Go back to—"

"You've been ill?" she asked, more anxiously than she'd intended.

"No, no, I'm fine." Her hands were folded demurely on the table, and Mikal's own hand rose reflexively, then fell back in his lap. God, how he wanted to touch her, just her hand. But he had to send her away, and she had to go directly. He was walking on eggshells as it was. Hidalgo was one thing, but Guerrero, General Castillo's hatchet-faced enforcer, was something else. Mikal leaned forward and willed her to understand the gravity of the situation. "There's really not much you can do for me here. I need you back on the home front, holding down the fort."

Morgan dug her heels in. She'd come this far and she was not going back to the waiting routine. She searched for a plausible line. "There are several pressing matters to be discussed, Mikal. I need direction. The Levine matter has reached a critical stage, and besides that..." She looked to the colonel, who had turned from the window to take a pointed interest in the conversation. "We've been out of touch with Mikal and Yuri Romanov for almost two weeks, Colonel. Our organization simply cannot function this way. If you could allow me some time here, just to work on some details that have nothing to do with—"

Mikal's hands shot across the table and he squeezed her forearm to silence her. "There's no need for that. Give me a written briefing, and I'll get back to you in writing or by phone—whatever I can manage."

Colonel Hidalgo took a step nearer the table. "You must understand, Miss Remark, that we are in the process of determining who our friends are. We allow very limited access to the palace, but if you have a reason to be here..."

"She has no reason to be here, Colonel." Mikal pushed himself away from the table and came to his feet, towering over everyone else in the room. "She's just a secretary." He gave Morgan the first chilling look she'd ever received from him. "Indispensable at the typewriter, but you know how it is with women. They start thinking you can't tie your shoes without their help."

Morgan found Hidalgo's slow smile only slightly less aggravating than Mikal's comment, but at least it was warmer

an the hand Mikal had laid on her arm. "She came a long
ay just to tie your shoes, Mikal." He turned to McQuade,
ho had become an impartial observer, and nodded to-
ard the door. "I could use five minutes of your time,
cQuade."

When the door closed behind the two men, Morgan
ondered whether she was, even then, truly alone with
ikal. Was there a microphone in the bookshelf? A tape
corder behind the wall? Stiff and impassive, he stood there
ad stared down at her. She came to her feet, hoping to
inimize her disadvantage, and waited for some indication
at it was safe to talk.

He spoke slowly and deliberately. "What, in the name of
l that's sensible and practical, are you doing here, Mor-
an?"

Her hands fluttered a little. "I'm not sure. I wasn't cer-
in how far I could get, but each time I made it a step
oser, I decided I'd try one more."

"Why?"

She looked up at him, amazed. Where was the sensitivity
at had been his hallmark? Why wasn't he as relieved to see
er as she was to see him? "Because my father is here, and
ou're here, and no one knew whether either of you was
fe."

"Your father is safe, and you did well not to reveal any
lationships. We're walking a very thin line here, with some
olatile personalities." He worked to tighten his internal
old on his emotions, reminding himself that it would be a
istake to take her in his arms.

"Hidalgo?" she asked.

"No. General Castillo has two advisers. Hidalgo is the
oice of sanity here. It's Colonel Guerrero's influence that
e're working to overcome."

"Are you free to walk out of here, Mikal?"

His shoulders sagged a bit. "No. Not without the oth ers."

"Is that *your* choice?"

He shoved his hands in his pockets. "It was my choice to come here. I wasn't 'detained' like the others. But, no, I'm not free to come and go as I please." He gave her a hard look. "You won't be, either, if Guerrero finds out anything about you. He thinks he can rule the world with an M-16."

"Do you think they're watching us now?" she whis pered. "Listening?" He shook his head, and she wanted to say "Touch me, then," but she recalled how cold his fin gertips had been and she chose reason over emotion. "I'm going to ask the colonel to let me see you on a daily basis just for a few minutes, just to assure our organization that you're safe and well. It would be in their own best interest to—"

"You'll do no such thing. You're walking out of here in three more minutes, Morgan, and you're not looking back until the plane takes off with you on it." Because he saw no sign of agreement on her face, he took her shoulders in both hands to shake her, to communicate his desperation. "You've got to get out of here. I don't want you here. I don't want to see you every day. I don't want..." Because he had touched her, he was lost. He pulled her into his arms and laid his cheek against her hair. "Oh, God, you're the most beautiful sight I've seen since I left Philly, but you can't be here, Morgan."

"Who says?" Her voice was raspy. Her throat burned as she reached around to offer a crushing embrace of her own.

"Your boss says." He slipped his hand beneath her short jacket and smoothed the cotton blouse that covered her back. "How much am I paying this invaluable secretary who types and ties shoes?"

"Nothing." Her lips grazed his neck, and she whispered, So I've come to get a raise out of you."

He tightened his hold on her and growled near her ear, "If t a raise, certainly a *rise* out of me." Stretching to her es, she rubbed herself against him with all the subtlety of hungry cat, and he groaned. "Morgan, five minutes isn't ough, and you have to go." He caressed her back, trying get his fill of her without touching her intimately as he nged to do.

"It's so warm here. Why are your hands cold?"

Gripping her shoulders, he put her away from him, let- ng her see his regret. "Because I've been cold with fear nce I walked into the room and found you here, Morgan. can't believe you did something this crazy."

"I can't believe my father's a hostage, or a detainee, or hatever the latest word for it is. I can't believe we're to- ther on this lovely little island, and we can't go down to e beach and lie in the sun." She reached up to cup his eek in her hand. "You look as though you haven't had uch sun recently. You have been ill, haven't you?"

He shrugged, letting his hands slide the length of her arms hold her hands. "I knew better than to drink the water, t I forgot about ice cubes. Listen, I'm okay. I want you to back and tell David that."

"Mikal, I'm not—" The door behind her opened slowly Mikal released her hands.

"Please don't argue," he said quickly.

Colonel Hidalgo cleared his throat. "I will have some- e see you and McQuade to the gate, Miss Remark."

Morgan turned, knowing that Hidalgo and McQuade ere waiting. She couldn't leave without looking back, but s expression was impassive once again. "I'll be back in the ates very soon," he told her. "Meanwhile, let's put ev-

erything on hold." She nodded and walked out witho
saying goodbye.

"Would you like to have your 'secretary' with yo
Mikal?" Mikal turned from the tall, narrow window. H
was beginning to regard Hidalgo as his ally, and he kne
that the man had not been fooled. "It could be arranged,
the colonel promised.

"You could also arrange to have her flown out of here th
afternoon."

Hidalgo arched an eyebrow. "You don't think she'll lea
on her own?"

Mikal sighed, shaking his head in wonder at what she ha
accomplished already. "I don't know. I would never ha
expected her to take such a risk. Ordinarily she's a ve
sensible woman."

"A paradox, then. That makes her a fascinati
woman—the only kind that would interest a man like Mik
Romanov. And, of course, she's beautiful."

"She won't be detained," Mikal insisted in a quiet, ev
tone. "She'll be free to go."

"If she chooses to leave, I see no problem at this point

"But you won't arrange for her departure, either," Mik
concluded.

Hidalgo smiled, his dark eyes sparkling. "I admire h
ingenuity. It will be interesting to watch her next move."

It was not McQuade's habit to try to influence a decisi
that wasn't his to make. He made his living working f
people who were determined to beat the odds, and he s
dom discouraged them from trying. Morgan Kramer had
intention of leaving the island yet, and McQuade didn't a
gue with her. He helped her find a room at La Casa Blanc
which was a comfortable hotel. He made inquiries for h

d he served as a sounding board. Two days after their visit
the palace, McQuade headed for the hotel with an offer
om Hidalgo, and he knew Morgan wouldn't be asking for
vice once she heard what he had to say.

Mike had described her as a "sensible, practical woman,"
d McQuade would have agreed, to a point. She had a way
making everything she did sound practical, and he had no
ubt she'd convinced herself that it was perfectly sensible
r a naive teacher type from the Midwest to fly down to De
olores and pretend there was something she could do
out the hostages in the palace. It amused McQuade that
e worked so hard at this sensible posture when it was as
ain as the nose on her face that she was there because her
art wouldn't let her be anywhere else. Knowing Mikal
omanov, whom he considered to be the most admirable
an he'd ever met, McQuade understood Morgan's predic-
ent. As long as Mike was on the island, McQuade felt
at he couldn't be anywhere else, either.

Within the hour McQuade was sharing a table in the ho-
l lounge with Morgan. He'd already drained one beer and
as starting on another. She was still sipping on a soft drink
hen he launched his news. "Mike seems to trust Hidalgo,
I guess we can, too. I just got word that you can go over
ere this evening and see Mike if you want. The invitation
me from Hidalgo."

Morgan's eyes widened as she let the plastic straw slip
om her lips. "If I *want!* When? What time?"

"Simmer down, now. I'll be taking you over. I want to see
idalgo's face—make sure I'm delivering you into his
ands. So we'll go in a little while."

At the thought Morgan's heart rate jumped into a higher
ar. "If we have a chance to talk privately, I should be able
get a clearer picture of where Mikal's negotiations stand,
d I can report back—"

"Report back?" McQuade laughed. "You're going i
there to see Mike, lady. I'm not *sending* you in there, and
don't even know whether to expect you back or not."

Morgan looked incredulous. "But it's important that w
establish better contact and let the State Department c
somebody know where things stand."

"Yeah, well, I have a feeling the State Department ha
some idea. What Mike's doing is being done quietly, whic
is the best way to keep people alive in a situation like this.
Stabbing a finger in the air for emphasis, McQuade leane
toward Morgan. "You, Miss Remark, are going in there t
see Mike. I don't know what kind of visit it will be, and
figure it's none of my business, but don't think I'm sendin
you, and don't think of yourself as some kind of envoy
You're not. You want to see Mike? You're getting you
chance."

Morgan studied the candle that burned between then
"You don't mince words, do you, McQuade?"

"I don't see any point in it when we're all voluntaril
perched up here, straddling the cutting edge of somebod
else's blade. You and I know damn well that as long as w
stay here, they can come and get us any time they want. W
ought to be honest with ourselves about our reasons for be
ing here." She looked up at him, and he smiled. "Tha
makes it easier to be honest with each other about how w
want to proceed. You want to change your clothes before w
go?"

"Yes," Morgan said quietly, offering no smile in return

Mikal waited in the shadows of the garden, where h
could see the terrace and the door she would come through
There was a silver slip of Caribbean moon in the sky, an
the garden was sweet with floral fragrance. If he couldn

give her an afternoon at the beach, he could give her a rendezvous in a tropical garden. Hidalgo had told him that she had stayed and that she continued to try to see him. If she wouldn't leave, he couldn't keep her safe. They could pick her up any time. And if Guerrero found out who she was and why she was there, he might do just that. If, if, if—she had to know, had to be warned, had to come to her senses.

And he had to see her, had to touch her, had to fill his head with the sound of her voice. For two nights he'd lain awake thinking of nothing else.

The light in the atrium came on and Mikal could see her with Hidalgo, who ushered her through the French doors to the terrace. Then the other man went back inside and closed the door and the light went out.

There she stood, her long, dark hair bright with moonlight, her white dress a beacon. Mikal indulged his senses in watching her as she crossed the tiled terrace toward the reflecting pool. The singing of insects seemed to fade for the moment as her sandals made a delicate clicking sound in the quiet of the night. Her dress was soft and loose, and it fluttered with the night breeze as she walked, as did her hair. She'd left it down, the way he liked it best.

Near the reflecting pool stood a shrine with a small mahogany carving of some saint—one whom Mikal imagined had taken pity on him this night, so he had filled the little candle holders and lit two dozen candles. Their bobbing flames, sheltered by flowering greenery, were reflected in the pool among the water hyacinths. The shrine drew Morgan, as Mikal had known it would.

She was made for candlelight. He watched her take an unlit candle from the rack and touch its wick to one of the flames he had put there to greet her. Light and shadow caressed her face, and the white spikelike flowers of an acacia fluttered around her head, paying her tribute with their sweet scent as she set the white taper in one of the few remaining holders.

"I hope that one's for me." Morgan looked up and saw him standing in the shadows. He always seemed comfortable with his surroundings; his smile came easily, as always. Morgan felt tension ease from her stomach, and her eyes brightened with her smile. In his white bush jacket and slacks, he could have been an advertisement for a safari vacation. "I've been keeping him in candles for weeks now," Mikal said. "Figured I needed a friend."

"You have me," she said, her voice barely audible. "I've kept your candle burning, just as you asked."

"I know," he whispered. "I've felt it." He reached for her hand and pulled her into the shelter of a stand of fringed palms. Lacing his fingers through hers, he teased the hollows of her palms with his thumbs while he poured fiery, slow, open kisses over her upturned face and whispered, "Hottest . . . damned . . . flame . . . oh, Morgan, you should go, you should go. . . ." He tasted her temple with the tip of his tongue, and she shivered with a thrill that passed to his own body. "Stay, please stay, Morgan . . . Morgan . . ."

His mouth captured hers and held it, offering no quarter. He plundered her with his flickering, plunging tongue, and she caught her breath, shocked, singed, seduced. She felt his heat, and she arched into it with a small sound, proclaiming her own tart, belly-puckering need, sweet, breast-swelling need. This was Mikal, whose way was always gentle; this was Mikal, whose strength ran deeper than the corded muscle she caressed from waist to shoulder. What dream could match the sound of his quickening breathing, the touch of his hand, or the taste of his kiss? Morgan was grounded in reality, and she would have Mikal ground himself in her.

Morgan's cotton gauze dress moved easily beneath his hands as Mikal reveled in the feel of her. She wore something between the dress and her skin, something smooth and feminine, something that didn't bind the firm curves of her bottom or the softness of her breasts that were pressed tightly against him. With both hands he held her hips closer to himself, and she rose on tiptoe to accommodate him as she invited him to deepen their kiss. Perhaps, he thought fleetingly, he would let her drive him to distraction, and then he could enjoy this heightened awareness of her to infinity.

Mikal lifted his head at last with a tortured groan. "Morgan, you're not safe here," he rasped.

Then she knew that for her there could be no safety. She pressed moist lips high on his chest in the vee of the shirt he wore with the short-sleeved jacket.

"I'm a selfish man. I know I should talk them into arresting you and putting you on a plane bound for the States," he whispered, but his embrace didn't slacken. "What's wrong with me? Why can't I do that?"

"I've come too far," she whispered.

"So have I," he confessed, cradling her face in his hands and tilting it up to his. "Forgive me for allowing you to risk this."

"You take your risks; I'll take mine." And she kissed him again. She fastened her senses on him, ignoring the scent of gardenias and the call of a night bird. She wanted only to fill herself with Mikal—the catch in his breath that her kiss caused, the citrus smell of his after-shave, the smoothness of his cheek beneath her hand. She held him close, wanting more of him. "Colonel Hidalgo says... before daybreak I have to go."

Mikal swallowed hard, closed his eyes hard, felt hard, and knew this was insane. "The room they gave me is close by," he whispered into the soft comfort of her hair.

"Take me there."

Chapter Ten

Morgan followed Mikal through the garden and down some tiled steps to a lower level of the terrace where another set of French doors opened to his room. He drew the drapes, throwing everything into pitch darkness. He gave her hand a quick squeeze before he released it, then fished a book of matches from the breast pocket of his jacket. He found his way to the bureau and extracted a match. Striking it, he located the candles he'd planted there earlier.

"Not enough light to draw any attention." When three candles were aflame, he tossed the matches aside and turned to Morgan. "But enough so I can see you."

"You have such a thing for candles."

He went to her, gathered her in his arms and turned her profile to the light. "I have such a thing for your face bathed in candlelight." His kiss was slow, controlled, tantalizing. He whispered, "Your face bathed in sunshine." Another slow kiss, another quiet bit of praise. "Your sweet face bathed in anything. Morgan, I have such thoughts."

Her stomach tightened and her knees grew weak. "Thoughts of what?"

"Thoughts of bathing you." His breath flowed hot against her neck. "But I can't run the water in the tub. Someone would hear."

"The pool outside..."

"Someone would see."

"...would be so nice. It's hot."

"Because you're wearing too many clothes."

Her dress was gathered at the neck, but when he released the string that held it, it slid past her shoulders easily. He kissed the curve of her collarbone. "Was it cold when you left home?"

"Yes," she whispered, trying to remember what cold was, what caused it. "Bone-chilling wind."

"Chilled these beautiful bones, did it?"

"Mmm-hmm." Her dress dropped to the floor, leaving her in a satin teddy.

"And you missed me?"

"My bones did," she managed. He admired the full length of what he'd uncovered, lovely Morgan in a small wisp of satin, and the light in his eyes became a heated glow. He covered her breasts with his hands, and she quivered inside.

"Where else did you miss me, Morgan?" His gentle coaxing hardened her nipples beneath the satin, and she whimpered. "Tell me," he urged.

"My breasts missed you."

He kissed her, letting his tongue drift between her lips. "Ah, Morgan, they did." One hand strayed lower, smoothed her flat belly and dropped between her thighs.

"And here," he whispered thickly. "Did you miss me here?"

"Oh, Mikal..."

"Yes, you did."

"Mikal..."

"I'm going to bathe you with my tongue," he promised. "I could bathe you inside, Morgan, but I'm not prepared for you this time."

She put her arms around him and held herself against him, testing his need. "You're such a gentleman, Mikal Romanov," she told him in a voice hoarse with tenderness. "I prepared myself for you." She looked up with soft, bright eyes. "But I appreciate the thought."

"Sure?" She nodded. "No more thinking, then."

"No more," she whispered as she pushed the jacket back from his shoulders. "Have you missed me?"

He shed his jacket. "Let me show you." The metallic clink of his belt buckle was followed by the click of a snap. "Let me show you how many ways I've missed you."

He showed her a hundred ways, and she responded in a hundred more. She was as gentle as he was; she was as wild. She was so lost in passion she had no idea where she was. She hadn't surveyed the room, and she didn't care. There was a bed, and Mikal was with her. She'd found him, and now she joined with him, greedy for the part of him that could not be taken back once given. She believed that with her heart, and her mind condoned the belief for her heart's sake.

Later, when they lay together quietly, their bodies glistening in the candle glow, Mikal said, "This is the way I think I missed you most."

"Hot and sweaty?"

He gave a low chuckle. "When I saw you teaching that class in the school gym, the way you threw your whole heart into those exercises, I had fantastic fantasies of other ways to get you hot and sweaty.''

"They worked." She tasted the salty sheen of his shoulder. "Both ways."

"I beg your pardon, ma'am, but there were at least seven ways that worked quite nicely." He braced himself on an elbow and trailed a finger along her arm. "Very, very nicely."

"It's amazing how long you were able to sustain that..."

"Optimum pulse rate," he filled in, grinning.

"And without much warm-up."

"Instant warm-up when I saw you on the terrace. As you see, there's no cool down."

"We can't open a window, can we?" He shook his head, and she pushed her hair away from her neck. "I should tie my hair up."

"Don't you dare." With splayed fingers he combed it back from her face and let it spill in dark swirls over the white bed sheets. "The way I missed you most is relaxed and sated with our lovemaking. You're a paradox, you know." He tickled his chin with a hank of hair, then made a loop of it and rubbed it over his cheek. "You're beautiful with your hair up, very prim, very sensible, very much in charge, but a little distant. Just out of reach, as though you were guarding some part of you." He smiled. "Now I know what it is."

"What part am I guarding?"

"The passionate lioness with the long, flowing mane. You pin up your hair to keep her in check."

"I pin up my hair to keep it off my neck and out of my way," she insisted. "Coming to this island is the wildest thing I've ever done, and I came with my hair pinned up."

He chuckled as he stroked her hair back again. "The lioness came dressed as Miss Dove so she wouldn't scare anybody."

She glanced up with a quizzical frown. "Do I scare you?"

"Sometimes."

"Why?"

Tenderly he caressed her cheek with the back of his hand. "Such delicacy makes me feel awkward sometimes, afraid to touch. The flip side of that is your fierce passion. You won't release yourself to me completely, but there are times when I get the feeling you want to drain me thoroughly."

"I want to give you . . . satisfaction," she said carefully.

"Believe me, you do. But there's more to it than that, I think."

Morgan stiffened. "I'm not making any demands on you, Mikal. Let's just be good to each other now and part friends when the time comes."

"Part friends?" She'd stepped into a hornet's nest to be with him, and she talked about parting as friends? Mikal wondered when the woman would ever know herself.

"What I mean is that I don't expect . . ." With a sigh, she told herself to relax, and she reached to touch the tousled hair that fell over his forehead. "You think like a poet, Mikal. Dreams are your reality. You even talk like a poet— about making love, and about lionesses and paradoxes. That's just your normal, everyday way of *talking.*"

"Is it bad?" he asked seriously.

She gave her hair a quick toss and laughed as she pulled him into her arms. "It's beautiful. It's magic. I love the way you talk, the way you put things. It's Mikal, no one but Mikal."

"Actually, Miguel called you a paradox. 'A fascinating woman,' he said." The curves of her back and her buttocks served as a playground slide for his hand. "I had to remind him that I'm bigger than he is."

"Who's Miguel?"

"Colonel Miguel Hidalgo." Mikal lay back on the pillow and cradled Morgan in his arm. "The man who's keeping us all alive right now."

"I thought the man in charge was General Castillo."

"Theoretically, he is. This coup was a party they held in his honor—supposedly. The general is a popular man, a grandfatherly type, whose instincts tell him to back down on this hostage thing and throw in with the West. Nobody liked the last regime much—they spent a lot of money they didn't have on stuff they didn't need, and the people stayed poor. So the Castillo faction came to power without a fight, and our State Department would recognize them with no problem, if he could just put a cork in Guerrero."

She'd heard the name before, and she knew it inspired genuine feelings of dread. "Who is this Guerrero, anyway?"

"He's Castillo's nephew and heir apparent. He's a user. He worked for the old regime, then jumped sides when it was convenient, and now he has the general's ear and a good deal of influence over what army they have here."

"This island seems too small to have much military power," Morgan observed. She'd seen automatic weapons, truckloads of soldiers, and wary civilians, but nothing resembling heavy artillery.

"Guerrero doesn't know that. He envisions himself as a cigar-chomping Caesar with a military empire. Thanks to Hidalgo's diplomacy and Castillo's popularity, the State Department is sitting on hold."

"And the hostages?"

"They're on hold, too. It's a tug-of-war with Guerrero on one side and Hidalgo opposite him. The hostages are the rope."

Morgan sighed. "Why don't we call in the marines?"

"Because then the rope breaks, Morgan." He lifted her chin and tilted his head for a look at her face. "You want the leathernecks instead of the silver tongue? No faith in me?"

"I don't understand exactly what you do, Mikal." And then she added quickly, "But I do understand that they're armed and you're not. That's scary."

"You'd feel better if I stuck a gun in my belt."

"Maybe one of those little derringers inside your boot."

He laughed, hugging her. "I don't own a pair of boots. Besides that, they search me quite thoroughly before they let me anywhere near Castillo, and I mean *quite* thoroughly."

"Oh, Mikal, this is crazy. The secretary of state should be down here taking care of this. They're not going to kill the secretary of state."

"They're not going to kill me, either."

She braced herself on his chest to launch her barrage. "How can you stop them, Mikal? With words? You're a poet. Who's going to retaliate if they knock off one dreamy poet with a head full of beautiful words?"

His chest rumbled as he laughed. "If they could see the look in your eyes, we'd all be on our way home tomorrow. My ultimate weapon—my lioness." He tucked a stray lock behind her ear, thinking how much he loved that fall of hair. "I want you right there beside me, purring like a harmless kitten, the next time I have a session with Castillo and company."

She tossed her hair again and smiled. "I'll show them balance of power."

"Right on."

"Cold war, détente, no holds barred—whatever they want, I'm ready."

"We'll rewrite *High Noon*."

"And I won't have to sit home twiddling my thumbs and waiting for—" their eyes met, and their smiles faded "—news." She closed her eyes and settled over him, resting her cheek against his chest. There was no music sweeter than his heartbeat.

"I'm not much of a poet, Morgan, but I'm a pretty fair novelist. A few people might care if I got 'knocked off' down here. Freedom International commands some respect, as well, so we've got *something* going for us."

"Something bigger than a derringer?"

"God, I hope so."

Hope springs eternal, she thought, especially in the mind of a dreamer. "What do you talk about in these sessions?"

"It depends. Castillo likes to talk about women, foreign aid, the price of pork and the CIA. Guerrero wants to impress me with his party line and his knowledge of weaponry, and Miguel wants to know what kind of school my son goes to and where he could get a grant to remodel the hospital here in La Primavera. Sometimes Miguel turns me loose in the kitchen and talks politics and philosophy while I cook us a decent meal."

"For heaven's sake, Mikal, what about the hostages?"

"That's what I choose to discuss, and the trick is in bringing them up whenever everyone's being reasonable. Miguel wants to let them go as a goodwill gesture. Castillo sees them as insurance."

"And Guerrero?"

Mikal sighed. "Guerrero is a fool." The truth was that Guerrero was a madman, but he chose not to use the word.

"He's willing to kill people," Morgan assumed.

He's *anxious* to kill people, Mikal amended silently, but aloud he offered hope. "Miguel Hidalgo is a reasonable man, though Guerrero's relationship to Castillo puts him in better standing with the old man. Miguel was educated in the States, and he knows what we have to offer. Right now, though, he has to play down his American sympathies, because independence fever is running pretty high."

"Then Castillo is just a pawn?"

Mikal shook his head. "I wouldn't say that. He's a wily old buzzard who's weighing his options."

It struck Morgan as an outrageous absurdity. A tiny island paradise, an uncontested coup and some men drunk with sudden power had the State Department "on hold," while some innocent people waited to go home if sanity prevailed—or to be shot if it didn't. What messes these dreamers get themselves into, she thought, and the thought gave her a queasy feeling.

"Why are they holding my father?"

"Basically, I think it's because Guerrero doesn't like missionaries. I gather he had some experience with mission schools when he was a kid. Anyway he says your father was in thick with the old regime. He's holding a young teacher under the same pretense."

"And the others?"

"A reporter, two college kids supposedly suspected of drug possession, a doctor—and then there's the woman with the haunted eyes."

"Are you being poetic again?"

"Can't think of any other way to describe her," he said absently as he pictured her. She'd reminded him of a trapped animal. "The others are American, but I'm not sure about her. She won't talk. She's terrified of Guerrero."

"Is she pretty?"

"She's beautiful." He enjoyed Morgan's even, controlled stare for a moment before he gave way to a smile and allowed a twinkle to creep into his eyes. "But plain as a pilgrim next to you."

She kissed the middle of his chest, catching a bit of soft curly hair between her lips for a playful tug. He only laughed. "Do you have any idea how beautiful you are, Mikal Romanov?"

"I'm dreamy," he reminded her. "You said so yourself."

"I meant that you're a dreamer. Purely insatiable, and I have a terrible weakness for your kind."

"Oh, really?" He rolled with her in his arms, and she looked up at him. "I didn't think there were enough like me to make up a whole 'kind.'"

"Dreamers," she said with a sigh. "Idealists. If you've met my father, you know what I mean."

"I've met your father, and I admire him. Was there someone else who fell into that troublesome category?"

"It's not a matter of being troublesome. It's a matter of being impossible to live with." This was not the time for this discussion, she thought. All she wanted was to be close to Mikal for a few hours. She turned, settling her shoulder back, letting her attention drift to the shadowed ceiling. "There was Jeremy," she said quietly. "But we had sense enough to realize it wouldn't work."

"Your good sense has served you well. Artists can be such eccentrics." He caught her incredulous glance and grinned. "Really. You're much too sensible to get hooked up with some crazy artist."

"I certainly have taken leave of my senses, haven't I?"

"I wouldn't say so." He was thirsty, and the only thirst quencher at hand was in the fruit bowl someone left for him each day. He reached behind him and located the bowl. "I' say coming to this powder keg of an island is perfectly sane. I did it myself. Have a grape.''

A bunch of purple fruit dangled above her nose. Morgan stretched her neck and captured a grape with her teeth. The skin burst and filled her mouth with sweet juice. She bobbed for a second one. ''Delightful.'' She watched him put several into his own mouth before he offered her another chance. ''Is this the forbidden fruit?''

Lips glistening with grape juice, Mikal offered a slow smile as he reached to the bowl, keeping his eyes on her. He came up with another offering. ''This,'' he whispered suggestively, ''is the forbidden fruit.''

''What is it?'' Morgan tested the smooth skin with her lips and found that it had more give than an apple. It felt cool, and she took a healthy bite. Sweet juice escaped the corner of her mouth.

''It's passion fruit.'' He swept up the errant dribble with his tongue. They shared the plumlike fruit, and when they were done, they shared the flavor that lingered on their lips.

''Do you have any idea how beautiful you are?'' he asked.

''No. Tell me.''

''Let me show you.''

Morgan found herself standing before the mirror and she saw the reflection of three flickering candles and two nude people. One was tall, broad-chested and breathtakingly handsome, and in front of him was a dewy-eyed woman who looked so completely content with her natural state that Morgan hardly recognized herself. Her breasts peeked through a cascade of dark hair, her mouth was moist and puffy from his kisses, and her skin bore a satiny sheen.

Mikal moved the fall of hair behind one shoulder and cupped her breast in his hand. She gave his reflection a saucy smile. ''What metaphor comes to mind? Grapes or passion fruit?''

He dipped his head to kiss her shoulder. "A flower," he murmured. "An orchid. So pretty. Such a soft, sweet petal here." She watched the mirror as though it were a movie screen, reminding herself that the sensations were real. "And here," he whispered, and she watched. The delicate caresses were being applied under her breast, over her belly, along her thigh, and her breathing became tremulous. "And here." Mikal lifted her hair and kissed the side of her neck and then the curve of her ear. "So pretty," he said again. "Open up for me, Morgan. Let me get deep inside you."

"You have." She gasped when he slid his hand from one thigh to the other, lingering momentarily at the intimate bridge between them. "Oh, Mikal, you will again."

"Only physically, unless you decide to trust me with more." He brought his hands to her shoulders. "Look at us, Morgan."

She did, and she giggled. "We're both stark naked."

"That's an honest observation. That's what the little boy in the crowd said when the emperor paraded through town in his imaginary clothes. The boy was a realist. I see naked people, too, but my mind's eye sees all kinds of possibilities."

"That's what makes you a dreamer. I'm like the little boy. I say we're both stark naked." But beautiful, some part of her insisted. As ludicrous as the situation seemed when she put it in plain and simple terms—that they were standing nude in the middle of an armed camp of revolutionaries—they were beautiful, as was the moment. She found wonder in that fact.

"And I say I like us that way," he said, turning her in his arms. "But I also like the possibilities." He gave her a gentle kiss.

"What kind of possibilities?" she mumbled.

"The best kind, Morgan." He pressed the heels of his hands along the firm ridges of muscle in her back and soared on sensation when she swayed against him. "We have wonderful possibilities."

Morgan's head dropped back with the intensity of their next kiss. If it were possible to become one with him now, she knew she would be whole. Her senses short-circuited, sparked and crackled with the need to be connected to his. She rose on tiptoe, pressed herself against him, tightened her arms around him, and sent her tongue to meet his. Suddenly his lips weren't there anymore, and he clamped his hand over her mouth. Morgan reeled with the shock.

"Don't make a sound."

She struggled to make sense of the hot warning in her ear. His face, tight with tension, came into focus. Wide-eyed, she nodded.

Mikal licked his thumb and forefinger and snuffed the candles. Moving quickly and quietly, he stood Morgan in the corner of the room behind the heavy drapes and breathed one more warning in her ear. "Stand perfectly still."

She assumed that he returned to the bed, though she heard no sound. Probably, she realized, because her heart was pounding so loudly in her ears. She flattened herself against the wall, trying to become part of it. What had he heard? They'd been kissing, and she'd been aware of nothing but their erratic breathing. Now the staccato thump of her heart filled her ears and she thought her temples might burst.

A door opened. A light came on. A man voiced what sounded like a string of demands in Spanish. A second voice chimed in. Then Morgan recognized Mikal's sleepy, *"¿Qué pasa?"*

What was going on, indeed? It was one of the few Spanish phrases Morgan recognized. She heard other doors opening and closing, presumably the bathroom and the closets, while Mikal and the men conferred. A strange voice drew closer, and Morgan held her breath. She imagined herself being discovered, and she thought, *Oh, God, not stark naked!* Lowering only her eyes, she realized that the drapes allowed a smidgen of light to pass beneath them, which meant that even though she was standing on her toes, her heels braced against the wall, there might be a sliver of exposed flesh. She gripped the sill of the window with her right hand, and she prayed. Rivulets of sweat streamed down the sides of her face as she listened to a conversation she couldn't understand and hoped that her heart's drumroll couldn't be heard beyond the curtain.

Mikal's effect on the other two men was discernible even from behind the curtain. The demands became more civil as his tranquillity prevailed. He sounded thoroughly unruffled, and the other voices became calmer.

"Lo siento, señor." The man was apparently satisfied, even apologetic.

"No importa."

The door closed and the room was dark again. Still, Morgan was unable to move. When Mikal drew the curtain back, she fell into his arms.

"This was crazy, Morgan. We've got to get you out of here."

His urgency scared her. "But Colonel Hidalgo brought me here, and he's one of the men in charge."

"Guerrero came along and found no sentries in this wing." He led her to the bed and found her clothes. "He stationed one, and the guy thought he heard something, so he brought the other one along to back him up."

"Do you think Hidalgo..."

"I think he'll meet us in the garden when he said he would, and you're going to wait for him there. The atrium is part of his suite. There's little chance of anyone snooping around. This is the only other room with access to the garden, and to get through here they'd have to get through me."

"Mikal..."

In the dark he caressed her cheek with a reassuring palm. "They *won't* get through me."

"But, Mikal..."

"Trust me." He kissed her softly.

"But can we trust Hidalgo?"

"We have to. If he double-crosses us, you're in here with the rest of us."

"Mikal, I want to see my father."

He was quiet for a long moment as he combed her hair back with his fingers and then cupped her cheek in his hand again. "Please don't try, Morgan. He's as well now as he would be if you saw him, and there's nothing you can do to help. The opposite, in fact. Please, go home."

She covered his hand with hers and tried to think sensibly. She tried to remember what practicality was. Her blood pounded in her ears, and all she could think of was that her father was there, and she loved him. Mikal was there, and she loved him, too. She turned her lips to his palm. "I'll call David and tell him I've seen you again," she whispered.

"Thank you."

She dressed quickly. He kissed her soundly, swallowing the lump in his throat that told him she would be gone from the island within hours, and whispered, *"Vaya con Dios, cara mia."*

Carrying her sandals, she slipped out into the night. The cool air was a blessing. Keeping to the shadows, she took the stone steps two at a time and found a hiding place in the garden where Mikal had waited just hours before. The candles in the shrine had gone out. Ears fully alert, she watched the atrium door.

Darkness obscured the identity of the man who came through the door sometime later, but he crossed the terrace with a purposeful stride. He clearly knew that she was there. Morgan stiffened where she stood behind the acacia.

"Miss Remark?" He reached the shrine and stopped, peering into the lush greenery. "It's Hidalgo. I heard what happened."

Relieved, Morgan stepped from behind the tree. "Why did they search his room like that?" she whispered. "Is Mikal a prisoner or not?"

Hidalgo sighed. "I'm hoping he's a bridge. I had told the sentry that I'd provided him with some, uh, distraction for the evening and that he was to turn a deaf ear. The man apparently decided to desert his post and find his own distraction." Hidalgo shook his head. "A young recruit with little training. He should be in school. With any luck, he soon will be."

In his jeans and cotton T-shirt, Hidalgo hardly looked the part of a military man himself. Mikal trusted him, and instinct told her that Mikal was right. They were birds of a feather, Morgan decided, two dreamers of the same kind.

"McQuade should be waiting for you outside the gate. I'll escort you past the guards. It will appear to them that you were...my companion this evening." Morgan nodded, and Hidalgo gestured toward the terrace.

They passed two uniformed men in the foyer, and Hidalgo hooked his arm around her shoulders. He mumbled something to her in Spanish, then laughed. She giggled, but her blush was real. The act was repeated twice more before they passed through the gates, crossed the street and strolled two blocks. They found McQuade, waiting under a street sign. As the two approached, he took one last pull of his cigarette and ground it beneath his heel.

"What are your plans now, Miss Remark?" Hidalgo asked. "Are you ready to go home?"

"Colonel . . . I have a confession to make."

McQuade's grip on her shoulder was less than gentle. "The colonel isn't a priest, Morgan, and this is no time for any revealing confessions."

Morgan shrugged away from McQuade's grasp as she searched Hidalgo's face for some sign of understanding. She decided she saw it in his eyes. "I'm not who I said I was, Colonel Hidalgo."

Miguel chuckled. "You're not Mikal Romanov's secretary?"

"No, I'm not. Mikal and I—"

"Morgan," McQuade warned.

"Your devotion to him is obvious, Miss Remark." Miguel offered McQuade a relaxed smile. "Do you think I'm blind, McQuade? I have a soft spot in my heart for romances such as theirs."

"My name is Morgan Kramer, Colonel. You're holding my father."

The smile dropped from Miguel's face. "You shouldn't have lied to me." He slid a cutting glance at McQuade. "Nor you."

McQuade shrugged. "I thought she'd be satisfied after a visit with Mikal and go home. Being Kramer's daughter shouldn't change anything. Nobody's threatening anybody here, or so you keep telling me."

"Mikal is a guest. Reverend Kramer is . . . somewhat suspect."

"You don't suspect him any more than I do," McQuade reminded him.

Miguel turned to Morgan again. "This is a delicate situation, Miss Re—Kramer. The fewer the complications, the better for all of us."

"I want to see my father." She knew she sounded like a spoiled American, but at the moment she didn't care.

"It wouldn't be wise," Miguel told her.

The night crowded close around her, and feelings jostled in her brain. She had opened herself for Mikal, whether he knew it or not, and suddenly she was just a mass of feelings. Feelings she'd been harboring for a long time now had a name, and though she knew that loving Mikal was as foolish as loving her father, still, there it was.

"I haven't seen my father in years, Colonel, and he's my only family. I don't know what you people plan to do with him, but I'm here and I want to see him."

"He'll be home soon. You can see him then."

"Can you guarantee that?"

Miguel Hidalgo was nothing if not an honest man. "I'll do all I can."

"I'm sure you will. He's an old man, Colonel. If all you can do isn't enough . . . and if Mikal's efforts fail . . ."

"Mikal has the general's ear. He's listening," Miguel assured her, "and I truly believe—"

"I want to see my father, Colonel."

Chapter Eleven

"General, the man's health is failing." There was no sense of urgency in Mikal's approach. The health of one aging missionary was not of major concern to General Castillo, but his international image was. "If you were to send Sidney Kramer home now, the gesture would be well received in Washington."

"It would be taken as a sign of weakness."

Guerrero's gravelly voice never failed to command attention. When he spoke, the natural lilt of the Spanish language became guttural. It was said that a boyhood injury to his throat had damaged his vocal chords, but that was only conjecture. Guerrero never offered any personal history. Mikal had heard two different stories about the four-inch scar that bracketed Guerrero's left eye and several explanations for the black pigskin gloves he always wore. Mikal was convinced that Guerrero had designed an image of villainy for himself and that he was more than a little melo-dramatic in dressing the part.

"I think we need to be realistic about our strengths and weaknesses, General," Miguel Hidalgo countered. "And I think we need to move toward establishing who we are now."

Mikal's relaxed posture was deceptive as he studied the three men who shared the table with him. In discussions with them, he was never relaxed. He chose every word carefully and analyzed every reaction. Guerrero sat to Castillo's left and Hidalgo to his right. Mikal wondered where Guerrero had gotten his medals. He knew about the man's participation in other Latin American insurrections, and he wondered whether the medals had been awarded or whether Guerrero had claimed them for himself. In either case, Mikal suspected that Guerrero slept in his uniform, complete with decorations.

Hidalgo, on the other hand, resisted such trappings. He wore the short-sleeved khaki uniform with its insignia of rank, but no medals, no epaulets or gold "scrambled egg" embroidery, rarely even a hat. Mikal suspected that Miguel was somewhat embarrassed by the pompous claims such finery would make for a colonel who had never been a captain. He knew that the general required the uniform, and Miguel deferred to the old man's wishes.

"I agree," Guerrero said, eyeing Hidalgo with disdain. "We are an independent Caribbean nation. Following Cuba's example, we must demonstrate that land mass and power are not synonymous."

Mikal checked mentally through his hand, looking for a card to play. "Sir, this man is a missionary, a man of the church. Not only that, he'd old. The world will sympathize with him almost as it would with...a defenseless woman or child." The comparison fit the general's concepts, but Mikal almost choked on the "defenseless woman" part. Morgan's image came to mind with the very word *woman,* and the phrase became absurd. "You are a man who defends the defenseless, General. That's why your people look to you for leadership."

"The general's concern is for the fate of the many—men, women and children. The people of De Colores, Mr. Romanov," Guerrero said, as though he were rehearsing lines, "are the general's only concern."

"I have to be concerned about our image abroad, as well," the general said, settling his bulky body back in his chair. If his white beard had been longer and a bit fuller, Mikal thought, the general could have exchanged his khaki uniform for a red one at Christmastime. The general tried to placate Guerrero with a fatherly smile. "That's why I rely on the two of you to keep me centered. You are my muscle, and Miguel is my visionary. I am just an old farmer."

Mikal's smile came easily. "I have the greatest respect for old farmers. My father is one, as was his father. His feet are firmly planted in the earth, along with his wheat."

"And you, I suspect, are his visionary."

"He would be hard-pressed to find so kind a word. You, General Castillo, are the visionary. You understand the need for balance between muscle and compassion."

"Yes, I do." The old man sighed as he checked his watch and then searched for the pills in his breast pocket. "I need water, Miguel." Hidalgo pushed his chair back from the table, and the general continued. "I tend toward the compassionate, myself, so I must defer almost entirely to my advisers for muscle. And I must weigh every move I make carefully. I cannot afford to think with my heart." He smiled sadly at Mikal as he tapped two fingers against his chest. "It's tired and doesn't do its job so well."

Miguel was back with a glass of water. "You should rest now, General."

"Ah, *siesta*." After swallowing his medicine with a long drink of water, the general wagged a finger at Mikal. "You cannot construe my afternoon naps as weakness, Mikal Romanov. Not on this island. Here, *siesta* is part of the good life."

"I know that, sir." Mikal stood in deference to the older man, who used the arms of his chair for leverage as he came to his feet. "The easygoing attitude here is just my style. I'm thinking of taking up permanent residence."

"Who knows?" the general responded, his eyes twinkling. "Maybe you already have."

Mikal returned to his room, dreading the prospect of meeting with Yuri and the others that afternoon. He knew that if he could meet with Castillo without Guerrero's presence, the old man would agree to a release of all detainees. Morgan had the idea that weapons made the difference, but Mikal had been at this long enough to know that wasn't true. Guns would not gain him any friends, nor would ten armed men keep him safe. Being unarmed didn't scare him. Guerrero was a man who was incapable of reasoning, and it was that fact alone that was frightening.

A blast of heat rose from the tiled terrace when Mikal opened the French doors. Leaving the confines of his room, he headed for the coolness of the garden. He took the steps three at a time. At the higher level he found a breeze that made the afternoon air a little less heavy. He was a man of the high plains. Humidity drained his energy, and he had to fight to keep it from draining his spirits.

Mikal noticed the remains of the candles he'd burned four nights ago at the little wooden shrine. Shoving his hands in his pockets, he let his head drop back, closed his eyes and smelled the garden scents, the passionflower and the acacia. He teased himself with the idea of opening his eyes and seeing Morgan.

"She's still here, you know."

Mikal turned sharply and found that Miguel had sought the solitude of the garden in advance of him. Mikal joined him on the wrought-iron bench in a shady spot near the pool. The two men had a tacit agreement to speak English when they were alone. "Since you hadn't told me otherwise, I thought she probably was."

"She wants to see her father."

Mikal was surprised. Until now Miguel hadn't mentioned his knowledge of Morgan's identity. "She can't come here again, Miguel. It's too risky."

"I'm inclined to arrange it for her at this point."

"Why?"

Miguel lit a cigarette and watched as a gray cloud of smoke floated toward the palms. "Castillo is just what he says—a farmer turned revolutionary. And I'm a teacher turned revolutionary."

This would have something to do with Morgan's request. It was Mikal's genius to know that, and to wait for the man to come to the point, however long it took. In the process, he would learn more about the men who held those whom Mikal had come to regard as *his* people.

"I hadn't figured you for a teacher."

Meeting Mikal's smile with a shrug, Miguel began, "There have been few fortunes made on this island, but my father was one who made his. He lives in Switzerland now. Our lives contrasted sharply with those of most of the islanders, who are generally poor. I was educated at the University of Massachusetts, taught there for two years, and then came home. I became a teacher, then an agitator, and finally a revolutionary." He chuckled with the memory. "Those in power were fat and complacent, and the plum was ripe for picking. It fell into our hands. Guerrero was hoping for more resistance.''

"And what was Guerrero before he became a revolutionary?'' Mikal wondered.

"Guerrero isn't a revolutionary,'' Miguel said quietly. "He is a brawler who's found the niche of his dreams. He is suddenly a hero, and he has the army in his pocket. If Castillo were not father, grandfather, or godfather to half the people on this island . . .'' Shaking his head, he returned his cigarette to his mouth and puffed angrily. "Castillo was the grandfather, and I was the teacher. In the evenings we would sip rum and plan all the improvements we would make. When the opportunity presented itself, we took it.''

"With the help of your friend with the muscle.''

"That's right. Castillo's nephew.''

How much will he tell me? Mikal wondered. How far can we go with this? "One or the other of you will succeed him,'' he mused. "Are you ready for that?''

"I'm a teacher.'' Miguel's tone was flat, and his stare was empty of expression.

"And Guerrero is . . . a brawler? I think that's an understatement.''

Miguel was quiet, reflective. "I need time.''

"How big is the army?''

Miguel looked at Mikal and smiled as his attention focused again on the present. "I would be a traitor if I told you that, my friend. But you didn't expect me to, did you?'' Mikal offered a lopsided grin, and Miguel laughed. "You are a master, Mikal. I would promise you a job in my government, but when we become a quiet little tourist spot again, there will be little need for your talents.''

"My talents run to writing, Miguel. Maybe I could write travel brochures.''

They laughed together now, trading fantasies. "We'll let you review our restaurants, if you won't be too critical."

"Maybe I could open my own—Mikal's Place."

"Miguel's," Miguel corrected. "We have the same name."

The same name, Mikal thought, but worlds apart. Mikal would soon return to the Midwest, where he would once again be the eccentric writer down the block who was always speaking up about some cause or other. Miguel faced a day of reckoning here, and no one could predict when that day might come.

"Then help me, Miguel, for the sake of—" Mikal opened his hands in a beckoning gesture "—our common name. Help me get these people home."

Miguel's gaze strayed to the pool as he took one last drag on his cigarette before crushing it beneath his shoe. "Kramer is ill, Mikal. You know that."

"That's why it's important that we start with him."

"I find it hard to refuse to let a daughter visit a father who is not well."

Mikal drew a long, slow breath. "I do, too."

"I'm not in a position to make any promises about the detainees, Mikal, but I can bar her from the palace if that's what you want."

He wanted her to go home, he reminded himself. He wanted to go home with her. He wanted to crawl under a blanket with her and listen to the North Dakota wind howl outside his window. He wanted to see her.

"Can you keep her clear of Guerrero?"

"I can try."

Morgan followed Miguel down the corridor she knew led to Mikal's room. She had been warned that her father was not well and that her visit would be brief, but she had some ideas of her own on that score. She had dressed in a loose black, gauze dress and covered her hair with a lace mantilla, as she'd been instructed to do. She looked like a nondescript nocturnal visitor, but she'd decided that if her father's condition warranted it, she could become something more. A smaller voice reminded her that she hadn't decided what.

Mikal was waiting for her.

"I'll go ahead of you and clear the way," Miguel instructed, pointedly eyeing first one American, then the other. Mikal and Morgan had eyes only for each other, and Miguel wondered whether he would have to remind them that this was not the time. "Ten minutes, Mikal, and then bring her back here. I'll expect her to be out of there by—" he checked his watch "—nine-thirty. The guard will be back at his post by then. Pay close attention to the time."

With three fingers he told them to give him as many minutes to prepare the way, and then he closed the door softly behind him.

Mikal laid a hand on Morgan's shoulder, and she swayed, turned and let him steady her in his arms. "I should be angry with you," she told him as her arms surrounded his waist.

"Why?" he whispered into her hair.

"You didn't tell me he was ill."

"High blood pressure. You knew that, didn't you?"

She shook her head.

"Dr. Kelsch, one of the other hostages, has kept close watch on him, but this whole ordeal has taken its toll."

The slow, soothing circles his hands made over her back told her that he knew the full extent of the toll it was taking on her. "Does he know I'm here?" she asked.

"I told him you'd gotten some help from Freedom International and the Red Cross. I didn't tell him about the risk you're taking."

It seemed ridiculous, she knew, after all the years of little communication between them, but it was important that she see her father now. In fact, if she could take him to safety, she thought she could be at peace with him. It occurred to her that the world's practical people had a duty to look after dreamers, whose heads had gotten so far into the clouds that their enemies had a clear shot at them.

"I just need to see him," she said.

"Yes, I know. And it's time."

They walked together along a hallway, down a flight of steps and through another hallway. Responding to some instinct for defense, Morgan took note of everything—the wrought-iron sconces and colorful woven wall hangings, the red tile, the white walls, and the absence of any sign of people. If she needed to, she would know her way out, she thought as she ventured deeper into the heart of the palace.

They passed through an anteroom, where Mikal told her at least two guards usually stood watch, often over a hand of cards or a game of checkers. Though the room was temporarily vacant, Mikal knew there would be guards at either end of the corridor. He tried the handle of a heavy wooden door and was half surprised to find it open. He motioned for Morgan to follow him.

The large room was dimly lit by a corner lamp. Furniture and other trappings faded out of focus for Morgan as Mikal hurried her past several people, all men, all staring vacantly as she passed. Her presence posed no threat, offered no promise. They sat in chairs or on pallets spread over the floor. The fourth face she saw she recognized. Yuri! He smiled, and she opened her mouth to speak, but Mikal tightened his grip on her arm. "Quickly, Morgan. Through here."

The room was small, but the open window allowed the evening breeze to keep the air comfortable and fresh. In the shadows a man sat on a bed, waiting.

"Morgan."

At the sound of her name, Mikal's hand eased away from her, but she caught his arm, wordlessly asking him not to go far.

"They tell me you've been ill," she said quietly. She fought the urge to be a little girl again, to give him a joyous hug.

"Not so ill that I couldn't handle a kiss."

His voice seemed only slightly less than pulpit strong, which Morgan found encouraging. She had once imagined that even if his whole body disintegrated like the Cheshire cat's, his voice would still be there. She sat beside him on the bed and gave him a peck on the cheek, while Mikal stood watch near the door. It was strange to find that her father was gray and frail rather than robust and hearty, as he had been when she'd last seen him—how many years ago? So little time, she thought. So much to say.

"Mikal will make them listen, Father. I know he will."

At his post, Mikal smiled to himself. When had she decided that? he wondered.

"Mikal and Yuri are good men," Sidney Kramer remarked as he patted Morgan's hand, "but they risk too much by being here, and so do you."

"I think it's some game these people are playing," Morgan offered. "I don't think they mean to harm anyone."

"Neither do I." They sat in silence for a moment before he asked, "What made you come?"

"I couldn't get a straight answer from anyone," she said. *And you were here. And so was Mikal!* But she didn't dare suggest such a foolish reason aloud.

"So you came looking for the answers yourself. You were always one to take charge."

Her father's small chuckle sounded hollow. It was unlike the deep, resounding laugh she'd always associated with him; this one issued from his throat rather than his chest. "How are you feeling . . . really?"

"Better now that I've seen you, Morgan, but when I know you're safe, I'll be just fine."

"By this time tomorrow she'll be stateside." With a shoulder braced against the doorjamb, Mikal cast her a pointed look. "Right, Morgan?"

"My father should be in a hospital, Mikal."

"He will be, just as soon as I can manage it. Right now—" Mikal tilted the face of his watch toward the light "—you've got one minute."

"Is there anything you need? The Red Cross can surely see that . . ." Morgan touched her father's arm. "Do you have medication?"

The old man nodded. "Our basic needs are taken care of. I need prayers."

Morgan's chin dropped in deference to the suggestion he'd offered ever since she could remember. It was a reminder that traditionally brought a twinge of guilt, because she'd usually been too anxious to get the job done on her own to remember her father's training. "Of course," she said quietly.

Sidney Kramer lifted his daughter's chin in his hand, and she looked up at him. "I need your forgiveness."

Morgan was shaken by the simplicity of the words and the enormity of their meaning. "You did what you had to do with your life," she said. "But I've missed you."

"Thank you for coming here to tell me that."

She hugged his neck briefly, feeling awkward, but also relieved, and she responded to Mikal's quiet reminder by pulling herself away abruptly. "You'll come to Bismarck when they release you?"

Her father lay down almost as soon as Morgan had given him the room to do so. "Yes," he said. "Now go with Mikal. We don't want to press our luck by running over their time limit. Take care, Morgan."

Morgan moved past Mikal as she left the room. She heard her father call Mikal back, and the weakening sound of his voice alarmed her. But it was Mikal he'd called, and Morgan stood rooted to the spot. Within moments Mikal reappeared at the door and signaled for Dr. Kelsch, who hurried to the minister's bedside.

"What's wrong?"

Mikal's expression was tightly fixed. "Nothing new. We have to get you out of here, Morgan."

"I want to know what's wrong." A door opened at the other side of the hostages' common room, and from the corner of her eye Morgan noted the faces of first one woman, then another. They didn't concern her. It was her father's need for the doctor that worried her, but Mikal was pushing her toward the big wooden door, where Yuri stood, listening. She jerked her arm away. "Mikal!"

"Your father is as stubborn as you are," Mikal barked; then he remembered himself and lowered his voice. "He doesn't want to be released without the others. He thinks his condition brings some pressure to bear, and it sure as hell does. On *me*. Because he's sick, and because he's *your* father, and because you're—" He snatched her arm again and propelled her toward the door. "You're going home, and he's next. Then maybe we can get something done here."

"He called you. You called for the doctor. I want to know why," she demanded, struggling.

"Mikal!" Yuri motioned them back as he inclined his head toward the door.

Mikal closed his eyes briefly as he pulled Morgan back against him and muttered, "What the hell am I going to do with you now?" But in an instant he moved in the direction of the room where the women slept. "Stay here," he ordered, and closed the door.

Morgan stared dumbfounded at the two women whose faces she'd glimpsed only briefly before, and they stared back. A blonde with a short, pert hairstyle stood by the room's only window. She'd apparently just closed the blinds. From Mikal's description Morgan recognized the slender young woman who sat on the bed as the beauty with the haunted eyes. One long, dark braid was hitched over her shoulder, and her eyes, startlingly blue, were sunken and underscored with dark circles.

"You're Mr. Kramer's daughter?" the blonde asked. Morgan nodded, thinking there probably wasn't time for a chat. "I'm Judy, and this is Elizabeth. And you're crazy to sneak in here like this."

"So I'm told."

"Dr. Kelsch agreed to come here because one of the college kids got his shoulder dislocated when they arrested him," Judy reported, "and they never let him go."

"Why do you think they're continuing to hold you?" Morgan asked as she took inventory of the room. She could hear voices on the other side of the door.

"Some kind of politics."

"Guerrero's madness."

Elizabeth's voice was surprising. She had a slight accent, much like Hidalgo's, and though her tone was flat with despair, there was a rich depth to it. Morgan was intrigued by the woman. "Are you—"

Judy interrupted. "I don't know where you can hide in here, but we'd better think of something in case—"

"Stand behind the door, Miss Kramer." Elizabeth stood and indicated a spot between the door and a tall bureau. "Judy and I are curious about the commotion out there. They'll see an empty room behind us."

From her risky hiding place, Morgan peeped over a door hinge to see three soldiers who were talking with Mikal in Spanish. A fourth followed the two colonels, Hidalgo and Guerrero, into the room. Guerrero was barking angrily, while Hidalgo spoke calmly, apparently asking questions. Mikal directed his comments to Hidalgo.

"Mikal insists that Mr. Kramer must be moved to a hospital at once," Elizabeth translated, ostensibly for Judy's sake. "He says that Dr. Kelsch can't stabilize his condition unless he can get him to a proper medical facility."

The discussion continued. Although Morgan understood none of the words, she saw that the power of Mikal's will had a visible effect on Guerrero's expression. That will needed no translation. The look in Mikal's eyes brooked no argument, and his stance was completely confident. At this critical moment, when a choice had to be made, Guerrero's bluster held no sway over Mikal's incontrovertible conviction. Hidalgo quietly dispatched two soldiers, who returned shortly with a litter. Morgan watched while her father was taken away.

Mikal followed Dr. Kelsch, and the whole contingency of captors trooped out with them, leaving Morgan behind with the captives. Yuri came to the door of the women's room as Morgan crept out from behind it.

"There's a good chance Mikal will be able to get them to fly your father to Miami now that they've allowed him to be hospitalized," Yuri said. "Obviously they don't want a corpse on their hands. That's a good sign."

Morgan shuddered. It wouldn't be just any corpse. "How can we get word on his condition?"

"If we get word, it will have to be through Mikal. He's become quite friendly with Hidalgo." Seeing her fear, Yuri gave Morgan's shoulder a comforting squeeze. "Stay in this room for now. The guards come and go in the common room, but they rarely bother the women. I think they're not so sure of Elizabeth's position here." He smiled at the other woman, who lowered her eyes without comment. "Mikal will come up with something."

It was nearly an hour before Mikal returned. In the meantime Morgan learned that Judy was a teacher. She'd been arrested following the coup because she was an American employed by the former regime and she was suspected of collusion. Judy explained that one of the other men was a reporter who had been vacationing on the island when the coup took place. There were also two college students being held because one of them had had a small amount of marijuana in his possession when they were searched by the police.

"They offered to let Elizabeth go, but she wouldn't take them up on it." Morgan turned a questioning glance at the dark-haired woman, but Elizabeth only stared down at the hands in her lap. "They won't let her take her baby," Judy added quietly.

"Why not? What kind of—"

"Guerrero is his father."

Elizabeth's bombshell was allowed to reverberate for a moment and then lie quietly. Morgan couldn't bring herself to ask any of the obvious questions. A rap on the door broke the silence.

"It's Mikal," his voice announced through the door. Judy hastened to admit him, and then she and Elizabeth left the room.

Mikal closed the door and leaned back against it. "He'll be flown to Miami with Dr. Kelsch as soon as it's safe for him to make the trip."

An overwhelming sense of relief washed over Morgan. Her father would get the care he needed and, as a blessed bonus, he would be safely away from the island. Relief gave way to concern as she looked at Mikal, searching his face for some sign of triumph and finding none. She'd watched him from her hiding place, and she'd seen the essence of his strength. Now she saw his fatigue. One of his worries had been taken care of, but one still stood before him. She went over and took him in her arms as she laid her head against his chest.

"Thank you, Mikal." He stroked her long hair, planted a kiss in its center part and said nothing. She was a burden to him now; she knew that. "When I heard he was ill, I was afraid if I didn't come, I might not see him again. It was a selfish move on my part."

"And selfish of me to allow it," he reflected. "I wanted to see you, even for ten minutes. Even for two."

Leaning back, she held his face in her hands and smiled through gathering tears. "Isn't it silly? The chance of seeing you keeps me here on this godforsaken island. When I think about going back while you're still here…" She shook her head, because she didn't have the words to banish the sensible thought. She hardly knew herself anymore.

"It's foolish to try to be together here."

Her laugh, however small, was incongruent with the tear that spilled to her cheek. "It looks as though you're stuck with me now, though, doesn't it?"

He took the tear in the palm of his hand and swept it to her temple, lacing his fingers into the soft hair he loved. "I'll get you out of here, Morgan. I swear I will." Gripping a handful of hair, he lowered his mouth to hers, pressing hard, piercing the space between her lips, revealing the only personal need he'd felt compelled to satisfy in recent weeks—his need for her. It took monumental effort to get a grip on her shoulders and pull back.

"I have a meeting with the general. I think we've made some headway, and I want to press the advantage." Mikal traced Morgan's hairline with his fingers, while he savored the beauty of her face, committing each feature to memory. "Miguel maneuvered some slack time between guard shifts to get you in here. Now I want you to borrow Elizabeth's dress, put it over your own and wear that black mantilla. I think we can pass you off as her. She's allowed to see her baby sometimes, so that's what I'm going to suggest to Miguel."

He smiled and kissed her softly. "Stay in this room until Miguel gives the word." Another kiss, longer and even more gentle. "And light a candle for me," he whispered. Then he was gone.

Morgan changed, and then she waited for what seemed like an interminable length of time, chafing and sweating in a double layer of clothes. Judy chattered, while Elizabeth retreated to a corner and offered little comment. When Yuri came to the door, Morgan jumped at the opportunity to move on, however risky the move might be.

Miguel, dressed in his uniform, was waiting in the common room with more instructions. "The guards are seated to the right. You will stay on my left side, and we'll cross the room quickly, while Yuri talks to the soldiers. Keep your head down and this—" he indicated the lacy mantilla "—pulled around your face."

"The talks—" Yuri began.

"The talks are over." Miguel jerked his chin toward Morgan. "This one is my concern right now. If she's discovered, it's a new ball game, all new rules." He turned to Morgan. "When I speak to you in Spanish, just nod."

Morgan gauged her pace by Miguel's, nodding after what sounded like a question and keeping her eyes riveted to the floor. She was aware of Yuri's presence and his halting words to the guards in bad Spanish. As she neared the anteroom door, she reminded herself not to rush her exit, which she felt a sudden drive to do. Just five more steps, three more...

They retraced the route through the darkened hallways, stopping only once at an alcove, where Morgan stripped off Elizabeth's dress and stuffed it behind a small table. Miguel made a mental note to retrieve the dress as soon as he deposited Morgan with McQuade. Morgan hesitated at the door to Mikal's room, but Miguel told her, "He's not there. When we pass anyone, I'll be telling you I don't have time for you tonight, and you have to go home. You should look... disgruntled."

Morgan pulled her mantilla close around her face and managed the role with considerable flair. The news about the talks being over sounded discouraging, and she let real anger take her through her performance.

McQuade was waiting for her on the same street corner as before. He was wearing a familiar rumpled khaki bush jacket, and she wondered if he were smoking the same cigarette. A wild notion flashed through her mind that perhaps some projectionist was rerunning a film that she'd somehow gotten herself mixed up in. She stood back and watched as McQuade offered Hidalgo a cigarette. Smoke curled above their heads, and she wanted to suggest that they break for lunch. Perhaps they could have Mikal's quiche, if these two were sufficiently secure in their masculinity to try it. Why were these two men huddled on the street corner, while Mikal, a man whose design for living was entirely peaceful, was facing armed lions in their den? The absurdity incensed her.

"What will you do now?" she demanded. The two men turned to her, Hidalgo with a frown, McQuade raising one eyebrow as he smoked. "My father and Dr. Kelsch are out, and now the talks are over. Why? What's going to happen to the other seven people in there?"

"Understand that only five of those people were detained by our government," Miguel pointed out. "The other two asked to be here."

"Mikal is a prisoner in there and you know—"

"Wait a minute," McQuade interjected, halting Morgan's accusations with a wave of his hand. "What do you mean, the talks are over? I got word about Kramer and Kelsch, but I was told... What's going on with the others?"

"Mikal was in excellent form this evening," Miguel reported, assuming an official posture. "The general was moved when Mr. Kramer's health obviously took a turn for the worse, partly because the general himself—"

"Yeah, yeah, come on, Miguel. What's going on?"

"Your State Department will be notified that the charges pending against all detainees have been dropped, and that Yuri Romanov will accompany them by plane to Miami tomorrow."

"What about Mikal?" Morgan and McQuade chimed almost simultaneously.

Miguel took a final drag on his cigarette, dropped it to the sidewalk and ground it beneath his heel. Expelling the smoke with a sigh, he reverted from official to friend. "Mikal will stay with us until we're satisfied—until *Guer-*

rero is satisfied—that the threat of foreign intervention is no longer a factor."

"Stay with you!" McQuade shot back. "What the hell does that mean?"

"It means that Mikal Romanov has negotiated a trade."

Chapter Twelve

Mikal's accommodations had been changed. He'd returned to the common room to discuss the plans for the release with Yuri, but it was clear that when the others left, he would go no further than the anteroom. The area of the palace he was now in was the easiest to secure.

He'd known he didn't have much to trade. Although Castillo refused to call anyone a hostage, Mikal had pointed out that, should the need for a hostage arise, it ought to be someone the world might want back—someone like a novelist of some renown, someone important to an organization like Freedom International, whose Nobel Prize he mentioned more than once. A couple of college kids and a reporter would hardly be missed. More releases could only boost the new government's image, he'd said. As soon as De Colores had reestablished its diplomatic relations with the U.S., he would expect to be on his way.

Yuri had been in closer contact with the detainees than Mikal had, and he was chosen to explain the conditions of the release to Elizabeth. Mikal rose from his chair when Yuri emerged from the women's room with Elizabeth and Judy behind him.

"Elizabeth agrees," Yuri said.

"I'm sorry, Elizabeth," Mikal offered, seeking contact with her downcast eyes. "They said it had to be all of you or none, and there was nothing I could do about your son. Guerrero was..."

"I know," she said, almost inaudibly. Then her voice gained strength. "Guerrero is Guerrero."

"Maybe when this situation stabilizes..."

"Contempt for him will grow," she predicted. "He won't always have this power. I'll come back for my son."

"And I'll come back for you," Yuri promised Mikal, glancing behind him at the pair of soldiers who had come to escort the group to the next checkout point.

"Give me a few days, Uncle Yuri. Miguel's behind me, and Castillo's tired of the whole thing. I think I can finish this up without an incident."

Yuri shook Mikal's hand, and since that wasn't enough, he gave him one of his burly bear hugs. His pride in Mikal had the old man fairly bursting at the seams. Despite the unexpected complication Morgan had introduced, Mikal had done a wonderful job. As Yuri saw it, delaying Mikal now was just a face-saving gesture on Guerrero's part. Just a little hitch. Mikal would be home soon.

"I don't know where Morgan is."

Yuri leaned back and read the worry in Mikal's eyes. "Miguel will keep you posted. I'm sure she—"

"I haven't seen Miguel this morning. I don't know for sure what happened to her after she left here. She thinks she can just waltz in and out of this place whenever she... Check on her if you can, okay?''

Yuri nodded. Mikal needed a woman like his own Helen, Yuri thought. One who would stay put while Mikal did the work he was meant to do. ''I expect that McQuade has gotten her into the hospital to see her father,'' he suggested.

''With any luck they'll be flying out on the same plane. You'll call David as soon as—''

''As soon as I get to a phone, Mikal. And there won't be a sound in this palace we won't hear,'' Yuri promised. ''We have many ears.''

Mikal stood to the side and watched as the doors were opened and ''his people'' were ushered from their prison. They looked anxious, unsure that freedom was really theirs for the taking. Too quickly the doors were closed behind them, and, despite the warm weather, Mikal felt cold.

''You won't be able to get in to see him, Morgan. Miguel won't help you, and neither will I, so be grateful for the arrangements we've managed to make, and get the hell out of here.''

McQuade leaned across his desk and gave her his darkest scowl. Even Morgan was intimidated. She turned away, shrugging helplessly. She was frustrated with the constraints of the tiny office. She wanted to pace. ''He's being deserted,'' she protested. ''Even if I could just see Miguel, get some assurance from him...''

''Who do you think you are, Miss Kramer? Some ambassador, for God's sake? I'll see Hidalgo, I'll get some assurance, and *I'll* stick around until they let Mike go.'' He moved to her side of the desk, giving himself a moment to reform his thoughts. She wouldn't take kindly to the words that kept popping into his head, and if he didn't get this woman on the next plane out, he'd be stuck with her. And could she come up with schemes! He managed a smile. "He isn't being deserted, Morgan. He's got me."

"Humph. You think *you're* some ambassador or something? You're the reason I had to come down here in the first place," she grumbled as she allowed him to usher her out the door. "If you had kept the line of communication open, McQuade..."

"Yeah, I know. Now, remember, you're with Freedom International. You're accompanying Mr. Kramer back to Miami."

"What do you do for a living, McQuade?"

McQuade squinted as they stepped into the sunlight. "I'm a guardian angel."

Morgan flew to Miami with her father. His hospital stay there would last several days, and Morgan decided to stay with him. In her years with the school system, she had used very little of her leave, and now was the time to take advantage of it. She called David each evening. McQuade called Morgan to report that he had seen Mikal. Things were going well, be said.

Things were going well, she reminded herself. After three days of good medical care, her father looked much better. Already he was talking about a little mission church that might need him on an Indian reservation. He'd forgotten his promise to return to Bismarck. He would work until he dropped, Morgan realized, and nothing she could say or do would change that. She'd been at his bedside for three days, and she'd been learning about him.

"Why did you ever marry?" she wondered. There was no hostility in her voice. She was simply curious.

"I loved your mother," he answered just as simply.

"But not enough."

"How much is enough?" He covered her hand with his. There were things he would have managed differently if he could have, but he knew his life was as it was, and he had never felt it was his to do with as he pleased. "I loved your mother, and she loved me. We had one dream when we started out, but in later years, when you were older and needed more... more practical things, she said... well, she was right. She had to make a choice."

"Between you and me?"

"No, Morgan, between Bismarck and—what was it at the time? Kenya, wasn't it?"

"Then you made a choice, too," Morgan said.

Sidney Kramer shook his head. "My choice had been made for me long before that. I was who I was, what I had to give."

There was little left for me, she thought. And for her mother... "She died loving you, you know."

"Yes, I know. We were never without love for each other, Morgan. There came a time when we couldn't live in the same place, but there was never a question of not loving each other."

It was a strange arrangement, Morgan decided, and certainly not one she wanted for herself. Perhaps Mikal's choices had been made for him, too. She had seen who Mikal was and what he had to give. Loving him for what he'd already given her, she would wait for his release, and she would be there when he set foot on safe soil. She would be there to see for herself that he was truly home. But Morgan knew she couldn't live as her mother had. The relief she longed to experience in being able to touch him again would only be temporary, and that wasn't enough for her. There would be more missions and greater risks. Mikal would go where he was needed, do what he did so well. And Morgan would quietly withdraw from the fringes of his dreams. They were too big for her.

The Miami airport was full of white suits and white dresses. There were the crisp, white, nautical uniforms of cruise line employees waiting for "snowbirds" to fly in from points north. There were chic white linens and crumpled white cottons, long sleeves pushed up to elbows, and jackets with bright white T-shirts underneath. Morgan stood near the gate, because she was impatient with sitting, and she watched the bustle of people. Every few minutes she glanced up at the clock. The plane was late, but Mikal was on his way home.

The plane's arrival from Mexico City was announced, and Morgan saw that Yuri and Freedom International attorney Alex Steiger, who'd been deeply involved in a discussion for almost an hour, were moving toward the door. There was a man from the State Department there, too, but he seemed content to stay out of the way for the moment. Two television cameramen took their places, while several reporters jostled for position. Morgan stood back, wondering whether she'd even have a chance to say hello.

McQuade came through the door first, and Mikal followed. The reporters started right in.

"Were you held on the island against your will, Mr. Romanov?"

"Were there any demands?"

"Were the demands met?"

"Were you traded for the group they released last week?"

Mikal smiled and promised a statement later as he scanned the crowd. Yuri shouldered past reporters, slapped McQuade on the back and hugged Mikal, while Alex followed with handshakes. But Mikal continued to search.

"Is she here, Uncle Yuri? I thought you said she was still . . ."

He saw her at last, standing alone, dressed in a light blue blouse and white tailored suit, her hair primly bound up at the back of her head. He wanted no one else but her. He wanted to drive this crowd back before he went to her, because he wanted no intrusions. He wanted to be home, and he saw home, sky blue and snowy white, waiting quietly by herself.

McQuade gripped Mikal's shoulder and muttered, "I'll run interference with the press." Mikal nodded.

"Mikal—"

"I'll talk to them all later, Uncle Yuri." Handing Yuri his bag, he added, "Communiqués and dirty socks. You and Alex sort them out."

Morgan's heart soared when Mikal stepped away from all the others and came to her. She felt too much just then, and there were too many people there. Her vision clouded as she clutched her purse tightly and smiled. "Mikal" was all she managed to say.

He put his hand at the top of her arm, then slid it down to hold her hand discreetly between them as he guided her down the concourse. He'd seen the promise of glad tears, and he didn't want to share them with anyone. "Hold that thought until we get into the cab," he said. "How fast can you walk?"

"As fast as you can."

The afternoon daylight was waning. They commandeered a cab and fell into each other's arms as soon as the door was closed. Unconscious of the man at the wheel, the meter, or the motion of the car, they shared a kiss. In the middle of it, Morgan heard the man's voice, but took no interest in what he said. Her mind was absorbed in the taste of Mikal's mouth.

It was Mikal who drew back into reality first. "Where are we staying?"

"Where? Oh . . . the Marriott."

"You have a room for me?"

She closed her eyes, nuzzled his neck, and whispered, "I have a room."

When they arrived Mikal used Morgan's phone and put in a call to his son. The sound of David's voice superseded all third-and-fourth-hand messages. Mikal knew he'd have to answer a thousand questions before he left Miami, but his son's single question came first. The answer: he would be home the following night.

For now Mikal was safe. Morgan had waited for him. There were no other questions. He drew the drapes and tossed his jacket on a chair. Morgan hung hers on a hanger with her skirt, then kicked off her shoes and lined them up neatly with the sandals that were already there. When she turned, Mikal was beside her, already stripped down to his briefs. Morgan saw the pile of his clothes on the chair. Indeed there were no questions.

"Whenever I felt the urge to lose my cool, I planned this moment," he told her. "I've been over it in my mind a hundred times in the last few days. I'm giving you a shower first." Smiling, because the fantasy was so close to becoming a reality, he unbuttoned her soft blue blouse. "And I don't give a damn who hears the water running."

"Do I need a shower?" she asked innocently.

"I do, and I'm not letting you out of my sight while I take one." She let him slip the blouse off, but she caught it and hung it up when he would have dropped it to the floor. "That wasn't part of my plan," he teased. "I saw a trail of clothes."

"Okay." She swept her slip over her head. "Let the fantasy start now." The slip fell to the floor, along with their last articles of clothing. The next part of the plan was a long, hot kiss, followed by a long, hot shower.

They made each other clean with loving caresses given by soap-filled hands. They tasted each other, tested each other. They drove one another to the brink, then stood poised under the warm water, every nerve tingling as they consented to another brief retreat from fulfillment.

They came out of the shower and dried each other with thick towels. He took her wet hair down and dried that, too. But when she tried to do the same for him, standing over him as he sat at the edge of the bed, he trapped her in the vee of his long thighs, tongued her nipple, then took one in his mouth, and put an end to retreating. She straddled him as he suckled her, and they clung to each other, pushing up their pulse rates until he laid her across the bed and buried himself deep within her. He said her name the same way she'd said his when he'd come to her at the airport. It was all he could manage.

But she said, "Welcome home."

He held her as they lay in bed and allowed her the freedom to touch him wherever she would, which seemed, at the moment, to be her fondest pleasure. It was as though he was the Christmas gift she'd thought unaffordable, and she had to examine every angle for authenticity and then simply touch, again and again, in appreciation. He understood. He had the same need, felt the same pleasure in touching her.

"Miguel said you traded yourself for the others," she said at last. "Is that what you did?"

"Not really. I agreed to stay behind."

"Were you so certain they'd let you go?"

"I was sure at least two out of the three wanted to let all of us go. The odds were in my favor."

She turned her face to his chest and kissed his flat nipple. "I hated coming back without you."

"I hated your being there, Morgan—the better part of me did. But there was a part of me that celebrated because . . . You're a paradox, you know that? You set aside all your good sense, and you came because I was there."

"I love you," she told him simply.

He let the words settle in his breast. He knew they were true. He knew, too, that she didn't want them to be. "That's not practical," he said, testing. "I'm a dreamer."

"I know." She sighed, and then repeated, "I know. The worst kind of dreamer. And the best. What you did took a rare kind of courage . . . and rare talent."

"I couldn't persuade them to let Elizabeth have her baby." His sigh echoed hers. "She made a trade, too, for the others. *That's* rare courage."

"I don't have that kind of courage, Mikal."

He laughed, and his voice rumbled in his chest beneath her ear. "My sensible coward. I couldn't believe my eyes when I saw you there at the palace that first time. Miss Remark! Whatever made you do such a crazy thing?"

"Not knowing made me crazy," she confessed. "Temporarily."

"Temporary insanity?"

"I don't want to be asked to make sacrifices like yours and Elizabeth's. I'm not that noble. I went to that island for purely selfish reasons."

"Love?"

"I'm selfish about the people I love," she said quietly. "I want them with me."

"All the time?"

"Most of the time." She considered, then amended, "At least, *some* of the time. It doesn't matter with dreamers, anyway. Even when they're with you, they're not *really* with you, if you know what I mean."

"No, I don't know what you mean. I have a lot of dreams, Morgan, and lately most of them include..." With two fingers he tilted her chin up as he bent his head to give her a firm kiss. "Am I really with you now?" he demanded.

"Yes." She wouldn't argue. This was the piece of him she knew was hers. She made it hers every time they were together this way.

"Good. If I'm in for an out-of-body experience, I don't want to have it right now." He shifted, cuddling her along his side. He wanted to toy with her hair and admire what he could see of her face in the dim light spilling from the bathroom.

"The boys from the State Department can have exactly one hour tomorrow," he decided. "No more. We're going home for Christmas. Will your father be ready?"

"Tomorrow, yes." She didn't tell him that she'd already made arrangements for going home. She'd made her reservation at the airport shortly before he'd arrived, allowing herself just one more night with him. This was her weakness, she decided, this most beautiful of all dreamers, even though he wasn't for real. Dreamers could never be mistaken for the real thing, for possessors of to-have-and-to-hold-from-this-day-forward dependability. As long as she knew that and recognized that he was, indeed, her weakness, she could afford to give herself one more night. Her weaknesses were few enough, she told herself, and she inhaled deeply of the heady scent belonging to this most cherished one.

"What made them let you go, Mikal?"

"I asked them to," he said, his eyes glistening with pleasure as he watched her hair sift through his fingers. "I told them you were waiting for me."

"No, really, Mikal."

"Okay, really." He tucked her head under his chin and held her close, so she couldn't see his face. "I held them at gunpoint, Morgan. I got the drop on Guerrero and threatened to expose him for the wimp he is if he didn't get me on the next plane out. I held a gun to his head while he drove me to the airport. You should've seen their faces when I sprayed them with my M-16 before I hopped on the plane and ordered the pilot to take off."

Morgan swallowed. "Really? Where was McQuade?"

"He was the tailgunner."

"Tailgunner?"

"We had it all worked out. Plan B. You should've seen me, honey. I was magnificent."

"Tailgunner? You came in on a 747."

His laughter was soundless, but his body shook with it.

"Mikal! Now, *really.*"

"*Really,* she keeps saying. You liked the second story so much better than you liked the first, Miss Remark." He kissed the top of her head, then laughed again. "McQuade will love it. My heroic moment."

She squirmed, pulling back to look up at him. "I saw your heroic moment, Mikal, probably one of many. You made Guerrero back down. You made him let my father go. I don't know what you said, because I don't understand Spanish, but I know you got the upper hand somehow, without a gun, without any tailgunner. What did you do?"

"Psyched him out, I guess. I knew you'd risk exposing yourself in order to get medical help for your father, so I had to get him out of there."

"How did *you* get out, then?" she asked again.

He gathered her back in his arms. "I told you," he said. "Castillo's pretty sentimental anyway. I spent a lot of time with him, talked farming, family and poetry, and he agreed to make some diplomatic overtures through me. And I told him—" he traced her jawline with the back of his hand and her collarbone with his thumb "—about my lioness. About the way she nuzzles my neck and purrs. About the way she usually takes a pretty practical position on life in the jungle, but that there are those days—" his hand slid to her breast, and she took a deep breath and filled his palm "—when she arches her back and digs her claws in—" he groaned as she ran her nails lightly along his back and sank them into his buttocks. "And, oh God, can she be a passionate handful then."

Mikal had an early-morning session with people from the State Department, which he suspected would take more than an hour. Yuri came to the hotel with Alex to pick Mikal up, but then, to Morgan's surprise, he stayed behind. He invited Morgan to have breakfast with him, and she accepted.

After the last cup of coffee was served, Yuri got to the point, for which Morgan had politely waited. She knew he was as practical in his own way as she was in hers and wouldn't have stayed behind without a reason. "I have not married with good reason," he began. "It would interfere with my work. Some men have space in their lives for both. Others don't. If they marry and the work claims them as it is meant to, they feel guilty." He eyed her carefully and with a hint of sympathy. "We don't want that for Mikal, do we?"

"Mikal has been married before," Morgan said evenly. She would not make this easier for Yuri by telling him it was unnecessary. She would make him ply his trade as he endeavored to free Mikal.

Yuri nodded. "And he has a son. Children adjust as the demands become greater. Women like you do not."

"Women like me?"

"You're a woman who can't sit home and wait, can't merely be ready when your man has time for you and be patient when he doesn't. That's the only kind of woman for Mikal now. He's too good at what he does."

"Have you thought about what *Mikal* might want?" she asked.

"You've read his poetry," Yuri reminded her. "You know his vision. He'll give his life for the things he believes in."

Morgan gave the old man a level stare. He was formidable, but she knew who she was. "I have a life, too, Yuri. I have work that I believe in. What's between Mikal and me is our own, and I doubt that you know as much about it as you think you do." She laid her napkin by her cup and stood, enjoying the fact that Yuri looked surprised as he followed suit. "Don't worry. I understand who Mikal Romanov is, and I won't tamper with that."

She was packed and ready to leave when Mikal returned to the hotel at noon. He saw her bags, and she read the confusion in his eyes. "I can't leave until tomorrow," he said, reaching for her. She backed away, and the confusion deepened. "I called David and told him tomorrow for sure. Can you wait another day? We'll go back together."

Morgan shook her head. "I need to get back. My father's ready, and so am I."

Mikal shoved his hands in his pockets and took a step back, giving her space. "Okay. I'll see you at home, then."

"I doubt that my father will stay around Bismarck long," she said quickly. "I want to spend as much time with him as I can, so I probably won't—"

"What's this all about, Morgan?"

In defense, Mikal let his confusion become his quiet form of anger. Morgan decided she could handle that with coolness. "It's not 'about' anything. You have business to take care of here, and I have mine at home. I appreciate all you've done for my father, Mikal."

"For your . . . father?"

Heaving a sigh, she reached abruptly for her suitcase, but when she leaned across the vanity for her purse, Mikal snatched it up first. They stared hotly at one another for several seconds, and then, without glancing away, he took several folded papers from his jacket pocket. He stuffed them into her purse before handing the bag to her and turning to leave.

"Let me know if you're ever free," he told her quietly, and then he closed the door behind him.

Morgan resisted looking at the pages Mikal had given her until her father had fallen asleep next to her on the plane. She opened her purse slowly and peered in, as though she were afraid to touch the papers—as though they might be hot. She felt them gingerly, ran a finger along the thick fold, and finally drew them out. She felt her throat tighten as she unfolded them and found several pages of Mikal's poems, each one dated. That was his book of hours, the difficult ones he'd spent at De Colores. These were the thoughts and fears he'd kept to himself, the frustration and the loneliness. And here was his love for her. He had remembered her and kept himself sane. He had talked to her, praised her, wondered, worried, called her his.

Know me, dark-haired lady
Trust me with your untried passion
Take my constancy to your soft breast

And see the man who loves the paradox in you.

Morgan's hands trembled as she folded the papers carefully and returned them to her purse.

His poetry haunted her. He reached for her with it across time and space, touched her with it, made forgetting him impossible. Dreams, she thought. She couldn't live dreams. She was a practical, down-to-earth woman. But her dreams of him were sweet things—milk and honey—nourishing and earthy. She feasted on remembrances of Mikal's smile, equally charming with his dazzling tux or his favorite sweater, of Mikal's light, easy touch as he prepared a gourmet dish or swept her hair back from her face, and of the sound of Mikal's voice, smooth and commanding in a room teeming with people, or husky and powerful in her ear. There was nothing ethereal about her memories of him. Even as she plunged back into her routine, he was with her, at her shoulder in every move she made. She wasn't sure whether she'd made him part of her reality or become a dreamer herself. Either way, the memories she cherished were of an earthy man whose single fault was that he dreamed. But now, it seemed, Morgan Kramer had learned to dream, too.

Morgan could smell Mikal's marinara sauce. If she'd had any reservations about ringing the back doorbell, they floated away as the aroma drifted to her nose. Tomatoes and oregano and Mikal's magic. She pressed the button.

The porch light came on, and David peered through the glass. Morgan was glad he opened the door so quickly. It was a still night that had already plummeted deep into the frigid temperatures of a typical Dakota January. He pushed open the storm door and offered an eager, "Miss Kramer! Come on in."

Morgan stepped over the threshold, just avoiding a large pair of running shoes, which David snatched out of her way. "Hey, what a surprise. Dad'll really be—Dad!" he called over one shoulder. To the armload of running shoes, David added a broom and a small collection of newspapers, which he gathered as he backed into the kitchen. "He wasn't expecting you, was he? I mean, it's great you're here in time for supper and all, but..." He gave a skinny-shouldered shrug. "We could've picked up a little."

"I'm barging in unannounced because I couldn't resist the smell of that sauce," she told him with a smile. "I don't want to cause any—"

"Hello, Morgan."

The sight of him, the sound of his voice, his very presence, made it hard for her to breathe regularly. "I came to wish you... a happy New Year."

He grinned. "The same to you. How's your father?"

"He's fine."

"Spending a lot of time together, are you?"

"Y-yes."

He moved closer, still wearing that grin, this time along with a rust sweater that looked comfortably Mikal. Dazzlingly Mikal. Charmingly Mikal. "Let me take your coat, Morgan. You'll have supper, I hope."

Morgan fumbled with her buttons. "It smells wonderful." When the last button was undone, Morgan raised her head slowly, taking a deep breath, more for courage than enjoyment of the aroma. His blue eyes were soft with understanding. She smiled, quietly adding, "And I *am* free."

Arms piled high with an assortment of misplaced articles, David rounded the corner behind Mikal and disappeared down the hallway. He was back in a moment with his own coat. "Scott just called, Dad. He asked me to stay over tonight, and he's got that new computer. Would you mind?"

"What about supper?"

"We're making pizza. So it's okay? Great seeing you, Miss Kramer. Eat my share." The back door closed on David's last words, "You'll love the marin—"

Mikal was laughing, and Morgan joined in gratefully. "It probably isn't that great seeing me. He just saw me in school today, and I got after him about being tardy."

"How tardy?"

"Not very."

"I guess I have to get after him now, too. About lying."

He'd put her coat over a chair, and now he was looking at her as though she might be the marinara sauce. Her tongue felt awkward as she tried to keep up her end of the conversation. "About what?"

He took her face in his hands and searched her eyes. "Did you hear the phone ring?" She shook her head. "Neither did I. I think he invited himself."

"So did I. You'll have to get after us both."

He smiled. "You first."

Their kiss was a deluge after too long a drought. It washed them over, swirled over hard, dry surfaces, splashed and sluiced, and finally soaked in, drawing them with it, deeply, to soothe aching roots. At last they were able to draw back, to hold and touch and look at one another.

"I love the poems," she whispered. He dipped his chin in acknowledgement. "I brought them back. You probably want to publish them."

"If you love them, they're yours, Morgan. I write poetry for love. Remember?"

"They're beautiful. You should share them."

"I did."

She hugged him close, pillowing her cheek against his sweater. "I see it differently now," she said. "It wasn't something you sought for yourself."

"I wanted to be home," he told her, pressing his hands against her back. "With my son and with you."

"But you'll go again if you have to."

"If I have to," he agreed.

She closed her eyes and breathed deeply of the smell of him. "If you said otherwise, you wouldn't be Mikal. And I love you."

"I'll be around the house and underfoot most of the time, Morgan. And I'm not exactly tidy. You'll be glad when Yuri persuades me to go on a mission, so you can get organized."

"As long as I never have to do any cooking."

He chuckled. "That goes without saying."

She tilted her head back and smiled. "Everything about you is too big for me. Especially your dreams. Are you really Freedom International's heir apparent?"

"Who said that? Yuri?" Morgan nodded. "I'm an idealist, yes, but so are you, lady. You're a teacher, aren't you? I believe in Freedom International, and I'll help out, but I'm a writer by profession. I want to be Steinbeck's heir apparent."

"I've missed you terribly," she confessed.

"It's been hard to stay away. I wanted to go after you and make you love me."

"I've loved you all along." She kissed his chin. "But you're such a dreamer."

"And you say *everything* about me is too big for you?"

"Maybe not *everything*."

One by one, he took the pins from her hair. "I'd say you were due for a little awareness rally."

Pressing herself closer, she soon made him groan with delight. "For your sake, we'd better make this a private rally. One thing about your awareness, Mikal Romanov—" she slipped her thumbs inside the waistband at the back of his jeans "—it's easily raised."

Mikal laughed as Morgan stood on tiptoe, angling for another kiss. He lifted her in his arms, and Morgan Kramer found joy in what once would have felt like a precarious position—her feet dangling above the floor and her head in the clouds.

* * * * *

MORE THAN A MIRACLE

Kathleen Eagle

For Christopher—
Thanks to my youngest,
I'm never at a loss
for hugs and kisses.

Chapter 1

McQuade stood on the landing and surveyed the crowd beneath the Purple Parrot's whirling ceiling fan. It was a mixed bag of locals and tourists, who were easily distinguished by their pink flamingo T-shirts with *Miami* splashed across the top. This wasn't a place he would have chosen for a meeting, but the woman involved had offered no choices.

He'd seen her only once before, and from that memory he was able to spot her immediately. She softened the space around her, creating her own niche of translucent blue-white in the middle of the smoky violet atmosphere. Her booth near the end of the bar was a little island, a haven at the edge of the din. McQuade wondered whether her isolation was self-imposed, or whether the boundaries were generally obvious and universally respected. It occurred to him that he might be the fool rushing in where wise men from near and far feared to tread.

The only reason he'd agreed to this meeting was that Mikal Romanov had called and asked him to. He would even give some consideration to taking whatever job the woman offered him, just because Mike had asked him to hear her out. Mike was the only true humanitarian Mc-Quade had ever met, and the only man he ever did favors for. Otherwise his services were costly, and he wondered whether this woman could afford him.

McQuade drew a pack of cigarettes from the pocket of his denim jacket, shook one out and stuck it in his mouth. If he'd waited until he got to her table he would have had to ask. He was capable of being at least that civilized. Something told him she would have been gracious about it. She was the kind of woman who seemed to float several feet above everyone else, and what the teeming masses did would not affect her. He drew deeply on the cigarette and squinted through the smoke, thinking he would take his time and size her up from here.

She looked up, saw him and knew him instantly. She offered no cheery wave, no beckoning hand. Huge brown eyes dominated her face, and her gaze was riveting. For a moment he was back on the small, troubled island of De Colores, where he'd seen her in the cool of the Caribbean morning nearly a year ago. They hadn't spoken when he'd helped her with her bags as she and four other hostages of the island's new government were escorted to their plane.

The other hostages had been American, but she was a native of the island and had been headed for exile. The aloof dignity of her bearing had set her apart. It was common knowledge that her husband, a member of the new three-man junta, was sending her away, but beyond that information, no one had discussed her situation. Little was said to her, mostly because no one had the proper words to give her, but also because her proud bearing had invited no questions, no expressions of sympathy.

McQuade watched her and wondered when she would look away. He could almost always evoke a revealing reaction from a woman right from the start, simply by staring. Within fifteen seconds he could usually tell what she wanted from him. He watched her while he took another long, slow drag on his cigarette, but her expression remained unchanged. She, too, was watching.

He made his way to her table, pausing at the corner of the bar to crush his cigarette out in an ashtray. She kept track of him every step of the way, a tactic that made the skin on the back of his neck crawl, because it was one he normally used himself.

Taken off balance, he did something that was unusual for him; he offered what he thought would probably pass for a friendly smile as he extended his hand. "Mrs. Guerrero? I'm McQuade."

The smile she returned was tentative and didn't quite reach her wary eyes. She offered her hand. "Please sit down, Mr. McQuade. I am Elizabeth Donnelly now. I am divorced."

"Donnelly?" He knew of a Donnelly who'd had some dealings in the islands, and as he extended a firm handshake he promised himself that if she was related to *that* Donnelly, he would promptly tell her goodbye, even though he found his fingers lingering around hers. Her hand was slight and cold and seemed to need his warmth. Before the moment became awkward, he slid into the booth beside her.

"Yes," she said, confirming his suspicions with the word. "My maiden name carries almost as many thorns as my married name."

"Why didn't you change it altogether, then?" He turned to find the bartender standing by his shoulder, and he ordered bourbon and water. The man didn't move until Elizabeth asked for a glass of white wine and gave him a nod.

"Your bodyguard?" McQuade asked after the bartender had moved on.

"My friend," she said. "And to answer your question, it wouldn't matter what my name was. My father was con- victed of drug trafficking, and my ex-husband is part of the new military government of De Colores, so I'm well-known to any and all authorities." She gave him a level stare. "And to answer the question you haven't asked, I had nothing to do with my father's business and very little to do with my father. Mikal Romanov was able to convince the U.S. gov- ernment of that fact. I've been granted political asylum, and I've applied for citizenship. My mother was, of course, De Coloran, my father American. The island was apparently a convenient place from which to do business, and my mother and I were . . . conveniences, too."

"He got sent up about two years ago, didn't he?" She nodded. "Is your mother still on the island?"

"No. She's dead." The look she gave him constituted a dare. "Am I too hot to handle, Mr. McQuade?"

He laughed. It was such a funny phrase coming from her, especially when he thought of her cold hand. "You may well be, Miss Donnelly. You may very well be."

"I had hoped that Mikal Romanov and Freedom Inter- national would be able to take care of this for me. They freed us, you know, those of us who were detained after the coup. Mikal gave me your name the last time I called him. He said he'd done all he could."

McQuade remembered Mike's call the previous day. "She's got a plan that's right up your alley, McQuade. Real cloak-and-dagger stuff. Freedom International can't really touch the problem, because there are no prisoners involved anymore."

Because Mikal Romanov was the man he was, McQuade surmised that he himself was this woman's last resort. Mikal preferred to use diplomatic methods, while nobody had ever accused McQuade of being diplomatic. Freedom International worked for the discharge of political prisoners, and Mikal had done a beautiful job of negotiating the release of the hostages on De Colores after the sudden military coup that had taken place there a year before. McQuade figured he was about to hear of a problem that diplomatic methods had failed to solve.

"What do you want from me, Miss Donnelly?"

"I want a miracle, Mr. McQuade."

McQuade raised an eyebrow. He'd been called the miracle worker by some because his business was, among other things, finding missing people, and he'd been known to "raise the dead." If the lost were anywhere on God's green earth, chances were McQuade could find them, or, at the very least, find out what had become of them. He considered private detective agency to be too mundane a term to describe his business, so he was listed in the phone book simply as McQuade, Inc.—the Inc. for tax purposes. His clients were always referrals who came to him from any number of sources.

Lovely as this woman was, she was still a prospective client, and McQuade was a man who put first things first. "Miracles don't come cheap, Miss Donnelly."

"I can pay you," she told him.

"Pay me for what?"

"Guerrero has our son—*my* son. I want him back."

"Get in touch with General Castillo. Of the three honchos, he's got the final word there on De Colores, and he strikes me as a fairly sentimental old guy. Tell him—"

"You haven't heard, then. The general died of heart failure two days ago. It's just the two of them now. Miguel Hidalgo has taken charge of health, education, welfare of the people and internal matters, while—"

"There! That's even better. Hidalgo's a good man. He'll listen—"

"—while Guerrero commands all transportation, all military forces and all police."

McQuade considered the information for a moment, remembering Guerrero, a man who wouldn't be satisfied until he'd armed every schoolboy on the island and taught them all to goose-step. "You're asking for more than a miracle, Miss Donnelly."

"I've tried the Red Cross, the State Department, even the Church. They tell me that this is a family matter, that Guerrero is a father with legal custody. Custody! Who determined that?" Her soft brown eyes suddenly hardened. "We will have to kidnap my son."

McQuade gave a short bark of laughter. Not that the request was funny, nor was it the first time he'd heard it. He'd run into a hundred kinds of desperation in his line of work. He'd run into a hundred kinds of madmen, too, and he'd judged Colonel Rodolfo Guerrero to be one of the worst he'd seen. This woman had to be Mrs. Madman, divorced or not. With Guerrero in charge, the presidential palace at La Primavera, the island's capital, would undoubtedly be a well-armed military compound by now.

His laugh drew an icy stare from the lady. "Mikal Romanov recommended you highly, Mr. McQuade. I'm surprised you lack the courtesy to even take my predicament seriously."

He moved his arm aside as his drink was delivered to the table, and he waved her complaint away after he'd paid the bartender, whose stare was as cold as Elizabeth's. The whole situation was thin-ice territory, McQuade decided. "Look, I wasn't laughing at your predicament, but you'll have to admit that the idea of kidnapping Guerrero's son is a little—"

"*My* son," Elizabeth repeated.

"Guerrero's his father, right? You just admitted that." The woman nodded solemnly. "And since he's half the government down there, he decides who's got custody. I guess I assumed you had a deal when you left—you got your freedom, he got the kid."

"When it was decided to release the other hostages, Guerrero ordered me to leave. I was not allowed to take my son."

Once again he saw the tragic dignity he'd noticed in her face the day she'd left the island. Her dark eyes were clouded with pain, but she held her pointed little patrician chin high. He couldn't imagine why any man would mind having her satin slippers stashed under his bed.

"Why'd he kick you out?"

It was Elizabeth's turn to laugh, but her amusement was brief. She took a sip of her wine and shook her head as she swallowed it. "It's a very long story, Mr. McQuade, one that would bore you, I'm sure. I was more than pleased to terminate my relationship with Guerrero, but I had hoped to be allowed to live quietly with my son near La Primavera, in the house where I was born. Guerrero decided to take my home and my son from me because I am not..."

He waited for her to finish, interested in knowing just what she was not. When it finally appeared that she'd decided against telling him, he prodded. "You're not what?"

There was a hint of defiance in her eyes as she straightened her shoulders. "According to Guerrero, I'm not one of the people his so-called government represents. My mother was, in his words, an aristocrat, and my father is an American criminal." She gave another mirthless little laugh. "All Americans have become criminals in Guerrero's eyes, but in my father's case—" she shrugged "—it's actually true."

"So why did he marry you?"

"Times and Guerrero's fortunes were quite different five years ago."

His real question was why had *she* married *him*, but he would let that one go. He found himself feeling a greater measure of sympathy for her than he'd planned to allow himself. Get the facts, weigh the odds, and take the job or leave it, he told himself.

McQuade leaned back and rolled his half-empty glass between his palms. "I guess you know how particular they've gotten about who gets on and off that island," he said.

"I wouldn't be able to enter the country by ordinary means anyway. We would have to—"

He glanced up quickly. "Lady, if I took this job, you wouldn't be able to go, period."

"If you took this job," she said quietly, "I would accompany you. That would be a requirement."

"When I take a job, I determine the requirements."

They stared at each other with firm conviction. "We are talking of my son, Mr. McQuade. He is only two years old. I will not have him taken from his home and smuggled to this country by a stranger."

"Then you probably won't have him at all, Miss Donnelly. It won't be a piece of cake, getting him out of that compound, and you won't find—"

"I have a plan."

"You look like you have a plan. And I look like a Boy Scout whose motto is Be Prepared for Ladies Who Have Plans." Wit like that called for another drink, and McQuade signaled the bartender.

Elizabeth frowned as she bit back words. She needed this man's help, and she wouldn't get it by telling him what she thought of his smug attitude. The words would keep until she had her son back. Mikal Romanov had assured her that she could trust McQuade, and Elizabeth held Mikal's recommendation in high regard, despite the chauvinistic smirk on the face she was carefully surveying. It was chiseled, with an angular jaw, a slightly irregular nose that might once have been broken, and gray eyes. There was no mistaking his masculinity, and Elizabeth didn't doubt that he had a typically masculine ego to match. She decided she could work that ego to her advantage for a change.

"I don't think you look like a Boy Scout, Mr. McQuade." She turned toward him, bracing her elbow near the edge of the table, and touched two fingers to her chin as she appraised him. "You look like a risk-taker. A man like you makes his own plans when a lucrative opportunity presents itself. You strike me as a man who's prepared to challenge the odds if the rewards promise to be worthwhile."

She was a classic. McQuade took a quick mental review of the women he'd known in the past, but he couldn't recall feminine poise that could rival hers. Worse, he couldn't call up the features of any other face as he looked at hers. She was a classic, all right. He summoned every ounce of cockiness he could muster.

"What's your offer, Miss Donnelly?"

"Ten thousand in advance. Forty when my son and I are safely back in the United States."

"That's only money." The look he gave her was loaded with other suggestions.

"Yes, it is," she said calmly. "If you thrive on adventure, I'm sure this job will provide you with that, also."

McQuade chuckled as he plucked a purple book of matches from the ashtray on the table. "Money and adventure, huh? You add bourbon, broads, cigarettes and rare steak to the list, and I start thriving pretty well."

"I'm sure fifty thousand dollars will go a long way, Mr. McQuade. Those things are all for sale." She gave him a pointed stare. "Are you?"

"I'm for hire, Miss Donnelly, when a job feels right to me. So far, this one doesn't fit. It feels tight." He bunched his shoulders in a gesture that suggested he felt constrained by his jacket, which was actually neatly tailored for his broad build. "Will we have to stop at the bank in La Primavera to make a withdrawal before we make our getaway?"

"I have the money, Mr. McQuade. And I bank in Switzerland."

"Don't we all? How'd you manage to keep Guerrero's hands off your money?"

"My mother did, actually, though her concern when she set up the trust fund for me was to keep my father's hands off the money—*her* family's money. When I reached the age of twenty-one, I allowed Guerrero to use some of my inheritance, but I had the sense to shelter the rest of it. He didn't realize that." She smiled, taking satisfaction in her small victory, but McQuade seemed unimpressed with her foresight. He must have enjoyed so many small victories that he couldn't appreciate this one, she thought. But she knew what he would appreciate. "I do have the money."

The arrival of another drink for McQuade and a second glass of wine for Elizabeth eased the moment. After a couple of quiet sips she asked, "Don't you want to hear my plan?"

McQuade settled back. Elizabeth Donnelly was easy to look at, and his second drink was sliding down even slicker than the first. "Why the hell not? Let's have it."

"I've arranged for a private plane."

McQuade acknowledged this by raising his eyebrows. "Nice. Where do we land this plane?"

"I'm not sure. I thought you'd probably have some ideas on that."

"Mmm. I even get to have ideas. Okay, so we land this plane somewhere. Then what?"

Elizabeth lifted a slender hand. "Then I have relatives, friends who will give us refuge. We'll make our way toward the palace."

"Umm-hmm."

"And you'll slip in . . . under cover of darkness."

"Oh, yeah, I've seen that done."

"If Tomás has the same nurse . . ."

"Tomás. That's the kid."

"Yes. If he still has the same nurse, she'll help us. I'm sure she'll still be there. Guerrero doesn't realize that she's my great-aunt."

"That's a plus."

"You'll bring him out, and we'll make our way back to the plane, or possibly to a boat, and we'll . . ."

McQuade's brow was furrowed, but amusement made his mouth twitch. "I think there are some holes in this plan, Miss Donnelly."

"And I think fifty thousand dollars should plug them up." Her smile was a mere wisp. McQuade wasn't quite sure he could even call it a smile, except that there was a sudden hopeful sheen in her eyes. He wondered whether she really believed money had that much power. "I can understand why your services come dear," Elizabeth added smoothly. "Mikal Romanov said he knew of no one else who knows the island, is familiar with the palace and has the expertise that you have."

She was making him sound as good as he was beginning to feel. He wondered how much of that had to do with her and how much had to do with his second drink, which was turning out to be a real kicker. "What kind of expertise did Mike credit me with?"

She lifted one shoulder and waved a hand to indicate that he surely must have been aware of his reputation. "A lot of local connections, a bloodhound's nose, an ability to defend yourself and others, the kind of cunning that—"

McQuade laughed. "Good God, why don't they make a movie about me! I sound terrific."

"He said you're the best there is, and that's what I need. You helped Mrs. Romanov."

He remembered how Mike's new wife had looked when she'd come to McQuade's cubbyhole of an office on the island, trying to find someone to get her into the palace to see Mike. Morgan Kramer had had *teacher* written all over her face and *woman beside herself with worry over her man* etched in her eyes. McQuade had been working with the Red Cross and Freedom International at the time, locating people who'd gotten lost in the shuffle of the coup, but he'd been able to dig up some information for several clients of his own in the process. With the Red Cross it was charity, and with Mike it was friendship, but he was also in this business for profit. And this woman was offering...

"Fifty thousand, huh?" He raised his glass, eyeing her over the rim as he took another drink. Best damned bourbon he'd ever tasted, and, if anything, the lady's bartender friend had skimped on the water.

"It's *respectable* money, Mr. McQuade. As I've explained, I inherited it from my mother."

"I'm not real fussy about where you got your money, lady, as long as it was printed by the U.S. Treasury Department." The bartender replaced McQuade's empty glass with a full one. McQuade flashed a questioning glance at Elizabeth. "Did you order this?"

"On the house, sir." The burly man took the white dish towel off his shoulder and took a swipe at the ring of water on the table. "The lady's a good customer."

McQuade made a point of surveying the Purple Parrot, from the gaudy papier-mâché bird that hung over the bar to the cashier, whose black-and-orange jungle-print sheath was backless to the waist. He raised an eyebrow at Elizabeth as he slid his complimentary drink back and forth over the pockmarked wooden table. "Strange hangout for a lady."

Elizabeth's survey took the same path as McQuade's. The place offered her the kind of distraction she needed. There were people everywhere. She didn't know them, but they were there, and that was something. She looked back to find McQuade staring at her oddly. "I don't know anyone in Miami," she explained. "As soon as I have my son, I'll probably move to New England. I went to school there, and it's the only part of the country I know. But for now..."

Her thoughts drifted away, and McQuade felt strangely bereft. He wanted her to talk to him. "Where are you staying?" he asked.

She smiled. Perhaps the question indicated a spark of interest in her situation. She sensed that so far he'd been put off by the mere fact that she was who she was. "I've taken an apartment and part-time job tutoring immigrants in English. Matt, the bartender, lives in my building."

McQuade glanced back over his shoulder and caught one of the many stares he knew had been trained on him since he'd sat down. He waved a single finger at the dusky-eyed man, who turned away without responding.

"I think he'd sooner break both my legs than serve me free drinks," McQuade decided.

"He's been a good friend to me," Elizabeth said quietly. "He wouldn't harm a fly."

McQuade nodded, smiling as he pictured the big bartender armed with a flyswatter. "Sure. Unless that fly came buzzing around you. Why don't you take Matt to De Colores and send him into Guerrero's little fortress?"

"He's offered to do that. If you think you need another man, I could ask him to come along."

"Instead of you?"

"No. I intend to go with you, regardless."

"I wouldn't need another man, and I certainly wouldn't need to drag you along, either. A job like this is best done quickly and quietly by a single person who knows how to handle himself." His hard look challenged her to argue with the sense of that.

"I would follow your directions, Mr. McQuade. I'd help, I'd stay out of your way—whatever you said. But no power on earth could keep me from going with you."

He saw her resolve in the way she clasped her hands in her lap and squared her shoulders. She had a slight build, somewhat tall—willowy, he decided. She had a strong will going for her, and she was determined to find her son. Hiring some muscle seemed to be important to her. She'd need some firepower, too, considering who she was up against. McQuade figured a flyswatter would be about all the firepower Matt, the bartender, could handle. He tossed back the rest of his drink and decided that Matt did, however, have a way with bourbon.

McQuade set his glass down and leaned forward. "Look, I'll give this some thought, Miss Donnelly. I want to talk to some people, find out what really happened to Castillo and what's going on down there now that he's out of the picture, see what my chances are of getting on that island without being noticed—details like that. I'll give you my answer in a couple of days."

"I'd like to leave tomorrow."

She had a delicate way of being demanding. McQuade saw the hunger in her eyes and knew that she was fighting to cover it up. She was striving for a look of serene dignity, one that said nothing could touch her. It wasn't working, but McQuade couldn't take much pleasure in that fact. The look in her eyes was having too strong an effect on him. He glanced away and noticed that another drink had appeared at his elbow.

"I can't believe the service around here," McQuade mumbled, tasting it. "Again the good stuff."

"Matt knows I need your help," Elizabeth explained. "It must be his way of saying— What's wrong, Mr. Mc-Quade?"

He scowled at the drink in his hand for a moment, then carefully placed it on the table as though it might have a life of its own. Then he turned hooded gray eyes on Elizabeth. "Tomorrow's too soon. Listen, company's been great, proposal's interesting, can't ask for more than drinks on the house, but I have to think it over." He slid out of the booth abruptly and offered his hand. "I've got your number. I'll give you a call."

Stunned, Elizabeth watched McQuade thread his way among tables and people as he headed for the door, walking a little less fluidly than he had when he'd come in. He tipped over one empty chair, caught it and set it back, then moved on.

"Where's he headed?"

Elizabeth looked up to find Matt, his arms folded around his barrel chest, glowering after the retreating McQuade.

"I don't know. All of a sudden he'd heard enough."

Matt shifted a toothpick from one side of his mouth to the other and made a clucking sound as he watched the door close behind the man Miss Donnelly wanted to hire. "If you'd 'a kept him here a little longer, I'd 'a had him passed out cold, and you could 'a dumped him in the plane and taken him where you wanted him.''

"What?''

Matt grinned at the lady's wide-eyed shock. "He won't get far as it is. Surprises me he could walk out like that. Hope he's not driving.''

"Matt!'' Elizabeth shot out of the booth and grabbed her purse. "Did you put something in his drinks?''

"It's an old recipe, Miss Donnelly, nothing—''

"Not drugs,'' she hissed. "You didn't—''

"It's just booze,'' Matt said with a shrug. "Goes down easy, but...''

Matt grinned as he watched Elizabeth shoulder her way through the crowd. If Mr. McQuade was still on his feet, he was about to have himself an embarrassing moment in front of Miss Donnelly.

Out on the sidewalk, Elizabeth frantically scanned the street for McQuade. Oh, God, she thought, he's gotten behind the wheel. Then she spotted him across the street. On slightly unsteady legs, he was headed for the wharf. She gave the traffic only a cursory glance before she hiked her straight skirt above her knees and made a headlong dash across the road.

Squealing brakes and the scream of a horn pulled McQuade's head around. Whatever he'd been drinking sure played hell with the mind, he told himself. Through the headlights he thought he saw a gorgeous pair of legs and Elizabeth Donnelly's face. What was in between was blotted out by glare until another car skidded to a stop and she sprinted past it. God, yes, Elizabeth Donnelly, skirt up around her thighs and running across the street, looking incredibly graceful and long legged.

"You're gonna get killed!" he shouted, and a man in a cab yelled something about where he was going to leave his tire marks. McQuade responded in kind, feeling in the right mood to shout down even a cab-driver. He reached for Elizabeth and hauled her over the curb as the cab whizzed by. "What the hell are you—"

"You mustn't drive, Mr. McQuade," she gasped, grabbing the front of his denim jacket for support.

"You think I don't know that? I need some air first. That's some drink your buddy, Matt..." Gripping her arms, he pulled her face closer to his. "What the hell— I can't believe I let you slip me something, lady."

"I didn't. I swear it. Please, let's walk, Mr. McQuade. Unless you feel—"

"What was I drinking?" He tightened his grip and the terror that flashed in her eyes surprised him. "Just tell me," he said evenly.

"Matt said it was just liquor, some kind of recipe. He wouldn't hurt you, I'm sure of it. He was trying to help me."

"By getting me drunk? What for?"

She shook her head, and her long dark hair swished about her shoulders. "I guess he thought it would be easier to get you on the plane that way. I'm sorry, Mr. McQuade. Matt didn't mean any harm."

He released her slowly, but she continued to stare at him, wide-eyed, like a night creature mesmerized by headlights. "I think I just need some air," he told her. "I'm gonna walk out on the pier for a minute."

She watched him stumble twice on the steps that would take him from street level to the wharf. He'd fall in the water, she told herself, and she hurried after him. "Let me go with you, Mr. McQuade," she called.

He turned and waited while he put a cigarette in his mouth and struck a match.

"Did you come in your own car?" she asked, approaching him cautiously. He had a right to be angry, she realized, and anyway, anger was what she had learned to expect from men.

"Yeah. Parked it in a lot. Hate to leave it in a lot down here overnight, but since I don't know what in hell it was I drank..." He blew a steam of gray smoke and started toward the pier. It was quiet down there. Maybe his head would clear.

"I'll drive you home, Mr. McQuade."

He turned to her, and she stopped in her tracks. She stood there, looking up at him in the lamplight, her chest fluttering with the unsteadiness of her breathing. She was scared, and McQuade wasn't sure whether the dash across the street was the cause or whether he was. Yet she had offered to drive him home. "Then how would you get where you're going?" he asked.

"I'd take a taxi."

"You've got a driver's license?"

"Of course."

He smiled at her bravado. "I don't want to be inside anything right now," he told her honestly. "Especially not something that moves. How about sitting out on the pier with me for a little while? Looking at the lights?"

She brushed at her skirt and then squared her shoulders, once again the lady with poise. "That would be very nice."

They found a spot where they could sit in near darkness and listen to the water lap at the sides of the boats moored nearby. A bridge stretched over the bay, and its lights were draped in scallop formation across the sky. McQuade finished his cigarette in silence, then flicked it into the water.

"I think I could get to the island myself," Elizabeth mused aloud. "They got Mrs. Romanov out of the palace by disguising her. Maybe I could get in the same way."

McQuade swung his head around and looked at her. She was staring off across the water, and he knew her brain was ticking in high gear. "You'd try it, wouldn't you? You'd give it a shot on your own."

She turned to him. "My son was just toddling when I saw him last. He only knew a few words. He might not even . . . know me right away."

"Is Matt's recipe for sale?" he wondered. "I've got some friends I'd like to try it on." His smile came slowly. "Your ex-husband, for one."

"You'll help me, then?"

McQuade sighed. This was another look he couldn't resist. Woman beside herself with worry over her kid. "A boy oughta be with his mother," he said quietly.

"Tomorrow?" she asked, brightening there in the dark.

"Not tomorrow, honey." He chuckled. "I'm going to have a record-breaking headache, so I'm gonna have to turn you down for tomorrow."

"I could drive you to the airport, Mr. McQuade, and you could sleep all the way to—"

"I can't be ready by morning, Elizabeth. I really have to check some things out before I jump into this."

"But the plane—"

"You let me talk to your pilot. I don't think I want to fly directly to De Colores, anyway. I'm gonna let you drive me home and pick me up in my car tomorrow. Then I'll meet this pilot of yours." He rolled his eyes toward the stars. "I hope he isn't related to your bartender."

Elizabeth smiled to herself, reserving her comments. "I'll have your advance ready tomorrow, Mr. McQuade."

He said nothing. He didn't want to discuss money with her now. He only hoped he could get off the pier without falling into the water. One more cigarette, he decided.

"Do you have a first name, Mr. McQuade?"

He drew deeply on the smoke and held it, then expelled it, remembering. "Yeah, but I never use it."

"May I?"

He shrugged. "Sure. It's Sloan."

She turned her face up to him, and in the dim light he saw that look again. She spoke in a pleading tone. "Help me get my son back, Sloan."

Chapter 2

Whoever the hell you are, you press that thing one more time and I'm coming down to break your finger.''

Elizabeth drew her hand back from the buzzer as though she'd been burned, and then she checked her watch again. Hadn't he told her to pick him up in the morning? Eight o'clock was surely reasonable if he intended to get anything done today.

She stepped closer to the intercom and spoke quietly. ''It's Elizabeth Donnelly, Mr. McQuade.'' Elizabeth tried to match her memory of McQuade's stony face to the agonized groan she was hearing over the intercom, but she couldn't get them to fit together. ''I'm not too early, am I?''

''I take it you know what time it is.''

''Yes, of course. I thought we should get started now.''

''Oh, yeah?'' The mirthless chuckle fit her picture of him well. ''Come on up, then.''

He was just another man, Elizabeth told herself as she stepped into the elevator. He couldn't help being so obnoxious, and she was prepared to be tolerant of simple obnoxiousness for Tomás's sake. Given the previous night's circumstances, he was probably even entitled to a few hours' foul mood. She would make it a point to be pleasant as long as he wasn't abusive. But the face that appeared at the apartment door after she knocked could have wilted a cactus. Elizabeth took a deep breath.

"I brought your car, Mr. McQuade. I wasn't sure how early you'd need it."

He gave her a cold, low-lidded stare. "Why the hell would I need a car? I've got my own freight train running through my head, thanks to Matt, the harmless bartender."

"I'll just leave these with you." She extended long fingers and a palm full of keys. The door swung open.

"Bring them in here so we can get on with whatever we're supposed to start in the middle of the night."

He stepped around the door, and she saw his white terry cloth bathrobe first, and then his bare feet. She wasn't sure why she wanted to giggle. "It's eight o'clock in the morning, Mr. McQuade."

"I resisted the urge to report that to you, Miss Donnelly. Do me the same favor."

"Perhaps if you had some coffee," she suggested as she stepped into the darkened room. The jacket he'd worn the previous night was lying on the carpet beside a leather chair.

"Perhaps if I went back to bed." He turned to raise one eyebrow at her, which took some effort. The skin grated over his skull. "Care to join me? I think I need to start this day all over again, with something more soothing than the sound of a doorbell buzzing." He managed part of a smile. "Can you think of anything?"

"Coddled eggs?"

His mouth turned down as he turned his back, grumbling, "Sounds slimy. You want coffee, you can make it. I'll be in the shower."

Elizabeth hoped he'd find that soothing. She opened the drapes and saw that the living room was in good order except for the clothes he'd shed the night before. She found the kitchen in good condition, too, with the makings for coffee stored in logical places. She didn't come across an abundance of groceries, but there was enough for a bacon-and-egg breakfast, and she proceeded to go to work. Sloan McQuade would be no good to her until his health was restored.

McQuade knew what the lady had cooking the minute he stepped out of the bathroom. It never bothered him when a woman got that domestic urge the morning after, but this wasn't a morning after. There was no feeling of exhilaration and no reason to believe he'd be welcome to walk up behind her and pat her bottom while she flipped his eggs. Worse yet, there was no reason to think his stomach wouldn't reject the eggs outright. He remembered what he'd gotten himself into the night before, but as he slipped into a pair of jeans, he couldn't remember why.

When he saw her standing in his kitchen with a plate of toast in one hand and a jar of jelly in the other, his memory came up with a flash of glaring headlights and beautiful legs. He watched as she gave the refrigerator door a nudge with her backside, and he knew this was the morning after a significant something had occurred. But he had the sinking feeling it was the beginning of something other than his customary after-breakfast farewells. With her long black hair, sleek as a seal's, setting off her soft white slacks and top, she seemed an unlikely domestic. More like an angel, he thought, then told himself to squelch such dangerous comparisons.

"So, Miss Donnelly, if you haven't made plans for breakfast, how about my place?"

Elizabeth turned, expecting to see him restored to the man she'd met the previous night, but his bare chest and faded jeans shocked away the pleasant answer she'd had ready for him. She stood in the middle of his apartment with his breakfast in her hands, and his smile said that he'd dressed with her in mind. His long, wiry torso looked hard and spare, which surprised her, because the simple lines of a shirt and jacket had softened him somewhat. She'd wanted him to be hard, of course, harder than Guerrero. She'd gone shopping for just such a man, and she hoped she'd found him, but that hardness—the stony face and those eyes and that chest—that hardness was as frightening to her as it was essential to him and his ability to do his job. Necessary for her, too, she reminded herself. She was going with him, and she, too, would have to be hard.

"Satisfied?"

Elizabeth raised her eyes to his, then looked away. He had an American smile; there was a playful hint of boy within the man. "I didn't mean to stare, Mr. McQuade, but that's an unsettling way to come to the table."

"I'm not unsettled. Are you?" He laughed, looking up at her with a mischievous twinkle in his eyes. "And I wasn't planning to come to the table, but make yourself at home. *Mi casa es su casa.*"

Elizabeth carried the toast and jelly to the table she'd already set, while three steps below her in the living room McQuade tossed his jacket on the sofa and plopped himself into the chair. "You speak Spanish, then," she said. She poured a cup of coffee and took it down to him.

"Not half as well as you speak English." He eyed the cup. "One sugar, no cream."

She took the coffee back up to the table, added his sugar, and put one piece of toast on a plate. Perhaps he'd start with that. "Do you take jelly on your toast?"

"Peanut butter, usually," he told her. It made him uneasy when she started for the kitchen. "But not today. Just that, that's fine. Really, that's all I can—" He accepted the coffee this time and set the plate of toast on a table beside him. "Look, I told you I'll take the job if I still think I can pull it off after I do a little checking. None of this is necessary. I'll make some calls, and I'll meet your pilot this afternoon. I promise."

"I asked Ronnie to meet us at the airport at nine-thirty. I thought you'd want to see the plane." She sat on the edge of the chair across from him and watched him sip his coffee. His wet hair was plastered against his head in tousled coils. "I thought you'd feel better if you ate something. I'm sorry about those drinks."

Her eyes were so wide with contrition, her face so pretty, that he was persuaded to reach for half a piece of toast just because she'd made it. "Guess I met my match. That stuff had one hell of a kick to it."

"I wouldn't have taken advantage of you, Mr. McQuade."

The idea made him laugh. He hoped she didn't expect the same nobility on his part, since they were about to spend a lot of time together, and that fresh flower scent she wore was making him want to follow his nose to whatever she'd dabbed it on.

"It's important to me that you believe that. I know I'm asking you to risk your life."

He saw how serious she was, and he decided to make it easier for her—and for himself, as well. "You're paying pretty well for it."

She nodded. "Would you like more coffee?"

"I think I'd like to watch you eat, too. What's on the menu besides coddled eggs?"

She smiled as she rose to her feet, and he knew he'd have to follow her to find out.

Ronnie Harper was not the man McQuade had expected. He wondered if she thought she was fooling anybody by shoving her pale red hair under a baseball cap. She wasn't going to make it as a man, and if she didn't get rid of those shapeless khaki shorts and high-top gym shoes she was liable to miss the mark as a woman. As it was, she could have passed for a Little Leaguer. McQuade offered her a nod and a handshake, but when Ronnie headed for her twin-engine Cessna, beckoning her prospective passengers to come aboard for a tour, McQuade grabbed Elizabeth by the elbow and grounded her where she stood.

"This *kid* is supposed to fly us to the island?" Elizabeth pulled her arm from his grasp, and he scowled as he leaned in closer. "It's bad enough that I have to take you along, but I'm not getting into this with some kid. We're not flying into a friendly situation, if you'll remember."

"I remember."

He closed his eyes and huffed. This woman had a way of looking at him that forced him to modify his worst retorts. "Okay, look." He laid a hand on her shoulder, but she chafed under that, too, so he shoved it into his pocket. "I'll look around for a plane, and I'll split the difference with you if I can't find as good a deal as you must have gotten on—"

"I've already hired her, Mr. McQuade, and I've paid her half in advance." She gave him a moment to roll his eyes and make a gesture of frustration. "I've spent months looking for a pilot. Most of them refuse to go near the island. Those who *are* willing want to be paid a king's ransom in advance, and they remind me of people who worked for my father. I believe we can trust this woman.''

They turned their heads toward the airplane. Ronnie Harper was sitting, chin in hand, in the open doorway, watching.

"She doesn't look like the type to be running drugs or illegal aliens," McQuade admitted, "but you can't go by looks."

"She's flown Red Cross supplies into De Colores with Miguel Hidalgo's blessing."

"What about Guerrero?"

Elizabeth laughed. "Blessings from Guerrero? Not for St. Francis himself, Mr. McQuade."

The flash of mirth in her eyes was a nice change. McQuade knew his resolve was softening. "She looks like a kid," he repeated stubbornly.

"As you just said, you can't go by looks. She's twenty-seven, she's been flying for eight years, and she's logged hundreds of hours in the Caribbean. I've investigated her thoroughly."

McQuade raised one eyebrow as he glanced at Elizabeth. He considered the plane again. "Thoroughly, huh? We'll see." With a shrug, he started toward the plane. "Let's get on with the interview."

McQuade's first meeting with Ronnie Harper convinced him that it was worth his while to consider her, but an interview with her was only the beginning. As always, he had some calls to make. After he dropped Elizabeth off at her apartment, he went about the business for which he was handsomely paid, though few clients knew the degree of care he took in checking all the angles. They paid him for results. This was how he got them and lived to tell about it.

* * *

Elizabeth Donnelly's apartment building didn't fit McQuade's image of her. He took the first three flights two steps at a time, but the last two flights slowed him down. On the way up he heard one squabble in English, two in Spanish and a chorus of crying babies. The island princess should have been spending her exile in a penthouse, preferably one with a limited-access elevator. She opened the door before he could knock twice.

"I was beginning to worry. I was afraid you'd changed your mind."

She had that fear in her eyes again, and McQuade stepped past her, resisting the niggling urge to reassure her with promises and other comforts. "The pilot's okay. I checked her out. I called a few people I thought might know something about Castillo's death, but it's all pretty vague. He did have a bad heart, and they're saying natural causes. Sounds like an uneasy partnership between Hidalgo and Guerrero."

"They are very different men."

Having moved inside, he turned to look at her in this unlikely setting. This was where she lived, in this sparsely furnished walk-up, but nothing of her was here. The white paint, brown carpet and red vinyl were not part of her; she could have been standing in some department store kitchen. She wore the soft white she seemed to favor, and her dark hair was caught up off her slender neck. She was white gardenias touched by an evening breeze. He suddenly realized he'd lost track of her last comment.

"Did you check me out, too?" she asked.

"Yeah. Yeah, I did." He glanced out the window, not bothered by the fact that he'd done his job, but embarrassed by what he'd been thinking and feeling a moment ago.

"Because of my father or my ex-husband?"

"Both."

"And are *you* satisfied?"

He turned to her and smiled. "You look okay to me. I went back and had a talk with Ronnie. We leave early in the morning."

"Before eight o'clock?"

"I'll pick you up at five. I've taken care of everything we need except your personal gear—whatever you can fit into a duffel bag." She nodded, and he felt good about the new expression in her eyes. He'd given her hope. "I'm changing the itinerary. We're flying into Arco Iris, and then we're taking a fishing boat from there."

"Why?" She'd sailed to the little island of Arco Iris many times. It was Mexican territory, but the two islands, De Colores to the west of Cuba and Arco Iris still farther west, shared the fishing waters between them.

"I don't want Ronnie to risk anything going in. A plane is more suspect than a fishing boat. She'll fly on to De Colores with her usual load of supplies for the Red Cross. We'll connect with her there, and she'll fly us out."

"How will we find a fisherman who's willing to take us?" She thought for a moment, then shook her head. "I might know someone in De Colores, but Arco Iris..."

"You leave that to me. I know people, too. That's why you hired me."

"It will take longer this way." She moved to the open window and looked down at the street. A group of small children were playing with a ball in the alley across the way. "I'd hoped we could be there tomorrow."

"The trick is to get there and back." He followed the direction of her gaze and watched, chuckling when one child bounced the ball off the back of another's head. "Looks like incubator alley down there. They sure have a lot of kids in this part of town."

"Don't you like children, Mr. McQuade?"

He shrugged. "Sure, I like kids. Who doesn't?"

"It's important to me that *you* do. I don't want my son left on that island under any circumstances." He turned to her and saw nothing of the fear he'd seen moments ago. Now her dark eyes burned with determination. "I'm paying you to see him safely away from De Colores and out of Guerrero's reach. I want to be sure you understand that."

Frowning in response to what appeared to be instructions for the feebleminded, he leaned one shoulder against the windowsill and folded his arms across his chest. "I understand what you've hired me to do, but I want you to understand something. You've complicated the job by insisting on coming along."

"I can't stay behind."

"You should also know that snatching a kid from his father can be sticky, and I've never tried it with a kid whose father is a head of state."

"But you have done this sort of thing before?"

He nodded. "For a woman who had custody, but the ex-husband skipped the country with the kid. You've got no custody, no laws on your side."

She turned away from him and watched the children again. She knew how bad the odds were; she didn't need to be reminded that she had no legal rights. In a way it bothered her that he was willing to help her. A man who could be bought, even at such a high price, could not be trusted. Yet if anything happened to her, she had to trust him with her son.

"Why didn't you move into a better neighborhood?" he asked. "This place isn't safe for a woman alone."

"My tutoring job pays the rent here," she told him. "I knew it might take everything I had to get my son back." Sparing him a sidelong glance, she added, "Especially since I have no laws on my side."

McQuade sighed as he straightened and stepped back from the window. Those eyes would be the death of him. "You've got me. What more can you ask?"

She smiled. "I'll be waiting at five."

McQuade arrived the next morning at the appointed time. He could tell she'd been up long before five. She was wide-eyed with anticipation, but she said little as they drove to the airport. McQuade felt as though he were accompanying a pilgrim on some holy journey, and he wished there was some way to protect her from her own high hopes. She'd followed his instructions by packing her personal items in a waterproof duffel bag, and she'd dressed in jeans and running shoes. She was ready to do the impossible, and determined that it would be done.

McQuade assigned Elizabeth to sit up front with Ronnie while he slept. He made a habit of sleeping when there was nothing better to do, and he judged that Elizabeth's adrenaline would keep her going for another twenty-four hours. When he woke, the women were chatting like old friends. He was glad Ronnie had gotten Elizabeth to relax.

"Arco Iris," Ronnie announced. Elizabeth leaned forward in her seat. They were making their descent, and the island had become a discernible dark spot in the blue sea.

"Look, Sloan! We're halfway there."

He'd begun to wonder whether she'd forgotten his name. Not that it mattered. McQuade was all anyone ever called him, even if that someone was whispering in his ear. But the sound of his given name made him sit up with a smile on his face.

"No kidding? This is a great little place," he said, searching out the spot for himself. "Nice beach, nice take-it-easy people."

"And at least one nice fisherman, I hope," Elizabeth wished aloud as she watched the island draw closer. "With a nice, fast boat."

The fisherman with the fast boat was not at the top of McQuade's priority list when he stepped off Ronnie's plane. He wanted a room, a shower and a stiff drink, which meant the first thing to do was look up Felix Santiago. Felix would grant those first three wishes instantly and immediately start locating the fisherman. All McQuade had to do was head for the Oyster Shell.

It was one of Arco Iris's three guest houses, and the sign above the front door proclaimed it a favorite haunt of Ernest Hemingway. The tiny lobby sported the obligatory ceiling fan, rattan furniture and mahogany reception desk, as well as a little old man whose black hair, slicked straight back from his face, gleamed with telltale hints of green. Felix Santiago did not plan to let his age show.

"I wasn't expecting you, McQuade. You don't tell me you're coming, I don't save your room." Felix shook a finger, but his eyes teased. "You should have let me know."

"This is just a quick trip, Felix. Anything you've got is okay." He dropped his big, green army duffel bag at the base of the desk.

Felix glanced at the two women standing behind McQuade. "How many rooms? One? Two?"

"Three."

"Oh?" Pity was evident in Felix's frown. "You're slipping, my friend."

"Yeah, well—" McQuade shrugged "—it happens. If things work out, it'll only be for a couple of nights."

Felix grinned. "That's right, McQuade. Think positive."

"Our stay. We'll be heading out after I make some arrangements with one of your many cousins." McQuade tossed some folded bills across the desk. "So what have you got?"

"I'll give you what I got left, McQuade. Two pretty nice rooms, one not too nice—you can make do." He palmed the bills with a thoughtful smile. "As for the cousin . . ."

"Just give me the keys. I'll explain later what kind of cousin I'm looking for."

Felix produced three keys from a drawer and handed two of them over. "Be a gentleman and give these to the ladies. You take this one." McQuade nodded, distributed the keys and shouldered his duffel bag. Felix closed the drawer and flashed another grin. "Don't worry, McQuade. I got all kinds of cousins."

Elizabeth opened the louvered doors and discovered that her room had a small balcony overlooking the sea. She filled her lungs with salty sea air and thought of home. The sand was a little whiter there, the sea a brighter shade of azure. De Colores was paradise, and she'd cast out because she'd had a tryst with the devil. The minute she set foot on the sands of her home, she would be an outlaw, a fugitive in hiding. What messes we make of our lives, she thought. She watched a curling wave toss itself over the beach and remembered. Not my son's life, though, she promised herself. She would not let Tomás suffer for her mistakes.

She walked to the bed, opened her duffel bag and extracted the one dress she'd brought. Her mother had always insisted on a dress for dinner. The loose-fitting white cotton would be comfortable. There was no need to worry about what Felix Santiago's cousins would think of her clothes. As long as there was one among them with a sturdy fishing boat, Elizabeth refused to concern herself with what McQuade expected for his generous tips or the degree to which Santiago was anxious to accommodate him with cousins. As long as McQuade did his job...

There was a rap on the door accompanied by Ronnie's voice. "Elizabeth? Ready for dinner? McQuade's waiting."

Ronnie sat on the bed and watched Elizabeth fasten the straps of her sandals.

"I thought McQuade would be getting acquainted with one of the Santiago cousins by now," Elizabeth said, surprised to hear the catty tone in her voice. She quickly added, "Of course, part of his job is to make those contacts. We'll need help from these people."

"The only contact he's made so far is with me and Felix. We decided I'd leave for De Colores in the morning." Elizabeth sat up and was greeted by Ronnie's knowing smile. "He's planning on dinner with you. Said he wanted to return some favor and make sure you eat something, which we've both noticed you haven't done all day."

"I'm too excited." Elizabeth dismissed the idea of food with a wave of her hand. "You've made more plans already?"

"I'll be looking for you guys at that little village about half a mile from the airfield."

"El Gallo?"

"That's the one. There's a cantina there where we'll touch base, McQuade says. After he gets your son, I'll fly you guys out." Ronnie's blue eyes sparkled as she leaned back and happily offered encouragement. "Easy as pie."

They were nearly the same age, but Elizabeth felt the weight of difficult years on her as she envied Ronnie's optimism. Ronnie's strawberry-blond hair and petite figure seemed more suited to the cheerleaders Elizabeth had seen at American college football games than to a woman who piloted her own plane. The world could be Ronnie's for the taking, Elizabeth thought as she returned the smile. "Easy as apple pie."

"Why do I say that?" Ronnie wondered. "Pie isn't easy. I couldn't make a pie to save my life." She hopped off the bed and reached for Elizabeth's hand. "Come on, I'm starving. McQuade might want dinner with you, but he's getting us both."

McQuade had had his shower and his talk with Felix, and he was on his second drink when the woman on his mind walked through the door. Her black hair draped prettily over her smooth, tanned shoulders, and her eyes were magnetic. The shapeless dress she wore did nothing to disguise the fact that she was a polished jewel.

"I figured the three of us might find something to talk about if I tagged along," Ronnie said brightly.

McQuade snapped out of his trance. "Ronnie. Sure. That's what I had in mind." He grinned, gesturing toward the third chair at the table. "A strategy session."

"You've made a number of plans already, from what I understand." Elizabeth took a seat. "I know I promised to follow your instructions, but I'd like to be present when plans are discussed. My son's safety is at stake."

"Yeah, I know. So is yours and mine. I'm looking for a hit-and-run mission. I'm the hit, and Ronnie's the run." A dark-eyed waitress sidled up to McQuade, and he raised an eyebrow at Elizabeth. "White wine?"

She refused to be anticipated. "Rosé."

"And orange juice for the kid." He shrugged and added for Elizabeth's benefit, "That's what she drinks."

"You'll be grateful for my clear mind and sound judgment when I get you off De Colores safe and sound."

McQuade flashed Ronnie a thumbs-up, and they shared a laugh.

"Have you discussed cousins with Mr. Santiago yet?" Elizabeth asked. She didn't like this cocky soldier of fortune routine. Her son was at the other end of this so-called hit-and-run.

"He's out shaking the family tree. He'll get me what I need."

"He said he had all kinds of cousins," Ronnie recalled as she surveyed the menu. "Must be a big family."

"*Cousin* is a general term for all kinds of relationships here," Elizabeth explained. "It's the same with the villagers at home. It's hard to keep everybody straight, so they're all cousins."

"I hope you've got a few," McQuade said. Elizabeth cast him a questioning look, and he added, "A few relatives. Friends. Sympathizers. Anybody we could trust."

"Everyone is afraid of Guerrero. We'll be fortunate if no one knows me besides my great-aunt."

He had no idea what other family she might still have, or what friends had turned their backs on her. She held her chin up as she talked about what amounted to being cast adrift, and McQuade felt an uncomfortable pinching in his chest. When the waitress delivered their drinks, he was glad to be able to toss off a casual, "Thanks, honey. You do good work. Now, if you can find me a nice piece of beef, something real tender and juicy, I'll pay whatever price you ask."

The waitress's smile said she was anxious to accommodate him.

They had finished their meal when Felix brought another chair to the table and joined them. "My cousin Rico will take you and the lady fishing the day after tomorrow, McQuade. He will ask too much money, but you can reason with him."

The discussion of the boat didn't interest Elizabeth. So long as they had one, she didn't care how much the fisherman asked. Her attention strayed to the door of the kitchen, which the waitress had left open, and Elizabeth watched a woman turn from her sink full of dishes to a toddler at her feet. The woman dried her reddened hands on the white towel that was wrapped around her waist and bent to lift the child into her arms. She kissed his chubby cheeks, and he laughed and grabbed a fistful of her hair. Chattering to him, she disappeared to another part of the room, and then the kitchen door swung shut. Elizabeth felt a warm hand cover hers, and she turned to find that Ronnie had sensed her need. She let Ronnie see her gratitude, while the men talked of boats and the prospect of fair weather.

Rico Santiago's prosperity was evident in the size of his belly, but not in the condition of his mouth. He was missing his front teeth. Still, he grinned with pride as he showed off his fishing boat. "Everything up-to-date," he kept saying. "Engine works good, generator, icebox—everything A number one." Elizabeth noted that the paneling inside the cabin had recently been varnished, while McQuade turned a knob on the radio and got static. "Radio works sometimes," Rico admitted with a shrug. "Who needs it?"

"We won't be making any announcements," McQuade said. "When was the last time you put in to De Colores?"

"Last week."

"Any trouble?"

"Never no trouble." Rico grinned as he rubbed his belly absently. "I got lots of friends."

"Good for you. We'll be heading for a little cove on the south side of the island where there's—"

"No port," Rico finished, shaking his head. "Nothing but rocks."

"You can get us in close enough. We'll use an inflatable raft. And then, as far as any of your friends are concerned—" McQuade clapped a hand on Rico's shoulder and returned the smile "—you don't know anything about any Americans." He was promoting the assumption that Elizabeth was American, too.

"Ignorance can cost a great deal." The spaces in Rico's smile might have been filled with dollar signs as his eyes glistened with greed.

"You'll be well paid," Elizabeth assured him, and she turned to McQuade. "I'm pleased with the boat."

His scowl was enough to set her back a step. "You're easily pleased." He gestured toward the steps that led to the deck. "After you. Let's go out for a smoke, Rico, and talk this over. It's a wise woman who hires a man to do business for her."

"It's a wise woman who appreciates quality." Rico followed his prospective passengers as he sized them up mentally. He would be a hard sell, but she had the money.

"That's what I told her when I hired on." A fresh breeze greeted them on deck as McQuade shook two cigarettes out of a pack and offered Rico one. "We're paying two thousand just before our raft hits the water and another three when we've accomplished our mission and gotten back here." He expelled a lungful of smoke, and the breeze carried it away. "If we're picked up on that island, it won't speak well for somebody's ignorance."

Rico considered the wonderful American cigarette between his fingers and told himself that five thousand American dollars was a lot of money. Felix had said that

McQuade didn't make mistakes. Rico had a good chance of getting the full amount. If not, even two thousand . . .

"McQuade!"

All three heads turned to watch Felix march purposefully over the pier's weathered planks. "McQuade, I have bad news," he shouted as he reached for the hand McQuade offered him. When he stood before them, he shaded his eyes against the sun and announced, "Miguel Hidalgo has been assassinated."

Chapter 3

"The deal is off, McQuade."

McQuade stood his ground, hands on his hips, legs apart, as he braced himself against the easy rocking of the boat. "What do you mean, the deal's off?" he bellowed at Rico. "We haven't even got a deal yet." He tried to keep an eye out for Elizabeth, who was quietly separating herself from the group, as he turned to Felix. "Where'd you get this story about Hidalgo?"

"It was announced on the radio. Guerrero blames a rebel faction. He claims to have those responsible in his custody."

"Rebel faction, hell." McQuade shook his head. "Poor damn bastards'll be dead before the day's out, and Guerrero's home free." Elizabeth stepped off the boat and onto the pier, and McQuade scowled as he watched her shoulder her way past two men, narrowly missing a collision with a third. "Hey, lady, we've got a problem here," he shouted. She kept walking.

"De Colores is too damn hot now," Rico said. "With Guerrero in control, suspicion is enough to put a man away for good. I could lose my boat."

McQuade surveyed the deck. "What's it worth to you?"

Rico dragged a fishing net off the deck and busied himself with it, finally shaking his head. *"¡En absoluto!"* he mumbled. The sound of his own refusal brought new conviction. *"¡Ni de vainas! ¡Ni bamba!* Not for love or money, *señor."* He squeezed his eyes shut for a moment, then shook his head harder. "The money is good, but not that good."

"Could be better, huh?" McQuade laid a hand on the man's shoulder and waited until Rico looked him in the eye. "The greater the risk, the greater the reward. I could double that reward for you, Rico."

Rico sighed, still wagging his head as though he were dragging a ball and chain with it. "Maybe in another few weeks, after things cool down over there, but not now, McQuade. I got too much to lose." He gestured widely from where they stood on the port side of his boat toward the bow. "A boat like this? They would be waiting for the chance to confiscate it and give it to some fat colonel's mother-in-law."

McQuade knew when he had his man—and when he'd lost him. He turned away from Rico and caught a glimpse of Elizabeth, who was hurrying toward the beach. "Get me somebody else," McQuade told Felix as he stepped over a coil of rope. "Somebody who hasn't got so much to lose."

He vaulted over the side of the boat and hit his stride. As people saw him coming, they moved out of his way without comment. He broke into a jog and bounded down the wooden steps to the beach. When he caught up with her he slowed his easy, loose-limbed gait, and they left boats and fishermen behind them.

"There are a hundred other fishing boats around here that can make the trip," he told her as he fell into step beside her. The breeze carried her hair back from her face and flattened the neckline of her batiste top against the curve of her breast. He wanted to turn around and walk backward just so he could look at her. She seemed not to notice him, so he tried again. "All we have to do is find a fisherman who doesn't listen to the news. We'll find a ride to De Colores."

"I'm sure these people have reason to fear Guerrero, too." She walked faster, planting each step more firmly in the sand. "He spent time here while Miguel and the general prepared for the coup on De Colores. He was like the fighting cock who has to be restrained when he smells the arena. He couldn't be trusted not to—to jump the gun, as you say."

"Where were you then?" It was one question in a long list of them that he already wanted to put out of his mind. He'd seen enough of Guerrero to know that this woman didn't belong with him, and he needed to know how she'd gotten mixed up with that madman in the first place. Whenever he thought about it, the scenes he conjured up weren't the kind he liked imagining for her. He told himself not to get personal, not to anticipate any answers, but he did it anyway.

"I was on De Colores with my baby." She turned her eyes toward him, defying him to judge her, and she kept walking. "I was allowed to return home when my pregnancy became... burdensome. Before that, I followed him."

"By choice?"

"In the beginning, yes." With the admission, her pace slowed, and the stiffness went out of her shoulders. "It was my choice," she said almost inaudibly, then spun on her heel and faced the sea. "Poor De Colores. Miguel was your last hope."

McQuade thought he heard tears, but he found none when he looked at her face. He shoved his hands into his pockets and let his gaze follow hers out to sea. It was not the time to pry into her soul with his eyes.

"Miguel was a teacher, you know. We were both among the fortunate few who could afford to go to college." Edging closer to the water, Elizabeth allowed the tongue of the next wave to slosh over her sandals, and then she watched it retreat, pulling a collar of sand around her heels. It was a soothing feeling.

McQuade stood close behind her and waited for her to tell him more. He lit a cigarette for something to do in the meantime, thinking he was the closest thing she had to a friend right now, but that patience wasn't his long suit. He had found that whenever she gave him a scrap of herself, he devoured it and had to bite his tongue to keep from asking for another.

She stood there, letting the water slip over her feet as she reviewed her memories. Finally she took a step back and tossed her hair, letting the breeze carry it away from her face. "I was several years younger than Miguel, and by the time I was a freshman, he had finished graduate school and was teaching at the University of Massachusetts. He could have forgotten all about De Colores, except, perhaps, for a convenient place to vacation. But he brought his fine American education home and offered it to his people. Those with foresight loved him for it."

"And you?"

She smiled, remembering. "He was my first hero."

That was a scrap he could have done without. He didn't like hearing about the first, and he sure as hell wasn't going to ask about the second, who had somehow become her husband. "What about those who lacked foresight?" he wondered instead. "I take it they didn't appreciate his efforts."

"The former government saw no need to make students out of what had been cheap labor. There had always been some schooling for the younger children, but as they got older, they were needed in the cane fields, or on the fishing boats, or even in the market, to weave straw goods. Miguel dreamed of a high school education for every child."

"Can't argue with a dream like that," McQuade admitted, flicking his cigarette into the water. "I'd say go for it. Take over the government."

She didn't hear his sarcasm. When she turned to him, he knew she hadn't heard him at all. "They killed him for that," she whispered. "Guerrero killed him. For that dream and all the others."

Suddenly the pain of her loss filled her, and she was drowning in it. But she didn't cry. There was no room in her eyes for tears, and none in his mind for sarcasm. A man who thought he had no patience for tears stood waiting for them to come from a woman who refused to share them. He wanted her to lean against him, and he wanted to hold her. He reached for her even as he told himself not to. When she backed away, he looked down at his own empty hands and felt like a fool.

She held her head high, and her hair blew back from her face. "I mourn without falling to pieces, Mr. McQuade."

"Mr. McQuade" struck him like a dart. "I can see that." Raising his hands in quick surrender, he took his turn at backing away. "Don't let me interfere. God knows I'm no saint. For a minute there I just thought you might need a friend."

Elizabeth watched him head down the beach in the direction of the Oyster Shell. The waves soon ate up the tracks he'd left on the beach. His long legs scaled a sandy dune without breaking stride. He was an arrogant man, she told herself. He assumed too much—that she needed something from him, that she wanted to be touched by him. He disappeared over the incline, and she stood there watching the crest of the hill and listening to the sea.

Felix was a welcome sight. McQuade needed a man to talk to about the job he had to do. He needed to get his mind on a neat set of priorities—a boat, a clandestine drop-off, a chance to slip into the palace and snatch the kid, a rendezvous, an airlift. He wanted to start the images rolling around in his mind so he could make them click into place. Felix was bound to make more sense than Elizabeth Donnelly did. One minute she was practically serving McQuade breakfast in bed; the next she was pining over her ex-husband's political cohort but shrinking back from any expression of sympathy McQuade might have offered. Who could figure the woman? He joined Felix at the bar and ordered a drink.

"I got other cousins, McQuade." Felix tossed a book of matches across the bar. McQuade snatched it up and lit a cigarette.

"Braver than Rico?"

"Oh, sure," he said with a nonchalant gesture.

McQuade blew a quick stream of smoke past Felix's shoulder. "Show me one."

"Give me a few hours. I've got feelings out."

"Feelers." Felix gave him a confused look, and McQuade laughed. "You've got *feelers* out. And I sure as hell don't want to talk about *feelings*. I want to have a couple of drinks, talk man to man, blow a little smoke in your face and never once mention anybody's feelings." He took the drink out of the bartender's hand and tasted it. "No special recipe, right? Just bourbon and water?"

The young man nodded, looking to Felix for support. Felix waved him on his way and grinned at McQuade. "A man who comes to the islands with two women is asking for trouble."

"One left this morning, and she wasn't a woman, she was a pilot who happens to be female. The other one's a client who also happens to be female. So neither one of them is a *woman*, Felix, they're just—" he waved a hand in exasperation "—just female."

"The more dangerous sex of most species."

"Yeah. So let's not talk about them, either." McQuade settled the bargain by raising his glass. "Let's talk about cousins."

"Male or female?"

"Anybody you know who's got a boat," McQuade grumbled.

"And some measure of . . . guts?"

The two men grinned, man to man. "We're talking male equipment here, right, Felix?"

Laughing, Felix leaned toward McQuade and laid a hand on his shoulder. "Rico was a poor specimen. Without male equipment."

"Damn right. The hell with equal opportunity. Find me a *man* for this job, my friend."

They laughed together. "A man for business, and a woman for pleasure. It's sad to see Americans in such a state of confusion these days."

"Hemingway would've packed up all his gear and moved here permanently by now," McQuade decided. He drained his glass in silent tribute.

"Without question. And this was his favorite place to stay—this very place." Felix pointed to the floor and beamed.

When Felix beckoned one of his cousins to join them, McQuade offered to buy her a drink. Her name was Anita, and she softened and melted just the way McQuade figured a woman was supposed to do.

Elizabeth had walked for hours. The night was cool and calm. She'd watched one family clean the day's catch and joined another at their invitation for a fish fry on the beach. She'd refused all the while to think about Miguel's death or McQuade's assumptions. It always helped to lose herself among strangers. They could carry on with their lives around her, and she would be safe for the time she was among them. She could even pretend she belonged. But now it was time to go back.

There was a crowd at the Oyster Shell. She had intended to slip through the foyer and go upstairs without taking note of it, but she heard the rich sound of a familiar laugh, and it drew her inside. There was Sloan McQuade with, not one, but two women at his table. Neither one looked like a fisherman, and together they looked as though they could keep him up all night. The grin on his face made it apparent that such a prospect would be to his liking. That *was* her concern, she thought as she found herself headed for the table where the threesome was seated. She was paying this man well for his services.

"Come on and join us, princess! We're waitin' on one more cousin."

"I should think that two cousins would be company enough." It bothered her to see him with a drink and a cigarette in one hand and a woman's shoulder in the other. Her dignity would best be served by discussing business, she told herself. This cozy scene bothered her only because it might distract the man from doing his job. She stepped up to the table but ignored the chair he'd halfheartedly offered.

He shrugged. "If three's a crowd, four's a party. What're you drinking?"

"I'm not drinking anything, Mr. McQuade. Will we be able to get on with our business tomorrow?"

"I'm working on it right now, honey. Felix and me." Pulling his arm away from Anita, McQuade described a vague arc with his hand. "Felix is around here somewhere. We're putting our 'feelings' out." The expression struck him as funny again.

Elizabeth stiffened her back and braced herself against a rising tide of feelings of her own. "I'm not paying you to put out *anything*, Mr. McQuade. If you feel compelled to spread yourself around here, please come back and do it on your own time. We need a boat, and we need—"

"We need an understanding, Miss Donnelly." His back easily matched hers for stiffness as he set his drink down and crushed his cigarette in an ashtray. "You're paying for results, but you don't dictate the process. If you want to prance around here like a princess with a poker up her back, you go ahead. I don't have to feel friendly toward you to get the job done. But if I feel friendly toward anybody else—" he jabbed a finger in the air for emphasis "—you've got nothing to say about it, lady."

"Your so-called friendliness is of less interest to me than . . . than the time of day in Cincinnati! Make a public spectacle of yourself if you must, Mr. McQuade, but get something done about this boat."

"Look who's making a public spectacle!" he shouted at her back as she walked away. "The island princess herself!" The surprised expression on Anita's face reminded him to settle down, keep it light. He came up with a conspiratorial grin. "The fancy barracuda."

Anita giggled and repeated, "Barracuda." Playfully punching his shoulder, she reminded him in Spanish that she didn't speak English. He realized then that *barracuda* was the first Spanish word he'd said since Elizabeth had walked in.

"Con permiso," he said. "Forgive my rudeness. The barracuda made me forget my manners." She'd made him forget that he'd been quite comfortably situated for the evening, too. He thought about whether to immediately press his advantage with Anita or hold off and light up another cigarette. He cursed himself as he busied his hands with a match. The best way to keep things light was to hang around lighthearted people. Anita had a ready smile for him. He checked to be sure, flashing her one of his own. "Another sangria?"

Yes, there it was, full of bright-eyed promise.

"Do you think we have time for another one, Mc-Quade?"

He was waiting for Felix. Tipping his glass to his lips, he stared over the rim at the foyer and the stairway beyond it. She'd marched up those steps like she was right on time to meet the queen. God, she had nice calves. Especially for a barracuda.

"I have another name, you know. A first name."

Anita stroked his forearm. "May I call you by your first name?"

He'd heard it twice lately, but both times Elizabeth had ensnared him with it, pulled him in close with a single intimate word. Who the hell did she think she was, calling him Sloan and beckoning him with that doe-eyed look all the time, and then pulling away as though he had scales for skin?

"No, McQuade's good enough. Look, have another drink. How about you, Lila?"

"Lola," the other woman corrected as McQuade signaled the bartender.

"Nice name." Nice, hell, he told himself. If he'd been interested, he would have remembered it. And if that woman hadn't strutted in and interfered with his train of thought, he could have gotten interested. The drinks appeared, and he pushed his aside. His brain would have to soak up a lot of bourbon before it would let Lola or Anita replace Elizabeth in its tenacious cells. Damn the woman for spoiling his night.

"Enjoy your drinks, ladies. Here, you can flip a coin for mine." He dragged a handful of bills and change from the front pocket of his jeans and tossed it on the table. "I think I'll do me a little barracuda baiting before I go out and track Felix down," he muttered in English as his chair scraped across the floor.

Anita understood enough. The "barracuda" had gone upstairs, and McQuade's attention had been on those stairs ever since.

It was a surprise when Elizabeth admitted him to her room without putting him through any verbal indignities. She'd kicked off her sandals, and she'd obviously had to put some clothes on when he'd knocked, because he'd had to wait a minute for her to open the door. Her hair was wet, and she was wearing the same walking shorts with the same cotton top she'd had on earlier. There was one difference, and it caught McQuade's eye immediately. No bra. She closed the door and turned to him with an expectant look, which prompted him to ask his most pressing question.

"What the hell do you want from me, lady?"

Her chin shot up as she squared her shoulders and pierced him with a frown.

"Look, I'm sorry your boyfriend's dead. I liked him, too. He seemed like a good man. I was trying to—"

"He wasn't my boyfriend," she said evenly.

"Okay. Your hero, or whatever." He waved his hand toward the window as he recalled the scene on the beach. "I wanted to offer you a shoulder back there, just between friends. You weren't about to let me touch you, but you came unglued when you saw me with my arm around somebody else. What's with you?"

Elizabeth folded her arms over her chest. "Your romantic activities don't concern me in the least. I came unglued, as you put it, because I saw that you'd been distracted from the job I'm paying you to do."

"That won't wash, lady. You saw me sitting there with two women who obviously enjoyed my company, and you didn't like it."

She turned away from him and took a moment to search for a reason. "I was embarrassed for you."

McQuade laughed. "Embarrassed! Next to you, they were the best looking women in the house. I was doing okay."

"Then go back to them, Mr. McQuade. I don't care whether you drink yourself into a blind stupor. It's a small island, so no matter where you find yourself when you wake up, you should be able to stumble back here, but I suggest you check your valuables at the desk before you go anywhere with those women."

McQuade stared in disbelief. Had he left the price tag on the seat of his pants or something? "Is that what you think I'm gonna do? Get rolled?"

"I'm sure that pair down there has gotten the best of better men than you." She tossed her wet hair behind one shoulder and settled her hand at her hip.

"No kidding?" He wondered if she realized how increasingly transparent her blouse became with each wet spot her hair made. Was she posturing for him, or was she utterly absorbed in this asinine conversation? Intentionally or not, she was definitely turning him on. He took a step closer. "How can you be sure? How can you be sure better men than me even exist?"

"One can only hope. You came highly recommended, but I'm beginning to think my expectations were too high."

The soft curves of her breasts with the small, dark shadows of her nipples teased him from beneath the wet cotton, and when his subtle glance became a frankly appreciative stare, it was too late to cover herself. He'd already caught her in his arms.

"We expect to get what we pay for," he told her, ignoring her look of surprise as he lowered his head. "You're entitled."

He felt her resistance, but he closed his mind to it. He told himself that she fit against him too well to be less comfortable with it than he was. Her mouth was warm, and if she wouldn't move her lips against his, he'd coax them. He steadied her head with his hand, and he varied the pressure of his kiss, making a strong statement, gently asking a shy question, then pressing the issue again. He'd trapped her hands between them, and he felt her fists on his chest.

Like a willow, her slender frame bent, refusing to break under the strength of his embrace, but the rigidity was there. When he moved his hand along her spine and massaged the small of her back, he felt some of the tenseness melt away. Her lips responded then, just slightly, just enough to allow him to feather his tongue without their bounds. She relaxed her hands, and his chest expanded involuntarily as he sucked in the flowered scent of her.

God, she was sweet! He wove his fingers into her wet hair and kissed her hard, sliding his hand over her buttocks to press her tightly against him. He felt his breath catch, felt the fists form again. When he slid his kisses along the side of her neck, she drew a tremulous breath. Every muscle and tendon in his body hardened at the sound.

"I didn't . . . I didn't mean it that way," she whispered.

Mean what? he thought. He was dimly aware that her voice had a strange edge to it, and he wanted to reassure her. He took her mouth again and kissed her, finding his way deep into her mouth and relishing the intimacy he found with her there. This was the way *he* meant it. He dragged his head away when her small whimper pierced his own fog of rapidly spiraling passion.

"I won't fight you," she said quietly, her chest heaving against his. "Just please . . . don't hurt me."

He lifted his head to see her face. The fear that blazed in her eyes shook him to the core. It took him a moment to realize that his hand was tangled in her hair, and he opened it as he relaxed his embrace. "I'm sorry," he said and wondered where the sandpaper in his throat had come from. "Was I . . . did I pull your—"

"No," she said quickly. "No, you didn't."

"I wouldn't hurt you, Elizabeth. You know that."

She nodded, but her eyes told him that she knew nothing of the kind.

He gave her some space, taking a moment to steady her on her feet. "Hey, look, I'm not forcing anything. That's not my style. But you've gotta admit—" he adjusted the neckline of her blouse before he let her back away "—*your* style's pretty provocative."

She looked down and covered her chest with a trembling hand. "It's wet," she whispered. "I wasn't thinking."

"So why start now?"

He stood there with his hands on his hips, making no attempt to conceal the physical effect she'd had on him. He figured she deserved the opportunity to be embarrassed for herself rather than on his behalf. He had nothing to be ashamed of. His was a man's response.

Elizabeth blushed and turned from him. "I'm sorry. I overstepped my bounds." She glanced back. "We both did."

"I don't know what your bounds are, lady, but I know I didn't overstep any. I didn't do anything you didn't want me to do."

"You flatter yourself," she said dully.

"Maybe." He took her chin in his hand and kissed her again, but it was over before she had time to raise her defenses. There was no battle—just a brief kiss. "Yeah, you turn me on," he said quietly. "But I can go back downstairs, and they'll have the same effect. So don't you flatter yourself, either." He started for the door, then hesitated and raised one finger of warning. "Don't play games with me, Elizabeth. Because I'm not playing any with you."

For long moments after she'd watched the door close behind him, Elizabeth stood in the middle of the room, her eyes fixed on the latch. She held on to herself, arms around her middle, waiting for the shaking to stop. It wasn't only the fear that had her trembling; it was the battle she'd waged to keep her arms from going around his neck. It was the way his kisses made her feel and the way she'd wanted to kiss him back. She'd been in control of her own life for a year now, and she didn't want that fragile state of affairs threatened. The old terror still held too much sway over her. She'd shown a woman's weakness when she'd promised not to fight him.

He'd said he wouldn't hurt her, and she wanted to believe that. Sloan McQuade was not Guerrero. And although he liked women, he'd made it clear he wasn't fussy, even if she did have a slight edge over the two ladies in the bar. If they were still downstairs, he was undoubtedly set for the night. She had to stay out of his private life. If she wasn't careful, she could end up actually caring what he did on his own time.

An hour later there was another knock at Elizabeth's door, and she leaped off the bed to answer it.

"It's McQuade."

His voice was a welcome sound, but she opened the door cautiously. He gave her a sheepish grin when she lapped a denim jacket around her chest. "I'm not looking for any more trouble, either," he promised, raising his right hand to attest to the fact. "I just thought you'd like to know— we've got a boat."

Chapter 4

Emilio Gomez had the face of a choirboy, but he was a working man. He had been a fisherman since he was five years old. Since his father's death, Emilio had had his own boat, which was small enough to be handled with the help of his seventeen-year-old wife and his thirteen-year-old brother. When Emilio introduced McQuade and the beautiful *señorita* to his family and his boat, *La Paloma*, his pride was as evident as Rico's had been in his fancier vessel.

Elizabeth glanced at McQuade as she extended a hand to Luisa Gomez She hoped he realized that somehow they would have to persuade Emilio not to take his pregnant wife on the trip. It was expected that at thirteen a boy would do a man's work and take life's risks upon himself, but Elizabeth would not endanger this woman's unborn child.

McQuade put his hand on the young fisherman's shoulder and took him aside. Emilio was a head shorter than McQuade, but years of hauling nets had built muscle in his arms and chest. The two men were an artist's contrast as they stood together at the end of the pier, McQuade's golden head bent over Emilio's shock of straight black hair.

"You didn't tell me your wife was pregnant."

Emilio met McQuade's expression of concern with one of indignation. "You did not ask, *señor*. Why should it be of interest to you?"

"I told you there would be some risk involved. We're not welcome at De Colorés. We won't be announcing our arrival to the officials at La Primavera."

"I understand that. But my wife goes with me—always."

McQuade reached for a cigarette and realized he was out of them. He hated scenes like this. Ordinarily he let people make their own decisions, just as he made his. The wife wanted to go along, and the husband knew the score. Fine. But there stood Elizabeth, sending him distress signals. She was worried about the baby. Okay, he didn't like it much himself, but these people had a life to live, too. On these islands, only the princesses like Elizabeth Donnelly took time off to be pregnant. Luisa Gomez would labor beside her husband until she labored with her child.

"How about if I put her up at the Oyster Shell?" McQuade suggested hopefully. "Give her a little vacation until you get back."

"My wife is a respectable woman. She does not stay at the Oyster Shell alone."

"Does she have a girlfriend who could stay with her?"

The idea was clearly repugnant to Emilio. "My wife does not stay at the Oyster Shell, *señor*."

McQuade gave Emilio an understanding pat on his bare shoulder. "I don't think this is going to work out, *amigo*, but I appreciate your position."

Luisa took two tentative steps toward McQuade. "We were going to De Colorés anyway." Her husband gave her a sharp look, but she continued. "My sister lives there." Her smile was hopeful. "My sister is married to Emilio's brother. We visit often." Her hand went to her small, round stomach. "I have three months to go."

"Luisa!"

"Emilio, these people are worried about me!" She turned to Elizabeth. "There is no need to worry. You need a way to get to De Colores, and we are going there."

"Here, *amigo*." McQuade offered Emilio a thick wad of money. "Get your boat ready. I want to be on the island tomorrow night. Your wife is your business."

Elizabeth thanked the couple and preceded McQuade down the pier, offering him a sidelong glance when they stepped onto the sand.

He raised one eyebrow. "Your pilot, my fisherman."

Adrenaline gave him a heightened sense of personal power when he prepared for the final leg of a mission like this one. McQuade didn't see himself as a silver screen commando, but he did arm himself when the job required it, and he was proficient with all the weapons anyone could name. The 9mm semiautomatic pistol he was turning over in his hands as he sat on the edge of his bed fitted the bill for this job. He reached for the can of gun oil, the rag and the cleaning rod he'd set out on the nightstand.

He knew the real challenge lay in accomplishing his mission without firing a shot—getting in and out of a hot spot without anyone knowing about it until he was long gone. The exhilaration he felt after the slick, clean execution of a mission was what kept him coming back. He grinned at the sleek weapon that lay in his hand. That thrill and the money. There could be no better reason for...

"Mr. McQuade? May I speak with you for a minute?"

That thrill, the money, and a mother who wanted her kid back. "Come on in."

Elizabeth's eyes widened visibly when she stepped into McQuade's small room and saw the weapon in his hands. He waited for her reaction, and when it came—"Is that the biggest gun you have?"—he tipped his head back and enjoyed a hearty laugh.

She wasn't sure why he was laughing so hard. "What if you have to face something . . . something bigger?"

McQuade examined the pistol and worked hard to control his mirth. "Maybe you'd better tell me what Guerrero's got."

"He may have a missile by now for all I know."

McQuade sputtered, and Elizabeth smiled at the idea that he found her suggestion so entertaining. "He might have it pointed right at Washington," she added, thinking she was on some kind of a roll.

"Better at them than me." Forcibly straightening his face, McQuade held the pistol toward her. "This is not a gun, honey. This is a Browning Double Action Hi-Power. It's a semiautomatic pistol. Have you ever used one?" She shook her head. "Then give it a chance before you dismiss it for lack of size. I'm not going to get too far in La Primavera with a submachine gun hanging over my shoulder."

She stood beside him and looked down her nose at the weapon. "I hope you don't have to use it at all. I wondered if there was anything I should be doing—preparing. I need to . . . to *do* something."

McQuade patted the place next to him on the bed. She hesitated, and his eyes softened with boyish innocence. "Relax, Elizabeth. I swear I won't bite you. This is business. We're getting ready to do a job together. We're going to have to learn to trust each other, you know."

She sat down as though she weren't sure the bed woul·
hold them both. "I know that. I don't know why I behave·
the way I did last night." She sighed, tilted her head bacl
and let her shoulders sag a little. "There was no excuse fo·
the way I spoke to you downstairs. That was your busi·
ness."

"Well, I know why I behaved the way I did, so I guess I'n
one step ahead of you." His smile offered no censure, an·
the one she returned made him feel lighter inside. "Anx·
ious to get this thing under way?" She nodded. "Kind·
makes you feel itchy inside, doesn't it?"

"Maybe if I could help you—" she tipped a long, slen·
der hand toward his lap "—polish your weapons?"

"This is it," he told her. "This and a little .38 Special tha·
I thought might come in handy if you..." Her eyes wid·
ened. "And a hunting knife. Disappointed?" She shook he·
head quickly, and he laughed. He rubbed the rag over th·
pistol and laid it in her hands, watching her reaction. Sh·
stared at it as though he'd pulled the pin on a grenade an·
handed it to her. "You must have been around them be·
fore."

"I've lived with violent men," she said quietly. She'd ex·
pected it to be heavier. Its dull matte finish gave it the lool
of death, but the metal was warm from his hands. "But I'v·
avoided their guns."

"There isn't much to it." He reached over to point out th·
mechanism. "You pull the trigger, it fires a bullet. Pull i·
again, it fires another one, just like Old Faithful. With th·
chamber loaded it'll deliver fifteen rounds before you hav·
to change the clip to reload. This one has a pretty strong re·
coil, which takes some getting used to, but the .38 is smalle·
and doesn't have as much kick to it." He wrapped her han·
around the butt of the pistol as though he were molding clay·
"It's not loaded, Elizabeth. It can't hurt you. If you're go·

ng to insist on sticking your pretty little neck out, it wouldn't hurt for you to get comfortable with one of these."

"I could never be comfortable with it," she said. She touched the trigger with the tip of her index finger.

"You have to think of preventing harm to yourself. Nobody wants to think of killing somebody."

"I've thought of it." Her fingers curled around the crescent shape of the trigger. "Many times."

The idea was all the more chilling because it came from her. He sat very still, anticipating an explanation. Such delicate, clean hands were incongruous with the piece of steel she held in them. The breasts he knew were round, soft and fully feminine rose and fell on a heavy sigh as she studied the weapon. Then she handed it back to him, almost reluctantly.

"That's why I couldn't be comfortable with it." She looked up at him, and he felt himself drowning in the depths of her dark eyes. "You said I had to think about preventing harm to myself. But when I'm afraid, I *can't* think. I can only feel. I can only be afraid." She glanced away. "But later, after the fear goes away, then I start thinking. I think about having a gun like yours. I dream of having your courage, your confidence, your body."

McQuade swallowed hard and reminded himself that she hadn't really meant what she'd just said. After last night, though, he sure as hell wanted to have *her* body. But there was more to it than that. He had a queasy feeling now, born of the realization that she was telling him about someone else who'd wanted her body. Some man who'd shown her enough cruelty to make her wish him dead. Someone like Guerrero. He could deal with the bile rising within him as he guessed the source of Elizabeth's fear. McQuade would repay Guerrero. Harder to handle was the growing urge simply to shield her with his body and protect her from the world.

He searched for a remark to cover himself, and he found a cocky grin to go with it. "That's why you hired me, honey. Don't go wishing for a man's body. Yours is great just the way it is."

Elizabeth watched him stow his pistol in an aluminum frame backpack. She'd said too much. There was something about this man that made her reveal more about herself than she intended. It was just as well that he'd managed another of his one-dimensional male remarks, to remind her to get back to business.

"Are we in need of any kind of provisions?" she asked. "Perhaps I could go to the market."

"I've sent someone out with a grocery list." He set the backpack on the floor beside the bed, propped a pillow against the headboard and leaned back. "Mind if I have a cigarette?" She shook her head, and he struck a match. "It'll be hardtack, jerky and stolen bananas most of the time, so eat hearty tonight." He turned his head to send a stream of smoke toward the open window. "I'm going to ask you to make room in your pack."

"Of course. I wish I had one like yours." His hiker's backpack held a small sleeping bag and a foam pad tightly rolled and strapped to the bottom. He'd stashed his pistol in the nylon compartment in the middle, and there was a larger compartment on top with a couple of smaller pockets. She was sure that one was reserved for cigarettes.

"You do." McQuade hopped off the bed, stuck his cigarette in the corner of his mouth and pulled his big green duffel bag out of the closet. From it he produced another black nylon pack. "Smaller version for women. Think you can handle it? Here, try it on."

Elizabeth put her arms through the straps and watched him adjust them. "How thoughtful. I could have—"

"You hired an outfitter for this little trek, sweetheart. I come complete with brain as well as brawn." His eyes twinkled when he drew a laugh from her. "Looks great on you. Matches your hair. You'll have to carry the grub, since I'm totin' the guns," he drawled.

"That's fair." She slipped out of the nylon webbing and examined each zipper and buckle. "Where do you get these things? Army surplus?"

"You go to army surplus, you get weight and plenty of it. You want efficiency, you get into sporting goods. Those wheat germ lovers know how to take a hike." He took a long drag on his cigarette, then crushed it in an ashtray on top of the bureau. A cloud of smoke dissipated around his head while he dug into one of the pockets of her backpack.

"Look at this." He came up with a handful of canvas that he unfurled with a flick of his wrist. He held the child carrier toward her by the straps, and she set the backpack on the floor to take a closer look at the next gadget. "You can use it in front or in back, but it leaves your hands free—*my* hands free. I expect to be carrying him when we're on the run." He didn't know what to make of the dazed look on her face. "It's for Tomás," he offered, his voice gentling on the name.

Elizabeth came to her feet slowly and reached for the carrier. In what seemed like another lifetime she remembered buying a tiny sleeper and imagining the baby she would bring home from the hospital in it. The sleeper had helped to make his imminent birth really seem possible. She hadn't seen him for almost a year now, but she would soon take him home in this child carrier. The scrap of canvas somehow made that a certainty. McQuade had provided something to carry her son in. She looked into his eyes and warmed to his reassuring smile. It made all the difference to know that he, too, believed it would happen.

There was a knock at the door, and a woman spoke Spanish through the crack she boldly provided for herself.

"I brought the things you asked for, McQuade. Is it safe to come in?"

They drew apart. Elizabeth turned her back on the door and rolled the canvas back up as McQuade let Anita in. She handed him a package, and he sorted through the contents.

"Good. You found that powdered stuff. And . . . what's this?" He sniffed at something wrapped in paper. "Dried fish?"

"Smoked and dried. I do good work, don't I, McQuade?"

Elizabeth stiffened at the suggestiveness she heard in Anita's tone. She tucked the carrier into its pocket and held the backpack in her arms like a cradle board. "I'll go pack my things," she said.

"Not so fast, lady." McQuade rustled through his duffel bag again and came up with several handfuls of neatly wrapped plastic packages. Elizabeth stood holding her backpack, while he stuffed the middle pouch with provisions. "Food, first aid kit, batteries," he said, checking off items on a mental list.

"I think I've got an overgrown Boy Scout on my hands." Elizabeth took perverse pleasure in speaking English. She glanced at Anita to see if she felt sufficiently excluded.

She did. "*Tienes un cigarrillo,* McQuade?"

He offered a quick smile over his shoulder. "Sure. *Sí. Un momento.*" Turning back to Elizabeth, he asked, "Shall we have one more good meal together before we head out?"

"I've already asked to have something brought to my room." She wanted to invite him to join her, but Anita was holding fast to her station by the door, reminding Elizabeth that she would be waiting after he left Elizabeth, as she had no doubt been waiting the night before. "I know I should get as much sleep as I can."

"Yeah." His voice was flat. "It'll be a short night even if you can get to sleep." She nodded. He zipped the pouch and dropped his hands to his sides, asking her with his eyes to change her mind. When she didn't, he backed away and found his keep-it-light tone again. "Don't stuff that thing too full. I'll be knocking on your door when it's time."

As she walked down the hall, she heard Anita's sweetly intoned, *"Gracias."* Elizabeth hoped the woman would gag on McQuade's cigarette.

Much later, Elizabeth lay in bed and recanted every unkind thought she'd ever had toward Anita or anyone else. She forswore all bad habits and promised Tomás to the priesthood if only she would be allowed a few hours' sleep. She closed her eyes and tried to remember her baby, but she'd learned long ago to put him from her mind to save her sanity, and now she harbored a superstition against thinking about him too much. Fate had a way of holding something good out to her and then twisting it into something terrible just before she touched it. She mustn't let fate see the pinnacle of her hopes anymore. She must, she decided, shroud that pinnacle in mist and not even think of it herself.

But how bleak a life was without dreams! She closed her eyes and listened to the sea fling itself against the sand, hoping the sound would lull her to sleep. She pictured each wave, and soon she began to doze.

She felt cool water around her feet and warm sunshine at her back. She was sitting on a small dock, waiting for the man who was walking along the beach carrying a child in a sling strapped to his back. He waved, and she waved back.

Sloan was bringing Tomás to her. Her heart swelled with joy when she recognized their smiling faces—both of them! Then a shadow fell across her own face. She turned as a man sat down beside her, and she saw the mark that identified him.

The scar was as red and angry as the eye it bracketed. Cold terror stilled the blood in her veins. He was talking to her, but she couldn't make out his words. His voice was the sound of gravel washing over sand. He jerked his chin toward Sloan and Tomás, waving his hand in their direction. And in his hand he held a deadly, dull black pistol. Elizabeth tried to reach out, but her arms wouldn't move. She tried to call out, but she had no voice. Horrified, she watched him take aim . . .

Elizabeth sat bolt upright, peering into the darkness. Her heart pounded wildly, and her whole body trembled. The walls were too close around her. She threw the sheet back and scrambled from the bed. The cotton shift she'd planned to leave behind came into her hand first. She pulled it on over her short nightgown and fled from the room on bare feet.

McQuade sat astride the wooden seat of a swing that hung from a big steel pipe frame on the stretch of beach belonging to the Oyster Shell. His habit of sleeping when he had nothing better to do wasn't helping him at all tonight. He'd had dinner and a couple of drinks with Anita, and then he'd sent her on her way. Things hadn't clicked with her, which was fine with McQuade. He was looking down the barrel of a high-energy situation, and he was feeling pretty good. Wait a minute—not *this* good. Not good enough to conjure up the moonlit mirage that had just glided into view.

His left hand slid down the swing's heavy chain. His right, holding a forgotten cigarette, was braced on his thigh. He sat perfectly still and watched her. Padding across the sand, she hurried toward the water as though it were her lover, her long hair wafting around her on the night breeze. The white dress he'd once thought shapeless hugged the front of her body and fluttered behind her. Luminous against the Caribbean sky, it suggested the shape of her breasts and the curve of her thighs.

This woman clicked with him. Her gears meshed with his and caused a humming in his head. God help him if this became a permanent hookup on his part; so far it was pretty damned one-sided. He helped himself to a lungful of smoke, thinking maybe it would pollute the whole works and break this crazy connection he'd come up with. He bent to bury the cigarette in the sand and came to his feet with the gears in his gut still shooting sparks to his brain.

"You can't sleep either, huh?" Her body jerked at the sound of his voice. He touched her shoulder as she turned quickly. "Sorry. I didn't mean to scare you."

A thick strand of hair blew across her mouth, and she brushed it back. "You move quietly, Mr. McQuade." She looked down and saw that his feet were bare, too. As she watched, the water washed over them and soaked the lower three inches of his jeans.

"I have a talent for sneaking around." He shoved his hands into his pockets just up to his knuckles. "Didn't Mike Romanov tell you that was one of my talents?"

She smiled, thinking of Mikal's description of this man. It hadn't begun to capture him. "Mikal thinks you have many positive attributes."

"And what do you think? Have you noticed any?" He didn't know what to make of that mystical smile, and she didn't give the affirmative answer he was hoping for. He shrugged off his disappointment. "Course, you have to hang out with me for a while before you get the full picture.''

She turned her face back to the sea. "We'll be hanging out quite exclusively together for the next few days, won't we?"

"Looks that way. Unless I can talk you into staying here while I go get the boy."

"You can't." She swished her foot in the retreating water.

"Did you get any sleep?"

She shook her head. "Not the kind I wanted."

"You've got a lot on your mind." She nodded, pressing her lips tightly together. "Bad dreams?" he asked gently.

She wanted to tell him how bad. Perhaps in the dark of night, with the calm sea lapping at her, making her feel a little cleaner, she could tell him some of it. With the darkness around them, he wouldn't see the awful black scar her marriage had left on her.

"It's Guerrero, isn't it?"

"Yes." She was glad he'd said the name for her. She never liked to say it in the dark. "He's like a parasite under my skin. I scrub, and I scrub, but the taint remains. He haunts my sleep. Sometimes, when it's dark, I can even smell him."

McQuade's jaw tightened. His heart thudded against the walls of his chest, and he drew a long, deep, controlled breath. "What did he do to you, Elizabeth?"

"Don't ask me to tell you about those things. Let them be my secrets." *Don't ask me to put the worst part of myself on display for you.* She smiled up at him. "Let them be part of the mystery about me. Aren't men attracted to mysterious women?"

"Men are attracted to everything you've got, lady. The mysterious part is—" he shrugged, searching for the word "—worrisome. It keeps you bottled up and . . . and scared inside.''

Best to keep ugliness in a sealed container, she thought, even if she had to serve as the vessel herself. "What's worrisome is what he might do to Tomás."

"Would he hurt a kid that young?"

"He's not above it, by any means. And, like most fathers, he wants a child who will follow in his footsteps." She gave a weary sigh and thought about that prospect for a moment. Then she said, "He would make a monster of my son."

"He won't get that chance."

There was a hard potency in his voice, and she tagged her hope to his power. A retreating wave dragged a large piece of coral along the side of her foot, and she bent to claim it.

"What kind of a family do you have?" she asked as she held her hand out. He took the coral and bounced it in his palm. "The regular all-American kind?" she wondered aloud.

"Not exactly. I had an old maid great-aunt who raised me. She died when I was twelve."

"What happened to your parents?"

"I don't remember my mother. When I was a baby she told Aunt Bertie she was going to look for my father, who'd split before I was born. We used to say she'd come back one day, but I don't think either of us really believed it." It was his turn to drift on a distant smile. "Aunt Bertie was a good ol' gal."

"What did you do after she died?"

"I lived in foster homes and boarding schools until I was old enough to join the marines. I was hell on wheels until that outfit got hold of me." He drew his arm back and pitched the coral at a cresting wave.

"Is that where you learned this trade you have now?"

"This trade?" He laughed. Sometimes he didn't know what to call it himself. "That's where it started. I was part of a Special Forces rescue team."

"Are you... What would you call yourself? A detective?"

"I have a private investigator's license." He knew that was misleading. "I still call myself a specialist."

"Mikal Romanov called you the miracle worker. He said you've even found people who'd been declared dead."

McQuade chuckled. "Mike should talk. He's the one who makes miracles happen. He could talk the Hatfields into donating to the McCoys' scholarship fund."

"And he said *you* could recover the Golden Fleece. You should both go into advertising." They'd begun to walk, swishing their feet as the waves lapped gently at their ankles. "Did you ever try to find your mother yourself?" Elizabeth asked.

"Sure. But I'm my own worst client. That lady did not want to be found." A wave splashed high against his leg and spattered his T-shirt. He liked the feeling. "Either that, or she fell into the Amazon River and was eaten by piranhas."

"Maybe she tried to get back to you."

He shrugged. "I doubt it. Sometimes I like to imagine the piranhas."

"Oh, Sloan..."

"It isn't the same with you and your son." He stopped and touched her shoulder. "Believe me, it isn't."

"He offered no alternatives. If the hostages were to be released at all, I had to go with them. I had no choice." She lifted her hand to cover his. "Maybe she didn't want to leave you. Maybe she had no choice, either, Sloan."

He turned his palm to hers. "Tomás will know how hard you fought for him. If he ever doubts it, you just tell him to give McQuade a call."

"I'll do that." The promise came out as barely more than a whisper.

This is getting too heavy, he told himself, and he tugged at her hand. "Wanna swing? I'll give you a push."

They padded over the wet sand, then plunged across a dry stretch toward a stand of palms and McQuade's swing.

"Have a seat," he offered, gesturing with a flourish. The look she gave him said she wasn't sure she should do this, and he wondered how long it had been since she'd played at being a child. "Tomorrow I get serious," he told her. "Have some fun with me tonight."

She smoothed her skirt under her and sat carefully.

"Ready?"

"A *small* push."

"Got it." He pulled her back, saying, "This is my smallest push," and sent the swing on its first arc.

The wind took her breath away. On the second arc it took her cares away, and the years dropped away on the third. She pointed her toes and speared the night sky, loving the way her hair flew back. Her billowing skirt didn't concern her. Each time McQuade's strong hands sent the seat forward, she leaned back and stretched her long legs toward the stars.

"Higher?"

"Oh, yes!"

"How much higher?"

"As high as we can go!"

His laughter echoed hers. Her hips filled his hands, and he thought only a crazy man would push them away. He felt crazy, though, *good* and crazy.

"Oh, Sloan, it's not fair. I'm the one having all the fun!"

"I wouldn't say that."

"You have to take a turn. Let me push you."

It wasn't a bad thought, but he had a better one. He caught her high in the air and eased her to a stop. "We'll ride it double. Remember how that works?"

She hopped out of the swing with a smile that set her eyes aglow. "Show me."

He sat in the swing and indicated the margin of wood on either side of his hips. "Sit facing me and put your legs through here."

"Sit in your lap? Like this?" Suddenly trusting and without inhibition, she climbed on the swing and straddled him, deftly bunching her skirt in the V of her legs. "How do we get started?"

He took two steps backward and set them in motion. "Just rock with me."

"This way?"

"Mmm."

"I don't think we can get very high like this."

"Ohh, baby, I think you're dead wrong."

"Let's do it, then."

"Hang on."

They pumped until the chain went slack at the height of each arc. Elizabeth's breath caught high in her chest, and then she laughed. McQuade watched her lose herself in the free-flying feeling as he himself was lost in the sweet torture that was centered in the fulcrum they made together. She leaned forward, the wind at her back, and she saw the pleasure in his eyes. It was a pleasure she shared. He raised his chin, she lowered hers, and they kissed just as a wave lapped the beach not far away. Cool and wet became warm when he touched his tongue to hers, and when he drew it back slowly over the roof of her mouth. The swing slowed, swayed, and finally stopped, but the undulating sensation lingered where their bodies met.

"Elizabeth? That was one hell of a nice ride."

Chapter 5

La Paloma skimmed over the smooth-rolling sea like a song. The sun was high, and it scattered white sparkles over the surface of the water. Emilio hadn't been able to resist doing a little trolling on such a fine day, and they'd made a nice catch. McQuade was glad to lend a hand to keep busy, but it surprised him that Elizabeth had joined in, too. He'd watched her toss slippery fish around like an old salt and wondered if Emilio noticed the way Elizabeth had made a point to move Luisa aside and take over for her when the nets were hauled over the side.

Luisa used her time below decks to make the noon meal more special. It was a wonderful blend of Mexican and island flavors—spicy panfried fish, rice, corn bread, and fried plantains with rum sauce. Thinking of the leathery-looking dried fish he might have to resort to within the next few days, McQuade had eaten his fill. Now, content, he lounged in a folding chair, enjoyed a cigarette and watched Luisa and Elizabeth emerge, one after the other, from below decks.

More than a Miracle

Emilio was tending to his nets, but he looked up from his work and smiled when he saw his wife. McQuade looked from one to the other and was touched by the pride they obviously shared in the coming baby. Together they would become three. Luisa turned to Elizabeth and whispered something. They glanced at each other and giggled. McQuade imagined Elizabeth as she must have appeared with the same small round belly, and a warm feeling for her spread though his own.

He beckoned her with a glance as he left his chair and stepped up to the boat's railing. She came to stand beside him, and he turned his back to the sea, braced both arms behind him, closed one eye and grinned at the sky. "Wouldn't this be the life? Sun and sea every day. Fantastic."

"If it could be like this every day, then this would indeed be the life." She smiled at the way the sun glinted in his hair like a wealth of copper pennies. He wore a dark blue short-sleeved shirt, jeans and blue running shoes, and she thought he should have been grilling steaks on a patio in some suburb of Miami.

"It's like this today, and this is it for me. My day as a Caribbean fisherman. I love it." He gestured broadly toward the couple at the bow of the boat. "Look at Emilio. The sea is his home. He's got his wife by his side. Who cares about the price of fish?"

"Whatever it is, they work hard for it. And for Luisa, it can only get harder."

His face became sober as he pursed his lips and nodded. "That's true. Men get off easy when it comes to having babies." He turned to her, curious. "How did you do?"

The question took her off guard. "Do? I did all right, I guess."

"I mean, you know . . . was it hard?"

He seemed genuinely interested, even concerned, and she wondered whether Luisa's condition suddenly bothered him. She found herself smiling to reassure him. "No matter how hard the pain is, it's forgotten the minute you take your baby in your arms. Your getting off easy has its drawbacks."

Emilio raised his voice to Luisa just then, and McQuade jerked his head around and straightened his back, scowling. Luisa had stumbled over some rope. As he caught her, Emilio scolded her for being clumsy.

Elizabeth touched McQuade's shoulder. "He worries, too," she said quietly. Unaware of his audience, Emilio covered his wife's abdomen with his strong brown hand, and Luisa's face became as radiant as the sun above her head.

"If I ever have a baby, I won't miss a thing," McQuade mumbled as he watched the young couple. "I'll be right there the whole time." He felt Elizabeth's stare. His face got hot, and he knew he was treating her to a rare sight. Sloan McQuade was blushing.

Damn it, McQuade, you might as well look her straight in the eye and get it over with. You just blew yourself right out of the water.

She was smiling.

"It's gotta be—" he shrugged, searching for a word—*any* word "—fascinating as hell."

"And then some."

Shaking his head, McQuade turned to lean his forearms on the railing and face the sea. He couldn't restrain a self-conscious grin. Elizabeth laid her hand on his shoulder and leaned close to his reddened ear. "I never know what to expect from you," she said.

He laughed. "Lately, neither do I."

"Disarmed, you're completely disarming." He cast her a sidelong glance, his gray eyes sparkling. "Really," she assured him.

"Hell, I oughta just deep-six the Browning and the .38 Special, then. I'll be so disarming I won't need them. What with your big brown eyes, this pregnant woman, and your kid waiting in La Primavera, you guys have all my weaknesses covered."

She lifted an eyebrow, incredulous. "What about the bourbon, the cigarettes, the steaks and...what else was there?"

He knew he'd probably said "broads" if he'd run down the usual list for her. "I can buy all that stuff, remember?"

"Oh, yes." Her tone stiffened, along with the expression on her face. "Money."

He looked straight ahead at the blue-on-blue horizon. His blush had gone the way of her smile. "Yeah. That was it."

They stood together in silence for a time, and then Elizabeth decided to try another subject. "I know a place on the south side of the island where we could hide."

"Where?"

"Southeast. We'd put in at the cliffs above El Gallo."

McQuade remembered where the little village was situated, cane fields to the north and, at its back, a mountainous region thick with tropical vegetation. "On the southeast end? That's sheer rock face."

"I know a way up to the top," she told him. "I explored a lot as a child. There's an old pirate lookout point up there, the ruins of a tower. What's left of it is overgrown—"

"And probably home for hundreds of slithery critters."

"Then we'll ask them to vacate." She folded her arms across her chest and gave him a look that challenged him to match her nerve.

"You sure you remember the way up? I've got goggles that'll improve our night vision, but we'd be in deep trouble if you couldn't locate the trail."

"I know exactly where it is," she assured him.

With Luisa at the helm, *La Paloma* hovered as close as it could to the rocky beach, while Emilio and his brother tethered the rubber raft alongside and handed McQuade's gear down to him. They lowered Elizabeth into his hands last, and with genuine concern for their safety, Emilio commended them both to God's care.

It was a moonless night, which McQuade counted as their first blessing, and they paddled the raft toward a rock formation high on the cliff that Elizabeth used as her landmark. There was little talk between them as they made their way toward shore, the hour approaching midnight. Waves splashed against the rocks as they slogged through the shallows in their running shoes, which protected their feet from the coral. When Elizabeth stumbled and scraped her leg, she was grateful for her soggy jeans.

McQuade let the air out of the raft once they were ashore, and then he made a tight bundle of the rubber and tied it to his backpack. No trace of their arrival could be discovered on the beach.

Elizabeth had no trouble finding the trail. They scrambled over a rocky incline and squeezed through some places that had once been easy passages for a child to negotiate. Behind what appeared to be solid rock was a rocky path that she remembered as a young girl's dream for climbing. Using hands and feet, they were soon on their way up the mountain.

McQuade had to hand it to her; she was as agile as a ten-year-old on the steep, rocky path. At the top there were trees growing thick and lush. They disturbed them as little as possible as they picked their way through the bushes until, shrouded in a dense copse of banyan trees, Elizabeth rediscovered her secret pirate hideout.

One set of stone steps led the way to a pile of rubble surrounded by a crumbling circular wall. There was no promise of shelter at first glance, but Elizabeth picked her way through the rocks and found another set of stone steps. "There's an underground room here," she whispered. In the dead of night it seemed inappropriate to raise her voice in this place.

McQuade lowered his backpack to the ground and removed the revolver and a handful of cartridges. He loaded it, rolled the cylinder into place and reached for the flashlight he carried in a sheath on his belt next to the knife. "Wanna place any bets?" he asked on his way down the steps.

"My money's already on you," she reminded him.

The passageway to what once must have been a storage room smelled like rich, dank humus. McQuade heard something rustling in the larger room ahead, and he approached with his back to the wall. He flashed his light from corner to corner and flushed out an iguana, which scurried over his foot and out the door. Feeling a little jumpier, he did another survey. Cobwebs were abundant in the room, which seemed to have been carved out of rock. A small pile of rocks stood in the corner.

McQuade felt more than heard the presence at his back, and in an instant Elizabeth was squinting into the beam of the flashlight. McQuade lowered the barrel of the .38 and sagged against the wall.

"Don't ever sneak up on me like that, Elizabeth. Not when I've got a loaded revolver in my hand."

"I'm sorry. I called, and you didn't answer."

"I didn't hear you."

"I didn't exactly *call*. I sort of hissed."

He groaned. "I could have mistaken you for a snake and shot you."

"Then you would only have gotten my foot. What did you find?"

He turned the light back on the room. "A hole."

"Oh, look! My gold!" She stepped into the light and pointed toward the rocks. "It's still here, right where I hid it."

"Great. Let's blow this joint and buy the island, lock, stock and baby."

"Scared?" It was a question she always asked sympathetically.

"Hell, no. This is perfect. Real cozy once we get rid of the wildlife." With his flashlight he took a swipe at a drift of cobwebs. "You actually came here to *play*?"

"I came here to hide my treasure," she said lightly as she slapped more cobwebs down.

"If you were young enough to be hiding treasure, you were too young to be up here alone."

"Probably. I'll go get your backpack."

He handed her the flashlight. "I'll get it. Remember, no lights outside."

The instant he was out of sight, she stopped breathing, and she couldn't draw breath until he returned.

"Turn it out of my face, honey."

"I'm sorry."

Her voice was thin and tremulous. It would have been unfair to taunt her with "Scared?" The place gave him the willies, but she was battling with something much deeper. He offered his hand, and she grabbed it and held on tight.

"It hasn't always been like this for you, has it?"

"No." She took a deep breath and exhaled slowly. "I'm fine. I just don't like being alone in a place like this."

"Hell, neither do I. Who would?" When she was done with his hand, he thought, he would set his backpack down. He wondered if she had any blood left in her fingers.

"I used to play alone all the time—eat alone, study alone. I've become such a baby." She sighed. "At night, sometimes I have to leave my bed and go outside."

"I hope you won't do that here. If you get the urge, let me know."

"Sometimes . . . I'm afraid I'll suffocate."

It was such a quiet confession that he had to strain to hear it. "If you feel like that during the night, wake me up. We'll go outside together."

She released her hold on him slowly. "How many flashlights do we have?"

"Two. And power to spare."

"Then I'll keep one close by."

McQuade opened the deflated rubber raft and spread it down as a mat. Elizabeth set about making her bed. As long as she knew he was there, she was all right. She decided they needed conversation. "I guess what you've been calling me isn't far from the truth."

"What's that?"

"Island princess. My grandmother had a plantation west of here, and I spent a lot of time exploring in these hills and along the beaches."

"She still there?"

"No. She died, and my father sold most of the land. The money I got from my mother was put in trust before my grandmother's death, though, and my father had nothing to say about it. We still had a house, but Guerrero laid claim to that."

"Along with everything else," McQuade added. "I've got one question."

"Hmm?"

"Where do you want me to sleep?"

"Right next to me." She gestured toward the spot, then looked up at him, quietly adding, "If you wouldn't mind."

"Mind? You kidding?" He unrolled his foam pad and lined it up next to hers. "I just had a thirty-inch lizard run over my foot."

Moments later she stiffened when she heard him start to unzip his jeans. She turned reflexively, and his hands stilled. "Look, my pants are wet, Elizabeth. Now, you can watch, or you can face the other way."

She did a quick about-face, then realized hers were wet, too. She flicked at the snap. "Are *you* looking the other way?"

"Hey, *I* gave *you* a choice." He laughed and then said with a gentlemanly drawl, "My eyes are averted, Miss Elizabeth."

Shucking her jeans with all the awkwardness of someone in too much of a hurry, she muttered, "I don't know if I can trust you quite this far, Sloan McQuade. You and all your weaknesses. I just can't be sure...."

She refused to look at him until she'd scooted into her sleeping bag and covered up. Then she risked a glance. Naturally he was smiling.

"You said you wouldn't look."

"I said my eyes were averted, honey. They were."

"How much did you see?"

"Not as much as I wanted to."

"Boorish American. I should have—"

"Can we turn off the flashlight?"

"Certainly. You can smirk in the dark."

She lay there in darkness for several moments listening to his breathing, concentrating on an awareness of his presence. It wasn't enough.

"Sloan?"

"Hmm?"

"Do you think we could touch somehow?"

"Touch . . . each other?"

"Shoulders or . . . or hands."

He sighed, muttering, "All my trials . . . come over here, princess. Lift up a little. Put your head on my shoulder. Better now?"

"Yes. Are you comfortable?"

Comfortable? Was she kidding? "Sure. You'll be okay. Just picture a nice sunny day. A bright sunshiny field full of . . . full of grazing horses. You like horses?" She nodded against his chest. "Lots of sun, lots of flowers. Mares and their colts. Can you see all that?"

"Mmm-hmm."

"Good. You go to sleep thinking sunshine and flowers and horses in the field." He kissed the top of her head and closed his eyes. *While I lie awake feeling sorry for the poor jerk in the stud barn.*

"No!"

McQuade shot up. The pistol came into his hand immediately, and he stared into the darkness for an instant before it came to him that the voice was Elizabeth's. Easing himself back on his elbow, he exchanged the pistol for the flashlight, aiming it at the wall above their heads. He leaned over her, but when he touched her, she tried to push him away.

"No, no. No más, por favor," she mumbled, whimpering like a child in pain.

"No more what? You're dreaming, honey." He touched her cheek and then drew her into his arms, gently rendering her struggling useless. "It's Sloan. Wake up, Elizabeth. Look at me. It's Sloan."

"No más." She groaned, pushing against his chest.

"I won't hurt you, baby," he whispered and pressed his lips against her forehead. "I could never hurt you. You're okay now. You're with me."

"Sloan?"

"Yeah." He leaned back so she could see his face.

She saw gray eyes instead of dark fury, golden hair rather than black, caring rather than cruelty. With two trembling fingers she touched his lips to be sure they were real. She closed her eyes, grateful for the solid feel of him.

"Oh, Sloan, you must think I'm loco."

"I think you're scared."

She sighed. "He won't let me sleep."

"How can I help?" He traced his thumb along her jaw. "What can I do for you, honey?" She stared at him. "We could zip the sleeping bags together."

"No."

"If I just held you . . ."

She was out of her bed and lunging for the door before he could protest.

"You sure you wanna go out there like that?" She froze. "Catch." He reached for the jeans she'd draped over her backpack and tossed them to her. "You stay by those steps till I get there," he warned as she faded into the dark passageway.

McQuade pulled his jeans on, tucked the pistol in the back of his waistband and reached for his backpack. "I need a cigarette. Look at me," he said in disgust. "I'm talking to myself." He stuck the end of the cigarette between his lips mumbling, "Maybe I'm the one who's loco."

Smoke curled around his head as McQuade fanned the match and pocketed it. Elizabeth was sitting on the low stone wall, and he joined her there. "I wasn't looking to compromise your innocence when I suggested—"

"I have no innocence to compromise." She took the cigarette from his hand, and he watched while she puffed on it with the ease of a lifelong smoker.

She handed it back to him, and he chuckled. "Is that the clincher? Would it corrupt you further if I offered you a whole one?"

"No, thank you. I stopped smoking when I became pregnant. I stopped being innocent long before that."

"What are you supposed to be guilty of?"

Hooking her bare foot over her knees, she brushed a troublesome pebble off her sole. "The original sin. I know too much."

He studied the perfection of her profile, the soft curve of her hair as it lay against her cheekbone, and the guarded look in her eyes. "You sure as hell couldn't prove it by me."

"And what do you know, Sloan McQuade?" She turned to him, squaring her shoulders. "What have you seen in all your travels?"

"I know loneliness." He lifted his shoulder invitingly. "I know what it's like when you need to be close to somebody."

Lowering her foot to the ground, she yielded to him, but didn't move any closer. "You talk like a woman sometimes."

"Don't knock it. Some of my best friends have been women." He took a quick, hard pull on the cigarette and spat out the smoke. "So how do men usually talk?"

"Without sympathy. They use vulgarity instead."

"Would you prefer that?"

"I would understand it better."

"Okay, I'll put it to you this way." He turned, bracing his hand on his thigh. "I wasn't looking to get laid back there, although if you'd offered, I sure as hell wouldn't have turned you down. You were scared, and I wanted you to settle down so I could get some sleep. And if you're so damn worldly, how come I feel like Jack the Ripper every time I put my hands on you?''

Elizabeth's eyes narrowed as she nodded. ''That's more like it, Mr. McQuade. That sounded very masculine.''

If there had been more light in the sky, they would have seen the light in each other's eyes and then the dawning of smiles. As it was, a duet of laughter broke the ice, and McQuade flicked his cigarette into a pile of rocks.

''So how should I talk around you, Miss Worldly Wise?''

''It might as well be your way, Mr. Macho. I'll expect the unexpected.''

''Good.'' He sobered, catching her cheek in his palm, and her laughter faded, too. ''Here comes the unexpected.''

Their kiss was sweetly serendipitous. Elizabeth took one deep breath and leaned closer. The unexpected was supremely gentle. For all she'd come to know about men, she knew little of this. His arms were comforting. His strength posed no threat. He took her breath only after she'd used it, and he traded it for his. For all her experience, she hadn't known a kiss like his. It was an offer, not a demand. It was a sip of fine wine, a whiff of its bouquet. She tipped her head back and sampled, rolling the taste of him over her tongue and finding it to be smooth and wonderfully full-bodied. How dangerous would it be to ask him to fill her glass?

But that was not offered. When he drew back he suggested simply, ''I want to hold you through the night, Elizabeth.''

She smiled. There was such softness in his eyes, and that, too, was unexpected. ''Will you tell me more about the horses in the pasture?''

* * *

Elizabeth had purchased a full cotton skirt and a loose blouse in Arco Iris. She had fastened her hair in a bun at the nape of her neck, and she hoped to find a broad-brimmed straw hat in the village. McQuade was an all-American tourist, from his loose-fitting shirt to his blue jeans. Only the pistol tucked in his pants under his shirttail spoiled the image. They walked into El Gallo without causing much of a stir.

McQuade knew most of the cantinas in De Colores, and La Gallina was one of his favorites. Antonio was a friend. And then there was his hot-blooded daughter, Chi Chi. As he held the door for Elizabeth, McQuade hoped that, with any luck, Chi Chi had forgotten him.

"McQuade! Man of my dreams! Ohhhh..." The dark young woman with the cherubic face lowered her outstretched arms, frowning. "You brought another woman?"

"I have another woman, yes. And you were going to get married to—what was his name?"

"Carl, I think. He was going to take me to Miami."

"Always Miami." Antonio appeared from the back room, offering a handshake. "McQuade! Our troubled island has seen little of you this past year."

McQuade took a seat at one of the cantina's three tables and pulled a chair out for Elizabeth as an apparent afterthought. They'd agreed that she would be a silent shadow during this visit.

"I've got some errands to run for the Red Cross, plus a little private investigating for a client back home."

Antonio dragged a chair close to McQuade and prepared to be included in his friend's wonderful secret dealings. Antonio loved American television, especially the detectives shows, and McQuade's visits were the highlights of any season. He flashed a conspiratorial grin. "What can I do for you, *amigo*?"

The question came as a surprise. "Nobody's been here looking for me? A woman named Ronnie Harper?"

"Another woman?" Antonio winked broadly. "I envy you, McQuade. They can't resist a man of action."

Antonio was one of McQuade's most reliable sources, but he wished the man would just answer his questions. He caught an icy glance from Elizabeth.

"The woman's a pilot, Antonio. She brings in supplies for the Red Cross. She was supposed to leave a message here for me."

"A message?" Antonio's eyes brightened as though the word suggested a gourmet delight.

"She's kinda cute," McQuade offered. "Boyish dresser. Reddish blond hair. She should've been here in the last couple of days."

Chi Chi piped up from behind the bar. "Doesn't sound like your type, McQuade."

"Has the woman been here, Chi Chi?" Antonio demanded. "You're not to handle McQuade's messages. That's *my* business."

"There have been no Anglos here for months, Papa. If one had set foot in the village, we would have heard about it."

The fact that the news disturbed McQuade also disturbed Antonio. "This secret message is for your client, no?"

McQuade was studying a pair of initials carved in the table. Ronnie had seemed pretty straight to him. Either he'd had her pegged wrong, or she was in trouble. He would have to do some checking, and that would take time—time he hadn't allotted in his plan.

"Ronnie Harper was my ticket out of here, Antonio. Can you find out for me if she was here? She island-hops in a Cessna."

"Security is getting tighter," Antonio said. "Since Colonel Hidalgo was killed, the police question every move anybody makes."

"Who do you think killed him?"

Antonio shrugged. "The government questions us, but we don't question the government." He leaned closer. "I think Guerrero worried about Hidalgo's popularity. But Guerrero says it was the CIA."

McQuade figured the CIA would have to double its forces to manage all the activity they were credited with, even the likely stuff—which this certainly wasn't. "Listen, Antonio, I need some information about Guerrero's kid. My client wants to know where he is, who's taking care of him, whether he's eating his vegetables—stuff like that. Who might know?"

Antonio glanced at Elizabeth and then flashed McQuade a grin. "That's easy, *amigo*. A girl from this village cleans the house where the boy stays. He's not at the palace. He stays with an old lady."

"Maria Adelfa?"

Both men turned to Elizabeth. "Yes, that's the one," Antonio said. Elizabeth nodded and quietly returned her attention to her hands, which were folded in her lap. "You can talk to the girl," Antonio offered. "She's Chi Chi's friend, but quiet as a mouse. You can trust her."

"You'll arrange that for me?" Antonio nodded vigorously, and McQuade laid a hand on the man's shoulder. "I trust you like a brother, Antonio. You're my eyes and ears in De Colores—you know that." Antonio beamed. "And I'm undercover this trip. Not a word to anyone about this woman or me."

"Of course not. You hear that, Chi Chi?"

"Keep your voice down, Papa, or the whole village will hear." She leaned over the bar, her arms forming a frame to enhance the deep cleavage in her full bustline. "I don't want nothing bad to happen to McQuade."

"Then how about serving up some dinner?" McQuade suggested. "I'm fading fast."

By the time they left the village, McQuade had learned that Ronnie Harper's Cessna had hardly been on the island long enough to refuel. It didn't make sense to him; if she'd planned to skip out on them, why had she flown into De Colores at all?

His ace in the hole was Emilio, who had arrived at his brother's house that morning. Antonio had brought Emilio to the cantina and left the two men to talk privately. He had also arranged for a meeting with Juanita, the nurse's housekeeper. Things were falling into place nicely.

As they hiked through the underbrush toward their mountain retreat, McQuade figured he faced two major problems. One, the barometer had dropped suddenly, and he felt the heavy stillness of a tropical storm in the air. Two, he faced another night in close quarters with Elizabeth.

Chapter 6

The sky had lost its color. It appeared above the trees in eerie patches, neither gray nor blue, as though watercolors had run together in a painting and gotten muddled. Elizabeth knew the signs. Islanders accepted the warning as a matter of course, and they prepared themselves and their property as best they could. She knew better than to begrudge nature her timing, but the bitterness that rose in her breast as she neared the top of the mountain could not be reasoned away. It couldn't happen now. No power on earth should be allowed to stand in her way now that she'd come this far.

"If this blows over, I'm going to go in after Tomás tomorrow," McQuade told her. They reached a small clearing, and he stopped to take another survey. "Feels like this could get pretty serious, though."

"Why couldn't we go now, tonight?"

She looked hard, determined and dangerously emotional. She avoided looking up at the sky, although he knew she sensed the ominous signs as intensely as he did. They were in for one hell of a storm.

"I figure that I can make the slickest snatch at siesta time. Juanita's willing to help for a small fee." He raised an eyebrow her way. "And you aren't going anywhere near that house, so don't get any ideas. You'll be waiting on Emilio's boat."

"What if this doesn't blow over?"

"Then we wait it out."

"And what if—"

He took hold of her arm. "Don't give me any what-ifs at this stage, Elizabeth. You and I both know that if this island gets hit with a real hurricane, it'll be a whole new ball game."

"You'll back out?" she accused, pulling away.

"Hell, no, I won't back out. You think I'm . . ." Furious, he started up the hill again.

When he felt her walking close by his shoulder, he began calmly. "You learn to adapt in this business. You count on your own wits, not your plans, and you don't waste time worrying about the things you can't control." He glanced at her to see if he was making any impression, but he couldn't tell. She was staring ahead with a resigned, vacant look in her eyes. "Life is full of variables, Elizabeth, and the weather is one of them. But we're going to deal with that."

Her look told him that *she* certainly would. He decided to go over everything with her that night. If he laid it all out for her, it might boost her confidence in him. This was turning out to be the stickiest job he'd ever taken, and it was beginning to make him feel a little edgy. It wasn't the risk; he'd gone into the backyards of adversaries who were better trained than Guerrero's little army and far better supplied. It wasn't changing plans, and it wasn't the weather.

He knew damn well it was his client who was making him nervous, not his opposition. When somebody paid him fifty thousand dollars to do a job, that was usually all he needed as a vote of confidence. So why did he worry about this woman every time she got that look in her eyes? It was a complicated look, and he liked to keep things simple. Whether for a client or a bed partner, he liked to think he supplied a service and got what he wanted in return. He'd gone through thirty-six years that way, and he'd counted on sailing through at least another thirty-six with the same no-strings philosophy. And then along had come Elizabeth Donnelly.

They stopped to wash themselves in a mountain stream, giving each other the space they needed mentally as well as physically. Then they climbed to the top of the cliffs over-looking the sea, but neither of them made a prediction about what might come next. The threatening sky hung low over white-capped, slate-colored waters, making clear what was about to happen. The wind was picking up. Now was the time, Elizabeth told herself. Just before the storm hit. If she couldn't get back up here, she could find another place to hide with her baby, and no one would be able to search for her.

"I love to watch a storm brew," McQuade said absently. "The power grows right before your eyes." He shoved his hands into his pockets as he turned to her. "We should be okay down in the hole. The water should run out the side of the stairwell and down the hill." She nodded. "Storms bother you, too?" he asked gently.

"This kind of storm kills people," she reminded him. Her hair blew across her face, and she pushed it aside. "Yes, they bother me. I don't enjoy watching them brew." She walked away from him, her full skirt hugging her buttocks and the backs of her legs as it billowed out in front of her.

Her hair flew forward, looking like the long leaves of the palms that bent above her in the wind.

"You're not going inside yet, are you? No telling how long we'll be stuck down there."

"I'm going to take the canteens and fill them in the stream," she shouted back.

He turned to the sea again and let the wind blow in his face. As he watched the storm clouds roll in, he realized that he was bothered by the way she had shouted at him without turning around. He hadn't seen her face when she'd told him where she was going. He looked up at the sky. Fill the canteens? Hell, they were about to be deluged with water. He broke into a dead run, mentally calculating the head start he'd given her.

She was easily followed. He was able to catch up with her and close in quietly. By the time she heard him, he was close enough to reach out and grab her by the arm.

"The stream's back this way."

Elizabeth stiffened and refused to turn around. "I've decided to go down there myself, McQuade."

"And do what?"

"Get my son."

He turned her to face him, keeping a firm hold on her upper arms. "I can't let you do that, Elizabeth."

Even in the near-darkness, he could see the fire in her eyes. "What lengths would you go to stop me?"

"I won't hurt you." He moved quickly and smoothly to sling her over his shoulder. "But I won't let you hurt yourself, either. Comfortable?"

"McQuade!"

"If you're worried about my back—"

"This—is—an—outrage!"

"—don't trouble yourself."

"Put me down!"

"I can bench press—"

"I—will not—tolerate this."

"—at least two of you. No problem."

McQuade's understanding of colloquial Spanish was stretched beyond its limits. He gave up counting the number of colorful words Elizabeth used to describe his depravity as he carried her up the hill. When the rain started, it came down in torrents, and he set Elizabeth on her feet, grabbed her hand and sprinted the remaining distance with her at his side. By the time they reached the ruins, the wind had them staggering like two drunks.

"Get inside!" McQuade shouted as they made their way down the steps.

Elizabeth flopped back against the wall just inside the entryway and fought to catch her breath. McQuade worked feverishly to clear the pile of rocks and debris that threatened to trap water in the stairwell. He sent the offending rubbish down the hill by handfuls until the water's path was no longer blocked. As he straightened from his work, the branch of a tree was caught by the wind and suddenly smacked the back of his head. Elizabeth gasped at the sight and plunged back into the wind to help him.

McQuade rubbed his head, hoping the flashing red and green lights he was seeing weren't signals for a blackout. He dropped one shoulder against the wall and fought to clear his mind. He felt a tentative hand on his back and another touch his hair.

"Is it bad?" she asked.

If he turned around, he knew he would yell at her. His head throbbed. "It's okay," he answered tightly. "Can you get the flashlight?"

"It's bad, isn't it?"

"Just get the flashlight, Elizabeth. I'll be okay in a minute." He listened to the sound of cautious footfalls and knew she was battling her fear and winning, at least for the moment. "It's straight ahead," he called out to encourage her. "Keep going. You'll run right into our stuff." He heard a rustling and hoped it was Elizabeth and not the iguana. His ears welcomed a click. "Great. A light at the end of the tunnel. Please don't shine it in my face."

She came to him. "Do you feel dizzy?"

"Not really."

"Not *really*?" She slipped her arm around his waist and draped his over her shoulder. "You're not really sure you won't fall flat on your face, are you?"

"To show my good breeding, I'm going to cooperate with you." He didn't lean on her, but he let her steady him, adding, "Just to show you how cooperating is done."

"That was outrageous, Sloan, to carry me that way."

"Yeah, yeah."

"It was boorish."

"Where the hell did you get a word like that? Does it mean anything like stupid?" He sat on the floor and propped his back against the wall. "Because that's what you were being. Plain stupid."

She knelt in front of him. "Obviously I would have turned back when the storm hit."

"Obviously you might not have made it." She shone the light in his eyes, and he turned his face. "Cut that out!"

"I want to see if your pupils are dilated, Sloan. Open your eyes." He complied, and she was relieved to find that his pupils immediately became black pinpricks in a field of stony gray.

He touched the back of his head again. "I've got a real goose egg back here. It's a good sign if it swells up right away like that."

"We need something cold to put on it." She reached into her backpack and came up with a bandanna. "I'll be right back."

Taking the light with her, she went to the door and returned with the bandanna soaked by the cold rain. He held it against the back of his head and closed his eyes, tempted to let the inky swirls behind his eyelids take him where they would. When he looked up, he saw Elizabeth, shivering in the shadows. Her hair was still partly knotted at her nape, partly plastered to the sides of her face. Her skirt and blouse were sopping, as well.

"Change your clothes," he ordered gruffly. "You look like a drowned rat."

"Yours are wet, too." She stood there hugging herself and waiting for the roof to fall in. It amazed her to watch him contain his anger. She hadn't known men who were capable of such control, and she hadn't intended to test this one's limits. There had been a storm coming, Tomás had been just out of reach, and, Lord, she'd only wanted her baby.

It had been a foolish move; she knew that now. She regretted the pain she'd caused McQuade, and although she expected rage any moment, she stepped closer, holding out her hand. "Let me take that out again. It has to be cold."

He came to his feet slowly, unsure of his balance. What did she think he was going to do? She looked like some frightened waif. Hell, he'd brought her to safety, and she looked as though she expected to be thrown to the wolves. He offered the bandanna, but he seized her hand when she tried to take it from him.

"What were you trying to do, Elizabeth? Scare the life out of me?"

Her heart hammered with fear. "All I could think about was Tomás—that he was so close."

"This damned hurricane was closer."

She made a gesture of entreaty with her free hand. "He's just a baby, Sloan. That house could blow away."

"Yeah," he said, nodding. "Yeah, maybe. And what were you gonna do if it did? Don't even think about that, Elizabeth, because if it happens, there's not a damn thing you can do about it. Chances are he's safe." He gripped her wrist more tightly then he intended. "Do you know what *your* chances were out there?"

"Please, let me go," she whispered.

He grabbed her shoulder in his other hand. "What if I hadn't found you? You know what I imagined?" He shook her once. "This delicate little body smashed against a tree somewhere."

"Don't. Please."

"Don't what?" he roared. "Don't sling you over my shoulder like a *boorish* American or whatever the hell else you were calling me out there?"

"Don't shout," she pleaded.

"Why not? Afraid I'll wake the neighbors?"

"I'm afraid—" she closed her eyes "—for my son."

"I told you I'd get him, Elizabeth. Don't you trust me yet? Don't you believe—"

"Yes, I believe," she whispered. "Please, let me go."

He released her, and she took a step back. The look on her face sliced through him, and the pain it caused glistened in his eyes. "God Almighty, woman, do you think I'd hurt you? Don't you know there's only one way I can think of touching you?" He reached for her and pulled her into his arms. "One way," he growled. "And that's *this* way."

She responded to his kiss without reservation because there was no time to think. There was only the need to share, and there was no mistaking his need, nor was there any denying hers. His tongue probed, and hers answered, *Sloan,*

you taste good, and if you would nourish me, I would de-
vour you.

He demanded her body's full attention as he held her
flush against him and ground his need against hers, as if to
say, Elizabeth, I'd fit you so well, and I'd make your body
weep for joy and send your mind soaring.

She lifted her chin and asked for more of him, pulling at
him with her arms, her hands, her mouth. This was a dream
changing into demanding need—the need to be kissed pas-
sionately and touched gently. And gently he touched her at
her back, her bottom, her shoulders. Even with his hands in
her hair, there was no pain.

Wet clothes, he thought absently. They have to go. He
longed for the feel of her skin against his, the chance to
make her warm. He pulled the blouse over her shoulders and
down to her waist, hoping she would do the same for him.

She froze.

When he hesitated, she pushed herself away from him,
covering herself with one hand and tugging at the elastic
neckline of her blouse with the other.

"What's wrong?"

"You can't do this!" Her voice rose with fear.

"Do what? Make love to you?"

She moved away again, and this time McQuade turned his
back on her rejection of him. "There's a word for you, lady.
How do you say *tease* in Spanish?" Tossing his wet shirt
over his backpack, he dug out a pack of cigarettes before he
lost his temper out of pure frustration.

He stood at the doorway and mopped the back of his
head with rainwater, letting it sluice down his neck and over
his back. He needed to soak his whole body in a cold bath.
He had let her get to him again. Had he stopped using his
head altogether? He was breaking all his own rules—good,

solid rules that had kept him out of trouble for years. He draped the bandanna over his neck and lit a cigarette.

Dropping his head back, he leaned against the arch that formed the entry to the underground passage and he dragged smoke deep into his lungs. *Rule number one: A female client is not a woman. Never confuse the two.* He exhaled and remembered *rule number two: Emotions cloud the clearest thinking. Don't indulge in them.* His brain had been clicking along fine, stacking up contingency plans, adding in the variables, and then she'd bolted. God in heaven, he'd drawn a mental blank. He'd raced after her like a lunatic rather than the calculating professional he considered himself to be. Then, when he'd looked at her back there, and she'd flashed him those big brown eyes full of fear... *Rule number three: When you remember the color of her eyes, you're in too deep.*

He laughed aloud, and the wind howled back at him. In too deep? Hell, that was all he really wanted, wasn't it? He wanted to bury himself in her to the hilt. That would satisfy him. She could flash those big brown eyes all she wanted, but once he'd had the satisfaction of breaking the ice barrier, she'd be dealing with a man who was fully in charge of his faculties again.

A tree limb suddenly crashed across the steps above him, and McQuade drew back into the passageway. Then he heard a soft noise at his back, which startled him even more. It sounded like a strangled sob to him, and his first thought was: not Elizabeth, Elizabeth doesn't cry. But the sound tugged at him like a rope. He flicked the cigarette butt into the night's chaos and went to her.

He found her huddled against the wall, clutching the flashlight and crying. When she saw him, she sat up quickly, breathing deeply in an effort to calm herself. She was swiping at her tears with the backs of her fingers when he knelt beside her and gently moved her hand aside. She closed her eyes and let him swab her cheeks with the cool, wet bandana. The hand he held was cold. He massaged it, giving warmth as he absorbed her tremors.

"I'm sorry," he murmured. "Forget what I said. It was . . . it was boorish as hell."

"No, it wasn't. It was true." She rolled her eyes toward the ceiling and gave a shaky sigh. "In a way it was true," she amended. "I didn't intend to tease you, but it worked out that way, didn't it? And I don't even do that well. Before you can succeed at teasing, you have to succeed at being a woman, and I've . . . lost touch with that, I think."

"Lost touch with being a woman?" His voice rose in disbelief.

Her eyes were swimming in tears again when she looked at him. "It was so good on the swing, Sloan. I felt free, and our kiss felt like something I could have had once."

"It was something you *did* have, Elizabeth. *We* had it. It was good for me, too. What happened tonight?"

"You were angry." She dropped her head back against the wall and tried to remember the look in his eyes.

"Honey, I was mad as hell. You scared the living daylights out of me."

She saw the echo of that look even now. Anger out of fear, she thought. How strange. "I encouraged you when you kissed me tonight. I know that. I had no right to turn you away after that."

No right? He turned the words over in his mind. They didn't sit well with him, even though he had to admit he had always believed that what she'd said was true.

"Who says?"

The question took them both off guard. Had he really voiced it? Had she really heard it? Elizabeth sniffled, and McQuade handed her the bandanna. "What I mean is that

I liked the feeling I got when you...when we kissed," she said.

"I could tell."

"But when you started to..."

No innocence? Like hell, he thought. "To take your blouse off," he supplied as he shifted and sat down beside her.

"Yes," she said quickly. "I felt differently then."

"Scared?" She nodded. He took the bandanna from her, set it aside and held her hands in his, massaging her palms with his thumbs. "Your hands are always cold, you know that?" Again she nodded. "Why do you think that is?"

"I don't know. I think I'm a cold person."

"You also think you've got all this worldly knowledge, and I don't think you know beans."

She gave him a sidelong glance. "Beans?"

He shrugged. "Just an expression. It means you don't know a damn thing."

She forgave him his arrogance because he couldn't have known what ugliness she carried in her head. If she could shed the years, the pain and the scars right then, there would be no fear, and she would open her arms to him.

"I want to ask you something about your husband."

"Don't—"

"Did he ever kiss you?" She looked at him quizzically, and he didn't like the feeling that he was trespassing where she didn't want him to go. He liked the thought of Guerrero doing anything with Elizabeth even less, but he had a hunch. He swallowed hard. "I mean, you know, like...like I did."

"No."

"He never...started out by—"

"No. He never did." Her tone said that that was the end of the discussion. She would tell him no more.

But he wasn't willing to accept that.

"How did he start out, then?" She closed her eyes and shook her head. "By pulling off your clothes?"

"Sometimes," she said in a small voice.

"Like I just did?"

"Not . . . not exactly. You were kissing me."

He nodded, letting the image sit in his brain for a minute. He was inclined to ask more questions, but he knew he'd already taken something she hadn't wanted to give.

"I want to do something for you, Elizabeth." He stood and drew her to her feet. "You're cold because your clothes are wet, and I want to help you take them off."

"I can do that myself," she said quietly. The fear came back into her eyes instantly.

He held her gaze with his, willing her to see that he had no hidden intentions as he lifted his hand to the back of her head. With great care he took the remaining pins from her hair. "I want to help you put dry clothes on. And I want to kiss you. And that's all. I promise."

The only warmth she knew at that moment came from his bare chest. She longed to touch him there, to cover his nipples with her fingers, but her hands felt like buckets of cement hanging by her sides.

He combed through her hair with his fingers. "Have I shown you anything to trust in me?" he asked.

"Yes."

"Tell me it's okay, then. I'll stop whenever you say."

"Sloan—"

"I know. You're scared. I want to help you stop being scared."

"I can't. . . ."

"Try," he whispered as he eased her blouse over her head. She hadn't worn a bra because the De Coloran women generally didn't, and she'd dressed as one of them. She hadn't worn one the night on the swing, either, and he'd been tantalized then as he was now. He freed her breasts, but he avoided looking, avoided touching.

"You okay?" he asked. She nodded, wide-eyed, and he smiled. "Breathe, then." He held her shoulders in his hands, and when she'd allowed herself a breath, he covered her mouth with a soft, easy kiss. He slipped his thumbs inside the elastic waistband of her skirt and found her panties in the same motion.

She stood perfectly still while he slid both garments the length of her legs. He figured that only a eunuch could do this with his eyes closed, and, as his eyes passed over each soft curve from breast to knee, he became painfully aware that he was no eunuch. She stepped out of her clothes, but he gripped the fabric in both hands for a moment longer, just to keep himself occupied. Then he brought jeans, panties and a shirt from her backpack. He slid the panties into place first, and then the jeans. His hands weren't quite steady on the snap.

"I've never done this in reverse," he muttered. A brief giggle brought his head up. The wariness was still evident in her eyes, but there was a spark of something warmer, and there was the shadow of a smile. He reached for her shirt and offered her one sleeve at a time as he tried to look anywhere but at her breasts. The challenge was impossible. He pulled the shirt together in front and buttoned it with deliberate motions.

"Are *you* okay?" she asked gently.

He held up his hands, his job done. "Hey, I'm cool as a—" he swallowed the word *cucumber* and fumbled for another choice. He came up with *fruitcake*.

Now she could laugh. "What strange expressions you have, Mr. McQuade."

Her eyes were still red, but there was a smile in them now, and he was smiling back. Under pressure.

"Yeah. Well, it's kind of a mixed metaphor, which means I, uh, need a cigarette. When I come back—"

"You don't have to go out there to smoke."

"Yeah, I do. I'll just take a minute. See if you can find us something to eat. When I come back, we need to talk." He reached up to smooth his hand over her hair. "Friends?"

Sharp tears sprang to her eyes. She nodded and pushed the word past the tightness in her throat. "Friends."

Their underground refuge had become a wind tunnel. McQuade's head still throbbed, and his cigarette wasn't doing that situation any good, but at least it was taking his mind off the rest of his body.

The problem was that he couldn't forget hers. Only a poet could describe the grace of its form and the poignancy of its slightness. He wanted to have her fitted for armor while he sharpened his sword, all for her defense. She brought out such an array of instincts in him, both lofty and base, that he was finding it impossible to conduct himself normally. Normal for him had always meant going with his instincts. He groaned inwardly. Had she screwed those up, too?

She was sitting cross-legged in the middle of her sleeping bag. She'd spread the beds out side by side again, and he settled across from her. Her backpack was close at hand, but she hadn't taken any food out of it.

"Doesn't dried fish catch your fancy?" he asked.

"No. Would you like some?" She reached for the zipper. "I'm sure you must be hungry."

"One of the agreements we made was that you'd follow my instructions on this little jaunt, Elizabeth. Now, I've noticed that you don't eat enough to keep a canary alive, and I've gotta tell you, it shows." She looked surprised and a little hurt. He smiled apologetically. "I couldn't help it. I tried to avert my eyes, but they wouldn't stay averted. You've got to eat something, honey."

"I did," she reminded him. "I ate Chi Chi's paella. I think she outdid herself for you."

"Is that why you picked at it like you weren't sure the shrimp were dead?" She made a face, and he gave her knee a teasing squeeze. "Thought I might have to kiss the cook, huh?"

"It wasn't that good," she said stubbornly.

He reached for the backpack. "You're going to eat, Elizabeth. It's risky for you not to. Beef jerky." She accepted the offer grudgingly. "It's delicious."

"I get along on very little food." In response to his admonishing glare, she tore off a piece of the dried meat with her teeth. "Especially when I'm away from home."

"But this *is* your home," he said over a mouthful of jerky. "Not this pit, but this island."

Elizabeth nodded, chewing slowly as she considered the idea of "home." "It was once. It was my mother's home, and my grandmother's. But my father didn't belong here. He used this island as a base for his activities, and he used my mother." She swallowed, then studied the food in her hand. Her look of distaste was not for the meat.

"He thought she gave him legitimacy, a plausible reason to be here, and that having a child made him a family man. All for the public eye. But he had no more respect for marriage than he had for the law. He was gone a lot of the time."

McQuade had a strange, tight feeling inside, the kind he got when he knew he was on the verge of learning a key piece of information, the one that would take him straight to the heart of a case—or, perhaps, a person. He was afraid to move, afraid she would become self-conscious and back off from telling him more.

"It was important to him that his daughter have an American education," she continued, "so I attended prep school and college. He planned to use me as a pawn, to arrange a marriage for me that would give him the berth he wanted in American society." She smiled slowly. "But I spoiled his plan."

"How?"

"I married Rodolfo Guerrero, the rebel." Her short laugh was mirthless, and the sound of it made McQuade feel slightly sick. She continued on a sardonic note. "I showed my father, didn't I? I married one of my own countrymen, a man who had risen through the ranks of the old regime and then boldly denounced its tyranny."

"You're talking about *Guerrero*?" With his thumb McQuade drew a slash beside his left eye and lifted a questioning eyebrow. The scar was Guerrero's most unforgettable feature.

"The same. He was always the same." She sighed, shaking her head. "Only in my *mind* was he ever a man of principle. He left the old regime because the president had agreed to cooperate with the U.S. Drug Enforcement Agency in an investigation of top De Coloran officials. Guerrero called it American intervention, but I know now that he was corrupt. He knew someone would be made a scapegoat to satisfy Washington, and he decided it wouldn't be him."

"Did Castillo and Hidalgo know all this when they teamed up with him?"

"General Castillo was Guerrero's uncle. In De Colores, relatives are forgiven their little shortcomings. Especially the young men, who are expected to make a few mistakes. The general blamed the system for Guerrero's corruption and offered him a chance to redeem himself."

"How about Hidalgo? Was he a relative?"

"No."

"Then what's his excuse?"

"He didn't know." Elizabeth tipped her head back and searched the ceiling. Her eyes glistened. "But more to the point, what was my excuse?"

McQuade touched her knee, which was only a fraction of the gesture he wanted to make. He had to let her come to him for comfort; otherwise, she would back away. She needed no excuses with him. He could blame Castillo, Hidalgo, the whole damned population of De Colores, for being taken in by Guerrero, but not her. And he didn't want her to tell him anything that would change his mind.

"Elizabeth, what did he do to you?"

She smiled at him as though he were a child who had touched her heart with an innocent question. "He didn't force me to marry him. I knew him socially. He must have seen my need to rebel, and the idea of defying my father along with the other powerful men on the island appealed to me. It also appealed to me. We fled to Central America and were married there. That was five years ago."

"When did he get hooked up with Castillo and Hidalgo?"

"About three years later. He had become quite the revolutionary by then."

"And you?"

She lifted her chin in the dignified way that had once put him off. "I followed my husband until my pregnancy became a burden."

"Oh, God, Elizabeth."

She covered his hand with hers. "I made that choice, Sloan. It was a life I chose when I went with him."

"Elizabeth," he began, and he waited until she looked at him. "Why is such a strong woman so terrified of that man?"

"Are you speaking of me?" she asked. "I'm a very weak woman. Surely you see that." In her shame she glanced away and quietly confessed, "I left my son."

He turned his palm to hers. "He was taken from you, and you were sent away."

"The fact remains—"

"The fact *is* that you are here now in spite of your fear. This is the craziest stunt I've ever seen any woman pull, Elizabeth." His voice grew hoarse. "Every kid's mother should want him that much."

With her free hand, she touched his cheek. She'd watched him shave that morning, and she remembered wondering why he'd gone to such trouble in this situation. With or without stubble, his face invited this gesture. It had become so dear to her.

"I want to make love to you," he whispered. She closed her eyes and gave her head a quick shake. He caught her hand before she withdrew it from his face. "It was your idea to touch me," he said in a low voice. "Don't take that back. I want that."

"You want sex."

"I want to make *love* with you, honey." She shook her head again, and he brought her hand to his mouth and kissed her fingertips. "Why not?" he asked, watching the wildness grow in her eyes. "Tell me why not."

"I couldn't stop you. You know that."

"Yes, you could. All it takes is a word."

"Not when you get..." She scanned the wall behind him, looking for a way out.

"Not when I get what?"

"Not when you get angry," she whispered. "There's nothing that can stop you then."

"And what would I do if I got angry?"

She risked a glance at his face. "You might hurt me. If I didn't do... what you wanted."

McQuade held both her hands, caressing her palms. He struggled to remain outwardly calm. "What do you think I'd want you to do?"

"I don't know," she managed. "I don't remember."

"You don't remember?"

"I couldn't respond," she said quickly. "I hated...I hated..."

"It's okay," he encouraged. "Tell me what you hated."

"It. *Him*. Everything, everything, everything..." She doubled over as if in pain, and he pulled her into his lap. Against her will, she put her arms around him and buried her face against the side of his neck. "I hate myself for being so weak, but I want you to hold me."

"That's not a weakness."

"It is when you want someone else to take care of you, to protect you from—"

"From what?"

"From a choice I made." She tightened her hold on him. "Just hold me," she begged. He did, and she relished the feel of his strength.

"Tell me the rest, Elizabeth."

"I can't."

"You have to tell someone," he said gently. "It's eating you up inside."

"I don't want you to know how weak I am, Sloan." Her voice had become a small thing, and the wind outside seemed to drown it out. But McQuade would have heard had she only mouthed the words. "I don't want you to be disgusted."

"Disgusted?" He was lost in her pain and couldn't think of the right words. "I'm no saint, honey. Why would I be... ? Whatever it was, it wasn't your fault."

"If I told you . . . in your mind, you would see me as—"

"Honey, it doesn't matter," he insisted.

"—totally debased. It matters."

Though she shed no tears, he held her close to his chest and rocked her as if she were crying in torrents. He was afraid his own tears would break loose if he uttered even a single word. Finally she squirmed in his grip. "I have a terrible fear of being smothered," she confided, and his embrace slackened, though he continued to hold her. "If I cried out, he would cover my nose and mouth with his hand or a pillow or something. I blacked out sometimes. He always seemed to know how far he could go without killing me, without breaking a bone or scarring my face. He said . . . he promised he would never scar my face."

McQuade took a deep breath and exhaled slowly. He couldn't speak.

"You see, Sloan," she whispered. "You don't want to hear any of it. It's disgusting. And weakness—tears and cries for help—those things just bring out more anger in a man."

"Oh, Elizabeth," he groaned. Hot pain warred inside him with cold rage, and he felt almost disoriented. "*You* are not disgusting, and *you* are not weak. And, God help me, I want to tear that bastard limb from limb."

"No. You must never get near him." She remembered the dream, and she hugged him close. "Please, Sloan. There's too much goodness in you, and none in him."

"Don't you believe that good wins out over bad?"

She gave a heavy sigh. "I did believe that, a long time ago, when I was innocent."

"When you can believe it again—" he kissed her forehead and laid his cheek against it "—then I'm sure the nightmares will stop."

"Do you think so? Then I won't be afraid to be alone in he dark."

He reached behind him and flicked off the flashlight. She ook a deep breath and held on tight.

"It's dark, and you're not alone," he assured her. "You're not alone at all. You've got good ol' McQuade ere."

"Sloan," she said softly.

He chuckled. "Sloan. Right. Who'd have thought it? But f you say I'm good, hell, I'll believe it. And I'm gonna beat he hell out of Rodolfo Guerrero."

Chapter 7

Chapter 7

Sloan held Elizabeth through the night, while outside the hurricane did its worst. By midmorning they were enjoying the eye of the storm, a couple of hours of relative calm. The wind was still strong, but they were able to venture outside to wash themselves and get a breath of fresh air. Trees had been uprooted, and the stream had overflowed its banks.

They didn't talk about the destruction the sea must have caused in the low-lying areas. They didn't speculate about conditions in La Primavera and El Gallo, nor did they venture to guess whether there would even be a boat to get them off the island. It occurred to Elizabeth that she might owe Sloan an apology since "his" fisherman had come through for them and "her" pilot had not. It occurred to Sloan that his lack of judgment in allowing Elizabeth to hire Ronnie Harper probably deserved some mention. The girl had probably been scared out somehow. He should have known that cute little tomboy wasn't up to this kind of a job. But neither of them spoke of Ronnie. Neither wanted to risk an argument. This was only the eye of the storm, and there was more violence to come.

Elizabeth found some undamaged breadfruit and coconuts near the fallen trees that had produced them. Fresh delicacies hadn't seemed important before the storm hit, because they'd been able to go to the village, but they craved them now. They hadn't planned to spend this much time in the ruins. The hit-and-run that McQuade had envisioned was not to be.

When the storm unleashed its fury once more, McQuade looked for ways to keep his hands busy. He cleaned weapons that were already clean and smoked the rest of his cigarettes. He put his hands into his pockets and paced. When he found himself craving another cigarette, he shoved a stick of gum into his mouth and paced some more. Finally he let himself take an interest in the activity Elizabeth had going in the middle of the floor. Along with the fruit, she'd gathered some palm fronds, and she was making something with them.

"Would you like some gum?" he offered as he squatted beside her on the sleeping bags. She looked almost content, if not happy, and he thought he might bribe her to include him.

"I wondered when you'd offer. Thank you."

He stretched out across from her, propping himself on an elbow. "God, I hate this dead time. So what are you up to?"

"I'm weaving a hat. I thought you might like a souvenir of your vacation on De Colores."

"Hell of a vacation. Rained the whole time we were there." He watched her work the palms, weaving them in and out as a circular form took shape. "How do you do that?"

She moved over a little, setting the whole process up under his nose. She demonstrated the basic pattern, and then indicated that he should give it a try. "Do you think your guns are clean enough yet?" she asked.

"The whole arsenal's in great shape," he told her. "I would be, too, if I weren't going stir-crazy. Show me that part again. Like this?"

Her long fingers manipulated the palm leaves, pausing for him to follow, and then went through the motions slowly once more.

"I've got it now," he told her. She let him take over so she could start another one. "Think we could go into the hat business?" he said, snapping his gum with the confident grin of a kid showing off for his coach.

Elizabeth smiled down at her project. "It depends on how long we're stuck in this cave."

"Hey, we could do cave paintings," he suggested, his voice on the rise. "That's how the cavemen spent the winter. What could we use for paint?"

"What did the cave dwellers use?"

"Hell, I don't know—berry juice, clay, blood, maybe." His eyes lit up. "Iguana blood! We'll set a trap."

"This stir-craziness seems to bring out your primitive instincts."

"No kidding." He glanced up, wondering whether she knew how close to the truth she was, but she kept working. "Listen to that wind out there, Elizabeth. Imagine how that must've sounded to a caveman."

"About the same way it sounds to me."

He watched her for a moment and then tried to remember whether he was looping over or under. "So they found something to distract themselves, like making spears, arrows, babies—stuff like that."

"Be careful, Sloan." She raised a prim eyebrow. "You promised to remain as cool as a fruitcake. No Freudian slips, please." She gestured vaguely in his direction. "Keep that part up."

His youthful innocence had vanished, and he gave her a slow, glittering grin. "That's just the trouble, honey. Why do you think I've been wearing a hole in the carpet?"

She reached for the end of the frond he held in his hand. "This," she directed with exaggerated patience. "Up. This loops under." He was still grinning at her. "You're absolutely outrageous, Sloan McQuade."

"You've heard of the spears and arrows of outrageous fortune?"

"*Slings* and arrows," she corrected.

"No way, lady. This is my Freudian slip, caveman style, which calls for *spears*." She shook her head, but he thumped his bare chest with his fist in triumph. He had her laughing. "Let's sacrifice an iguana and paint the walls with naked women wearing palm hats. Otherwise I'm about to become as nutty as a cucumber."

"Cucumbers aren't nutty, not even American cucumbers." McQuade rolled over on his back and gave his whole body over to laughter. "I ought to know," Elizabeth insisted. "I had them by the dozens in Miami."

"Did you, now?" He rolled his head and grinned up at her. "You're playing with me, aren't you? I love it."

She offered a coy smile. "I'm teaching you to weave hats, but you're a very inattentive pupil."

"You're right." Affecting seriousness, he sat up and attended to what he was doing. "We've got to get this done before winter sets in. Probably won't need too many spears and arrows."

"Not with the automatic revolver and whatnot."

"*Semi*automatic *pistol*, and who's an inattentive pupil?" A light dawned in his eyes. "Hey, that's what we should do!" Tossing her hat aside, he reached for his backpack. "How about a munitions lesson? I want you to be able to load and fire the .38."

Her hands stilled as she watched him take a handful of bullets from a box, arrange them in a row in front of him, and then bring out the revolver. "I don't think I want to," she said quietly.

He glanced up at her and dismissed her objection. "Look, if I have some confidence in your ability to protect yourself, I can concentrate on protecting Tomás. Make sense?" With a sigh, she nodded. He patted the place beside him on their pallet. "Come on over here, then." He adjusted the beam from the flashlight while she settled next to him.

With a click of the release, the cylinder swung into his hand. "Slide the cartridges into the chambers, slick and easy. You get six shots, see? This is the safety. It's on now, so you can't shoot anybody. Off, it's ready to fire." He glanced up to see whether she was following him. Satisfied that she was he continued, manipulating each feature as he explained its purpose. "You use the ejection rod to unload the cartridges, like this. You always check to see if it's loaded, even if you think you're sure. You don't take my word for it, or rely on your memory. You check it out. Understand? I don't want you to hurt yourself with this thing." She nodded. "Okay, load it yourself, then, just like I showed you."

He handled the weapon as easily as he would a bottle of bourbon, but in her hands it became a delicate object, a piece of fragile equipment. She went through the motions carefully, and he decided she might be able to return fire half an hour after somebody had shot at her. She worked at it for a while, and then they took a break, trading their gum for the taste of coconut milk. Returning to the lesson, he made her repeat the loading process until she could do it in a matter of seconds. When she no longer handled the revolver as though she were trying to balance a handful of fresh eggs, it was time for step two.

"Now for some target practice," McQuade announced.

Elizabeth scowled at him. "I'm not shooting this thing in here."

"Unload it, and show a little respect. It's a revolver, not a thing, and it could save your life. Or mine, or Tomás's, if you're covering us." The stony look he gave her made her shiver. They were no longer playing. "We're all in this together, and we can't afford the luxury of being squeamish."

"I am not squeamish. I'm just..." She squared her shoulders as she snapped the empty cylinder into place and checked the safety. Then she lifted both her chin and her gun hand purposefully. "I need a target," she said, looking toward the doorway.

He aimed the smaller of the two flashlights at the wall, and then he moved behind her. "Are you right-eyed or left-eyed?" he asked. She turned a frown his way. "I suppose you wouldn't know that, huh? Let's close the left and sight down the barrel with the right. Both arms straight, the left supports the right. This is the sight, right here." He touched the metal tab on the nose of the barrel and steadied her arm. "You can pull the hammer back with your thumb for more accuracy, or just use the trigger. Try it."

She cocked the hammer and pulled the trigger, producing an empty click. He wasn't satisfied. "Just squeeze with your finger, honey, not your whole hand. When you fire, it makes a lot of noise, because it has a short barrel, but it won't recoil too much, because it's a small-caliber weapon. You have to be fairly close to the target. Try again."

He enjoyed laying his cheek next to hers, sighting down the barrel with her, taking physical control and leading her step by step. He got her to stand up and go through the process again. "Just squeeze with your finger," he repeated. "You're not milking a cow. Deep breath and hold it. Do it like you mean it. This isn't a toy."

He would have liked to be a toy in her hands himself about then. She was beginning to relax with the weapon and move smoothly, and that excited him. If she would only squeeze him instead, he could promise he wouldn't recoil. He bit off the suggestion he wanted to make by nuzzling delicately at her jaw, just beneath her ear. "You're doing great," he muttered.

"It's not so bad," she decided, examining the .38 once more. His breath felt deliciously warm against her neck. As long as he stood behind her that way, she would have practiced until her arms fell off.

"Of course, it *is* unloaded," he admitted.

"And the target is only a beam of light. If it were a man . . ."

"If the man had a gun, Elizabeth, and if it were pointed at you—" he took her shoulders in his hands and turned her to face him "—or Tomás, or even me . . ."

"I would have to shoot, wouldn't I? I would have no choice." No choice, she thought, wondering if such a situation truly existed. "Does it make it any easier later, when you think back on it, to know you did it because you had to?"

He wanted to freeze the moment. His answer would have come easily if she'd asked if he'd ever killed a man. That he had, was a matter of record. But she'd asked him how he felt about it, and the answer to that wasn't on record anywhere—yet.

"It's never easy to think back on it," he confessed quietly.

"How do you ever know? When you look back, how do you know that you *had* to do something?" He hung his head, and she knew he didn't have the answer, either. "If our lives were in danger," she ventured. "Tomás's, yours, or mine..."

"You could use it, then?"

"I think so." She looked up at him, and, just for a moment, he saw past her eyes and into her soul. "When something unspeakable must be done, we block it out, and we go through the motions to survive." She touched his cheek. "Don't we, Sloan?"

"Yeah. I guess we do."

He took the revolver from her hand and studied it while unwelcome images, some vivid, some shadowy, flickered through his mind. He'd lived thirty-six years, and he'd done his share of living. There was a lot he didn't like thinking about, a lot he wouldn't tell her, because he wouldn't want her thinking about it, either. Tucking the .38 into the back of his waistband, he looked down at her again, his eyes mirroring that touchstone of the human condition, the skeleton that rattled in every mind's closet. He understood now that it was enough to be able to admit to another person simply that it was there. He didn't need the details of her memories, and she didn't his.

"I don't spend too much time looking back anymore," he told her. "I know it sounds like that's easy to say. It's not." He lifted her chin in his cupped hand. "You've got your nightmares. I've got mine. But I'd gladly kill that bastard, Guerrero, and take on another one if it would set your mind free."

"That's not the answer," she whispered. "Just get me my son."

"I will. And then what? That's not the only answer, is it?"

"I don't know what you mean."

"Yes, you do. There's more to this nightmare of yours, and we need another answer." He drew her into his arms and lowered his head, promising, "I'm damn well gonna find it."

He took her to their bed and made her dizzy with his kisses, but he made no demands as he held his needs in check. His lips moved over hers slowly, savoring her like a discriminating gourmet. Her lips parted for him, and the kiss sweetened. Oh, she was good. But he told himself it was enough just to touch her, to have her reach around him of her own volition and lay her cool hands on his back. He knew the answer he was looking for lay in giving, not making demands.

She stilled his hand when he unbuttoned the top button on her shirt, but he bade her, "Trust me. I just want to kiss you, honey. I just want to touch you and give you pleasure."

"There is no—"

"Yes, there is. Let me show you." He waited until she released his hand, and then he freed her breasts, caressed them, kissed them, made them harden with need. It was impossible not to touch her gently. Her femininity made his masculine protectiveness surge to the fore. He would let no harm come to her, least of all at his own hands, and she would learn that no part of his attentions needed to be dreaded. Then she would respond to him fully, and, please, God, she would respond without fear.

She moaned, and his name on her lips became a plea. For what? For more? For mercy? His body reminded him of his own needs, and he struggled to contain them. He loved a challenge; scaling the wall of Elizabeth's fear was the ultimate test. Each time he touched her in a new place, she stiffened against him.

"Easy, baby," he whispered when she stopped him from unzipping her jeans. "It doesn't have to hurt. Let me show you."

She shut her eyes tight against the war going on inside her. His gentle touch was an alien thing, but it claimed to be her body's friend. Her senses were not to be believed, she decided. She had to get away from him, yet she wanted to become part of him. Experience had taught her to be still, to endure. But an untried part of her wanted to enjoy.

"Don't try to prove anything," she ground out. "Just get it over with."

Something inside him was angry. Something else was hurt, and something was sad. He moved past all those things, because caring consumed all else and gave him power over his impulses. Pressing himself against her hip, he let her feel his need while managing to deal with it in his own head. Her need was greater.

"Get it over with? Put your arms around my neck, and I will," he promised. When she complied, he whispered, "Kiss me, and I will." She opened her lips to his kiss as he slid his hand under her jeans and over her belly. He found soft fabric, softer skin, and the contrasting coarseness that protected the place he most wanted to touch. Skilled fingers made her moist, made her moan against his mouth, made her arch into his hand and call his name. The plea was unmistakable this time.

"Come to me, sweetheart." He watched her. Her eyes were closed, but the tension drained from her face as she gave herself over to him. She was lovely.

"It feels . . . oh, Sloan . . ."

"Good," he whispered, and he kissed the corner of her mouth. "It's good."

Her arms tightened around his neck, and she affirmed, "It's good."

"You want me to... get it over with?"

"No," she breathed. Then, "Yes! It's too..."

"Too good? Go with it, honey. I'm with you... all the way."

"Too good," she said, and her overwhelming shudder took her with him. The smell of her, the feel of what was happening under his hand, the flushed beauty of her face, gave his body leave to share. Ordinarily he might have cursed. Tonight he kissed the woman who had given him more than pleasure. She had trusted him.

"That's never happened before," she said shyly.

He smoothed her hair back from her face. "It will again. I promise. When you're ready."

"But what about you? What did you get?"

"I don't have to 'get.' I want you to give."

"What if I can't?"

Smiling, he slipped an arm beneath her shoulders and lay down, holding her in his arms. "Too late. You already have."

The rain ceased, and the wind blew itself out by midmorning. The rushing stream chased the effects of inertia from McQuade's body and made his skin tingle. For Elizabeth, a heightened awareness of her skin's sensitivity had blossomed hours before. She was afraid to speak of it lest she lose it in the light of day. The cold water brought delicious renewal.

Now she faced a day of reckoning. The trek down the mountainside bred pure dread. It was as if huge jaws had torn the lush tropical island to shreds and spat it out in a shambles. Many buildings had been damaged, some totally razed to the ground. McQuade watched as Elizabeth took everything in, and he shared her fears in silence. They reached the road to El Gallo, and at a spot that had once been a picturesque overlook, they stopped to survey the town.

The cantina looked unscathed, as did the sturdier structures—the community center, the one small store in town and a few of the houses. But the rest—the storage Quonset, the tin-roofed huts—were all in varied states of destruction. So much of the vegetation was in shreds that it looked as though a herd of huge beasts had grazed there.

At the sound of an approaching vehicle, they dove into the brush for cover. A truckload of armed soldiers rumbled by them. When it had passed, Elizabeth moved to stand, but McQuade caught her arm. They waited while two jeeps and another truck sped by. After several quiet minutes had lapsed, McQuade turned his attention to El Gallo again. He realized that it was now crawling with soldiers.

"Elizabeth," he began, "I'm taking you back to the ruins. I want you to wait there for me."

"I'm going with you."

Her chin was high, and her jaw was set. He knew she wasn't going to make this easy. "If we're picked up, you can forget about rescuing your son. If I'm alone and I'm picked up, I've got Red Cross identification and people who'll vouch for me." He took her by the shoulders and made her look at him. "You agreed to do as I said, and I'm saying you can't go down there. I'll check in with Emilio and see if he's still got a boat. Then I'll find Tomás." She lowered her eyes, doubting him, and he tightened his grip on her. "I swear I will. For God's sake, have some faith in me."

"I do," she said softly. "If it can be done, you'll do it."

"It can be done. This won't be easy on you, I know, but you'll have to wait—" he cast a glance at the mountain "—up there."

"Sloan—"

"You're going to handle this, honey, and I'm going to know you're safe. I'll get Emilio to pick us up on the other side of the mountain, where he let us off."

"What if his boat was damaged by the storm?"

"I'll find another one." He knew he was asking her to believe the myth that he could work miracles. Right now, he needed to believe it himself. "I'm taking you back. You with me?"

On impulse, she slid her arms around his waist and held him close. His arms came around her, too, just for a moment, and then he said, "Let's go."

Leaving her at the ruins wasn't any easier on McQuade than it was on Elizabeth. She kissed him hard before he set out again, and the desperation in that gesture shook him. She was counting on him. He'd always taken his jobs seriously, but he took this one to heart. The loss of his objectivity put a new wrinkle in the execution of his plan. Ordinarily he reserved the option of pulling out when the risk factor became too overwhelming. This time he knew damn well he was going in without allowing himself that option.

He was challenged by two soldiers when he entered the village, but his Red Cross identification got him past them. Outside the cantina he ran into Emilio.

"I am getting ready to leave, McQuade. According to the reports, the hurricane bypassed Arco Iris and is headed for Florida."

McQuade clamped a hand on the shorter man's husky shoulder. "That must mean *La Paloma* is still seaworthy."

"My brother and I beached her before the storm hit," Emilio told him. "He was going to help me scrape her hull in return for a load of fish. She was in a sheltered place."

McQuade cast his eyes heavenward and grinned. "Somebody up there likes me."

"But we're putting out to sea before the army decides to confiscate her. So many of the boats here were destroyed."

"Listen, Emilio, I'm going to make you a rich man." Emilio made a move to back away, but McQuade tightened his grip. "I'm going over to La Primavera to find the child we came here for. Elizabeth is waiting for me on the mountain. You meet us in the same spot where you dropped us off. Pick us up about midnight. You'll have to paddle ashore for us. Do you have another raft?"

"I can get one," he said hesitantly. "A child?"

McQuade nodded. "It means his life, Emilio." The man who anticipated becoming a father was not about to refuse. "I'll help you get your boat out of here, *amigo*."

Within another hour McQuade was on his way to La Primavera. He'd seen Emilio's fishing boat safely out to sea and had secured a pack of cigarettes from the cantina as an afterthought. He avoided roads, but every moment was precious now. He couldn't expect Emilio to risk waiting for them, and there was so much to do by midnight. He found a town that was reeling from the shock of a hard blow to the gut. People were picking through the rubble of what, just days before, had been an easygoing life-style. Soon they would pull together and begin licking their communal wounds, but now they were dazed.

The army was out in force. McQuade had to produce his identification twice as he made his way through the narrow streets toward the address he'd been given for Maria Adelfa, Tomás's nurse. He had the child carrier in his pocket and his pistol tucked at his back in the waistband of his pants.

A police car cruised by, announcing over its loudspeaker a five o'clock curfew and the locations of shelters for those whose homes had been destroyed. The officer slowed for a second look at the tall Anglo whose short-sleeved bush jacket billowed behind him. The policeman was looking for potential looters, and the jacket could easily be concealing a weapon. He paused to get a look at the man's face. Then he smiled.

"McQuade! *¿Qué pasa?* This is no time for a vacation, *amigo*. The bars are all closed."

"Hey, Felipe! I forgot to check the weather report before I came down here." McQuade remembered the young man as one who had generally been on cussing terms with the law, but he'd also usually been good for cheap bits of information. The car crawled along beside him as McQuade continued to walk. Felipe was apparently anxious for a friendly chat, and McQuade didn't want to arouse any suspicions. "How the hell did you get into a cop's uniform?"

The man shrugged. "New government, new opportunities. What brings you down this time of year, McQuade? You know it's hurricane season."

"Came in with a load of Red Cross supplies." At least it had started out that way, he thought. "My pilot took a powder. Cute little redhead—keeps her hair tucked up under a baseball cap. Ronnie Harper. What do you know about her?"

"Not a thing, man. Maybe she took off with a load of something a little hotter than Red Cross supplies."

"Nah, I doubt it." He'd considered that possibility, too, but he'd rejected it simply because he refused to be that wrong. They were nearing the Red Cross office, where he hoped he'd find the one woman in the world he knew damn well he could count on. "This looks like my stop, Felipe. I'll try to stay out of trouble."

"You do that." He lowered his voice and leaned out the window. "If you're doing any snooping around, Mc-Quade, my advice is—don't."

McQuade stood to watch the patrol car pull out into the street and continue on its way before he ducked into the Red

Cross office. It was busy, but he managed to corner the small, gray-haired lady who was in charge and spirit her into the back room before she could sputter her initial question too loudly.

"McQuade! What are you doing here?"

He closed the door to the little room he'd used more than once as his office in De Colores. He and Dorothy had an understanding: she gave him a legitimate reason to be there, one that was seldom questioned, and he helped her with her list of concerns, which generally involved detainees or missing persons.

"As far as the government is concerned, I'm working with you guys," he said. "I flew in on a puddle jumper before the storm hit," he lied.

"And why are you really here?"

He could see the worry in her face, and he knew some of it was for him. Dorothy liked to think of herself as an adoptive mother, and of McQuade as one of her many children. "What's it been like here since Castillo died?" he asked.

"Everything's happened so fast. First Castillo, then Hidalgo. I see more uniforms every day. If you're up to something Guerrero might take exception to..." She shook her head. "But then, he takes exception to everything. There are new directives every day, and he declared martial law the day Colonel Hidalgo was assassinated. Don't do anything foolish, McQuade."

"I'm here to find a kid for his mother."

Dorothy's eyes widened. "Not...not Guerrero's child? The mother was—"

"Exiled. Right. I need a favor."

"McQuade—"

He held up his hand. "Just leave the back door unlocked. If the kid objects to keeping company with me, I

may need a sedative for him. Will you handle it for me?"
Dorothy hesitated. "The kid needs his mother, Dorothy.
And Elizabeth needs him."

The very act of uttering her name had softened Mc-
Quade's normally stony face.

"I take it this Elizabeth has become important to you."

"She's a client," McQuade claimed.

The woman gave him a maternal smile. "Uh-uh, Mc-
Quade. This is Dorothy, who knows you well."

He rolled his eyes and tried to shrug her concern off, but
she wasn't buying. "Okay, yeah, this job's different. Without that kid, she'll never be able to—" McQuade shook his
head, hoping to clear it of emotion. "She left her son, but
she's gone to a lot of trouble to come after him. There isn't
much time, Dorothy, and we need your help."

She took a small ring of keys from her pocket and handed
him one. "I'll watch out for you," she promised. "But a
man carrying a crying child shouldn't arouse too much suspicion out there. People have been bringing them in all day."

Bouncing the key in his hand, he tossed her a wink.
"Thanks, beautiful."

Several blocks from the Red Cross office, McQuade
found Maria Adelfa's house, or what was left of it. The roof
had caved in, and at the sight of the wreckage, McQuade's
chest nearly did the same. He stepped over a piece of picket
fence, dreading what he might find behind the door.

"Señor McQuade!"

The voice came from around the corner of the house.
Dusk was falling on the tattered island, and McQuade
turned to peer into the shadows of what had been a small
garden. He saw a woman looking at him. He immediately
recognized her as Juanita, Maria's housekeeper and Chi
Chi's friend.

"Antonio sent me. I was here when we evacuated, but I went home to El Gallo right after the storm."

"Evacuated? Where?"

"Maria's daughter lives in a house made of poured concrete," she told him. "She took the boy there."

McQuade glanced at the wreckage and shuddered. "Guerrero doesn't care much what happens to his kid, does he? Why didn't he take them to the palace?"

Juanita shrugged. "Maria always goes to her daughter's at the first sign of bad weather. Guerrero might not even know where they are."

Things were looking up, McQuade decided. If he got a move on, he might make it to the boat on time. "Show me the way, Juanita."

Halfway there, Juanita spotted an old woman hurrying down the street with a child bundled in her arms. It was nearly dark, but the woman's familiar waddle caught the girl's attention. "That's her!" She ran ahead of McQuade calling, "Maria!"

McQuade followed, pulling Juanita back to his side as they approached the woman. "Let me handle it," he said quietly as he reached inside his jacket for his identification. "Señora Adelfa, I'm with the Red Cross."

While the old woman peered uncomprehendingly at the papers, the child in her arms studied McQuade, who smiled automatically. Tomás, he thought. Elizabeth's Tomás. Eyes like big black saucers gave a look that said, "So, who are you, mister?"

"She can't read, *señor*," Juanita said.

McQuade's attention snapped back to the old lady. He pointed to the paper. "Here, can you see the cross? It's past curfew, *señora*. You should return to your daughter's house. I'm afraid yours is . . . heavily damaged."

"My house?" Maria looked up at him, desolation in her voice as she repeated, "My house?"

"I'm sorry, *señora*. I came to get the boy. We're inoculating the children first. Typhoid, you know."

Maria looked at the child as though she weren't certain anymore who he was. "Typhoid?"

"The disease, *señora*. Typhoid. The water system—" The woman turned her blank stare back on McQuade. "*Señora*, I must take the boy to the clinic. His father, the, uh, general—" He glanced at Juanita and knew he had it right. Guerrero had promoted himself. "The general asked me to see to this personally. This is Tomás Guerrero, right?" The old woman nodded. When McQuade reached for the child, Tomás turned away, squealing, but Maria relinquished him automatically, as if she were too stunned by McQuade's news to realize what she was doing.

"My house has been . . . destroyed?" Maria moved past them in a daze, while Tomás squirmed in McQuade's arms and whimpered.

"Go back to your daughter's house, *señora*."

Maria ignored McQuade's instructions. "I'll take her back," Juanita promised. "You take the boy. *Tenga cuidado.*"

"You take care, too," he said. "You forget my name, I'll forget yours."

Tomás's whimpers were turning into pathetic sobs. McQuade kept moving, talking quietly all the while, and by the time he let himself in the back door of the Red Cross building, the sobs were hiccuping little whimpers again.

"Here we go, tiger," McQuade crooned. "We'll get you something to help you sleep, and then I'll take you to your mom. How's that?" He pulled the shade down and turned a desk lamp on. "What else do you need, hmm? What do you wear for shorts?'' A pat on the baby's bottom reassured him. "You're a big boy, huh?''

Dorothy appeared at the door. Tomás reassessed his situation, looking from the strange woman to the man who held him, and decided to bury his face in McQuade's jacket. McQuade's chest tightened, and he chuckled as he covered the child's back with a comforting hand.

"It's okay, son. She's a kindhearted old battle-ax.''

"He won't think so when I give him this.''

McQuade grimaced at the sight of the syringe. "Can't you give him a pill or something?''

"How much time have you got?'' Because she knew the answer, she dug under the boy's blanket and found his thigh. "It'll just take a second. Hold him still.''

Tomás's howl was thin and brief.

"Sorry, tiger. It's all over now. She won't hurt you again.'' McQuade ruffled the thick thatch of soft black hair and glanced at Dorothy. "I need some wide adhesive tape.''

"And a diaper,'' she decided.

"Hey, come on, he's got his pride.'' McQuade looked down at the teary brown eyes. "You wouldn't leak on me, would you?''

"You've got a lot to learn about babies, McQuade.'' But she had the feeling he was willing.

With the sleeping Tomás strapped to his back in the canvas baby carrier, McQuade slipped through the darkened streets of La Primavera and into the bush. He'd put tape over the baby's mouth to muffle any cries, and he moved quietly toward the mountain. As he traveled, he thought of Elizabeth. His night goggles helped him find his way, but it was dark on the mountain, and, even with a flashlight, Elizabeth was bound to be battling her terrors. She had the revolver, and she knew how to use it, but this must have been an awful day for her. She was one gutsy lady, he thought. One beautiful, gutsy lady.

The closer he got, the faster he traveled. Anticipating her joy, he moved on cat feet, eating up ground in stealthy silence. The night breeze was a gentle echo of the howling wind that had passed. The climb became steeper, and he knew he was on the last leg of the journey. Elizabeth would be waiting at the top of the hill, and McQuade was about to make her a very happy woman. That knowledge made his heart feel light enough to float him to the crest of the mountain.

He flew down the stone steps calling her name, but when he reached the entry, he realized there was no light inside. An icy feeling crept over him. He drew out his pistol and his flashlight.

''Elizabeth?''

Except for their belongings, the underground room was empty.

Chapter 8

McQuade carefully searched the area surrounding the ruins. He brought his panic under control and summoned his skills, combing the territory in widening circles as he risked calling Elizabeth's name. She wasn't there, and time was short. She was either in El Gallo or La Primavera. He worked hard to drive the image of Elizabeth in Guerrero's hands from his mind. He had to be able to think straight—with his brain, instead of with his seething gut. More than once she'd reminded him that she was hiring him to get Tomás off the island no matter what else happened. If he was to accomplish that safely, it had to be done now. Once the boy was discovered missing, he would become one hot property.

His slight hope of finding her waiting for him on the beach was dashed by the same waves that washed the empty shoreline. The child he carried on his back still slept as McQuade climbed down from the rocks and searched the dark horizon. The boat was there. He signaled with his flashlight, and the signal was returned. Fifteen minutes later Emilio paddled a rubber raft to within a few yards of the shore, and McQuade waded out to meet him, carrying his pistol high over his head, the child on his back.

"I have a small life jacket for the baby," Emilio announced. "Where's the woman?"

McQuade searched his brain for the least alarming answer as he backed up to the raft. "Take him, Emilio. We got our signals crossed. I have to go back and find her. Can you wait?"

Emilio worked at the straps on the baby carrier. "I've seen one patrol boat already. We cut the engines and drifted, and he turned back. We have to get out while we can."

McQuade stood waist-deep in the water and felt as though he were drowning. "Can you wait just a couple of hours?"

Taking the baby in his arms, Emilio gave his answer gently, knowing what it meant. "For my family's sake, I must refuse, *señor*."

McQuade hauled himself over the raft's inflated rim and tucked the pistol away. "I'll help you get back to the boat. I need to talk to your wife about taking care of Tomás." He supported the sleeping child between his legs while he put the life jacket on him. Emilio watched, impressed by the care the big man took in peeling the tape away from Tomás's mouth.

Cradling the child in the V of his thighs, McQuade took up a paddle. "If you need the raft, you'll have to paddle me back in. I'm in no mood for a midnight swim."

"You're staying?"

"I'm sure as hell not leaving her here."

Elizabeth had put up a valiant struggle against the encroaching underground walls, but they had finally overwhelmed her. Outside, she'd huddled next to a crumbling wall and watched the night draw down and envelop her. Sloan had been gone too long, she decided. Something had gone wrong. She had no idea how long it should have taken, but the waiting had become unbearable. She needed to move, to act against her fears. She knew where Emilio's brother lived, where the boat had been docked and where Maria Adelpha's house was. She dressed in her skirt and blouse, covered her hair with a scarf and returned to El Gallo.

No one would speak of Emilio, and Elizabeth couldn't locate Antonio. Everywhere people were busy sorting through the rubble and tacking their lives back together with hammer and nails. In La Primavera the story was different. Policemen cruised the streets, and soldiers patrolled, but Elizabeth witnessed several acts of looting as she hurried to her destination. There were other witnesses, as well, but, like Elizabeth, they had more pressing matters to attend to. The cries of those whose houses were unprotected were less urgent than of those who were homeless.

Elizabeth heard such a cry as she approached Maria Adelpha's battered house. The old woman's monotonous moaning drifted softly over the ruins. Elizabeth found Maria bent over a hutch that had been overturned by the winds, its contents smashed over what had once been her porch. Elizabeth's heart forgot its own troubles for a moment and yearned toward her great-aunt.

"*Tía*, you mustn't stay here." She reached for Maria's shoulders, but the old woman ignored her, refusing to straighten. "There are thieves running all over the city, *Tía*. It's not safe for you to be here. These things are all broken."

"All broken," Maria echoed. "All gone."

"*Por favor, Tía*. Where is Tomás?"

The old woman stood then and looked at Elizabeth for the first time. Perhaps because there was so little light, she decided it wasn't worth the effort of trying to figure out who the younger woman was. She sighed heavily and gave all her efforts over to the name. "Tomás?"

"The little boy you're caring for. Where is he?"

Maria shook her head slowly. It was too hard to think about these things now. "Some men took him," she said finally.

"Men in uniforms?"

Maria shrugged and bent down to the ground. As she began sifting through unrecognizable pieces once again she repeated, "Some men."

Elizabeth regretted leaving the old woman in the rubble of her home, but her time was growing short. She had no doubt that Guerrero had sent "some men" to get Tomás and take him to the palace. McQuade might have gone there, too. The risk was awful, but she would have to go herself. She could only hope that pandemonium ruled there, as it did in the streets.

Elizabeth kept to the alleys at first. A door flew open as she hurried along, and she jumped behind a rack of garbage cans. She heard a scuffle, and she flattened her back against the cool stucco wall behind her. There were shouts, the report of gunfire and retreating footsteps. When it was quiet again, she ventured forth and found a man's body lying near the open door. Elizabeth turned and ran.

On the street once again, Elizabeth whirled toward the voice on the loudspeaker. She ducked into a doorway as a police car crawled by. The man might be alive, she thought. Someone should be told.

"*¡Escuche!* Listen! The five o'clock curfew is in effect. All citizens must go home or find shelter. Violators will be arrested."

Then she couldn't tell the police. She couldn't allow herself to be arrested. Moving on, Elizabeth dashed from doorway to doorway, taking a few seconds in each one's dark shelter to check behind her and scan ahead. Power for the street lights had obviously been lost, but the night sky was bright with stars, and occasional headlights flooded the street as a patrol car or an army jeep cruised by.

"*¡Ay! ¡Ay!*"

Elizabeth jumped back in shock from the soft thing she'd stepped on in the narrow doorway of a corner shop.

"*¡Discúlpeme, por favor!*" she whispered, begging a pardon from whoever lurked in the shadows.

"Get out of here! This place is mine."

"A man has been shot in the alley back there," Elizabeth said quickly. "I don't know whether he's alive, but—"

"Take your trouble somewhere else, woman. Go on!"

She rounded the corner in terror. A beam of light flashed in her eyes, and she covered her face with her hands.

"Identify yourself."

"M-Maria An-Antonio," Elizabeth managed.

"Prove it."

"I can't. My house is a shambles. I've lost—"

"You are in violation of the curfew."

Elizabeth squinted into the light, trying to see the face that went with the harsh voice, but she saw only the outline of a hat. "I . . . can't find my—"

"We have orders to arrest all violators, *señora.*"

"But I must—" Elizabeth stiffened when the man seized her arm. "*Por favor,*" she whispered desperately.

"As soon as your identity is confirmed, you will be assigned to a shelter," he assured her, his voice softening on a note of sympathy.

"Where are you taking me?"

"To the presidential palace."

Assisted by two young soldiers, Elizabeth climbed into the back of a canvas-topped lorry and took a place among the looters and other curfew violators. She was grateful for the soldier who helped pull her into the truck and then ordered a man to get off the bench so she could sit down. Her knees felt as though they might give way beneath her. Raw terror churned in her stomach and threatened to make her physically ill. No one spoke as the truck lurched into motion. The passengers pitched from side to side each time the obviously inexperienced driver shifted gears, but in the intervals they tried to keep their shoulders from touching. It was dark, and they were all strangers.

The truck was unloaded in the palace courtyard. Elizabeth surveyed her surroundings as she was lifted from the truck by the same soldier who had found her a seat. The courtyard lights were off, but several areas were brightened by battery-operated spotlights. Elizabeth avoided those, immediately seeking a dark corner where several women huddled with their children. She could see light in some of the palace windows, which told her that the emergency generator was working. Were they keeping Tomás in the family wing? she wondered. If so, the best route for her would be through the darkened courtyards and gardens, since the troops seemed to be occupied out here in front.

A booming loudspeaker brought all the bowed heads up. "You will all be questioned in due time. Be prepared to prove your identity."

A stout woman near Elizabeth whined, "I have no identification. My purse was stolen."

"It serves you right!" another returned. "You were too busy stealing from my shop."

"One bracelet, and it was lying out in the street. Here, take the worthless thing."

"No," the shop owner said stubbornly. "It is evidence."

The large woman turned to Elizabeth, holding the gold bracelet out to her. "I *found* it," she insisted. "I didn't steal it."

Elizabeth looked at the shop owner. "If all she took was this, the kind thing would be to take it back and say nothing. We've all suffered enough."

The shop owner eyed the bracelet in the other woman's beefy hand, peered into her round face and then accepted the return of her property. "You'd better stay out of my shop," she muttered as she turned away.

"*Gracias,*" the woman whispered to Elizabeth. "I am Serita Martinez, but I can't prove it. Who are you?"

"I am Maria Antonio, but I can't prove that, either."

Serita looked back over her shoulder and then turned a saucer-eyed look at Elizabeth. "Do you think she'll tell?"

"I don't think so. These are dangerous times, Serita. You must be careful."

Serita nodded sadly. "It was so pretty. If I hadn't picked it up, it might have been kicked into the gutter."

"She's lucky you found it for her."

Offering a tentative smile, Serita asked, "What do you think they'll do to us here?"

"I don't know." But Elizabeth had some idea. She'd been held with a group of detainees almost a year ago, and she remembered how persistently they had been interrogated. Miguel Hidalgo had been alive then, and General Castillo had been in charge. Now there was only Guerrero. Unless she could somehow slip away before she was recognized, she was certain he would kill her.

A little girl in the crowd whimpered.

"Whose child is this?"

"Not mine."

"I don't know. Where's your mother?"

"Are you all by yourself, little one?"

The barrage of questions made the child cry harder, and Elizabeth lifted her into her arms.

"Keep the children quiet!" An officer, threading his way through the crowd, shook a finger at Elizabeth. "The general wants the children quiet."

"Sit down, all of you!"

The gravelly voice pierced Elizabeth's senses, laying her open like a tree struck by a bolt of lightning and exposing her terrorized core to cold fear. She knew that voice well. Along with the others surrounding her, she sat down where she stood, holding the little girl in her lap. Her voice trembled as she buried her face in the child's matted hair and whispered, "Shh, little one. We'll be fine."

"I'm hungry," the girl whined.

"We'll eat soon. We must be very quiet so they'll bring food."

She kept her head down as she watched the tall black boots come toward her. People squirmed to make way, because those boots demanded a path; they would not take the trouble to step over anything. One woman pulled her hand out of their way just in time. The boots were headed straight for Elizabeth. Nausea swirled in her head as she clutched the little girl to her breast.

"I have no time for your petty attempts at trickery," came the guttural warning. "I have no patience with those who take advantage of my generous nature. I gave you a chance."

Oh, God! Staring at the boots, Elizabeth was paralyzed. A blackjack dangled menacingly in the gloved hand that swung near his thigh as he approached. Elizabeth refused to lift her eyes to his terrible face.

The toe of his boot struck her knee as he passed by.

"I assigned a shelter to every area, and I told you to report there by five o'clock. If you're here, it's because you disobeyed that order."

The voice continued to rumble at her back, but it was retreating. The boots were walking away.

"Rations are being distributed at the shelters. You'll get nothing here. Those of you who are charged with looting will find that guilt is easily proved. Think of that while you sit here on your worthless haunches and await my pleasure."

For several moments Elizabeth could not move. The child in her arms seemed to sense that becoming invisible was necessary for survival, and she, too, sat very still. Finally Elizabeth allowed herself one deep breath, and then another. Suddenly a hand touched her shoulder, and she squeezed her eyes shut and prayed for one more act of deliverance.

"I believe this is the woman, captain. I recognize the scarf."

Sloan! His deep, rich voice could have been a choir of angels singing. She lifted her head slowly and looked up into gray eyes that lit with joy when he saw her face. "Yes, this is the one. Please come with me, *señora*."

He extended his hand, and she laid hers in his warm palm. "In her confusion she ran from us," McQuade explained to the captain. "Her house was demolished, and most of her family was killed. She's totally disoriented."

Elizabeth caught his meaningful look and said nothing as she rose to her feet.

"This isn't your child, *señora*," he told her as he took the little girl from her arms and handed her to a woman sitting nearby. "We've found your baby. He's safe."

She looked at him, and her eyes filled with tears. It was as though fear had left her with a hangover, and she wasn't sure she understood what was being said, but she fastened her hopes on his dear face. McQuade nodded, smiling. "I'll take you to him."

He turned to the captain. "We have her child at the Red Cross office. He's an infant, in need of his mother."

"I can see that this isn't a criminal case," the captain said. "Allow me to escort you to the gate."

As she turned to leave, the little girl called her back with a cry of, "Mama!"

Elizabeth wrenched her whole body toward the cry, but McQuade put his arm around her shoulders and pulled her along. "No, *señora*. This is no time to look back. Your son is waiting."

Tomás! her heart sang. Could he really be telling her that he had located her son? She covered her face with her hands and let her head drop against McQuade's chest as he led her through the crowd. Guerrero could neither see her nor touch her, she thought. She had magic. She had a miracle! She had McQuade.

He flashed his identification at the gate, shook hands with the captain and was hustling Elizabeth across the street when they overheard another announcement from the loud-speaker.

"General Guerrero's son is missing. Male Anglos are to be arrested and brought to the palace for questioning."

The captain turned toward the courtyard long enough for McQuade to duck around the corner, dragging Elizabeth, who had paused in confusion just as the captain had.

"Sloan! Tomás is missing."

"No kidding." Keeping up a steady jog, he switched her hand to his left and pulled the Browning from under his jacket with his right.

"You already have him, then! Where—"

"Shut up, sweetheart, and run like hell!"

They heard shouts behind them, but they didn't look back. Like all small island towns, La Primavera provided a maze of winding back streets. McQuade and Elizabeth soon discovered what the looters already knew: rubble provided good cover. They could only be followed on foot, and their pursuers had gotten a late start.

They hid in a building with a partially collapsed roof until the searchers moved on. Then McQuade led Elizabeth down a dark side street. They were about to dash across the main thoroughfare when a police car came screeching around the corner. McQuade fired two shots, smashing both headlights. The driver put the car in reverse and rapidly disappeared around the same corner.

After they dashed on and took refuge in another alley, McQuade allowed himself a chuckle. "Cop, hell. Felipe's still looking out for number one."

"Sloan, please tell me—"

"Tomás is safe." He glanced back over his shoulder. "You go ahead and let me cover the rear. Hundred-yard dash, honey, all the way to the end of this alley."

Elizabeth hiked up her skirt and let herself go, sailing over all the hurdles in her path. She slowed down when the end of the winding street was in sight, and she turned to find McQuade close behind. He jimmied the lock on the back door of the last shop and ushered her inside.

"I know this place," he explained as he closed the door and locked it. They were both breathing hard. Elizabeth peered into the dark room and realized that it was a bar. "It's always been a cozy port in a storm. Looks like it weathered this one pretty well."

"We're not stopping for a drink, are we?"

McQuade grinned as he flicked the safety on his pistol and tucked it behind his back. "They keep all the good stuff downstairs. Come on."

"McQuade!"

Despite the urge to protest, she followed him through the back room to a basement stairway. It was pitch-dark. She grabbed his arm, and he produced a flashlight. The storage room at the foot of the stairs was filled with liquor boxes, cases of beer, and small, scurrying wildlife. McQuade flashed the light at the unfinished ceiling and disturbed a tiny lizard.

"Hope my buddy, Ed, still keeps his key in the same spot." He found the niche in the floor joist above him and felt around until he sounded a delighted, "Bingo!"

The key opened the lock on another door, which McQuade also secured behind them. Beyond that door was a long passageway filled with kegs and racks of bottles. McQuade gestured with a flourish and announced, "The good stuff."

"Sloan—"

He moved slowly along the passageway, taking careful survey of the racks. "You like really good wine? How about some Château something-or-other?"

"Sloan, where is Tomás?" Elizabeth demanded.

McQuade couldn't suppress his grin. He felt as though he had a great big gift-wrapped box waiting for her under the Christmas tree. "Emilio's got him. Am I a miracle worker, or what?"

"Oh, Sloan." He spread his arms for her, and she went to him gladly. "You are a wonder." She raised her head quickly. "But it's after midnight!"

"And *La Paloma* is on its way to Arco Iris with your son on board. Of course, we're not putting up any signs to advertise the fact." His grin faded as he noted the smudges of fatigue under her bewitching eyes. "What happened, Elizabeth? Why didn't you wait for me?"

She laid her cheek against his shoulder. "I waited forever. I was sure something had gone wrong. Without you there, it was so quiet up on that mountain." She lifted her head again. "Are you sure it was him?"

"Juanita and I found old Maria on the street. I told her I was taking him to the clinic for shots." He laughed, remembering the way Tomás had hung on to him when Dorothy walked into the room. "He's a real cute kid."

She hugged him again. "Now how will we get out of here?"

"I'll think of something. Most of the troops have been pulled back from the village to La Primavera, so I think we'll head for El Gallo." He slid his hand over her bottom. "With me covering the rear."

"You're outrageous," she reminded him.

"Nicest rear I ever covered. Although I oughta paddle it for not staying put." She gave him a wary glance. He hastened to add, "But that's pretty far down on my list of priorities of things to do with you." The warmth in his smile made her stomach do a cartwheel. He shrugged. "I'd be about as effective at paddling as Felipe is at being a cop. Did you see him gunning the car down the street in reverse?"

"You knew the policeman in that car?"

McQuade laughed. "Yeah, I knew him. *Well.*" Sobering, he touched her cheek. "Antonio will find us another boat. We'll be out of here before you get fully geared up for a good worry."

"But so many of the boats were damaged by the storm."

"He'll find us one. You don't know Antonio."

She touched his chin in return. "I know you."

He swallowed, and his voice dropped to an intimate level. "I was scared I wouldn't find you."

"You should have gone on Emilio's boat with Tomás."

He shook his head. "No way."

"If you were with him—" she laid her hands on his unshaven cheeks and looked into his eyes "—I would know he was safe. I would know . . . he would have a good life with you. You take your job ser—"

His mouth came down hard on hers, and she rose to meet his kiss with open lips and a welcoming tongue. He hadn't left her. She indulged herself, rejoicing in that fact. She reveled in the kiss that promised to wipe away fear and pain, and in the touch of hands that would not, *could* not, hurt her. He held the flashlight against her back as he spread his other hand over her bottom and pressed her into him. She arched, rubbing against him like a cat, and he groaned.

"How long can we stay here?" she whispered when he lifted his head. Her pulse pounded, and she was short of breath.

He looked down at her and saw the invitation in her eyes. Her need was as great as his. He closed his eyes and gave his head a quick shake. "We can't stay. We have to get to the village by daybreak."

He moved to put her away from him, but she held him tighter. "Why did we come in here?"

Drawing an unsteady breath, he smoothed her hair back from her temple and kissed her there. "This passage takes us across the street to another bar, owned by the same guy— Ed—" his explanation was punctuated with soft kisses feathered over her forehead "—this guy I know. We're near the edge of town, and, honey, I'm damn near the edge of my sanity."

"I want to know more of you, Sloan." She closed her eyes against the tears that burned to be shed, not from fear, but from a need she'd never experienced before. "If we're caught after we leave here, I never will."

For a moment he just held her. He was afraid to move, afraid to breathe, because the emotion that had suddenly filled him might spill out. Slowly he took her face in his hands and made her look at him.

"Then we can't get caught." His voice was hoarse with feeling, but he managed a smile. "Because when we make love, we're going to take our time, Elizabeth. We're going to get to know each other very, very well."

"You'd made love to me already," she whispered, her throat burning, too. "In a way."

"I can do better than that," he promised. "We'll make it, honey. You have to believe we'll make it." He clearly intended his prophecy to include all the promises for the future it could possibly hold. She closed her eyes and nodded. "Ready for the home stretch?"

"I'm ready."

"That's my girl." With an arm around her shoulders, McQuade led Elizabeth through the dark, bottle-lined passageway. "Ever gone barhopping underground? Some setup, huh? Ed'll have a fit when he finds the door locked and no key around." He gave her a gentle squeeze. "Take it easy, honey. Just take it easy. Don't cry."

Elizabeth dropped her head against his chest as they walked. She let the tears slip silently down her cheeks, amazed that he knew she was crying even in the dark, even though she had made no sound. She had lived in emotional isolation for a long time, but she found that she could keep nothing from this man. And nothing she gave him seemed to turn him against her. Their plane and their boat had both left, and Sloan was still there. She had messed up his plan, but he hadn't gotten angry. He had found her and delivered her from the jaws of her worst nightmare. He was almost too good to be true.

"Here we are," he announced when they reached another door. "Heaven's Gate. I think that's the name of this place." There was another storage room on the far side and, next to it, a stairway. McQuade turned the flashlight off when they reached the top.

"We're only a couple of back streets away from the edge of town." Moonlight from the window drew a halo over the top of Elizabeth's head. Smiling, McQuade touched it. "I don't suppose you've frequented these alleys much."

"I have an idea where we are," she told him.

"There's a little farm on the outskirts near here, and then we hit the boondocks." He peered out the window at the quiet street. "I think we lost 'em. Ready?"

She squeezed his hand. "I'm ready."

They made their way quickly and quietly through the back alleys and ran when they reached a small orchard at the edge of town. Secreting themselves in the tropical underbrush, they doubled back and headed for El Gallo.

Chapter 9

"You should be gone from here, *amigo*." Antonio shook his head in reproach. "Long gone." He hadn't minded being dragged out of bed before dawn—working with private investigators meant being ready for anything—but he'd hoped McQuade had gotten himself and his charges safely off the island by this time.

"Yeah, well, things got a little complicated, and we missed the boat." For Elizabeth's sake, McQuade shrugged off Antonio's concern. She was sitting on the tall stool next to him, looking very tired. "The baby made it, though, and we'll make it the next time."

"It's not so easy now. Their security is tightening." Antonio set three glasses on the bar and brought out a bottle of rum. "I can't sell it, but there's been no directive against giving it away."

"As long as you're giving it away, how about a little bourbon?"

Antonio's laughter rumbled in his chest. "Rum is the drink of the islands, McQuade." He reached for another bottle and set it next to McQuade's glass. "Haven't you gone native by this time?"

Day was dawning, but with the window louvers closed the three were in near darkness. McQuade grinned past the trio of candles that flickered between him and Antonio. "I'll eat your food and . . . wear your flowered shirts, Antonio, but I won't drink your damned rum."

The line had changed. Antonio remembered it being "eat your food and love your women," and a stronger expletive had usually described the rum. With a chuckle, he glanced at the woman who had induced McQuade to mind his tongue. He knew who she was. There had been much speculation about her exile, and it was the general consensus among the islanders that she had suffered. She had risked her life to return like this. Now the child was safe, and the mother was back in the lion's den.

"They'll start taking the fishing boats out again soon." McQuade poured himself a generous shot of bourbon, thinking he had definitely gotten his days and nights turned around. If he had a sack to hit, he knew he would be out like a light. "They'll have to. These people have to eat."

"Our general is more interested in tight security than in full bellies." Antonio sipped thoughtfully at his rum. "Now that we've lost Castillo and Hidalgo, I think this government will go sour."

"I think it already has."

Elizabeth's quiet statement took both men by surprise. They watched her drain her glass.

"I'll find you a safe place to sleep, *señora*. You need food and rest."

Elizabeth offered a grateful smile, but McQuade raised his palm in refusal. "We'll take the food, but I think we're better off hiding in the jungle, Antonio. And you're better off without us around.''

"You think I worry about Guerrero?" Antonio tapped McQuade's shoulder. "You and I are two of a kind, *amigo*. We love to take chances. Besides, you cannot leave here again until nightfall."

The sound of a laboring motor brought the conversation to a halt. Antonio blew out the candles and swept the bottles and glasses from the counter. McQuade glanced at the door to Antonio's living quarters, but decided on the curtain behind the bar. At his signal, Elizabeth slid from the stool. Without a word, they hid behind a stack of boxes. Antonio proceeded to build another stack to enclose them.

The door rattled as someone outside pounded on it, demanding, "Open up!"

McQuade drew his pistol, and Elizabeth listened as the latch was drawn and the door swung open.

"*Buenos días, señor*. We are here to remind you that you are not permitted to open for business today."

Antonio yawned loudly. "I was closed until you dragged me out of bed, captain. How long is this going to last?"

"Until the directive is lifted. We also have orders to look around."

"What for?"

"There's been trouble in La Primavera."

"*¡Ah, eso!* City people! Here in the village we simply want to get on with our lives. Help yourself, then."

McQuade and Elizabeth heard a louver squeak on its hinges, and then another. One set of footsteps crossed the floor, followed by a second. A door opened, and there was an exchange of words before it was shut again. The back room brightened as the curtain was drawn. A flashlight beam bounced from corner to corner. Darkness shrouded the room again.

"Remember, no liquor sales. Martial law is still in effect."

The door closed, the latch was drawn, and both louvered windows clattered shut. "Martial law," Antonio grumbled. "Is that what they call it?" He ducked behind the curtain. "Stay where you are," he whispered. "When they're tired of nosing around, we'll have breakfast."

McQuade sat with his back to the wall and his legs outstretched. He helped Elizabeth to the floor, settling her between his legs and easing her back into his arms. "Rest now," he whispered close to her ear. "This might take a while."

Under different circumstances he would have slept, too, despite the lack of comfort, but he was a sentinel now, alert to every sound. For Elizabeth, the rum had been a sedative. She drifted into sleep, while McQuade waited, wishing the floor was softer and the small, slatted vent high above him was down closer to his face. He could hear the village coming to life beyond his wall of boxes. The captain's door-pounding was soon drowned out by the pounding of hammers. The people were rebuilding. McQuade wondered how long independent islanders like Antonio and his neighbors would tolerate Guerrero's interference in their lives.

Minutes ticked away in his head. An hour and a half, he judged. He wanted to take his jacket off, but he couldn't without disturbing Elizabeth. A runnel of sweat slid down the side of his face. He lifted his shoulder to wipe it away, but it was a losing battle. His shirt was sticking to his back. He was sure his muscles had felt stiffer, but he couldn't remember when.

"Ow!"

McQuade clamped his hand over Elizabeth's mouth. "Shh. You're dreaming again," he whispered.

She shook her head, and he lowered his hand. "Something bit me!" she said, gasping for air.

Grateful for the chance to shift positions, he chuckled. "I suppose you thought it was me."

"I'm serious." She rubbed the back of her calf.

"Keep your voice down."

"We have to get out of here, Sloan. There's something back here."

"Hold still," he ordered as he took off one running shoe and came to his feet slowly. "I think I see your attacker."

High on the stack of boxes, where the slatted vent cast strips of light and shadow on the cardboard, a big brown spider was attempting his escape. McQuade squashed him.

Feeling the small, repulsive creature burst open gave him a strange sense of satisfaction. "That's one ugly bastard who won't bother you anymore," he muttered. He knelt beside her and slipped his hand under her leg, touching the spot she'd been rubbing. "Packed quite a wallop, huh? He raised a welt on you."

Her heart was racing. The place where she'd been bitten throbbed. If she didn't get out of this corner soon . . .

The top two sections of their wall fell away, and Antonio's face appeared in their place. "You can come out now. Peace is restored to our village, and the army lives to fight another day." When his wit went unappreciated, Antonio took another look. "Is something wrong?"

"I don't know, Antonio. Elizabeth—"

"It's just a little sting," she said quickly. "I'll be fine. Antonio promised us breakfast."

"Yes, you must be famished by now. I'll prepare it myself." He lifted another box out of the way. "With the cantina closed, Chi Chi is hard to keep track of."

El Gallo did not miss the loss of electricity. Only the cantina, the general store and a few homes had it, and they had gotten it only recently. Antonio still had a small brazier, which he used to produce a hearty hot meal. McQuade hardly looked up from his plate until he'd consumed enough sausage, bread and beans to feed the troops that had just left the village.

Then he took note of Elizabeth's plate.

"I thought you were hungry for a change."

"I can't keep up with you," she muttered into her plate. She took a small bite of bread.

McQuade lowered his fork. "You okay?" She shook her head. "What's wrong?" It took her forever to chew and swallow the bread. All he needed was one look in her eyes. "Elizabeth?"

She lifted her chin and then her lashes, and he knew she was in pain. "It was just a spider. I've been bitten before, stung, whatever...." She shrugged, feeling at a loss to explain the pain. "I thought I had pretty thick skin by now."

He slid his chair back from the table. "Let's have another look. I have a feeling ice is going to be hard to come by." He pushed her skirt up to her knee and ran a gentle hand down the back of her calf. "You've never had a reaction to anything?"

"Never."

The welt on her leg was circular and reddening, and the area around it was beginning to swell. McQuade heard Antonio come in from the kitchen. "You've got some first aid stuff around here, haven't you, Antonio?"

"Sure, I've got the big, deluxe chest you mount on the wall with the—" Antonio put away the clean glasses he'd brought from the kitchen and came around the end of the bar. McQuade was kneeling by the woman's chair. "Trouble?" Antonio asked.

"Do you have any cold packs?"

"I don't know. I've never let anyone use anything out of my big, deluxe chest."

"Now's your chance, Antonio. Break it out."

"Sloan, I need to lie down," Elizabeth pleaded. He looked up quickly. Her face was becoming chalky even as he watched.

"Good Lord." He came to his feet. "We need a bed, too, Antonio."

"Take mine. Perhaps hot brine..."

McQuade scooped Elizabeth out of the chair and carried her through the door his friend held open for him. "Bring me the whole damned chest, Antonio. Rip it off the wall."

Antonio found the cold packs and hurried after McQuade, hoping his prized emergency kit could stay where it was. "Perhaps a little brandy..."

"Perhaps, perhaps." The bedsprings creaked under McQuade's knee. "Maybe you oughta spray the back room," he grumbled.

"Sloan, please. The man is trying to help us." Elizabeth fought to keep her mind firmly in the present. She felt the chenille bedspread under her palms and saw two bare bulbs in the overhead light fixture. She knew there should only be one, and she concentrated on them until they merged. Something cold was wedged under the knot of pain in her leg.

"Elevate it," Elizabeth suggested. She had a vague notion of a flurry of activity around her, but her own body felt as if it were moving sluggishly through thick air. "Do you think it would be all right...if I slept...just a little while?"

"I don't think I'm going to be able to stop you."

She saw him clearly, his face, looming above hers, softened by a sympathetic smile. She saw herself touch him, saw him kiss her palm, and then she drifted away.

* * *

"I don't suppose you've got a doctor around here."

Antonio shifted his gaze from the woman's sleeping face to McQuade's dark scowl. He would have done anything to accommodate this man. One of life's joys was being able to put just the right source or resource at McQuade's disposal. Unfortunately the village had only one healer, and that one would not be to the Anglo's liking.

"There is only *Tía* Teresa."

McQuade sat on the side of the bed and wearily rubbed his hands over his face. "What is she? Some kind of midwife?"

"No." Antonio was hesitant to elaborate. He looked at the woman again. He didn't know what kind of spider had bitten her, but there were poisonous ones on the island. Part of her was of the island, and perhaps that part would connect with *Tía* Teresa's mystical ways. "But she *is* a healer," he attested finally.

"Some kind of folk medicine?"

"I have seen her bring about marvelous cures."

McQuade looked down at Elizabeth and touched the back of his hand to her forehead and cheek. "She's exhausted. Get me some soap and water and some antiseptic. We'll keep the cold packs on her. When she wakes up, we'll ask her if she wants any of that herb stuff."

When McQuade stretched out beside Elizabeth and covered his face with his arms, Antonio took it as his cue to hover elsewhere. He would have to consult with *Tía* Teresa. As a rule she was unwilling to share her curative powers with outsiders. He would have to convince her that Elizabeth was truly an islander and that McQuade was simpatico. He found Chi Chi and instructed her to be on the lookout for soldiers. Taking along the offering of rum the old woman would demand in return for a consultation, Antonio headed for the small house that stood alone at the edge of the village.

McQuade came awake with a start when he was touched decisively, delightfully high on the inside of his thigh. His surprise gave way to a groan of pleasure as he turned to Elizabeth. It disappointed him to discover that she wasn't awake, but disappointment faded as his alarm grew. Her pallid face felt hot and clammy under his hand. He sat up quickly and examined her leg. The cold pack and the pillows he'd propped her leg on had fallen to the floor. Her calf was swollen down to the ankle, the skin stretched taut. He replaced the pillows and applied a fresh cold pack, but beyond that he didn't know what to do.

She moaned.

"Elizabeth? Wake up, honey. We need to talk."

She turned her head aside and moaned again.

McQuade stared for a moment. "You've got to be kidding," he muttered. Filled with an overwhelming sense of helplessness, he sat back on his heels and tipped his head back. "Hey, up there! You've got to be kidding me!" Planting his elbows on the side of the bed, he clenched his fists together and rested his forehead on them. "Now what am I supposed to do? No doctor around, just some superstitious quack, and how in hell can I hide you when you're like this?" He raised his head to look at her again as he knelt beside the bed. "Can't very well stash you behind a pile of boxes in the back room now, can I?" He lifted a long strand of her hair away from her cheek. "If you weren't so damn pretty—"

Antonio knocked as he opened the door and stuck his head in the room. "McQuade, *Tía* Teresa is willing to treat Elizabeth. We'll have to take her over there, though."

"Doesn't she make house calls?"

"House calls?" Antonio selected his words carefully as he came into the room. "McQuade, there is one thing you must understand about *Tía* Teresa. She has no sense of humor. If you try to joke with her, she will be offended."

McQuade sat on the side of the bed. "I'm not feeling very funny, either. We need a doctor, Antonio, not some mumbo jumbo. With my luck, Guerrero's men will come snooping around while this woman is in the middle of some incantation."

"The soldiers would not intrude." McQuade lifted a questioning eyebrow, and Antonio explained, "No one interferes with *Tía* Teresa."

"You mean they wouldn't search her place?"

"No one goes there except for treatment. Her house is inviolate." Antonio shrugged. "Call it superstition, if you will. It's wise not to disturb the sleeping viper."

"Viper! Listen, Antonio—"

Antonio raised his hand against the objections. "The antidote for venom is more of the same."

"You don't think Guerrero's boys want to mess with this lady?" Antonio shook his head. "Let's get her over there, then. I'm not superstitious. I've handled some pretty feisty witches in my time."

As she was lifted into his arms, Elizabeth reached around McQuade's neck. "Sloan?" She reminded him of a sleepy child. "Is it time yet?"

"Relax, honey. I'll get you there. Don't worry about the time."

Unlike most of the older island women McQuade had seen, *Tía* Teresa was thin. Her slightly round-shouldered stance and her frowsy hair gave her the look of a palm tree, with two coconuts slung low on her chest. Her skin was desiccated, like an old piece of fruit. She offered no greeting when she answered the door, but waved the group over her threshold with a long, withered hand.

Turning her back on them, the old woman gestured vaguely toward the back of the house, the papery hand fluttering at the end of her arm. "Put her back there."

McQuade ducked through a curtained doorway, and Antonio followed. The house smelled of balsam and incense. A kerosene flame burned in a red glass lamp in the corner of the room. The bed looked comfortable, and the room was stark but neat. The mattress dipped under McQuade's knee only slightly more than he would have liked as he laid Elizabeth on the bed.

"Leave her to me, now," the old voice said.

"Antonio is leaving, *Tía*, but I'm staying with her."

The old woman scowled first at McQuade, and then at Antonio. Antonio swallowed hard. "This is McQuade, *Tía*. The one I told you about. A man of courage."

Teresa crackled. "More courage than you have, anyway, Antonio. You can't wait to get out of here." She motioned impatiently. "You go out with him," she instructed McQuade. "I'll see to your girl."

"I can't leave her, *Tía*." McQuade searched for the right excuse. "I made her a promise."

"A promise, you say?" She eyed the sleeping woman and chuckled. "Suit yourself. Maybe you're sick, too. Healthy people usually keep away from me." Taking both men by surprise, she whirled toward Antonio. "Out with you! Go cower somewhere else."

Antonio backed away. "If you need anything, McQuade, just, uh, just send word."

"Paper and pencil," McQuade said quickly. "And ask Juanita if she'll do an errand for me."

After the front door had closed behind Antonio, Teresa went to a cupboard and took out a sheet. "Take her clothes off," she ordered.

McQuade turned to her, surprised. "All of them?"

"Cover her with this," she said, tossing him the sheet. "You might as well be useful. She's fevered. She needs to be sponged. You can help with that."

"Yeah, right," McQuade grumbled in English as the old woman left the room. Stripping off his jacket, he stashed his pistol under the mattress. Then he began with Elizabeth's blouse, lifting her to pull the garment over her head.

McQuade sponged cool water over Elizabeth's face, neck and torso, while Teresa applied a pungent-smelling poultice to the swollen leg. She showed him how to pay particular attention to the backs of their patient's knees and to her underarms, where a little rubbing would release more heat. Together they force-fed Elizabeth a brew of herbal tea, massaging her throat to induce her to swallow. Finally Teresa burned incense, fanning the smoke over the bed while she chanted something in a strange tongue.

McQuade figured the smoke and the chants couldn't do any harm, and he hoped the same went for the woman's other efforts, but he had his doubts about what *good* any of it would accomplish. In light of his doubts, he sat near the lamp and drafted a note on the paper Antonio had sent over.

Dorothy knew every ailment on the island, and she had cures for most of them. McQuade figured she'd been with the Red Cross for almost half a century. His note didn't reveal any names or locations, but he described the problem and asked for medication and instructions. His second request came harder. It was a carefully worded appeal for her to contact Mikal Romanov. He wanted Mike to recover the "canvas bundle" he'd acquired recently and keep it for himself if anything should happen to McQuade and his client. He had told Dorothy that they were headed for Arco Iris when he and Tomás had taken refuge in her back room. Shrouded clues would tell her that only the child was there with the fisherman, Emilio. It was the best provision he could make for little Tomás.

Juanita agreed to deliver McQuade's message and return with the medication. She folded the note into a narrow strip, stitched it into the waistband of her skirt and promised not to take any unnecessary risks. When she returned, she would be carrying first aid supplies for the village.

"It was a brown spider, you say?"

Teresa's question brought McQuade's head around. He'd been watching over Elizabeth from a chair beside the bed and noting that she seemed to be resting more easily since she had drunk the tea. Coming to his feet, he unbuttoned his shirt and reached for the cloth he'd left floating in the basin of water.

"Yeah, brown." He sponged his face and neck, letting the water run freely down his back. "Is that bad?"

The old woman raised her eyebrows as she jerked her chin toward Elizabeth. "For her it was." She stood at the foot of the bed and worked with a mortar and pestle as she talked. "We have many varieties of spiders here. What is important is not the spider's poison, but the victim's susceptibility. Your woman's blood is too thin."

"Oh, yeah?" He glanced at the small cup in Teresa's hands. "Is that some kind of thickener you're working on there?"

"This will attack the poison itself," she explained. "Dried snake."

"Dried snake," he repeated slowly. "What do you do with that?"

"I make a paste of it and apply it to the wound."

"Oh." He nodded as he mopped his chest with cool water, unconcerned about the way it trickled over his belly and into his pants. He was relieved that the old lady didn't have plans to make Elizabeth take the stuff internally.

"It would do no good to feed it to her yet," Teresa added, eyeing McQuade perceptively. "We'll wait until the tea has had some effect."

"Yeah. Good plan." He wondered how long it would take Juanita to get back with some real medication. "What's in the tea?" he asked, plunking the rag back in the basin.

"A blend of herbs."

That sounded harmless enough. He took up his position in the chair again, leaned forward and stroked Elizabeth's damp hair, letting his fingertips linger on her forehead. "How long do you think she'll be like this?" He was willing to give the woman some measure of credit. No doubt she'd seen a great deal in her time.

"Until she recovers or dies." He gave her the look she expected from an Anglo—the fierce denial of the obvious alternatives. In return she offered a cold stare. She would not be accountable to one so ignorant. "Whatever fate decides."

So much for the folk healer, McQuade concluded. Fatalism wasn't to his liking, and he had to make a conscious effort to keep that fact from registering on his face. He would strike a diplomatic balance—trying to avoid offending the old woman while fending off the powdered snake.

"You must leave now," Teresa ordered. "I see that your attitude toward my power is not good."

McQuade straightened his back slowly. "What do you mean not good? I brought her here to get help, didn't I?"

"Since she is one of us I might be able to help her, but not with you watching us."

"I'm not watching you," he said evenly. "I'm watching her. I gave her my word. Now, I don't know anything about this power of yours, but I'm willing to move heaven and hell to see that this woman recovers." He caught the glimmer of surprise in her eyes. "Yeah. Heaven and hell. Which is it, Teresa?"

They glared at each other for a moment, but it was Teresa who backed down and left the room.

McQuade moved to sit on the edge of the bed, needing to be closer to Elizabeth. The tea had had a drugging effect. She was sleeping peacefully, with only the fine mist of perspiration covering her pale skin to betray her illness. Her hair spilled across the white pillow in dark waves, framing her face like an eerie portrait in pallid shades. If she looked otherworldly, there was no question in his mind which world she favored.

"We'll get you through this, angel," he whispered, taking her hands in his. They were cold, and her palms were moist. "The snake powder doesn't sound too promising, but reinforcements are on the way." He took up the cloth from the basin again.

McQuade dozed in the chair next to Elizabeth's bed. The smell of incense and balsam roused him, and the sight of old Teresa waving her palm fan over Elizabeth brought him fully awake. "What's going on?" he grumbled, rubbing a hand over his eyes.

"Be still," Teresa said. "You would not understand. Just watch, and be satisfied that what I'm doing can help her."

McQuade sat up, squinting. The acrid smoke made his eyes burn, but aside from that, he figured it couldn't hurt anyone. Elizabeth turned her head and groaned.

"Have you looked at her leg?" he asked.

"Yes. It's the same."

"Has the swelling gone down any?"

"No, but it's no worse."

"Great." He planted his elbows on his knees and ran his hands through his hair.

"You *should* be grateful. I've seen them swell like a watermelon."

"What happens then?"

"Sometimes they burst." He arched an eyebrow, and she flicked her fingers, spreading her withered hands as she cackled.

"Listen, Teresa, I haven't quite figured out whose side you're on, but I wouldn't be too surprised to find out that you really are a witch." She dropped her hands, her mouth drew up in a tight line, and it was McQuade's turn to chuckle. He tossed the sheet back from Elizabeth's feet and had a look at her leg for himself. Teresa was right; there had been no change.

"Sloan?"

"I'm here, honey." McQuade knelt beside the bed, fussed with the sheet and held her hand. "Feeling any better?"

"I had a bad dream." Her voice was thin and unnaturally high.

"Fever dreams," he confirmed. "They're always bad."

She blinked, trying to bring his face into focus. "Have you had them?"

"Sure." Teresa slipped a fresh basin of water onto the stand next to the bed, and McQuade nodded his thanks. "Are you thirsty?"

"Mmm-hmm."

Teresa took the cue and left the room. Without taking his eyes off Elizabeth, McQuade fished the cloth from the basin, squeezed it out and began bathing her face. It was a service he enjoyed performing, not a task.

"I can't imagine you being sick," she mused in a thick voice. "When was the last time?"

He shrugged. "I don't know. It's been a while."

"Who took care of you?"

"My Aunt Bertie, when I was a kid. And then ... I took care of myself."

She lifted her hand to his cheek. The gesture felt so tentative that he quickly covered her fingers with his own. "Next time I'll take care of you," she whispered.

Her promise warmed him on the inside like a sip of whiskey. He turned his lips to the center of her palm and kissed her there.

"You need a shave."

He smiled and kissed her again.

"Sloan, I want you to go back to Arco Iris ... now. Today. I'll come when I'm better." She clasped his hand and pulled it to rest between her breasts. "Please."

"When I go, you're going with me."

She shook her head. "Please, Sloan. For Tomás."

"I haven't forgotten about Tomás." He smoothed her hair back with the damp cloth. "Dorothy will get word to Mike Romanov. I trust him like a brother, Elizabeth. He'll get Tomás to the States, and he and Morgan will take good care of him until we ... until you get back."

Pressing his hand between her breasts, she smiled. "I chose the right man for this job, didn't I?"

"Damn right." Her heart fluttered against his palm, and his throat went dry.

"I want to know that you're safe, Sloan. That Guerrero can't touch you with his hideous, filthy—"

"Shh, shh. He can't touch us, honey." He glanced up at Teresa, who was standing beside him holding a cup. He shifted positions so that he could prop Elizabeth up against his chest. "Look at all we've got going for us," he whis-

pered to her in English. "The Good Witch of El Gallo—
Gracias, Teresa—and good old Dorothy."

Teresa stepped back and watched the man minister to his
woman. She was weak, but she drew on his strength. Antonio had said that the woman was half Anglo and half De
Coloran, but she belonged to this man completely. Let him
heal her, then, Teresa decided. If she lived, fine; if she died,
then it meant his power was not so great. Teresa left the
room and returned with a package, which she handed to
McQuade.

"Your girl delivered this earlier," she grumbled.

"Juanita?" He set the cup down and lowered Elizabeth
to the bed.

"She wanted to give it to you personally, but I scared her
away."

Tearing into the package, McQuade found Dorothy's instructions inside a roll of gauze bandaging.

"I scared the soldiers away, too."

He looked up and saw a hint of mischief in Teresa's dark
eyes. McQuade grinned. "What the hell's wrong with those
guys? Don't they know about the Good Witch of the
South?"

Chapter 10

"Teresa, if you don't get out of here with that stuff, I'm going to dump this on your head!''

McQuade set the basin aside and peered through the smoky haze at the old woman, who had burned one spice or herb after another over Elizabeth until the room reeked of warring scents. His eyes were teary from it, but *Tía* Teresa stood firm in the midst of it all, glaring at him like a stone gargoyle. With a weary sigh, he snatched his jacket off the back of the chair and pulled his cigarettes from the pocket.

"Hell, you'd probably melt," he grumbled in English. "You make your smoke, I'll make mine." He adjusted his tone of voice to a more civil request in Spanish and came up with an apologetic smile. "Would you stay with her while I take a break?"

"If you think you'll return in a better mood."

He looked down at Elizabeth, whose fitful tossing had ceased for the moment. "Just keep on doing what you're doing," he said. "It seems to be helping."

It was a thinly veiled offer to let the old woman keep up appearances, and he knew she saw through it. It seemed to satisfy her, though, perhaps assuaging her pride. He'd followed Dorothy's instructions and injected Elizabeth with a serum that he prayed would soon take effect. Teresa mumbled continually, and he wasn't sure what she was praying for or, for that matter, to whom she was praying, but he'd decided it didn't much matter as long as she gave them refuge. He'd put his real trust elsewhere.

He flattened his back against the rough stucco next to the front door and watched his stream of smoke dissipate into the night. The cool air felt good on his damp chest. The storm had apparently skirted *Tía* Teresa's little house. There were still blooms on the hibiscus near the front window.

But that back room was hotter than blazes. Heaven and hell, he thought. He'd sworn to move both. He realized that was a pretty brazen claim, but he figured Dorothy might have a little pull with heaven, and heaven might nudge hell aside for Elizabeth's sake. For his part, he could only follow his instincts. Dorothy's note had advised patience. Give the treatment time to work. Patience. Time. *Damn.* He lifted his cigarette to his mouth and drew the smoke deeply into his lungs. He had precious little of either commodity.

"She calls for you again."

McQuade pushed himself away from the wall as he dropped the cigarette and ground it into the dirt. Teresa held the door open for him, and he stepped past her.

Elizabeth looked like a small, wild creature trapped in the untidy thicket of her hair. Her eyes blazed at him when he pushed the curtain aside.

"Get away from me!" she snarled. "I have a gun."

For a moment he thought she might have found his pistol, but his eyes adjusted to the light, and he saw that her hands were empty. He knelt beside the bed and laid his hand on her forehead, easing her head back to the pillow as he whispered, "It's okay, honey. It's Sloan."

"Sloan? I thought you'd gone."

"I just went outside for a smoke." He covered her with the sheet, feeling a little guilty about her appearance. Even when they were living in what amounted to a cave, she'd been perfectly groomed. As soon as he could, he'd fix her hair up for her. "I'm right here," he told her.

"It's too dark." She searched his face as though she weren't convinced of his identity. "Sloan?"

"Yes." He brought her hand to his fuzzy cheek. "Same old Sloan. See? I still haven't shaved."

"Very nice," she whispered, exploring his jaw, his cheekbone, touching his lower lip with her thumb. "The sweetest face. The sweetest, sweetest mouth."

"Shucks," he drawled, smiling. "I'll bet you say that to all the guys you hide out with. Feeling better?"

"I'm very...thirsty."

"Teresa! Bring some tea," he ordered. Then he added, "Please. Not too hot."

Elizabeth grabbed his shoulder with sudden desperation. "Sloan, don't let him take me!"

He saw the wild confusion in her eyes. "Nobody's going to take you from me, Elizabeth." She reached for him, and he caught her against his chest. "You hear me?" He buried his face in the tangled mat of her hair and swore fiercely, "Nobody!"

Her delicate gasp told him that he was squeezing the breath out of her. "I'm okay," she assured him as he settled her back on the bed. "It's strange. Things weave in and out." With a fluttering hand, she described the motion. "Everything seems real, and I'm not sure anything is."

"I'm real. This heat is real." He adjusted the wooden louvers on the small ventilating windows near the ceiling and floor, but it didn't seem to make any difference. Teresa pushed the curtain aside. "Here comes some real tea," McQuade announced, "but I can't vouch for the old lady. She might be mythological."

"I should throw you out of my house and let the vultures have you," Teresa grumbled as she stood waiting for McQuade to adjust Elizabeth against his shoulder.

"Who said *Tía* Teresa lacks a sense of humor?" He grinned as he reached for the cup she'd brought him. He squeezed the old woman's hand and confided, "I think she's better, *Tía*, don't you?"

"We'll see," Teresa muttered, shaking her head as she shuffled out of the room. "We'll see."

"You make damn good tea," McQuade called after her. He held the cup to Elizabeth's lips, and she sipped. "Fit for an island princess," he added as a quiet afterthought.

"You are an impertinent young man," came the answer from beyond the curtain.

McQuade laughed and whispered to Elizabeth, "The woman's crazy about me. Are you jealous?" Elizabeth offered what might pass for a smile and nodded. "Yeah, and you're one sweet old lady," McQuade said, raising his voice so it could be heard in the other room.

"Mind your manners," Teresa snapped back.

"Be careful, Sloan," Elizabeth whispered. "Don't press your luck."

"She's just like the rest of us—likes to be ribbed a little. You don't believe any of that supernatural power stuff, do you?"

"I don't know." She closed her eyes, and her head lolled back against his shoulder. "I believe in darkness and light," she muttered. "When the darkness slides over me . . . something bad . . ."

She was drifting again. He laid her back down and turned up the flame on the kerosene lamp. "Teresa, let's get more light in here. Elizabeth hates the dark."

Teresa was accustomed to darkness. Nonetheless her back room now blazed with the light from three lamps. She stood in the doorway and squinted in the brightness at the man and woman who slept peacefully together on the narrow bed. The white sheet was tucked under the woman's arms, covering her breasts, and the man slept in his jeans. He'd combed the woman's hair, taking pains to untangle the dark mane lock by lock with the kind of patience she had thought only a woman could have. Then he'd braided it, washed the woman, washed himself, lain on his belly at the edge of the bed and finally allowed himself some sleep.

One of his arms dragged on the floor and the other guarded the woman. Not from her, Teresa realized. He was an Anglo and was too ignorant to fear her. She was strangely willing to forgive him that. Something in the way he treated her had put a chink in her crusty defenses, and she was willing to let this man get away with his insolence.

He scoffed at the source of her power; she knew that. She was used as a last resort even by those who believed, and then they could never quite look her in the face. They scurried away as soon as they could, and they gave her a wide berth when times were good lest she harm them. This man had brought his woman to her because he feared the soldiers. He trusted her poultice and her tea, but her friends on the dark side were of no consequence to him. She might live to regret it, but she was inclined to allow him his irreverence.

She'd watched him fuss over the woman, harkening to every sound she made, fretting over her pain. The medicine he dispensed might not do any more good than Teresa's herbs. Who could say? They'd used both. What interested Teresa was his power as opposed to her own. She'd beckoned in the darkness, and nothing had happened. It was as though he'd scoffed it all away. So be it, Teresa thought as she watched them sleep. His power was all that was left. Did he think he could love his woman back to health?

If such a thing was possible, she would be glad to let this man accomplish it. Seldom had anyone turned to her with acceptance rather than fear, looked at her and not made her feel repulsive. All his teasing was good-natured, and when he looked at her, he often had a smile on his face.

McQuade caught himself just as he was about to roll off the bed. Cursing, he rolled instead to a sitting position, shielding his eyes with his hands. "What is this, the Super Bowl?" he grumbled. "Who turned on the floodlights?"

"I wondered the same thing."

He twisted around sharply, blinking back the brightness.

"I thought it was probably you." Elizabeth offered him a smile, and her eyes glowed anew.

"Hey..." McQuade's face softened as he returned her smile. "How're you doing?"

"I'm not sure." She tilted her head to look at him from another angle and gave a little laugh. It lacked gusto, McQuade noted, but it was laughter. "Is there really a naked man with very wild hair in bed with me?"

McQuade sat up and stuck his thumb in an empty belt loop. "I've got my pants on, lady. I'm decent!" Laughing, he ran his hand through his unruly thatch of hair. "What you see is what you get."

"Then I must be doing okay." She spoke softly, slowly, as though she hadn't used her voice in a long time. "I think I see an angel."

"Hey, let's not rush it, honey." He took a quick inventory, touching her forehead and her cheek, catching her hand in his. "This is one time I don't mind noticing how much you've cooled off. How's the leg?"

"The one you bit? It still hurts." She lifted a hand to his hair, letting an errant lock tickle her palm. "How long has it been?"

"I lost track." He shrugged. "Couple of days, I guess."

"There's a woman—"

"*Tía* Teresa. Her bark's worse than my bite, but don't let that fool you. She's a good ol' gal."

Her hand slid back to her own shoulder and came to rest on her thick braid. "Who braided my hair?"

"Same old dog who bit you in the leg. How'd I do?"

The tears sprang to her eyes so quickly that she didn't have time to hide them. She could do nothing but wrap her arms around his neck and whisper his name with wonder as she wept.

"That bad?" He held her, half laughing, half wanting to cry himself. "I can fix it, honey. I can do better."

"No, no, no," she said, smiling through her tears. "That good. Sloan, you're that *good*. You took care of me." Leaning back, she took his face in her hands and filled her mind with the sight of his soft gray eyes. "I've never known anyone like you," she whispered.

Her face was lovely and frail and full of tears, and McQuade thought he would burst just from looking at her. He wiped a tear away with his thumb and found just enough voice to tell her, "You gave me a hell of a scare, lady."

"I'll be back on my feet soon. I promise."

"Not unless we get some food in you. Good Lord, you're wasting away." He slid his hand over her shoulder, and the sheet slipped below her breast. That much had not wasted away. He replaced the sheet, but not before her nipple had puckered under his scrutiny. Lifting his gaze to hers, he whispered, "Sorry."

Clutching the sheet, she lay back against the pillow, smiling wistfully.

"Could you eat something?" he pressed.

"I could try."

A desperate squawk silenced them both. A whacking sound drew McQuade's eyebrows down, and when he heard a thud, he had his pistol in his hand. He drew the curtain back. The front door was open, and he saw that it was daylight. There was Teresa, her back to him, with the freshly decapitated carcass of a chicken lying on a stump just outside the door. He could see the neck dangling over the edge.

"Oh, hell, what is she up to now?"

"What is it, Sloan?"

"I don't know, but if she's got any sort of voodoo in mind..." McQuade tucked the pistol at his back as he crossed the front room. He braced his shoulder against the doorjamb. "Teresa, what are you going to do with that poor bird?"

Without turning around, she waved a knife at the ground. "Do you see the head there? Do you see the condition of the entrails?"

"Come on, Teresa, let's not—"

She cut him off with a cackle as she plunked the carcass into a pot of water. "Now the scalding cauldron," she chanted, "makes the feathers fly."

"Teresa, I don't think we need to do anything drastic. Come see for yourself. Elizabeth is—"

"Ha!" She whirled around with more agility than he'd thought possible and held the bird aloft, inches from his nose.

McQuade jumped back before he took a second look. It was plucked. "What the he—"

The old woman's eyes were alight with mischief in a way she rarely shared with anybody. "Now we cook him. Your girl has to eat, doesn't she?"

McQuade's shoulders shook with laughter. *"Bruja,"* he called her. "What a sweetheart of a witch."

While Elizabeth rested in Teresa's care, McQuade searched for a way to get them off the island. Many of the fishing boats were under repair, and most of the fishermen were wary. Guerrero was issuing directives against this and demanding permits for that. No one dared make a move without first getting a military stamp of approval. The village fishermen were an independent breed, but they were still licking their wounds from the hurricane. Word had gotten around, and when they saw Antonio coming, they would shake their heads and wave him back. They shrugged off McQuade's monetary offers with, "Got no place to spend it," or, "Wait a while. Maybe when things settle down."

Discouraged, McQuade sat alone in the cantina, nursing a glass of bourbon and a cigarette. He heard a key rattling in the back door and prepared himself for more bad news from Antonio. But what came was worse. It was Chi Chi in all her buxom glory, and she was moving toward him with a decidedly lascivious grin that made her dark eyes sparkle. Expelling a last lungful of smoke toward the ceiling, he stubbed the butt out in a plastic ashtray.

"What's up, Chi Chi?" McQuade let one foot slide from the rung of the bar stool to the floor and stretched his back. His shirttail was stuffed into his jeans, but the buttons were undone. It was too hot for formality. "What did you do to your hair? It looks...different."

It looked as though she'd washed it in blood, but he wasn't irritable enough to put it quite that bluntly.

Hiking her straight, plum-colored skirt above her knees, she gave herself a boost on a rung on the bar stool next to McQuade's and gradually slid her rump into place on the seat, smiling at him through the whole process. "You like it? It's called Hot and Sassy. I did it for Miami."

McQuade chortled. "I'm sure you'll blow a fuse on their scoreboard, sweetie, if you can just find a way to get there."

With a slow hand she smoothed the skirt over her thigh. "I made myself a new skirt, too. What do you think?"

"Nice." He planted his elbows on the bar and lifted his glass. "Here's to the new Chi Chi."

"*Gracias.* I hope Juanito shares your enthusiasm."

"Juanito?" He could have sworn the act was for him, but he'd been wrong before.

"I call him Juanito because he's just about this tall." The hand she extended indicated a height of less than five feet. She smiled sweetly at the space under her hand, as though a cute little person were standing there. "Not macho like you, McQuade, but still, he's a man, and he's always willing to do *anything* for me."

"Oh, yeah?" McQuade sipped his bourbon. "Is he a Miami fan, too?"

"He has a boat."

McQuade slid his gaze her way and smiled. "Oh, yeah?"

"Oh, yes, McQuade." She propped herself prettily on the bar and posed with a pout, eyeing the dusting of light hair on McQuade's bronzed chest. "Little Juan has a big boat. Big enough to take you and me and that scrawny friend of yours all the way to Miami."

Swiveling on the stool, he faced her as he set his glass down. "What will it cost me for tickets to this cruise?"

She slid to the floor and stepped closer. "I believe the polite question is what will it cost *me*?"

"Well, look—" The hand she slipped inside his shirt was bad enough, but the one on his thigh reminded him of the need he'd felt for Elizabeth in recent days. "How about we work a trade?"

Chi Chi lowered her lashes and smiled. "Mmm-hmm?"

"I've got season tickets to the Dolphins' games."

The smile became a scowl. "Do you think some football player with fake shoulders and a thick neck could take the place of the man of my dreams?"

"You mean Juanito?"

McQuade took a not-so-playful fist in the breastbone. "I don't have to introduce you to my friend, McQuade."

She'd managed to slip the strap of her skimpy blouse off her shoulder. McQuade smiled as he slowly slid it back into place. "How soon can you arrange it?"

"I'm seeing Juanito this afternoon. We can meet you here around nine."

"I'll be here," he promised.

She snaked her hand behind his neck. "You can make your plans, and then Juanito will go back to get his boat ready. And then you and I . . ." Craning her neck, Chi Chi pressed her mouth against McQuade's.

His body responded because she was female, and Lord knew he'd been hungry for one. But not this one. His brain clicked into autopilot as he went through the motions of kissing Chi Chi. He wanted Elizabeth. More than that, he wanted Elizabeth *safe*, and he'd do whatever he had to do to see to it. Even this. Even more than this. The thought occurred to him that when he'd used women for himself it had never bothered him. But the idea of using anyone for Elizabeth's sake made him hurt inside.

McQuade wiped the back of his hand across his mouth as he walked back to Teresa's house. A couple of kisses had left his lips feeling gritty. The sky was clouding over, and he hoped it would rain right now and get it over with. Since it didn't, he went to the side of the house and filled the metal tub with rainwater from the cistern. Stripping to the waist, he gave himself a bath.

He found Teresa preparing to go out. He hadn't known her to leave her yard before, but she seemed anxious to be gone and impatient with him for dawdling in the water and letting his hair drip on her floor.

"Do you think I've got nothing better to do than tend to this woman?" she grumbled. "She thinks she's well enough to wash clothes and meddle in my kitchen, and I've had all I could do to keep her in bed this morning. That should be your job."

He almost missed the twinkle of mischief in Teresa's eyes. "Yeah, well . . ." He grinned when he caught it. "Maybe someday. You think she could travel pretty soon?"

"I thought that would be the next thing on your mind. She's as frail as a newborn."

"We've gotta get out while the getting is good, and you just said she was trying to—" He frowned. Teresa had hung several bags made of woven sisal over her arm, and she was tying a scarf over her frowsy hair. "Where do you think you're going, old lady? It's going to rain."

"It rains often, but I have things to do."

"Like what?"

"That woman drinks my tea, uses everything in the house. I have to make a new collection." She pointed to the top of her cupboard. "Hand me that bottle."

"How long do you think you'll be gone?" He took the bottle down and gave it to her. "I'm telling you, it's going to rain."

"You'll be gone tomorrow, won't you?" she asked.

"Probably, if things work out."

"I won't be here. But you must take some of that—" she pointed to a jar on the shelf "—and make her tea twice a day. And that's the salve for her leg. You know what to do with it."

"What do you need more stuff for now?" McQuade demanded. "You're going to be out there in the jungle all night?"

Ignoring his bluster, she handed him the bottle. "This is witch hazel."

Snatching the tall glass container, he gave it a disdainful once-over. "What, you've got her in a bottle?" He offered Teresa a teasing grin. "I suppose she's your sister."

"Your impertinence will bring you to no good end, young man. You use this on that woman."

"That woman's name is Elizabeth."

Teresa looked up at him, her eyes dancing. "She's a pretty little thing, too. You rub this on her back. She's been lying in bed too long. This will make her skin tingle."

"Oh yeah?" McQuade chuckled as he took another look at the bottle. "Why, you sly old—"

"You do your job now." She poked him in the chest and fluttered her hand toward the back room. "I have to be about my business." When she actually smiled, McQuade thought he saw the young woman Teresa must once have been. "Your power has been good for her," she confessed. "Better than mine. Go on now. Take care of her. Let her take care of you."

McQuade heard the door close quietly behind her as he drew the curtain aside.

Elizabeth was lying fully dressed on the bed, and she reminded him of a child who'd fallen asleep waiting for someone to come and take her somewhere. He hoped he'd be able to take her somewhere soon, but he didn't want to get her hopes up until he had a firm offer. Her bare feet peeked at him from under the hem of her full yellow skirt. Like a swatch of black silk, her braid fell across the front of her white peasant blouse. Sitting at the edge of the bed, he laid a possessive hand on her hip, and she stirred lazily.

"Hi." McQuade smiled as she rolled over on her back and blinked at him. "Dressed for a date?"

"I hope so. Do we have one?"

"I'll check my calendar." He drew the bottle from behind his back and held it up in front of her. The clear liquid inside reflected the light from the lamp that burned near the foot of the bed. "Do you know what this is?"

"If you're drinking it, it must be bourbon," she guessed. She sat up and scooted back, clasping her arms around her knees. "And if we're having a party, I'm ready. I'm going crazy."

"Feeling frisky, are we? Teresa said you were trying to overdo it today."

"Teresa wouldn't allow me to do anything," she informed him. "I was fortunate to be able to bathe myself and wash my hair."

"You would have been more fortunate if you'd waited and allowed me to do that. But never mind." He took the cap off the bottle and sniffed. "Hmm."

Elizabeth leaned forward and took her turn. "Let me guess. It's one of Teresa's brews."

He snapped his fingers. "Right you are. Guaranteed to make the lady's skin tingle and her toes curl. I have the witch doctor's instructions to rub this stuff—" he slid her a crooked smile and relished each word "—all over your body."

Elizabeth laughed, and the sound came from deep in her throat. "Witch hazel, I'll bet. Where's Teresa?"

"She rode off on her broom." Cocking a teasing eyebrow, he raised his forefinger. "But I heard her exclaim as she rode out of sight, 'Make her happy, McQuade.'"

Elizabeth's smile faded, and her dark, trusting eyes met his. "We're alone, then?" He nodded. "And she actually said that?"

"Words to that effect." He was no longer smiling. His voice turned husky. "Turn over on your stomach. I'll start with your back."

"No. Not my back."

She lowered her eyes and would have retreated if it had been possible, but he wouldn't allow it. He set the bottle on the table beside the bed. "Your back," he said firmly, "is as beautiful as your front, and, believe me, I'm qualified to make that statement."

He saw the signs of capitulation as he persuaded her with gentle hands to lie down again. It wasn't what he wanted, but it was the only response she knew. Today he would teach her another one.

She lay facedown on the bed and thought of all the care he'd taken with her, all the tenderness he'd shown, and she knew he wouldn't hurt her. This was Sloan. She would be still for him.

He sat at the edge of the bed, moved her braid aside and slipped her blouse over her shoulders. The flat bones in her back protruded at odd angles as the muscles around them tensed, but she made no move to stop him from pushing the blouse to her waist. He took some of the liquid in his hand and began smoothing it over her shoulders. His palms tingled with it.

"I think we've got a good thing going here," he decided. "How does it feel?"

"Good," she said tightly.

"That's all I've got in mind." His hands moved in small circles, and he spoke to her quietly. "I just want to make you feel good."

"Sloan . . ."

"I used to wonder why my mother left me and never came back," he told her, his soft, rich voice stroking her even as his hands did. "I used to worry about it. Was it because she didn't like me? I wondered if it showed, if I affected other people the same way, if they could tell by looking at me that my own mother didn't want me."

He felt some of the tension dissolve under his hands. She opened her eyes and concentrated on the empty chair next to the bed, and her thoughts turned from herself. "I don't know why she did what she did, but I know it had nothing to do with you," she said. "Looking at you, I see only beauty and . . . and kindness."

He chuckled. "You saw that from the very first, did you?"

There was some hesitation. "No. Not the first night."

"Nor even the day after that, right?"

The cooling witch hazel made her tingle under the warmth of his caressing hands, and she relaxed more. "I see it now," she told him. "That's what matters."

The caresses moved to her lower back, and then he pushed her skirt below her waist, and his hands stilled. Elizabeth couldn't draw breath. She knew what he was seeing. His lips touched the place just above the swell of her hip, the only physical mark of her shame, and she squeezed her eyes shut.

"I saw this the other night when I was bathing you," he told her. There was no hint of shock in his voice, no horror. His kiss was like a touch of satin against her, and his breath warmed the cold, white mark. "It made me angry, but I'm glad you didn't see that. You might have thought the scar itself displeased me."

"It's an ugly thing." Her voice was small and thin, and the pain in it pierced him.

"What he did was an ugly thing, and my anger was for him, and for myself for not being there to stop him."

"But you didn't know me then."

"I do now. That's what matters." He kissed her again, and he heard a trembling intake of breath fill the hollow, lonely places inside her. He wanted to fill those places with something warmer, and this was where it would start. With a deep, cleansing breath. "I don't know why he did what he did, Elizabeth, but it had nothing to do with you."

He peeled her clothes away, sliding them over her legs, and he stroked her back and her buttocks, telling her over and over how beautiful she was. She turned to him, her eyes brimming bright with tears, arms reaching for him. He slid over her and covered her mouth with his. She dropped her head back and drank in his kiss, letting his tongue have access to the soft, moist cavern of her mouth. When he raised his head, the tears had slid from the corners of her eyes, and her lashes glistened.

"You're the *most* beautiful," she said, smiling up at him.

"Not from where I'm sitting."

"I wish—"

"Shh, don't tell me what you wish." He touched the damp spot where the tear had trailed into her hair. "I can't change the past. Tell me what you want right now."

"I hardly know." And that truth frightened her, too.

"Then trust me. Let me give you something new."

He kissed her, made her mouth soft, and moved his lips over her neck and her breasts, testing her as he tasted her. If she seemed to hesitate, his touch became tentative, teasing her until she thrust her breast into his palm and filled his mouth with her tongue. He groaned and pulled her body against his, so that she would know how it was with him, and how much of him he was asking her to trust. In answer, she drew his head back to her breast and invited him to suckle her. It was her turn to give, and he took satisfaction as he gave breathtaking delight.

When he kissed her mouth again there was a gathering of heat between them, a systematic building of energy, one impulse exciting another. She writhed against him, holding him, exploring, finding the button at the top of his jeans and tugging it loose.

"Elizabeth?" he whispered.

"You're what I want, Sloan."

"Are you sure?" He slipped his hand between them and caressed her on the soft curve of her inner thigh. He knew damn well it was an unfair question, but he was past the point of being fair. He'd settle for being the best thing that had ever happened to her if she'd just say . . .

"Oh, Sloan . . ."

He touched her and found a readiness that made him harder than he had been. She arched her back, surging into his hand, and he touched her again.

"Please, Sloan. Make love to me."

He unzipped his pants, and she slid her hands over his hard, smooth buttocks. Growling, he shucked the jeans in one quick movement and knelt between her thighs, bracing himself over her on unsteady arms. She reached for him, held his hips in both her hands, and he came nearer to her cautiously, by slow degrees. She gasped as she felt him fill her.

"Is it okay?" he asked.

He knew it was. He could see it in her face, but he wanted to hear her say . . .

"Yes."

He moved inside her, slowly.

"Oh, yes!" This was Sloan, and she couldn't be still. She remembered the swing, the way he had pushed and she had flown, and she said, "Yes, Sloan, yes."

He slid deeper inside her, and then he remembered the swing, too, and he whispered, "How much higher, honey?"

She raised her knees—higher—lifted her hips—still higher. "Oh, Sloan—as high as we can go!"

McQuade held her until she went to sleep. Then he slipped out of bed, pulled his jeans back on, and made them some supper. After they'd eaten, they made love again, and then they lay in each other's arms and listened to the rain pinging softly on the corrugated metal roof.

He'd unbraided her hair, and he sifted his fingers through it, letting it fall like corn silk against his arm. "I have to meet some guy over at the cantina in a little while," he said hesitantly. "I'll be back just as soon as I can."

"Does this guy have a boat?" Elizabeth asked, trying not to sound too hopeful. She knew that, if he did, Sloan had kept that information from her for a reason.

"He's supposed to. We'll see." With a sigh, he dropped his head back to the pillow and stared at the ceiling. "He's a friend of Chi Chi's, and Chi Chi's kind of...spacey. You never know."

"But you are the man of her dreams," Elizabeth teased as she toyed with the springy hair on his chest.

"Yeah, well, this guy's supposed to be sort of a boyfriend, so I guess I've been replaced." He kissed the top of her head. "You'll be okay for an hour or so?"

"Of course." She pulled his head down and stretched her neck to offer him a reassuring kiss, running her hand along the growth on his cheek that was fast becoming a beard.

He groaned with pleasure. "Do me one more favor."

"What?"

"Say my name again."

She nuzzled his neck and said it softly, deep in her throat. "Sloan."

He smiled at the sound. "You're the only one who calls me that anymore."

"Does anyone else even know it's your name?"

"I don't think anyone else ever asked." Wrapping her in his arms, he drew her close for another moment. He didn't like the idea of leaving her to go out in the rain.

He liked the idea of meeting Chi Chi at the cantina even less.

Chapter 11

Guerrero's directive was posted on the cantina door.

> Liquor sales prohibited. Martial law has been declared during this state of emergency by order of General Rodolfo Guerrero. Violators will answer charges before the military tribunal.

McQuade stared at the stamped signature and considered what he would give for ten minutes alone with its owner. No hardware, no witnesses. Just one-on-one.

The louver in the window was lifted, and an eyeball appeared in the crack. A stage whisper followed. "Come to the back door."

McQuade played along. He hadn't walked up to the front door without checking around the premises first, but Antonio's game had its rules. Somewhat to McQuade's surprise, it was Chi Chi who led him through the tiny kitchen and past the bedroom, where a kerosene lamp burned beside the bed.

"My father is out," she whispered, smiling. "He probably won't be back tonight."

It occurred to him that that kind of smile wasn't as attractive to him as it once had been. "Is your friend here?" he asked.

"Just as I promised." She took his forearm in both hands and pressed her finger gently downwards, as though testing a piece of fruit for its ripeness. "And I heard my father say that he's been planting a story about a certain child who's missing. Some clever Anglo made off with the boy in a little Beechcraft airplane. You have nothing to worry about, McQuade." The lambent look she flashed told McQuade otherwise. "We are looking after you very, very well."

Juanito waited in the corner of the cantina, where one candle provided a dim circle of light on the low ceiling above the little wooden table. He was a short man, but he had the beefy shoulders of a net-hauler. He greeted McQuade with a hearty handshake and the kind of straightforward attitude that gave McQuade a pang of regret. Juanito was getting a line from Chi Chi, and McQuade had to feed into that, at least initially. If he cooperated completely, though, Juanito would be well paid.

McQuade returned the friendly grin and cast a meaningful glance at Chi Chi. Island custom excluded women when the men sat down to talk. "You ready to talk business, *amigo*?"

Chi Chi looked from one man's face to the other, posturing with her hands at her hips. "Going to Miami is my business. *You* said you'd get me across the water." She pointed a red fingernail at Juanito's head, then turned it on McQuade. "And *you* will get me into the city. Just so you know." She turned on her heel and marched behind the bar.

"I'll get you drinks, but I'll be listening to every word. That's the way they do it in Miami, you know."

Juanito chuckled. "I like a little fire in a woman. Don't you, *señor*?" Leaning over the table, he added from behind his cupped hand, "But this one is some big handful, if you know what I mean."

"I think I can sympathize." McQuade pulled out a pack of cigarettes and offered one to Juanito. "You've got a boat that can get us as far as Key West?"

"Miami!"

"We'll drive to Miami, Chi Chi." McQuade lit Juanito's cigarette, then held the match to his own. "The woman who's with me has been sick. I need to get her out of here as soon as possible."

Smoke swirled around Juanito's head. "I was fortunate to have been in Arco Iris when the storm hit. My boat wasn't damaged. But these are troubled times, *señor*."

"And transportation is at a premium," McQuade finished for him. "I'm well aware of that. What's your price?"

"Five thousand American dollars."

Hell of a bargain, McQuade thought, but he didn't let the thought register on his face. "You got a crew?"

"My son and I can handle the boat."

Damn. Another kid. "How old's your son?"

"Eighteen. And big for his age." Juanito held his hand several inches above his own head.

McQuade smiled. "Look, we're running a risk here. If you want to leave your son out of it, I can crew for you."

"Just being alive in these times is risky. We have taken chances before." He gave a conspiratorial wink. "You are not the first to come to this island, or leave it without going through the port authority."

Chi Chi delivered three drinks to the table and lifted her glass with a cheerleader's enthusiasm. "Here's to Miami, where all the action is!"

As Chi Chi had planned, Juanito left soon after her toast to prepare his boat for an early morning departure, but she hadn't planned for McQuade to leave with him, in the interest of scouting things out. It was disappointing to be left alone to blow out her lamp and wait until it was time for her to go down to the dock. Her only consolation was the promise of big city lights to come—the kind she would never have to blow out.

Elizabeth sat in the chair by the bed and waited. Every sixty seconds made a minute, every sixty minutes made an hour, and every sound outside made her lose count. Waiting alone in the house took every ounce of control she had. McQuade's face in the doorway was the most beautiful sight imaginable. She came out of the chair like a shot and fell into his arms.

"Hey, I'd say we're recovering nicely." He basked in the warmth of a smile that suggested nothing but joy at his return.

"I waited, Sloan. It seemed like forever, and I thought I heard... I don't know what I heard, but I waited."

"You did fine, honey." Far from patronizing her, he was proud. He rubbed her back affectionately. "This is a spooky place. How's the leg?"

"It itches."

"Can you walk on it?" She nodded hopefully. "What do you say we blow this joint, then?"

"Chi Chi's friend will take us?"

"Chi Chi came through. And according to her, word's out that Guerrero's son was kidnapped by an Anglo, who managed to fly him out of here in a single-engine Beech-craft.''

''But that's...''

McQuade smiled. ''Antonio has a wonderful way with rumors.''

''So they're not looking for us?''

''I think Guerrero's got his hands full keeping order in the city. If we can get by the patrol boats, we should be okay.'' He hesitated. ''And then there's Chi Chi.''

''Chi Chi?''

McQuade took Elizabeth's flowered scarf from the bed-side table and draped it over her head. ''Chi Chi's going to have to miss the boat again,'' he said as he tied the scarf under Elizabeth's chin. Wrapping her in his jacket, he added, ''There's no way I could get that woman past customs. Besides, Miami has enough problems.''

Juanito was waiting for them at the dock. Wordlessly they followed him past the boats in various states of disrepair that bobbed in the water like so much flotsam. Gentle waves slapped against the hulls and washed ashore, and worn wood creaked with the motion. It was a warm night, with a slip of a new silver moon brightening the starry sky.

The agile little fisherman hopped onto the deck of his boat and lifted his brawny arms as McQuade handed Elizabeth down to him. ''I have a place below where you can rest,'' Juanito told her. ''We'll be on our way soon.'' He gestured to the lanky young man who had apparently been sleeping in a chair on the deck. ''This is my son, whose name is also Juan.'' The boy rose obediently and dropped the army blanket he'd been wrapped in back on the chair. He stood more than a head taller than his father. Juanito clapped a hand on his son's back. ''I guess he'll be Big Juan, and I'll be Little Juan, right? This way," he invited, and Elizabeth followed him below deck with McQuade in tow.

Once she was settled, McQuade followed Juanito up to the wheelhouse.

"If we get stopped, there is a compartment right here—" Juanito popped open a door that blended in with the woodwork just below the wheel "—that hides a man quite nicely. We'll just say the woman came along with my son, and Chi Chi—" He checked his watch. "Chi Chi is holding us up." Frowning, he peered through the window toward the dock.

"Chi Chi is under the impression that she has another hour or so to get her act together." McQuade positioned himself carefully between Juanito and the door. "I'm afraid Chi Chi's not going to make this trip."

"Oh, but this was Chi Chi's idea. She'll be very—"

Juanito turned and found McQuade's pistol pointed at his belly. "Tell Juan to cast off," McQuade said quietly.

He was glad Elizabeth wasn't there to see him pull a gun on this man. Juanito's eyes bulged as he glanced up at McQuade's face and then in his son's direction. He swallowed convulsively, without quite closing his mouth, then cleared his throat and called out to the boy. "Let's cast off, Juan, while the coast looks clear."

Young Juan complied without comment. The engine rumbled, and the small fishing craft pulled away from its mooring, leaving the village of El Gallo in its wake. The boy went back to his deck chair, trusting his father's judgment as the boat churned through the inky water in search of open sea. McQuade didn't like himself much for giving the idea that the boy was part of an insurance package, but he had to consider Elizabeth first.

Juanito maneuvered across the little harbor. If they were stopped, it would happen near the channel, a fact which was on the minds of both men as they scanned the horizon.

McQuade was so absorbed in his act of piracy that Elizabeth's voice gave him a start.

"What's happened, Sloan?" McQuade's head came around only long enough to catch the look in her eyes. It wasn't one he wanted to deal with just then, and he turned his attention back to Juanito.

"Nothing, honey. We're on our way."

"What has this man done?" Her voice betrayed confusion and disbelief.

"He's left his girlfriend behind."

"But why the gun?" Elizabeth insisted.

"Saves questions," McQuade offered. "Simplifies matters, and gets us on our way. We're not going to Key West, Juanito. We're headed for Arco Iris."

Juanito shrugged. "That's fine with me. It's closer."

"It wouldn't have been fine with Chi Chi."

Juanito lifted his eyebrows in assent. "Chi Chi could almost smell Miami this time. Me? I like the smell of the islands better. I took this job for the money, *señor*, not for Chi Chi."

"Oh, yeah?"

"Please, Sloan," Elizabeth entreated. "I think we can trust this man. No more guns."

"Understand me, Juanito. This woman has a little boy waiting for her in Arco Iris. I intend to see that she gets there."

"I have a son, too, *señor*."

"Yeah." Somewhat chagrined, McQuade put his weapon away. "There was no way in hell I was taking Chi Chi to Miami," he mumbled as he fished in the breast pocket of his shirt for a cigarette.

"She's probably pacing the length of the dock right about now." Juanito's laugh was hesitant at first as he allowed himself to relax a little. Then he pictured what he'd described, glanced at McQuade's empty gun hand and laughed again. "I can always tell her you held a gun on me. But you, *señor* . . ."

The man's laughter was contagious, and McQuade couldn't resist. "God help me if that woman ever does find a way to get to Miami." He offered Juanito a cigarette.

Juan's lean face appeared in the doorway. "Patrol boat coming, Papa."

McQuade moved away from the window and nodded at Juanito to take a look. Juanito confirmed the news. "I can't outrun them. That's our best bet." He indicated the compartment he'd shown McQuade earlier.

McQuade allowed himself a glance at Elizabeth. She braced herself visibly and smiled as she lifted a hand to touch his bearded cheek. He took her hand to warm it in his and shifted his glance to Juanito. All the advice he'd given Elizabeth about trust came back to haunt him. Trust *me* had been easy to say. Trust her life to the good graces of some fisherman he'd just met? It was almost unthinkable.

"Don't make any mistakes." McQuade shoved the cigarettes back in his pocket as he riveted Juanito to the deck with a cold stare. "If anything happens to her, Juanito, I'll get you before they get me. I promise you that."

"Sloan." The sound of her voice softened him inside, and when he looked at her, his fear showed. "That's not the way," she said quietly.

He lifted the scarf, which had slipped to her shoulders, and tied it over her head. "You've had a fever," he reminded her.

"I'll be all right."

"She will if you get out of sight, *señor*." Scowling, Juanito jerked his chin toward the compartment again.

As the cruiser approached, its searchlight flooding the deck of the fishing boat, Juanito cut the engine. Elizabeth joined Juan on deck. She had her role to play. Juanito had given her a pair of shapeless paints that she'd rolled to midcalf, a faded sweatshirt with a hood and a pair of canvas deck shoes. With her thick braid tucked inside the sweatshirt and the scarf over her head, her identity, her age, even her sex, became almost indeterminate.

"Getting an early start?" The voice from the cruiser echoed through a bullhorn.

"Yes, sir," Juan called out. He took the cue to drape a protective arm around Elizabeth's shoulders as Juanito appeared on deck.

"Not much competition for territory these days," the voice said. "Everybody else is beached."

"Getting a jump on those Mexicans from Arco Iris," Juanito shouted back. "People have to eat."

"Papers in order?"

"You see my tags."

A beam of light flashed over the bow of the fishing boat, where the evidence of his registration was fastened.

"Just you and your kids?"

"My son and his betrothed. Pretty hard to put together a crew lately."

"Forecast looks good for today. Save us a nice piece of marlin."

The three stood silently, bracing themselves as the little fishing boat rolled over the retreating cruiser's wake.

"I owe you, Juanito." McQuade came down the steps from the wheelhouse. "Starting with an apology."

* * *

The edge of the world lightened gradually with the promise of a new day. McQuade braced his forearms on the railing and looked out over the stern at the horizon. He took a final deep drag from his last cigarette. Then he flicked it overboard and watched it arc high before hitting the water. The sun was coming up, and they were nearly home free. Elizabeth had said nothing to him since the patrol boat had given them a reprieve.

She would have Tomás back soon, and then hadn't she once said she'd be moving to New England? He figured the five thousand he owed Juanito would take the rest of his advance, since he'd already given Emilio five thousand. Realistically the trip hadn't cost him much except his time, and he could afford that. They were getting down to the wire, and it was time to take an objective look at himself and the emotional vise he'd willingly put himself into.

He felt her beside him before he turned to see her there. The scarf had slipped from her head again. Even the oversize clothes could do nothing to diminish the dignity in her bearing. McQuade decided he wouldn't take any final tallies of what this trip had cost him until she said goodbye.

"Do you have another cigarette?" she asked.

He shook his head. "Fresh out."

"Too bad." She shrugged, shoved her hands into her pockets and leaned against the rail. "I had a sudden craving."

"Just as well I ran out. You should be resting."

She shook her head, letting the wind take the loose wisps of hair away from her face. "I can't take any more cramped quarters. Besides, I wanted to watch the sun rise on this day."

He'd been watching the pink streaks gather above the calm sea, gaining in intensity like a musical prelude. "It's going to be a beauty, all right."

"I know you did what you felt you had to do," she said quietly as she gazed out at the sea. "But seeing you hold a gun on that man..."

"I've been carrying it since the first day, Elizabeth. I use it when I have to."

"But he wasn't threatening us. For a moment I was on his side and not—"

"Not on mine. I noticed."

"He had agreed to help us."

"He'd agreed on certain terms, and I changed the terms. When you don't have time to argue, you play your ace. It's as simple as that."

McQuade straightened, held the rail in both hands and drank cool air from the salty rim of morning. He didn't feel clean, but he told himself that all he needed was a shower and a shave, and he'd be fine.

"Would you have shot that man?" she asked him finally.

He gave her a long, hooded look. "I don't pull a gun on a man unless I'm willing to use it. I know it, and I make sure he knows it. Nine times out of ten, that's all it takes."

"You mean the threat is usually enough."

"That's right." Folding his arms across his chest, he turned to face her. "Why did you hire me, Elizabeth? Remember all those qualifications you thought I had? You could handle the gun yourself. I showed you how—remember? But you didn't know if you could use it." He tapped his fingertips against his own chest. "You hired me because that's what I do. When the chips are down, all the channels are exhausted and everybody's hands are tied, people come to me because I'm willing to use the gun if I have to."

"But with Juanito—"

"I couldn't be sure, and I didn't have much time. There are no superheroes, Elizabeth. You wanted the Lone Ranger? Well, all you got was me." He knew what she was thinking. How were his tactics any better than Guerrero's? She would have to sort that out for herself, he decided. "Anyway, we're headed for Arco Iris, and your kid's waiting there for you."

She turned her face toward the rising sun and smiled. "So the day begins."

"So you have arrived, my friends." Juanito watched his son tie the boat to a piling. He turned to McQuade and cocked his hands on his hips. "You are safe. I am still alive, since you found no fault with my services. When I see Chi Chi again, well..." He shrugged and gave his head a dramatic shake. "That condition may change."

McQuade laughed. "Take her a present, *amigo*. You've got a bonus coming. Fix her up with something sparkly and she'll probably let you off easy." Sobering, McQuade offered his hand. "We owe you our lives, Juanito. I only did what I did because—"

Juanito accepted the handshake with a broad grin as he glanced at Elizabeth. "I know. For this lady, I would have done the same."

"Thank you, Juanito," she said.

"I will see you with your son before I leave here, *señora*," he said. "I have thought of nothing else all day long—to see the happiness on your face."

"Yes." An irrepressible smile burnished her dark eyes. "Yes, you will. As soon as I—Sloan..."

"The first thing we do is get to the Oyster Shell, so I can take care of Juanito, get cleaned up and find out where

Emilio lives,'' McQuade said. "I'll meet you there later, Juanito. First round's on me.''

McQuade reached for Elizabeth's hand. He felt the tremors of excitement ripple through her body as he helped her plant her feet firmly on the weathered boards of the pier. The slanted rays of late afternoon sunshine were still warm, and the lush green, lazy little island basked in them. McQuade slung his jacket over his shoulder and fixed his mind on a long drink and a large, rare steak. The idea reached his stomach, which seconded the motion with an audible growl.

Elizabeth favored her injured leg as she tried to set a faster pace than she could handle. "I can't wait for you to do all that,'' she complained.

"And I'm going to get a doctor to take a look at that leg.''

"After we get Tomás. Oh, Sloan, do you think he'll remember me?'' She looked down at her skirt, then grabbed her braid and examined that, too. "Maybe a shower and some clean clothes.''

"Might not be a bad idea.'' He slid her a loaded glance. "They say a mother's scent is the first thing her child learns to recognize.''

"McQuade! Are you saying I might ... smell?''

He laughed. "Not to me, lady. We've been hanging out in the same rat holes.'' He watched her adjust the scarf, which had slipped to her shoulders again. For once she looked a little disconcerted, her dignity bruised, and he took a perverse enjoyment in that look.

Felix Santiago was overjoyed when the two bedraggled guests presented themselves at the desk in the lobby of the Oyster Shell.

"McQuade, my friend! I was beginning to wonder whether you'd be back to pay your bill. I've been holding your rooms. At ninety dollars each a night, that's—''

"That's a hell of a way to greet an old friend," McQuade interrupted. They shared a laugh and pumped each other's hands.

"Emilio Gomez had a harrowing story to tell," Felix said as he handed two keys over the desk. "We were afraid we'd have to count you among the missing at De Colores."

"Is Tomás all right?" Elizabeth asked anxiously.

"The child?" Felix smiled. "He's fine. You might have some trouble separating him from the Gomezes, though. They've become quite attached."

"I left a few things in the room, Felix. Are they still there?" she asked as she edged toward the stairs.

"Everything is as you left it," Felix assured her. He turned to McQuade. "What can I get you, my friend?"

Watching her push herself up the steps purely on adrenaline, McQuade decided to postpone the drink and the steak. "How about a razor?"

McQuade walked Elizabeth to the Gomez home. It meant climbing a hill, and he fought the urge to lift her into his arms and carry her along the gravel path. A chunk of wood or a flat rock served as a step every few yards. When at one steep spot she bent over, seeking a rock for a handhold, he gave up the fight and swept her off the ground.

"Sloan, no, I can . . ."

He made an effort to sound matter-of-fact, to look into her eyes without betraying himself. "Elizabeth, I won't have you crawling up this hill."

"It looks outrageous, but I guess we're beyond that," she admitted as she settled her arm around his shoulders.

"No kidding," he said drily and proceeded up the hill.

The little house overlooked the bay. From it, Emilio could keep an eye out for his boat, the weather and the temperament of the sea. When they arrived, Luisa Gomez was taking her laundry off the line. A white sheet flapped under her outstretched arms. At her feet, a dark-haired little head bobbed above the rim of a basket.

"Tomás." Elizabeth's voice was barely audible.

McQuade lowered her feet to the ground. His throbbing heart found its way into his throat as he watched her take three tentative steps toward her son. When she saw them, Luisa stepped away from the basket.

"Tomás?" Elizabeth approached slowly and spoke to the child in quiet, melodious Spanish. "Don't be afraid, little one. It's me. It's... it's Mama."

She knelt beside the basket, her white cotton dress billowing around her. Her hands trembled as she reached them, palms up, toward the boy. McQuade shoved his own into the pockets of his jeans, embarrassed even though no one else noticed, that they weren't steady, either. Tomás stood up, holding onto the basket's rim, and looked into his mother's eyes. His own were as big as saucers.

"Do you remember me, Tomás? Will you come to your mama?"

He wrapped a chubby hand around her fingers and searched her hand for some kind of offering. Finding none, he looked into her face again. The rim of the basket failed to support him, and he tottered off balance into his mother's waiting arms.

"Oh, Tomás, I've missed you. I've missed you so much!" The toddler grabbed a handful of his mother's thick hair, and she laughed through joyful tears. "Can you say Mama, little one?"

"Mama?"

"Yes!" She hugged him close and rocked him as she had dreamed of doing for almost a year, while she crooned, "Yes, it's Mama. Yes, yes, yes..."

McQuade watched, sharing her joy, yet distanced from her by it. He'd brought the two of them together, the mother and her son. Elizabeth and Tomás. God, how he wanted to be part of this reunion. It was his reunion, too; he'd made it happen. But he'd lost contact. He stood at the edge of the little yard, saw that Luisa spoke to them, heard their voices, but registered nothing of what was said.

The women would probably find a lot to talk about, he told himself, and he had an appointment with a steak and a bottle of his favorite bourbon. He turned back to the hillside path.

"Sloan!"

Turning again, he squinted into the evening sun.

"Please wait."

"You guys need to get acquainted," he said, somehow managing to speak the words easily. "Take your time. I have to take care of Juanito's account and my stomach. I'll come back for you later if you want."

"We'll take care of them tonight, *señor*," Luisa offered.

Elizabeth took a step toward him, her confusion evident. "Juanito's account is mine to deal with."

"We'll settle up later. Don't worry about it." He nodded at the child in Elizabeth's arms. "Cute kid. He needs looking after. I'll see about a doctor for you. You can plan on an examination before you check out of here, lady."

"Sloan . . ."

"Keep her off that leg," he told Luisa. "I'll check in with you tomorrow, then."

He struck off down the hill, as if steaks really did make appointments and bourbon could really fill the aching hollow in his gut.

Elizabeth rapped softly on the door to McQuade's room. No answer came. She knew it was early, but she had slipped away before Tomás awoke. She tightened her fist and rapped with more determination.

The suggestion that came from the other side of the door would have been anatomically impossible for her to follow. She was trying to come up with an appropriate reply when the same gruff voice added, "Any comments can be dropped off at the desk."

"I'm afraid I'm speechless, Mr. McQuade."

The next grumble was muffled, and then, "Hold on. Lemme find my pants."

In a moment Elizabeth heard the faucet running. When the door swung open, she could tell that he'd dunked his face in water and hastily combed his hair. "Do you have a watch, lady?"

"No, but I believe it's—"

"Spare me. I've got one. Come on in."

She saw where he'd slept and knew the sheets would still be warm. And she saw, to her relief, that he'd slept alone. His clothes, other than the jeans he wore, were scattered on the floor along with damp towels and several sections of *The Miami Herald*. His pistol lay on the nightstand next to a glass tumbler, which contained the dark remains of a drink.

"Did Felix manage to find you a good steak last night?" she asked.

"Fair."

"And a good bourbon and water?"

"Several."

"Is that why you didn't come back?"

He raked his fingers through his hair and shook his head. "Luisa said they'd look after you, and Tomás was probably confused as it was. He didn't need to deal with another person. He would probably have remembered it was me holding him when he got stuck with a needle."

She smiled. "You'll be surprised. He's not shy. He seems to know me, and he likes Emilio. He won't have any trouble getting used to you—unless, of course, you greet him the way you greeted his mother this morning."

"Yeah, well . . ." He shrugged. "His mother's got a bad habit of looking me up too early after a rough night."

"Is that so?" She stepped closer to him, then reached up and touched his cheek. "I was beginning to like the beard."

"Yeah?" He smiled, relishing the contact, wanting more. "I thought it looked like hell."

"It was part of the face that chased all my demons away. I owe you such a debt of gratitude, Sloan McQuade." She let her hand slide to his chest, admitting, "Of course, I owe you more than that, on top of what you paid Emilio and Juanito."

He caught her hand in his. She looked up into his eyes and found a curious scowl. "Your debt was canceled when we made love, Elizabeth."

"I don't pay my debts that way." She tried to draw her hand back, but he tightened his grip.

"You know what I mean. I couldn't take money from you now. The advance paid most of the expenses, so let's call it even."

"We aren't even. You did your job. You deserve—"

"I deserve money, right? You needed a little muscle, and I provided that. You didn't always like the looks of it, not when things got muddy and you weren't sure who was wearing the white hat. But I did the job, and I deserve to be paid for it. Is that what you're trying to say?"

"We had an agreement," she reminded him. He was squeezing her hand too hard, but the look in his eyes wasn't threatening. He might have been willing to shoot Juanito, but he wasn't willing to hurt her.

"The terms of the agreement changed somewhere along the way, Elizabeth. Figure it out. We had to bring Tomás home. It wasn't a job anymore. It was the way it had to be."

"Why?"

"Because it was right. Because the kid needed his mother, and because his mother—"

He pierced her with the sharp edge of a glittering scowl, the muscles in his jaw working as he drew a long breath. The look she gave him was as good as an invitation, and he damned himself for wanting one more kiss even as he pulled her into his arms and slanted his mouth across hers. She took his kiss as hungrily as he gave it. He could smell salt air in her hair and a citrusy scent on her skin. Everything about her was clean and fresh, and he wanted the fresh taste of her on his tongue and the feel of her clean hands on his body. He dipped his head to kiss her neck and tangled his fingers in her silken hair.

"Just a simple thank-you, Elizabeth," he whispered into the hollow of her neck. "That's enough."

She flattened her palms against his back and drew herself against him so that he could feel the points of her breasts and the curves of her thighs. "It isn't enough, Sloan. Is it?"

He lifted his head, and she looked up at him, repeating the question almost inaudibly. Without fear, without any reservation, she wanted him. She gave him a look that set his blood on fire.

"God, no," he groaned. "It isn't. Damn you, it isn't."

"Let me give you—"

He lowered her to the bed. There was no time for preliminaries or slow undressing. He pushed her dress aside, and she helped him with his pants. They found each other with trembling hands, touched each other with shuddering need.

"I want—I need to be—"

"Let me love you, Sloan."

"That would be enough," he whispered as he slipped inside her.

"That . . . oh, yes, that—"

"If you could love me, Elizabeth . . . oh, honey, if you could love me . . ."

"I could love no one else," she promised. "Only you."

Tangled together in sheets and clothing and long black hair, they touched and exchanged soft looks. She wouldn't take the child and leave him now. He wouldn't take the money and run. She touched his lower lip with her middle finger. He smiled and nipped the fleshy pad. It was a time of wonder.

"I want to be touched," she marveled.

"I want to touch you."

"I had forgotten what it was like not to be afraid."

"You know I couldn't hurt you. Not intentionally." He slipped his hand beneath her dress, caressed her belly and cupped her breast. "I want to protect you, Elizabeth. I would do anything to keep you from harm. Go to any lengths."

"But I know you wouldn't have shot an innocent man."

He kissed her hair and said, "No, I wouldn't have," but he knew he was simplifying the matter for her sake. It might be something she would never understand. He'd made a split-second decision to force an issue at the point of a gun. It had been a power play, and he knew she would never sympathize with that. But, unlike the man who'd tormented her, his power was tempered with mercy, with conscience, with the capacity to care. Surely by now she'd learned that much about the man who loved her.

"Where's Tomás?" McQuade asked.

"He was still sleeping when I left. Luisa's probably given him breakfast by now." She snuggled against his shoulder.

"I don't want to go back to Miami for a while. I want to stay in this quiet place and get to know my son again." She traced a provocative circle around his flat nipple. "Aren't you due for a vacation, McQuade?"

"I'm due for another advance from you, lady." She raised a questioning eyebrow, and he smiled. "On all that love you promised me. I've got a hell of a lot of it stored up for you."

"Oh, but I'm due for a rest," she teased.

"I haven't forgotten about the doctor, either." He smoothed her hair back and tucked it behind her ear. "And then we're going to collect Tomás from Luisa. You think he'd let me teach him how to swim? Or should I wait a couple of years on that?"

She remembered the dream she'd had of Sloan playing with Tomás on the beach. "I trust your judgment, Sloan." She kissed him and whispered, "I trust you."

Afterword

The islands of De Colores and Arco Iris are lovely figments of the author's imagination. To get to them, one must launch a little boat called *The Silhouette* from the east coast of the Yucatán Peninsula, set a course by the stars and sail straight on till morning.

*   *   *   *   *

PAINTBOX MORNING

Kathleen Eagle

For my sister, Jill.
It's going to be a bright, sunshiny day.

Prologue

The bright white glare from the noonday sun was almost as troublesome as the man who persisted in poking the barrel of a pistol in Miguel Hidalgo's back. Miguel's eyes were light-sensitive, and he had lost his sunglasses. And now it appeared that his sensitivity to .44-caliber bullets was about to be tested. He knew his skin would puncture as easily as Julius Caesar's, although the three men who accompanied him in his final walk were hardly senators. The island's fledgling government had not advanced that far.

Miguel paused to turn his face to the salty breeze. His escort prodded him between the shoulder blades, and they continued on. His senses were heightened now, and he wanted to absorb an overdose of his island home—the rhythm of gently lapping waves, the gritty feeling of sand in his shoes, the smell of hibiscus and seawater and the sun-bronzed face of his fellow islanders. Even the three who were bent on killing him.

They were young enough to be idealistic but possessed of enough naïveté to be totally misdirected. They were soldiers, and they had their orders. They had chosen to put their trust in the man who appeared to be the stronger, a man whose very name was a threat. Rodolfo Guerrero would soon claim to be the solitary authority in De Colores. Miguel remembered the beginning of it all—the three of them: Castillo, Guerrero and Hidalgo. Suddenly Castillo was dead, and Guerrero was clearly wasting no time ridding himself of his other partner. Miguel's dying regret would be that he was leaving his little homeland in the clutches of a tyrant.

The stretch of sand became rocky as they approached the cliffs. With his hands tied behind him, Miguel's balance was unreliable. He cursed the smooth soles of his shoes as he negotiated the rocks. When he stumbled, one of the soldiers reached reflexively to steady him, while another jabbed him in the side with a pistol. "Move along," their companion ordered.

"Where are you taking me?"

Miguel's question was ignored until they stood beneath the dark cliffs, and the man who held the gun to his back announced, "This is far enough."

They spun him so that his back was to the sea. The man who held him at gunpoint had a lean face and hungry eyes. He gave an impatient wave with his pistol, and the other two clutched at Miguel's shoulders like a pair of buzzards and ripped the oak-leaf clusters from his khaki shirt. To Miguel the rank had always been a sham, and he was relieved to feel the weight of it lifted from his shoulders. He had shunned the ribbons and gold braid with which Guerrero had decorated himself so generously. But when the small embroidered shield bearing the rainbow-hued emblem of De

Colores was torn from its place above his breast pocket, he flinched.

"Why are you doing this?" he demanded.

"We are ordered to strip you of all symbols of the country you betrayed," said the man behind the gun.

"Betrayed?" Miguel's blood heated at the sound of the word. "*Betrayed!* I may be guilty of many sins, but not treason." He looked from one anxious young face to another. "Am I to be tried here on the beach? Is this Guerrero's latest idea of judicial process?"

"You have already been found guilty, *señor*. We do not question the general's orders."

"'*Señor*,' is it?" Miguel gave a short, mirthless laugh. "And Colonel Guerrero has promoted himself to general. Is there a promotion in this for the three of you, as well?" Miguel read the answer in their silence and suggested quietly, "Beware of rank that comes too easily. You see how easily it may be stripped away."

The lean-faced soldier jerked his head, and the other two moved away from Miguel as they pocketed the bits of metal and cloth they'd torn from his clothes. Then they unsnapped their holsters and withdrew their pistols.

"Were you present at my trial?" Miguel asked in a smooth, low voice. "If I've been found guilty, there must have been a trial. There must have been specific charges. Do you happen to know what they were?"

"Our orders came from the general himself. That's all we need to know."

They needed to know how to kill a man, Miguel thought. Guerrero had work to do if he expected to build his military machine from boys like these. Miguel watched them ready their pistols. The smooth-faced one on the right turned his head and made an attempt to spit in the sand, but his mouth was apparently all but dry. The one on the left wiped a palm on the leg of his camouflage pants. Miguel doubted that either of them would be his murderer, but the man in the center with the lean face might be able to manage it. Miguel decided to die facing the sea.

"Perhaps it would be easier for you if I turned around," he suggested, and he did so.

"Front, back, it makes no difference."

Miguel heard the breech bolts slide back and forth on two of the pistols, and he filled his lungs with a salty breath. One assassin's voice cursed his companions as the words of a well-rehearsed prayer floated across Miguel's mind in time with his heartbeat. The sound of an incoming wave washed across the rude reports of gunfire, and a ball of white heat slammed into his back. Blue water, he thought as he sank to his knees. Blue sky, blue heaven . . . blue . . . gray . . . black.

Chapter 1

This was not the way Paulo Torrez had envisioned his career. De Colores had never had much of an army, but Paulo had seen movies, and true soldiers did not spend day after day patrolling the beach in a rattletrap jeep. Paulo didn't even get to drive. His cousin Raphael claimed that privilege because he was two years Paulo's senior. Blue sky, endless sea. Everything was calm. Paulo longed for some kind of action.

"Pull over," Paulo demanded as the jeep labored toward the top of a grassy overlook. He spotted a couple of scraggly bushes that would serve his limited modesty.

"What for?" Raphael asked, reluctant to be distracted from his reverie of a young woman he'd met the night before.

"What do you think? You've bounced me in this seat long enough, *hermano*. I'm about to disgrace my uniform."

Raphael grinned as he turned the wheel. "I guess I did

promise your mother I would look out for her *niño*, and *niño* is what you are.''

''*Bored* is what I am,'' Paulo said as he climbed down from the jeep. ''I would rather clean fish with my father than ride around in this poor excuse for a vehicle from morning till night.''

''All right, all right,'' Raphael grumbled. ''I'll let you drive a little while. Just hurry up.''

A wide grin split Paulo's boyish face as he spun on his heel and trotted up the hill toward the bushes.

''*Niño,*'' Raphael said to himself. ''You're too young for this army life.'' But Paulo had been his shadow ever since Raphael could remember, and Raphael would have had it no other way. If the great battle Colonel Guerrero was always predicting ever came to pass, Raphael would trust no one else in Paulo's foxhole. Personally, Raphael hoped the peace would hold, and that it would not be too late for Paulo to get the education Colonel Hidalgo had promised. Paulo was smart. He'd finished the eighth grade. That was probably why he had deserted his father's fishing boat and followed his cousin into the New People's Army of De Colores. Paulo wanted adventure, but what he really needed, at the tender age of seventeen, was more education.

Something below the bluff had caught Paulo's eye. Raphael slid from the seat as he watched his cousin drop to the ground and peer over the edge. Paulo motioned for silence and signaled Raphael to join him. Raphael snatched up the automatic rifle and was hurrying to join Paulo when he heard the report of gunfire below.

Paulo was struggling to get the pistol out of his holster as Raphael dropped to his side. On the beach below, three men converged upon the body of a fourth. Raphael stilled Paulo's hand with his. ''They're out of your range,'' Raphael whispered.

"But not yours." Paulo nodded at the M-16 in Raphael's grip. "Raphael, I think that was the colonel they shot."

"The colonel?" One of the men knelt in the sand and made a hasty examination of the body.

"It looked like Colonel Hidalgo," Paulo insisted. "Shoot them, Raphael. They've murdered the colonel!"

Raphael looked at his young cousin and saw the outrage in his face. He looked down again. The three were dragging the body across the sand, and he realized that these were men he knew from the barracks. "*Dios*, Paulo, they're . . . they're on *our* side. I can't just shoot them."

"They shot the colonel!"

Raphael shouldered the rifle and sighted down the barrel. If he pulled the trigger, he wasn't sure what he'd hit. "If he's dead, he's dead, Paulo. We don't know what's going on here."

The three men and the body disappeared into a small cave in the cliff near the water. Paulo cursed his cousin. "I know what I saw. You should have cut the bastards down where they stood, Raphael. What is the matter with you?"

Raphael stared at the entrance to the cave. "We can't go around shooting people just because we carry guns. I have to think about this, Paulo. I have to figure out what's going on. Our own men—"

"There they are! They left him in the cave."

"The tide's coming in," Raphael observed as the three below them moved quickly to quit the scene of their crime. "If the water reaches that cave . . ."

"The body will be washed away, and we'll have no proof of what we saw." Paulo gestured helplessly. Had the rifle been in his hands, he would have taken a shot at *something*.

''We'll wait until they're gone, and we'll remove the body,'' Raphael said patiently. ''Those three may be renegades.''

''Then we should go after them!''

''On the other hand, there may have been another takeover. We must be careful, Paulo.''

They moved the jeep to a sheltered spot near a path they knew would take them directly to the beach. It would be a steep climb carrying a corpse, but at least they would not be out in the open. They had to hurry. The tide was already approaching the mouth of the cave.

The body lay facedown in the sand. The cave was dank and filled with the scent of fresh blood. In the dim light Raphael was able to locate the wound in the man's back, while Paulo knelt beside his head and brushed the sand from his face.

''It *is* Colonel Hidalgo.'' Paulo's awed pronouncement echoed within the close walls. ''Why did they do this?''

''I don't know,'' Raphael said as he cut the rope that bound the colonel's hands. ''Help me turn him over.''

As they rolled him onto his back, Paulo pulled the colonel's head into his lap. He had seen Colonel Hidalgo at a distance many times, and once, not even very long ago, on the anniversary of the fall of the old regime, the colonel had visited his barracks and shaken his hand. The soldiers had seen more of Colonel Guerrero than they had of Colonel Hidalgo, and many of them were impressed with Guerrero's flashy uniform and tall black boots. His quick temper was also impressive to some, who took it as a sign of power. But Paulo remembered how proud he'd felt when Colonel Hidalgo, whose head now lay so still in his lap, had taken the time to greet him.

"Paulo, I think he's still alive!" Raphael lifted his ear from the colonel's chest and looked at his cousin with wide-eyed hopefulness.

"*¡Dios!* Alive?"

He felt for a pulse on the side of the colonel's neck, taking care not to press too hard. "My own heart is pounding so hard, I can't tell whose is whose, but . . . yes, I think so."

"What can we do?"

"So much blood. Give me your shirt, Paulo."

"Mine?" His camouflage uniform was Paulo's pride and joy. Only those who had special assignments, like patrolling the beaches, were issued uniforms. So far the uniform was all that had made the job worthwhile.

"Your undershirt. I'm not wearing one."

Somewhat relieved, Paulo unbuttoned his shirt.

"Tear it in half. I think the bullet went right through him."

Raphael joined their makeshift canvas belts together and tied them around the colonel's chest to hold the folded pieces of shirt in place over the entrance and exit wounds. Then he lifted the colonel's shoulders, Paulo took his legs, and together they carried him up the side of the mountain. Their years of hauling nets full of fish had prepared them for the job. When they laid him on the back seat of the jeep, he groaned.

"Colonel?" Raphael waited a moment, hoping the colonel would open his eyes. "Bring water, Paulo." No sooner had Raphael uttered the command than the canteen, with its cap dangling open on its chain, appeared at his elbow. "Can you hear me, Colonel Hidalgo? Take a sip of water. Open your eyes and tell us what to do."

There was sand in his mouth, and then there was water. It was the sea. The sea had claimed him. A muffled voice called to him above the water's depths. When he tried to answer, the water filled his mouth again. Struggling with heavy eyelids, he managed to lift them for a brief flash of sunlight, and then everything became murky. Cold. Disjointed. Heavy. Crushing weight on his chest.

"Colonel Hidalgo, please . . ."

Please what? Please die? Not now. Not yet. Not with the name of . . . Traitor . . . Guilty . . . Cold, cold . . .

"Open up that canvas, Paulo. Cover him. He's cold."

Traitor . . . traitor . . . I'm not a traitor, Paulo.

"Paulo didn't do this to you, sir. Me and Paulo, we saw them. We couldn't stop them. We were . . . too far away."

The young face was clear, just for a moment. Dark, anxious eyes. Trembling mouth. Kindness, even in the killer.

"You're not dead, sir. Not yet, anyway. You need a doctor."

No doctors. No hospitals. No police . . . no soldiers.

"Stay with him, Paulo. Keep that tarp over him. We need a place to hide him."

The little landing strip was used only occasionally. It was one of the few spots on the island where fuel was available, albeit at a steep price, and few questions were asked. For a price, security could be relaxed, as well. Raphael remembered a shack that stood at the edge of a sugarcane field adjacent to the landing strip. He thought the colonel might be safe there until Raphael could decide what should be done. He left Paulo in the shack with the wounded man while he went to the village for food and bandages, leaving the jeep well hidden in an overgrown ravine.

As he cut across the field toward the shack, he considered the situation while he surveyed the cane and the stand of trees nearby. He couldn't trust anyone now, and that, more than anything, frightened him. Paulo wanted to shoot first and ask questions later, but Raphael felt the weight of cautious instincts. In addition to buying food and bandages, he had been anxious to hear some bit of conversation that would explain the attempt on Colonel Hidalgo's life. He'd heard nothing.

Paulo stuck his head out the door just as Raphael reached for the latch. "The colonel has regained consciousness," Paulo announced, his eyes bright with the news. "He says the wound is not so bad." Anxious for his cousin to see the improvement for himself, Paulo took the rifle from Raphael's hand and set it against the wall as Raphael closed the door quickly. "The bleeding has stopped," Paulo said, as though he had accomplished it himself.

Raphael cast an apprehensive look at the man who was propped up on the folded tarp. Colonel Hidalgo met Raphael's look with a dark, unemotional stare. Without looking away, Raphael extracted a package from his knapsack before handing it to Paulo. What had this man done? Raphael wondered. In his delirium, the colonel had mumbled something about not being a traitor. Who dared to accuse such an important man? Whose side had Raphael and Paulo taken by rescuing this man from the tide, and against whom were they siding?

"What is your name?" the colonel asked in a low, strained voice.

"Raphael Esperanza." Raphael ripped into the package containing the few medical supplies he had been able to find as he took a step closer. "Corporal Raphael Esperanza."

"You were not with the three who shot me?"

"No. We were on patrol." Raphael cast a quick glance at his cousin, then knelt beside the injured man. "Paulo and me—we were on top of the cliff. We saw them drag you to the cave, but... they were our own men. You had already been shot. We... we didn't know..."

"It's all right," the colonel said. "You acted wisely. Guerrero holds all the cards at the moment."

Paulo stepped closer. "Colonel Guerrero *himself* is responsible for this?"

The colonel closed his eyes and nodded. "I understand he's made himself a general now. He may have caused Castillo's death, too. I don't know."

"Ay," Paulo groaned. "We should have killed them. I knew it!"

"No," Raphael said. "If just one of them had gotten away, they would be combing the island for us by now. As it is, they think the colonel's body has been washed out to sea."

"Where are we?" the colonel asked. His dark eyes probed Raphael's for more than the answer to that question.

"We're near the village of El Gallo. There's a small landing strip." Raphael jerked his chin toward the door. "My uncle's cane field stands out there."

Colonel Hidalgo nodded. "I know the place. It's a good choice, Raphael. There's the possibility of . . . a plane." His features tightened with the strain of his agony.

Raphael reached for the buttons on the man's tattered shirt, then hesitated, asking permission with his eyes. Now that the colonel was conscious, there was his rank to be considered. Hidalgo simply closed his eyes, and Raphael dispatched the buttons quickly. He eased the bloody wad of Paulo's shirt away from the low chest wound.

"Colonel, I must get you to a doctor. All I could find in the village besides some bandages was an antiseptic for the injuries of children." He tossed the cotton aside and examined the wound, from which blood was slowly seeping. Paulo's claim that the bleeding had stopped had been premature. "This wound is serious, too serious for us to—"

"Do the best you can with what you have. With any luck, you will have my undying gratitude."

"What I have—it's not enough," Raphael protested as he examined the small bottle of medicine. When he saw the colonel make a vain attempt to moisten his own lips, he signaled impatiently to Paulo for the canteen.

"It has to be, Raphael. My life is in your hands now."

The very idea chilled Raphael. He held the canteen to the colonel's lips and whispered, "Drink slowly, sir."

"Colonel Guerrero is the wrong man to lead this country," Paulo said quickly. "You must recover from this, Colonel Hidalgo, and we must raise an army, and we must—"

The colonel pushed the canteen away and swallowed as he looked at Paulo. "You must return to your posts. You have already risked too much." He turned to Raphael. "Do what you can to plug up the holes. If you could leave me some food, perhaps a gun... I might turn hijacker if the right plane—"

"We won't leave you, colonel."

Miguel Hidalgo studied the faces of the two young soldiers who watched him so anxiously. They were just boys. Boys had tried to kill him, and boys had saved his life. All of them should have been working on their fathers' fishing boats or in their uncles' fields. Better yet, they should have been studying in a classroom. But, if Guerrero had his way, they would all carry guns. The boy was right. He had to recover from this.

He took the canteen from Raphael's hand and tipped it to his mouth to slake an overwhelming thirst. Grateful for some measure of relief, he turned his commanding gaze first on Paulo, then on Raphael. "If I am still your colonel, then you will do as I say. Is that clear?" Both nodded. "Good. Then you will do what you can to get me on my feet. If we accomplish that, it will be reasonable to formulate some kind of plan.''

The sound of a distant engine cut the conversation short. They listened. They looked at one another, hoping they were all hearing the same sound. A plane!

Paulo crouched behind a pile of old tires as he watched the pilot tend to her plane. She was clearly American. Her hair was tucked into a baseball cap, and her loose-fitting khaki shorts and shirt almost camouflaged her sex. It was obvious that she was no stranger to the island. She knew enough to refuel her plane immediately and be ready to fly. She was alone, she was quite small, and she was perfect, Paulo thought. If she would only go inside the ramshackle gas station and stay there for just a minute or two.

Paulo waited while the woman scrutinized every inch of her twin-engine Cessna. Sweat streamed from his face to his neck as he prepared to take advantage of the first opportunity. Raphael was bandaging the colonel's wounds, and the colonel had agreed to eat what he could of the food Raphael had brought from the village. The colonel was a strong man, Paulo reminded himself. He would survive the trip. There! She'd gone inside. Pistol in hand, Paulo made a dash for the door of the plane.

Miguel slipped his arm into the sleeve of what was left of his shirt as Raphael, kneeling behind him, held the garment up. Miguel took the fact that he could sit up on his own as an encouraging sign. Every move he made cost him precious strength, though, at this point, the show of what strength he had left was for the benefit of the two boys who wanted so desperately to believe in him.

"You and Paulo must return to your posts and tell no one—'' urgency glittered in Miguel's eyes as he looked up at Raphael "—*no one* about anything you have seen or done today. If I'm captured, you will not interfere. There are only two of you, Raphael."

"There will be more," the young soldier promised.

"Don't do anything foolish. Please. I'll come back as soon as I'm able. I'll go to El Gallo and I'll get word to you."

Raphael nodded. "I joined in General Castillo's coup last year because I believed he would bring freedom to De Colores," he said. "He promised land, and you talked of a new life for everyone. But Colonel Guerrero is no different from *El Presidente* and the rest of the old regime."

"He's different," Miguel said quietly, thinking what uneasy bedfellows the coup had made of the three of them. "He's more dangerous."

"I want what you've promised us, Colonel Hidalgo. A life without fear. Jobs. Schools for boys like Paulo."

Miguel turned away so that Raphael wouldn't see the amusement in his face. *He* wanted schools for boys like *Raphael*, too. "Teachers are always pushing for schools," he said. "And I'm a teacher. This uniform doesn't fit me."

Raphael eyed the tattered shoulder of the colonel's shirt, where the symbols of his rank had been ripped away. "You don't need the uniform, Colonel Hidalgo. Just come back and lead us. We'll follow you."

The boy's faith in him made him shudder inwardly. Through the triumvirate, Miguel had unwittingly helped Guerrero gain unlimited access to power. What if he couldn't come back? What would happen to these boys and others like them? The answers crowded into his mind along with the pain, and all of it made his head swim. "Take a look outside," he said gruffly. "See what's taking that cousin of yours so long."

Ronnie Harper felt uneasy. There was only one small window in the place, and the quarters were too close for comfort. She'd contracted to fly into this hornet's nest to help some people escape, and the sooner she could take on her passengers and hightail it out of here, the better she'd like it.

From a dark corner of the building a radio was blasting a mixture of static and calypso music. Ronnie handed a roll of bills to the man behind the pile of crates that made up the counter in this so-called gas station. She had included the mandatory "tip" as payment for no questions asked, then informed the little man that she'd brought Red Cross supplies. He smiled as he examined the American currency. As long as the money was good, he obviously didn't care what she'd brought.

"I'll move my plane to the other side of the strip," she told him in Spanish. "I won't be here more than a few days." *I hope,* she added to herself.

The dark-haired man shrugged as he pocketed Ronnie's money. When the music was interrupted, he wiped his hand on his oil-stained T-shirt and turned the radio up. The announcement of an emergency bulletin caught Ronnie's attention, and she concentrated on separating the Spanish from the static and making sense of the message.

"Sad duty to report...Colonel Miguel Hidalgo's death...assassinated by a rebel faction...state of emergency..."

"Ay," the dark-haired man groaned.

Damn, Ronnie thought. The hornet's nest had become a snake pit. *"Es una verguenza,"* she sympathized. And it certainly *was* a shame. Her written permission to fly supplies in from the Red Cross came from Hidalgo. Of course, she had no permission to fly her passengers out, which was one of her reasons for choosing this particular airstrip—that and its proximity to El Gallo.

"Yes, it is a shame," the man agreed. "Now we have only... the one."

Ronnie knew little about the three men who had overthrown the island's old regime, but "the one" inspired a fearful tone even in this man's voice. Two down and one to go. It sounded as though dictators were dropping like flies. She decided to make herself as inconspicuous as possible while she waited in El Gallo for her passengers to show up. Meanwhile, she did have supplies to deliver to the Red Cross office in the capital city, La Primavera.

"I don't suppose you have a phone?" she asked. The man shook his head. "I'll move my plane, then."

Wearily, Ronnie walked outside and climbed into the cockpit. She'd logged a lot of flight time in the past couple of days, and she was glad for the delay in one respect—she could get some rest. Then she heard a deadly click behind her head, and cold metal rested against her warm neck. The thought of rest flew out the window.

"Don't turn around, *señorita*. Take this plane to the end of the runway. Do as I say, and I promise not to hurt you."

"Which end?" Ronnie asked calmly.

"The east end. Near that shack."

Ronnie did as she was told. She didn't need to turn around. She could tell by his voice that the man who held the gun to her head was young and scared, a dangerous combination. She turned her head slightly and watched two men emerge from the shack. They were soldiers. The young, lanky one wore camouflage fatigues, and the older man was dressed in tattered khakis. Ronnie's attention was drawn to the latter, the trim, broad-shouldered man, who had apparently been injured. He held his hand tightly over his left side, and he refused the young soldier's assistance as they walked quickly toward the plane. When the injured man stumbled, the man with the gun started a bit, but the young soldier on the ground lent a steadying hand. The door to the aircraft was flung open, and Ronnie sat quietly, listening as the wounded man struggled to climb aboard.

"Move back, Paulo," a rich, deep voice said. "Let's let our pilot turn around. Very slowly, please."

Ronnie turned to face a man who looked as haggard as he did handsome, sitting in the back seat between two teenage boys who were dressed up as soldiers. The boys were scared, but the man appeared to be calm. His dark eyes betrayed fatigue, but no emotion.

"Give me your pistol," he told the man who had accompanied him to the plane. The young soldier slid the clip from the butt of the gun and satisfied himself that the weapon was fully loaded before handing it over.

Ronnie willed her voice to sound confident as she eyed each man's face. "What's going on?" she asked quietly.

"You're taking me for a ride," the injured man said.

"Where?"

"We'll discuss that as soon as we're in the air."

"I think I should go with you," the man who'd commandeered the plane said. "You might—"

The wounded man shook his head. "I've given your cousin my orders. You are to follow them to the letter."

"But I can't leave the island just yet," Ronnie blurted. With three pairs of dark eyes and the black muzzles of two pistols staring her in the face, she knew she was in no position to lodge an effective protest. "I, um...I have papers signed by Colonel Hidalgo himself," she explained. "Permission to deliver Red Cross supplies. If I could just..."

The injured man managed a crooked smile. "I'm afraid those papers will no longer do you any good, *señorita*."

"Well, there's something else. I have another very important job to do, and if you could just wait a couple of days—"

"I don't have a couple of days." The older man motioned the other two toward the door, but his attention did not waver from Ronnie. "Go on, now." The two young soldiers obeyed immediately. "And be careful," their leader told them as they jumped down from the plane.

"Get this crate in the air," the man demanded in slightly accented English.

"You don't look like you're in very good shape to me," Ronnie returned. "What if you—"

"I won't," he assured her smoothly. "And unless you turn around in your seat and fly this plane, you may find yourself in poor shape, as well. I believe I could handle this machine myself."

Ronnie assessed the dark look in his eyes and the equally black hole in the muzzle of the gun. Then she turned her attention to the controls.

Chapter 2

Ronnie retracted the landing gear and prayed that the man with the gun would pass out soon as she watched the nose of her plane point toward blue sky. She knew he couldn't hold out long. He was already half dead. Of course, she didn't want him to go all the way, but if he would just lose consciousness and drop that gun, she would feel a lot better. Gripping the wheel, she eased the nose down for a normal climb. The controls were in her hands, but the gun in his made her uneasy. She wanted to hear it fall to the floor and know that her passenger was out cold. When he climbed into the seat beside her, her hopes slipped a notch. But glancing to the side, she saw the pallor in his face and they rose again.

"You will take me to Florida," he said. His voice was strong, but his exhaustion could not be masked.

"That's ridiculous. What would I do with you? You can't expect to get past customs."

"I'm sure you can find a discreet place to land this plane so that I won't have to deal with that problem."

Ronnie glanced down at the gun, which was no longer pointed directly at her. He held it loosely, almost as though he'd forgotten about it. "Let me take you to Arco Iris. You know, that little island west of here. It's Mexican territory. You should be safe there."

"I *should* be safe in De Colores," he said. "I'm not, which means I'm not safe anywhere."

"I didn't know there was any fighting going on there." Ronnie waited for an explanation of his situation, but he studied the gauges and offered no comment. "Arco Iris is closer," she continued. "I have passengers waiting in De Colores—or, at least, they will be. They're depending on me. I could just drop you off on Arco Iris and go—"

"We're going to Florida." Miguel knew he needed help, and he knew someone in Florida who might help him. After all, McQuade owed him a favor after Miguel had helped the private investigator and his friend, Mikal Romanov, get a group of hostages safely off the island and out of Guerrero's reach. "Your other passengers can wait a couple of days."

"If I'm not there when I'm supposed to be, they could be in as much trouble as you are." Ronnie cast a pointed look at the man's wounded side. "Who's after you, anyway?"

"My partner, I guess."

"Nice guy." Her gaze traveled from his bloodstained shirt to his dark eyes. "I heard about Hidalgo's assassination. Were you with him?"

Miguel lifted the corner of his mouth in an attempt to smile. "You have my signature on your papers but we have never met."

"Miguel Hidalgo's signature is on my papers, and he's dead," Ronnie insisted. She had gained the altitude she wanted and was leveling off smoothly. "I heard it on the radio."

"The news of my death came a bit prematurely."

Her eyes widened. "You're *Hidalgo*?"

She was an American, he told himself, with an American conscience—that wonderful aversion to kicking a man when he's down. She delivered Red Cross supplies. She was concerned about the passengers she'd left behind, who were probably also on Guerrero's hit list.

He decided to trust her. He knew he had no choice. "I regret having to introduce myself to you with a .45 in my hand, Miss Harper."

"I don't think you regret it half as much as I do, colonel. It takes all the fun out of flying."

He smiled indulgently. "And what would you do if I put the gun away?"

She glanced away from him. "Three people are depending on me to fly them off that island. I'd go back for them."

"I thought you would."

"Colonel—"

"I'm no longer a colonel, Miss Harper. As you can see, they stripped me of that burden prior to my execution."

"Pretty sorry excuse for an execution, if you ask me," Ronnie grumbled. His weakened condition was evident even in the sound of his quick laugh. Ronnie found herself wondering how much blood he'd lost and wishing she had some way of replenishing it right there on the plane.

"I can't be held responsible for that. Guerrero's in charge of military training." He dropped his head back against the seat and sighed. The sun's brightness hurt his eyes, and he wanted to shut it out somehow. "The three who were chosen for the job of shooting me are obviously in need of more practice. Would you have me offer them my back again? Perhaps they can get it right the second time."

"No, of course not. If your boys had just explained what was going on, I probably could have gotten everybody out safely."

"There was no time. Believe me, Miss Harper, there was no..." Miguel jerked his head up. He'd nearly fallen asleep. Or passed out—he wasn't sure which. "Those two boys would have been killed, too, simply for helping me," he said quickly. "It isn't that my life is more valuable than anyone else's. But I have to try to stop Guerrero."

"In the shape you're in, you'd have trouble stopping a mosquito." She raised an eyebrow in his direction. "And any blood sucked out of you at this point would probably push you beyond the brink."

"Such blunt words from such a sweet face," he muttered, studying the gauges again. He'd lied when he'd said he could fly the plane himself, but he knew something about the instruments, and he could tell that they were on course. He wanted her to believe that, if need be, he could handle the craft as skillfully as she did.

"Sweet?" Ronnie laughed uneasily. Kids were sweet. Baby faces were sweet. He looked at her and probably saw both. And he was...classy, she decided. His clothes were tattered, his face drawn with pain, and he was a fugitive from his own government. Yet he bore himself with imperturbable dignity. *And* he was about as handsome as any man Ronnie had ever met.

"Kind," he amended quietly. "You have a kind face. I believe, Miss Harper, that if I hadn't the strength to fight off a mosquito, you would take it upon yourself to chase it away."

She added the word *charming* to her mental assessment, and she had to remind herself that this classy, dignified, handsome, charming man was pointing a gun at her. Well, *almost* at her. She reached behind her seat and found the lunch she'd packed for herself that morning before taking off from Arco Iris. She saw that his hand tightened around the grip of the gun. Matching bracelets of raw skin suggested that his wrists had recently been bound.

"I don't carry a gun, Colonel—*Mr.* Hidalgo. But I do carry—" she extracted a bottle from the paper bag "—orange juice. You'd better drink all you can."

When he hesitated, eyeing the screw cap, she shook the contents, opened the bottle and offered it again. He took it with his free hand. "Miguel," he corrected as he raised the bottle to his mouth. The juice was not cold, but it was wet, and it tasted good. His look was grateful as he repeated, "My name is Miguel."

She smiled, and her azure eyes glowed softly. "I'm not afraid of you any more, Miguel. I really don't think you'd shoot me."

"Please don't put me to the test, Miss Harper."

No, she wouldn't. She wanted to persist in her belief without conducting any tests. "Ronnie," she said quietly.

"Ronnie," he repeated.

She offered him a sandwich, and he accepted it hoping he could quell the light-headedness he felt, but he could only eat a few bites. He held the gun with one hand and his wounded side with the other and struggled to remain conscious. There were moments when the instrument panel became blurry, and he'd blink several times in an effort to refocus. His chest throbbed, his back burned, and he took shallow breaths, hoping to disturb the holes in his body as little as possible. He knew he was losing the battle. God help him, he couldn't pass out.

"Miguel." Her voice seemed distant. He concentrated his energy on looking at her, keeping his head up and his eyes open. "I'm taking you to the Keys," she said. "To my house. It's in an isolated spot. You'll be safe there."

"Good," he managed to say, though the word sounded like a grunt. In an attempt to keep his act from falling apart, he tried again. "That's good."

"Let me have the gun now."

It was a gentle order. A soft command. He felt the pistol slide from his fingers, and he couldn't close his hand. It didn't matter, he thought as he rested his head against the back of the seat. He could never have shed her blood, and she knew it. The act was over.

Ronnie removed the ammunition clip from the pistol and dropped it in the paper bag, along with the remainder of her lunch. The pistol itself she stowed in the pocket of her jacket. She could do anything she wanted with this man now. He was completely helpless. She could open the door and shove him into the sea if she wanted to. After all, he was a hijacker. He'd held a gun on her. He'd messed up an important job.

His head lolled to one side, and she reached quickly for the hand that lay limp on his thigh. His pulse was not strong, but it was steady. He needed a doctor. He needed to be in a hospital. She'd promised to take him to her house, but there was no doctor on the island she lived on. There was Becky Gordon, her neighbor, but Becky was a retired nurse, not a doctor.

There was another promise she had to keep, and that was the one she'd made to Elizabeth Donnelly. Elizabeth had hired a man named McQuade, who was some kind of high-priced troubleshooter, to help her get her baby son out of De Colores. Elizabeth and McQuade were going to hire a fishing boat to take them to the island, and Ronnie was to meet them in El Gallo and fly them out. She wasn't sure how long it would take them to get there or to find the child, but her instructions had been to leave word at the cantina and to wait for a message from McQuade. They had paid her well, but, more than that, she had come to think of the beautiful woman as a friend, and Ronnie Harper never deserted her friends.

They wouldn't have reached the island yet. Ronnie figured she had a little time. She didn't know much about the politics in De Colores other than that it had been ruled by a three-man junta until just recently. The death of one of those men and the attempted murder of another within a few days' time seemed a little too convenient for the third. She decided she had time to get help for this man.

Miguel's seat seemed to roll beneath him. His first thought was of the sea, but the roar of the plane's engines crowded that thought from his mind as he fought with heavy eyelids. When he succeeded in lifting them, the light speared his eyes. He covered them quickly with his hand and rubbed them with his fingertips and his thumb.

"How are you feeling?"

It was the soft, melodic voice of a woman. He lowered his hand slowly and opened his eyes, letting them adjust to the light. Ronnie, he remembered. The American woman. She'd taken off her baseball cap, and her reddish-blond hair fell past her shoulders. It looked as soft as her voice sounded.

"A little seasick," he mumbled.

"We've run into some low-level turbulence. Nothing major." She hadn't radioed ahead for clearance yet, but she'd decided on a new flight plan. She had an emergency on her hands. "I'm going to take you to a hospital, Miguel. You need medical attention."

As he struggled to sit up, he remembered that he was unarmed. As he'd lost consciousness, she'd taken his gun. She smiled at him, but not, as he might have expected, in triumph. It was a reassuring smile. She intended to help him, but she had her own ideas about the best way to do that.

"If you take me to a hospital, I may very well be sent back to De Colores," he told her, "where I would be killed."

"But not if you tell them what happened. You can ask for political asylum."

"Guerrero has declared that I'm a traitor. I'm told there was even a trial of some sort. He'll demand extradition."

"But, Miguel, surely the United States government wouldn't turn you over to Guerrero after what he's done to you."

"I can't take that chance." It took a great deal of effort simply to shift in his seat so that he could observe the expression on her face. "Guerrero thinks I'm dead. I was left in a cave on the beach, and the incoming tide would have washed me away if Raphael and Paulo hadn't come along when they did."

Ronnie stared at him for a moment. "You do know that without the proper medical attention, you might die anyway."

"Given a choice," he said evenly, "that is the chance I would prefer to take. Even if I am granted asylum, Guerrero has many contacts. I would be dead before the week was out."

"My God," Ronnie said. "What am I going to do?"

"You said . . . you would take me to your house. I would try very hard . . . not to die in your bed." He tried to smile, but he wasn't sure his face was cooperating. His vision was cloudy.

"Don't even suggest it. Where would I..." She turned to him and scowled. "Don't you pass out on me again! Miguel, is there anyone I could notify?"

He closed his eyes and rolled his head back and forth on the back of the seat. "I have no family. Except . . . my father. Lives in Geneva. His name . . . Roderigo."

It was after sundown when Ronnie landed her plane on the strip near her beach house. She had radioed Marathon Airport that she was having engine trouble and was making an emergency landing, which meant that she would have to pay a customs official overtime to come out and clear her. She would have time to get Miguel into the house and invent some kind of engine trouble.

The plane's touchdown roused Miguel. He lifted his head and peered out the side window, trying to make sense of the shadows in the twilight. Water and trees seemed to whiz by the window in shades of gray. He turned to Ronnie, his face a reflection of his muddled mind.

"It's all right," she said, sparing him only a quick glance. "This is where I live. Ordinarily I use Marathon Airport, but I told them I had to make an emergency landing." She knew this strip of ground, but she knew the low light could play tricks on a pilot's eyes. "We'll get you into the house before the agent comes. Can you walk?"

"What agent?"

"Customs," she said as easily as she might have said mail carrier. "I've been outside the country. I have to get clearance." She shut the engines down and turned to him. "Don't worry. You'll be safe in the house. If we can get you there, that is."

He sighed. "I can walk."

"I'll have to rig up something to make it look like I really had engine trouble, and . . . I do have to get you some help, Miguel."

"Just get me some bandages," he said wearily, "and some kind of—"

"I have a friend who's a nurse. I trust her."

"I'm supposed to trust her because *you* trust her?"

Ronnie grabbed her jacket and the paper bag. "You don't have any choice," she informed him over her shoulder as she opened the door. "I've got the gun now."

Miguel leaned heavily on Ronnie's shoulders as they made their way to her front door. She tossed her jacket and lunch bag on a chair and turned a light on. The only bed in the house was at the top of a flight of narrow steps in the little garret bedroom. Miguel made heavy use of the handrail and Ronnie's surprisingly plentiful strength in getting up the stairs. In near darkness she did her best to ease him down to the bed, but when his legs finally buckled and he collapsed, she went down with him. Her arm was trapped under his back, and when she tried to lever herself away from him, he groaned and shoved her hand away. Down she went again.

Her hand was wet, and her heart was pounding. His chest heaved beneath her head as he struggled to gain control. A terrible shudder rippled through his body, and he rolled his head to the side, where she lay very still. She listened to the air rush in and out as his panting became shallower, and she knew he was fighting off a blackout.

"I'm sorry," she whispered, now frightened for him rather than of him. "I made it start bleeding again."

"No...not you. The walk..."

His shirt was damp with sweat. When he turned his head more, his chin rested against her forehead. His face was wet, too. She stopped trying to pull away and simply let her arm be around him, let her head rest against him and let her body absorb his trembling. "I was carrying medical supplies for the Red Cross," she said quietly. "They're still on the plane. Becky will be able to fix you up."

"You can...*you* can take care of me yourself."

Ronnie eased herself away from him and helped him get his legs on the bed. Then she turned the switch on a table lamp. Miguel put his hand over his eyes, shunning the light.

"I can't," she said finally. "I don't know how." She went into the tiny bathroom at the other end of the garret and took two clean bath towels from a shelf above the commode. Returning to his side, she sat on the edge of the bed and unbuttoned his shirt as she talked. "Listen, you're not in a hospital *yet*, so just be grateful for small favors. But you need help. *I* need help. I'm not sure I even want to look at this."

She drew the shirt back from his chest. The thick pad of gauze and the strips of bandaging holding it in place were red with the spreading evidence of more bleeding. Ronnie lifted her eyes slowly from the wound to Miguel's face. His eyes were glazed with pain.

"It looks awful."

"You haven't seen anything yet, Miss Harper. And there's another one in back just like it."

"That must be a good sign." She glanced down and then up again. "The bullet must have gone right through you."

"I find that encouraging." He realized that his throat was as dry as the remark.

"But there's no telling what it might have ripped through along the way." She leaned across him to open the little window above the brass headboard. The smell of his blood was making her head spin.

A request for water had been on the tip of his tongue, but when the front of her loose-fitting khaki shirt drooped close to his face and one white button brushed the tip of his nose, the words vanished. Beneath the shirt, smooth, honey-toned skin disappeared into a vee of unadorned white cotton. From his vantage point the cleft between her breasts looked like an arch through which a man might pass on his way to heaven. He wondered whether this was a sign that he was on his way.

"There, that's much better." Ronnie sat back quickly and caught his wistful smile. Her hand flew to her chest, pressing her shirt tightly, and she felt her face grow warm despite the cool breeze from the window.

"Thank you," he said in a voice as mellow as the look in his eyes had become.

"I have to get back to the plane before they come." She glanced around nervously, saw the towels and snatched them up. "I'd better get some sterile supplies off the plane before I take this bandage off. Was this stuff sterile?"

He lifted one corner of his mouth. "I forgot to ask."

"Can you lift up a little?" She tucked one towel under his back and laid the other on top. "Hold this." When he didn't move, she took his hand and pressed it against the towel. "I think if you could apply some pressure here, it might help."

He nodded. "How long will you be gone?"

Ronnie studied his face. His dark eyes glittered, and his jaw was set. Black hair tumbled over his forehead, which glistened in the lamplight with a fine sheen of perspiration. He knew more about the extent of his injuries than she did. He had to. He could feel the pain. His question was the first hint that he might be afraid of what he knew.

"I've got to make it look like we had an oil leak or something. Most of the agents know who I am. I won't have any problem with clearance. Then I'm going to get you some help."

"Please don't involve anyone else."

"Listen, mister." She cast a look at the pitched ceiling and inhaled deeply. Then she expelled a long, slow sigh as she looked at him again. "I'd have a heck of a time coming up with a good explanation for your corpse."

"I'm not dead yet," he pointed out. "It must not be very serious."

"Yeah, right," she tossed back as she pressed her small hand over his. "Hold this tight, okay?"

"May I . . . have some water?"

She saw a flash of fear in his eyes, and her breath caught in her chest. "Of course." She moved quickly, coming back from the bathroom with a glass of water and a damp washcloth. He started to raise himself on his elbow, but she was there before he'd expended much energy. She slid her arm beneath him and supported his head on her shoulder while she held the glass to his lips. "Slowly," she warned when she saw how thirsty he was. "I don't know why, but they always say that when people get hurt."

"Who says that?" he asked when she lowered the glass.

"People in movies." She smiled at him. "I like to go to movies. Especially movies about the past, with lots of gorgeous costumes." She lifted the glass again. "More?"

He turned his head and grunted, which she interpreted as a decline of the offer. "If this were a movie, you would take out your mother's embroidery basket and repair whatever the bullet ripped through," he told her.

Carefully she withdrew her support, and he settled his head back on her pillow. "If this were a movie, your shirt would be covered with catsup instead of blood," she countered as she daubed the cool cloth over his forehead. "Besides, my mother died long before she had a chance to teach me anything about sewing, so you're just going to have to trust my friend Becky."

She avoided his eyes as she swabbed the sweat from his neck. His eyes never left her face. She felt their heat, and when she stood up and took a step back, she was reminded of the sensation she had stepping back from stoking a fire. She cleared her throat. "I'd better hurry."

"Is that catsup on your shirt, or is it more of my blood?"

She glanced down at the red stain. "Oh, gosh, I'd better check the seats out there, too." She pulled the closet door open and snatched another shirt off a hanger. Her fingers froze on the top button of the shirt she wore, and she glanced furtively to see whether he'd noticed the reflex. His attention was fixed on the bathroom door.

"Do you need . . . anything else?" she asked as she edged toward the stairs.

"No," he said quietly. And as she started down the steps he called to her. "Don't worry, my little angel of mercy," he said. "If something goes wrong, I won't forget to tell them that you agreed to all this at gunpoint."

"Nothing's going to go wrong," she promised. And then she was gone.

Ronnie had a lot to do and not much time to get it done. Buttoning her clean shirt with one hand, she used the other to stuff her stained shirt under the lid of the compact washer in the kitchen, spray cleaning fluid on a rag and take a flashlight from the cupboard. With her buttons in order, she hurried back to her plane.

The yellow beam from the flashlight revealed blood smeared like fingerpaint over the tan vinyl seats, both front and back. Ronnie cleaned them thoroughly before turning to the motor. She drained the oil from the left engine, dribbled it around generously to fake an oil leak and set up a repair scene for the benefit of the driver of the boat that was just putting in at her dock. She proceeded to bewail her troubles to the customs agent as she explained that she'd dropped two passengers off in Arco Iris and headed for De Colores. She showed him she'd returned with all the cargo she had intended to deliver to the Red Cross office in De Colores.

"Didn't they want it?" the agent asked.

"They're all in a tizzy down there." Ronnie shut the cargo bay and opened the side door, gesturing for the agent to have a look inside. "Some colonel got himself assassinated, and they wouldn't clear my plane. I was lucky they let me refuel and come home."

"Guess so." The sandy-haired young man took a seat and filled out his forms under the plane's interior light. "Too bad about your leakage problem. How long since you had your gaskets checked?"

"It isn't a gasket," she said as she braced her hand on the doorway. "It might be the fuel-pump seal. I'll take care of it tomorrow."

He signed his name with a flourish and handed her a copy of her customs clearance with a smile. "Long day, huh?"

"It's been a killer," she admitted. "Or damn near."

Ronnie had lived on the little key with no name for as long as she could remember, and Becky Gordon had always owned the small cottage with the red roof, the one Ronnie could see from her kitchen window. There was a time when Becky only spent summers there, but that was long ago. Ronnie sometimes thought Becky had retired from nursing just to help Ronnie survive adolescence, which hadn't been an easy time for a girl living with a house full of men. Her father hadn't known quite what to do with her until he had hit upon the idea that she wasn't really that much different from her two older brothers, and had begun to treat her as such. When she'd needed to know more about what it meant to be female, Becky was there to help her.

Ronnie had never needed Becky's help more than she needed it now, and once again she found herself knocking on Becky's door with a head full of questions. Her heart pounded, and she knew she was just as fearful of the answers as she had been when she was twelve years old.

Something was terribly wrong. Blood scared her, and she'd never seen so much blood.

A tall, slender woman with short gray hair appeared at the door in her bathrobe. Her frown disappeared as she raised her brow in amazement. "Back so soon? I thought you said you'd be down in the islands for a week or more."

Ronnie backed the woman inside and closed the door. "I need your help, Becky. I've got a friend. He's... he's been hurt really bad."

Becky was a nurse by nature as well as by profession. Retirement hadn't modified her reaction to the news that someone was hurt. Her scuffs flapped against her heels as she headed for the bedroom untying the sash of her robe. Her questions trailed behind her. "Where is he, honey?"

"At my house."

"What happened?"

"Somebody shot him."

Becky tossed her robe on the bed and turned back to the young woman who stood in the doorway. "Somebody *shot* him?"

"Yes, Becky, he's been shot. Please hurry." Ronnie spotted a pair of Becky's shoes under a chair, and she lunged for them. "He was shot in the back...sort of to one side...came out the front, I guess. There's just so much blood, and I don't know—"

Becky tied a wraparound skirt over her short nightgown and took the shoes Ronnie handed her. "Is he conscious?"

"Most of the time." Ronnie swept Becky's favorite white cardigan off the chair and held it up for her.

"What we need to do is get him to an emergency room. Have you called—"

"I can't, Becky." Her eyes met the older woman's over the sweater's shawl collar. "He's in trouble."

If Ronnie was willing to help him, Becky was, too. And if Ronnie was willing to protect him, Becky didn't have to ask whether the trouble was of his own making. "I don't have much to work with," Becky said regretfully. "I've got my old Africa bag, but it's been a long time since—"

"I'll get it," Ronnie said as she turned toward the closet. She'd always loved Becky's stories of the time she'd spent nursing in the missionary outposts in Africa. The medical bag was kept on a high shelf in the closet, still just beyond Ronnie's grasp.

Becky reached over Ronnie's head and took the bag down. "But I don't have any kind of antiseptic, no sterile bandages, nothing for . . . wait a minute." She went to the medicine cabinet in the bathroom, took a couple of bottles down and dropped them into the bag. "They don't do me much good, anyway," she muttered.

"I've got a bunch of stuff on the plane," Ronnie called out. "Stuff the Red Cross ordered."

Becky emerged from the bathroom. "This man had better not be some drug runner, missy."

"He's not. I swear." She took Becky's elbow and scooted her along. "I'll tell you everything I know, but we've got to hurry. I think he's pretty bad off."

The sound of voices swirled around the fringe of Miguel's elusive consciousness. When he became aware that the voices were somewhere in the house, he tried to sit up, but he struggled in vain. He gave up, lay still and watched the top of the steps. A gray head appeared first, a woman carrying a black bag. A doctor? God, he needed a doctor. He'd almost be grateful, even if it meant the young woman had betrayed him.

"I'm here to try to help you," the woman said as she approached the bedside. "Miguel, isn't it? Ronnie tells me your name is Miguel."

"Yes," he managed to say over a dry tongue. He was still clutching the towel against his side as Ronnie had instructed. "Miguel."

"I'm not a physician, Miguel." The woman set her bag on the table near the bed and sat down in a straight-backed chair that had appeared near her hand. When she was seated, he saw Ronnie standing behind her. "I want you to understand that. I am a nurse practitioner, long retired. You'd be much better off if you'd let us send for a doctor."

"You know my situation?"

"Ronnie tells me you have some powerful enemies." Becky opened her bag as she spoke.

"It's important that I return to De Colores. I can't afford the complications that doctors and hospitals might cause."

Becky moved Miguel's hand and took the towel away. "We're going to need those supplies, Ronnie," she said over her shoulder. "Bring in everything you've got, and let's hope we can put together the right combination."

Returning with a large plastic garbage bag full of packages, Ronnie overheard Becky's use of a word that meant more trouble. "Surgery?" she croaked as she let the bag slide to the floor. She noticed a pile of bloody bandages lying on a newspaper beside the bed. "You can't be serious."

Becky turned from her patient, eyed the bag and then looked up at Ronnie. "I was just explaining to Miguel that I did all kinds of surgery when I was out in the bush. Lots of times when it needed to be done, there was no one else to do it. Sort of like now."

"Can't you just sew him up?"

"Essentially, yes, but this man is in a lot of pain, and there's a lot of blood here." Ronnie went around to the opposite side of the bed, and Becky turned to Miguel. "I think the bullet might have nicked the bowel, which means that has to be sewn up, too. I haven't done anything like that in a long time."

"At least you've done it," Miguel said in a tight voice. "My friend here tells me she knows nothing about sewing." He looked at Ronnie and offered a thin smile. She read the message in his eyes. He needed a friend, and she was all he had.

"I've got some more bad news," Becky continued. "We don't have access to any controlled drugs, and I can tell you right now, there aren't any in that Red Cross shipment. Which means no painkillers and no anesthetic. All I have is what I take for arthritis, which might give you some relief after we're done." Miguel closed his eyes and gave a nod of understanding.

Ronnie braced herself on both arms and leaned closer to him. "This would be a good time for you to stop fighting it and just pass out."

Becky examined her own gnarled fist. "I used this once. In those days I packed quite a wallop." She acknowledged Miguel's attempt to smile, and then she had another idea. "Ronnie, don't you keep some whiskey around for your dad?"

"I think there's some." She got to her feet quickly. "I don't know how much."

"How much would it take for you to reach the feeling-no-pain stage, Miguel?" Becky asked.

He groaned. "At this point, just the smell."

"Did you see anything in that bag labeled sterile bandages?"

Becky's question stopped Ronnie before she reached the stairs. "Yeah, lots of it."

"Toss me a package of it."

Miguel welcomed the whiskey as a thirst-quencher as much as anything else. It didn't take much to separate him from what little grip he had left on his sense of reality. With his head pillowed on Ronnie's shoulder, he began to drift, and he decided that the shoulder of this angel was a pleasant conveyance for drifting. She fed him little sips, and he tried to ignore the woman who had removed his shirt and was swabbing his side with something cool.

"Your eyes are the color of the sea," he told his angel. His tongue was thick, and he took pains to enunciate each word slowly so that she would understand. "Both green and blue. More green with indignation. Blue steals across them softly with your compassion."

Ronnie smiled. The whiskey was working. The man was definitely hallucinating.

"You've got yourself a smooth talker there, missy."

Ronnie glanced up at Becky, who was working on Miguel's belt buckle. "You're not going to take his pants off, too."

"They're filthy," Becky muttered. "When you've seen as many naked men as I have, they all start looking pretty much alike."

"Becky, for heaven's sake," Ronnie whispered.

"And we'll have to tie his hands to the bed. Probably his legs, too. We can't have him—"

"No." At the sound of the word, Ronnie looked down, and Miguel searched through the encroaching haze for the blue in her eyes. He remembered his last walk on the beach. The rope that bound him had rubbed his wrists raw. "You won't tie my hands."

"Just to keep you from thrashing about, you understand. You might think you can stand the pain, young man, but this could be one heck of a . . ."

Ronnie tuned out Becky's warnings and allowed Miguel to draw her into the depths of his dark eyes. Within a few short hours Ronnie had become his ally. He was being stripped of all his clothes before two women he didn't know, and in a moment one of them would fillet his flesh and lace it up again. All he asked was to be spared the indignity of being trussed like an animal.

"There'll be no need to tie his hands," she told Becky. "I'll hold them."

Chapter 3

Miguel's thick, dark eyelashes were hovering at half-mast, but his eloquent way with words, even when the words were slurred, impressed Ronnie. He praised her hair, her good sense, her smile and her skill as a pilot. He could have almost convinced her that she had relatives on Mount Olympus had she not been determined to put every beautiful word he said in perspective with the situation at hand. The man was at her mercy as he lay there bleeding all over her bed while she poured whiskey down his throat. Still, she enjoyed the words. Never before had so many pretty ones been directed her way.

"Forgive me for frightening you with the gun," he said.

"I wasn't scared." She had helped him turn on his side, and she sat beside him on the bed with her back to Becky's preparations. Miguel was covered from the waist down with a clean sheet, and Becky had boiled her instruments while Ronnie rigged a mechanic's trouble light over the bed.

Miguel offered a sleepy smile. "Not even at first? Tell me the truth."

"That young soldier scared me when he popped up in the back seat. I'll have to admit that."

"But I didn't?"

"What would you have done if I'd refused to follow your orders?" she asked, half teasing.

His eyes slid closed, and he sighed. "I don't know."

"Are you ready?" Becky asked.

The ominous question brought Miguel fully awake. He fixed his gaze on the place where the pitched roof met the wall. "Go ahead."

His whole body tensed with the initial shock of another steel-tipped assault. His head came up off the pillow, but he held fast to his focus on the wall. The muscles in Ronnie's stomach tightened as she read the pain in his face. She laid her hand on his shoulder. As the seconds ticked by, he began to tremble. Beads of perspiration shone brightly on his tanned face.

"Try to relax, Miguel," Becky said. "Try not to move at all."

Ronnie started to look over her shoulder.

"Don't!" All the fire and fear in his black eyes met hers. "Don't . . . watch her . . . carve me up!"

Ronnie touched his forehead, let her fingers slide into his damp hair and gently pushed his head back against the pillow. "I won't," she promised.

He closed his eyes and worked to control his breathing. "Talk to me, angel." Looking up again, he pleaded quietly, "Talk to me."

Distract him, he meant. Dear Lord, how could she? What could she say? She leaned closer, curling around him to shield his face from Becky's work. "The whiskey didn't help much, did it?" she sympathized as she combed his thick black hair back from his face. "The first time in my life I've ever tried to get a man drunk, and he refuses to cooperate."

"Next time," he grunted. "But give me...better cause."

"This cause is a good one, Miguel. Becky's going to fix you up, just like new. Hold on, now." She stroked his face, trying to smooth away the strain. "It'll be over soon. You're doing fine. You're doing just fine." She caressed his shoulder, kneading the hard ridge of muscle.

"Liar," he gasped, and he snatched her hand and crushed it in his.

"No, no, I've never seen anyone...so strong..." His head came up off the pillow again, and she wasn't sure whether the groan she heard was his or her own. "Oh, dear God," she whispered as she scooted her knees beneath his head and pulled his face against her belly.

"This part's going to hurt," Becky muttered.

This part? Ronnie braced herself for the pain as Miguel's free arm encircled her hips. His other arm was trapped beneath his body, but he groped for a second handhold and found her ankle. Ronnie's breath caught in her throat. His groans were muffled in her lap until he finally slipped into blessed unconsciousness.

"Is he out finally? Thank God," Becky said.

"Thank God." Ronnie sighed, feeling physically relieved. She continued to hold him, shutting out the smell of sweat and blood as she stroked his hair.

The Red Cross was the unwitting supplier of tetanus serum and antibiotics, both of which Becky injected into her patient. She would have traded the gross of thermometers for a couple of pints of blood and the wherewithal to match and transfuse it. As she taped his bandages in place, she gave Miguel a silent order to step up the manufacture of his own blood. Finally, she leaned back and flexed her aching hands.

"What have you got to drink in that poorly stocked kitchen of yours besides whiskey?" Becky asked.

Ronnie hesitated to give up the task of washing Miguel's upper body. It was a task she'd assigned herself while she'd watched Becky do the bandaging, and she found it comforting because she told herself it gave him ease, even in his unconscious state. She could have sworn she'd actually felt the blade bite into her own side, the needle puncture her own skin. His pain had become hers, and now she shared in his relief.

"There's coffee," she said as she dropped the cloth into the bowl of warm water. "And orange juice, of course."

"Coffee for me, and orange juice for you." Becky stood and rubbed the kinks out of her back. "If you're going to nurse this boy back to health, you're going to have to feed him real food, honey. You never have anything in that refrigerator but orange juice and shriveled carrots."

"I'd hardly call him a boy," Ronnie said as she admired the broad back of the man who now rested peacefully in her bed.

"They're all boys when they're sick. And this one's going to be laid up for a while." Becky frowned. "Do you think his enemies would have any way of tracing him back here?"

"I don't see how." Ronnie came around the bed and linked her arm with Becky's. "I'll make you some coffee if you'll help me solve my next problem."

"Which is?"

Ronnie stepped aside and let Becky precede her down the steps. "I've got to make a quick run to De Colores, which means—"

"Which means you want me to watch over this fellow. Now listen here, missy, this old girl retired from dressing wounds and carrying bedpans a long time ago."

"Bedpans?" Ronnie wondered how she would improvise an article like that.

"You don't like the sound of that too much, do you?" Becky grumbled as she approached the descent slowly and at an angle, in deference to her creaking joints. "Every time you brought home a stray puppy or a lost kitten and your dad got after you for it, you always brought it to my house. And then who ended up taking care of the darn thing?"

It had never occurred to Ronnie that Becky might turn her down. The old woman never had. Ronnie explained the problem of her soon-to-be-stranded passengers over sandwiches and coffee. Since McQuade and Elizabeth had planned to take a fishing boat from Arco Iris to De Colores and they hadn't yet hired one when she'd last seen them, she figured she had another day or two. But she'd promised to be there for them when they needed her, and she couldn't risk cutting it too close. She wanted to leave the following afternoon. Becky agreed to stay with Miguel while Ronnie was gone, but she was bent on retiring again, at least for the night.

After Becky left, Ronnie climbed the stairs to her room. The house that had once housed four people now had only one bedroom. It had never been big enough for four, but after her brothers had left home and her father had moved to Marathon Key, she had turned the bedroom downstairs into an office, and remodeled the attic, adding a small bathroom up there. The tiny room that had once been hers was now used for storage. She was comfortable now, but her redecoration hadn't provided for guests.

Miguel hadn't moved. Ronnie took the small upholstered rocker from its place by the far window and put it beside the bed. She'd had less comfortable sleeping arrangements. This wouldn't be so bad. As tired as she was, she figured she could probably sleep standing up.

A hot shower melted the tension from her shoulders. She wrapped her hair in a towel and dressed in a comfortable pair of pink jersey pajamas. Then she slathered her face with the same camphor-scented cream she'd been using since she was thirteen. The thought of the pretty things Miguel had said about her made her wonder whether it was time for a new scent. She'd doubled her age since she'd first adopted this one. She remembered Elizabeth Donnelly's faint aura of tropical flowers, and the way McQuade's eyes had glittered whenever Elizabeth entered a room. Would Elizabeth have piqued the same interest if she'd smelled like camphor?

Ronnie reminded herself that she was not the flowery type. There wasn't a flower in her wardrobe. She liked to see them blooming by the doorstep, but she wasn't inclined to wear them. That wouldn't be Ronnie. Anyway, what difference did it make? She sat in the rocker and kneaded the coiled towel to blot the water from her hair. She wanted to help this man who had hijacked her plane. That was her choice to make, and it had nothing to do with whether he liked her scent or the color of her eyes.

She liked the color of his, she remembered. But now that they were closed she liked the way his black hair teased his forehead in sexy disarray and the way his long, dark lashes hid the telling circles under his eyes. He looked younger now, free of pain. It was hard to imagine him as a leader in a military coup. Belief that such a man had suddenly ended up in her bed came harder still. Men didn't end up in her bed, nor, for that matter, did she end up in theirs.

Ronnie dropped the towel on the floor, dimmed the lamp, propped her feet upon the bed and rocked gently. The rocker's rhythmic creaking would soon lull her to sleep. The thought flitted across her mind that she had no business sleeping when she had given her word to two people who trusted her. At this moment she was supposed to be somewhere else. But her energy was gone, her mind was drifting and she had no other choice right now. Her body demanded sleep.

Hours later she was awakened by a tortured groan. Miguel had rolled onto his back, and was fighting with the sheet, which was wrapped around his hips like a sarong. Ronnie sat next to him on the bed and called his name, but there was no response. She took his face in her hands and found that his skin was warm and dry. The cool breeze from the open window touched her still damp hair, and sent a shiver through her shoulders.

She fetched a washcloth and a bowl of tepid water from the bathroom. The faint smell of whiskey plagued her as she pressed the cool cloth against his face. Already she regretted the hangover that would add to his discomfort when he awoke, and she couldn't believe the alcohol had spared him any pain. He groaned again as he turned his face away from her.

"Sediento," he muttered.

He was thirsty. She slid her arm beneath his head and reached for the glass of water she'd left on the nightstand. "Drink this, Miguel."

He swallowed several times before he turned his head away again. *"Gracias."*

She laid his head down and wondered whether she should try to give him something for fever. Not yet, she decided. Aspirin was all she had, and it probably wouldn't be good for someone who'd been bleeding the way he had. His eyes were closed, and the water had left his lips looking moist and sensuous. Ronnie imagined herself comforting him with a tender kiss.

The image was absurd, and she shook her head to dispel it. The man was in need of practical nursing, a job she'd never thought she would be much good at. Tomorrow she would turn him over to Becky, and then he would have the best. Ronnie had done what she could for him. She had flown him to a safe place.

He tried to shift his position again, but the sheet effectively restrained him. Ronnie wondered whether it hurt him to lie directly on the wound. She tucked two small pillows under his right side, above and below his bandages.

"Caliente," he whispered between quick, shallow breaths.

Ronnie reached for the washcloth and gave it a squeeze. "I know you're hot," she told him as she began bathing his chest. "You're fevered, and I'm not sure what to do about it. When Becky comes back..." The thought disturbed her. Becky would come back and take care of him while Ronnie replaced the oil she'd drained from the plane's engine. Each woman would perform the task she knew best. Ronnie would feel the oil between her fingers, but she would remember the feel of Miguel's warm skin.

She didn't like the idea of turning him over to another woman, not even Becky. Her thoughts would be with him as she returned to the place where he'd been hurt. She would see to the safety of those who had paid for her services, but she would worry about Miguel, who had gotten her attention with a loaded gun. It didn't make much sense, but there it was. This man's life was in her hands now, and she *wanted* to help him.

She continued to bathe him until he slept quietly again. Then she returned to the rocker, tipping it back and rocking very slightly as she watched him, taking note of the combination of masculine features that made him so handsome. Even before she slept, she drifted in dreams.

Becky arrived at the crack of dawn to check on her patient. When no one answered the door, she let herself in and climbed the stairs to the bedroom. The scene at the top didn't surprise her. Ronnie was curled up like a cat in the rocking chair, and Miguel slept in a feverish sweat.

The touch of Becky's hand on her shoulder interrupted Ronnie's sleep with a start. "What's wrong?" she asked, pushing herself upright as she tried to shake off overwhelming grogginess. "I thought he was doing better. I just . . . dozed off for a minute."

"He's all right," Becky assured her. The pat on Ronnie's shoulder was intended to settle her back into the chair, but it didn't work. Ronnie was already sitting beside Miguel and testing the heat of his skin with the back of her hand. "There would have been nothing wrong with you lying down next to him and getting some decent rest," Becky pointed out. "You're not going to be in any condition to fly today."

"Yes, I am," Ronnie said absently. "What are we going to do about this fever, Becky? He's been like this for hours."

"I'm going to take care of it while you get some rest," Becky proposed. "Why don't you go on over to my house where it's nice and—"

"He's burning up with it," Ronnie said, ignoring Becky's suggestion. "I was afraid to give him any aspirin, but I don't like this fever at all."

"Neither does he." Becky had long since learned to save her breath when Ronnie wasn't listening. She took the glass from the nightstand, refilled it and handed it to Ronnie. "See if you can get him to drink some water. Dehydration could cause real trouble now."

"Water . . . poses a problem also." Miguel's quiet statement took Ronnie by surprise. His eyes were still closed. His face was damp, but his lips were dry. "There's a bathroom close by, isn't there?"

"In your condition, it'll have to be brought to you," Becky said offhandedly as she turned her attention to the boxes of Red Cross supplies. "We'll give him an aspirin substitute."

"I'll find it," Miguel muttered, pushing himself up gingerly. He wasn't talking about the medicine. By the time Ronnie moved to the opposite side of the bed, he was sitting on the edge, clutching the sheet at his waist.

"What are you trying to do?" Ronnie demanded. "You can't—"

"Trying to spare us all—" he closed his eyes and waited for the room to stop spinning "—further embarrassment."

Becky's chuckle rose from the floor in the corner of the room. "I've seen it all, honey. The last time I remember being embarrassed by any of it was in 1938."

"Spare myself, then." When the dizziness did not subside, he opened his eyes and saw the young woman with the beautiful aquamarine eyes. She stood over him, and the way she squared her shoulders and ducked her head beneath the roof's steep pitch gave him the feeling that she sought to steady the undulating surroundings, much like a tent pole on a windy day. "I can make it," he told her.

"I'll help you," she said, and she lent him her strength once again. He tried to keep himself covered, but the effort was wasted, and the sheet was left trailing over the end of the bed as he leaned heavily on Ronnie for support. She transferred his weight to the sink on one side and a towel bar on the other. She kept her eyes on his face. "You think you can manage, um . . . by yourself?"

"When we hear a big thud in there, we'll know he managed to pass out," Becky predicted.

Miguel's chest heaved with the effort of his breathing, and his face, drained of color, glistened with sweat. "I need a moment's...privacy," he said, laboring over the words. "If you'll just give me that, you'll hear nothing."

Ronnie nodded and closed the door. The man had suffered enough humiliation, and Ronnie knew how the need to salvage what was left of one's pride could create strength where it seemed there could be none left.

"I'll go down and see what I've got in the house to feed him," she told Becky. "What do you think? Soup? Or juice. He drank some juice yesterday."

Becky examined the label of a plastic bottle as she rose from the floor over the protest of morning-stiff joints. "See what you've got. His stomach might not tolerate anything yet, but—" She raised an eyebrow toward the bathroom door. "We'll have to start getting something in him pretty soon."

Ronnie went to the kitchen and rummaged through her cupboards. She found a can of beef consommé that had probably been sitting up there for a year. Leaning across the sink, she drew the blue gingham café curtain back and took time for a good look at the morning. Still rouged by the risen sun, the sky promised her smooth flying. That was good. She wanted to do her job and get back just as soon as she could. She was needed here, too.

She found a pair of clean shorts and dressed quickly in the downstairs bathroom before padding up the stairs on bare feet. Miguel was in bed, braced on his elbow, the glass somewhat unsteady in his hand as he washed down the tablets that had come from Becky's plastic bottle.

"Do you think you could eat something?" Ronnie asked. Easing himself back on the pillows, he offered her the glass. Her cool, steady fingers met the vibrating heat of his, and he hesitated in releasing the item that brought about the contact. His eyes were glazed, and his face looked like a clay casting of itself in an unnatural tone.

"Not now." He tried to smile as she set the glass aside. "It seems I haven't the stomach for this surgery . . . in the field, as it were."

"Maybe you just can't stomach my dad's brand of whiskey."

"He needs rest," Becky said. "I've given him something to bring his temperature down."

"I did tell you I'd be leaving today," Ronnie reminded him. She knew her urge to apologize for leaving him was silly. She had a commitment, and he had interfered with it. Still, the apologetic tone was there. "I really must get back to the people who hired me. They could be in serious trouble, just like you. I'll be back as soon as I can." Her face brightened with another idea. "Maybe I can get the scoop on who knows what about your untimely—"

"No!" He gripped her wrist with more strength than she'd thought he had. "I can't stop you from going back there, but you are not to express an interest in my fate to anyone. Do you understand? You will not hint of any association with me."

"I can't see how they could possibly find you here, Miguel. You'll be perfectly safe—"

"But you won't be."

Ronnie wondered whether his grimace reflected physical pain or something else. "I've been down there lots of times," she assured him. "I know people there. I'll be okay."

"How do you know?" He gripped her tighter, and the dark heat in his eyes betrayed his anxiety. "We know nothing for certain. You heard a radio report of my assassination. I was told that I had been tried and was to be executed. I may have been seen, and I'm not certain who my enemies are. Someone may have reported your plane." He paused, allowing time for the gravity of the situation to sink in. "What you're doing is foolish."

"Those people are counting on me."

"Send someone else."

She laughed at the very idea. "I'm nobody's boss, Miguel. There's no one to send."

"There must be other planes for hire. Other people who do what you do who wouldn't be—" he closed his eyes and gave a weary sigh "—putting themselves in such danger."

"I was hired for this job, and I'll get it done." He released her, and she stood up. "I have to undo my simulated oil leak and service my engines, but I'll try some of my cooking out on you before I take off today. I'm sure you'll be impressed."

"I'm sure I will." The resignation in his tone was clearly born of complete exhaustion, and he was drifting. "I've been quite impressed so far."

This was not the time for engine trouble. Ronnie had replaced the oil and restored everything she had tampered with for the customs agent's benefit, but the engine refused to crank. She checked lever adjustments, circuits, connections—everything was intact. Left with the sinking feeling that her airplane was in need of major repair, she headed for the phone. Norm Keller, her favorite mechanic at the Marathon aircraft maintenance shop, agreed with her suspicion that she needed to have the starter repaired or replace it with a new one. She knew she couldn't repair it at home, but it wouldn't take much to install a new one herself. Naturally there was not one available at the shop. Norm promised to track one down for her and get back to her as soon as he could. She clapped the receiver down in frustration and turned to find Becky standing in the kitchen doorway.

"Sounds like you might be stuck here a while," Becky observed. "How about some lunch?"

"Is he asleep?" Miguel had become such a constant presence in her mind that she didn't even think to name him.

"He is." Becky smiled knowingly as she passed Ronnie on her way to the refrigerator. "I don't know much about his politics, but I'd say you've rescued yourself a real looker there, missy. Soon as he gets his color back . . ."

"Oh, Becky!" Ronnie used the toe of one gym shoe to push off the heel of the other one. "I don't care about his looks or his politics. The man was shot in the back. I couldn't just . . . open the door in midflight and push him out." She remembered considering it, and smiled as she pulled off the other shoe.

"He's right about your going back there, you know. It's too risky."

"I've been paid to take the risk." Ronnie set her shoes and socks near the back door and moved to the sink to wash her hands. "De Colores is just a risky place to be right now, that's all. That's why I probably couldn't get anyone else to do it for me even if I wanted to." She reached for a nail-brush and looked over her shoulder at the woman who knew her better than anyone else. "The woman who hired me had her child taken away from her before she was deported. She's taking an awful chance going back there."

Suppressing the urge to repeat herself, Becky opened the can of consommé and poured it into a sauce pan. If Ronnie couldn't get the plane started, maybe the problem would solve itself, at least on this end. As for Ronnie's passengers in De Colores, well, Becky didn't know them. She hadn't mothered them into adulthood. Ronnie was convinced that their lives depended entirely on her, but Becky had lived long enough to know that no human being truly carried such a burden. Of course, Ronnie hadn't experienced that revelation yet, and she would keep trying.

"It'll all work out." It was, Becky knew, one of those truisms the young were bound to misconstrue or just ignore.

"Of course it will. I'll fix the starter, and we'll be back in business." Ronnie flipped the hand towel over the cabinet door beneath the sink and turned to give Becky a peck on a cheek worn by the years to powder softness. "I don't know what I would have done with him if you hadn't been here, Becky. You're amazing, you know that?"

"He's not out of the woods yet. And I might as well tell you, missy, if he takes a turn for the worse, I'm calling for help."

"He's not worse, is he?" Ronnie's eyes widened as she started backing toward the door to the living room. "Didn't that stuff help his fever any? Has he lost any more blood? Is he vomiting? What?"

"I'm just warning you, now. Actually, he's just been—" Becky shook her head as Ronnie took the steps two at a time the way she had when she was twelve "—sleeping."

Ronnie sat on the side of the bed with her bare feet tucked under her. Even with the cross ventilation from both windows, the garret room was warm. Miguel's muscled torso glistened. She laid her palm against his cheek, and his eyelashes lifted slowly. "My angel is back," he said in a voice that sounded rusty.

"Got my wings clipped," she told him as she drew her hand back. "But only temporarily. I just need a new part."

He took a sleepy stab at smiling. "I see no part in need of replacement."

"Yes, well—" She pulled on the legs of her shorts and covered up a few more inches of thigh. "You haven't heard what the Cessna's doing when I turn the key."

"What is it doing?"

"Nothing."

"Ah," he said. "Does that mean you can't fly off to put your neck in Guerrero's little noose?"

"You're the one he's after, buddy, not me. How are you feeling? Does your—" She cast a pointed glance at the bandages that bisected his torso. "Does it hurt much?"

"Not if I don't breathe." He closed his eyes. "I'm very thirsty."

Ronnie brought him a glass of water and helped him prop himself up for a drink. He rested the back of his head against her shoulder, and she felt his hair's dampness through her shirt. "Becky says you've got to try to eat," she told him. "Just some clear soup for starters. How would that be?"

"Hot," he said when he had drained the glass. "I would prefer something cold and tasteless. Like more water."

"Water won't build your strength back up." She settled him back against the pillows and set the glass aside. "If you start slipping away from us, Becky's threatening to call in medical reinforcements, so you'd better follow orders."

"I had just gotten used to the idea of giving them. Have you seen a newspaper today?"

"No." She smiled and dared to tease him. "Want me to check the obituary column and see if you made it yet? You just want to see if they said nice things about you, right?"

"I would prefer to attend the funeral. The eulogy should be interesting. Guerrero deferred to me for Castillo's, and I spoke of loyalty, honor . . . dreams for the future." He tried to shift his weight for some relief from his pain. "Guerrero will not come to praise me, and he won't have anything to bury."

"Maybe he's already commissioned a monument." Ronnie reached for a pillow that had fallen on the floor and tucked it behind his shoulders. "Or maybe he's hired someone to erase your name from the history books. Either way, surely he'll give you a decent funeral."

"He'll do his peacock act and perhaps cremate me in effigy." He lifted his hand in a gesture that dismissed the whole idea. "History books are Guerrero's last concern. He'll put guns in the children's hands before he'll give them books."

Becky bellowed from below. "Lunch will be served in the loft if someone's willing to help me carry it up there."

Ronnie was too busy urging Miguel to drink his soup to worry about the sandwich Becky had made for her. For Miguel's part, sleep was more tempting than food, and he finally finished the contents of the mug in the hope of being allowed to drift off again. Another dose of the fever-reducing tablets was all that was needed. Ronnie sat with him until he was sleeping quietly.

She busied herself with Miguel's laundry, taking note of his sizes so that she could pick up a change of clothes for him when she had the chance. The afternoon dragged on with no word from Norm Keller. She finally called him, and found that he was having trouble locating a starter for her particular model. He suggested that if she wanted to hedge her bet, she should pull hers out, bring it to the shop and let him try to repair it. In the meantime, if he found a new one, all the better.

Every bolt, every wire, every screw in the Cessna's ignition assembly became the object of Ronnie's verbal assault as she took it apart. By the time the work was done, it was too late to get the faulty part into the shop before morning. She revised her plans accordingly as she headed back to the house. After they had changed Miguel's bedding and all three had eaten again, Ronnie sent Becky home for a good night's rest with the reminder that her next shift would be a long one.

Miguel had lost track of time and touch with reality. Dreams of hot white sand and the glare of the sun off the water washed over damp white sheets beneath him and the sharp pitch of knotty pine above his head. He heard the report of a pistol one moment and the soft voice of a woman the next. Time was measured not by ticking, but by the constant pulsing ache in his side.

She looked different each time he saw her, and the images blended in his mind. She was at once a candy-sweet girl in pink pajamas and a sassy strawberry blonde making light of his trouble in an effort to make him smile. The sound of the shower had awakened him, and he sorted through all the images he had of her, making bets with himself on which one would emerge when the bathroom door opened. He became impatient with the sound of the hair dryer, enchanted with her lilting, snatchy rendition of an old movie theme and anxious when, for a moment, there was no sound at all.

Then she appeared in a cloud of steam, gowned in white batiste, her hair, gleaming with a freshly washed patina, falling softly to her shoulders. Backlit by the bathroom light, the feminine line of her body was defined in silhouette. Too soon she flipped the wall switch, and the definition vanished. He continued to watch her as he wondered whether this aspect would disappear, too. Her blue eyes brightened with surprise.

"I woke you up." She opened the closet door and took a white duster from a hook. "I'm sorry I made so much noise."

He was sorry to see her add another layer to the airy cotton gown. "I'm glad you did. I can't seem to stay awake."

"It's the fever," she told him as she came to the bedside. "Soon as we get that licked, you'll start eating better, and then I have a feeling there'll be no holding you down." She sat next to him and touched his face. She hardly needed a thermometer anymore, so sensitive had she become to the slightest variation in his body temperature. "I think it's a little better."

"You smell as good as that shower sounded," he said. "It would be good just to feel clean again."

"I've bathed you...some." She tucked her hands into the white cotton folds in her lap. "It helps bring your temperature down."

His eyes were bright black and hot with an intensity beyond feverishness, beyond the heat of the night. He held her gaze for a long time. Without touching him again she felt the dampness that clung to his skin and knew the dryness in the back of his throat. She said nothing, but went to the bathroom for water—a glass of it that was cold and a bowlful that was warm. She brought a washcloth, soap and a towel, and when he had drunk his fill of water, she turned him to his side so she could start with his back.

It was impossible not to admire him physically. Becky had said that all men looked the same to her, but Ronnie knew no other man could look like this one. His skin was tan and smooth, and the muscle beneath it was hard. When he lay on his back he closed his eyes, and she told herself it was just as it had been when she'd done this before. But it wasn't. His faint smile told her that what she was doing gave him pleasure. That was fine, she thought. His comforts were few and not to be minimized. She spent much time soothing his face and his chest with water.

A bottle of hand lotion caught her eye. Setting the water aside, she squeezed a dollop of lotion into her palm and rubbed her hands together, releasing the aloe scent. She began kneading the muscles in his shoulders, and his eyes opened sleepily. There was no mistaking the gratitude she saw in them. His skin felt silky as she slid her hands from one group of muscles to another and let her fingertips urge him to relax. He needed real rest. He needed peace of mind. He needed to stop tensing against the pain.

As her thumbs pressed along either side of his spine he groaned and gave in to the relief she offered him. Dream or not, she was a wonder, and such a blessing was not to be questioned or analyzed. The quality of her mercy was unrestrained.

She assumed he'd fallen asleep again, but when she started to move away, he caught her hand. "Tell me your name," he said. "Your true given name."

The soft look in his eyes laid claim to her heart, and her answer came in a whisper. "Veronica."

"Perfect." He closed his eyes again, floating on a dream, the shape of which he managed to verbalize. "Lie beside me, Veronica. I want to be close to you."

Chapter 4

The scant two-foot space on Miguel's left was certainly tempting. Two feet of firm, flat bed. The six-foot length was not quite enough for Miguel, but it was plenty for Ronnie. Her tired body yearned toward the promise of such luxury. He had all the pillows, but she wouldn't need one. Once she achieved a horizontal position, she knew she would be out like a light.

The thought of being that close to him through the night, even when he was in this condition, was somehow very disturbing. His chin, made no less attractive by two days' growth of dark stubble, had dropped to his left shoulder when sleep claimed him. His well-groomed hand, having clutched at the bedding moments ago, now lay relaxed at his side. His legs were too long for the bed, and one foot, extending beyond the mattress, peeked out from the white sheet. But even in this disheveled state, he was clearly a man of distinction. She'd never known a *personage* before—someone whose name cropped up in world news from time to time—but here was one lying in her bed, suffering and sighing, just like any human being who'd been shot in the back. Miguel Hidalgo was a real man. Too real.

For the time being, she had charge of him, but there were moments when she wondered how much charge she had over herself. There were moments when she felt drawn to touch him without any real purpose. There were instances when she caught herself looking at him simply because she enjoyed it. If she let this continue, she was probably in for trouble, she thought. Without really planning to, she gradually lowered her head to the mattress, stretched one leg slowly and eased the other alongside it. Her last conscious thought was of the amount of heat his very real, very human body radiated and how, even from a distance of several inches, she felt it envelop her.

She turned her head, dragging her face across the mattress, and his hand slid from her hair to her cheek. Even half awake, she knew it was Miguel's hand. Her nose was within an inch of his side, and the sheet had slipped to the level of his hipbone. During the night she had managed to scoot halfway down the bed and curl up into her usual fetal position. She moved his hand, carefully setting it on the bed, and raised herself on her arms. He touched her cheeks with the back of his hand, and she felt the warmth of her blush as she looked up at him.

"Good morning, Veronica."

She caught her lower lip between her teeth. Her hair tumbled in her eyes, and she was afraid to imagine how she must look. How *this* must look. She pulled the edge of her duster together between her breasts and sat up quickly, pushing her hair back with her free hand.

"How are you feeling this morning?" she asked.

There was a warm smile in his eyes as he caught the hand coming away from her hair. "Usually when you ask me that you put your hand on my face, like this. How do I feel?"

"Better." She cleared her throat and added, "Not so hot."

He chuckled. "Didn't you just contradict yourself in American terms?"

"Maybe. Better can still be not so hot, and, in your case, not so hot is better." She smiled because, regardless of the wordplay, his face felt good under her hand. "Are you hungry?"

"Yes."

His eyes told her that that exchange was open for interpretation, too. Her thumb stirred involuntarily against his cheek. "You could use a shave."

"That I could."

She jumped up suddenly and whirled away. "Would poached eggs be okay? One of the things I need to do today is get groceries."

"Eggs would be fine." He watched her pull open a drawer and dig through it as though she'd just realized she had an appointment elsewhere. "Did I do something to scare you away?"

"I have to get moving," she answered too quickly. "I have to get to Marathon with that starter and just pray Norm can fix it. We've got to have some food around here, and El—" She cut herself off before divulging the name of the woman who'd hired her. "My passengers are waiting for me. Do you need anything besides a change of clothes?"

"Sunglasses," he said flatly.

"Ah, we're going to convalesce incognito. Anything else?"

"I don't suppose you're a smoker."

"Not a chance." She glanced up. "I suppose you are." He nodded, and she shrugged as she went back to her digging. "I'll get you some cigarettes, then. I would think a man who's just been pointedly reminded of his mortality would swear off—"

"Where did you put my pistol, Veronica?"

She pulled a pair of olive-green shorts from the drawer and looked up slowly. "Why would you need that?"

"Because you are leaving me here with a defenseless old woman, and there are people who want me dead."

"As far as we know, only four people know you're alive," she reminded him.

"As far as we know," he repeated. "Anything we don't know could threaten Becky's life as long as she is with me." He propped himself up on one elbow and looked at her earnestly. "She saved my life. I need the gun to protect hers."

"And your own," Ronnie pointed out quietly.

"Yes. Mine, too."

She opened the closet door. The jacket she'd had with her on the flight from De Colores hung there, and its deep side pocket sagged with the weight of the pistol. She took the weapon out and studied it a moment. She remembered disabling the gun by removing the clip, and then... Where had she put that clip? Her eyes met Miguel's again.

"I think Becky should have the gun," she decided. "If anyone does come after you... well, at least Becky's ambulatory. If I leave her the gun, she won't be defenseless. And she'll defend you." *If I can find that ammunition clip.*

"I don't want her to defend me."

"You weren't anxious for her to carve you up, either, but we were lucky she was here." She laid the pistol on top of her folded clothes and closed the drawer. "Need some help getting to the bathroom?"

After she had Miguel settled back in bed, Ronnie took her clothes downstairs to dress. While she was preparing breakfast, she remembered her lunch bag. It wasn't in the living room, where she remembered dropping it. As she thought it through, she realized that she hadn't hung her jacket up, either. She dug through the trash in the kitchen and pulled out the bag, which yielded the ammunition clip. The eggs were ready. Thinking that she'd tell Becky about it later, Ronnie dropped the clip into a drawer full of odds and ends, then hurried upstairs with breakfast for her patient.

When Becky came to take her shift, Ronnie took the small boat she shared with Becky and delivered her faulty starter to Norm Keller. She shopped for jeans, shirts, underwear and tennis shoes for Miguel. At a revolving display she tried on several pairs of men's sunglasses, peering at herself in the little mirror and imagining Miguel's Latin features in place of her own. Then she bought groceries, cigarettes and a copy of the *Miami Herald*, and returned to the shop for the bad news that the starter was shot. Norm promised to call her as soon as the part he had ordered for her arrived.

The image of Elizabeth Donnelly's hauntingly beautiful face troubled Ronnie as her little boat bucked the easy rolling water across the channel toward home. Elizabeth must have lost faith in her by now, and McQuade must have been heaping curses on her head. She probably deserved them. Maybe she should have tried to find someone else. But Elizabeth had made it clear that she was not in a position to trust many people, and McQuade, hard-boiled man for hire that he was, trusted no one. What a mess! Ronnie told herself she was crazy for getting mixed up with any of these people as she juggled an armload of packages and shouldered her way through the front door.

"Your father's on his way over."

Two packages fell to the floor as Ronnie unloaded the rest on the small kitchen table and turned a wide-eyed stare in Becky's direction. "Right *now*?"

"He called about an hour ago. Said he stopped in at the shop, and Norm told him UPS had just delivered your part." Becky gave a mock-sweet smile. "He wanted to see you anyway, so he thought he'd run over with the part. You must have just missed him."

Ronnie checked her watch. "I don't suppose it would be a good idea to try to get him over to your house even if we had the time. Not that he'd have any reason to go upstairs, but you never know with Barnaby." Ronnie had followed her brother's lead in calling their father by his first name, and they had all been Barnaby's "buddies." She grabbed a sack of groceries and plunked it on the floor near the refrigerator. Wagging a finger at Becky, she warned, "Don't you dare ask him to stay for supper."

"He'll think it's a little funny if I don't offer."

"I don't care." Hand over hand, Ronnie stashed packages of meat, celery, milk and oranges into the refrigerator in hurried disorder. "Let him think it's funny. He can't just drop in any time he wants and expect people to drop everything. We've got lives, too."

"What we've got is some kind of political fugitive laid up in *your* bed." Becky propped her hip against the counter and stuck her hands in the pockets of her white cardigan sweater. "Maybe you should tell your father about him. I'm not sure we know enough about this man to—"

"No." Ronnie stood up and closed the refrigerator door. "Barnaby would have to report him." She had made her commitment to this man, and she faced Becky with a look of unwavering conviction. "From the little I know about politics, it seems to me that possession of power is nine-tenths of the law. I can't take the chance that Miguel might be sent back to De Colores, or that Guerrero might send some kind of a hit man after him.''

''I think you're taking a very big risk for a man you hardly know.''

''I know enough.'' Ronnie picked up the empty paper bag and folded it up. ''How is he?''

''The wound itself looks pretty good. I got him to eat some solid food and gave him what I had for pain. He should be sleeping.''

''I guess I'd better warn him about Barnaby.'' She gathered the packages of clothing and started toward the door. ''Oh,'' she said, doing an about-face when she remembered the cigarettes. ''If you see anything else that might start him asking questions, hide it. You know what he's like when he starts playing detective.''

Miguel was awake. He watched her ascend the top three steps and cross the room with her armload of packages. Propped up against a pile of pillows, he was wearing his khaki pants and lying on top of the coverlet. It occurred to Ronnie that if she'd had a wounded wolf stranded in her garret, this would be the look in its eyes.

''It's so dark and dismal in here.'' She dropped her packages in the rocker and reached up to give the cord on the blinds behind the headboard a quick jerk, thereby flushing the shadows away. ''Isn't that better?''

He shielded his eyes with his hand and muttered, ''I think I may have been a mole in a previous life.''

''Is it something serious?'' she asked, concerned.

''The doctors say that my eyes are unusually sensitive to light.''

''I've got just the thing.'' Ronnie fished around in one of the bags and produced the black-framed sunglasses she'd finally selected for him. Before handing them to him, she bit off the piece of plastic that held the price tag. He put them on and looked up at her. She tipped her head to one side and smiled. "I knew those were the right ones. They're the kind Fernando Lamas would wear."

"Do I look like Fernando Lamas?"

"A little, especially now that you've shaved." Shaving was something she had imagined herself doing for him, and she wondered if Becky had helped. She pulled out a pair of jeans, followed by a short-sleeved shirt. "But your hair is darker. Actually, you sound like him."

"Perhaps I should forget about that wretched little island and make my way to Hollywood."

"Sounds like a healthy idea if you stay off the freeways out there. Think these will fit?" She set the jeans on the bed and held the shirt up to her own shoulders.

"If you like the voluminous look." He noticed that she had applied a bit of mascara to her blond eyelashes, and, if he wasn't mistaken, she'd enhanced the peachy glow in her cheeks. "The turquoise is very becoming," he said and refrained from adding that it looked much better than the tan shirt she was wearing.

"I wasn't sure about the color." She tossed the shirt across his lap and dropped packages of white T-shirts, briefs and a sweatshirt on top of it. "All I know is that you wear uniforms and don't like them. I couldn't picture you in palm trees and flowers."

He laughed. "Why not?"

"I don't know. It just wouldn't come together in my head." She headed toward the clothes. "Are the sizes okay? I've got tennis shoes and socks in another bag."

He flipped through the pile and checked the jeans. "You did very well. Thank you." He looked at her in earnest. "I will repay you, Veronica. For everything."

The idea made her uncomfortable. She knew that even a friend would expect to be repaid, but she didn't want that.

She simply wanted to do this for him. She pulled two packages of cigarettes from the pocket of her shorts and tossed them on the nightstand. "That's the only part of it I want to be reimbursed for. They're not part of the rescue operation."

"I appreciate your thoughtfulness, and I promise to use them only in case of emergency."

"Speaking of emergencies—" Ronnie knelt beside the bed and began folding the clothes and stacking them in a pile "—we don't want to panic, but we may have one coming up. I'm going to put all this stuff under the bed for now. I'm really short on drawer space."

"What kind of emergency?" he asked calmly.

"Barnaby Harper." She stuffed the bags under the bed, too, and then planted her elbows on the bed and tried to muster a reassuring look for Miguel's sake. "My father. He called while I was gone and said he was coming with my engine part. I must have just missed the delivery. And, of course, he just happened to stop in at the shop after I'd left and thought he'd do me a favor."

"It would not be a good idea to tell him about me," Miguel said, and he covered her hand with his. He suspected that it was not easy for her to keep anything from those who were close to her.

"I know." His hand was warmer than hers, but his touch made her shiver strangely inside. She glanced up, and he removed the sunglasses. "My father is the county sheriff."

"I see." He smiled wistfully. "I had better watch my step around you, hadn't I?"

"I don't wear my father's badge." She stood up, drawing her hand away quickly. "Just be very quiet up here, and I'll get rid of him as soon as I can." She started for the stairs and paused. "Try not to listen . . . I mean, don't pay attention to anything . . . to the way he sort of treats me like . . ."

She sighed and shook her head as she started down the steps. "Just try to ignore him, okay?"

Barnaby Harper's physique had the look of something formed by a trash compactor. He had a big square chest, short, heavily muscled legs, no waist or neck to speak of, and his white hair was trimmed into the four right-angled corners of a flattop. Totally incongruous with the rest of him, his expressive blue eyes and his finely cut features were the only physical evidence of his relationship to the young woman who greeted him at the door.

"Hello, Barnaby."

"Hiya, kid." Neither offered to kiss the other. "Hear you're having a little trouble getting that puddle jumper started."

She took the box he handed her and set it on the kitchen table. "How do you always manage to be in the right place at just the right time?"

"Intuition." He turned to Becky, who was cracking a tray of ice in the sink. "How's it going, Beck? What have you got there? Iced tea?"

"Would you like some, Barnaby?"

"Love some." He dragged a chair away from the table and sat down. "I don't suppose you're cooking supper, are you, Beck? If you are, I'll consider staying."

"We weren't planning anything special." She glanced at Ronnie as she reached into the cupboard for glasses. "Were we, Ronnie?"

"We sort of had a late lunch," Ronnie told him. "But if you're hungry, I could fix you up a little something."

"That's okay. Your little somethings aren't much better than mine, kiddo." He laughed as his daughter handed him a glass of tea. "Why didn't you ever get Becky to teach you how to cook? Say, are my eyes playing tricks on me, or do I detect a little face paint there?''

She felt her cheeks get warm, and she knew there was no need for any face paint now. ''You've needed to get your eyes checked for years, Barnaby. Last chance, now. You want a sandwich or something?''

He waved the offer away and drank deeply. ''Did you hear about Dan's latest?''

Ronnie shook her head, knowing that her father would tell her about her oldest brother's most recent achievement, probably in his work as a police officer, which Barnaby considered to be the noblest of professions. Her older brother, Rory, was an officer in the Navy, the second noblest profession. Ronnie had always thought she would have ranked somewhere near the top if she had been a Navy pilot.

''He made detective,'' Barnaby retorted. ''What do you think of that?''

''I think it's wonderful.'' She couldn't remember a time when Dan had fallen short of wonderful in her eyes. When she was younger, she'd lived the game of follow the leader, allowing Rory to take the lead whenever Dan wasn't around. She had never pretended to be a boy, but she felt certain there was a female version of her wonderful brothers, and that was who she had tried to be. It had been a futile, frustrating exercise. Finally, with Becky's help, she had given it up and let herself be Ronnie.

''He's gonna clean up in Miami, that son of mine.'' Barnaby planted his elbow on the table with a forceful thud, extending his forearm straight up in the air and positioning his beefy fingers for a hand clasp. He waved at the chair opposite him. ''Sit down here and give your old man a go. You can use two hands. Let's see if I can get a takedown in less than a minute.''

Ronnie was mortified. What served Barnaby as a normal speaking tone would have carried all the way to Key West. The beautiful man upstairs who had given her eyes such lovely praise was hearing all this!

"I'm not twelve years old anymore, Barnaby," she said quietly. "You win by default."

Grinning, he lowered his arm. "Remember the first time Dan beat me?" He laughed. "'Course, he had the crowd with him. You and Rory really had his adrenaline going." He shook his head, remembering, and then the box caught his eye. "Why were you in such a hurry for this thing? You got a tight booking?"

"I've got passengers waiting in De Colores," she told him as she stood by the counter and stirred her own tea, watching the sugar crystals whirl inside the glass.

"Haven't you heard the weather report today, kiddo? De Colores is in for a bout, and we're gonna have a fair share of wind and rain off the tail end of it."

"You mean . . . a hurricane?"

He closed his hand around the glass, but his attention was on Ronnie as his brow drew down into a scowl. "What's the matter with you, Ron? You're usually the one telling *me* about the weather. I was gonna suggest you and Becky come on back with me. At the very least, you can count on a power failure out here."

Ronnie turned to Becky. "You go ahead. I want to put this starter in and maybe move the plane to a safer spot."

Becky returned a meaningful look. "You're overdoing it in the risk department, missy."

Ronnie's eyes glistened like polished turquoise, and her lips were pressed into a firm line. "If it looks bad, I know the way to the shelter. You go on back with Barnaby." She pointed to the blue sky out the window. "I've got time to make my repairs and move my plane," she insisted.

Barnaby opened the refrigerator door and did a deep-knee bend. "Got an orange or something just to... here's one." He tossed the orange in the air and caught it. "Yeah, you've got time. De Colores is out, but you've got time to batten down the hatches here." He reached for a drawer. "Where do you keep the knives?"

Her hand shot out instinctively to block his intended move. "Not that drawer!" They looked at one another for a moment, Barnaby assessing the roundness of Ronnie's eyes. She willed her body to relax as she reached for another drawer. "The knives are in here."

"So what's in there?" He jerked his chin toward the guarded drawer as she handed him a paring knife.

"Junk," she said, "but it's *my* junk. Stuff I save. Stuff you'd probably laugh at."

He did just that without even knowing what it was. He could just imagine. "Such a pack rat. Drawers full of worthless little stuff."

She smiled, mostly with relief. "I never had any room for saving worthless *big* stuff. Except Mama's trunk."

"Yeah." He turned away. The subject of Mama was closed, as always. "Listen, Beck, I'll help you secure your place, and then we'll head for higher ground."

Becky had done all she could for Miguel. The rest was a matter of convalescence, and Ronnie knew how to manage that now. Becky sympathized with Ronnie's other dilemma, but she knew if she left, the decision would be made. Ronnie would not make any foolhardy attempts to race against a hurricane if she were the only one left to take care of Miguel. Her concern for Becky's safety had forced Ronnie's hand. Like everyone else, the couple in De Colores would have to wait out the storm, and Ronnie would become the woman in charge of Miguel's recovery.

"I never did like riding in those light planes," Becky said. "You talked yourself into a job, Barnaby. I always have trouble closing those shutters."

After Barnaby and Becky left, Ronnie took the ammunition clip from the junk drawer, dropped it into her pocket and bounded barefoot up the steps to her bedroom. When she saw the pistol lying on the bed under Miguel's hand, she laughed, releasing an hour's worth of tension, and held the clip up for him to see.

"I know," he said, contemptuously eyeing the useless gun in his hand. "This was all I had. I felt like Jim Bowie lying in his bed and listening to Santa Ana storm the Alamo."

"You couldn't have bluffed Barnaby Harper as easily as you did his daughter," she said as she dropped the clip into her pocket again and sat beside him on the bed. He moved over to give her room.

"It was loaded when I pointed it at you," he reminded her solemnly. He knew he would always cringe inside whenever he thought of the time he'd held her at gunpoint.

"You wouldn't have used it, but, of course, I didn't know that then."

"You don't know that now."

"Yes, I do." She hadn't asked him about his temperature, but he was her patient, which meant that she could touch him without asking and without fear that her action would be misinterpreted. She touched him only to help him. He accepted it because he knew that. No big deal.

His face was as warm as the look in his eyes. "There's a storm coming," she said. Her voice had gone husky.

"I know." Her hand felt cool against his cheek, and he wanted her to keep it there. Earlier in the day when he'd gone into the bathroom to shave and wash up, he'd fought off wave after wave of dizziness with thoughts of her hands on him, cooling him, soothing him, driving the pain away. She had a healing touch. He wondered if she knew that.

"How long has it been since you took something for the fever?"

He caught her hand before it slid away. "Check my chart."

"You know, that's not a bad idea." It took real concentration to think of anything but the effect his handclasp was having on her pulse rate. "We should have a chart, or at least a list—"

"I think you'll find one in the drawer there." He nodded toward the nightstand. "Becky's been making notes of some kind. I assume they're of a professional nature."

"She thinks of everything. I should probably try to get her to stay, at least until you're—"

"I'm sure I'll get along quite well under your care." He turned her palm up and filled it with hard, cold metal. "You said you were going to leave this with Becky."

"I know. I forgot about it."

"It's useless anyway without the clip. If you're to be the keeper of the gun, then load it and keep it in a handy place." He smiled as he folded her fingers around the weapon's grips. "You see? Something inside you is still not quite sure of me."

"It isn't that," she insisted.

"It *is* that. It is that I threatened you, and now I must work harder to earn your trust." His hand stirred over hers. "I intend to do that, Veronica. You've more than earned mine."

She rose from the bed, took the clip from her pocket and fitted it into the butt of the pistol, which was set on safety. "I can't hit the broad side of a barn with one of these," she told him as she slid the pistol into the drawer of the nightstand. A piece of paper caught her eye. "My brother Dan tried to teach me once, but I never got the hang of it." Her eyes were fixed on Becky's notes as she added, "Just don't shoot my father. I don't have room for another patient."

"Veronica." She looked up. "You must understand that I can't allow anyone to detain me here. If you leave the gun there, I'll use it to defend myself if I have to."

"My father's going back to Marathon." She considered the intense look in his eyes. "My father's not the one you're worried about, though, is he?"

"No. He isn't looking for me."

"Probably no one is."

"Even if he were, he wouldn't harm you. I think . . ." He touched her knee and saw the flash of surprise the touch of his hand brought to her eyes. He moved his fingertips back and forth to soothe, to persuade. "I think you should go with Becky and your father. I know I can't go anywhere for a couple of days, and I'm afraid it's not safe for you here . . . with me."

"I thought you intended to earn my trust."

"I do. You, the two boys who put me on your plane, and Becky. Beyond that, I don't know who my friends are. And I don't want my friends caught between me and my enemies."

A knock at the back door was followed by Becky's call. "We're leaving now, Ronnie."

"If you're gonna get that starter put in, you'd better get moving, kiddo! That front's moving in."

Ronnie flew to the steps, casting a quick glance over her shoulder as she started down.

"Go with them," Miguel urged, merely mouthing the words.

Within ten minutes she was back, carrying a newspaper and two glasses of orange juice. "They're gone. I've got some work to do, so I thought I'd bring you something to read.'' She set the juice down and handed him the paper with a smile. ''Do you like seeing your name in print?''

''Is it extolled or maligned?'' he asked as he unfolded the paper.

''I would say that it's extolled for the moment, but soon to be disgraced. Fortify yourself with this.'' She handed him a glass of juice, and he took it without looking up from the front page. ''You'll need it. You're definitely past tense. Assassinated by a rebel faction.''

''Three boys,'' he corrected as he scanned the news. ''What did he do to them?''

''Supposedly they're in custody. There's some suggestion that you may have been involved with them, and they turned on you. The investigation continues.'' Ronnie took her seat on the edge of the bed and sipped her juice.

''He killed them,'' Miguel said tightly. The pages rustled as he searched for more information. ''He'd have to.''

''But *they* shot *you*.''

''They did what he told them to do.'' He tossed the paper aside and stared at the window at the opposite end of the garret. ''At least, they tried to.''

''Miguel,'' she said quietly, ''we're not talking about going on maneuvers. Those men attempted to murder you. How could they possibly have thought a legitimate execution would be carried out—''

''We are talking about three boys who know nothing of due process.'' He watched the gathering of gray clouds and avoided her eyes. ''They know how to cut cane or gut fish or take handouts from tourists, and they know how to do as they're told.''

''What about the two boys who helped you?''

He smiled, remembering their faces. Raphael and Paulo. ''They were not ordered to kill me.''

"They seemed quite devoted to you. I don't think they would have—"

"There's no point in speculating, is there?" He turned to her and realized that her face was as dear to him as any in his memory. "Make me strong, little angel. Strong enough to go back to them."

The rich sound of his voice shimmied through her. "Drink your juice," she told him. "That's my best prescription."

"You're going to fix your plane now?"

She nodded. "Try to get it done before the weather gets bad."

"You're not still thinking of going to De Colores," he warned. "Not now."

"No, not till the storm passes. I checked with the weather bureau, and Barnaby was right. De Colores is getting socked, and without much warning."

"The losses will be great. Homes will topple like houses made of cards." He drank his juice and set the glass on the nightstand. "It's safer for you here, Veronica. Even after the storm is over, you can't go back there."

"There's no point in speculating now, is there?" she said, echoing his remark. She went to the bathroom and brought him a glass of water and a dose of Becky's prescription. "Try to rest while I get my repairs done and move the Cessna to a more sheltered place. Then, if you're really brave, you can take your chances with my cooking."

"I look forward to it. So far it's been excellent."

"Canned soup and orange juice?"

He closed his eyes and smiled. "Excellent."

The sky was dark and heavy when Ronnie returned to the house. She looked like a diesel mechanic. She couldn't even go upstairs without showering in the bathroom downstairs first. Once that was done, she realized that all her clean clothes were upstairs. All except . . .

Wrapped in a thick white towel, Ronnie went to the storage room off the kitchen, where she kept her mother's trunk. She knelt slowly and opened the lid. The scent of the cedar lining caused her to draw a deep breath while she settled back on her heels. Sometimes she opened the trunk just for that smell. She had no real memories of her mother, but she had the trunk. She remembered the day Barnaby had decided to get rid of it, and she had tearfully pleaded with him to let her keep it. The tears seemed to take him off guard since, coming from Ronnie, they were quite rare, and he relented after securing her promise to keep it out of his sight.

The trunk contained pictures, jewelry that was valuable only because it had belonged to her mother, and dresses, including a white wedding gown that attested to the fact that Ronnie shared her mother's size. And there were keepsakes. Trinkets and programs, seashells and satin sachets. Things that were never really needed but were worth saving.

Ronnie unfolded her favorite dress from her vintage collection. The soft shades of tropical jade and turquoise seemed too pretty to wear, but she loved the way the yards of voile fluttered when she shook it out. She'd tried it on many times in private, and it made her feel . . . different. If she wore it for Miguel—not that she would, but if she did— would he tease her? She remembered Barnaby catching her in it when she was sixteen and dying for a certain someone to ask her to the high-school prom. Barnaby's comment had made her feel like a fool, and the certain someone had asked another girl. A girl who didn't look like ''a goose trying to be a swan.''

Ronnie pushed her damp hair from her face as she stood with her back to the door and held the dress to her shoulders. Smiling to herself, she closed the trunk and turned, clutching the dress and the towel to her breast, thinking that it wouldn't hurt just to...

She glanced up, and her entire body froze. Supported by the door frame across the kitchen, Miguel stood watching her.

Chapter 5

P ut it on."

Ronnie whipped the dress behind her back, nearly losing the towel in the move. Wide-eyed, she clutched the terry cloth between her breasts and sputtered as though she'd been caught in some terrible act. "It's just an old thing. I...didn't have anything else handy, and I didn't want to wake you."

"It's pretty. You would look very..." He slumped against the door frame, pressing his hand to his side. She noticed the gun in his other hand.

"Damn you." Ronnie grumbled. The dress fell to the floor behind her as she hurried to help him. "What are you doing up, anyway?"

"I heard someone down here." He straightened and tipped his dark head against the white wood. "When you come into the house, you must tell me you're here."

"Who else would be using my shower?" she demanded,

adjusting her towel as discreetly as she could manage right under his nose. Thunder rolled in the distance.

"I didn't hear the shower. I seem to drift in and out." She put her arm around him, and he leaned heavily on her shoulders as he tucked the pistol into the back of his pants. "Perhaps if I ate something substantial, I wouldn't feel so..." He waved his hand in front of his face.

"Dizzy," she finished for him. "You lost a lot of blood, Miguel. You're bound to feel dizzy. You can't be walking around any time you please."

"I didn't hear anything. All of a sudden I knew someone was in the house." He shook his head. "I can't take any more of those pills. They make me too groggy."

Struggling between Ronnie and the railing, Miguel managed the stairs. His breathing was labored, his balance not quite steady. Ronnie imagined the strain was enough to keep him from noticing the warm contact between so much of his skin and such a generous amount of hers.

It wasn't. The fresh smell of soap on her smooth skin and the dash of lemon in her damp hair swirled around in his tipsy brain. He remembered the way they'd fallen in a heap the first time she'd helped him to her bed, and the whole vision tumbled over and over in his head—soft skin, cool, damp hair, a towel unfurled and the tangy scent of lemon. He felt a tugging at his back and heard the pistol clatter in the wooden drawer. The spinning stopped when Miguel's head hit the pillow. No one tumbled, and no one lost her towel, but the delicious daydream made him smile and reach to touch the smooth curve of her shoulder before she could draw away.

She sat next to him with her knees pressed tightly together and her arms wrapped around herself and her towel. She felt as though every muscle in her body had formed a compact ball, but the touch of his hand was an appeal to relax, to let go. "I'll get dressed and fix something substantial for us to eat." She stood, and the motion was slow and stiff. "Could you eat beef? Like maybe a steak?"

A crack of thunder shook the stiffness out of her and made her jump. Watching her get hold of herself made Miguel smile. She managed it quickly, refusing to indulge herself in a moment of fear. "If you shared it with me, I think I could," he said.

She backed away, her laughter lacking its usual easy flow. "Once you taste it, you'll probably make me eat the biggest share."

"If I do, it will be my loss, I'm sure."

Ronnie emerged from the bathroom wearing her customary tan shorts and a cotton knit shirt that was a darker version of her peach skin. The boxy shorts seemed to be her uniform, and after she disappeared down the steps, Miguel lit a cigarette and imagined gauzy turquoise and jade spiraling around her slight body like the smoke that curled above his head. He had a strange longing to play Pygmalion, to help her set her femininity free.

She wanted it to be good. *Anybody* ought to be able to broil steaks and bake potatoes, Ronnie told herself. She thought she was doing pretty well until another overhead rumble gave way to a resounding crack, and the lights went out. She hurried to the foot of the stairs.

"Miguel?" she called out.

"I'm still here."

"The electricity went off, but don't worry. I've got plenty of candles."

He laughed. "I appreciate your concern, Veronica, but moles are quite comfortable in the dark."

"Moles?" She remembered his aversion to bright light. "Oh, yes, moles. Well, I just didn't want you to be alarmed." Under her breath, she added, "And sneak up on me with a gun."

"The pistol is right where you left it," he assured her.

She scowled. How could he have heard that?

Back in the kitchen, Ronnie resorted to Plan B—the gas grill. Her father always had good results with the grill, and Becky was a grilling marvel. Ordinarily Ronnie would opt for raw hot dogs rather than take the thing out and try to regulate the heat. It wasn't a fancy model. She wasn't a fancy cook, she reminded herself as she carried the steaks out to the porch, where the hot, black jaws of the grill stood open, ready to destroy her efforts. While the food cooked, Ronnie took candles upstairs, arranged a small cluster on her dresser and a few on the nightstand, then promised to be right back with dinner.

One of the steaks looked like tar paper, but the other was perfect. Uneven heat, she decided as she mounted the steps with a tray containing a hearty meal for one. It wasn't really her fault. But there was no way that Miguel would ever see that other steak.

Ronnie set the wicker bed tray over his lap and settled herself in the rocker. "I guess I was pretty hungry," she said, eyeing his food. The smell of charcoaled beef was tantalizing. "I couldn't stop nibbling all the while I was cooking. I just..." She shrugged, unable to actually make the claim that she had already eaten. "So now it's your turn."

"It is." He smiled appreciatively as he moved the napkin to his lap and took up the knife and fork. "I think you've resurrected my appetite. It looks wonderful." More than the aroma of the food, he savored the anxious gleam in the eyes that were the color of his beloved Caribbean. "Come here and sit beside me, Veronica."

"Oh, but I don't want to...crowd you while you eat." She nodded toward the tray. "Is there anything missing?"

"Yes." The warmth of his smile beckoned her. "You promised to share this with me, and I'm going to make you keep your promise." He patted the place on the bed right next to him. "Come to the table."

She moved, tucking one leg under her bottom as she sat down. "I knew you were basically a cautious man. But, I warn you, I have a pretty strong constitution, so you won't be able to tell anything by trying it out on me—" he filled her mouth with a bite of steak, and it took a moment before she could finish the sentence "—first. Hey, that isn't bad."

"Of course not." He cut himself a piece and popped it into his mouth prepared to relish rather than test. "*Delicioso*, Veronica. I've never tasted better."

"Well, neither have I," she marveled. "Isn't that incredible?"

"Not at all."

"I don't do much cooking," she said, the blush of pleasure in her accomplishment rising in her cheeks. "I used to try to make something for Barnaby and my brothers once in a while, but they always gave me so much flak about how bad it was."

"Who took care of you after your mother died?"

"There was a variety of sitters and housekeepers until we got old enough to fend for ourselves. And then there was Becky." Ronnie accepted another bite of steak as she thought about what an understatement she'd just made. *Thank heaven, there was Becky.* "She let Barnaby know right away she wasn't for hire, and then she became part of our family, sort of like having a mother for a neighbor. Crazy, huh? I used to wish Barnaby would marry her so she could move in."

"Why didn't he?"

She shrugged. "I don't know. I guess because he always had another girlfriend. But that didn't stop me from wishing."

"And it didn't stop her from being a mother to you."

She watched him sample the salad she'd made. The candles near the bed cast his face in bobbing light and shadows, and she imagined sitting across the table from him in the dark, private corner of an elegant restaurant. The reverie was like a black-and-white movie, or perhaps an old photograph. And in the photograph the woman was...

"My mother was very beautiful," she confided. "Barnaby says that none of us kids got our mother's looks, but I know from pictures that my hair is the same color as hers was, and I must be about the same... height." She had almost said build, but she knew that fitting into her mother's clothes didn't give her the feminine shape of the woman she saw in the pictures. She wondered why she was telling him any of this. Was it because she didn't fit into the picture of an intimate candlelit dinner with Miguel Hidalgo?

"Did your mother have eyes that change color like the sea?"

She hadn't realized how closely he'd been watching her. "My mother's eyes were green," she said.

"Plain green?"

"*True* green."

He smiled and repeated, "*Plain* green. Not like yours."

"My mother had beautiful eyes," Ronnie insisted.

"I'm sure she did." He cut off another piece of steak and offered it to her. "I like yours."

She took the meat into her mouth and chewed slowly while he watched. He found her frank look of appraisal to be almost as disturbing as the way her lips moved against one another. She was clearly weighing the probability that he was simply flattering her against the chance that he might be expressing himself as candidly as she was in the habit of doing. It took her forever to say, "Thank you."

He knew the art of flattery. He had perfected it and used it with a certain Old World flair. The women he'd known had expected it and taken it for what it was. It had been part of the ritual, a piece of the armor. It surprised him to realize that the compliment he'd paid her had been genuine. Still more unexpected were the hundred others that formed, less of mind than of heart, as he admired the red-gold candle glow in her hair.

"Were you able to fix your engine?" he asked, shifting the conversation to a less personal topic for both their sakes.

"Yes, but not soon enough," she said with a sigh.

"Better to be grounded here than down there." He raised his brow and lifted one bare shoulder. "Unless, of course, you have an affinity for hurricanes."

"Those people were counting on me," she said stubbornly. "I enjoy a reputation for being totally reliable. I don't want to have that ruined by some dumb storm."

"Or some dumb political fugitive." He filled his mouth with a forkful of potato and his eyes sparkled.

"I can't blame you now for being in a hurry to take off when you were bleeding to death," she allowed. "But I do feel pretty queasy inside when I think about letting those people down."

"It's been a long time since I've met someone who took such fierce pride in being dependable. It's a commendable attribute." He reached for the glass on his tray and took a sip. Orange juice with everything, he thought. Strangely, he was beginning to like it. He also liked the way the candlelight flickered across her face. "Providence has a way of looking out for sparrows and for desperate souls," he told her. "Even the dumb ones."

"*Especially* the dumb ones. What I can't figure out," she added after a moment, "is how someone who's as smart as you are could be so dumb about someone like Guerrero."

"And what makes you think I'm so smart?" he asked.

"The way you talk. Spanish is your native language, but your English is better than mine."

He lifted one shoulder. "I have an American education."

"So do I, but I think yours is a few years up on mine."

"I'm a few years up on you in more ways than one," he said, cocking a finger at her. "But there's nothing wrong with your English."

"How old are you?"

Because she had asked so directly, he laughed and answered in kind. "Thirty-seven."

"Really? I never would have guessed."

"I'm dumb for my age," he quipped with a bright glance out of the corner of his eye.

"Only about Guerrero," she hastened to add. "And who am I to say? He was probably a nice guy until the power went to his head."

"I don't think so," Miguel said as he stared thoughtfully at the pink center of his steak. The ominous sound of rolling thunder reminded him of Guerrero's temper. "I've never heard anyone apply the term 'nice guy' to Rodolfo Guerrero. It was Castillo who started our movement. The old farmer whom everyone loved. I followed him because his dreams matched mine, although—" he looked up at her and smiled "—I was not a man of the soil."

"What were you before you became *Colonel* Hidalgo?"

"I was *Professor* Hidalgo." At the word, laughter bubbled in her throat, and he assumed an expression of mock offense. "You laugh? Only a moment ago you said you detected some signs of intelligence. I'll have you know that I was an associate professor of history at the University of Massachusetts before I took up arms against the old regime in De Colores and became a rebel. Then I became a benevolent dictator's right-hand man, and now I'm a fugitive. All in a day's work, I guess." He laid his fork down and started to lift the tray, but Ronnie stopped him.

"Oh, no, you don't. I've eaten more than you have." She situated herself purposefully, crossing her legs Indian style, and began sawing on the remaining steak. "If you ask me, anyone who's studied history should know better than to get mixed up in this revolutionary stuff."

"Really?" He opened his mouth for the bite of meat she was pushing at him, mostly to get it out of his way. "What would you have done in 1776, Miss Harper?"

"That was different."

"Uh-huh. How was it different?"

She scowled as she pondered the question. "Well, for one thing . . . there was no Rodolfo Guerrero."

"There was a Benedict Arnold."

"And this was a whole big . . . This wasn't some tiny little . . ." Her gesture changed from wide to narrow, and then she frowned, exasperated. "What's a *benevolent* dictator, anyway? You know very well there's no such thing."

"Do you realize how much power your president has in time of war?" he countered. "After a war, whom do you elect to be your next president? Your generals, of course." Piqued by the topic, he fell naturally into the roll of lecturer. "A coup is accomplished by force—military force, although, in our case, it was on a rather small scale. Nevertheless, wartime conditions did exist for a time, and a show of force may have been necessary to restore order. Despite Guerrero's objections, I had written a constitution, and we were ready to form a new government. There would have been elections very—"

"You *wrote* a constitution? You mean you just sat down all by yourself and *wrote*—"

He headed off another mouthful of food by taking the fork from her hand. "What do you think General Mac-Arthur did for Japan after the Second World War? And where do you think the United States got its constitution? It was not a divine gift etched on stone tablets. It was written by men."

"Men," she repeated. "Not one man."

"I used it as a model." He saw her face brighten, and he smiled. "I think even Ben Franklin would have approved. Does that give me some measure of credibility in your red, white and blue eyes?"

"It's just so hard to believe that I'm sitting here eating steak with a man who's written the constitution for a whole *country*." She took the fork out of his hand and resumed her work on the steak.

"Just a *tiny* little country," he reminded her, and she winced when the words came back at her. "What's hard to believe is that you insist upon hand feeding the man who's written a constitution for a whole country." But he did accept another bite.

"A man who was an associate professor of history at the University of Massachusetts," she recited happily.

"Turned rebel," he added.

"Now hunted fugitive." She laughed. "The whole thing is impossible."

"It's impossible for me to eat another bite." He held his hand up, and the expression on his face pleaded for mercy. "Truly. My *stomach* may become rebellious."

Ronnie set the tray aside and reclaimed her seat, planting her elbows on widespread knees and her chin on clasped hands. "Where's your constitution now?" she asked.

"It was in the top drawer of my desk." Miguel settled back against the pillows and hooked one arm behind his head. "By now it has no doubt been reduced to ashes, along with the rest of my papers."

"But you can always rewrite it," she encouraged.

He smiled, enchanted by the way her eyes glistened with excitement. "I think I remember the gist of it, yes."

"Shall I get you some paper?"

"Now?"

"I want to watch you write it. I want to tell my children about it. Or... my nieces and nephews, anyway." She straightened her back as the excitement grew. "I'll hang a sign outside. 'Miguel Hidalgo slept here.' We'll get the house listed in the guidebooks, and we'll have parchment facsimiles of the De Colores constitution for sale in our gift shop."

"Parchment!" He couldn't help laughing, and he winced when it made his side hurt. "I used a word processor."

"Oh, gosh, don't tell anyone that. It'll ruin everything." It was good to see him really laugh, and she laughed along with him.

"Bring me every pen and pencil you can find. I'll make them all collector's items."

"I'm serious, Miguel." She was smiling, but not to tease him. "The idea of actually writing a constitution for your country..." She shook her head. "That's really something."

"None of it will amount to anything unless I get back to De Colores."

Reality brought an end to the merriment. "What will you do then?" Ronnie asked.

"I'll fight Guerrero," he said, knowing it wouldn't be that simple. "There are those who will join me."

"And if you win?"

"There will be none of this interim military government. Castillo was wrong in letting it drag on, and we paid the inevitable price for such a mistake. If I win, I'll offer the people a written constitution, and we will hold a plebiscite. If the constitution is approved, we will elect a president."

"What if you lose?" she asked quietly.

His smile was almost apologetic. "If I lose, your attempts to save my life will have been in vain."

"Then you can't lose." She smiled, her eyes brightening with the promise of his success. "I didn't go to all this trouble over you for nothing."

Before she took the tray downstairs Ronnie put candles in the bathroom and offered Miguel a sink full of hot water and assistance if he needed it. He would have enjoyed soaking in a tub and then letting her lather every inch of his body, but he knew that wasn't the kind of assistance she had in mind. When she returned, he asked her simply if she would wash his back, which he couldn't reach.

Ronnie closed the lid on the toilet and directed him to sit with his back to her. She snipped off the gauze bandaging and removed the pads that covered his wounds. In the dim light she could see the puckering stitches just below his rib cage. "Does it hurt very much?" she asked as she prepared to clean the area with antiseptic.

"The holes persist in letting me know they're there."

"They're not holes any longer. Pretty soon they'll just be a pair of scars. Battle scars," she named them as she daubed around them with cotton. He flinched. "Stings, huh?"

"Mmm, a little." On the end of a chuckle, he added, "When I became a teacher I thought I would miss out on such things as battle scars."

"If you had stayed on campus, you might have. But think of the fun you'll have showing them off. The, um . . . the ladies in your life will be quite impressed."

He smiled secretly. "Ladies?"

"Or the *lady*," she tossed out as casually as she could manage. "Is there just one?"

"At the moment, there is none."

She, too, smiled secretly as she filled the sink with fresh water, took up the bath sponge and applied it to his broad shoulders and smooth-skinned, tapering back.

Miguel closed his eyes and let the water soothe him even as the touch of her hands and the womanly scent of her filled his head with stirring images. At the moment, he amended mentally, there was actually one. He braced his hands on his thighs, which were spread wide over the seat, and let his head fall forward. There was his angel of mercy who had saved him, sheltered him, seen to his repair and now sought to comfort him. Did he impress her? She washed and rinsed him, and the warm water trickled over his shoulder, down his chest and his belly, and disappeared into his waistband toward the place where, God help him, he was as hard as any lusty youth. One tender angel, and he had no intention of tarnishing her halo.

She set the sponge aside. The muscles in his back were tense—probably, Ronnie thought, the result of being stuck in bed so long. He looked as though he'd made it his practice to be physically active. She was untutored in the skill, but she managed to massage him, clearly to his satisfaction, just by attending to his responses. The starch in his shoulders gradually melted under her hands. Finally he dropped his head back and muttered, "*Bueno*, Veronica. It feels so good."

"You've gotten stiff."

His eyes flew open, and when he saw candlelit innocence in her eyes, he chuckled. "More so than I'd realized."

"You're not ready for anything strenuous, but you do need a little physical activity."

"Whatever you prescribe." She could do anything she wanted to do to him right now with those hands, he thought. Her hands were magic.

"We'll get you up more tomorrow," she promised. "And even while you're in bed, there are things you can do."

"I have no doubt." But he rejected his own most pressing suggestion.

"And, of course, things I can do for you."

"You've already done more than you know," he mumbled as he tilted his head to the right. "But far be it from me to discourage you at this point."

"Are you feeling light-headed again? Let's get you to bed. I can do the rest there."

"The rest?"

She looked down at him and smiled. "The bandaging. You look tired."

"So do you." He held on to the sink and stood up slowly. It was best to put an end to such exquisite pleasure before it became painfully tempting to see it through to its natural conclusion.

"Lean on me," she said. "I'll be careful not to touch—" She looked up at him, and the look he returned made her mouth go dry. She swallowed hard, and added almost reverently, "The place where you were shot."

She bandaged him while he sat on the edge of the bed and smoked a cigarette. Miguel watched the pale smoke disappear out the window into the rain-drenched night, and he thought of the rain and wind that were battering his island home. What would the people do when it was over and their homes were gone? There would be so many needs, and Guerrero would take an interest only in the needs he could exploit. There was no one to stop him now. The rain splashed on the windowsill and began streaming down the wall. He put his cigarette out in the ashtray she'd set on the nightstand.

"I'll have to close that," Ronnie said as she followed the direction of his gaze. She pressed the last piece of tape against his skin and moved within reach of the window. "This damp draft wouldn't be good for you, anyway."

"It feels good, but the floor..."

"It's hardly wet." She turned from closing the window and found him watching her. "Rest now. I'll give you some medication after I get ready for bed."

She emerged from the bathroom in her white batiste gown and robe a few moments later. She took him some pills and a glass of water, and she noticed the pants he'd been wearing had been tossed over a chair. He was covered to the waist with the sheet. Soft light and shadow played across his face as he handed her the glass.

"Good night," she said. She took a candle in its holder from the group of three on the nightstand.

He frowned. "Where are you going?"

"Downstairs. I'm going to sleep on the love seat tonight."

"It's made of wicker," he reminded her.

"I know, but—"

"You need rest as much as I do, Veronica." Holding her gaze with his, he spread his hand over the extra space on the bed. "Sleep here."

"Oh, no, I'll be fine down there. I only stayed close by the last two nights because—"

"You'll be fine up here," he promised. "I will be on my best behavior." He gave her a reassuring smile. "I'm in no condition to behave otherwise."

"It isn't *that*," she said, too quickly. "I'm not worried about... It's just that I'm such a squirrelly sleeper."

"Squirrelly?" The comparison amused him. He could almost see her scampering barefooted up a tree, a silky, pale red ponytail bouncing behind her.

"I move around a lot. I might keep you awake."

He shook his head slowly. "I feel just as tired as you look. Nothing could keep me awake." He moved to give her more room. "Stay beside me, Veronica. It's good to know that you're close by."

She could not deny him that measure of comfort. She blew the candles out, lay next to him on top of the sheet and pulled the bedspread over her.

A sharp crack shattered his sleep. He shouted and sat bolt upright. Pain as jagged and sharp as the lightning that streaked across the sky gouged his side. He clutched himself, groaning, knowing he'd been hit again. Quick light filled the room and was gone before he got his bearings. He shuddered with the sound of cannon fire overhead.

"Miguel," a soft voice called. Puffs of breath warmed his back, and a gentle hand caressed his arm. "Miguel, it's all right. It's the storm."

Stifling another groan, he turned his head toward the voice. She was a dark shadow framed by the window behind her. A flash of lightning formed a curve of white light over the top of her hair. "Veronica?"

"Yes," she whispered as she pressed his shoulder back. "Be careful. You'll hurt yourself."

"I've been...shot." He laid back on the pillow and closed his eyes in his confusion. "My own people...shot me."

"No, Miguel," she said, her soothing voice gradually claiming the operative track in his dream-muddled mind. "Guerrero's people shot you. Are you okay? Did you—"

"It happened again."

"You were dreaming." She stroked his face and found him feverish. "I'll get you some aspirin."

He grabbed her wrist when he felt her moving away. "No, don't go. I'll be on my best . . . behavior."

"I'm not going far," she promised, petting his shoulder even as she disengaged herself. "I'll get you some water. Your throat sounds dry."

He took the aspirin and eagerly drank the whole glass of water, but he wouldn't let her leave the bed a second time. She set the glass on the nightstand and lay beside him again. Another flash of lightning brightened the pattern of knots in the pitched ceiling, and a report of thunder followed.

"It sounds a little like gunfire, doesn't it?" He asked the question hesitantly, dreading that his notion would sound utterly foolish if she disagreed. But he took the risk because he needed her affirmation. A moment ago he'd experienced it all again. The reality had been a nightmare, and the nightmare had seemed absolutely real. He was still shaken, still not certain he could separate the two.

"It does," she said. In the dark, her voice didn't sound as though it belonged to her. It was someone else lying next to this beautiful, haunted man. "It scares me, too."

He was older, stronger, wiser, more experienced—it was important that she believe in him. He wasn't sure why, but, at the moment, reasons were immaterial. "Would you mind if I held you?"

"No," she said quietly. "I wouldn't mind."

Chapter 6

The storm wrapped a gray curtain around the house. Without electrical power, the day seemed like a throwback to another time. There was little to distract from the pane-rattling wind, the sheeting rain and the day's heavy darkness except the company of another person. But the two people who shared the sanctuary had slept together the night before. Throughout the day they were aware of little else.

In daylight, gray as it was, it all looked different. They made careful conversation or sat together in uneasy silence. Miguel refused to be bedridden, but his energy was limited. He dressed in his new jeans and a white T-shirt and ventured downstairs to look for reading material. Ronnie behaved like a clerk in a bookstore—a friendly, helpful stranger. And Miguel was equally polite. He asked permission to open the window behind the wicker love seat and have a cigarette, and Ronnie quickly assured him that would be fine.

It was too dark to read the coffee-table book about the air war in Europe in 1942. Miguel's mind drifted, like the curling thread of smoke from the cigarette he held between his fingers, toward something fresh. Veronica. Lying against his good side, she'd been a balm for his wounded one. In her sleep, she'd turned to him, nestling, and he'd felt her heart beating close to his. He'd thought of opening the cotton robe she'd worn to bed and letting the tips of his fingers slide down her throat, her chest, beneath her nightgown in search of her breast.

It was foolish to tease himself that way. They had offered one another comfort when the night and the elements had joined forces to play tricks on the mind. He knew that, by morning's light, she'd realized that in the dark of night, she'd come too close for comfort. She was a sensible woman. Giving comfort in the dark was risky, and Veronica had already taken more than enough risk in helping a man whose destiny linked him with a viper.

He watched the smoke slide quickly through the narrow window and heard a clattering in the kitchen. She was tempting, and he had to remember that she didn't mean to be. She had no idea how lovely she was. When she wasn't feeling wary, as she obviously was today, she was beautifully natural and naturally caring. Then she was vulnerable. He'd seen the way she looked at him sometimes, and he knew how many ways a man could use that vulnerability to his own advantage. On the other hand, a man could hold it dear and make every effort to let her see herself in the mirror of his eyes.

"Is the book any good?"

Miguel turned from the window and looked up at her as he reached past the arm of the love seat to put his cigarette out. "It has nothing new to say." He'd actually read very little of the book that lay open in his lap.

"It's one Barnaby left behind," Ronnie explained. "There are others around. Barnaby is a real military buff."

Miguel closed the book and set it on the table. "Do you need any help in the kitchen?"

"Nothing works." She busied herself unloading a pile of magazines from the chair across from him. "Isn't it amazing how many things you forget are electrical? It's a good thing I've got that gas grill."

"There's room for you over here." She hugged the magazines to her chest and lifted her chin, but she made no move in his direction. "I think we need to put an end to this awkwardness," he said. "We have to talk."

Ronnie put the magazines in the chair and took the seat beside him. "How are you feeling? Are you . . ."

He took her hand and pressed it against his face. Her fingers felt cool against his skin even though he was no longer fevered. "I've come to expect you to touch me when you ask that," he said in a smoky tone.

Her fingers moved slightly against his smooth-shaven cheek. He released her hand, and hers lingered a moment before she drew it back. "There was a time when you couldn't answer. Now that you can, there's no need for, um . . ."

"There's a need." She looked straight into his eyes with more curiosity than surprise, and he responded with a hint of a smile. "You're a desirable woman, Veronica. I would be less than honest if I didn't tell you that. Because I don't think you know it."

"I'm a woman, and at the moment—" she lifted one shoulder "—I don't have much competition."

"We could go to any city you care to name. In a crowd of women, I would single you out and offer you a seat next to me."

She gave a toneless whistle. "Wow!" It took a quick shake of her head to clear it of the rich echo of his voice. "I *would* get stuck here without power, without any lights, all alone with some guy who looks like he belongs on the cover of *Gentleman's Quarterly* and talks like Rudolf Valentino."

Miguel tipped his head back and laughed. "Valentino! He didn't even talk."

"That's because his lines were too good to be true, just like yours, professor." She was smiling, more relaxed now, her eyes alight with her teasing.

"Consider the situation from my point of view," he suggested, his smile becoming a counterpoint to his instructional tone. "Like you, I find myself stranded with someone who is both physically attractive and perfectly charming. But I have been literally shot full of holes. A trip to the bathroom is a major achievement. I'm lucky to be able to chew my own food." He wagged his finger at her when she giggled. "Don't laugh at me, woman. You'd do it for me if I asked you to, and you know it."

"I would not!"

"Ah, my sweet angel, you know very well you would. I'm getting stronger, thanks to you, but not strong enough, not yet." The laughter in his eyes disappeared, and it was replaced by soft, bittersweet regret. "And when I am," he said, "when I *am* strong enough, I will leave you unharmed. I promise. We've shared some very intimate moments, you and I, but our circumstances have left us few choices. Please don't be embarrassed, Veronica. Don't be afraid to look at me or talk about what happened last night. We shared a bed."

Her merriment dissipated, and she glanced away. "We can't do that again."

"Why not? It's the only one in the house."

"It's too..." She took a deep breath and expelled it slowly. "Too much. It's just too much."

"Too much what?"

"Too much you. Too much me. Too close together."

"I enjoyed being close to you, Veronica." She gave him a look that invited him to touch her, and there was nothing he wanted to do more. He resisted. "You're much more than a desirable woman." With a shrug he gathered his cigarettes and matches from the side table. "It wounds my ego to admit it, but my lack of physical strength renders me totally harmless."

Her smile was back. "Heaven help us, the man is wounded again. We'd better get you back to bed."

"Oh?" He watched her stand up, then accepted the hand she offered him. "To tend to which of my wounds?"

"All of them." She tugged on his hand. "Your body needs rest, and those dark circles under your eyes can't be good for your ego."

"Nonsense," he said as he hooked his arm over her shoulders. "They're like the battle scars. They garner feminine sympathy."

He woke to the sound of her footsteps on the stairs, and his first thought was that she was wearing shoes. The rain was still washing against the window pane, but it had grown dark, and there were more candles burning on the dresser. He'd slept through the afternoon again and hadn't heard her moving around until now. Ordinarily a light sleeper, he was almost embarrassed by this uncharacteristic behavior. Worse, it left him feeling disoriented, and he was uneasy because so much time had passed while he lay completely unaware of everything that was going on around him.

The sight of her banished all thoughts but one. Veronica. She could have been dressed in sea foam. The dress was like a frothy watercolor, a blend of jade and turquoise that crossed over her breasts, was cinched at the waist and then became a waterfall of fluttering fabric over her slender hips. Her hair curled softly at her shoulders, and the heels of her sandals clicked against the floor as she brought the dinner tray to the bed. As she came closer, he saw the uncertainty in her eyes.

"Forgive me." Miguel spread his hand over his bare chest as he braced himself on one elbow. "I'm not dressed for dinner."

"You told me to put it on." She set the tray on the bed and stepped back. "Tell me the truth. Do I look silly?"

"Am I laughing?" She saw the appreciation in his eyes and knew that it was not for the food. He hadn't even looked at the tray. It was she who laughed as she shook her head and sat beside him on the bed. He said the words he knew she'd heard too seldom. "You look beautiful."

"I'm sure it's out of style."

"Beautiful can never be out of style."

"It was my mother's. That's how outdated it is." She smiled easily now, her nervousness gone. "I like to put it on sometimes when nobody's looking, just for fun. Do you like chicken cooked on the grill that way?"

"Chicken?" He looked down at the tray and pushed himself up straighter. "Oh, yes, it looks delicious."

"If we had electricity, I could have made lasagna. I'm pretty good with lasagna."

"There's only one plate."

"But lots of food." She smiled as she scooted closer. "I could only fit one plate on the tray."

"And one fork?" He picked up the utensil as if to examine it, then raised a teasing eyebrow as his mouth twitched with the urge to break into a broad grin.

"Gunshot wounds aren't contagious, and I'm trying to keep the dishwashing chores to a minimum."

"I offered to help."

As she watched him puncture the breast of chicken with the fork, Ronnie prayed that nothing red would gush forth. She breathed easily when he sliced into the meat with his knife and it proved to be done. "This was your first day up, and I didn't want any mishaps," she told him. "You were pushing pretty hard as it was."

"I slept all afternoon. Forgive me for taking the first bite, but this is irresistible." He filled his mouth and reported an enthusiastic "Mmm, *excelente*!" as he cut a piece for her. "You can stop apologizing for your cooking, Veronica. You have no electricity to work with, and still you're able to serve a wonderful meal."

Her eyes were soft with gratitude. "Maybe I should just chuck the stove."

"Maybe you should disregard past criticism and take the word of a man who appreciates fine food."

"Okay," she said hesitantly, "but don't expect this every time. Sometimes it just doesn't turn out. Besides, we'll have to rely on canned stuff pretty soon. The frozen food is thawing out, and it won't keep."

"The storm can't last forever." The look they exchanged spoke of mutual regret. The storm had prevented her from leaving him, and they were enclosed by it now, together. No matter what havoc it had wreaked outside the walls of Ronnie's house, it had served their own two-person world quite well.

"You need more time," she said. "I know you're thinking about going back, but you need more time."

"Perhaps another day or two."

"And you'll need help. You can't just storm the presidential palace with two men."

He lifted the glass of ever-present orange juice. "I'll have to find some means of transportation first."

"I'll fly you down there when you're—"

"No, you won't, Veronica. It's too dangerous for you. I know a man in Miami who might be able to help me." He trusted Mikal Romanov, but Mikal lived somewhere in the Midwest. McQuade, who had stood by Mikal during the hostage crisis that Guerrero had engineered a year ago, lived in Miami. Mikal had negotiated the release of the hostages, and McQuade, working with the Red Cross, had been on hand to run interference for him. Miguel thought he could trust McQuade, too.

"We've got plenty of time to talk about it," Ronnie said lightly as she took a turn with the knife and fork. "It'll be a while before you can hook up with anyone from Miami."

"Yes," he agreed, anxious to turn the conversation back to the present. "A while."

They finished their shared meal with no more references to the future. By the time Ronnie set the tray aside, she had kicked off her shoes and become Miguel's vision of a barefooted sea nymph. The lighthearted sound of her laughter drove thunder into the background, and her honey-toned skin glowed in the candlelight.

"No one ever calls me Veronica," she told him. "It always seemed like kind of an elegant name, and I always thought if I ever wanted to be elegant someday, I might use it."

"Do you mind if I use it for you?"

"Oh, no. It sounds so pretty the way you say it," she assured him with a gamine smile. "Say it."

"Veronica."

"Veronica," she repeated with a flourish, and he laughed at her version of his voice. "My mother named me," she said. "Maybe she thought I'd be a movie star or something."

"I thought perhaps you were named for a saint. We De Colorans name our children for saints, and we believe the name influences the child's life." He reached for a cigarette, then thought better of it. He didn't want her to back away from him. "Yours certainly has."

"Has it?" She moved to the side of the headboard and opened the window. The scent of rain-fresh air drifted over them. "Was there a Saint Veronica?"

"Legend has it that when Jesus bore his cross through the streets of Jerusalem, Veronica came forward to wipe the sweat from his face. She was a courageous and compassionate woman." Ronnie took the cigarettes from the nightstand and handed them to him. His warm gaze met hers as he accepted the package. "And you are very much like her."

The strange notion tingled in her system like a message of great import sizzling along telegraph wires. She tried to remind herself that this was just the way Miguel talked, but a stubbornly romantic part of her refused to listen. The compliment was too beautiful to be ignored.

The unlit cigarette was halfway to his mouth when he paused with it. "I don't want this to drive you away," he said.

"It won't. My father always liked to have one cigarette after supper." The quick flare of the match released a familiar sulfur smell that reminded Ronnie of past suppertable scenes. The tip of Miguel's cigarette glowed in the shadows as he drew the smoke deeply into his lungs. Watching made Ronnie's own chest hurt. "I grew up in a house full of men." Even as she said it, she was unsure what that explained.

He turned his head and directed his smoky breath toward the window. "You have one brother who is a very good policeman."

Recollections of her father's recent visit made her blush. "As far as my father is concerned, my mother was the only real woman in our family."

"Then your father is a blind man." Miguel shifted his position just enough to ward off the stiffness that was setting into his side. "Perhaps he chooses to be blind rather than to be reminded of his loss."

"His loss of what?"

"Your mother. You undoubtedly remind him of her. Perhaps he protected himself by thinking of you as one of the boys." He watched her consider the possibility as he brought the cigarette to his lips again. "How many brothers do you have?"

"Just two. And they were right, you know. I was never much good at girlish things."

"What girlish things?"

"Well, like makeup." She smoothed her skirt over her thigh.

"You don't need it."

"It's a good thing." Her eyes sparkled as she laughed, letting him know his words gave her a good feeling. "I used to experiment with it and come out looking like a clown."

His smile was warm. "The dress is beautiful on you, Veronica. It makes me think of dancing."

"Dancing?" She said it as though she didn't recognize the word.

"In the islands, beautiful women and dancing simply run together in a man's fantasies."

"Hey, I can rock and roll like nobody's—"

He shook his head, laughing. "You'll ruin the fantasy. I want to hold you in my arms and move with you to the music."

"I used to practice moving to the music in front of that mirror over there." She nodded toward the full-length mirror attached to her closet door. "When no one was looking, of course."

He blew a stream of smoke past the ashtray as he leaned over to stub out his cigarette. "Wouldn't you rather dance with a man than a mirror?"

"Now?"

"No one is looking."

She glanced over her shoulder as if she weren't sure. "But there's no electricity, no mu—" Her eyes brightened and her hair swished past her shoulder as she turned excitedly back to him. "I've got an idea," she said. "Wait here."

He chuckled as he watched her fly to the stairs on small bare feet. "I'll have to. I can't move that fast."

The quick patter of her feet announced her return moments later. Her skirt fluttered back as she hurried to the bed carrying a silver box in both hands. "Needs no batteries," she quipped as she set the old-fashioned powder box on the nightstand. "It was my mother's. Actually, my *grand*-mother's." She lifted the lid and released the tinkling tones of "The Skater's Waltz."

Miguel swung his legs over the side of the bed and stood up slowly, willing the insidious wave of dizziness away. He took Ronnie's hand and raised it to his lips while his dark eyes sent a tender message. "Will you do me the honor of dancing with me, *señorita*?"

He took her in his arms before she could answer, and she felt as though she had stepped out of her body and into a form that defied gravity. She lifted her chin and found her lips to be a hairbreadth from his smooth shoulder. "I'm not wearing any shoes," she whispered, half thinking that might explain why she felt so light.

"Neither am I." He smiled down at her. "We're both safe."

He wasn't wearing much of anything, and she was profoundly aware of that fact. She glanced past his arm and caught a glimpse of the seat of his jeans as they passed the mirror. It seemed strange that such elegant steps could be taken in jeans. On the next turn, she saw the dim reflection of a woman with flowing hair, floating skirt and shining eyes. She actually felt feminine enough to *be* that woman.

"You must have practiced waltzing in front of the mirror," Miguel said close to her ear. "You do it very well."

"I'm waltzing?" Her body was doing whatever his suggested and feeling decidedly ardent about it.

"We're waltzing. I hope you'll pardon my attire, but I thought that since dinner was informal . . ."

"Denim and gauze are in this year," she assured him. "Especially for the gentleman who's convalescing."

"*Most* especially if he's convalescing in the lady's boudoir."

Ronnie relished the sound of his deep chuckle, and she closed her eyes and found herself smiling against his shoulder as she pivoted, her bare foot brushing against his.

"*Perdone,*" he offered gallantly. "Excuse my clumsiness, *señorita*. One would think I'd been shot in the foot." He turned his lips to her hair and savored its lemon scent.

She caught her breath for a moment, then managed a lighthearted comeback. "Such flawless manners, *señor*. You'll soon have me thinking I could replace Ginger Rogers."

"I've never danced with Ginger Rogers," he said in a voice that sounded throaty so close to her ear. The notes from the music box were winding down, and they moved with them in slow, hazy motion. "Does her hair smell like lemon?" he whispered.

"It probably smells like something more—"

"You replace no one, Veronica." With the final tinkling note he placed her hand on his shoulder and lifted her chin in the curve of his finger. "Your own place would be empty if you did."

The candlelight shone in her eyes, and he thought of moonbeams in a calm sea as he lowered his head. A brief kiss, he thought, just to show her, tell her... taste her, ah, feel her lips... such soft, eager lips. Like an unexpected shock, the kiss caused a quick spark, and each looked to the other. *Did you feel that?* Her eyes said yes, and he dipped his head with no equivocating notion in his brain. There was only the need for another kiss. Hard, wet, open, demanding. A jagged shaft of white heat shot through them, and then the resounding report seemed to echo in the night.

Ronnie gripped the warm, solid ledges of his shoulders as she rose on tiptoe to meet his kiss. His arms tightened around her, and he moved his feet apart to allow her to step between them, bringing them closer still. He moved his hands over her back, now caressing her through the thin fabric of her dress, now dipping into the deep vee to touch the long, sleek indentation of her spine. He kissed her until she was dizzy with it.

So was he. He raised his head and drew a deep, unsteady breath. "*Gracias, señorita.* You're a wonderful dancer."

"I'm beginning to believe you." She opened her eyes and smiled. "It's almost like flying."

"I think I must make my landing soon."

"Oh, Miguel," she sympathized, suddenly coming to her senses as she ushered him back to bed. "You keep trying to overdo it, and I'm obviously not helping matters. Becky said that what you had was just like major surgery, and here we are—"

"Dancing." He eased himself against the pillows and drew her by the hand to sit beside him. "Another ego-wounding experience. One turn around the dance floor and I'm—"

"Kissing." She made him look at her, made him listen. "We were kissing, Miguel. That's a step beyond dancing."

"Yes, it is." He pressed his lips against her fingers. "Another kiss. You warm my heart, Veronica, and I want to kiss you. But my word is good, you know. I won't hurt you."

She glanced away. "A gentleman of the old school."

He ignored the remark. He had been raised a gentleman, but he had never felt the concerns he felt for this woman. He wanted to don armor. "Nor would I allow harm to come to you if it were in my power to prevent it." He chided himself immediately, but, by God, that was the way he felt.

"Pretty big talk for a man whose color just drained from his face after a couple of minutes of dancing." This was the time to assume a casual posture, she thought. The man had moved from a kiss's heady promise to talk of not hurting her within the space of a few breaths, and she wondered if she'd missed something along the way. Was she supposed to feel threatened? Perhaps it should embarrass her that she didn't.

"Kissing," he reminded her. "Much energy is expended in kissing a beautiful woman."

"More than you could spare, obviously." He was still holding her hand as though the contact came naturally to them. The butterflies in her stomach reminded her that it didn't.

"Get ready for bed." He smiled as he moved his thumb across her knuckles. "And you must put this dress in your closet, Veronica. Don't bury it in a trunk."

Her ears were still stuck on *Get ready for bed*. Beyond that, she heard only the wind as it whistled under the eaves. Without even giving it voice she rejected the idea of sleeping downstairs. She wanted to be with Miguel. She wanted him to hold her through this stormy night, and she wanted to rest in the knowledge that he was all right. His health had become her responsibility, her focus. She would stay close and watch over him.

She dressed in her pink pajamas and returned to the bed after blowing all the candles out. Miguel had fallen asleep. A spring groaned beneath Ronnie's cautiously planted knee. She took such care in easing herself down beside him that the kiss he nuzzled at her temple took her by surprise.

"Sleep well, *mi angel*."

She tried to wake him as carefully as possible, but he heard the urgency in her voice even before the words, "Miguel, wake up," made sense to him.

He sat up quickly, and the pistol materialized in his hand. He groped for his bearings and demanded, "What is it?"

"Not—no, it isn't that, Miguel." Ronnie laid a reassuring hand on his forearm. "I'm sorry. I didn't mean to alarm you. It's just that it's stopped raining, and I want you to see the sky."

"The sky?" He leaned back on his elbows with a belated awareness of the stiffness in his side. Blood pounded up the side of his neck, and his temples throbbed. He lowered the gun. *Dios. The sky?*

He noticed, as Ronnie rushed to the closet and pulled out a shirt, that she was already dressed. "Put this on," she insisted, tossing him the shirt whose color reminded him of her eyes. "Hurry, or it'll be gone."

"The sky will be gone?" He struggled with a combination of stiffnesses—his body's and that of the new cotton shirt.

"No, the...you have to see it," she insisted as she helped him with the shirt.

"Where did you put my shoes?"

"No time for shoes." She dragged him to his feet. "On second thought," she said as she snatched the tennis shoes from the dresser on their way by, "you might catch a chill."

She forced herself to contain her enthusiasm and slowed her steps to match his pace. She maneuvered him out the back door and across the sandy yard, where tufts of thick-bladed grass were the only growth hardy enough to survive. Sea oats, already on the rebound from the pounding rain, sprouted along the path to the beach. Not a tree meddled with the expansive melding of sea and sky. A single pelican stood in silhouette atop a purple dune, and beyond him the sky was lightening in rosy hues. Harmless lavender clouds billowed above the deep magenta crack above the horizon, which spilled a river of pink into the calm blue-violet waters.

"A paintbox morning," Ronnie said, her voice as soft as the surrounding colors. "Isn't it worth getting out of bed for this?"

"A paintbox morning," he echoed, thinking this woman the only person capable of originating such a delightful expression. "Beautiful."

"Feel up to a short walk? Let me help you with your shoes."

She was down on her knees before he realized what she was doing, and he bent to help her to her feet, raising his voice to object. "Veronica—" He caught himself. Sudden movement troubled his injury.

"I don't want you sitting down in this wet sand," she insisted. "Balance yourself on my shoulder and lift your foot." At a glance she could tell this embarrassed him. "Come on, now. When you get better, you can try the glass slipper on my foot."

He smiled as he straightened and gave her one bare foot. "Did you lose a slipper at the dance last night?"

"Come to think of it, I was barefooted. No wonder the prince never comes looking for me."

She brushed her fingers over the bottom of his foot, releasing sand and tingling sensations. Miguel had trouble holding up his end of the conversation. "I'll pack one of your shoes with me when I leave."

She looked up as she guided his foot into a shoe. "You won't have to try it out on too many people. No one else would want to claim my old gym shoes."

His smile broadened. "Especially not from a rebel who was stripped of the rank he never earned and left for dead."

"Some days it just doesn't pay to get up in the morning," she quipped as she finished her task.

He reached for her hand. "This isn't one of them."

They walked hand in hand over the wind-rippled dunes and basked in the rising sun. The cool breeze would soon give way to a warm day full of welcome sunshine. As the sun gained height, the sea turned jade and turquoise, and Miguel thought of the dress Ronnie had worn the previous night. This morning she was back to tan shorts and a shirt she'd left unbuttoned over a salmon-pink top. Her shirt sleeves were rolled above her elbows, and the shirt tails fluttered as she walked beside him. The morning sun danced in her blond hair, glinting red-gold. It was the first time he'd seen her outdoors in the sunlight, and it struck him that the sun might have sired her. It gave her hair its own fire and made her skin honey gold, honey sweet. He noticed the dusting of pale freckles across her nose. There were more of them above the scoop neck of her top, and he imagined them slipping between her breasts.

He scolded himself for creating the image. He'd challenged himself to keep her dressed in his mind, just as she kept herself dressed in his bed—*her* bed. He didn't seem to be up to the challenge. His weakened physical state was, he felt, to blame for all this untempered longing. It seemed that no part of him could escape being touched by this woman's refreshingly unsophisticated beauty.

As they neared a huge, skeletal tree, weathered softly white and standing as a lone sentry on the beach, Miguel shaded his eyes with his free hand. Like the clouds overhead, the white beach now gleamed in the morning sun, and, as much as he loved the sea, such brightness was the bane of Miguel's existence. He felt a tap on his shoulder.

"Would these help?" Ronnie offered the sunglasses she'd bought him. "Just happened to have them in my pocket."

"Gracias, señorita." He smiled as he pushed the black bows through the thick, dark hair at his temples. "You're becoming intimately acquainted with all my weaknesses."

"If that's true, then I can vouch for the fact that you don't have many. It's only been a couple of days since I thought I might have to dig your grave in my backyard." He barked a laugh, enjoying the wonder of his narrow escape now that it was accomplished. "I'm not kidding," Ronnie insisted. "And now look at you. Strolling on the beach just as pretty as you please."

"I'm trying to keep up appearances because I'm with such a pretty girl."

"Time out," she said with a laugh. This man had a way of warming her insides from head to toe. "Time to take a rest. Prop yourself up against old Methuselah here." She indicated the smooth, ashen trunk of the bare-limbed, barkless tree. Its exposed roots undulated in and out of the sand, clutching at barren ground like the bony fingers of a dying man.

Miguel leaned one shoulder against the tree and looked out at the sea. The last time he'd stood this way, there had been a gun at his back. He'd said a quick prayer and prepared himself to die. Now he watched this woman, who'd held his head in her lap and eased his pain, as she walked a few steps away from him to let tongues of sea foam wash her feet. He was grateful to be alive, glad to be here with her, and if he had any sense at all he would stay with her and live to love her. He knew she cared for him.

"Is it cold?" he asked.

"Kind of. And it's usually clearer than this, but the storm churned it up." The water drew back and left a piece of brown sea boa clinging to her toes. She laughed and let the next surge carry the weed away.

"It's good to see the sun again." It sparkled in the water behind her, enhancing her very nature for his enjoyment.

"Even though it hurts your eyes?"

"It doesn't now. I've got my shades." It would hurt more than just his eyes to turn his back on her sunny smile, and he needed to prepare himself for that. Later. He extended his hand. "Come here. I want to tell you something."

She went to him and took his hand as she lifted her chin and let the breeze lift a hank of hair away from her hair. "I'm listening."

"*Bueno*, because I want to tell you how beautiful you look this morning." She smiled. He brought her arm around his waist and held it there while he touched her neck, insinuating his fingertips beneath her shirt collar. "You wear the sea as well as you wore that dress last night. The colors are perfect for you."

"I'm wearing brown shorts and an equally brown shirt." Still she smiled, and the challenge to flatter her more danced in her eyes.

"Immaterial."

"It *is* material. One hundred per cent cotton."

"No, no, *querida*, a moment ago the sea dressed you in aquamarine, the color of your eyes. The most exquisite shade of—"

"You know what I've concluded?" A step closer put her on top of an exposed tree root and brought her eye level near his as she slipped her other arm around his waist.

"What have you concluded?" Now that she had her arms around him of her own accord, he could explore both her shoulders with gently kneading fingers.

"I think it's just the way you talk. Even when you're half out of your mind with pain, you talk like that."

He moved his hands over her neck as though he were molding her out of clay, and he lifted her chin with his thumbs. "Like what?"

"You say pretty things." And she was getting mushy inside. She wished his eyes weren't hidden behind the glasses.

"Pretty things come to mind when I look at you. I need to remember . . ."

She watched his lips part slightly as he lowered his head.

"Remember." He brushed a kiss against her lips.

"Remember . . . what?"

"Remember me, *querida*."

He enfolded her in his arms and covered her mouth with his. Her balance on the root was tenuous, and she tried to grip it with her toes, but Miguel slid one arm around her hips and pressed them tight against his. She tried to keep her weight off his injured side, but he seemed unaware of any pain as he urged her mouth open and slipped his tongue inside. Hers greeted his, tentatively at first, then eagerly.

When his glasses got in the way, it was Ronnie who took them off.

"Just keep your eyes closed," she murmured against his mouth. With a groan, he slanted his mouth across hers again.

His eyes were still closed when he tipped his head back against the tree and put mind over matter to steady his breathing. She, too, was gathering her wits. He felt her body stiffen as she tried to regain her balance and take care not to lean against his bad side.

"Are you okay, Miguel?"

He turned one corner of his mouth up without opening his eyes. "Are you?"

"Too soon to tell."

"And too late to pretend."

"I think I'm much better than okay."

He looked down at her now, his eyes soft and warm. "I think so, too." He eased her away from him, steadying her as she stepped back from the camel-backed root. Then he moved his thumb slowly over her moist, full lips. "I will remember you, Veronica. Long after you've forgotten me."

Her protest died in her throat, stung by the threat of tears. She gave her head a quick shake, and he tucked her under his arm on his good side and started them on the walk to the house.

"I have to make a phone call." Whoever Miguel was trying to call was a busy man. Miguel left message after message on the answering machine. For two days he watched the phone as though he could make the right call come by sheer concentration, but the only calls came from Barnaby and Becky. Becky had decided to spend a few days with her sister in St. Petersburg and had gotten Barnaby to agree to drive her there. Ronnie recognized the effort for what it was and thanked her friend, assuring her that all was well on their little island. *Everyone* was just fine.

With each call to the answering machine, Miguel's mood seemed to darken. He became more withdrawn, spent more time sitting on the porch, smoking. Conversations were politely strained. He walked the beach late at night, and he made it clear that he preferred to spend the time alone. But when he came to bed, he insisted Ronnie be there. He persisted in holding her, there in the darkness, where he would recite to himself the litany of reasons he had to return to a place where people he loved might shoot him on sight. And there was another list to be etched on the brain—that of reasons to leave the one person he knew he could truly trust.

When the call finally came, Ronnie handed the phone to Miguel and turned to leave the room. But then he called the man by name.

McQuade.

Chapter 7

"McQuade!" Ronnie exclaimed as she edged closer. "Sloan McQuade? The one who—"

"Shh!" Miguel raised a hand for silence. "This is a bad connection. I can't—"

"Where is he? Is he in De Colores? Is Elizabeth Donnelly with him?"

Miguel scowled at Ronnie while he tried to put the pieces together and, at the same time, tried to make himself heard. "McQuade, can you hear me? Yes, Miguel Hidalgo. Yes, yes, the *late* Miguel Hidalgo. Cancel your order for funeral flowers, McQuade. No. As it turns out, my executioners were poor marksmen."

Miguel found it hard to laugh at McQuade's response and shake Ronnie off his arm at the same time. "Where are they, Miguel?" she asked. "Is Elizabeth with him? Find out if Elizabeth is with him."

"Elizabeth?" Miguel was having trouble deciding which way to direct his conversation. "Is Elizabeth with you?"

Ronnie watched the light dawn in Miguel's eyes as he listened to the voice on the other end of the line. It looked good. She held her tongue and crossed her fingers, but from the look on Miguel's face, Elizabeth was safe.

"I think I may be able to answer that for you, McQuade." Miguel surveyed Ronnie up and down, his eyes dancing. "Was your pilot a little over five feet tall, reddish-blond hair, blue-green eyes, usually wears— Yes, that's the one. I'm looking at her. I'm afraid I hijacked your rescue plane, my friend." McQuade's response brought another laugh. "I'm not familiar with that expression, McQuade. I'll have to brush up on your American street language. However, I'm alive and very nearly well in the Florida Keys, and you and Elizabeth are safe in Arco Iris. How long will you be there?"

"Did Elizabeth get her baby?" Ronnie demanded in a stage whisper.

Miguel nodded and gestured for her to hold her questions for just another moment. "I want you to help me get back to De Colores," he told McQuade. "No, but I'll find a way. Yes, as soon as I can." Miguel laughed. "Not to give *them* another shot. I was thinking of returning fire. You, too? I'm afraid you'll have to stand in line, amigo. Yes, I'll be in touch."

Miguel hung up the phone, and he and Ronnie stood looking at one another for a moment, sorting through the pieces of news. "Your passengers are safe," he said, almost reverently. "They got away on a fishing boat after the hurricane. Elizabeth is free of Guerrero, and she has her son."

"I didn't really know all the details. I take it Guerrero is the child's father."

Miguel smiled as he put his image of hard-shelled Mc-Quade together with the way the man had just spoken of Elizabeth. "I suspect the boy will soon have a new father."

"McQuade?"

"McQuade."

Again they looked at one another, and their smiles faded.

"And so you're leaving."

"I'll meet McQuade in Arco Iris, and from there—"

"Arco Iris is no problem."

His eyes became stony. "No, Veronica."

"Listen, I can take you that far. There's no risk—"

The touch of her hand was the problem. The risk lay in the way it made him feel. "No. It ends here."

"What ends?" She gripped both his arms now and felt her pride drain away as she looked up at him. "There's nothing to end, Miguel. Nothing ever got started. We shared a bed, but not... it was just..."

"Just what?"

"Just one of those things, as the song says." She cast around for words, wanting to tell him what it really was for her while she still had the chance. But she knew if she did, she would get nowhere with her offer. "Just a sweet interlude. Like something out of a movie." His dark eyes softened, and he brought his hands up slowly and curved them around her back, but he said nothing. "And no one got hurt," she added quietly. "So it's okay. There's no reason you shouldn't fly with me. There's no—"

His kiss unleashed the need he'd felt for days. He'd longed to fly with her, bury himself deep inside her and soar on and on with her. He plunged his tongue into the soft, wet warmth of her mouth, slid his hand to her hip and pressed her firmly against him, trying to content himself with a semblance of what he wanted. It was like trying to satisfy a terrible hunger with just the aroma of a delicious meal. He ended the kiss as abruptly as he had begun. She laid her head against his shoulder, and they stood together, holding one another close enough to share a heartbeat. For the hundredth time he entertained the thought of not going back. For the hundredth time he damned himself for a self-serving coward. He had to make a move, or he would lose his mind.

"How soon can you have your plane ready?" he asked finally.

Arco Iris was a bright little island whose population seemed to thrive on the business of enjoying life. The island shared De Colores's fishing waters but not her political problems. Because Arco Iris was Mexican territory, Miguel felt reasonably safe as he and Ronnie left the green and white Cessna at the airstrip and headed for the Oyster Shell, McQuade's favorite guest house on the island.

Felix Santiago made a habit of greeting every guest under the ever-creaking paddle fan in the rattan and potted-palm appointed lobby of the Oyster Shell, and he never forgot a face. The little blonde had checked in a couple of weeks ago with McQuade. As Felix recalled, she had flown McQuade in with Elizabeth Donnelly. He could have sworn he knew the man with her, too. Even behind the dark glasses and looking a bit leaner than he remembered, Felix was certain he knew this man. Of course, Miguel Hidalgo was dead, but the resemblance was remarkable.

"Two rooms, *por favor*," the man said.

Felix turned to Ronnie, who doffed her red baseball cap and shook out a profusion of strawberry-blond hair. "So you brought me another guest, Miss Harper. McQuade and his lady returned, you know, with the little boy. I think McQuade is—" he raised his eyebrows and gave a conspir-

atorial smile as he pushed registration forms across the desk
"—headed for the altar straightaway."

Miguel picked up a pen and began filling out a form.
"We'd like to see McQuade right away," Ronnie told Felix.
"He's expecting us."

Felix raked his fingers through his slick black hair and
abandoned any pretense of subtlety by twisting his head to
look at the name of Miguel's registration form. "Is Mc-
Quade a friend of yours, too, Señor... Fortuna?"

"Yes, he is."

"Where are you from, señor? If I may ask."

"Miami." Miguel took the key from Felix's hand and
picked up their two small bags. "Which room is Mc-
Quade's?"

"I can call him, señor, just..." The man behind the sunglasses did not wish to wait. "Room nine. Please tell us if
there's anything..." Miguel was on his way up the stairs.
Felix handed Ronnie the second key. "Anything you need.
He is a *friend*, you say?"

"Yes, very definitely."

By the time Ronnie stepped around the smooth curve of
the mahogany banister at the top of the stairs, Miguel was
already embracing the beautiful Elizabeth Donnelly with
one arm and shaking hands with McQuade with the other.
A dark-eyed toddler rode contentedly in the arm of the big,
blond private investigator, whom Ronnie never would have
imagined to look so natural carrying a child. She stood hesitantly on the landing, thinking the scene seemed quite
complete without her. She would have been satisfied to
sneak right past without having to answer to McQuade at
all.

"Would you look at this," McQuade announced.
"Amelia Earhart returns. I think you oughta hire a new
navigator, sweetheart."

"I'm really sorry, McQuade." Ronnie rubbed her palm over the polished wooden handrail. "There were these two guys with guns, and Miguel was bleeding all over the place. I tried to get back, but—"

"For what it's worth, this woman saved my life. Inadvertently, you two arranged for my rescue." Miguel stepped away from the couple and held his hand out to invite Ronnie to join them.

She accepted it, grateful for any moral support. She still had the feeling that somehow she could have been in two places at once, and that any excuse for her failure would sound lame. "I had engine trouble, and then the storm hit."

"Thank God you were able to help Miguel, Ronnie," Elizabeth said, and smiled. "Your untimely departure gave Sloan a chance to earn his outrageous fee."

"Yeah, well—" McQuade hooked his free arm around Elizabeth's shoulders and pulled her against him. "What with compound interest, it'll take you a lifetime to pay up, lady." They exchanged a secret promise as Elizabeth turned to look at him. "Did you guys get rooms?" McQuade finally thought to ask.

The answers came quickly, simultaneously.

"Yes."

"Yes, we did."

McQuade laughed. He remembered when intimate looks between people in love had made him edgy, too. Weeks ago, in another life. "Why don't you settle in, get cleaned up, and then we'll trade hurricane stories over dinner."

Miguel's room was right next door to Ronnie's, and she knew that the extra door joined them. The security chain dangled near the door frame. She started to fasten it, then changed her mind and let it drop. She didn't have to lock him out. She didn't want to. But they weren't alone together in her little world anymore, and there was no longer any excuse for them to share intimate space, to come and go as though their lives were one. Miguel would be resting in the other room. It had been a long day, and he'd looked tired. He had his bed, and she had hers.

Ronnie opened her bag and began unpacking toiletries and the few articles of clothing she'd brought. In a little while they'd go downstairs to the dining room, and there would be women wearing summer dresses having dinner with the men who admired them. She came to the bottom of the bag and knew even as she reached for it that she was being silly. The sea-foam dress, Miguel had called it. She lifted it high, shook it out and then held it up to her shoulders as she turned toward the mirror. She could afford to buy dresses. She just didn't. Oh, she had a couple of skirts in her closet for emergencies, but her life didn't call for dresses. This one was so outdated. Not that she knew that much about styles, but it had to be. She thought of the pretty yellow sundress Elizabeth had been wearing, and the warm way McQuade had looked at her. Elizabeth would look elegant in a flour sack, but not Ronnie. Ronnie could put on some high-fashion designer outfit, and she knew she'd still look like one of the guys.

She folded the dress and put it back in the bottom of the bag. This was an island resort, and her casual clothes were perfectly acceptable. She'd feel ridiculous trying to be someone she wasn't, especially in front of Elizabeth and McQuade. In private it had been one thing, but she wasn't about to take such a risk in public. Miguel would probably be embarrassed for her.

Miguel stood by the open window in his room and watched the sun sink toward the sea. He took a long, slow drag on his cigarette and blew the smoke away, watching it dissipate in the clear evening air. He had managed to pry McQuade away from Elizabeth long enough to enlist his help in finding transportation to De Colores. McQuade had made several contacts, and, with any luck, Miguel could be gone by morning.

Luck. He'd called himself Fortuna, which was a strange choice, indeed. He'd never believed in luck. He believed in reason. He believed that right would prevail because it was reasonable, and he could take that belief one step further to explain why his body hadn't been carried away by the tide. Raphael and Paulo had carried him from the beach because it was the right and rational thing to do. He wasn't alive because of luck. It was not reasonable for Guerrero to kill him. Guerrero's power on the island was an insult to reason. The only reasonable course of action for Miguel was to return and seek out the *reasonable* people, who would undoubtedly support him.

Miguel stuck the cigarette into the corner of his mouth and began unbuttoning his shirt. He was satisfied that he had it all figured out until he brushed his hand against the square bandage that was taped to his side—the bandage Veronica had put there that morning. Veronica defied reason, and calling her a stroke of luck would not fit her into a comfortable niche in his brain.

She had not happened along by chance. She had come to De Colores with a purpose, and he had spirited her away at gunpoint. But he'd been too weak to force her to make any further decisions. She'd made them all on her own, and, in view of the fact that he had diverted her from her purpose by force, none of her decisions had been reasonable. She had helped him. She had protected him from her own father. And she had brought him here. In all these things, she'd been motivated by kindness, not by reason. He plucked the cigarette from his mouth and smiled. His angel had a great capacity for kindness and, yes, for love. He believed in that, too. He also believed it would be a mistake for her to love Miguel Hidalgo right now. She was bound to make more unreasonable choices—choices that would be dangerous for her. And each time he held her in his arms, he felt his own reasonable resolve slip another notch. For her sake, he *had* to be gone by morning.

She'd been ready for some time when he knocked at the door. She looked so pretty that he thought he would have to launch a steady barrage of flowery compliments just to keep his mouth busy. He wanted to kiss her.

"How pretty you look."

"I suppose I could go out tomorrow and look for some sort of dress," she said as she glanced at herself in the mirror. She'd sent her tan slacks and her yellow and white striped shirt out to be pressed, and they looked crisp and neat. She'd washed her hair and made an attempt to fluff it up with a brush and a blow drier. She'd even used a little mascara on her nearly non-existent lashes. "You know, for dinner. With the four of us together, people will sort of think that I'm with you, and I didn't bring much to wear." She looked up at him as though she'd just stepped on his toe. "I thought I'd stay around for a few days and see that you, um—don't try to rush your convalescence."

"I didn't bring much to wear, either," he reminded her. "If blue jeans are prohibited in the dining room, I'm out of luck."

"I wore shorts the last time I was here." She wanted to tell him how wonderful he looked in his jeans, but instead she said, "I'm sorry. I should have gotten you some slacks. You're probably used to wearing—"

"I'm used to wearing a uniform, which never fit me. I can hardly remember what I wore before that." He smiled and offered his arm. "If you have no objections to dining with a man in blue jeans..."

Her smile made her face glow as she slipped her hand into the crook of his arm. "Actually, I kind of like the idea."

Elizabeth and McQuade had already been seated at a table for four. Ronnie had been certain that no one looked more beautiful than Elizabeth Donnelly with her black hair cascading past her shoulders, but now she decided she had been wrong. Elizabeth Donnelly with her hair in an elegant twist was equally beautiful. The same yellow sundress took on a whole new look, and Ronnie couldn't wait to hide her own slacks beneath the tablecloth.

"Where's the baby?" Miguel asked as he held Ronnie's chair for her.

"One of Felix's many cousins is sitting with Tomas tonight," Elizabeth said.

"We spent most of the day splashing in the surf," McQuade added. "I had him doing a pretty respectable dog paddle already. Wore the little guy out."

"Tomas tags after Sloan like a little tail." Elizabeth gave the image some thought and added with a laugh, "A tail that wags the dog. We're going to have quite a job unspoiling him once we get back to Miami."

McQuade saw the anticipatory gleam in their friends' eyes. "The woman has no choice but to marry me," he explained. "Gotta keep the tail and the dog together."

It was clear that Elizabeth had chosen a man who loved her this time. Ronnie remembered the sad, haunted woman who'd chartered her plane. Elizabeth deserved this happiness, and, from what Ronnie had heard of the difficulties she and McQuade had overcome to recover little Tomas, she had paid dearly for it. The stories the couple told filled Ronnie's mind with one thought: in a matter of days Miguel would be in the very trouble spot these two had left behind.

"How bad is the damage?" Miguel asked. He turned the stem of a goblet between his thumb and forefinger and watched the red liquid slosh in the glass.

McQuade sighed, laid his fork on his plate and looked up at Miguel. "It's bad, amigo. Villages went down like dominoes. Fishing boats were smashed in their moorings, trees beaten to the ground. I didn't have time to take any inventories, but I saw some pretty battered cane fields."

"Guerrero will ask other governments for aid." Miguel sipped the wine and then pressed his lips together, appreciating the bitter aftertaste. "If he gets it, very little will reach the people."

"He seems to have a penchant for military toys," McQuade said.

Elizabeth grew impatient with the way the conversation seemed to skirt the immediate issues. "There are soldiers everywhere. I know what you have in mind, but if you go back there now...Miguel, if you fall into his hands, he'll see you dead himself this time, and he'll take pleasure in it."

"I am inspired by your own act of courage, Elizabeth." The fierce look in her eyes brought a mirthless smile to his lips. She, too, had come to know Guerrero the hard way.

He did not doubt the quick tempered dictator had been a cruel husband. "I'm going to find out how many others in De Colores have the same kind of courage. Even while I devoted my attention to what I considered to be the real needs of the people, I was not completely out of touch with Guerrero's little army. They follow him out of fear."

"I can understand that," Elizabeth said quietly.

"But Veronica can vouch for the fact that I have at least two loyal followers."

Ronnie turned at the sound of her name and basked in his warm smile, which she took to be a gentle apology for having held her at gunpoint. "You left two loyal followers behind. I hope they're still there."

"They're waiting for me, and there will be others. It's partly because of my own stupidity that Guerrero has come this far. But he can be stopped. His ludicrous ego is a fatal weakness."

"The people you're counting on to help you are in desperate need of supplies right about now," McQuade pointed out. "The way he's got transportation sewed up, you're gonna have a hell of a time—"

"But I brought transportation." Ronnie was suddenly the center of attention, and she had the feeling she'd said the wrong thing. Even Elizabeth's expression indicated disapproval. Ronnie straightened her back and squared her shoulders. "Now, look, I've been flying Red Cross supplies for years. If they can get me clearance, there's no reason I couldn't smuggle a few—"

McQuade dismissed the notion lightly. "Don't even think it, kid. If I'd known what was waiting for us on that island, I'd have locked Elizabeth up someplace in Miami."

"And I'd have cursed you until your dying day."

"Aw, c'mon, honey." McQuade covered Elizabeth's hand with his. "You'd have changed your tune when I brought Tomas back to you."

Their contentment made Ronnie squirm. Their ordeal was over now, and they could afford to look back and say they would have taken fewer chances. But Miguel was climbing into the crater of a seething volcano, and Ronnie had only one practical kind of help to offer him. She didn't want to tip her hand entirely, so she searched for a casual response.

"Listen, you guys, I'm not just another pretty face. I'm a pilot. I do this for a living."

"Smuggling?" McQuade laughed. "You're as wholesome as your orange juice, Ronnie." He nodded toward her glass. "Drink up."

Without touching her, Miguel sensed the stiffness in her body. McQuade was unaware that he'd thrown a gauntlet at her feet. Her suggestion was not to be dismissed with a joke. "We'll talk about it later, Veronica. In fact—" he managed his most charming smile for the entire table's benefit "—I suggest we turn our conversation to more pleasant matters. This talk of a wedding, for example." He lifted his glass. "I hope I'm not too late to offer the very first congratulatory toast."

Discussion of her plan was not the only motive Miguel had for asking Ronnie to walk with him on the beach. There was the waxing moon in a sky hung generously with stars, and there were his needs—the need to be alone with her on this last night and the need to avoid the door between their rooms, the one he knew she hadn't locked. And there was the very practical need to see that she stayed awake most of the night so that she would sleep in the morning.

They had rolled up the bottoms of their pants and left their shoes behind. Small waves broke gently and lapped the sand, now washing their feet, now sliding away. Miguel slipped his arm around Ronnie's shoulders. "Do you mind if we walk like lovers?"

She put her arm around his waist. "It seems the thing to do on a night like this."

"In another world—another time and place—we would have shared more."

"Had you stayed a college professor, you never would have met me," she pointed out.

"I might have chartered your plane for an expedition. Research on the Aztec ruins in the islands of the Caribbean."

She slid a glance up at him. "Are there any?"

He smiled as he promised, "We would have left no stone unturned in our search for them."

"Really? Would you have taken the summer off?"

"I would have taken a year's sabbatical."

"Just to look for ruins?"

He stopped and turned her into his arms. "Just to fly with you," he said, and then he kissed the salt spray from her lips. He found her own delicious taste underneath, and pried her lips apart with his tongue, savoring it like a child seldom treated to candy. *"Muy dulce,"* he muttered. "Sweet, so sweet."

Ronnie curled her toes in the wet sand and pressed her palms against his back. He was so much taller than she was, even when she dug in and stood on tiptoe, that she had to tip her head back and let his kisses come to her. And they came, filled her mouth, filled her heart and made every part of her that touched him ache in sympathy with the need she felt deep, deep down. She felt the cool breeze on her arms, cold water on the bottoms of her feet and the warmth of his breath against her cheek.

"We could fly so much higher," he whispered. He nuzzled her ear and kissed her neck.

She opened her eyes, saw the white moon hanging just above his shoulder and gave a husky chuckle. "You have a good pilot at your disposal, Miguel."

"Mmm, yes." He nudged her collar aside with his nose and tasted her shoulder with the tip of his tongue.

"I could take you anywhere you wanted to go."

He lifted his head slowly, cherishing the offer. Her face was brightly moonlit, and he hoped his was sufficiently shadowed. "I don't want to leave, Veronica. If I could choose..." He shook his head, warding off any alternatives. "I have to go back, and I don't know how long it will take... to do what must be done."

"I'm going to get in touch with the Red Cross tomorrow."

"Why?"

He'd gripped her shoulders suddenly and assumed a wide-legged stance.

"Why not?" She clutched his arms, wishing she had the power to shake some sense into him. "The Red Cross will tell me exactly what they need, and they'll get me government clearance. It sounds as though food and medical supplies should come first. I'm sure you've talked to McQuade about guns. Once I've made a few routine deliveries, I should be able to—"

"No!" Miguel didn't believe what he was hearing. He'd anticipated her persistence in trying to help him get back, or perhaps trying to dissuade him from going back at all, but this plan was suicidal. Gunrunning!

"Miguel, I am a charter pilot. I've been making regular deliveries—"

"Contraband?"

"What?"

"Have you been delivering contraband, Veronica?"

"Of course not!"

He slid his hands to her upper arms and gentled his voice. "That's what you're suggesting now. Delivering guns to an outlaw."

"You're not an outlaw," she insisted. "By all rights you should be the law in De Colores."

"Soon after I return from the grave, I will be declared an outlaw, and anyone who aids me—" his voice grew softer "—comforts me—" and softer still "—consorts with me... Veronica, you saved my life. I will not have you die for me.''

''I won't.'' She saw the gleam in his eyes, and her throat went dry. ''I won't die. I'll be... careful.''

''As you were on your last trip to the island?'' He laughed and pulled her against his chest. ''*I'll* be careful. I won't let you get mixed up in this.''

How could he stop her? She'd never been mixed up in anything more deeply than she was with this man's life. She tucked in her chin and pressed her forehead against a button on his shirt. ''Are we going to make love before you leave, Miguel?'' He took a slow, deep breath, and her head rose and fell with his chest. No answer came. She leaned back and looked at him. ''Before you go off to start your revolution, will we...'' She bit off the words. ''Maybe we could save this argument for another time and just... walk along the beach like lovers.''

He put his arm around her again, and they walked without talking and let the water wash their feet.

And later, when it was almost time, Miguel slipped through the door that separated their rooms. She slept bathed in moonlight, the picture of the angel he knew her to be. Her head was pillowed on her arm, and her lips looked moist, as though he'd just kissed them. He wanted her to know how much he loved her, but nothing would stop her from following him then. His love would lead her into a hotbed of danger. He couldn't trade her safety for the ecstasy of making her truly his. She still had choices. For him, there was none. But if he could have chosen, made one claim, allowed himself one personal concession, it would have been Veronica.

Chapter 8

Raphael recognized the green and white airplane. Its wheels skimmed the cracking surface of the old airstrip without a bounce. He motioned for the men in his party to meet the craft on the field, but he reached for Paulo's shoulder and pulled him back before he could step away from the trees with the rest. "It's the *gringa*—the one who took the *jefe* to the States. He'll want to know she's here."

Paulo nodded and trotted off toward the village. He cradled the .22-caliber rifle as though it were an M-16. The next automatic rifle they got hold of would go to Paulo, Raphael vowed as he turned back to deal with the visitor from the north. Miguel had said nothing to Raphael about sending for the woman, but she'd flown in like she owned the place. In the three weeks since his return to De Colores, the *jefe* had said little about the time he'd spent away except that the woman had kept his confidence and seen to his recovery. But somehow she must have known that Miguel and his followers held the villages in this area, including El Gallo and this airstrip. Otherwise she surely would not have risked such a bold landing.

Miguel took a two-fisted hold on the canvas tent he'd been helping to repair and came to his feet slowly as the news sank in. He'd ignored the sound of engines in the air, assuming that, as usual, the plane was headed for La Primavera. "You've *seen* her, Paulo?"

"I couldn't see the pilot, but it's her plane. I remember the numbers on it," Paulo announced, hoping his astuteness would not go unnoticed. "Shall I drive you to the airfield, *jefe*?"

Miguel paused a moment to hand his side of the tent back to the young couple who owned it. The thought of her being there unnerved him, and he needed time to overcome his weakness. He turned to Paulo, who waited so anxiously to do his bidding. "Have her move the plane into the trees at the east end of the field," Miguel said finally. "Tell Raphael to camouflage it thoroughly. You are to bring *Señorita* Harper directly to my quarters."

"Yes, sir. Do you want me to tell her anything?"

"That she's up to her neck in hot water." Seeing the surprise in Paulo's big brown eyes, he laughed and shook his head. "No, just tell her you're bringing her to see me."

"Yes, sir." Paulo turned to leave.

"Take the jeep, Paulo. Show her we've got class."

Paulo grinned. "Yes, sir."

Class was not a scale-tripping advantage when they were up against superior firepower, but women liked it. Miguel realized the implications of that thought as soon as he'd formulated it, and he dismissed Paulo with a more impatient gesture than he'd intended. Was he actually entertaining thoughts of impressing this woman when she had absolutely no business being here? He turned on his heel and strode toward the far end of the gravel street and the metal

Quonset building, which served as a supply depot and his private quarters.

Ignoring a greeting from the crew assigned to salvage anything useful from the wreckage left behind by the hurricane, Miguel noted three more tents standing in one of the temporary camps. They meant either more recruits or more refugee families. Either way, there would be more mouths to feed.

He waited beneath the thatched shelter he'd built near the Quonset. Overturned crates provided seating, and a patch of dirt served as the drawing board for his strategy sessions. He remembered the massive mahogany desk in the office he had occupied in the east wing of the presidential palace, and realized that he liked this office better. It had no walls. From here he could see how his people fared. He picked up a stick and scratched the letter *V* in the dirt. For victory? Or for Veronica? At the sound of the jeep's roaring engine, he reached down and erased the evidence of his yearnings.

The red baseball cap proclaimed her identity. Surrounded by dark-haired, brown-skinned young men armed with various forms of weaponry, she bounced in the seat next to Paulo with only the cap occasionally rising above the top of the windshield. Miguel regretted the fuel he'd expended in this show of hospitality as he watched them approach. Raphael and Paulo escorted her to the shelter as though she had been granted an audience with a man of real power. For the sake of their morale, he allowed them that fancy. Their rebel band now had squads and committees, details and inspections. He claimed leadership, but he refused to claim rank.

"*Señorita* Harper's plane is loaded with medical and food supplies," Raphael announced as he ducked from the sunlight into the shade of dried palm thatching. "With your permission, we will transfer everything to Supply."

Miguel nodded, concentrating on Raphael's face and avoiding Ronnie's. What he could see of her in the periphery was enough to make his throat go dry. "Use Antonio's truck," he ordered. Even though the people of the village had generously made their property available for the good of the cause, Miguel insisted upon acknowledging private ownership. Guerrero had dealt with disaster by laying claim to anything he could use after the hurricane, and the people, already disgruntled, had finally begun to balk.

"No need to worry about gas," Paulo said proudly. "After I picked up the first watch and dropped off their replacements last night, we appropriated a full tank from one of the so-called People's gas pumps."

Miguel's scowl skittered past Ronnie as he turned to Paulo and demanded, "On whose authority?"

"On . . . well, I—" the boy shrugged, and his face fell "—thought we needed gas."

"Raphael, take this boy with you, and explain to him why we don't make raids on a whim."

"Yes, sir," Raphael replied, whacking Paulo's arm with the back of his hand as he backed into the sunlight again.

"Not even on the *People's* gas pumps, Paulo."

"Yes, sir," came the retreating, disappointed response.

Ronnie stood quietly under the rustling thatch and waited for Miguel to really look at her. She knew he was putting it off as long as he could. He watched the two young men spar with one another as they returned to the jeep and shook his head, speaking to himself rather than to her. "They ask for permission to unload supplies, but they wander beyond our lines on the spur of the moment to steal a tank of gas."

Wordlessly she watched him rake his fingers through his thick, black hair. She wondered whether his jeans were the ones she'd bought for him. If they were, he'd lost weight. His face, though more deeply tanned, looked drawn, angular. He finally turned to her, and he was able to maintain a hard, forbidding stare for a moment. His look challenged her to offer an excuse for being there, one that he could cut to shreds with imperious logic. But she said nothing, because excuses and reasons would add up to a lot of hot air. She was there, and that was that.

His dark eyes softened, and he almost chuckled, *almost* smiled. "And what am I supposed to do with you?" he asked finally.

"Nothing," she said quietly. "You're supposed to take the supplies I brought and put them to good use."

Her eyes were as stirring as he remembered, those cool facets of aquamarine drawing him closer, offering respite from all his cares. All but one. They refused to release him from the one that made the syllables of her name an integral part of his heartbeat. Supplies, he reminded himself. "You didn't bring any guns, did you?"

"No, I'm sorry. I didn't."

"I'm sorry, too, that you didn't." He saw a flicker of surprise in her eyes. She swallowed quickly, absently pressed her lips together to moisten them and waited. What was she waiting for? The question was foolish; he knew the answer well. He felt the same tingling on his own lips and longed for the same taste. He watched a trickle of perspiration follow the snaky path of a tendril of copper-yellow hair that was plastered to the edge of her face and smiled. "On the other hand, if you had flown in here carrying guns, I would have been furious with you."

"Does that mean that you're not?" she asked hopefully.

"It means that I need guns as much as I need fuel. But you are just as reckless as Paulo is. I should paddle you both."

"Before you even say hello?"

He lifted his gaze to the scene behind her. What had once been a sleepy fishing village was now an armed camp, and everything that happened here was his business. Raphael had taken the jeep across the street to the little gas station, now the motor pool, where tavern owner Antonio Moreno had recently been made quartermaster. Antonio's beloved twenty-year-old daughter, Chi Chi, had one eye on Raphael's squad and the other on Miguel's conversation with the bold and obviously female Anglo pilot. Nothing Miguel did escaped his people's notice. The only thing they could not see was the way his palms tingled with the thought of greeting this woman properly.

"Hello, Veronica."

The flash of disappointment in her eyes pierced a soft place inside him. Without explanation, he took her by the arm, led her to a door at the back of the Quonset and ushered her inside. He lifted the cap from her head and released her hair. It was damp and replete with her special brand of lemon scent. The cap fell to the floor as Miguel placed the tips of his fingers at her temples and moved his hands slowly, letting the silken strands slide through his fingers while she watched his eyes fill up with pleasure. Suddenly, swiftly, he took her in his arms and said hello again, this time with an urgent kiss. Ronnie felt a flood of relief pour over her, which manifested itself in an unusual, unexpected trickle of tears from the corners of her eyes. She parted her lips to touch his tongue with hers and greet him. He hadn't forgotten her!

Her hand skated over his back to the place she'd tended, and she felt the puckered flesh through his shirt. When he lifted his head, she caught her breath, then asked, "How are you, Miguel? Are you okay?"

"I'm healing very well, thank you." He brushed the track of her tear from her temple. "What's the matter, *querida*?"

"You're not angry." Her voice went husky on the last word.

With a brief kiss he took away the tears from the other side of her face and whispered, "Of course I am."

"It doesn't show."

He chuckled. "Are you disappointed?"

"Relieved," she said with a sigh. "Very relieved, and very, very glad to see you."

"You shouldn't be here, and I am *not* pleased to see you here." He pressed a kiss into her hair and hugged her possessively. "But it pleases me to hold you, *mi angel*."

"Oh, Miguel, I had to come. The news releases about you are so confusing."

"Nobody's asked me for an interview." He laughed, but when he leaned back to look at her he saw that she didn't share his amusement. "Our numbers are growing, and we're just beginning to pose a threat. Have we made network news?"

"They're not sure what to make of you. One day they say you're reported to be leading a rebellion against the Guerrero regime, and the next day the uprising is under control, and there are rumors of your arrest." She looked up at him and touched his face as if to convince herself that his flesh was warm. "Once they reported that your body had been discovered in the—" With a quick shake of her head, she dismissed the terrible vision. "But later they identified it as someone else."

She'd grieved for him. In her eyes he saw the remembered pain, and he touched her neck with gentle fingers and traced the line of her jaw with his thumb. "I'm sorry."

"They say you're hiding in the mountains and terrorizing the villages."

"We've liberated several villages, inviting anyone willing to fight to come and join us," he explained. "We've had a few hit-and-run skirmishes with government troops, but they aren't pressing us. Guerrero stands to lose even more men to desertion if he mounts an attack on these villagers. He's experimenting with propaganda at the moment."

Ronnie slid her hands to his waist. "And are you experimenting with starvation? You look as though you haven't slept or eaten a decent meal in three weeks."

"No one here is eating well."

"I know," she said. "I did get in touch with the Red Cross. And I did get someone to fly supplies into La Primavera for them, but I knew that wouldn't help you. McQuade found out that you had control of this area through his—" she waved her hand "—inexhaustible sources."

"Where is McQuade?"

Ronnie checked her watch. "I'd say he should be coming home to his wife right about now."

Miguel smiled. "They wasted no time, then."

"Neither did you." He looked puzzled. "Leaving Arco Iris, I mean."

He sighed and turned away. The room was too hot. He opened the door and leaned against the door frame. The building stood on a low bluff. Beyond it he could see the small, turquoise lagoon, and beyond that, the blue sea. "I thought it would be easier that way, Veronica."

"Easier for whom?" She found herself speaking to his back.

"For both of us."

"And was it?"

How could he answer that? The bittersweet taste of her kiss lingered on his lips, and he couldn't say whether it was worse to be with her, knowing it couldn't last, or not to be able to see her at all. "I haven't stopped thinking of you," he confessed quietly.

How did he think of her? she wondered. With gratitude? With amusement? Perhaps fondly. "At least you knew I was safe."

"I prayed that you were." He felt her close behind him and wished that she would touch him. "You *will* be safe, Veronica. As soon as the plane is unloaded, you'll be on your way."

"If you're so anxious to give me orders, Miguel, why don't you let me join you? I'm willing to fight. You said—"

"I said nothing about you!" He stepped over the threshold and into the sunlight, struggling to control the tone of his voice as he turned to face her. "Nor anyone who cannot call this island *home*. It is for *us* to fight for our freedom, Veronica. You have no part in this."

Rejection had a razor's edge. *You're* my part in this, she shouted, but only inside her head. She gripped the door frame and sought an impassive comeback. "Would you let McQuade help you?"

He sighed and shoved his hands into the pockets of his jeans. "You must know that I've asked for his help."

"I know that he met Mikal Romanov in Washington, and that Mikal is still there, on your behalf, I assume."

"I hope so," Miguel said. "But it won't do any good until we prove ourselves a force to be reckoned with. In order to do that, we must have—"

"Guns."

"That's right."

"Did you ask McQuade to get them for you?"

"No." He looked away and added quietly, "Not yet. I gave him my power of attorney so that he would have access to what money I have, but to ask him to arrange something that risky..." Miguel shook his head.

"You won't have to ask him. This is Elizabeth's home, too, Miguel. When I tell them what the situation is here—what I've seen—"

"You'll do that?"

"Yes, of course." She stepped closer to him and laid her hand on his arm. "Let's dispel the rumors, Miguel. I brought a video camera. Let's give Mikal Romanov something to work with, and let's let McQuade do what he does best."

Ronnie sat in the McQuades' darkened living room and watched Miguel on the television screen. She had never used a video camera before, and she was making mental notes of all the mistakes she'd made. McQuade seemed impressed. "This is great," he kept mumbling. "You could do this for a living, Ronnie."

"We wanted to show the people—there's Paulo, the one who hijacked me—and the destruction caused by the hurricane. See how Miguel's got everything organized? That's the motor pool."

"There's the cantina," Elizabeth said, pointing to the screen. "That's where I was attacked by that terrible spider."

"Oh, God, there's Chi Chi," McQuade groaned, sinking lower in his chair.

"McQuade! Man of my dreams." Elizabeth's apt mimicry of the flirtatious Chi Chi brought a sheepish grin to her new husband's face.

"This woman has a real jealous streak, I'll tell ya." He leaned forward, bracing his elbows on his knees, and listened more intently as Miguel recounted the attempt on his life and described his efforts to help the people gain their freedom. He explained that there was a shortage of supplies but no shortage of determination. He said that he was not asking anyone to intervene. He believed this was their fight, but he wanted the cause to be understood for what it was. The real terrorist, he said, was in the presidential palace, and the people would not allow Guerrero to stay there much longer.

McQuade moved from his chair to comfort Elizabeth on the sofa, and Ronnie saw that tears had prompted his attentiveness. Elizabeth buried her face in McQuade's shoulder, and he held her as he looked at Ronnie. "We'll express the tape up to Mike Romanov first thing in the morning."

"McQuade, he needs help now," Ronnie said. "Guerrero could decide to attack them any time, and they've got practically nothing to fight back with."

"I know. Elizabeth and I have talked it over, and we agree—" Elizabeth raised her head and took a swipe at her tears with the back of her hand as they exchanged a look. "Well, we're damn near in agreement," McQuade amended with half a smile. "She's staying here with Tomas, and I'm going to Arco Iris to take delivery on a shipment of the, uh, necessary hardware just as soon as I can solve the problem of—"

Elizabeth's pointed glare came too late. Ronnie was ready with, "Transportation?"

From the air De Colores looked like a peaceful little chunk of paradise, but McQuade knew better. Ronnie's skillful approach took them over the mountains and clipped the tops of the trees in an abrupt descent as she flew over what she hoped was still Miguel's airspace. When they drew fire from the ground, she knew some of it must be under dispute.

"Did they hit anything?" she asked.

McQuade tucked in his chin and looked himself over. "Nothing important on this side. You?"

"I'm fine. Are you sure Miguel's still in control of this field?"

"According to my sources he is, but it looks like somebody's playing a little king-of-the-road back there."

They touched down and taxied toward the east end of the field, where Ronnie had hidden the plane in the trees during her last visit. McQuade reached behind his seat and made contact with the steel barrel of his automatic rifle. He'd been here before, and the air felt just as sticky as ever.

"I'm sure they must have seen us," Ronnie said, scanning the trees.

"Somebody sure as hell saw us," McQuade grumbled as he checked what he knew to be a fully loaded magazine. He shoved it back in place and nodded toward the door. "We're gonna blow this crop duster and find out what we're up against here."

"There's Miguel!"

Leading a squad of men, Miguel strode out of the shadows and cut across the corner of the airstrip. Ronnie and McQuade climbed down and met the welcoming party beside the Cessna's tail.

"I should improvise a jail and arrest you for your stupidity, McQuade." Behind his dark glasses Miguel could have been one of the faces on Mount Rushmore.

"Don't use Antonio's back room unless you have it exterminated first." McQuade found himself laughing solo. "It's, uh...it's full of spiders, you know. Spiders?" No one was paying any attention to him, and he wasn't quite sure how to interpret the heated looks Ronnie and Miguel were exchanging. "Look, Miguel, she's been running back and forth here come hell or high water for a long time now. It doesn't matter what you say, what I say... You sent her after guns—she brought you guns."

Miguel shifted his cool stare. "I sent her to you, McQuade. You were supposed to bring the guns."

"In what? My little red wagon? She's been here twice in the last—"

Ronnie stuck her hands on her hips. "*She* is not out in the kitchen making coffee while you two discuss *her* air-charter business. I do this for a living, you know."

Miguel spoke through clenched teeth. "You do not smuggle arms for—"

"I do now." She shoved the key to the cargo bay under Miguel's nose. "This is not a gift horse you're looking in the mouth. You can pay me after you move into the palace. And I suggest you send one of the boys after the truck. This damned stuff is heavy." She turned on her heel and marched to the cockpit.

"You can't win with them anymore, amigo," McQuade confided. "I think they passed some new law that lets them have things their way about ninety-nine percent of the time."

"In America," Miguel amended.

"Yeah, well—" McQuade shrugged "—in that tape you said you were fighting for American-style democracy for De Colores. You're bound to end up with uppity women, just like that one."

Miguel shared a secret smile with McQuade as he watched Ronnie jerk the cockpit door open. "Your De Coloran woman is just as headstrong, my friend."

"What were the fireworks all about?"

"A government patrol trying to get a shot at you." He indicated McQuade's weapon with a jerk of his chin. "Would you care to shoot back?"

Miguel had no plans to send Ronnie back immediately. The plane had been fired upon this time. Seeing the troops take aim and knowing she was up there in that cockpit had filled him with rage. When the patrol had taken flight, his first instinct was to go after them. Instead, he had come to her.

Once they'd loaded up the assortment of automatic and semiautomatic weapons and the boxes of ammunition and explosives, Miguel fell in beside Ronnie and struggled once more with his instincts. He wouldn't allow himself any time alone with her. Not yet. Not until he was sure reason dominated his instincts once again. And he would have to plan for her departure, even if today was not practical.

Antonio was glad to see his truck. Chi Chi was glad to see McQuade again, and everyone was glad to see the new arsenal. Supper was served in front of the cantina, and even though rations were slim, there was a fiesta atmosphere. At the center of it all was the truckload of arms and ammunition, which was admired like a piece of metal artwork by everyone in turn. Families gathered with their children. Soldiers, some wearing parts of the uniform of the army they had deserted, clustered in small groups, discussing the merits of the new weapons and boasting of varying degrees of experience with them in the hope of attracting attention. Smokers shared cigarettes they'd guarded jealously. There was not enough of anything, but the *jefe* set an example of self-sacrifice that everyone was expected to follow. Observing it all, Ronnie shared an outdoor table with Miguel and McQuade, who were enjoying McQuade's cigarettes.

"*Bienvenida!* Welcome back, McQuade." Voluptuous Chi Chi with her bloodred hair sidled up to him from behind and draped an arm around McQuade's broad shoulders. "There must be some attraction for you here, since you keep coming back. What could that be, hmm?"

"Peace and quiet," he returned as he flashed Miguel a look of distress. "Nice place to get away from it all."

"Didn't you forget something the last time you left?" she asked sweetly.

He hadn't forgotten. He'd purposely left her standing on the dock while he and Elizabeth had made their getaway. "You don't want to go to Miami, Chi Chi." He gestured toward the yard full of men. "You've got everything you need right here."

"I bend over backward to help you and that skinny island *princesa*, and you repay me by leaving me behind." Her pout became a suggestive smile. "But now you're back, and you *are* the man of my dreams."

"Honey, you can dream all you want, but I've taken myself out of circulation. Permanently." He grinned up at her. "We're talking matrimony here."

"You *married* her?" Chi Chi pulled away in amazement. "That skinny—"

"Island princess. That's right. Didn't waste a minute after she said yes. Didn't want her to change her mind."

"*Que verguenza!* Such a shame, McQuade. I'm not interested in married men." She glanced at Ronnie as though sharing a bit of female wisdom. "They seem to lose their sense of humor when they get married."

McQuade chuckled as he watched Chi Chi join the crowd around Antonio's truck. "The truth is, they don't have to spend night after night pretending they're having a great time anymore," he muttered.

Miguel sent a stream of smoke into the evening air. "I have a plan that should put my forces on an equal footing with Guerrero's, and get you back to your wife within a couple of days."

"Oh, yeah? I have a feeling Guerrero's gonna be watching the skies for that plane now."

"Our next target is Guerrero's munitions dump. It looked like the only way to arm ourselves, and now, with the weapons you've brought us, we won't be committing suicide in the process. We'll take everything we can get our hands on and blow the rest up." He removed his sunglasses, placing them carefully on the table, and looked at Ronnie. "Once we throw La Primavera into an uproar, you should be able to get away safely."

Ronnie nodded, hoping he wouldn't ask her for any promises. She saw too many needs here, and she couldn't promise to turn her back on them.

Miguel turned to McQuade. "I'll need your help, my friend. I know the layout, but I know very little about explosives."

The thought of sending Guerrero's toy closet up in smoke put a look of pure joy on McQuade's craggy face. "I'm your man."

Someone decided the weaponry windfall was truly cause for celebration, and celebration in De Colores meant music. Guitars, bongo drums, castanets and carved flutes began appearing in the grassy village square as a new white moon rose to brighten the starry sky. Antonio stirred up a rum punch, and soon people were singing and dancing to the island's traditional rumba rhythm. Watching them, Miguel let himself forget what had prompted the celebration and simply enjoy the cool night air, the scent of the sea and the sweet-tart flavor of the fruit drink. Soon he emptied his head of all but those sensations, noticing the way lilting strings and insistent drums combined to coax the hips to roll naturally, male courting female, female beckoning male.

Miguel looked at Veronica. She laid her cap on the table and ruffled her silky hair. The sleepy smile she returned assured him that her head was filled with all the same things.

"Let me teach you another dance," he said, and he reached for her hand.

The invitation came as no surprise to her this time, and she offered no premature apologies. The music felt like something elemental inside her, and it moved her toward Miguel. It moved her *with* Miguel. All others faded away. There was nothing but the night and the music and two who moved as one. Steady, rolling, undulating, the beat kept them moving, hip to hip, thigh to thigh, belly to belly. Approach, touch, slowly slide away, sway together again. The subtler the friction the more sultry the heat. His hips moved like lapping water, and her belly undulated easily in a feminine version of his fluidity. On and on and on rolled the pattering drum.

Dancing was so much like lovemaking that one gave way to the other with little more than a whisper. In a moment they were truly alone, hidden by the branches of a breadfruit tree. Under the onslaught of Miguel's kisses, Ronnie braced her back against the trunk of the tree and added inches to her height by standing on its roots. The undulating continued to the beat of the drum, thigh to thigh, belly to belly. He bent his head to kiss her breast through the ribbed cotton of her tank top, and when he sucked her nipple into a small, straining knot, she wasn't sure whether the groan it brought came from him or from her. She plunged her fingers into his hair and held his head fast, unwilling to let the pleasure his mouth brought her slip away. He lifted her top and suckled her other nipple until she gasped for her next breath.

Swiftly he unbuttoned her shorts, slipped the zipper down, and slid his warm hand over her belly. She whimpered, and he reversed their positions, supporting himself against the tree and cradling her against his shoulder while he kissed her face and sensitized her with his hand.

"Miguel..."

"This is for both of us," he whispered, his breath as hot against her ear as the place, that deep place his fingers sought and found.

"Oh, Miguel," she groaned, making an awkward attempt to unbuckle his belt. She was without dexterity. Her body was liquefying. In agonizing futility she rubbed her hand over the stiff denim and found him to be wonderfully hard.

"Shh, *querida*, shh. Let me take care of it for you. Yes, relax. Mmm, I want to feel you quiver in my hand."

"Miguel!"

"Ah, yes, *mi amante*, my lover. *Bueno*. It's good."

"Miguel." She sighed, and then they shared a long moment of quiet. She kept her eyes closed, certain that if she opened them she would feel foolish with what had just happened to her. "Don't you want me, Miguel?"

"*Dios*," he groaned. He took her hips in his hands and placed her firmly against him. "Feel how much I want you."

"What you did was beautiful, but... I would still..."

"*Querida*, don't. I cannot think with nothing but rum in my belly and my arms full of you."

"Why must you always think, always..."

"Because it's what I am good for." He combed her hair back with his fingers and kissed her forehead. "Tomorrow I will lead these young men on a raid, our first serious attempt at taking out an enemy advantage, and I don't know if I'm any good for that. If I'm not, I don't want to leave you . . ." She looked up at him, and he saw her fear. It reflected his own. "I don't want to leave you."

"Miguel . . ."

"You'll be here when I come back," he whispered fiercely. "This time. Just this one time. Then you'll go home to your little island and be safe."

"From you?"

"From all of this. When it's over . . . when this is over, Veronica . . ."

It seemed too risky to voice the promise, so he covered her mouth with his.

He took her to his room, gave her his cot and told her that he had to spend time with his men, especially the less experienced ones, to let them know that they could trust him to see them through the mission. Then he went out into the night, and in the privacy of a sheltered place near the lagoon, he gave himself relief.

The following day ticked by slowly. Miguel held strategy sessions with individual squads and with McQuade. Plans were mapped out in the dirt, and each squad leader was drilled on his assignment. Raphael was involved with much of the planning, and Paulo was an assault-squad leader. Everyone in the village had been assigned a job, and Miguel met with each group he'd organized, reminding them of their commitment, of the chain of command and of the contingency plan to take refuge in the mountains if the order should come. Ronnie had been assigned to the first-aid station, but Paulo came to her with news of another assignment.

"The *jefe* wants you to move your plane to a more sheltered place and camouflage it well." He touched the shoulder strap of his new M-16 automatic rifle and grinned. "I'm ready to escort you and show you the place he's chosen."

They walked to the airstrip, cutting across a sugarcane field that had been devastated by the hurricane. "How dangerous is this mission, Paulo?" Ronnie asked as she adjusted the bill of her cap against the sun.

"The *jefe* has warned us that some of us may not come back. Everyone on the assault team volunteered for it."

"Why?"

The question surprised him. If she cared for the *jefe*, surely she knew why. "Because this will be the real beginning. Guerrero's only real advantage is that he is better supplied."

"That's a major advantage."

"Not *well* supplied," Paulo pointed out. "Just better supplied. Tonight we even the odds. Most of the men who have families chose to stay behind and defend our position. The rest of us—" He grinned with pride. "I was chosen because I've had training, and I know how to use this." He patted his weapon.

"And Raphael?"

"He will command the defense team."

Ronnie moved the plane as she was instructed, and she was satisfied that the new situation, away from the airstrip but with easy access to the cane field, was less visible. When she returned, she found Miguel in his room. A small arsenal was laid out on the cot, and he had dressed completely in black, right down to the combat boots.

"Come in, Veronica. I was beginning to think I would have to go looking for you. You've moved the plane?"

"Yes." Her voice sounded very small.

"Good." He took a pistol from a shelf above the bed and checked the clip as he spoke. "You'll leave with McQuade shortly after we've accomplished our mission. I don't want anything to happen to that plane."

When she said nothing, he turned to her and saw the reason. Her eyes were dry, but beneath the bill of that red baseball cap they were as wide as green saucers. At a distance she could be mistaken for a child, but there was no mistake when he took her in his arms and lifted the cap. This was his woman, whose version of his heightened sense of anticipation was pure anxiety. She would bear the burden of the wait.

He kissed her, and her throat burned with the sweetness of it. Then he took her face in his hands and searched her eyes for a message, something he could take with him that would supersede all words. "I want you safe, *querida*. I wish you could be home tonight having supper with Becky or maybe tinkering with your engine."

She managed a smile as she hooked her thumbs in the empty belt loops at the sides of his pants. "I wish *you* could stay and tinker with my engine."

"Be careful, *mi angel*. If that's an invitation, this is the only time I'll ever refuse it."

Her smile faded. "I want to go with you, Miguel."

"Don't talk like a child. You have a job to do here. Everyone has been..." He sighed and pulled her against his chest. "I couldn't do *my* job if you were there. As it is, I will worry about your safety until I see your face again."

"How long?"

"That depends on how they react. When you hear the explosions, you'll know it's half over." He drew away, touching her cheek with his forefinger. "Pray for us, Veronica. Your heart is as kind as your namesake's, and your prayers will be heard. Pray for a paintbox morning."

She watched him disappear into the trees in the waning evening light, and then she joined the others. There was little talk. There was little to do now that everything was prepared. The night's silence became maddening. Then suddenly it was shattered by a series of deafening explosions.

Chapter 9

After the initial burst of explosions, it was hard to tell how much gunfire was exchanged. Staccato rounds were punctuated by more detonations. The people of El Gallo gathered in the square and encouraged one another, speculating about each ominous report. Government troops were on the run, they told one another. Ronnie nodded with the rest of them, but she knew that her smile was just as thin as theirs and her eyes just as bright with fear.

Raphael appeared suddenly, shouldering his rifle as he came to them from out of the darkness. "Get back to your posts!" he shouted. They stared at him as though they weren't sure who he was. "What are you waiting for? A direct hit in the center of town?"

Finding their wits, the crowd scattered. Before Ronnie could approach him with any questions, Raphael was gone. On her way back to the sandbagged root cellar that had been outfitted as an aid station, Ronnie chided herself for the foolish notion that Raphael would know anything more than she did. *When you hear the explosions, you'll know it's half over.* There was no turning back now. That was all anyone knew.

An hour passed. The explosions stopped, and sounds of gunfire became more erratic and were seldom close by. Three men were brought to the aid station, two with superficial wounds and one older man who was beyond help. Ronnie watched the light go out in the man's eyes and heard his wife's grief-stricken wail, and she felt numb. This was what the furious noise in the night was all about, she thought. This was what it brought. She left the aid station in a daze and headed for the cantina in search of more water.

"The first assault squad has returned!"

Ronnie turned toward the hand that had grabbed her shoulder and found it to be Raphael's. "Is Miguel with them?"

"No. They were sent back with a truckload of arms and ammunition. You should see—they got a bunch of stuff! They said everything went like clockwork, and the rest of our men should be on their way." Flushed with the excitement of his news, he flashed her a grin as he backpedaled away. "The fox got into Guerrero's henhouse, and the chickens ran for cover!"

Another hour passed, and two more vehicles returned with stolen supplies. Finally, all but eight of the men were accounted for. Miguel had sent his own squad back to the village in an effort to support the defense teams as quickly as possible, but it was becoming apparent that Paulo's squad had gotten into trouble. McQuade and Miguel were with them. The city's sirens could be heard, and an occasional gunshot, but the battle was over. Those who had returned were talking excitedly about victory, hedging only when the subject of the missing squad came up. For Raphael, who cocked his head at every sound coming from outside the perimeter of the village, the promise of victory had lost its sweetness.

Ronnie felt as if her nerve endings had all poked through the surface of her skin. Maybe they were pinned down somewhere. Maybe someone was badly hurt. Maybe some were trapped, and the others were maneuvering to free them. Maybe, maybe, maybe. Miguel was all right, she told herself. As the minutes ticked by, her prayers became more desperate. Bring them back. Bring them back. Her heart thudded with the words.

The small group straggled in just before daylight. Six shadows. Only six. Four young soldiers. McQuade. Miguel. Ronnie took several deep breaths and blinked back the burning tears before running to him.

She resisted the urge to make a fuss over his injuries, but as he dropped a weary arm around her shoulders, she took an instant inventory. None of the scratches looked serious. A blistering burn on his forearm would need attention, but the burden of his responsibilities obviously made him oblivious to his physical wounds. He pressed trembling lips against her forehead as she slid her arms behind his back. "How are things here?" he asked.

"One man died," she told him. "Carlos Denuedo. He had a chest wound, and there was nothing we could do for him." She tightened her grip. "Miguel, where's Paulo?"

Miguel's eyes met Raphael's as the young man approached. "McQuade," he said over his shoulder. "Find the other boy's family and tell them what's happened." He gave Ronnie's arm a gentle squeeze. "I must speak with Raphael."

Ronnie felt bereft when Miguel stepped away from her. The loss she had dreaded had not occurred, but she'd had only a moment to rejoice in that. Grief would descend with another loss, and she felt vaguely guilty about the relief she'd felt when she had identified Miguel in the group, as if no one else had mattered. Miguel spoke to Raphael privately, their faces only a few inches apart. He gripped the young man's shoulder, and Raphael nodded several times. Ronnie watched them walk away together.

Miguel found her waiting for him under the palm shelter near the Quonset supply building. She stood quickly as though her name had just been called for an appointment. He ducked under the fringe of dry palms and took her in his arms.

"Paulo's dead, isn't he?" she whispered.

"I don't know. He and another man spotted a rocket launcher and went back for it. They got caught. The last time they were seen, they were alive." He sat her down on an overturned crate and took a seat beside her. "I want to get you out of here just as soon as I can, Veronica, but I have to ask you to wait a little longer."

"That's no problem," she said as she took his hand and drew his arm closer. "You know I don't want to go, anyway."

"I need McQuade," he explained. In the dark she was trying to examine the burn on his arm, which he didn't remember getting. "If there's a way to get to them, McQuade will find it."

She looked up, her eyes glittering. "Just the two of you?"

"I can't stop Raphael from going with us. He needs to be in on it, for his own peace of mind."

"You don't sound hopeful."

"I think we'll find them." He sighed. "My greatest fear was that someone would be taken alive. I told all of them that."

She held his hand and let him sit quietly for a moment. She sensed his fatigue. "Let me take care of this for you," she whispered, touching his arm near the place where he'd been burned.

"When I come back," he said. "We need to leave now, before it gets light. Guerrero has more patrols out now. We didn't have much trouble getting in and taking what we wanted. It wasn't until McQuade started setting off charges that they really knew what hit them."

"Do you know where he might keep prisoners?"

"Prisoners." On the bitter sound of the word Miguel glanced away, and his voice grew raspy. "Paulo always tries to go one better. He's too impulsive." He shook his head. "I should have known better."

"He's been with you since the start, Miguel. You knew his capabilities. He told me that he had the necessary training and was familiar with the automatic rifle." She moved her hand to his shoulder. "He volunteered. He told me that, too—that you gave everyone a choice." She sensed that Miguel found no comfort in that fact. "At least you know they're both alive. When this is over, you'll liberate the prisoners. And then you can reprimand Paulo for his impulsiveness and send him off to school."

Her naïveté came as no surprise to him. She was an American, and in America even prisoners had rights. In De Colores, Guerrero had become the law, which was to say there was no law. There was only the ego of a madman. They heard the sound of footsteps in the grass, and they knew McQuade and Raphael had come for him.

He pulled her to her feet and gave her a quick, hard kiss. "We're going to move carefully," he promised. "Don't expect us back before midafternoon."

It was late morning when the three men finally reached the outskirts of La Primavera. It was as though an agreement had been reached to permit themselves a few more hours to believe in miracles. They had not been in any hurry to confirm what each, in his own mind, knew they would find.

The spectacle had been arranged at a gas station at the edge of the city. McQuade shoved his grief-stunned companions into the wreckage of a small hut in an overgrown, wind-battered orchard. He knew that Miguel would recover his senses in a moment, but the *jefe*'s heart ruled his first response. This was what they had expected—a scene, nevertheless, for which they could never have prepared themselves.

The bloodied bodies of the two boys were propped against the stucco wall of the gas station. Their hands were bound, and their heads lolled toward one another as though, even in death, they could somehow offer each other support. Their blood reddened the whitewashed wall. Two soldiers stood guard.

"I cannot leave them like this," Miguel said quietly. His voice was expressionless, his eyes hollow.

McQuade looked at Raphael, who simply stared. "This trap was set for you, Miguel. Take a good look." McQuade gave them a moment, but he knew both men saw only Paulo. "That's all we're supposed to see. Two bodies and two guards."

"Their bodies must not suffer further indignity, McQuade. We must spare them that."

"They're beyond suffering now," McQuade said gently. And then he cleared his throat and said matter-of-factly, "It'll be easy to take those two out. They're just kids. Sacrificial lambs. Guerrero can sure pick 'em."

Miguel nodded mechanically, still staring vacantly at the scene. "So can I."

McQuade's jaw tightened as he cursed himself for having taken the wrong tack. In about a minute he could see both of these guys throwing themselves on the pyre.

"I know that one." It was the first comment Raphael had made, and it came in a whisper. His voice grew stronger as he explained, "The small one. Ernesto Ramal. We called him Raton, the mouse. He always wanted to play center field, but the ball would fly right over his head." He gave a mirthless chuckle. "We made a good catcher out of him. Paulo was our best pitcher."

While they watched, a group of a dozen people came around the corner of a building about a block away. Men, women and children approached the macabre display reluctantly as though they had been shoved on stage. They huddled near the gas pumps and hung their heads. In the center of the group several people made quick, subtle signs of the cross, while those at the back cast furtive glances over their shoulders.

"The people are expected to desecrate the bodies somehow, but look—" Miguel touched Raphael's shoulder. "They refuse."

McQuade was interested in other aspects of the group's behavior. "That's where the big guns are," he whispered. "Behind that building." He surveyed surrounding roofs and saw no evidence of artillery. "Amateurs. I'd have put them up there."

After a moment, the people moved away. Another moment passed, and the man Raphael still thought of as Raton said something to his companion, who shifted his attention from the nearby trees to the quiet city street. While Miguel, Raphael and McQuade watched, the young man lifted the body of the friend with whom he had once exchanged pitching signals and laid him down carefully. Raphael stiffened when he saw the knife removed from the sheath on Raton's belt, but Miguel gripped his shoulder with a strong hand. They watched Raton cut the bonds from Paulo's wrists and carefully place his hands on his chest. With one hand he closed Paulo's eyes while he blessed himself with the other.

"That kid's no mouse," McQuade said softly.

Raphael's shoulder trembled beneath Miguel's hand as he dropped his chin to his chest. He gasped, strangling on his grief, struggling to stem the flow of his tears. Finally his shoulders sagged in defeat, and the drops fell on his thighs as he sobbed.

McQuade reached for the rifle lying forgotten near Raphael's knees. "Let's get out of here."

Ronnie made herself useful by helping to reorganize the first-aid station and fill more sandbags while she waited for Miguel's return. It was nearly nightfall when the three men appeared without the two they had hoped to rescue. No questions were asked. Miguel visited briefly with two more bereaved families, while McQuade sat under the thatched shelter with Ronnie and chose his words carefully as he recounted the events of the day.

"I haven't told Miguel this yet, but I've decided to hang around a while."

Ronnie stared at him. "What about Elizabeth?"

"When you go back, I want you to go see her. Tell her I'm okay and that things are looking good here. We have to move quickly now, before Guerrero can replace his losses."

"We need food and medical supplies."

"Hey, look, you're not part of that 'we.'" He caught the direction of her thoughts and grabbed her elbow, intending to nip her idea in the bud. "Miguel about had my head for letting you transport the guns. You're going home to stay, kiddo. For his sake."

The idea was well past the budding stage. "It isn't for you to decide what I need to do for his sake."

"I know how you feel about him." McQuade sighed. "Some guys love power, and they'll do anything they can to get it. If a few people get hurt, well, that's part of the game. Miguel's not like that. From the beginning he's been in this only because he thinks it's right."

"I know that."

"You've gotta understand, Ronnie. He just came back from seeing what was left of two kids Guerrero got his hands on. And Miguel was in command of the mission when they bought it. If anything like that happened to you..."

"I'm not a kid, McQuade. Neither was Paulo. He made a choice, and he was willing to die for it."

They saw Miguel, his face shrouded by twilight shadows, striding toward the shelter. "Tomorrow you'll do what you have to," McQuade said quietly. "Just don't add to his grief tonight."

Miguel ducked his head and stepped under the shelter. "They're serving supper in front of the cantina."

"Wonder what a shot of bourbon costs at La Gallina these days," McQuade said as he stepped over a crate.

"I think it's negotiable," Miguel replied. "Antonio likes to hear your stories."

"Antonio's one of my main men." McQuade gave Miguel's shoulder a parting squeeze. "Take it easy, amigo."

Miguel and Ronnie looked at one another as they listened to McQuade's retreating footsteps.

He looked tired, beaten.

"Have you had anything to eat?" she asked.

She was warm, vital, and he saw solace in her eyes.

"I ate something this morning," he said.

His heart was breaking. She felt it in her own chest.

"McQuade told me what happened."

Her heart was open to him. She offered sanctuary, but he felt completely undeserving.

"Both of them. They were so young." He lifted his hands slowly, palms up. They were empty, just as he was. "I failed them, Veronica. I should have been the one to—"

She stepped into his arms and held him. She would not deny his pain by refuting it, but she would not let him be alone with it.

"I should have been teaching them *about* wars—*past* wars, over and done—not asking them to join me in making this one." His chest sank away from her cheek as he snorted in disgust. "What do I know about making war? *Dios*, I'm a teacher. Just a teacher."

"You know about freedom," Ronnie whispered.

"Freedom? Yes, of course. Did I tell you about the villages we *liberated*? And now the liberated souls of young men who should never have been allowed to—"

"I love you, Miguel."

"What?" His voice was hoarse, and he looked down at her as though she had taken leave of her senses.

"I said I love you." He appeared not to understand, not to believe. "I can't give you back what you've lost. I can only tell you that you're a good man, maybe too good for the job you've assumed, because you care so much. And I love you."

In his despair, he could have turned it all back on her, refused to accept any of it, except the last. He saw himself as a presumptuous man who had already made too many promises, except to her. He'd promised her nothing, but she loved him anyway. He needed her beyond all reason.

"They've wounded you again," she said quietly.

His hands were in her hair, holding her head still while he searched her face for some reflection of his need. "You've mended me before."

"Let me try again."

His kiss was a plunging plea for deliverance from everything that ached inside him. He'd been afraid his lovemaking might hurt her, but she molded herself to him and welcomed him with an open kiss, telling him how much she wanted it. She would ease the ache. She would restore his health. She would take him, broken as he was, and make him whole again.

They went to his room. He closed the door, and there was almost no light. The louvered ventilators near the top and bottom of the outside walls permitted them to see the outline of one another. But Ronnie didn't need light. She knew this man. She knew the way his flesh quivered with pain or with desire even as his mind controlled his responses. She knew the sure, sensual way he moved his body when he danced, the way he led her, reassured her, accepted her responses and made her feel at long last comfortable with her femininity. She knew what to expect.

He peeled his T-shirt off and dropped it. When she moved to do the same, he stilled her hands and brought them around his back. "Allow me that pleasure," he said, and he slid his hands beneath her tank top, unloosed the back hook on her bra and ran his hands up and down her back, pressing her hips more firmly each time he reached them as he arched against her.

His skin felt warm, smooth and waxy from the heat. She kissed the curve of his pectoral muscle, and tasted the saltiness of him with the tip of her tongue. "Don't keep yourself from me this time," she whispered without lifting her head.

"I won't," he promised. He moved his hands slowly to bracket her breasts. "I can't." But he eased her away from him and swept his thumbs over her nipples while he kissed her as if her mouth could supplement the little food he'd permitted himself.

She groaned when his touch left her breasts straining almost painfully for him. "Raise your arms," he whispered into her hair. She complied, and he pushed both garments up her arms as though the act were part of a sultry dance. At the top of his journey he caught her hands and lowered them to his shoulders, letting the clothing fall. He pressed his lips against her temple, her neck, and then entered her hot, wet mouth with his tongue, holding her so that her nipples barely brushed against him. She felt spongy from the waist down, and she worried vaguely that her legs would not support her.

He held her under her arms as he lowered one knee toward the floor. "I'm hungry, Veronica," he whispered against her breast. "So hungry."

Literally, it was true. He took her nipple in his mouth and suckled, and she thought wildly of what satisfaction she would feel if she were able to give him real nourishment at her breast. She tunneled her fingers through his hair and only regretted the time he lost in moving his mouth from one breast to the other. Then the waistband of her shorts went slack, and she felt his hard palms sliding over her hips, pushing the rest of her clothes out of his way. He knelt at her feet, freed her of shorts and shoes and then nibbled around her navel. He gripped one firm thigh in each hand to coax them apart. With his thumbs he teased her soft inner thighs, inching higher until she sucked her belly in with a quick breath.

Words of protest flitted through her mind like weightless moths chased by a steadily intensifying jet of need. He found the source of that need, and the jet shot to the place he touched with one deft thumb. And then he kissed her there.

He felt the bite of her nails in his shoulders, and h
stroked her gently in return. He supported her inconse
quential weight until he felt the fluttering within her that h
promised himself he would prolong. Steadying her in on
arm, he unzipped his pants and rose to his feet. He had
plan for putting her on the cot, but she caught him by su
prise, caught his buttocks in her hands and pressed hersel
against him. Her mouth made a moist foray across his ches
while she rolled her hips against him in a carnal rumba.

He followed her lead this time, their pulses providing th
drumbeat. She slid her hands inside the back of his pants
maneuvering denim and elastic until he slipped his han
between them and freed himself. Her hand followed har
upon his, but when she found him, she hesitated. He guide
her. "Don't shy away now, *mi amante*," he whispered int
her hair.

But in a moment he knew he was nearing the limits of hi
endurance. He stalled her caresses with one hand and tosse
his bedroll to the floor with the other. In another moment
all of his clothes lay in some unseen corner of the room, an
he was cradling her, moving to cover her body with his. "
shouldn't do this," he whispered as the back of his finger
skimmed one breast, lingering lightly against the nipple he'
made round and hard, and then sliding over the tightl
stretched satin of her belly. "*Muy hermosa*. So very beau
tiful. I shouldn't . . ."

She put her hand on his hip. "Don't shy away from m
now, *mi amor*."

He nudged her legs apart and moved between them
bracing himself over her and whispering of his needs i
Spanish, the language spoken by his heart. Their bodie
were slick with sweat. He whispered her name as he entere
her, and she gasped. He thought he had hurt her and drev
back, but she arched her back and held him inside her. H

moved slowly, and she followed the lead he gave her. He groaned, wanting more, and she reached, offered, arched, gave. He moved faster, and she led the way this time as she left the weighty part of herself behind and soared on the declaration of her love. He cried out in pain and joy. She joined him in celebrating both.

And when he had spent himself inside her, he buried his face in the comfort of her shoulder and hoped she couldn't distinguish his sweat from his tears.

Ronnie found herself on the cot when she awoke. She had no recollection of moving. She remembered lying on the floor feeling pleasantly warm and sated and safe, her arms and legs woven together with Miguel's, her mind drifting in sleepy satisfaction. In the dark she listened for the sound of his breathing, but the room was quiet. She slid down and felt her way across the floor, but she found only a tennis shoe and a blanket. In her groping she found her top but not her shorts, so she dragged her bag out from under the cot and dressed in the first thing that came into her hand—her sea-foam dress.

She suspected the lagoon's tranquil water might have drawn him to it the same way it lured her. The night was warm and still, and the stars were dimming. She stepped from prickly grass to soft sand. Her heels scooped out footholds on her way down the eroded bank. A cigarette glowed in the shelter of the palms some yards away, and she padded across wet sand in the direction of the small red beacon.

As Miguel watched her come to him he had a fleeting vision of her fanning the gossamer folds of her skirt with outstretched arms and fluttering over his head like a butterfly. He'd come to believe that she had her own wings. He imagined her reaching down as she passed, plucking him out of the trees and lifting him high, carrying him away under the expanse of her beautiful turquoise and jade wings. He shoved the cigarette against his mouth and sucked the smoke deep into his lungs. She was driving him crazy, filling his head with such wild . . .

"Is that you, Miguel?"

"Fortunately for you, *querida*, I'm not one of Guerrero's men."

She pushed past the fronds of waist-high vegetation and moved toward the shadowy form leaning against the trunk of a coconut palm. "If you're safe out here, then I must be, too," she said quietly.

"I'm not safe anywhere, but I did think to carry a pistol. Did you?"

"No." She stopped when another step would have taken her into his arms. "Why would I take a pistol along when I was looking for you?"

He turned his face from her and took a final drag on the cigarette. The smoke became part of the darkness. "Why, indeed?" he reflected as he dropped the butt and buried it in a hollow he'd scooped out of the sand with his bare foot.

"Have I done something wrong, Miguel?" She wanted to take that last step, but the distance between them suddenly struck her as a forbidding space. "When I woke up and found you gone I felt . . . I thought . . ."

He pushed away from the tree, took her slight shoulders in his hands and drew her against his chest. She sighed and slipped her arms around him inside his open shirt. His skin felt cool and damp. She found the pistol tucked into the back of his pants, and she flinched when she touched it. "Good grief, Miguel. If this thing went off, tending your injury would be a pretty indelicate proposition."

His chuckle came deep, rich and warm. "But I could trust you to work your delicate magic under the most indelicate circumstances.'' He kissed the top of her head. ''No, Veronica, you did nothing wrong. In my heart everything we did felt perfectly right.''

''And in your head?''

''My head,'' he reflected and made a clucking sound. ''My head won't let me sleep. That's where my conscience seems to reside, and my conscience tells me that every moment I spend with you is a moment stolen out of your life.''

''That's nonsense.''

''Is it?'' Even as he thought of putting her away from him, he crushed her closer. ''Like Paulo, you risk too much, *querida*. Your life is too much. Do you think that being a woman or being an American or... or simply being too young to die makes any difference? Do you think you can't be touched?''

''I *have* been touched, Miguel.'' She tilted her head back and lifted her hand to his cheek. ''I have nothing in my life that's more important to me than you are. You're worth whatever risk I may be taking.''

''But I have—''

''I know.'' She touched his lips with her thumb and she smiled. ''You do have something more important. I understand that.''

''Veronica, it isn't—''

''Shh.'' She pushed her fingers into his hair and found that it was wet. ''This is *my* time. Given or stolen, it's mine.'' She pulled his head down slowly and felt his body harden even as his resistance went soft. ''Isn't it,'' she insisted.

''Yes.'' His mouth came down in a hard kiss that would deny her nothing. He caressed the soft skin bared by the deep vee in the back of her dress and speared her mouth with his questing tongue. He moved his hands over the frothy fabric, past her waist and over her bottom, and it excited him to feel the lack of anything but her beneath the dress. Sliding his kisses to her neck, he pressed her tight against him.

"I love this dress," he whispered as he slipped it off her shoulders. She freed her arms, and the bodice fell to her waist. As the night lifted toward day it pearlized her skin with a smooth, shining luster. Her breasts were like the mica-bright sand of his home. Their dusky peaks beaded under his scrutiny. He touched them, almost shyly. "When I first saw you holding this dress against yourself after you'd showered, I was torn between wanting to see you in the dress and longing for you to drop the towel."

She sucked in a breath at the thrill of his touch. "Ah, Miguel, what do you want now?"

"I want you again, querida. Here on the beach. I want to come into you just as morning breaks."

"That will be beautiful," she whispered as they sank together to their knees. He peeled off his shirt and put it aside with the pistol. She watched him slide his pants down his legs and saw only beauty in a body that was becoming too lean. He moved over her, and she touched first the bandage over the burn on his arm and then the puckered scar under his ribs. He gave tenderness for tenderness as he sought his place beneath her skirt. When he came into her, she turned her face to the bright red crack on the horizon and whispered, "Miguel."

He loved her well, with the coming of the light spurring him on. She rose to meet him, and the colors they mixed for one another brimmed, quivered at the moment of overfill, and then spilled over in psychedelic hues too intense to last. Replete, they lay in each others' arms and heard the sound of lapping waves, liquid color fading to warm pastels, soothing, soothing.

Miguel braced his elbow in the sand and admired her face while he spread her skirt to cover her thighs. She offered a languid smile. "Your hair is wet," she said as she touched it.

"I went for a swim."

Her hand trailed down his chest and rested at his flat belly. "You must eat more, Miguel. You make too many sacrifices."

He pulled the gathered fabric of her bodice to cover her breasts. "I was unable to make the one I intended where you were concerned. I need you more than food or sleep or... But I will not sacrifice your life, Veronica. I beg you to—"

She silenced him with a finger over his lips. The promise he wanted to extract from her would be impossible to keep. "Let's not miss the sunrise," she said.

He pulled his pants on, and she shrugged into the straps of her dress. The amethyst sky scattered gold dust and powdered rubies across the lagoon's winking ripples. For Ronnie it was an irresistible trove of treasures. They walked to the edge of the water together, but when he stopped, she kept walking.

The water buoyed the sea-foam dress in a circle around her hips and bathed her privately within that curtain. Miguel could hardly breathe as he watched her. The water loved her as he did. The sky laced her hair with glinting jewels and would lure her from him with the promise of more. Jealous, he waded in after her.

She met him in thigh-high deep water with her skirt clinging to her hips. Her face was filled with dawn light. "How's this for a paintbox morning?"

"You fill my heart with these colors, Veronica." He took her in his arms and lowered his head to her. "You fill me," he whispered against her lips. "You fill me."

At breakfast Miguel and Ronnie sat together with Mc-Quade, Raphael, Antonio and others. Raphael ate quietly. McQuade offered his help in planning and executing the next raid, and Miguel refused it. Their discussion tied Ronnie's stomach in knots. McQuade insisted that they must press their advantage immediately, and that Miguel needed all the help he could get. Miguel wanted McQuade to return to his wife. Ronnie sympathized with that wish, but she wanted McQuade to stay. Miguel needed him. Yes, Elizabeth was her friend, but Miguel was fighting for the life of his country. He had to let people take their own risks if he were to stand a chance of winning.

She noted once again the scarcity of food. The hurricane had destroyed so much of the island's bounty, and there was barely enough for two meals a day. Beans, rice and fish, and none of it plentiful. They talked of another raid, and she knew how depleted the medical supplies were. She made her decision to leave without telling Miguel. He would only try to make her promise not to come back, and he would insist that McQuade go along. It was a scene she wanted to avoid because she had every intention of returning within a day or two with desperately needed supplies. While the men went round and round, Ronnie slipped away.

Miguel crossed the street on his way back to the Quonset building. McQuade was right. His skills were valuable, and put to proper use they could help bring an end to the strife before the bellies of the children became puffed with malnutrition. But he had to get Veronica out safely. He would promise her the moon and hope he lived to deliver it to her, but for now she had to go.

She was not in his room. He reached for the dress she'd hung on a hook earlier and let the soft, damp cloth slide through his hand as he smiled, remembering. He was in for another argument, but his capitulation to McQuade was the only one he would make today. And then he thought again how lovely she'd looked standing there in the...

The explosion rocked him, and he was not aware that he filled his fist with fabric and ripped the dress off the hook.

Chapter 10

Miguel bolted for the door and scanned the tree line, his heart pounding in his throat. Black smoke rolled skyward from what he knew, with icy certainty, to be the cane field. He saw nothing along the periphery of his path as he ran. He heard nothing but the buzzing in his ears and, as he drew closer, the mighty whoosh of flames. He had a fleeting notion that someone else's legs must have been carrying him, since his were paralyzed with fear. When he saw the wing tip, the tail and the ball of fire, a terrible, anguished sound ripped his throat.

Flames licked furiously at the Cessna's metal body. The cockpit had become an incinerator. McQuade shouldered his rifle and tore across the field. Miguel was running blind, a senseless moth headed for the flames, shouting, "Veronica!" McQuade managed to tackle him, bringing them both to their knees in the stubbled field. Heat rolled across the ground in waves.

"They've killed her!" Miguel clawed at the earth as he struggled to free himself. "My God, they've killed her, they've killed her, they've killed her..."

"Take it easy," McQuade pleaded as he hooked an arm over Miguel's shoulder and dug his heels into the ground. "Take it easy, amigo. How do you know? Maybe she wasn't in there."

"I was looking for her," Miguel panted. "I couldn't find her. She was gone. She was..."

McQuade felt the man's chest sag beneath his arm. He loosened his hold and squinted up at the raging fire. "You can't see a damn thing in there. There's no reason to assume... We've gotta back off now, before she blows again. C'mon!"

McQuade half dragged, half carried Miguel to a safe distance. As if on cue the auxiliary fuel tank exploded. The plane was blown apart, and pieces of metal scattered in all directions. The two men watched, helplessly mesmerized.

By twos and threes the villagers ventured forth. They knew their job. The defense measures that had been planned were put into action as the fire-fighting teams organized their efforts to keep the flames from spreading. Miguel stood silently and watched while his heart shriveled and burned before his eyes. The people lowered their heads in respect for his grief as they moved past him.

"We'll search for her, Miguel."

McQuade's voice seemed to come to him through a long tunnel. Miguel nodded dumbly.

"By the looks of it, I'd say they either tossed a grenade into the cockpit, or—" He sighed. He hated the second possibility. "They could have wired the ignition with a detonator."

"In which case, someone turned on the ignition and set off the charge." Miguel's voice was hollow, and his eyes were glassy.

"Yeah." McQuade squeezed Miguel's shoulder. "I'll... probably be able to figure out what happened when the wreckage cools off."

"I'm interested in only one piece of information." He turned to McQuade in dark anguish. "If she'd been anywhere in the area, she would have come running when she heard the explosion."

"We'll look for her."

Miguel knew the search was hopeless. He also knew that Ronnie would never have regarded it that way, so he searched, praying all the while for some sign of her and some piece of her optimism. He found neither. He had no tears. Tears were triggered by the heart, and he had watched his heart die in those flames. Those who loved him tried to console him, but he saw little and heard nothing. His mind spun like a child's top, and his chest was a cold, empty cavity. Finally there was only McQuade to keep the vigil with him in the waning hours of afternoon under the rustling palms of the shelter.

"You know we're going to have to hit our next target tonight," McQuade said. He picked up a stick and drew a line in the dirt at their feet. "We decided on the control tower at La Primavera airport. We should be able to get the job done, like you said, without civilian casualties. While they clean that mess up, we go for the harbor patrol headquarters, take out a few patrol boats." Miguel stared at him, and McQuade wondered whether he'd been heard. "Hell, I know it sounds callous, Miguel, but either you strike now or you lose your advantage. There'll be time to mourn them all properly when this thing is over."

"I want Guerrero," Miguel said in a flat, even tone.

"We'll get Guerrero," McQuade promised. "We go about this right, we'll have him inside a week, guaranteed. Nobody's backing him. Every day a few more of his regulars come crawling out of the woodwork and ask to join us."

"I want him dead, McQuade. I want to put his corpse on display the way he did Paulo."

Miguel's threat was so quiet, so deadly that it nearly masked his grief. "You'll get your chance," McQuade promised. "You'll have his head on a platter. And then it'll be up to you to dispose of it—" he waved his hand at the range of possibilities "—any way you want."

Miguel's face became murderous. "You think I won't do it?"

The anger was good, McQuade thought. It was better than the catatonic state the man had fallen into earlier. McQuade studied his friend's face. "I think you won't do it. I think you're not like Guerrero."

Miguel pointed to the ground. "If I had him groveling at my feet, defenseless and begging for mercy, I would cut his heart out."

"That's fair," McQuade said quietly. "That's what he's done to you."

Miguel's shoulders sagged, and he gripped his knees. It all seemed like such a nightmare, an absolute absurdity. Everything around him looked just as it had yesterday, but nothing could ever be the same again. He'd loved her and lost her within a matter of hours.

"I loved her, McQuade. She gave, and I took, but I loved her." Miguel turned his head slowly, and the pain McQuade saw written on that lean, dark face made him shudder. "What kind of a man lets his woman die without telling her he loves her?" Miguel asked.

"A man just like the rest of us, amigo." McQuade laid a brotherly hand on Miguel's back. "She knew."

"I wish—" His voice went hoarse, and he had to start
again. "I wish I had told her."

The airport control tower went up in flames along with
two cargo planes. Within hours, the harbor patrol headquarters was a pile of rubble. Miguel's men cleared people
out of the target area while McQuade set the charges. During the next two days Miguel's men kept government troops
on the defensive. Small bands of Miguel's guerrillas ham-
pered every retaliatory effort by the city-based government
troops, and the villagers protected their own. Striking re-
peatedly without allowing Guerrero time to regroup was
paying off. And it was the single objective of Miguel's every
waking hour. The prospect of defeating Guerrero kept him
sane.

McQuade watched Miguel toy with a shot of the bourbon that Antonio protected like a hoard of Liberty dimes.
It wasn't just the one glass of bourbon Miguel was considering. McQuade knew the look of a man who was mulling
over the prospect of getting drunk. Miguel certainly had the
look, and no one deserved a few hours of oblivion more
than he did. They had run out of cigarettes, and there was
little else for consolation. In Miguel's condition—tired,
hungry, emotionally twisted at the center of his gut—a couple of shots would be all it would take. But McQuade knew
Miguel wouldn't do it. In a moment, he would push the
glass aside and talk about tomorrow's raid.

At the sound of the back door creaking open McQuade
dropped his hand on the M-16 that lay on the bar.

"It's Antonio," Miguel said confidently.

McQuade was ready to shoot if it wasn't. Antonio saw
McQuade's reaction as he entered the cantina from his
apartment in back, and his eyes were momentarily a bit

rounder than usual. They looked at one another, and then everyone relaxed. Doubt was a sign of the times.

It was a gray, rainy afternoon. Antonio reached for a towel to dry his head. "I have news," he announced as he rubbed the back of his neck dry. He turned up the flame on the kerosene lamp so that the two men might appreciate every nuance of his tale. "Chi Chi's friend Juanita, who lives in the city now since the storm ruined her house— You remember her, McQuade. She did some errands for you."

"Yeah, I remember Juanita."

"Well, she was in touch with Dorothy Bartholomew at the Red Cross office in La Primavera, and she relayed a message to you—through me, of course." Antonio's eyes shone with his pride in being recognized as McQuade's contact.

"Dorothy's still around?" McQuade scowled. "Damn. I'd hoped she was safe and sound in the States by now."

"What's the message?" Miguel asked impatiently.

Antonio preened with the distinction of carrying a secret for important men. "It comes from Mikal Romanov. He says Freedom International is working for you. They have put together a report on Guerrero's activities, and the State Department is listening. He also says that Guerrero is getting nowhere with any government in his requests for military assistance."

A smile spread over McQuade's face. He looked at Miguel and saw nothing but cold satisfaction.

"It's good news, isn't it?" Antonio asked.

McQuade slapped Antonio on the back. "It's good news, my man. It means Guerrero is no more flush with ammunition than we are."

"It means we pick our targets carefully and end this nightmare as quickly as we can," Miguel added.

The front door opened, and Raphael stepped inside, also dripping wet. He, too, had news. His eyes were bright with it, but there was neither joy nor sadness in his expression—only excitement. He pulled a brown envelope from under his shirt and held it up. "A package from Guerrero. It's for you, *jefe*."

Miguel reached for the package, but McQuade got to it first. "Just let me check this baby out first," he muttered as he tested the envelope with uniquely perceptive fingers.

"Guerrero doesn't have the finesse for such delicate plotting, McQuade." Miguel sipped his bourbon and watched McQuade treat the envelope with studied care. He was almost amused. "I suspect he dreams of pulling the trigger on me in person next time."

"Ain't gonna be no next time, amigo." McQuade slipped the envelope's flap off the clasp and peered inside. His face dropped, and then his features froze.

"What is it?"

McQuade looked up and passed the envelope to Miguel as though it were, indeed, something that might blow the roof off the cantina. He bit his lower lip as he watched Miguel take a look, then reach inside.

With an unsteady hand he drew out the envelope's precious contents. A red baseball cap sporting the Boston Red Sox logo in a size that would accommodate a wealth of silken hair and a small, delicate head. The envelope fell to the floor.

"Who delivered it?" McQuade asked as he bent to retrieve it. "What did they say?"

"The man knows nothing, *señor*. He's just some terrorized merchant who is doing what he was told to do. He's supposed to return with a reply."

"Guerrero's probably holding the man's wife until he gets back." McQuade found a note at the bottom of the envelope. Without further comment he handed it to Miguel.

The words blurred on the paper when Miguel first held it up. Still clutching the cap, he laid the note next to the kerosene lamp on the bar, smoothed it out and willed his eyes to focus.

"It says they have her." The words danced mischievously in front of his eyes, and he wondered if they teased him deliberately. "It says... it says she's alive."

"What does he want?" McQuade asked.

"How do we know he's telling the truth?" Raphael put in.

"It could be any cap," Antonio added.

Miguel turned, his eyes alight for the first time in days. "It isn't *any* cap. It's *her* cap."

"That doesn't mean she's alive," Raphael said bitterly.

"It doesn't mean she's not," McQuade returned. "It just means they blew up a plane and got a baseball cap out of the deal. Maybe more." He turned to Miguel and asked gently, "Does he say what he wants?"

"He wants to talk. He says that I am to meet him at the gas station—the one where they had Paulo—at a time of my choosing. He will bring Veronica."

"Alone?" Antonio asked.

"I am to be alone."

"He won't be," McQuade said.

"*Jefe*, it's a trap." Raphael stepped closer. "Just like it was before." The *jefe* didn't seem to hear him, so he took another step. "You might find the same thing you found before. It's no good to see that, *jefe*. You'll hate yourself if you walk away, and if you don't..."

"I'm going to find out whether she's alive."

"How do you propose to do that?" McQuade demanded.

"We're going to take the palace, McQuade. We're going to end this thing."

"If they've got her, they'll kill her for sure if we try anything."

"I'm going inside." A thin, humorless smile reflected Miguel's mood. "In my mind I've gone over a plan for taking the palace a hundred times. Every detail. We do it by getting a team inside first. Only now there is an added detail. That team must get Veronica out."

"If she's there," Antonio insisted.

McQuade exchanged a hopeful look with Miguel. "We'll know soon."

"I need paper," Miguel said quietly. "Our merchant must be returned to his wife. Guerrero can plan on a meeting tomorrow. We will plan our strike for tonight."

He penned the message in a bold, even hand. Let Guerrero believe he would walk into this willingly, anxiously. The belief would be short-lived. He handed the note to Raphael. "Send an escort with this man, and tell them he is not to reach the city before nightfall. Antonio, I want you to bring me all our squad leaders."

As the two men headed out into the rain, McQuade took note of the distant look in Miguel's eyes. The *jefe* needed some privacy. "I wanna check supplies," McQuade said. "I'll be back for the meeting." He laid a hand on Miguel's shoulder and offered his customary, "Take it easy, amigo. I've got a strong hunch she's okay."

"I like your hunches, McQuade."

When the door was closed and the cantina was quiet, Miguel allowed himself another look at the red baseball cap. Hard-boiled as he was, McQuade was blessed with a touch of that American optimism, Miguel told himself. Not as generously endowed with it as Veronica was, but it showed through at times like this. It was almost tangible. Miguel liked the airy feel of it. Optimism. *Dios*, he could fortify himself with the taste of it and get through the next twelve hours on nothing but that, but the specter of Paulo's battered body would not leave him alone. He pressed the bill of the cap over his eyes and silently begged the awful image to go away.

The litany of her name became a hoarse chant as he rubbed the well-worn cap over his face and savored the scent, the feel, the slim but precious chance.

Miguel's plan depended on stealth, timing and teamwork. He knew the palace well. During the time he'd been there, he had taken an interest in its structure and its history. It had been built in the seventeenth century to house the Spanish viceroys. Remodeled many times over the years, it featured a whole system of hidden rooms and passages once used to conceal valuables and to protect inhabitants from any number of threats—storms, pirates, even rebellious De Colorans. This time the tables were turned. The palace's chief occupant had no interest in its history or its secret passages. The island's chief rebel did.

Miguel assigned Raphael and six small squads to the assault on the palace. Each had a primary and secondary target. The squads would converge once inside the walls. After disabling two sentries, Miguel led a seventh hand-picked squad over the garden wall. Now each man had his job to do. Two of the men who had once been palace staff would hit the armory while two others took out the two machine guns that were mounted on the roof. McQuade followed Miguel as he picked his way through the neglected tropical foliage that had once been a carefully tended garden. Their objective was underground.

Miguel paused between two palmetto palms, still dripping from the rain that had ended earlier, and looked around to assure himself of his bearings. The big cedar had fallen against the wall, but this was the spot he sought. The palmettos and the mango trees sheltered them from being viewed from the palace. Miguel began ripping the new growth of creeping vines away from the clay tile. He uncovered a handle and pulled open a wooden hatchway, which was tiled to match the rest of the terrace. Miguel followed the barrel of his rifle down the stone steps. When he reached the bottom, he flicked his flashlight on. McQuade joined him, closing the door behind them.

The passageway was cool and damp and smelled like fertile humus. An array of creatures, most of them heard but not seen, scurried for cover as the two men worked their way along the route that Miguel hoped only he and these creatures had recently explored. They came to a fork in the passage. Miguel pointed to the left. They passed a room, and Miguel flashed his light on a cache of kegs and bottles, hoarded by some Spanish connoisseur who had long since stopped aging. There were other rooms along the passage, but Miguel showed no interest in them. His sights were set on another set of stone steps and another trapdoor that led to an obscure storage room in the east wing. If Guerrero were holding a prisoner whose stay would be short, Miguel suspected that she would be kept in that wing, perhaps even in his old office.

Miguel pointed his flashlight at the steps and ran the beam up to the underside of the trapdoor. McQuade nodded, and they retreated along the passageway to the fork.

"This tunnel adjoins the sewer system." Miguel's hushed voice echoed softly. "The grate is directly under the front gate. I'll try to get her back to the tunnel before the charge goes off."

"If she's here," McQuade reminded him.

"Yes. If she's here."

McQuade gave a thumbs-up sign and headed down the dark passage. Miguel adjusted his rifle strap on his shoulder and hurried back to the stairs. The hallway was dark, but one light shone, and one sentry was posted near the door to the office suite Miguel had occupied in what seemed another lifetime. The sentry had to be guarding someone, and Miguel prayed that it was Veronica. If Guerrero was behind that door, he was a dead man.

The sentry turned his ear toward the door. "You need what?" he said. "I'm sorry, but I can't—" The young man gave a disgusted sigh and took a ring of keys from his pocket. Miguel pulled his pistol and moved closer. The soldier pushed the door open and stuck his head into the room. "What? No, no, I've made them as loose as I dare. The general assured you that this situation would only be tempor—"

Miguel struck the man over the back of the head, then stepped over the fallen body and into the room, his finger on the trigger of his weapon. In the next second he nearly dropped it.

"Miguel! My God, how did you—"

"Shh." He touched a finger to his lips and fought back blurring tears. She was tied to a chair, but she was alive. His angel was alive! He dragged the soldier over the threshold and closed the door. He dealt first with the bonds on her wrists. Her arms were stretched diagonally across the back of the wooden chair, with each wrist tied near the seat. He cut the ropes, but she couldn't make her arms move right away. Her bare feet were tied to the front chair legs. As the ropes fell away he tried not to think about the rope burns on her ankles that matched the ones on her wrists. He couldn't coddle her now.

"My arms," she whispered.

He looked up quickly and immediately wished he hadn't. A red welt underscored her right eye, and she grimaced as she tried to rotate her shoulders. "How bad?" he asked.

"I don't know. I've been sitting like this for so long."

"Do you think anything is broken?"

She shook her head quickly, but she really didn't know. Her arms protested her every movement with bone-splitting pain. He put his hands on her shoulders and massaged gently, and she groaned. "Try to get the circulation going, *querida*. We must move quickly."

He gathered the rope and moved to the unconscious sentry. "Did this one hurt you?" Ronnie shook her head. Setting his pistol within easy reach, Miguel quickly bound and gagged the man and dragged him into a closet, muttering, "You'll sit this one out."

Ronnie stood up slowly and flexed her ankles and her knees. "Come on, blood," she ordered, trying to ignore the rush of dizziness she was feeling. "Get pumping."

Miguel laid his hand on her shoulder. "We must move quickly and quietly. Are you able to manage?"

"Yes." She had to be.

"Can you use this?" He offered his pistol.

Sort of, she thought. I can't hit anything with it, but . . . "I know how to fire it."

"Good. Stay close."

He led her through quiet halls to the storage room. He removed the false floor covering and opened the trapdoor. "This is one avenue of escape," he whispered in the dark. "It leads to the garden, which will probably become a dangerous place in a few moments. You should be safe in the tunnel, but not in the garden. Not unless I come for you."

"What's going on, Miguel?"

"We're about to topple Guerrero's house of cards. McQuade is setting a charge under the gate. When that goes off, the attack begins."

He guided her away from the secret door and took a position facing the door to the hallway. He wanted to hold her, but he had to keep his priorities straight. His rifle was aimed at the door. The things he wanted to say to her would have to wait. If he started on them now, the rifle would soon be forgotten.

"Did you think I was in the plane when it blew up?" she asked in a voice that was barely audible.

"Yes," he answered tightly.

"I almost was. Then somebody decided I might be useful."

"Does Guerrero know . . . what is between us?"

She swallowed hard. "I don't think so. He just knows I brought you the guns."

"Did he . . ." This was not the time to ask, but he couldn't stop the question. "Did he hurt you, *querida*?"

"No, not . . . not really. He hit me and threw me around a little. I don't know what he thought I knew. How did you know I was here?"

Miguel's hands tightened around the grips of the automatic rifle. "He sent a messenger. He wanted me to meet him."

"He would have killed you."

"He would have killed both of us."

The explosion rent the night, and Miguel smiled to himself in the dark. It had begun. One blast followed another—on the roof, in the courtyard, in the west wing. He could identify them all by direction. The sound of footfalls on the stone steps made Ronnie stiffen. Miguel turned the rifle toward the trapdoor. "McQuade?"

"I think I really made a mess of your gate, *jefe*," was the answer from below. "Did you find her?"

"She's right here."

"She okay?" McQuade stepped out of the hole, clicking off his flashlight.

"I'm fine."

"Hiya, kiddo."

"Hiya, McQuade."

"So let's not let Raphael's boys have all the fun," McQuade quipped. "Let's see if we can find the snake's head and chop it off."

Miguel took hold of Ronnie's arm. "You are to wait at the foot of these steps. Anyone who comes for you will identify himself when he opens the door. If he does not, be prepared to shoot him."

"I'd rather go with you, Miguel."

"You were not in on the planning, Veronica." He pressed his flashlight into her hand. "Please do as I say this time."

"I will," she whispered. "I promise."

In total darkness he found her lips instinctively and gave one brief, hard, desperate kiss. Then he pushed her toward the secret door. "Don't use the light unless you have to. I'll come back for you myself if I can."

Ronnie found her way to the bottom of the steps and stood there for a moment, blindly trying to make sense of where she was. She didn't like it. It smelled like wet clay, and the air felt clammy. She ached all over anyway, and now the dampness crept into her bare feet. Above her she could hear gunfire, and she shivered. Dying, darkness, death. Was this the way it felt to be inside a tomb? Something ran over her foot, and she decided she wanted to be buried with her shoes on. She didn't want to be buried at all—what was she thinking? This was awful. Musty, dusty, surrounded by earth. She was a sky person! When she died, she was definitely going *up*.

She couldn't stand the suspense any longer. She flicked the switch and shined the flashlight beyond the steps. A tunnel, a scurrying squad of mice and a hole in the wall. She clicked the light off. This was hardly the Hilton. Maybe they could call it Catacombs Inn. Air-conditioned niches for a never-ending night's rest. Oh, God, people were actually shooting at people up there. Miguel was up there. Guerrero was up there.

Guerrero. That bastard. His best feature was the big red scar next to his left eye. The rest of his face was ugly and devoid of any spark of human emotion. Except when he was inflicting pain, she amended, and then his eyes were anything but human. She had tried to hit him back, but he had found her efforts amusing. She had seen people strike others before, and their eyes were always full of some combination of anger and fear. Behind Guerrero's fist Ronnie had seen black eyes gleaming with demonic pleasure. During her encounters with him, Guerrero had made it clear to Ronnie that the man he wanted most was Miguel Hidalgo.

Ronnie's whole body stiffened as her mind formed pictures of destruction for each explosion she heard. At her back, the earthen well shuddered with the rumble of man-made thunder, while behind her eyes bricks and mortar crumbled, and human bodies became part of the debris.

After what seemed an interminable time, the trapdoor was thrown open. Ronnie stuck the flashlight in her pocket and stepped back, holding the pistol in both of her trembling hands.

"Veronica, come quickly!"

She lowered the gun, took out the flashlight and mounted the steps. "You're supposed to identify yourself."

He laughed. "It's Miguel."

"Miguel, Miguel, Miguel," she chanted as she raced toward heaven. Her flashlight illuminated the hand he extended to her. "Miguel who?" she squealed as she grabbed his hand and sprang from the bowels of the earth into his waiting arms.

"Miguel Hidalgo, leader of the De Colores Freedom Fighters and rescuer of—" They shared a kiss in celebration, and he ended it with another joyous burst of laughter. "Beautiful, beautiful women," he finished.

"Is it over?"

"The fighting? Yes. We're searching the palace room by room, but Guerrero's troops have surrendered. We haven't accounted for him yet, but there are bodies yet to be—" He smiled when he realized that she was trying to check him over while he talked. He knew he must look like the devil.

"You're okay?" she asked.

He leaned down until his lips were close to her ear. "I can't be certain until my angel of mercy gives me a thorough examination. But that will have to come later."

"You're bleeding here," she said, touching his chin. "And here."

He closed his hand around hers and kissed her fingertips. "In turn, I intend to examine you. Are you all right?" She nodded, and he touched the bruise under her eye. "The thought of this makes me crazy," he said quietly, taking the flashlight from her hand. "I have a safer place for you now. We've secured the central offices."

They moved into the hallway. Dark and quiet, it seemed to be in a separate world from the distant shouting and the occasional gunshot that could be heard outside the building. Miguel doused the light and took the lead. When he rounded the corner at the end of the hallway an attacker charged out of the darkness, and Miguel's rifle discharged as it clattered to the floor. Ronnie stumbled backward, and something brushed her foot as it sailed past. The attacker and Miguel became entangled in one grunting, pounding, thrashing ball of fury. Ronnie had the pistol, but all she could see were dark shapes. It was like watching two men struggle inside a huge sack.

The flashlight! She had felt the flashlight hit her foot. She groped along the floor, cringing at the sound of bone-breaking combat. She knew well the sound of Miguel's voice, but she heard nothing that resembled its rich, smooth tone. The two men snarled like wild beasts. Their furious, incoherent shouts seemed to lend power to the body blows. Finally Ronnie's hand struck metal. She pivoted on one knee and edged closer. One hulk rose above the other, arm upraised.

"Miguel?"

"Get back, Ver—" The arm came down with a thud.

Ronnie flashed the light in the face of the towering figure.

His eyes were glowing coals, fires undaunted by a mere flashlight beam. In that split second he seemed to enjoy her challenge, although he could not see her face. The red scar mocked her. He knew she had a weapon pointed at him but that she dared not fire it. The man she loved was too close. With nostrils flaring, he savored the smell of her fear, and delighted in her dilemma. He knew she was afraid she'd miss. He knew she was equally afraid of hitting a human target.

Then his eyes popped with shock. He peered into the light in disbelief. His thin lips parted, but no words would come.

"*Diablo,*" Miguel hissed as he came up from his knees. He got a better grip on the knife he'd pushed into Guerrero's gut, and jerked it upward. The fiery eyes went wild. Guerrero gasped, and finally the devil's fire was extinguished.

Ronnie brought the light closer. Standing inches from Miguel's back, she could feel the trembling aftershock that racked his body. He drew several deep breaths, each one more controlled than the last, and then he took the flashlight and knelt beside the man he'd killed. The pistol dangled in Ronnie's hand. The hilt of the knife and the spreading red pool looked surrealistic at the edge of the circle of light. Ronnie thought she might have been watching a movie, except that she could smell the warm blood.

Footsteps echoed in the hallway. Ronnie touched the pistol to Miguel's shoulder as another flashlight beam rounded the corner.

"Jefe!"

Miguel dropped the lifeless wrist. "It's all over, Raphael. We've severed the snake's head."

The following day announcements were made. Rodolfo Guerrero was dead. The news was greeted with apprehensive silence. Miguel Hidalgo had once been dead, too, many of the people grumbled among themselves. Who could be trusted in times like these? The people were tired and hungry and past caring who lived in the palace as long as it was someone who would let them clean up the rubble and reopen their shops, get their boats back into the water and replant their small fields.

The villagers knew Miguel Hidalgo better than the city people did, and they helped spread the word that the reign of terror was over. Restoring order occupied Miguel's time and energy immediately. Guerrero's top aides were held in custody, and the island people breathed a tentative sigh of relief as they turned their efforts to rebuilding. Miguel sought emergency food and medical supplies, and relief agencies responded quickly. The constitution would come, the elections would come, but first he would staunch the flow of blood and feed his people.

The first shipment of supplies arrived from the United States within hours of the call, and Ronnie and McQuade were on hand to help Dorothy Bartholomew of the Red Cross set up aid stations and arrange for the distribution of food. The two were assigned the happy task of making the first delivery to El Gallo. They stood aside while Antonio and Chi Chi supervised the unloading of crates of powdered milk and eggs, farinha and Florida oranges.

"Breakfast is served," McQuade observed with a satisfied smile.

"Orange juice." Eyeing the Florida-stamped crates, Ronnie could almost taste her favorite drink. "Did you get hold of Elizabeth?"

The sound of the name made his eyes light up, and he nodded. "She'd already heard the news, and she and Tomas are on their way. She wants to help." He shrugged. "I guess it'll be sorta like doing a little stint in the Peace Corps. Hell of a honeymoon, huh?"

"Are you complaining?"

McQuade's grin completely erased his hard-boiled image. "If that woman wanted to honeymoon in Antarctica, I'd be shopping for snowshoes. How about you? Did you get through to your family?"

Ronnie nodded. "My dad was quick to point out that the insurance on the plane won't cover an act of war. Looks like I'll be working for someone else for a while."

"You going back?"

She nodded again.

"What about Miguel?"

"What *about* Miguel?"

"Nothing. Just that the man's crazy about you."

She looked down at the toes of her gym shoes. "Miguel has a lot on his mind now. When the new government gets organized, he'll be president. That sort of puts a different color on things, doesn't it?"

"What color is that?" McQuade asked.

She lifted her chin and gave him an incredulous look. "*President* of a country, McQuade. Presidents don't get crazy over charter pilots who wear high-topped sneakers and baseball caps."

"So change your shoes." The stars in his eyes told her that nothing could have been more obvious to a gumshoe who'd just married an island princess. "Listen, you see that little hut over there?" Ronnie turned her attention to the house he pointed out. "That's Tia Teresa's place. She's pretty antisocial, and she probably won't get in line for any of this stuff, so I'm gonna take the mountain to Mohammed. She helped Elizabeth, and I owe her more than a few oranges. So that's where I'll be when you're ready to head back." He smiled and gave Ronnie's shoulder a friendly tap with his fist. "Don't change a thing, kiddo. Get yourself a new baseball cap. Miguel loves it."

Ronnie pushed her fingers through her hair as she watched McQuade walk away. She would, she decided. She would get another baseball cap, but not because of Miguel. She needed it to keep the sun out of her eyes and her hair off her neck. It was practical. She was practical. And it was time, for once in her life, to be realistic, too. No president was likely to choose her to be his lady.

Miguel found her walking barefoot in the lagoon's white sand. Tan shorts, a salmon-colored tank top, and strawberry blond hair unfurled by the breeze were framed by rippling water glistening in the afternoon sun. The urge to put life's less pleasant demands aside and simply become one with Veronica was almost overwhelming. He had believed that she was lost to him, and he had never known such a feeling of emptiness. He started down the sandy bank and realized how uncomfortable his shoes were, so he pulled them off and left them lying in the sand beside his socks. With a sense of weightlessness he picked up his pace.

"I believe you dropped this, *señorita*."

Ronnie turned on the axis of her heart and found the promise of her own brand of heaven beaming at her through brown eyes. "Miguel!" She curbed her impulse to throw her arms around him and managed a little laugh. "You're forever popping in on me out of nowhere. I didn't even hear you walk up." She glanced down at the hand he held out to her. "Oh. My baseball cap." She reached for it as though she doubted its authenticity. "Where did you find this?"

"A man brought it to me thinking I might know its owner."

"Thank you." She studied the red cap, fingering its brim. "Funny, isn't it? The things we get attached to. My dad took me to Boston once. He asked me what I wanted to see most, and we looked in the paper. I picked a baseball game. He loves baseball." She looked up. "What do you think he'd have done if I had told him I'd always wanted to see a ballet?"

"I can only tell you what I would have done."

"You would have taken me." She smiled. "Always the gentleman."

"I would have taken you because you wanted to go. Had I asked you what you wanted to see most, you would have told me honestly." She glanced away, and he touched her arm. "Whether it was a baseball game or a ballet, you would have told me, wouldn't you?"

"Yes."

"Why?"

"Because . . . because you're too much of a gentleman to laugh at me either way."

He took her shoulders in his hands and made her look at him. "Because your happiness is important to me, *querida*. Your safety, your happiness . . . and your honesty. Why are you leaving me?"

She looked up at him in surprise. "Leaving you?"

"I came looking for you, and all I found was McQuade. He told me."

"Oh, well . . . in a few days, a week, whenever things settle down a little. I know there's a lot to do around here, but, of course, sooner or later I'll have to figure out what I'm going to do about—"

"I asked you why you're leaving *me*."

A hundred questions went unanswered in the looks they exchanged. Ronnie smiled bravely. "Maybe because you're too much of a gentleman to lay the cards on the table yourself."

"I'm not a cardplayer, Veronica. I'm a teacher. I prefer discussion."

Still clutching her cap, she laid her hands against his chest and spoke to him as softly as the quiet water splashing against their bare feet. "You are an important man with a very important job to do. You haven't had a moment for yourself since . . . since we—"

"Forgive me," he said just as softly. "I thought you understood. I should have—"

"No, I *do* understand, Miguel. What we had here in this quiet spot was very special to me, and I don't ever want you to apologize for it."

His brow beetled as he stared down at her. "You told me you loved me."

Her throat went dry, and her reply was barely audible. "I do. But you don't have to worry—"

"Worry? I never know what you're going to do, *querida*. I can't help but worry. You fly through enemy fire with a planeload of guns and explosives. You sneak away while I'm not looking, your plane goes up in a pillar of flame, and I die inside while I watch. When they brought me that cap and the hope that you were alive, I thought I might live again, too." He touched the fading bruise beneath her bright, teary turquoise eye. "I nearly went mad knowing what he was capable of doing, knowing he had you. I'm sorry for all you've suffered on my account.''

"It wasn't your fault," she whispered as a tear slipped to her cheek.

"It wasn't my intention. It wasn't what I wanted to give you. I didn't say the words because I was walking around with a huge target pinned to my back, and I had no right to love you. But I did. I do." He pulled her into his arms, and her tears were warm against his neck. "I love you, Veronica, and if you leave me, you will take the color from my life."

She hugged him with all her strength because her throat was full of tears and her heart was bursting. How else could she answer?

"I'll run for office, and I'll serve if it be the will of the people, but don't ask me to do it alone, *querida*. Don't ask me to do it without my angel. Before I met you, my mornings were gray."

"I don't believe that," she managed, half laughing, half crying.

"It's true," he insisted, leaning back while she lifted her face. "I was a stodgy old professor—bookish and totally unaware of the beauty, the many beauties... You're so beautiful. Tell me, Veronica. Say the words to me."

She smiled through her tears as she put her baseball cap on his bookish head. "What words?"

"The words that sound like gold and vermilion and every shade of blue in the Caribbean." He brushed his lips against her forehead and whispered, "Let me hear you say them, Veronica."

"I love you, Miguel."

Epilogue

Mikal Romanov followed his son, David, down the steps from the airplane. Mikal's wife, Morgan, was in the lead. This trip to De Colores was the family Christmas present, and Morgan had promised herself that *this* time she would actually get to enjoy the white sand and blue-green sea. The last time Morgan had visited the island, she'd had serious business to accomplish with the three men who'd been holding Mikal and her father hostage, but this time she was there for pleasure. They had left North Dakota's two feet of snow behind them for ten days, and Morgan was anxious to break out the suntan lotion. Mikal smiled to himself at the prospect of slathering it all over her. He had pleasure in mind, too.

"So what's the big grin for? You think we'll see any action down here this trip?"

"Action?" Mikal laid a hand on David's shoulder as they walked across the runway. David had a new look. Huge black-rimmed shades and long hair. Mikal loved it. It reminded him of the sixties. But he was afraid to ask what a fourteen-year-old boy's idea of action was these days.

"Sure. This place is like one headline after another. Maybe we'll get attacked by a gang of crazed Ninja dwarfs or something."

"Or maybe we'll attend a fairy-tale wedding and everyone will live happily ever after and absolutely nobody will drag your father into a crisis for the next ten days." Morgan Romanov slipped her arm into the crook of her husband's elbow. "You didn't leave any phone numbers, did you?"

"I told Uncle Yuri—"

"Oh, no."

"—that we were going to Tahiti."

"He'll almost believe that," David put in sarcastically.

"Mr. and Mrs. Romanov?" A young man stepped forward and offered a gracious smile. "I am Raphael Esperanza. President Hidalgo asked me to meet you. He said to tell you that your old room at the palace is waiting for you and that your son will have special accommodations."

The look Mikal gave Morgan made her blush.

McQuade lay stretched across the bed, his head propped up on a cocked arm, as he watched Elizabeth arrange her satiny black hair. His wife was the fairest in the land. The mirror in front of her could not lie. She was dressed in the same pale-pink dress she'd worn for their own wedding, and he felt just as awed by her now as he had the day she had exchanged vows with him. He still couldn't quite believe she was his.

"I'm glad you were able to get Tia Teresa to help with Tomas," Elizabeth said. "There will be so much to celebrate at the fiesta tonight, and I haven't danced in years."

"You mean I'm supposed to be able to dance?"

She turned, hands on hips, and gave a coy smile. "You did check dancing on the application, Mr. McQuade."

"You mean the application for the marriage license? I was so nervous, I checked everything."

"I certainly hope you didn't falsify any qualifications, *Mr.* McQuade." She sat beside him on the bed. "It would be such a disappointment to discover that I didn't get what I bargained for."

He laughed and reached for her as he rolled onto his back. "I'll dance your shoes off, lady. Then I'll toss you over my shoulder and haul you back up here so I can get what I bargained for."

"Boorish American." With a contented smile, she plucked at his T-shirt. "You'd better get dressed. We have a wedding to attend in less than half an hour."

He grinned. "How about another advance?"

Elizabeth McQuade lowered her head and happily allowed her husband to kiss her lipstick away.

Ronnie wished she could call the whole thing off. Miguel had told her she could have any kind of wedding she wanted, and she wished now that she had suggested a small ceremony in the palace chapel. Instead, she had planned a big public occasion, and now she had to face the music. The garden had been refurbished and was now in full bloom. The flames of a thousand candles were mirrored in the reflecting pool, and the guests were waiting to witness a wedding.

There was a knock at the door. "Are you ready, Veronica?"

"Al-almost." She took another hard look in the mirror. She'd probably overdone the blush. Yes, she definitely had. She looked like a clown. She snatched the last tissue from the box on the vanity. The rest formed a heap between the array of makeup and the brush and comb.

"May I come in, *querida*?"

"No!" She didn't want him to see her. "Yes." He was the only person in the world she wanted to see

He opened the door and stuck his head into the bedroom they would share that night. It was not his room, but one he'd designated the honeymoon suite because it was on the third floor and would give them privacy. He'd furnished one of the alcoves as a dressing area for her, and he could hear her movements but he couldn't see her. "You're not going to leave me standing at the altar, are you?"

She stepped into the room and took his breath away. Her dress poured the colors of the Caribbean over her body in a soft, feminine style that reminded him of a vintage forties film. She'd told him she'd decided against white in favor of a more flattering color, and she had chosen his favorite. Her hair was full and soft, and her lips were pink, glossy and ready to be kissed by her adoring groom.

He closed the door behind him, and she wondered if anyone so handsome could possibly be real. His black hair and dark tan were startlingly beautiful with the ivory tuxedo. His brown eyes glistened, and it occurred to her that she might be the cause.

They drank each other in.

"You look beautiful," they said in unison, and then each gave a nervous laugh. They stood several feet apart, uncertain about the next move.

"I'm scared," she said.

"So am I."

"They're all waiting, aren't they?" He nodded. "I should have let Barnaby give me away."

"You wanted to come to me on your own," he reminded her. "The way you always have."

She nodded, remembering how she'd planned it before she knew how scary it was going to be. "Becky fixed my hair," she said. "How does it look?"

He swallowed. *"Bello,"* he whispered, and then found a bigger voice. "Beautiful."

"Miguel, let's get the priest to come up here and just . . . marry us right here."

"That would be fine with me, but the priest might take exception." He smiled. "It was your idea to share our celebration. The next time I kiss you the fireworks will be real, not just in my head." He reached out for her hand, and she smiled as she laid it in his. "The idea is a good one," he assured her. "The people need a celebration. I just need you. You and your wonderful paintbox."

Hours passed before Miguel had *just* Veronica. After they had made promises, he had kissed her before all the world, a kiss that triggered a burst of fireworks and cheers throughout the city. They accepted all the good wishes and feasted and danced until the merriment was well underway. And then they slipped away.

They whispered more promises while they made love, and when they were too contented to do anything but lie in each other's arms, they pondered the night's wonders. The doors stood open on the balcony, and the fireworks display continued for their entertainment. Bursts of gold glitter and showers of pink stars adorned the canvas of night sky. The drums and guitars played dance after dance, and the air was filled with the voices of people enjoying life.

"Four years," Miguel said quietly. "Maybe eight, but I hope someone can be found to replace me after one term. Then I can be myself again. Professor Miguel Hidalgo. I want to build a small college here on the island."

"And we can go on that research expedition."

"By that time, we'll have to take the children."

"Mmm." She turned her head to plant a soft, wet kiss on his chest. "I don't know how I'll be with this first lady business, but I'll make a terrific mother."

"Making you a mother is my job." She nibbled at him, and he groaned. "And you have slipped into the role of first lady quite satisfactorily. Ah, look at the sky, *querida*!"

She turned in time to see the crackling splashes of blue, green, silver and gold. "That's how it feels when you make love to me," she said. "Those are the colors you make inside me."

"I promise to color our nights if you'll paint the mornings."

"It's a deal," she said, moving over him. "Get out your paintbox, *mi amor*."

* * * * * *

Witness what happens when a devil falls
in love with an angel

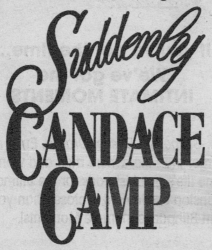

Suddenly

CANDACE
CAMP

Simon "Devil" Dure needs a wife, and Charity Emerson is
sure she can meet his expectations...and then some.

Charity is right, and the Devil is finally seduced by her
crazy schemes, her warm laughter, her loving heart. There
is no warning, however, of the dangerous trap that lies
ahead, or of the vicious act of murder that will put their
courage—and their love—to the ultimate test.

Available at your favorite retail outlet in February.

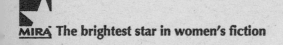

MIRA The brightest star in women's fiction   MCCS